# Megan

## JACK WEYLAND

**BOOKCRAFT**

SALT LAKE CITY, UTAH

*To Sherry*

*My companion for eternity and
the best part of every day*

The talk given by Elder Richard G. Scott, quoted on pages 259-60 in this book, was given in the October 2000 semiannual general conference. See "The Path to Peace and Joy," *Ensign*, Nov. 2000, 25-27.

Visit us at www.deseretbook.com

Library of Congress Cataloging-in-Publication Data

Weyland, Jack, 1940-
    Megan / Jack Weyland.
        p.   cm.
    Summary: Infatuated with an older boy who is not a member of her church, seventeen-year-old Megan, a Mormon, goes against the values she was raised with and becomes pregnant.
    ISBN 1-57008-732-6 (Hardbound : alk. paper)
    1. Mormons—Fiction. 2. Pregnancy—Fiction. 3. Conduct of life—Fiction.
I. Title

PZ7.W538 Me 2001
(Fic)—dc21

Printed in the United States of America          70582-6862
Phoenix Color Corporation, Hagerstown, MD

10    9    8    7    6    5    4    3    2    1

# 1

Megan, seventeen, a senior in high school, stared in the restroom mirror at Leo's Pizza and, with her black, almond eyes, scowled at her reflection. Her thick, dark brown hair was out of control. In the fluorescent lighting, the tan she had worked on so hard gave her skin a near-death, grayish tint. She was wearing the purple eyeliner that her older brother, Bryce, said made her look like she'd been in a fight. Now, in that light, she could see why he'd said it.

She stepped back and turned to catch her profile in the mirror. Her hip-hugging khaki pants fit really well, even though her mom thought they were too tight. Megan had bought them a week earlier with her paycheck from Burger King, where she worked part-time.

Underneath the oversized T-shirt she'd permanently borrowed from Bryce, she was wearing a black tank top. She'd bought it at the same time she got the pants but, up to then, hadn't had the courage to wear it in public. She was wearing it tonight just in case Kurt showed up.

1

*What if he doesn't come? But he will. Thomas said he was coming, so he'll be here. And even if he doesn't come, I'll have fun. I always have fun with Thomas.*

She took a deep breath, opened the swinging door, and entered the Friday night after-hours world at Leo's Pizza. Although the restaurant was closed, Thomas Marconi, her best friend from school, was one of the managers, and he often let his friends come in while he was cleaning up. They'd make their own pizzas, push the tables and chairs into a corner, and dance. On the weekends they'd be together until one or two in the morning and then Thomas would get them to help clean up and then he'd boot them out.

"Is this okay with Leo?" Megan had once asked.

Thomas laughed. "There is no Leo. The owner's name is Phil Silverstein, and he hates pizza."

Thomas was six-foot-two. His wire-rimmed glasses with small frames made him look intelligent, yet somehow detached, as if he were a dispassionate observer of the follies of mankind. His nearly black hair was so thick and coarse, it hardly ever got out of place.

"Well, then, is it okay with Mr. Silverstein?"

"I asked him once. He said it was okay as long as I take full responsibility for what happens and pay him back for what we use for our pizzas. One thing it does is reduce the chance of anyone breaking in."

Megan had known Thomas since seventh grade. Through the years they had remained devoted friends. In fact, because he knew Megan liked Kurt, it was Thomas who had invited him to drop by.

"Are you sure he's coming?" she asked.

"He said he'd come."

"I wish he'd hurry up."

"Me, too, so you'd quit bugging me about it. To get your mind off him, how about making me a pizza? Write a special message on it, just for me."

2

She suspected that rather than trying to help her, he just wanted a pizza, but, even so, she couldn't turn him down. He was her best friend. "I guess I will," she said.

"That's my girl," Thomas said, patting her on the arm as he sat down to enjoy watching his friends have a good time.

Of the ten people who came regularly to Leo's after hours, Thomas only let three or four actually make pizzas, people he could trust not to make a big mess. Megan was one of those few.

She remembered when Thomas had tried to teach her how to toss the pizza dough in the air to shape it. By the time they were through, she had an extra large, doughy crust draped over her head, and they were laughing so hard they had to lean on each other for support.

She loved working in the kitchen at Leo's because it was well-equipped, and people were always drifting in, asking when the next pizza would be done.

After getting Thomas's pizza ready to go in the oven, she decided to write him a message using chopped green peppers to make the letters. She thought of several possibilities, some of which would be funny, but then she thought about how much happiness he was giving to his friends and so, in the end, she decided to go with THANK YOU!

By the time she'd done THA, she realized she wasn't going to be able to finish the whole phrase, so she changed it to THANK U!

In her excitement to prepare this tribute to Thomas, she almost forgot about Kurt, but ten minutes before the pizza was done, she peeked out to where Thomas was sitting and saw Kurt at the same booth with him.

"Oh, my gosh! I can't believe he's here!" she said to herself.

Thomas and Megan had first gotten to know Kurt a year earlier in choir in high school. From the first time she saw him, she'd been attracted to him. He had great looking, dark

3

brown hair and brooding eyes and a terrific smile, when he chose to show it. But the thing that attracted Megan the most was his self-confidence. It was almost a cockiness that made it seem as though he didn't need anyone's approval.

Kurt was also into adventure. He loved to surf and camp and hike and scuba dive and sail.

Since their paths seldom crossed now that he'd graduated from high school, she'd cooked up this way to stay in touch. This might be her only chance with him. He was a moving target and might never return to Leo's.

She went to the restroom and took off her T-shirt to see how she looked in the tank top. She turned sideways and admired herself in the mirror. The tank top was tight, and it left her midriff and belly button exposed. She liked the way she looked, but because she'd never worn something that daring in public, she began to have second thoughts. *Well, it's not what I usually wear, but it's no worse than what they show on TV. Besides, this may be my only chance to get Kurt's attention.*

She stepped back to take in the overall effect. *Good thing none of my Church friends are here,* she thought with a cynical smile. *No worry about that. Their mommies wouldn't let 'em out this late. They're probably all home praying.*

*Heather would have a fit if she saw me in this,* she thought. Heather was her twenty-two-year-old sister, who was serving a mission in Montana. Heather wasn't like anyone else in the family. She was quiet and reserved and had an inner compass that caused her to always make good choices.

*The tank top's not really that bad. It just seems weird to me because of what I usually wear. But it's no worse than what everyone else is wearing these days.*

Megan remembered Heather going through her clothes just before she went to the temple, getting rid of anything that would be inappropriate for someone who'd been to the temple.

*She'd have gotten rid of this, if she'd had it*, Megan thought. *But so what? I'm not going on a mission, and I'm not going to the temple. At least not for a while, so why not wear whatever I want until then? It's like they say, you're only young once.*

She pursed her lips, trying to decide if she had the courage to leave the T-shirt off and just go with the tank top. *I bought it, so I might as well wear it. I'll probably get used to it after I've worn it a few times. Besides, it's not that bad.*

She took the pizza out of the oven, cut it into slices, and carried it out to where Kurt and Thomas were talking.

"Here's that pizza you ordered, sir," she said to Thomas.

Thomas's eyebrows rose at seeing her for the first time in a tank top.

*Please don't ask why I changed*, she thought. *At least not in front of Kurt.*

"Is this pizza any good?" Thomas asked.

She loved bantering with Thomas. "My friend, this is the best pizza that's ever been made!"

"I'll be the judge of that. And let me warn you, I have extremely high standards. Sit down and let's see how you did. Oh, you remember Kurt, right?"

She sat down next to Thomas, facing Kurt. "Oh, sure. Hi, Kurt. You want some of the best pizza in the universe?"

"How could a person turn that down? I'd better wash my hands though. I just got back from horseback riding."

"So you're the one who smells like a horse. I was wondering."

He seemed surprised by her boldness, but then flashed his trademark, understated grin, and left for the men's room.

"So, what's with the . . . uh . . . new look?" Thomas asked.

"Is it okay?"

Thomas was doing his best to avoid looking at anything except her face. "Yeah, sure, why not? It's just that, uh, it's not what you usually wear. So why did you change? For Kurt?"

She was blushing. "I just wanted to see how I'd look, that's all. Do you think he noticed?"

"Oh, yeah," Thomas said with a silly grin. "You can trust me on that."

"It was a dumb thing to do, wasn't it?" She folded her arms over her midriff because she felt self-conscious.

"You don't need to do anything, you know. You're great just the way you are."

"Yeah, right," she said with a scowl.

"I'm serious."

"Whatever."

"Why do you like Kurt, anyway?" he asked.

"Look at him. And because he's so sure of himself."

"He's like you then, right?"

"Do I seem that way?"

"With people you're good friends with, you are."

"That's what I want to be."

"That's what you are."

"Thanks." She kissed him on the cheek.

"What's that for?"

"For being my friend."

He raised his hand to fend her off. "Don't go thinking that kissing me is going to make me give you a better evaluation of your pizza. I can't be bought, you know."

She laughed. "Well, it was worth a shot."

"All right, it's payback time. I made you feel good about yourself. Now you do the same for me."

"You want me to lie?"

He grinned. "Yeah, pretty much."

"Well, you're my very best friend, and I love spending time with you."

"That's not a lie, though, is it?"

"No, it's the truth."

He put his hands behind his head and leaned back. "Tell some outrageous but flattering lies about me, okay?"

She ran her fingers through his hair and spoke in a husky, seductive voice. "You are, without a doubt, the sexiest guy in the world."

He chuckled. "That was okay, but this time try to exaggerate."

She mussed his hair with one swipe of her hand.

"Hey, don't mess with perfection, girl."

She folded her arms across her chest. "You think I'm dumb for wanting to spend time with Kurt, don't you?"

"Well, yeah, I do actually."

"Why?"

"Because Kurt doesn't need anyone. Not you, not me, not anyone. That's the way he's always been."

"I like that in a guy."

He shook his head. "Great then, if that's what you want."

"Are you jealous?" she asked, putting her hand on his arm.

"Maybe a little, but I'm not that worried. You and I will always be close. And Kurt will be out of your life before long."

"You're probably right."

Kurt came back and sat down. He looked at Megan as if expecting her to say something. "Well?"

Megan didn't know what he meant. "Well, what?"

"How do I smell?"

She leaned over the table and sniffed. "A lot better."

"Good. You ever try to wash up in a restroom? It's not that great. Especially trying to dry yourself with paper towels. The wet towels kept sticking to me. At one point I looked like a mummy."

She laughed. "I would've loved to see that."

"I should've invited you in."

"Actually, I usually stay out of men's restrooms."

"Except for when you clean for me after everyone else is gone," Thomas said.

"Oh, well, sure, but that doesn't count."

7

Thomas put his arm around Megan and patted her shoulder. "After our little party is over here, most everyone chips in and does a little work, but Megan stays around and works until everything's done. She saves me a ton of work."

Kurt gave a halfhearted smile. "What a trooper." He looked bored.

*He's going to leave now and never come back. What am I doing wrong?*

Kurt started to talk about his dad's sailboat. Megan leaned forward and tried to look very interested in everything he was saying, even offering animated comments like, "That sounds so fun!"

It must have worked. "You want to go sailing?" Kurt asked.

"Sure, when?"

"Now."

"Now?"

"There's a full moon, so we'll be able to see where we're going."

She didn't know what to say. She turned to Thomas. "I'd better stick around and help Thomas clean up after everyone else goes."

"No, that's okay," Thomas said. "You go ahead. I can get by without you."

To Kurt the decision had been made. He stood up, grabbed what was left of the pizza and a handful of napkins, and said to Thomas, "Sorry to take your best worker and the best pizza in the universe."

"No problem, man."

Megan felt like she was betraying Thomas. "Are you sure you don't need me?"

"No, you go ahead," he said with what looked to her like a slightly forced smile.

Kurt drove a late model, bright yellow Jeep Wrangler, complete with roll bars and with the top removed. He turned to his favorite radio station, started the engine, and turned to her and smiled. "You buckled up?"

"I am."

"Good," he said.

She worried, because of his reputation as an outdoors adventurer, that he'd drive like a maniac, but he didn't. In fact, she felt very safe with him. He didn't talk much while he drove, but that was okay. It gave her a chance to enjoy the ride.

An hour later he pulled up to a parking area next to the private dock where his father's boat was moored.

She looked at the clock on the dashboard. It was two o'clock. Her mother would expect her to be home by now. Her dad was a Scoutmaster and was on a camp out with the boys.

She knew she should call home and tell her mother what was going on but didn't because her mother would want her home right away. Megan didn't want to cut short her time with Kurt. She figured they'd be out on the water for maybe an hour, and then it would take another hour for Kurt to drive her home. But at least she'd have a good explanation of why she was late.

She decided not to tell Kurt she needed to be home.

It was a beautiful thirty-foot sailboat, sleek and long and slender.

"This is amazing!" she said as he extended his hand and helped her step onto the polished, wood deck.

"It's even better on the open water. Let's get to work. I'll need some help from you."

"Sure, what?"

"I'll tell you, but first we need to have a few lessons. Listen carefully because there will be a quiz afterwards."

"Sounds serious," she teased.

"It can be. If you mess up at Leo's, you end up throwing away a pizza. You mess up here, and you could die."

"Okay, teach me what I need to know."

"The right-hand side of the boat is called the starboard side. The left-hand side is called . . ."

"Wait a minute. Why not just call it the right side of the boat?"

"Tradition."

She smiled. "And calling it by the right name is going to save my life? I don't think so. I think you just want to impress me with how much you know."

He started laughing. "Well, I can see you've got me figured out."

"Not quite, but almost. I just need a little time."

"I think that can be arranged."

An old man with a flashlight walked down the dock toward them.

"Who's that?" she asked privately.

"Night watchman."

The man got close enough and then shined the flashlight in their eyes. "Kurt, I see you're at it again, hey?"

"It's a beautiful night for sailing."

"Yes, it is. And how is Samantha doing tonight?"

Kurt rolled his eyes. "Actually, this isn't Samantha."

"Oh, sorry. Who's this one?"

"Tell him your name," Kurt said.

"You don't know my name?"

"Sorry. I forgot."

"I'm Megan," she said to the night watchman.

"Oh, Megan. Well, good to meet you. I can't keep track of 'em all."

"Apparently, Kurt can't either," Megan teased.

"He brings a lot of girls out here, that's for sure."

"I'm sure you have other things to do," Kurt said, sounding annoyed.

"This is our first Megan, isn't it?"

"Yes, it is. It's been great talking to you."

10

"You're right. I need to go. Well, be careful out there. The sea is a vengeful mistress."

"We'll be careful."

"The sea is a vengeful mistress," Kurt mimicked as the night watchman continued on his way.

"So, how many girls have you brought out here?" she asked.

"What difference does it make?"

"Maybe you should have a guest book so you can keep track of 'em all."

"I haven't found what I'm looking for yet," he said.

"What are you looking for?"

"Someone I can talk to about things that really matter."

She could find nothing about his answer to make fun of. That was what she wanted, too.

The things Kurt needed her to do as they left the dock were easy enough—shining a flashlight ahead of them to make sure there were no hidden obstacles and steering the small outboard motor while Kurt rigged the sails as they left the inlet.

And then they were under way. It was a magical experience to be silently sailing under a moonlit sky with the lights of the city across the bay, shining like sparkling diamonds.

It was cooler on the water. She had goose bumps and wished she had something to put on over her tank top; but she didn't say anything about it. "It's so beautiful out here," she said.

He nodded. "This is where I come alive."

"I can see why."

"I'm happy to share it with you. Oh, there's some wine in a cupboard in the galley. Why don't you go see if you can find it and then pour us both a glass?"

Ordinarily she didn't drink. Just once in a while when it would be awkward to say no. But never to excess. For instance, she'd never been drunk. And she was always very

11

careful so her parents wouldn't find out. Even if she'd been drinking on a Saturday night, she always made sure she made it to church the next day because she didn't want her parents to get suspicious.

She knew what the Church taught about not drinking, but she couldn't see how a beer or two with friends once in a while was that big of a deal. It was like the boy who talked her into taking her first drink at a party two years earlier had said, "It's just one beer, okay? It's not going to kill you. C'mon, loosen up. You're ruining the night for everyone else."

She found the wine, located two glasses, and poured a little in each glass. Drinking wine on an expensive sailboat in the middle of the night seemed like a very grown-up thing to do.

On her way out of the galley, she saw a sweatshirt on a hook. It would keep her warm and make her feel less self-conscious, but she decided not to ask if she could wear it. Kurt was paying attention to her. She wasn't sure how much of that was due to the tank top, but she definitely didn't want to ruin everything.

She made her way back to Kurt and gave him one of the glasses. He took a small sip and set the glass in a nearby cup holder.

They sipped their wine and looked at the stars and at the lights of the city, enjoying the sound of the wake as the sleek hull knifed through the dark waves. In the distance she could see the Golden Gate Bridge in one direction and the Bay Bridge in the other. Megan could hardly believe it. Being here, alone with Kurt, was about the most exciting thing she had ever done.

"You love this, don't you?" she asked.

"I do. More than I can say." He seemed to be struggling to open up to her. "Out here is the one place where I feel . . . like I've found my place in life." He paused. "And . . . that I'm not a complete failure."

12

"It's hard for me to believe you'd ever feel that way about yourself."

He nodded. "I don't admit it to most people." He paused, then sighed. "Actually, I've never admitted that to anyone else." He smiled. "You know what? You're very easy to talk with. Not like the other girls I've brought out here."

"Why am I different?"

"With everyone else, it's like I'm putting on an act. My dad once told me, 'Never let 'em see you sweat.' I guess that's what I do with everyone else. But sometimes I get tired of it all and wish I could just find someone that I'd feel free to talk to about my hopes . . ." She was seated next to him as he operated the wheel, and he reached over and rested his hand on her leg just above her knee. " . . . and my dreams for the future. Maybe you're what I've been looking for . . . all this time."

She wasn't that comfortable having his hand on her leg, but she was reluctant to ask him to remove it when he was revealing his innermost thoughts and dreams for the future.

A moment later he removed his hand and asked, "Are you cold?"

"Well, maybe a little."

"You should have told me. Let me go get you something."

He brought out the sweatshirt she'd seen. "Here, put this on."

She put it over her head. It had that new sweatshirt smell she loved. Being warm again, along with the wine, made her feel relaxed and comfortable.

"The truth is, I don't have anyone . . . I can really open up to," he said. "About the things that really matter, I mean, like what I'm going to do with my life."

"What do you want to do?"

He sighed. "That's just it. I don't know. Oh, of course, my folks have plenty of suggestions. But it's all what they'd do if they were my age. Well, they had their chance. Now it's my turn."

"Have your folks ever said you had to be exactly like them?"

"No, not in so many words, but the message is always there."

"You don't have to follow in their footsteps."

He nodded. "You're right. You're absolutely right. You know what I'd like to do? Have a marine store and sell boats like this."

"Do it then."

"It wouldn't bring in much money."

"You don't have to be rich to be happy."

He smiled. "Now that's a new thought."

"It's true."

"Are you happy?" he asked.

"Most of the time."

He sighed and took another sip of wine. "You're doing better than me then, that's for sure. I'll go get us some more wine."

She didn't want any more wine but didn't tell him that because she didn't want to ruin the evening. When he returned, he brought the bottle. "Do you want me to fill up your glass?"

"Just a little."

She noticed a pattern in his drinking. He would fill the glass maybe a fourth of the way full as if he just wanted a sip, and then he'd take small sips occasionally, giving the impression he was just a social drinker. But then, a few minutes later, he'd repeat the whole process over again.

The more he drank, the more he confided in her. "I just want to be left alone to let me find out who I really am. Is that asking too much?"

"No, not at all."

"This is so great having someone I can talk to like this.

And this night, well, it's perfect. It's a gift, really, a gift made for us to share together."

She looked at her watch. "Well, that gift is going to have to end pretty soon because I've got to get home and get some sleep."

He put his hand on her arm. "Why go home?"

"Because my mom will be starting to wonder where I am."

"Any other reason?"

"I need to get some sleep, so I can go to work tomorrow."

"This is such a beautiful night. What if we stayed out here all night? You could sleep in the cabin. I'd sleep out here under the stars. It'd give us more time to be together."

"I can't stay here tonight with you."

"Why not?"

"Well, for one reason, my mom would freak out. And my dad, too, when he gets home tomorrow."

"Where is he?"

"He's a Scoutmaster. He's on a camp out tonight."

"Your dad is a Scoutmaster? You're not serious."

"He's been Scoutmaster for the past five years. He bought a Scout uniform when he first began. It fit then, but now his stomach spills out so you can hardly tell if he's wearing a belt or not."

Kurt laughed. "I guess I shouldn't complain. My life could be a lot worse. Like, my dad could be a Scoutmaster."

"He loves it."

"Good for him."

Kurt sat down next to her and reached for her hand. "I told you there would be a quiz about sailing tonight. So here it is. What if the wind were to suddenly die down and we were left stranded out here until morning? We'd have no way of getting back to shore."

"Except for the outboard motor," she said.

"Let's say we don't have an outboard motor."

"But we do."

15

"Pretend we don't. It's my quiz, okay?"

"Well, even if we didn't have an outboard motor, the fact is the wind isn't dying down."

"True, but your mom doesn't know that, right?" he said with a grin. Even in the darkness, his straight teeth glowed white.

"Well, actually, Kurt, I'm not comfortable spending the night out here with you."

"Hey, I know what you mean, but we need to get to know each other better. Nothing will happen, okay? Except we'll have a few more hours on the water on the most beautiful night for sailing I've ever experienced. Let's call your mom and tell her about the wind dying down and us out here with no motor. What is she going to do? Swim out here and rescue us? I don't think so."

Even though she still had reservations, Megan took his cell phone and punched in the numbers.

It rang several times before her mom answered it.

"Mom, hi, it's me. Don't get worried, okay? Everything's fine. I'm with Kurt. We were in choir my junior year."

She listened for a moment.

"Well, I met him at Leo's, he's a friend of Thomas, and he took me out on his dad's sailboat, but now the wind has died down, so we can't get back."

She glanced at Kurt, and he gave her a thumbs-up.

"So I won't be home until morning. I didn't want you to worry." She listened again.

"Yes, I know it's late. Sorry. There's nothing I can do about it now, though. We're stranded out here. I feel as bad about it as you do."

"Let me talk to her," Kurt said.

She handed him the phone, and he put his hand over the mouthpiece.

"What's your last name?" he asked.

"Cannon."

16

He put the phone to his ear. "Hello, Mrs. Cannon? I'm sorry about this, really I am. Don't worry about a thing. Megan will be perfectly safe here. We should be back around ten in the morning. . . . Yes, that's right. If you want, I can give you my cell phone number in case you want to get hold of us. . . . Okay, here it is." He gave her his cell phone number, assured her once again of Megan's well-being, then said good-bye.

"There's a bed in the cabin. When it's time, I'll make it up for you." He paused. "You'll be safe in there."

"Thank you."

They spent another hour sailing. At first she just stood next to him as he steered, but after a time he had her sit in front of him and he let her steer as he pointed out the lighted landmarks on the shore—Fisherman's Wharf, Ghiardelli Square, Coit Tower, and the big hotels on Nob Hill. Megan had never done anything so romantic and couldn't believe she was actually there with Kurt, cradled in his arms, listening to the wash of the boat's wake, the lights of the city reflecting off the water.

Finally, they went toward the shore and anchored the boat for the night, and then he showed her where there was an extra blanket, said goodnight, and closed the door to the cabin on his way out.

She was self-conscious about the arrangements and didn't think she'd sleep at all, but just after nine-thirty in the morning she awoke, sat up, looked out a porthole, and saw that they were under way.

She glanced into a mirror on the galley wall, tousled her hair with her fingers, and wished she had a toothbrush or some gum. Then she left the galley and climbed the stairs to the deck. Kurt was standing at the wheel. He smiled when he saw her.

"Good morning," he said.

"Good morning."

17

"Did you sleep okay?" he asked.

"Yeah, really good. What about you?"

"No problem at all, except I was a little lonely not having you to talk to. I can't remember when I've opened up so much to anyone. You probably know me better already than anyone. Thanks for being such a good listener."

"I enjoyed talking to you, too."

"You want to call your mom and tell her you're okay?"

"She's at work by now."

"She has a phone at her work, doesn't she?"

"Yes."

"Let's call her then. I don't want her worrying."

"What about your folks?" Megan asked. "Why haven't you called them?"

"They know where I am."

"How do they know that?"

"GPS tracking. They always know where I am when I'm out on the boat . . . or at least they could know if they wanted to. My parents and I have an arrangement. I stay within their limits of acceptable behavior, and they don't ask too many questions. It's a good arrangement. They're very busy people, you know, and very influential. They don't want any negative publicity about me, but other than that, I'm on my own."

"That seems strange to me."

"It's like being in a very big and very expensive prison. As long as I don't try to escape, things go well for me."

Five minutes later Kurt was talking to Megan's mother at work. "Hi, Mrs. Cannon. This is the guy who got your daughter stuck in the middle of the bay last night," he laughed. "I just wanted you to know that everything's fine. I didn't want you to be worrying about her. Also, we drifted a little during the night, so we're just a few miles from Sausalito. I was wondering if I could have your permission to take her to breakfast there before we head back."

This was all new information to Megan.

18

"Yes, thank you. Would you like to talk to her?"

He handed Megan the phone. "Hi, Mom. Everything's okay here. I'll be home soon. Okay. . . . Yeah, me, too. Bye."

She handed the cell phone back to him. "I need to be at work at one o'clock," she said.

"Where do you work?"

"Burger King."

"Can you get the day off?"

"No."

"Have you ever missed work?"

"Yeah, sure, when I'm sick."

"How long has it been since you called in sick?" he asked.

"About six months."

"Well, I think you're about to get sick again. C'mon, one day isn't going to make any difference. If you call now, your boss will be able to get someone to fill in for you."

"That's not how it works. If I'm not going to be there, I have to get my own substitute."

"Even better." He handed her the phone.

"Why should I sluff work?"

"Because this is going to be a spectacular day. And that should never be taken for granted. We'll go to Sausalito and have an early lunch, looking out at the bay while we eat, and then we'll walk through Vina del Mar Park and see the elephants and the fountain, and then we'll go back, have a snack, and come home. We'll be home about the same time you'd be getting off work. This will be our day in the sun. Everyone deserves a day in the sun, a time-out, and this will be yours. It's my gift to you." He was grinning at her. An inviting kind of grin.

"What about you? Don't you have a job?"

"I work for my dad, but my hours are my own."

"What do you do?"

"I write code for computer games. I do most of my work

19

at home, usually between the hours of eleven at night and two in the morning. I'm all caught up this week."

"Let me think about it while I get cleaned up, okay?"

"Sure, take all the time you need. We'll be at Sausalito in half an hour, but we can always turn around and head back."

She went into the boat's cabin, closed the door, and began to wash her face. As she did so, she thought about her job. She worked harder than any of the other student workers, and she was often called upon to fill in for them when they got sick.

It was hard work, and her boss hardly ever said a nice thing to anyone. The best part of the work day was when he left and put her in charge. They worked harder but had more fun when he was gone.

Her boss had grudgingly made her assistant manager but at no increase in pay. Three nights a week she closed and took care of the night depository.

She was tired of the people she worked with. Most of them told dirty jokes and made cutting remarks about the people who came in to eat.

*Kurt is right. I deserve a day off.*

A few minutes later she came back on deck. "I need to use your phone to try and get someone to go in for me."

He smiled. "I promise you won't regret it."

"I may not be able to get a substitute."

"I'm sure you'll get the job done."

It took six phone calls to get someone to go in for her. By that time they were pulling into Sausalito. After docking the boat, they walked along the waterfront and bought food for a picnic lunch, which they ate at a park.

"This is where I want to live someday," Kurt said. "I'll work from an office in my home. I'll work three hours a day and then spend the rest of my time sailing."

"How would it be?"

"It would be even better if you and I were enjoying it together."

"It sounds like it could be fun."

When they were done eating, they tossed their trash in a dumpster. "But right now it's time to go shopping. All the big stars from Hollywood come here. Let's go back to the boat. You can ditch the sweatshirt, and we'll put on sunglasses like we're rich and famous and don't want anyone to know who we are, and we'll walk through this town like we owned it."

As she followed his advice and took off the sweatshirt, she was still a little self-conscious about the tank top but felt more confident than she had when she first put it on the night before.

They spent an hour pretending to be rich and famous, wandering in and out of the quaint shops and art galleries, acting sufficiently bored, pretending to nearly buy artwork valued at over twenty thousand dollars and then, when they couldn't keep a straight face anymore, running outside and laughing about it all the way to the next shop.

Kurt had brought a digital camera from the boat. "Let's pretend you're a famous fashion model and we're here today on a shoot."

She smiled and shook her head. "Just take the stupid picture, okay?"

He took the picture. "Work with me, baby! Show me some good stuff!"

At first she was too self-conscious to do much more than just smile at the camera, but after a while, with Kurt's encouragement, she got into it. She told herself that she didn't know any of the tourists milling around and would never see any of them again. After that she tried to pose as if she really were a fashion model.

Kurt loved it. "Oh, yeah! You're hot now! That's it! Give me more of that."

When a group of Japanese tourists stopped to watch and

take their own pictures of her, Megan decided it was time to quit. "Kurt, I can't do this anymore. It's too embarrassing."

"Sure, I understand. Let's go someplace else."

They walked along the harbor front for a while, enjoying the view of the city across the bay, then sat down on the lawn in the warmth of the sun. While he lay on the lawn, half sleeping, she sang to him. After a couple of songs, he opened his eyes and smiled. "Let's do this every day for the rest of our lives."

"I think after a while my boss would catch on that I wasn't coming in to work."

"So what? It's a dumb job anyway, right?"

"But it's the only one I've got. We can't all have *rich* parents."

"Look, my parents aren't rich, okay?" He spoke with bitter resentment.

"How can you say that? That boat alone is worth more than the house I live in. Looks to me like you've got it made. You work, what did you say, three hours a day? I know this will be a surprise to you, but some people work eight to ten hours a day. Like my mom and dad. They both work hard every day."

He cupped her chin with his hand and turned her head so they had eye contact. "There's something you need to know about me."

"What?"

"When it comes to writing computer code for video games, I'm . . . well, . . . I'm one of the best. I'll just leave it at that. I know I go around looking like all I do is have fun, but that's just because when I do work, it takes so much concentration that I can only do it for a few hours at a time."

She didn't appreciate him lecturing her. "Okay . . . sorry if I made you mad. I didn't mean anything by it."

"It's kind of a sore point with me. All the guys I graduated from high school with think I'm totally irresponsible for not

22

going to college like them. But I'm already making more than they ever will, so why should I follow in their footsteps?"

"No reason to."

He sighed. "I'm glad you understand. Sorry if I came on too strong. Sometimes I just get tired of trying to explain to the world why I'm not like everyone else."

She was quiet for a moment. "That's why I like you."

He put his arm around her shoulder as they continued their walk. He whispered in her ear. "Do you have any idea how beautiful you are?"

She blushed. "No, not really."

"Well, you are."

"Thanks."

"Especially your eyes. Did you know they sparkle when you smile? And your mouth. I bet when you were a kid, you could give your folks a pouty face better than anyone in your family."

She stopped walking. "Excuse me? Are you saying I was a difficult child?"

"No, not at all. It was a compliment."

"Yeah, right," she laughed.

They stopped to admire the sailboats dancing on the water. "It's such an amazing day, isn't it?" he asked.

"It is."

"The sun, the water, the clouds, it's all just perfect. But even with all that, the most beautiful thing on this island is right here beside me."

"You're making me blush."

"What do you say we stay here tonight?" he asked. "We'll find ourselves a fancy hotel, and we'll call up room service and order every chocolate dessert they've got. How does that sound? You like chocolate, don't you?"

She was alarmed by how innocent he made it seem. "Kurt, I can't drop everything just to be your playmate for a day."

He kissed her cheek. "I think what we've got going here is

23

way more serious than just two people coming together for a day or two."

"You do?" she asked hopefully.

"Oh, yeah. Something like this doesn't come along every day. I mean, at least not for me. What about you?"

She cleared her throat. "I've never had more fun with anyone."

He gave her his confident grin. "I'm so glad to hear you say that. I was worried I was the only one who felt this way."

Megan was worried. This was moving way too fast. *I need to let him know what I believe. But where do I start?*

She cleared her throat. "There's something you need to know though."

"What?"

She paused. "Did you know that I'm a Mormon?"

"Let's see, did I know that? I think somebody told me that once."

"We're taught that life is more than just having fun," she said.

"Since when?"

She rested her hand on his shoulder. "Kurt, you have so much to give to the world. The reason you were sent to earth is to help others less fortunate than yourself."

"Helping others? You know what? I've never thought of that as a reason for living. Well, okay, Megan, if you really want to help someone, help me become a better person."

She smiled. It was the one offer she couldn't refuse.

# 2

On Sunday Megan went to church but found it hard to think about anything except Kurt. It was Scout Sunday, which meant the deacons and her father wore their Scout uniforms to church. It was an old ritual, and Megan had long ago gotten over being embarrassed about it. She just tried to pretend that the totally enthusiastic, nearly bald, middle-aged man with stomach protruding under his faded Scout shirt was not her father.

Sometimes she wondered if her dad actually thought they were close. *He might,* she thought. *That's because we never really talk. Or if we do, I try to say what he wants to hear. It's not that hard to do. Anyone can learn to do it.*

Megan's family always sat in the same place in sacrament meeting, usually the third row on the right side of the chapel. That allowed her mother, who was ward chorister, to sit with them after the sacrament until the closing song.

Megan always sat on the end of the row nearest the wall, with her fifteen-year-old sister, Brianna. Their father, Walter, sat next to Brianna, and Carolyn, their mother, sat on the end of the row, next to the aisle. Megan liked having Brianna serve as the buffer between her and her parents.

Her twenty-one-year-old brother, Bryce, didn't go to church anymore. At first it was because he worked Sundays at The Home Depot, but then, after a while, he quit coming, even when he wasn't working.

Because it was Scout Sunday, the deacons gave talks about the values of Scouting in their lives.

*I've heard these same talks every year since I can remember,* Megan thought.

She took the program for the meeting and drew four lines to set up a game of tic-tac-toe with Brianna. It was something they'd been doing for years. She showed Brianna the paper.

"Only if I can be first," Brianna whispered.

"You're always first," Megan answered.

"That's because I win. The one who wins gets to be first the next game."

"The reason you win is because you go first all the time."

Brianna smiled sweetly. "Who else have you got to play this game with?"

Megan shrugged, and they started to play, passing the paper back and forth as they made their marks.

A few minutes later, Brianna stopped their game long enough to listen to the special music. A girl Brianna's age sang a hymn.

"You're way better than her," Megan whispered.

Brianna smiled. "I know."

Megan studied her sister's face. They didn't look much like sisters. Megan was darker in complexion and had more of a dramatic look to her. Brianna was like the cheerleader for the whole human race. She talked with more energy and volume and enthusiasm than any of her friends. And she had a gift for comedy. Just watching her was enough to make anyone smile, even more so now that she had developed her own rap vocabulary.

Privately at least, Megan had begun to think of her parents as Walter and Carolyn. They were less threatening that way. *Walter and Carolyn*, she thought. *If you're named Walter, what else can you end up being but a joke to the rest of the world? How did those two ever get together? Mom says they became friends first and then they fell in love.*

Sometimes when they talked about their courtship, her father would say with a big smile, "You never know what a little friendliness can get you."

She'd grown up listening to her dad, a sales representative, talking on the phone, saying, "Good morning, this is Walt from Consolidated Industries. How's it going? Say, I was wondering . . ."

As critical as she was of her father, she found it difficult to be too hard on her mother. *She's still pretty, even though she's been doing her hair the same way for as long as I can remember. I remember when she seemed so tall, and now she's the shortest one in the family.*

The girl finished her song and the game of tic-tac-toe continued.

Brianna, when she won, which she always did when she was first, leaned over and whispered, "I took care of it, right?"

"You hottie," Megan whispered back, a phrase she'd learned from Brianna.

Megan skipped Sunday School because it was boring. She went to Young Women, though, because the news would get back to her parents if she weren't there.

Before Young Women began, Alexis, the Laurel class president, approached her. "We're having a presidency meeting right after church. Can you come?"

Megan was the secretary of the Laurel class. "I'm not sure. Probably not. Sorry."

Alexis paused. "I called yesterday morning but you were gone. I left a message."

"Sorry, I didn't get it."

"We could meet at my house later today, if that would work out better for you."

"No, you go ahead."

Alexis looked troubled. "Is anything wrong?"

"No, why do you ask?"

"No reason." Alexis looked directly into Megan's eyes.

"What?" Megan snapped.

Alexis pursed her lips. "Nothing. You just seem different today, that's all."

"I'm the same as I've always been."

In her Laurel class the lesson was about the importance of staying true to the standards of the Church. To keep her mind occupied, Megan took a piece of paper and wrote Kurt's name over and over.

As they drove home from church, her mother asked how their classes had been.

"Real good," Megan said.

"What was your lesson about?" her mother asked.

"Keeping the standards," Megan said.

All afternoon she stayed by the phone, hoping Kurt would either call or come over to see her, but he didn't, so she took a nap and then watched some reruns of *Friends*. She'd taped all the episodes so she could watch her favorite programs any-time she wanted. Someday, she wanted to have a life like the cast on the show.

◆　　◆　　◆

The family waited until Bryce got home from work before they had their big meal on Sunday.

He always entered a room like he was a cop making a drug bust.

"Hey, bro, what's happenin'?" Brianna asked.

"Don't talk to me about work! I hate working Sundays."

Bryce was the tallest one in the family. He had a high-domed

28

forehead and a strong jaw. He prided himself on his barrel chest and what he called his "washboard abs," something he had developed by buying every ab machine offered on infomercials in the past year. Most of them were now stored in the storage shed next to the house.

Bryce went to wash up before supper.

Brianna had gone to a dance the night before and wanted to talk about it as only she could do. "Well, this hottie Derin was talking to me, and I was like, 'Wow, he way is diggin' me,' so I was all, 'Hey, pap, what up, stud?' So he was all, 'Not much, mama, how you doing?' So we talked, right? And then when I was making my cool exit, I tripped. So I turn to him and I'm all, 'Good thing I didn't just trip and look stupid, huh?'"

"Please pass the mashed potatoes," Walter said.

Bryce returned to the dining room and sat down. "Why do you talk like that?" he asked Brianna.

"Like what?" Brianna asked.

"You know what I'm talking about. You think it's cool, but it isn't. It's stupid."

"How do you want me to talk?" Brianna asked.

"Like a normal person."

"Yeah, right," Brianna said. "Like you're the expert on normal."

"What went wrong at work?" Carolyn asked.

Bryce shrugged. "Sundays are when all the desperate women come out."

"Desperate women? I don't understand," Walter said.

"You show me a woman wearing tight jeans and a too-small tank top who says she needs a five-eighths socket wrench, and I'll show you a desperate woman."

"Are you saying a woman can't buy a wrench?" Megan asked.

"No, I'm not saying that. I can tell the ones who are trolling for men though. They've spent at least four hours

29

getting ready. They wander around the store looking like they're lost, hoping to find a man to help 'em. But they never buy anything. And some of them have left kids at home with a sitter."

"Are they looking for a husband?"

"They're looking for anything they can find. My favorite time to work is Mondays, where all you see are contractors buying supplies for the week. But not Sundays."

"If you didn't work Sundays, you could come to church," Carolyn said gently.

Bryce smiled. "I don't hate Sundays that much, but keep trying, Mom."

After they finished eating, they read one chapter from the Book of Mormon. It was a Sunday tradition.

"I'd like to interview each of my children today," Walter said.

"Count me out," Bryce said, getting up. "I'm going to help a friend sheetrock."

"Megan, how about if we start with you, and then I'll do Brianna."

Megan had grown up having monthly interviews with her father. The last time she'd been totally honest in talking to him had been when she was in the ninth grade. He'd asked if she had any questions about sex, and she'd asked him a question about something she'd heard in school that someone had done. It flustered him so much that he had to leave the room for a glass of water. When he came back, he said, "I really don't think you should be thinking about things like that."

"It's just something I heard at school, that's all. I just wanted to know what it is and what the Church teaches about it."

"The Church is against anything like that. That's all you need to know."

From that moment on, she began holding back from him.

And now she said very little that would let him know what her life was really like.

But, still, they dutifully went through the ritual once a month.

This interview always took place at the dining room table. Everyone in the family knew to stay away during these times.

"How are things going for you?" he asked. He would be going to a court of honor later that day and was still wearing his too-tight Scout shirt.

"Just fine, Daddy. Just fine." She looked at all the badges he had on his shirt and wondered why he insisted on disgracing himself so publicly.

"Your mother says that on Friday night you went sailing with a boy and when the wind went down you couldn't get back, so you and the boy stayed the night in his boat."

"Yes, Daddy, that's true. We both felt bad about it. Oh, in case you're wondering, nothing happened. We didn't even kiss."

"Well, that's good to hear. Some boys might have tried to take advantage of a situation like that."

"I know, but I'd never spend time with a boy like that."

"You can't always tell these days."

"I'm real careful, Daddy."

"Good, I'm glad to hear that." He cleared his throat. "There's one more thing. Your mother says she's not happy with some of the clothes you've been buying lately."

"Like what, Daddy?"

"She says you bought a tank top with your last paycheck."

"I did, and I know that doesn't sound very modest, but, the thing is, I'm going to always wear a T-shirt over it, so it's not that bad."

"Oh, I see. I didn't know that." He seemed puzzled. "If you always wear a T-shirt over it, then why'd you buy it?"

"It's what people are wearing these days. Except they wear it without the T-shirt. But not me."

Walter cleared his throat nervously a couple of times. "Sometimes a boy will get a certain . . . message when a girl wears immodest clothes. It might not be the kind of a message a girl like you wants to give."

"I know all about that, Daddy. We talk about it all the time in Young Women."

He gave a sigh of relief. "Well, good, I'm glad you know." He got up and got himself a glass of water. "You want any?"

"No thanks."

He took a big gulp and sat down. "One more question. How are you doing in regard to chastity?"

"Fine, Daddy. Everything's fine."

He seemed relieved. "Good. Do you have any questions for me?"

"No. Like I said, we cover all that in Young Women."

"What about the Word of Wisdom? Any problems there?"

"Not really." She chuckled. "Except . . . I shouldn't have had so much dessert today."

He laughed, patting his stomach. "Well, I don't think we want to get into that. If we do, I'll end up having to go on a diet."

"You're just fine the way you are, Daddy."

"Well, I should watch what I eat more than I do." He finished off the rest of his water. "I think we're done, unless you have anything you want to talk to me about."

"No, Daddy. Everything's going real good for me now."

"I suppose you'll be applying for college any day now, won't you? You think you might go to BYU?"

"I'm not sure my grades are good enough."

"How about BYU-Idaho?"

"I don't know. I guess I could try."

"Or if not that, you could go to a California school where they have a strong institute program."

"That's a good idea, Daddy. I'll look into that, too."

He stood up and hugged her. "You're growing up so fast. A year from now you'll be away to college. We'll miss you."

"Thank you, Daddy. I'll miss you, too."

"Go tell Brianna I'm ready for her."

"Yes, Daddy. Thank you for taking the time to talk to me."

"My pleasure. I know I'm not home much during the week, and then with Scouts I'm gone some Friday nights and Saturdays, but I want you to know you're my number one priority."

"I know that, Daddy."

She was relieved that was over for another month.

♦　　♦　　♦

Monday nights were usually slow after hours at Leo's Pizza, and the next day was no exception. The weekend had taken its toll on Thomas's friends, but Megan showed up. She wanted to spend some time with Thomas.

They worked in the kitchen cleaning up. She was on her hands and knees washing the worst spots while Thomas was scrubbing down the counters with soap and water. He always told her she didn't need to do the floors on her hands and knees, but she liked to do it the way her mother had taught her on their kitchen floor at home.

"So, how was it with Kurt?" he asked.

She tried being low-key. "It was okay."

"Just okay?"

She smiled. "Better than okay, actually."

"Tell me all about it."

Megan told him everything.

"So, you stayed the night with him on his boat?"

"Yeah, but nothing happened. I slept in the cabin, and he slept under the stars."

He grinned. "Yeah, right."

"It's the truth."

He quit smiling. "I believe you. I was just teasing. So, do you like him?"

"Yeah, actually, I do."

"What do you like most about him?" Thomas asked.

She thought about it before answering. "He really opened up to me. I mean once you get to know him, he's not anything like the way he comes across. At least not with me."

Thomas chose his words carefully. "Did he tell you that he was opening up more to you than anyone else he's ever known?"

"What if he did?"

"Well, that's great . . . if it's true. I mean it might just be what he says to girls to get them to trust him."

"He's not like that."

Thomas held back saying more. "Great then. I'm happy for both of you."

"You don't trust him, do you?"

"I don't know. I'm not sure what to think."

"I'll be careful."

"Good. I think you should."

She was standing next to Thomas at the sink while he worked. He was wearing a ragged, gray T-shirt. She slowly ran her hand down his arm. It was part of a running joke between them. The hair on his arms was like the hair on his head—dense and coarse. She'd once told him that if an ant ever fell on his arm the other ants would have to send out a search team to find him.

"Well, did you find that silly ant yet?" he asked her.

"No, it's still lost. What are you going to do after you graduate?"

"I guess I'll take some classes and work here at night. What about you?"

"I don't know."

"Harvard hasn't called yet?" he asked.

"No, they must have lost my number."

"Mine, too. You and me, we're pretty much average, right? No better, no worse."

"I want to be more than average," she said.

"Look on the bright side. We're way ahead of those who are below average."

She smiled. "You sure know how to cheer a girl up."

"Glad to help out."

They stepped back and admired the clean kitchen. "We're almost done here," he said. "We just need to wipe off the tables and take out the garbage."

"I can start on the tables."

A few minutes later, Thomas joined her in the eating area as they wiped the tables clean.

"Thomas, can I ask you a question? How come you don't drink?"

He shrugged his shoulders. "Drinking messed up my cousin pretty bad. He got drunk and ran his car into a bridge. So now he's in a wheelchair. I was nine years old when it happened. After that, I decided I wasn't ever going to even start."

"That's good. One other question."

"Okay."

"You don't go after girls like some guys do, you know, to see how much you can get."

"No, that's not my style."

"How come?"

"The girl I marry deserves better than that."

"You'd make a great Mormon. Better than me, that's for sure."

"Being religious isn't my style, either."

They finished up opposite each other, wiping up the same table. "Can I ask you a really personal question?" Thomas said.

"Sure, I guess so."

"You don't have to answer it if you don't want to. What are you going to do when Kurt suggests you sleep with him?"

"Thomas! We haven't even kissed yet. Besides, I'm not that kind of girl."

"It might be just a matter of time, though. So answer my question."

She shook her head. "I don't know."

"You'd better start thinking about it."

"I guess it would depend."

"What would it depend on?"

"If I really cared for him."

"So what you decide will be based on how you feel about him?"

"Yes, I guess it will."

"Sure, why not?" he said, walking away from her.

"You think I shouldn't?" she called out after him.

"I didn't say that, did I?"

"I know, but the way you're acting I can tell."

"Once you start that way with him, you'll never have time for me."

"That's not true, Thomas, I'll always have time for you."

He shook his head. "I know how these things work." He started for the kitchen again and then turned to her. "It's okay, though, as long as you're happy. That's the main thing, right? To be happy."

She wanted to assure him she'd always be there for him, but she wasn't sure she could guarantee it.

*I wonder how this will turn out*, she thought.

♦   ♦   ♦

From then on, because Thomas had raised the question, Megan tried to decide what she'd say if Kurt wanted her to sleep with him. Even after two weeks of dating him and thinking about it, she still couldn't make up her mind.

To help her decide, she picked up a copy of teen a magazine at a convenience store. An article entitled "Your First

Time" advised a girl not to rush into something like that but ended with "You'll know when it's right."

Whenever she watched *Friends,* the answer seemed to be, *If you like the guy and he seems really nice, and if your friends like him, too, and if you want to, then it's okay.*

She knew what the Church taught, but all the people who talked about chastity in the Church were old people with families—like her bishop, or her Laurel adviser. She couldn't imagine any of them being tempted. And it was gross to think about any of them making love. *Things are different now than when they grew up.*

*Kurt isn't even a member of the Church. If I start trying to change him, he's not going to want to spend any time with me. Is that what I want?*

After a lot of thought, she finally decided that if she felt that Kurt really loved her, she might agree to sleep with him.

When she told Thomas her decision, he got mad at her. "Are you saying that all any guy has to say to you is, 'I really like you,' and you'll sleep with him?"

"I didn't say *any* guy. We're talking about Kurt."

"How can you base a decision like that on what a guy says to you? Don't you know that some guys will say anything to get what they want?"

"Kurt's not that way."

"No, that's just it. He is. Why don't you base your decision on some kind of overriding principle, not just on your feelings?"

"You're just jealous."

"That's not true. I just don't want you to get hurt, that's all."

"I won't get hurt. I know what I'm doing."

"Why don't you talk to some of the girls Kurt's been with? Why don't you ask them what he's like?"

"I have," she lied.

"What did they say?"

37

"Nothing bad. Look, I can take care of myself, okay?"

"No, that's just it, you can't. You'll get hurt and then you'll come crawling back to me."

"That's not going to happen. I can take care of myself."

"Good-bye, Megan. I can't stand to sit by and let this happen to you. I can finish up here by myself tonight . . . and from now on."

Megan left Leo's Pizza that night for good.

♦　　♦　　♦

Megan continued to see Kurt. Sometimes when they were together, he opened up to her like he'd done the first night on his dad's boat, but at other times he seemed preoccupied.

"Is anything wrong?" she asked one night.

"No, not really. It's just that I've been working really hard writing code for a new computer game. After doing that for ten hours straight, it's hard to let it go. My dad's really excited about what I've done so far. He's thinking of us starting up our own company. So that'd be great."

There was one thing she could do to get him to focus totally on her, and that was kissing. At those times she had his undivided attention. She loved the feeling of having power over him. "You thinking about computers now, Kurt?" she once teased him.

"No, not at all."

"Really? What a surprise? So what are you thinking about?" she asked.

"You. Just you."

She grinned. "I know."

Sometimes things got a little crazy, but she was always able to stop what they were doing before it got out of control. And he never pushed beyond what she felt comfortable with. The only trouble was that the more time they spent together, the harder it became to hold the line.

She didn't worry about it too much when she was with him. But there were times when she worried where this was going. Like one morning when she woke up and saw her sister Brianna kneeling by her bed saying her prayers.

Brianna thought Megan was sleeping, and so she was saying her prayer out loud in a soft voice. Megan pretended to still be asleep and listened to the prayer.

"Please help me live the commandments," Brianna said softly.

*I never pray anymore,* Megan thought. *I should. It might help me. What would I pray for? To be happy. That's all I want out of life. Just to be happy.*

She didn't feel comfortable attending Young Women anymore because every lesson seemed to be on morality. *Why do they have to keep harping on that all the time? If I hear one more lesson about wilted flowers and the symbolism of white dresses, I'm going to puke.* She kept going, though, because if she didn't go word would get back to her parents, and she didn't want them to get on her case or be suspicious.

When she and Kurt first started seeing one another, Kurt preferred to pick her up at school or at her work, because then he didn't have to deal with her parents. But when her father found out she was continuing to see him, he said he wanted to meet Kurt.

"My dad wants to meet you," she told Kurt one night.

"Why?"

"He just does."

Kurt shrugged his shoulders. "All right, I'll do it. Tell me about your dad."

She told him more about his involvement in Scouting and about his job as a salesman.

That Friday night Kurt dropped by Megan's house to pick her up. Her dad answered the door, but her mother rushed in to have a chance to get better acquainted.

Megan wasn't quite ready when Kurt arrived. By the time

she entered the living room, he was telling Walter about how much he had enjoyed Scouting when he was a boy. Her parents were hanging on his every word.

"So, you're an Eagle Scout?" her father asked.

"Oh, yes, that's where I got my love for the outdoors."

"I can't tell you how many college-age, young men have come back to tell me their Scouting days gave them not only a love for hiking and backpacking but a solid foundation for life."

"That's certainly the case with me," Kurt said. "And not only that. What I know about patriotism, obedience to laws, respect for authority, and an appreciation for the spiritual side of life all came from Scouting."

Walter was fairly beaming.

Megan was standing in the doorway to the living room watching Kurt win her dad over. "Well, I'm ready."

Kurt stood up and shook hands with Walter. "I've really enjoyed getting to know you both."

"Since you have an appreciation for spiritual things, what would you think about hearing something about what we believe?" Walter asked.

"Well, that'd be great. Megan has already told me a few things about your church. It sounds very interesting."

"We'll see if we can arrange to have our missionaries come around sometime and teach you," her father said.

"Great. I'm looking forward to it."

A few minutes later, they were on the road. They drove to his dad's sailboat, then sailed out into the bay and followed the coast to a secluded cove where Kurt threw out the anchors and cooked them steak over a charcoal grill.

Megan sat in the boat, sipping wine and watching him. She loved the confidence and skill Kurt demonstrated as he prepared their food. And when she asked if she could help, he wouldn't let her.

After eating they drank some more wine and listened to music and watched a glorious sunset.

At nine-thirty they went swimming off the boat for half an hour.

While they held onto a float in the water, he kissed her and then whispered, "You know how I feel about you, don't you? I think about you all the time." He was nuzzling her neck with his lips.

The closeness made her shiver. "I'm the same way."

"Since we both feel the same way, and this is such a special night, why don't we do each other a really big favor?" He was smiling as he said it.

*This is it,* she thought. *I knew it was coming. I just didn't know when.*

There was just one thing left to find out. "Do you love me, Kurt?"

He laughed. "I think you know the answer to that, don't you?"

"Yes, I do."

"Let's go back to the boat then."

They swam to the boat, dried off, then went in the cabin, and she gave in to him.

When it was over, she wanted to stay in his arms all night and never leave him, but at ten-thirty he got up, dressed, and slipped out of the cabin and pulled up the anchor and prepared to leave.

"Are we leaving?" she asked a minute later.

"Yes. I think it's better if we don't stay out too late tonight."

"Why's that?"

"We don't want your parents to be suspicious, do we?"

On the way home, she wanted to talk, but he didn't say anything. She couldn't figure it out. She thought that what they'd done would bring them closer together.

She didn't know how to even begin a conversation. Finally she asked, "Are you really an Eagle Scout?"

He looked at her and scowled. "Why are you asking me that?"

"I just wanted to know."

"Well, it's a stupid question."

"Well, just tell me and then we'll talk about something else."

"What do you think?"

"I don't know what to think. That's why I asked."

"No, I'm not an Eagle Scout. I just said that to impress your father."

She wasn't sure why, but she felt very depressed. "That's what I thought."

"Then why did you ask the question?"

"I was just curious, that's all. It's not important."

She did have another question, though, but she didn't have the courage to ask it. The question was, *What lies have you told me just to set me up for tonight?*

"You do love me, don't you?" she asked.

She'd seen the look before. When he was upset or angry, he clamped his jaw tight. It wasn't easy to detect, but there was a set of muscles along his jawline, which became visible. Other than that, he left no clue how the question affected him.

He drove silently for a time and then turned to her, reached for her hand and kissed it. His jaw muscles were relaxed once more. "You know how I feel about you. It's even more now than ever before, because of tonight. This was your first time, wasn't it?"

"Yes," she said timidly.

"That makes it even more special to know that I was the first."

She nodded.

A minute later he looked at his watch, let go of her hand, and began driving faster.

They pulled into her driveway just after midnight. In spite of his assurances, she felt confused.

"Call me in the morning," she said as he walked her to the door.

"I've got a few things I have to do tomorrow, but I'll call you as soon as I can," he said.

He held her in his arms and whispered in her ear, "Thank you for a wonderful night. You're the best."

As soon as she got in the house, she hurried upstairs, took a shower, and then crawled into bed without turning on the light. Brianna was already asleep.

Megan couldn't sleep. She kept going over in her mind what had happened that night. At first she tried to focus on the closeness she'd felt with Kurt. But something else kept nagging at her. *I've done the one thing I've been warned all my life not to do. Now what happens? Do I go to church on Sunday and pretend nothing has happened? How can I sit through church anymore knowing what I've done? I knew this is against the teachings of the Church, but I did it anyway.*

*The reason I did it is because I love Kurt. And when you love someone, you want him to be happy. I knew that doing it would make him happy. And it did for a few minutes. And then he turned weird. Like he couldn't get rid of me fast enough. I don't understand that.*

At ten the next morning, a Saturday, thinking that Kurt might drive over and surprise her, she carried her phone into the bathroom. While she did her hair, she kept listening for his call.

At eleven-thirty she finished putting on her makeup and got dressed. She was scheduled to work at Burger King, at one-thirty.

At twelve o'clock she went in the kitchen and made herself a sandwich and ate it in her room. *He probably slept in this morning. That's why he hasn't called yet. But I'm sure*

43

*he's up by now. He's probably taking a shower and getting ready. And then he'll call.*

She half expected Kurt to drop by and see her at work, not to stay, just to say hello and maybe tell her he'd been thinking about her all day, and with a private wink telling her how much the night before had meant to him, and then asking when she got off work so they could spend some more time together.

But he never showed up.

She worked until eight and then went home. She asked if Kurt had phoned but was told nobody had called for her.

At nine-thirty that night, feeling abandoned because she hadn't heard from Kurt, she called his home.

"Is Kurt there?"

"No, he went kayaking with his friends," his mother said.

"Well, do you know when he'll be home?"

"He took his sleeping bag and camping gear, so I'd guess he won't be home tonight," his mother said.

"Oh."

"Would you like me to give him a message when he comes home?" his mother asked.

"Yes, please. Tell him Megan called."

"Megan, all right, I'll tell him. Are you the girl from the kayaking club?"

"No, I'm another Megan."

"Oh, of course. Look, maybe you'd better give me your number."

By the time she hung up, she was near tears. *How many Megans does he know? Did last night mean anything at all to him? Why doesn't he call? Will he ever call? Will I ever see him again?*

On Sunday she went to church with her family as usual. She skipped Sunday School but forced herself to go to Young Women, although it nearly made her physically ill to have to stand and recite the Young Women's theme. She wanted to

44

run out of the room and never come back, but she couldn't because Brianna would see it, or her Laurel adviser, a friend of her mother, would notice it, and questions would be asked.

Alexis sat next to her in Laurel class. "Can you meet after church for just a few minutes? We need to plan an activity with the priests quorum. It's coming up in two weeks."

"I can't meet. I have to go home."

"How about later this afternoon then?"

"No, we're having a family activity this afternoon."

"We can work around it. Just call me when it's over. We'll even come to your place if you want."

"Why do you need me?" Megan asked. "I'm just a secretary. Anyone can do that."

"You're not just a secretary. You're part of the presidency. And you always have such good ideas. I need your help."

"Sorry, but I can't help you," she said, feeling a sense of loss and estrangement.

The first thing she did when she got home after church was to check to see if there were any phone messages.

There were no messages.

At three-thirty, while she was taking a nap, there was a knock on her bedroom door.

*It's Kurt!* she thought excitedly.

"Yes?" she asked.

It was her mother. "Alexis is here to see you."

*I told her I couldn't meet with her. Why can't she get the hint? I don't want to have anything to do with her anymore.* She sat up. *If I don't at least talk to her, Mom might start getting suspicious.*

"Okay."

Her mother opened the door for Alexis to enter. "I'm sorry if I came at a bad time."

"It's all right. I needed to get up anyway. When are the others coming?"

"They're not coming. I came to visit you."

45

"Why?"

Alexis closed the door and came over and pulled up a chair next to where Megan was sitting on the bed. "I'm worried about you."

"There's no reason to be."

"You sure?"

"Of course."

"We are friends, aren't we? I mean, if you had a problem, you'd tell me, wouldn't you?"

"If I had a problem, I'd tell you. Right now my only problem is you grilling me about whether or not I have a problem. Well, I don't. I'm still the crazy, girls camp tentmate I was when we were Beehives."

Alexis gave a sigh of relief. "Good. I'm glad to hear it." She stood up. "Well, I'd better be going."

"Thanks for coming."

They walked outside together. While standing in the driveway, Alexis announced her plans for the summer. She would be leaving right after graduation to attend summer school at BYU. "What are you going to do after you graduate?"

"I'm not sure yet," Megan said.

"You should come with me to Utah. We'd have a great time together."

"We would. That's for sure. I'll think about it, okay?"

Privately, Megan was glad she'd soon be graduated and that Alexis was moving away and that she'd have the freedom to live her life the way she wanted to without any interference from anyone.

♦　　♦　　♦

On Monday, in school, she saw Thomas in the hall, but she turned her head and pretended not to see him because she didn't want to talk to him. Because if she did, he would find out what had happened. She could never hide anything from Thomas.

Kurt called on Monday night, at seven-thirty, just after family home evening. She had come very near to deciding not to see him again. She was not only mad at Kurt, but the guilt was eating her up. She'd have to go to her bishop and tell him what had happened and try to get her life back on course again.

Brianna answered the phone, then handed it to her. "It's for you."

"Who is it?" Megan mouthed.

"How should I know? It's a boy."

"Hello?" she said.

It was Kurt. "Hey, I just got back from my trip! I thought I'd call and see how you're doing."

"Okay, I guess," she said sullenly, taking the phone to her room so she could have some privacy.

"You don't sound all that great."

"Why didn't you call earlier?"

"Like I said, I went kayaking with some friends, and we were having so much fun we decided to stay an extra day."

"Oh."

"You should've been there."

"I wasn't invited."

"It's just an expression."

"I know."

"But if it's any consolation, there weren't any other girls there. Just guys."

"Oh."

"The reason I called was to see if you'd like to go sailing tonight. It'll be a perfect night for it. I can have you back by ten o'clock."

"I'm not really in the mood for sailing."

"What would you like to do then? Your choice."

She still felt betrayed. "I'm not sure."

"I just wanted to tell you that Friday night was really good for me."

She didn't say anything.

"How was it for you?" he asked.

The feeling of being abandoned afterward overshadowed any physical pleasure she might have experienced. But she knew he wouldn't understand that, and she didn't want to hurt his feelings. "It was really good," she lied, trying to sound as though she meant it, but, at the same time, feeling like she was not being honest with herself.

"For me, too," he said, then paused before adding, "So I was wondering if we could get together and do something tonight."

She wasn't sure what to do. The reason she had done what she'd done with Kurt was because she wanted to show him how much she cared for him. It wasn't just because she wanted to experience the physical act of love. She wondered if he would have been equally happy with any girl.

She had thought that giving in to him would make their love grow deeper, but now she wondered if all it had accomplished was that from now on, every time they got together, he would expect them to be intimate.

Even so, she was reluctant to stop seeing him because, if she did, it would mean that her decision to give herself to him the first time had been a mistake.

*I have too much invested in this to just quit now,* she thought. *Maybe in time he'll come to love me the way I want him to.*

"You still there?" he asked.

*I know what I'll do. I'll show him so much love he'll never want to leave me.*

With that decided, she said, "You know what, Kurt? I've changed my mind. I'd love to go sailing with you tonight."

"Good girl. You won't regret it."

Even then, she wasn't sure that was true.

# 3

I'm expecting a baby! Can you believe it?" Melissa
Partridge, barely twenty years old, who had been married
in the San Diego Temple only two months before,
announced to the other Young Women leaders in her ward
just before a presidency meeting.

"That's wonderful! Congratulations!" Colleen Butler, the
Young Women president, herself the mother of five children,
exclaimed as she hugged Melissa.

"It must have happened on our honeymoon!" Melissa,
red-faced, said with a huge grin. "Can you believe that? It
might have even happened on our wedding night! We were
totally blown away when we found out. We thought it'd take a
whole lot longer."

Ann Marie Slater, thirty years old, the tall, blonde, and
usually very in-control first counselor in the presidency,
fought to keep her composure.

Melissa continued. "When we were talking about getting
married, we talked about maybe having six children. But we
didn't think we'd start so soon."

The Young Women president and Melissa were still hugging.

*What if everyone else hugs her?* Ann Marie thought. *What will I do? I'll have to hug her, too. I can do it if I have to. I can do anything if I have to. I can go to baby showers. I can look at new babies when a new mother shows one to me. I can send little notes to new mothers. I can listen to a child cry and not rush over to pick her up. I can do anything. Anything except get pregnant, that is.*

To her great relief, the other counselor as well as the age group advisers did not hug Melissa, and so all Ann Marie had to do was force a smile and return her eyes to the agenda they would soon be covering in their planning meeting.

The meeting began with a prayer and minutes and then they proceeded through the agenda. When asked, Ann Marie gave her report on the upcoming service activity.

An hour and a half later, the meeting was over. There were refreshments, but Ann Marie made some excuse why she needed to get home.

She pulled into the driveway of her home ten minutes later, activated the remote, and closed the door of the garage.

She could hear Weston, her husband, cheering as he watched an NBA game with his thirteen-year-old nephew and ten-year-old niece from Utah, who were visiting with their parents from Pleasant Grove. They'd arrived in time for supper and would be staying three more days.

*I can't go in like this*, she thought. *I need a few minutes to try to get better control of my feelings. If I go in the way I am, I'll burst into tears.*

She cupped her hands to her face and permitted herself to have a few minutes of sorrow.

*All I've ever wanted from the time I was a little girl was to be a wife and mother someday. I never wanted a career like some of my friends.*

*Father in Heaven, what do you want from me? I never did*

50

*anything growing up that violated the law of chastity. I kept myself morally clean. I didn't even kiss a boy until I first kissed Weston shortly before we became engaged. We wanted a baby and, from our first night together on our honeymoon, didn't do anything to stop one from coming. So why won't you let me get pregnant when that's all I want?*

She ended her prayer. She'd said it all before, hundreds of times, and it never did any good.

*I'm not asking for anything. I've given up asking. God never hears my prayers. It doesn't matter how many times I ask. It never does any good.*

*When we were first married, being intimate with Weston was a celebration of our love for each other, but now it's something else.* She struggled with her thoughts. *Now it's a test, a test that I always fail at because I never get pregnant.*

They had gone to several doctors who specialize in helping couples get pregnant. They had kept a daily record of her temperature until she began to think of herself as a science project.

For the first couple of years of marriage, Ann Marie had stayed at home, fully expecting she would be getting pregnant soon. She wanted to be a stay-at-home mom, but after they'd purchased a home, Weston made an offhand comment that it would be nice to have a little additional income. And so, Ann Marie got a job as a secretary for an insurance agent. She worked full-time and soon became invaluable to her boss—efficient, careful, and friendly to everyone she dealt with.

"The best thing that ever happened to me is when I hired you," Burton McLaughlin, a portly man with an infectious smile, said to her nearly every week.

"I enjoy working for you, too," she said with a forced smile. *But it's not what I want. It's not what I expected my life to be.*

She searched in the glove compartment for a tissue but couldn't find one. She searched again through her purse to no

51

avail, so she did something she hadn't done for twenty years. She used her sleeve to wipe her face and nose.

*I am so pathetic, crying in the dark in a garage. I should go inside and sit down and watch the game with Weston's niece and nephew—both above average in intelligence, both extremely talented, both advanced for their age. And neither of them belonging to me or Weston.*

*It's not just me who's suffering from this. It's Weston, too. He's so good with kids. When he enters a room, they just gravitate to him. It's such a waste he's not a daddy.*

*I am of all women most grieved,* she said, quoting a scripture from the Old Testament, which now reflected her true feelings about her situation.

She used her other sleeve to wipe her face, then turned on the dome light and looked at her reflection in the mirror. Her eyes were puffy. *If I go in all cheerful and happy, then go to the kitchen and make some refreshments, nobody will notice.*

*I can't let them see me down,* she said. *In a couple of days, Weston's family will leave, and then I'll have a little time alone to feel sorry for myself.*

*But not now.*

*Melissa got pregnant on her honeymoon. It's not fair. Why couldn't God give that baby to Weston and me? Has he even heard our prayers? And if she was going to get pregnant so soon, why put her in our ward, and call her to work in Young Women, so I'd know about it? Why do I have to be around women who have babies?*

She sighed and opened the car door.

*I will put some of the cookies I made last Saturday on a plate. And make some lemonade. If I wait long enough, maybe by the time I go in the game will be over, and I can say I have a headache and go to bed.*

*And be asleep before Weston comes in.*

*Because I can't fake my feelings to him.*

*He always knows when I've had a hard day.*

52

She forced herself into motion, moved in the dark to the door leading into their house, and put on her best smile.

"I'm home!" she called out brightly.

# 4

MAY

Just after her eighteenth birthday, Megan had her annual interview with her bishop. Bishop Oldham was a giant of a man. Easily six-foot-four, he weighed well over two hundred pounds, and in his college days he had played basketball for BYU. But that was twenty years before. His only souvenir of his glory days was a pair of bad knees.

While some bishops might go on and on with small talk, Bishop Oldham, an engineer, although friendly, liked to get down to business right away when he interviewed.

"Any problems with the Word of Wisdom?" he asked.

"No, not at all."

"You understand what we mean by being morally clean, don't you?" he asked.

"Yes, of course," she said, her smile frozen on her face, hoping she was not blushing.

"What does it mean?"

"Bishop, I'm about to graduate from high school. I mean, it's not like I'm twelve years old. I do know what it means."

"Then tell me."

"Well, it means you don't watch bad movies, and you're careful who you date, you know, that they have good standards. And it means you don't let yourself get carried away with a guy, you know, physically. That's about it."

"You're dating someone now, aren't you?"

"Yes, I am. How did you know?"

"Brianna told me."

*What did Brianna say? Does she suspect anything?*

"I've been seeing a guy named Kurt off and on."

"Is he a member of the Church?"

"No, but he's really interested. He's talked about taking the missionary lessons."

"Tell me a little about him."

"Well, he's an Eagle Scout. He's a year older than me. He works for his dad. He writes code for computer games. He and his father have started their own company."

"Have you two had any problems with regard to chastity?"

"No, of course not. I'm usually home by eleven when I go out with him."

"So there's no problem with chastity?"

"No, not at all. Why do you keep asking?"

"I'm not sure. It's just, well . . . you seem a little nervous."

"Is my face red?"

"A little."

*Confess something,* she thought. *Something that doesn't matter.*

"Well, Bishop, to be perfectly honest, I did have a little bit of a problem with Kurt."

"What's that?"

"Well, about a month ago he talked me into having some coffee, just to see how it tasted. I knew that wasn't right, but I did it anyway. I feel really guilty about it now. But I just took a taste, that's all, and I'll never do it again."

The bishop seemed relieved it wasn't more serious.

A few minutes later, the interview was over.

55

When Megan left, she appeared cheerful and upbeat to him. But she only made it two blocks in the family car before she had to pull over. She felt sick to her stomach. *I can't do this anymore. I can't live a double life. It's tearing me up too much.*

And so, to get away from her family, a few weeks later, just after graduating from high school, she moved away from home into an apartment on the other side of town. She told her parents she was going to room with another girl. But there never was another girl. It was just a way to get them to agree to let her move out.

◆ ◆ ◆

## JULY

Megan sat hunched over a TV tray and ate her supper, a warmed up can of beef stew. While she ate, she watched one of her tapes of *Friends*. Her hair smelled of fried foods, and her skin felt greasy. All she wanted was to eat, take a shower, and go to bed.

She worked the morning shift at Burger King, and then, as her second job, assembled computers in a high-tech production line. It was mind-numbing work, tedious and boring.

She no longer went to church. It was easy to justify because she always scheduled herself to work Sundays.

*I wonder if Kurt will show up tonight. He'd better not. He knows how I feel about him showing up in the middle of the night and expecting me to welcome him with open arms.*

After watching *Friends*, she decided to clean up a little before taking a shower. She liked to keep her place neat and tidy. Kurt liked things that way. And she never knew when he'd show up.

The furnished apartment wasn't much, but it was all she could afford. On the outside the apartment building looked like it should be condemned, but inside it wasn't so bad. At first she had prided herself on making it look good. She bought posters to hang on the walls and hooked up her stereo. She had high hopes. She had even invited her mother and Brianna to come and see it. They came and were politely complimentary.

"Of course, it's not exactly what I had in mind, but I won't be here long. As soon as I get a better job, I'll move to some place better, some place overlooking the beach."

"Wouldn't that be nice," her mother said diplomatically.

The better job never came. With only a high school education and very few job skills, she was never considered for the jobs she really wanted.

Megan was always surprised how little was left over after a paycheck. Not enough to fix up her apartment. Not enough to take college night classes. Not enough to afford a better place to live. The old, beat-up car her parents had let her take always needed gas and repairs, and she couldn't believe how much the insurance cost.

She and Kurt had talked about getting their own apartment, but so far nothing had come of it. They'd looked at a couple of places but none of them seemed good enough for him. "It's probably better for me to stay at home," he said. "That way I can save up money so we can move into a really nice apartment someday."

Sometimes when Kurt dropped by, he stayed only part of the night because his friends and what they wanted to do always took precedence over her. At other times she didn't expect him, but he'd knock on her door, sometimes late at night, after she'd gone to bed.

The last time he showed up past midnight she told him it was too late for him to come in. He said he just wanted to talk to her for a few minutes. She gave in and let him in, and he ended up staying. But when she woke up the next morning, he was gone without even a note.

The closeness she had hoped for in their relationship wasn't there. They were, of course, close physically, but when that was over, it was to him almost like it had never happened. She was beginning to feel she was being used. *He takes me too much for granted,* she thought.

The company Kurt and his father had started was beginning to be very profitable. In many ways Kurt lived a charmed life. He could always get time off work, and he always had plenty of money. All his parents asked was that he stay out of trouble.

*What attracted me to him at first was that everything came easy to him. That was true of me, too,* she thought with a growing sense of bitterness. *I came easy, too.*

She turned off the TV and sat in her apartment in the dark and listened to the sounds coming from other apartments. Mr. Podolsky, in the apartment next door, was going through another of his coughing fits. He'd been wounded in the Vietnam War and hadn't worked since then. He'd been living in the same apartment since being released from the veteran's hospital in the mid-seventies. Mr. Podolsky still walked with a limp due to his war injury. He had no friends or family. He spent hours each day tending a small garden along the side of the building, not because it required that much care, but because he had nothing else to do. While he worked, he waited for someone to come by so he could lecture them about world events. He liked to talk about the corruptness of city, county, state, and federal officials. Megan had learned to avoid talking to him.

*He got lost in the system and nobody cares about him anymore, so now he's a prisoner here and will be until he dies, just like everyone who lives here. The same thing might be happening to me. What if I'm still here in ten years?*

In the other apartment next to her was Mrs. Capriatti, a dried-up, fragile woman in her eighties who never left her apartment. Megan had seen her once at her door, taking food from a boy who was delivering a week's worth of groceries to her in one small bag. Because Megan seldom heard anything from Mrs. Capriatti's apartment, she sometimes imagined the woman was dead but had not been discovered yet.

Once in a while she heard a man and woman on the floor above her arguing late at night, but she didn't know who they were.

*I hate living here*, she thought.

She felt betrayed. The only problem was she couldn't decide who to blame.

What she wanted from Kurt was not what she was getting. If anything, he was more detached now than before they'd become intimate.

*He's the master of putting his life in nice neat compartments*, she thought. *He's able to keep his life with his friends separate from his attachment to me. I'll never be a big part of his life as long as they're around. He's having too much fun to give them up. He likes having his physical needs met by me and spending the rest of his free time with his friends.*

*So what do I do? If I don't let him come and stay the night, then he'll quit coming around entirely. And if he does that, then what do I do? Move back home and admit to my family what's been going on in my life? I can't do that.*

*If we had our own apartment, if he'd give up going out night after night with his friends and spend more time with me. If it was more like we were . . .* She sighed . . . *If it was more like we were, well, married*, she thought. It was a bitter pill because it was what her mother had warned her about long ago.

*I'll make this work out. I won't let things stay the same. I'll get Kurt to go with me to find a place for the two of us to live, and then I'll be happy. Anything to get out of here. And then in a couple of years, we'll get married and everything will be fine.*

But even as she thought about it, she doubted if it would

ever happen. *Kurt wants the best of what life has to offer, but only if it requires no effort on his part.*

She brought strands of her hair to her nose and sniffed. She hated it when she smelled of greasy foods. *I'll clean up and then I'll take a shower and then I'll go to bed.*

In the tiny kitchen, she filled the sink with water to wash two days' worth of dishes. Because it was a warm night, she opened the window. It had begun raining. There was a screen on the window to keep the bugs out. Over the years its wooden frame had been painted permanently closed.

As she set the last dish to drain on the counter, she glanced out the window. In the light from the street lamp, millions of raindrops glistened, shooting out beams of colored light in all directions. It was the most beautiful sight she had ever seen.

Looking at the scene, she felt a longing for something she couldn't even define—something to fill the emptiness in her life. Tears welled in her eyes and, when she blinked, began running down her cheeks.

She dried the dishes and silverware while continuing to look out at the light show being put on by nature.

She wanted to pray. She closed her eyes and folded her arms the way she'd been taught in Primary. "Dear God . . ." she said quietly, then stopped because it sounded so out of place. "I can't even remember how to do this anymore. I used to pray all the time, but then I stopped because I was doing things that I knew were wrong. Thank you for the rain and the way the lights are shooting out. It's very beautiful. That's all I wanted to say. Amen."

Tears continued rolling down her cheeks. She realized she had more to say, much more.

She went to the bedroom and closed the door and fell to her knees.

"Oh, God, please help me. I'm trapped in this apartment and I'm trapped in my jobs and it seems like I'll never get out of this. I'm afraid I'll go the rest of my life trapped. Please, get me out of this. Please, dear God, please. Amen."

She ended the prayer, still embarrassed she'd done it. And then she sat down on her bed and tried to figure out where things had gone wrong.

◆    ◆    ◆

## AUGUST, FIRST MONTH

Megan stood in front of a display of home pregnancy tests in a mall drugstore. She'd come in just before closing, hoping there wouldn't be many customers. She didn't want to run into anyone she knew.

*It's probably nothing,* Megan thought, trying to subdue the panic that had been building in her over the past few days. *It happens all the time. Like that girl who sat next to me in English last year. She told me once that she missed all the time. All the time she was running cross-country, she missed every month. So missing once doesn't mean anything. It could be I'm just working too hard and not getting enough sleep.*

There were other signs, too, but most of them could be attributed to other causes. She was going to the bathroom more often than usual, and she felt sick in the morning when she woke up. Also, she seemed to be tired all the time.

She looked around to make sure nobody was watching her and then grabbed one of the packages and then almost as quickly returned it to the shelf. *I can't take this to the counter and have the clerk see it. I can't do it. There's no reason to even worry about it anyway. Women miss all the time. It doesn't necessarily mean . . .* she couldn't even think the words . . . *that there's a problem.*

Out of the corner of her eye, she saw someone with a shopping cart coming toward her. She panicked, moved ten feet down the aisle, reached for a package of foot powder, and then quickly walked in the same direction down the aisle so she wouldn't have to face the customer.

She waited at the far end of the store until the customer left the store. And then she walked quickly down the aisle and picked up a home pregnancy test kit and headed for the checkout counter.

*I can't have this be the only thing I buy because if it is, then the clerk might say something to me, and I couldn't stand that.*

She picked up some eyeliner and a copy of *Cosmopolitan* magazine.

Later that night, in her bathroom, she stared in disbelief at the results of the home pregnancy test, her heart pounding and her thoughts racing. *Oh, no! This can't be right! I can't be pregnant! There must be something wrong with the test.*

She felt like she was going to faint. She sat on the floor and fought the overwhelming panic.

*This can't be right! There must be a mistake! I must not have done the test right. That's it. That's what happened. It's because I've never done the test before. There must be some step I left out. I just have to find out what I did wrong and then get another test and do it again.*

She pulled out the directions and tried to read them, but she couldn't make her eyes focus. And then she broke down. She rested her arms on the side of the tub and sobbed. *What is Mom going to say? It will break her heart.*

Mr. Podolsky next door turned down his radio. "What's going on over there?" he yelled through the paper-thin walls.

"Nothing. Everything's fine."

"You sure?"

"Everything's fine. I just stubbed my toe, that's all."

The radio went back to loud again.

She washed her face and went into her room and crawled into bed and pulled the covers up. Lying there in the dark, she couldn't stop thinking. *I can't be pregnant. If I am, everyone will know. They'll think I'm a fool. I can't be pregnant. I'm not ready for this. And neither is Kurt. Someday we'll be ready to settle down and have kids, but not now.*

*I'm not worried about Kurt, though. If I am pregnant, we'll get married. He told me he'd take care of me if anything happened. It's just that we're not ready for this.*

*I don't trust these tests. I've got to find out for sure tomorrow. I've got to go to a doctor. I'll call in sick at Burger King, get the test, and then go to my second job. I'll feel a lot better once I know I'm not pregnant.*

♦　　♦　　♦

Megan's family had gone to the same doctor all her life, but she couldn't go to him because she was afraid it would get back to her mother, and she didn't want her mother to know about this. And so she picked a public health clinic out of the Yellow Pages.

She was hoping she would get there early enough that she wouldn't have to wait, but by the time she got there the waiting room was full. The woman next to her was there with four kids, all under six years old. The mother was impatient and spoke Spanish to them.

*I bet these people are all on food stamps. You can always tell.*

And then she began to wonder if anyone was looking at her, wondering why she was there. She looked around, but nobody seemed to be paying any attention to her.

She saw a girl her age, or maybe even younger, with a baby in her arms. Because Megan felt so isolated, she went over to sit by the girl, who wore no makeup and hadn't done anything that morning with her hair.

"Hello," Megan said.

"Hello," the girl said quietly, and then turned her gaze away from Megan.

"Busy place," Megan said.

"It always is."

"Really? This is my first time."

Megan tried not to be critical, but the baby obviously had a messy diaper. The smell was making her sick.

"Are you out of diapers?" Megan asked the girl.

"I brought two diapers, but he's gone through them already."

"Do you want me to go see if I can get you one at the desk?"

The girl avoided any eye contact but nodded.

Megan went to the desk to talk to the receptionist, a distracted woman who was shuffling papers.

"My friend has run out of diapers. Do you have one she can use?"

"We don't supply diapers."

"I know, but you must have one or two lying around. The thing is, it's stinking up the whole place."

The woman pointed to the end of the room. "You'll have to go see a nurse . . ." She pointed. "Over there."

"Thank you."

Megan walked to the back of the clinic. Finally, she found a nurse. "I need a diaper. It's for a girl in the waiting room. Her baby has a messy diaper, and it's smelling up the whole place. The secretary told me I could get one back here."

The nurse went into a storeroom and brought back a diaper and handed it to Megan.

Megan returned to the girl and gave her the diaper. "There you go."

The girl took it. "I have plenty of diapers at home. I just forgot to bring enough here, that's all."

"I understand."

"I am a good mother."

"I'm sure you are."

The girl went into the restroom to change her baby's diaper.

*That could be me in a year*, Megan thought but then quickly disregarded the thought. *No, not me. The worst that could happen would be that, if I am pregnant, Kurt and I will get married a little sooner than we'd planned. That's all. I will never be like that girl, alone, afraid, and dependent on government support.*

Forty minutes later a nurse with a loud voice that filled the clinic called her name. Hearing her name announced in a place filled with people she'd spent her life looking down on made Megan want to run away.

An hour later Megan was told by the doctor she'd been assigned, "Well, you are pregnant."

"Are you sure?"

"Positive. I assume you'll want an abortion. That's not something we do here, but I can give you some names of clinics where you can get it done."

"An abortion?"

"Yes. You're not married, are you?"

"No, but I'm sure that once . . . my . . ." She couldn't think of the right word. *Husband* wouldn't work. *Lover* seemed too intimate a word to use in front of a doctor.

"Your partner?" the doctor asked.

"Yes, once my partner finds out, he'll want to marry me."

The doctor raised his eyebrows. "Well, I'm not in a position to comment on that. But if it doesn't turn out for you, I'll give you a list of clinics where you can get an abortion."

Megan took the list and a short time later left the clinic and went out to her car and sat there in a stunned stupor.

*I've got to tell Kurt right away*, she thought. *He'll want to know. We have to talk about when we're going to tell our folks, where we're going to live, and when we're going to get married.*

She thought about waiting for Kurt to come around and

65

see her, but she didn't think she could wait that long because sometimes he didn't come by for days at a time. It was Friday, and on the weekends he was usually gone with his friends camping or sailing or hiking or whatever else they decided to do.

She didn't want to just leave a message because he never called back. He said it was because he never got the messages she left, but she was beginning to think that wasn't always the case.

She thought about going to where he worked and asking to talk to him, but she knew that would make him mad because he liked to keep each part of his life separate.

As she was trying to decide what to do, she realized her right hand was resting on her stomach. She looked down at her hand and tried to imagine what was taking place inside her, how many cells that would become her baby were being produced every hour, all of this going on without any conscious effort.

*Hundreds, maybe thousands, all coming together in some orderly way that nobody can understand. How can this be happening without me even knowing that it's going on?*

That helped her decide what to do. *I can't wait. I've got to see Kurt now. We need to talk. There's so much we need to do to get ready for our baby.*

She knew he wouldn't appreciate her interfering with him at work. She decided to call him first, so it wouldn't come as a complete surprise to him that she was coming.

She used her cell phone to call him.

He didn't say hello, just gave his last name.

"This is Megan. I need to talk to you . . . right away."

"Can't it wait until after work?"

"No, it can't."

"I'm in the middle of a big project."

"I know, but this is important. And it won't take long."

"What's it about?"

"We'll talk about it when I get there."

"What's so important you have to interrupt me at work?" He stopped, and then swore. He lowered his voice. "You haven't gone and gotten yourself pregnant, have you? I mean, is that what this is about?"

She was startled by the accusing tone in his voice. "I'll talk to you when I get there," she said.

"Because if you have—"

"I'll be there in ten minutes."

"I'll meet you at the front entrance."

"Bye then."

Even though she said she'd only be ten minutes, she couldn't drive right away because she was furious with him for the way he'd treated her over the phone. Her hands were shaking, and her face was flushed. She kept going over in her mind what he'd said. *You haven't gone and gotten yourself pregnant, have you? Like he didn't have anything to do with it. Like it's some germ you get if you don't wash your hands. Like everything is my fault.*

She showed up at the place he worked twenty minutes later than she said. She could see him through the front window, in the lobby, pacing the floor. *Good,* she thought, *let him sweat this out like I had to.*

"You're late," Kurt said the instant she walked in the door.

"Sorry."

"Let's get this over. I need to get back to work."

"Where can we talk?"

Kurt looked around. They were in the front office, but the secretary was away from her desk.

"Here's good. Say what you came here to say."

"Well, I went to the doctor today."

He rolled his eyes.

"And you were right. I am pregnant."

Kurt swore.

"I thought you'd better know right away so we can make preparations."

"Look, I'll pay for the abortion."

She was stunned. Her black eyes flashed, and she recoiled in horror. "Are you serious?" she asked, barely above a whisper.

"Of course, what else is there to do?"

"Well, we could get married."

"Forget it. I'm not marrying you."

"You said you loved me."

"I say a lot of things, but one thing I never said was that I'd marry you if you got yourself pregnant."

"Got *myself* pregnant? As I recall, you were there, too!"

He waved his hand in a gesture of disgust.

"You said you'd take care of me."

"And I will. I'll pay for the abortion."

"That's taking care of me?"

"Be reasonable, will you? The sooner you get this taken care of, the better off we'll both be. You don't want people knowing about this, do you? Your family? Your friends? It's best just to get it taken care of, and then we can both get on with our lives. That's the best way."

"The best for you, or the best for the baby?"

"It's not a baby. Besides, we never said anything about a baby."

"That doesn't matter now, does it?"

He threw up his hands. "Look, what do you want from me? Money? Is that it? How much? Just tell me and I'll get it for you . . . somehow."

"It's our baby, Kurt. Doesn't that mean anything to you?"

"It's not a baby, okay? It's just a growth that needs to be cut out, that's all, just a growth. People do this all the time, you know. It's not that bad. You go in, they take care of it, and you're back home the same day. And then there's nothing left to worry about. It's all taken care of. For good."

"How can you be so heartless and cruel?"

"I'm just looking out for myself. That's what both of us need to do now. For all I know, you got yourself pregnant to try to force me to marry you."

The secretary came into the office. Kurt took that as an excuse to leave. "I really have to get back to work now."

"Call me, okay?"

He waved her off and disappeared through the door to the carrels where everyone worked.

Megan left the office and went to her car, drove three blocks, pulled into a grocery store parking lot, and sat there stunned. She felt betrayed. And alone, with nowhere to go.

She sat in her car for two hours, and then, ten minutes before she was scheduled to show up at her second job, she called in sick.

Two hours later she was still there in her car outside the store. She might have stayed longer, but she needed to use the restroom. She looked at her reflection in the rearview mirror and tried to make herself look presentable, then opened the door and walked slowly toward the entrance of the store. She took her cell phone with her just in case Kurt came to his senses and called to apologize for the way he'd acted earlier.

As she slowly walked toward the entrance, it was like she'd been transported to a different planet. Everything seemed different to her, even things she'd taken for granted before. Like a mother with two kids coming out of the store with her cart filled with groceries, and one of the kids begging his mother to find the cookies they'd bought, and the mother saying she didn't know which sack they were in, and the boy, about five years old, asking her just to look because he wanted a cookie. And his two-year-old brother, perhaps only knowing a handful of words, but knowing the word *cookie,* who kept saying over and over, "Cookie? Cookie?"

The mother stopped and went through her groceries until she found the package of cookies. She opened it, gave a cookie to each of her boys, and, as a happy afterthought, took one for herself. Then, munching together, they made their way slowly to their car, happy with life.

Megan turned to watch them, paying particular attention to the two boys, both of them with light blond hair and a fair complexion. *A boy,* she thought, *I could have a boy. A boy like one of those two.*

She used the restroom and then drove back to her apartment. She fell asleep with the cell phone in her hand, watching *Friends.*

Kurt did not call all that week.

She continued to oppose abortion in principle, but there were times, when she felt sick to her stomach, or late at night when she couldn't sleep because of worrying about her situation, when she just wanted all her problems to go away, that she considered it as a possibility for her.

On Friday she was fired from her job assembling computers because she'd missed two days in a row.

With only her part-time job at Burger King in the mornings, she wouldn't have enough to pay her rent and buy groceries.

On Saturday morning she got sick at her job at Burger King and had to leave a customer in the middle of filling her order so that she could throw up. When she came back, her boss told her to go home until she was feeling better.

"I'm okay now."

"You don't look very good. I can't have you handling food if you're sick. Just go home. Come back when you're feeling better. I'll take you off the schedule for a couple of days."

"You don't understand. I need the money."

"I'm sorry, but I have to look out for my customers. I don't want you spreading germs."

Megan returned to her apartment.

*What am I going to do? The rent's due next week, and I don't have enough money. Where can I get it? I can't face this all by myself. It's too much. I can't tell my folks. It would kill*

70

*them to know. What other choice do I have but to go along
with what Kurt wants me to do?*

She called Kurt's parents' home at around two that afternoon. Kurt's mother told her he'd gone camping.

"This is Megan. He wanted me to bring him out some
climbing rope, but he didn't tell me where he'd be camping.
Can you help me?"

Kurt's mother said she wasn't sure where he was going
that weekend but did give her directions to where he and his
friends usually went.

Megan didn't feel well enough to travel right then, so she
took a nap.

When she woke up, it was late afternoon. She could hear
Mr. Podolsky coughing next door. He had his radio on.
Someone was talking about UFOs. " . . . and it was then the
spacecraft, or whatever it was, began hovering."

"What were you thinking when that happened?" the
moderator asked the caller.

"Well, I'll tell you, I was pretty scared."

Megan banged on the wall. "Mr. Podolsky, turn it down!"

He yelled back at her through the wall. "You should listen
to this. It's important to our survival."

"Turn it down!"

Mr. Podolsky turned the radio down.

She started to watch TV, surfing through the channels
until she had a familiar wave of nausea.

By the time she came out of the bathroom, she'd made her
decision. She'd go along with what Kurt suggested and get an
abortion.

An hour and a half later, she drove through the entrance
of the state park where Kurt's mother had said Kurt and his
friends might be spending the weekend. She drove slowly
from one campsite to another until she spotted his Jeep.

A group of maybe ten guys was sitting around the campfire, drinking beer and talking.

71

She knew Kurt wouldn't be happy to see her. He liked spending time with his friends, and she'd never been invited to go with him and his buddies. It was like a club, and no girls were allowed. She got out of the car and walked slowly toward the campfire. At first she didn't even know if Kurt was there.

They looked at her as if she were an intruder.

"I'm looking for Kurt," she said.

For a few moments no one said anything. Finally, one of the guys pointed. "He's down at the dock."

She turned away from the fire and walked slowly down a steep path, wishing she had a flashlight. As she approached the dock, she could hear Kurt talking to someone. It sounded very familiar to her. "Sometimes I just wish I could find someone I could really talk to about my feelings and dreams for the future."

"Really, Kurt? I feel the same way," a young girl replied.

Megan slipped on the graveled path and fell down on her seat, jarring herself.

"Someone's coming," the girl said.

Feeling stupid for falling, and angry, Megan stood up and forced herself to walk onto the dock. "If you want to talk about your hopes and dreams for the future, Kurt, I'd suggest you talk to me," she said, her voice sounding hollow and mechanical, like it was coming from a computer.

"I'd better go now, before my dad starts to wonder where I am," the girl said. She pushed past Megan and hurried up the path.

"Up to your old tricks again, right, Kurt?"

He ignored her question. "What are you doing here?"

"You said you'd pay for my abortion, right?" Megan asked.

"Yes, that's what I said."

"Good, because I've decided to do that. Can you write me out a check for it now?"

"I can't just give you a check now."

"Why not? You said you'd pay for it."

72

"Do you have insurance with your job?" he asked.

"No, I got fired."

"The insurance should still be in effect. I think you get thirty days, but I'm not sure. It's something you'd have to check out."

"Why bother? You said you'd pay for it."

"I will."

"Then give me the money. I want to get it taken care of tomorrow."

"I know, but if you have insurance and if they cover abortions, then I'd only have to pay the deductible. I mean there's no need to waste money over this, is there?"

"I don't want to wait. I want to get it done right away. Monday by the latest."

"I'm not sure we can get all this straightened out by Monday."

"Hey, I've got an idea," she said sarcastically. "Why don't you give up trying to come on to ninth-grade girls and playing 'Survivor' with your stupid friends for one weekend and help me get through this?"

"I don't see that there's any reason to rush this. I mean you can get an abortion anytime in the first three months, right?"

"It's making me sick. I can't work. I can't eat. And I'm about to lose my apartment. I want it taken care of right now. Even tonight, if I can find somebody who will do it. Just give me some money now, and we can sort out the insurance later."

"I'm afraid that with insurance it doesn't work that way."

"Are you going to pay for the stupid abortion or not?" she shouted.

"Not so loud. People can hear you."

"You think I care what your stupid friends think? Well, I don't. I want out of this. I want someone to make this all go away."

73

"Did you really think you could show up here and I'd just write you out a check?"

"So what are you saying, that you're not going to help me?"

"I'll help you, but only what your insurance won't pay. Do you know if your insurance will pay for it?"

"No, Kurt, I don't. Sorry. I hate to take up your valuable time like this."

"Sometimes you can get a doctor to bill you for something else that your insurance will pay for, like for appendectomy, and then he just goes ahead and does the abortion." He paused. "If you can find the right doctor, that is."

"How many girls have you had to do this for?"

He ignored the question. "I'm just saying you have to find out, first of all, if your insurance will pay for it, and then, if it won't, see if you can find a doctor that will charge you for something that the insurance will pay for."

"Why does all this fall on me?"

"Because it's your insurance policy, not mine. They won't give me information about your insurance. Look into it and then get back to me."

"Will you be with me when I . . . when I have my . . . my abortion?"

He pursed his lips. "Actually, that might be a problem. We're in the middle of a big project. One deadline after another."

She shook her head in disbelief. "Of course. I wouldn't want you to miss one of your deadlines."

"Get back to me when you find out about your insurance. I might be able to take half a day off when the doctor operates on you."

She started back up the path and then turned to glare back at him. "Can I ask you a question? Did you ever love me?"

He pursed his lips. "In my own way."

She nodded. "That's what I thought."

She drove much too fast down the winding mountain road leading to the highway, partly out of anger at Kurt and partly because she didn't care anymore if she lived or died.

◆　◆　◆

The next night, not wanting to end up in bed listening to Mr. Podolsky's radio, she decided to go to a movie. It was Sunday, but she decided to go anyway. Anything to get her mind off her own problems.

She ended up at a multiplex movie theater. There was a long line for the seven o'clock show. When she finally got to the front of the line, the gum-chewing ticket girl at the counter asked, "What movie?"

Megan had been so wrapped up in her own problems, she hadn't even thought about what movie she was going to see.

"Do I have to make a choice now?"

The girl rolled her eyes and gently slapped the counter with her hand. "Yes, I have to know. Otherwise we don't know when we've sold too many tickets."

"Well, what's showing?"

"It's up there, on the wall."

The first movie was an R-rated movie that, on the poster, promised to be a "raucous sex romp."

*That's part of the reason I'm in the fix I'm in now, because of movies like this one.*

The second movie was R-rated. "Is there much sex in that movie?" she asked, pointing at the poster.

The girl groaned and looked up at the ceiling as if seeking divine intervention. "Look, all I do is sell tickets. I'm not a movie reviewer."

"How long is this going to take?" the girl behind Megan asked.

75

One of the other movies was a Disney film. It seemed like the best choice. At least it wouldn't have any sex in it.

When she entered the theater, though, it was filled with kids and their parents. She found one seat at the far end of one of the side rows near the back of the theater. She excused herself and made her way past a family. The movie hadn't started yet, and after taking her seat Megan looked out of the corner of her eye at the family next to her. The father was a good-looking man with a well-kept beard. His wife was beautiful in an unassuming way, and they had three children—a girl, maybe three years old, her brother, a six-year-old boy, full of questions, and his sister, twelve years old, not quite sure if she was too old for Disney, alternating moment to moment between being a young woman and being a child.

Megan was sitting next to the twelve-year-old girl.

The three-year-old was taking all the attention of the parents.

"Must be a good movie, right?" Megan said.

The girl turned to Megan. "Excuse me?"

"I said this must be a good movie."

"Why?"

"Because of all the people."

"Whatever." The girl turned away from Megan, obviously not wanting to talk.

Megan looked at her watch, impatient for the movie to begin. She didn't like being around so many children.

A two-year-old boy in the row in front of her turned to face her. He was being fed popcorn one kernel at a time. He held out his hand to Megan and said, "More?" Except it sounded like "Moa."

"You want me to have this piece?" Megan asked.

"Moa?" he asked again.

Megan took the kernel of popcorn. The mother turned around. She was a young mother, not too much older than Megan.

"I'm so sorry."

"No, it's fine, really."

"Moa?" the boy asked, looking to see if Megan would eat the popcorn he'd given her.

"Thank you!" Megan said enthusiastically. She popped it in her mouth.

"Oh, gross," the girl next to Megan said.

The boy turned to his mother for another piece of popcorn, received it, and then turned to Megan. "Moa?"

Megan took the piece of popcorn and then ducked down behind the backrest of his seat, then popped up suddenly.

He started to laugh.

She ducked down again.

Same result.

The little boy laughed each time Megan appeared from behind the backrest of his seat.

The girl next to her wasn't amused. "Tommy, can I change places with you?" she asked her brother.

They changed places. Tommy joined Megan in the ducking game, ducking down the same time Megan did. The little boy in front of them was even more delighted and laughed even harder.

A few more minutes of that, and his mother turned around. "You can ignore him if you want," his mother said to Megan.

"No, it's okay. He's so cute! How old is he?"

"He'll be two next month."

"He's adorable."

The mother smiled and nodded. "I guess we'll keep him."

Megan felt a wave of embarrassment and shame. *That's more than I'm going to do. I'm having mine cut out of me on Monday or Tuesday. That's because it's only a growth, not a baby.*

"Moa?" the boy asked.

Megan shook her head. She'd had enough. This was too painful.

The theater darkened, and the coming attractions began showing on the screen.

"Moa?" the little boy asked.

Megan felt sick to her stomach. She stood up and made her way out of the row, past the family, to the aisle, and then up the aisle to the common hall linking all the movies being shown at the multiplex that night.

She went into the least offensive R-rated movie, wanting to escape from little kids who laughed at the silliest little thing.

The movie had already started, but she found a seat at the back, glad for the darkness.

A few minutes into the movie, a very good-looking guy and an equally glamorous woman ended up in bed together, although they'd just met.

She couldn't watch it. She walked out.

She stood in the hallway connecting the movies and tried to decide what to do. She looked at the gaudy signs for each movie, wanting desperately to be taken away from her own problems and to be transported into another world with different rules, to be someone else for even a few minutes, just to escape the reality of her own life.

She looked down the hallway to the choice of movies she had. *There's nothing here for me. Maybe I'd just better go back to my apartment.*

A few minutes later, she entered her apartment, closed the door, and began watching one of her favorite videotaped episodes of *Friends*.

*Why can't my life be like that? That's all I've ever wanted— to have friends and be free to do what I wanted to do.*

*Friends* had always worked for her before. In a way she felt like they were *her* friends. They were always there for her, no matter what.

78

But this time it didn't work.

She turned off the TV and all the lights in the house and sat on her couch and tried to think. She heard what sounded to be a shot or a car backfiring.

*Welcome to my world,* she thought.

Finally, she fell asleep.

When she woke up, it was four-thirty in the morning, and she wasn't sleepy anymore, so she splashed water on her face and brushed her teeth and went outside to take a walk.

Early on that Monday morning there was still very little traffic. The sun was like a timid actor in a grade school production, hanging in the wings until it was time to make his appearance, bringing light to the world in cautious degrees.

As she walked she thought about the little boy in the movie theater, how much happiness she had brought him in just a few minutes.

*I have a baby inside me. Well, not an actual baby, but he will be a baby someday. A boy or a girl. Whatever it is, it's not his fault, and it's not her fault. How can I take away the chance to be born just because I messed up? If I do, then who will hear the laughter? Who will hear him say, "Moa?"*

*It's one thing to say I oppose abortion when it's just talk, when it's not a choice I'm facing. But if I'm against it in principle, then I have to be against it now, for me, or else it doesn't matter what I believe. It's not what you believe; it's what you do.*

As she stopped to watch the sunrise, she knew she couldn't deny future sunrises to the baby she was carrying.

*I'm not sure what I'm going to do with my baby, but one thing I am sure of, I'm not going to have it cut out.*

She came to a McDonald's and ordered herself breakfast. Instead of her usual coffee and pancakes, she had eggs and orange juice.

For the baby.

79

# 5

Megan knew she had to tell her family she was pregnant, but she had a few days left before the rent was due, and there was still a little food in the apartment, so she hung on a little longer, hoping for some kind of miracle that would make all her problems go away.

On Monday Brianna called and invited her to Young Women Standards Night on Tuesday. "I'm going to sing. It's going to be way cool. Please come, Meggie, okay?"

"Well, I don't know."

"Please. I've worked *so* hard on my song. I want you to hear it."

*What else have I got to do?* she thought. *Haven't I watched enough episodes of* Friends *to last me a lifetime?*

"Okay, I'll go."

"You're awesome!"

On Tuesday night Megan sat with her mother on the second row in the Relief Society room.

*How many of these have I been to?* she thought. *And they're all the same. Every single one of them.*

She did like Brianna's song, though, and her sister looked so happy, Megan thought, *I'm glad I came. To show my support.*

Bishop Oldham was introduced. Big and tall, wearing a slightly rumpled suit, he looked a little out of place standing behind a table that had been covered with a lacy cloth and decorated with a vase of fresh flowers. He was obviously nervous, and just looking at him as he stood in front of them made Megan feel the same way.

"I'm sure you're all familiar with this," he said, holding up the *For the Strength of Youth* pamphlet. "How many have looked at it in the last six months? Raise your hands." He looked around. "Good. Very good. You can put your hands down now."

The bishop wiped his forehead and cleared his throat and looked down at the floor.

*Oh, great, he hasn't even prepared a talk,* Megan thought critically. *Way to go, Bishop.*

He looked out at each one of the girls. "How many of you have read it in the last month?"

Fewer hands went up.

"That's what I thought. Even though you think you know everything about this book, it is filled with things you need to review frequently."

*Why don't you just read it to us, Bishop? That way you won't have to make it obvious to everyone that you're totally unprepared.*

As if on cue, the bishop said, "Let me read some of it to you."

*How much time would it have taken you to actually prepare a talk?*

Bishop Oldham spent a moment silently reading, trying to find what he was looking for.

*You're wasting our time, Bishop. Why don't you just admit you're not prepared and sit down?*

81

He turned the page and continued to silently read. Megan looked at the Young Women president. She maintained her composure, but Megan wondered if she was getting frustrated.

He cleared his throat. "The first part is from the First Presidency. I'll read part of what they wrote."

*We can read, Bishop. We don't need you to read for us.*

"'You cannot do wrong and feel right. It is impossible! Years of happiness can be lost in the foolish gratification of a momentary desire for pleasure. Satan would have you believe that happiness comes only as you surrender to his enticement to self-indulgence. We need only to look at the shattered lives of those who violate God's laws to know why Satan is called the father of all lies.

"'You can avoid the burden of guilt and sin and all of the attending heartaches if you will but heed the standards provided you through the teachings of the Lord and his servants.'"

The bishop looked up from his reading. "I cannot emphasize too much the importance of living the standards talked about in this booklet. It can make all the difference in the world to you and your future happiness."

He set the booklet on the table. "Dear young sisters, these are the words of the prophets. I hope you can feel their concern. What they have done here is raise a voice of warning. I plead with you to pay attention to what they have to say. The principles they are trying to teach you are true. You may think you can ignore the warnings, that it doesn't matter how you dress and think and act, but I promise you that it isn't true. If you violate these standards, it will result in sorrow and regret."

He cleared his throat again and stared at the floor. When he began to speak again, his voice faltered. "I . . ." he pointed to the Young Women leaders, " . . . we . . . love you and hope for your happiness. We know that when any of us breaks the commandments, it results in heartache, and we want to help you avoid that kind of sorrow."

He paused again and then said, "Sometimes people think they can lie to me during an interview." He pursed his lips. "Well, I guess they can. I'm not that clever to tell sometimes if someone is telling the truth or not, but I can tell you this . . ."

His voice faltered again, and he stopped talking and looked down. "Excuse me . . ." he said, fumbling for his handkerchief. After wiping his nose, he smiled and said, "You ever wonder why women cry and men blow their noses in situations like this? It must be genetics, right?"

He continued. "Nobody ever volunteers to be a bishop. It comes out of the blue, totally unexpected. I'm an engineer, for crying out loud. What do I know about counseling people with problems? Not much. But I've been blessed greatly as I've tried to learn my duties.

"When anyone hides the truth from me in an interview, it's almost as if they are lying to the Lord. Not because there's anything special about me, but because the Lord has called me to be your bishop, and he needs you to be honest. Totally honest. The thing is, unless you're truthful, there's nothing I can do to help you."

Megan felt as if the weight of a truck was on her chest, making it impossible to breathe. She wondered if anyone was noticing how flushed her face was, and, if they were, what they were thinking.

The bishop picked up the booklet and tapped it on the podium. "There can be no deviation from these principles. None whatsoever. Doesn't he say, 'I the Lord cannot look upon sin with the least degree of allowance'? Well, that's the way I have to be when you come to me. You can't say, 'Well, I'm doing just a little of this or a little of that, but it's not that serious.' You can't say that, because that's what Satan wants you to think. Besides, we don't want you worrying about the consequences of misbehavior. Youth is a time to have fun and enjoy life. That's not possible if you are breaking the commandments."

Megan felt like running out of the room, but she was afraid that if she did everyone would know why, and she couldn't bear for anyone to know.

The bishop then talked briefly about the importance of dressing modestly and living the Word of Wisdom and dating good boys, preferably members of the Church. "You may think these are little things, but they often lead to much more serious transgressions."

*Please, just stop,* Megan thought. *I can't stand this. I don't care how bad things get, I'll never go to you. Not ever. I couldn't stand you browbeating me and making me feel like a fool for what I've done.*

The bishop said a few more things and then sat down. And then there was a song and a prayer, and it was over.

Megan had come to the meeting with her mother and Brianna, so she had to wait for them before she could go home.

"I'll be outside," Megan said to her mother.

"Don't you want some refreshments?"

"No, I just want to get back to my apartment. I've got to go to work early in the morning."

"We'll hurry."

Megan sat in the car and waited.

*When am I going to let them know I'm pregnant? I only have two more days until my next month's rent is due. Maybe I should tell them tonight.*

She shook her head. *No, not tonight. Not after this. Not after what the bishop said.*

She found a tissue in the glove compartment and wiped her eyes.

*This might be a good time, though, because Dad is out of*

town on a business trip. So I wouldn't have to face both Mom and Dad at the same time.

She shook her head. *I don't want to do this. I really don't want to do this. I wish I could just fall asleep and never wake up. But I can't do that. It's more than me now. It's a baby. I have to be good to my baby, no matter what.*

She tried to imagine what her mother's reaction would be. *What will I do if she tells me she knew this was going to happen? What will I do if she tells me I've disgraced the family?*

*And what will Daddy say? Not much, probably. He never says much. But I know he'll be disappointed in me.*

Her mother and Brianna came out to the car and got in. "Sorry we took so long," Carolyn said.

"It's okay," Megan said.

"Didn't Brianna sing well tonight?"

"I took care of it, right?" Brianna beamed.

"You did great," Megan said.

"And some people say I can't sing!"

"Who says that?"

"My choir teacher, but what does he know, right?" she joked.

"Right."

A few minutes later they pulled into the driveway of their two-story condominium.

"We can say good night here, if you need to be on your way," Carolyn said.

"Well, actually, I think I'll stay for a few minutes, if that's all right."

"Yes, of course, whatever you'd like," Carolyn said.

They ended up in the kitchen, with Carolyn loading the dishwasher, and Brianna having a piece of cake and some milk.

"Oh, we got a letter from Heather today," Carolyn said.

"How's she doing?"

"Good. They had a baptism last week."

"That's great."

"Here's the letter," Carolyn said.

Megan began to read.

*Things are really starting to pick up here. My new companion, Sister Lofgren, and I are really working hard. We've been teaching a family of four, the Gundersons. They're really doing well. Last Sunday they even came to church. We've set their baptismal date. It's in three weeks.*

*I am so happy out here. I'm so grateful to the Lord to be able to tell people about the gospel.*

*How is everyone doing? I want to hear all your news. I brag about you all the time.*

By the time Megan finished the letter, Brianna was in the living room, talking on the phone and watching TV.

Megan set the letter aside. "Mom, there's something I need to tell you," she said softly.

Her mom turned to look at her. "What is it?"

"You know I've been seeing Kurt, off and on. And, well . . ."

There was no easy way to say it. Megan took a deep breath and said, "I'm pregnant."

Carolyn stopped loading the dishwasher. She brought her hand to her mouth.

"Oh, Megan."

Megan couldn't stand seeing the pain in her mother's eyes and looked away. Neither of them said anything for a moment, then Carolyn asked, "Are you sure? Sometimes people think they're pregnant, but it's something else, like a tumor for instance. I've heard of that happening."

"I checked it with an in-home test and then went to a clinic. It's for sure."

Carolyn moved to Megan's side. "What are you going to do?"

"I don't know. Everything is still up in the air."

"Does Kurt know?"

86

"Yes, I told him."

"What did he say?"

"He made it sound like it was all my fault. He has no interest in getting married. Oh, he did offer to pay for an abortion, though. Well, actually, that's not true either. He offered to pay for whatever my insurance wouldn't cover."

"You're not seriously considering getting an abortion, are you?"

"No of course not. But get this, Kurt said some doctors will charge you for some other operation that your insurance will pay for. And then they just go ahead and do the abortion."

"That's not honest."

"Oh, Kurt doesn't care about that. He just wants to save a little money." She sighed. "It doesn't matter though. I'm not getting an abortion."

"So that means you're going to have the baby?"

"Yes, that's right."

"To keep?"

"Yes, of course. I could never give my baby away."

Megan's effort to hold in her emotions suddenly failed. "I'm so sorry, Mom," she whispered and buried her face in her arms on the table.

Carolyn came to her, raised her up, and wrapped her sobbing daughter in a long, tearful embrace.

Brianna came back into the kitchen. "What's wrong?" she asked.

"She needs to hear it from you," Carolyn said.

Megan cleared her throat. "I'm pregnant."

"No, you're not."

"I am."

"You sure?"

"I'm sure."

Brianna's perpetual smile collapsed, and tears sprang into her eyes. "How could that happen?"

"It just does sometimes."

Brianna put her arms around Megan and held her tight. And they cried.

"I've always looked up to you," Brianna said.

"I know. I'm sorry," Megan said. "I should have been a better example."

"I love you," Brianna said.

"I love you, too."

The phone rang.

"It's probably for you," Megan said.

"I don't care." Brianna pulled up a chair and sat next to Megan. "What are you going to do?"

"I'm not going to get an abortion. That's what Kurt wants me to do."

"No way."

"I'm serious."

"Did he tell you that?" Carolyn asked.

"He did. He makes it sound like it's all my fault."

"It's his kid, too, though, right?" Brianna asked.

"Yes, of course."

"He's trash then."

"He might change his mind," Carolyn said.

"Even if he does, it wouldn't make any difference."

"So, how did it happen?" Brianna asked.

Megan looked at her strangely, not really knowing how to answer the question.

Brianna slapped her own forehead with her open hand. "Good thing I didn't just ask my sister what made her get pregnant, right? I need to get back on my medication right away, right? What a stupid question. What I meant was . . ." She started to blush. "Was it just, like, you know, one time, where things got out of control?"

"Brianna, I'm really not sure you need to know those kind of details," Carolyn said.

"No, it's okay," Megan said. "The truth is, this has been going on since just after I met him."

88

"How could you go against the teachings of the Church like that?" Brianna asked.

"Brianna," Carolyn gently warned.

"What?"

"Not now."

Brianna shrugged her shoulders. "Okay. Well, answer me this then. Are you going to keep the baby when it's born?"

"I'm pretty sure that's what I'll do."

"You've got to keep it," Brianna said. "I'll help you raise it. I'm serious. I'll be the dad."

"You can't be the dad."

Brianna put her arms up and flexed her muscles. "Why not? I'd make a good dad. I can throw a ball, and I can hog the remote. Just ask Mom."

Carolyn smiled. "She's very good at hogging the remote."

"And I can spit. And I can lean under the hood of a car and hit the engine with a wrench. I'd make a great dad."

Just then Bryce came home from work at Home Depot. Seeing the three of them at the table, he stopped on his way to clean up. "What's up?"

"Megan's pregnant," Brianna said.

"Well, the hits just keep coming, don't they?" he announced, mimicking a radio announcer. "Way to go, Megan! Way to use your head. We're all real proud of you! Yes, sir! That's just great!" He started up the stairs to his room.

"Hey, come back here!" Brianna called out. "You're not at Testosterone City anymore, Bryce, so quit acting like a complete jerk."

"Don't you talk to me like that," he shot back.

"I'll talk to you any way I want to," Brianna answered. "I'm not afraid of you."

He stopped and came back down the stairs, glaring at Brianna. "What do you want from me?"

"What we don't want is attitude."

Bryce sat down. "All right. So you're pregnant. What are you going to do about it?"

"I'm not sure yet."

"What does Kurt want to do?"

"He wants her to have an abortion," Brianna said. "What a psychopath."

"I won't get an abortion," Megan said.

Bryce nodded his head. "All right. Next option. You could put the baby up for adoption."

"I know, but . . ."

"You're not thinking of trying to raise the baby by yourself, are you? That would be a dumb idea. You've already done one stupid thing, Megan. Don't make it two in a row." He stood up. "I've got to take a shower and clean up."

"Thank you so much for sharing your infinite wisdom with us mere mortals," Brianna shot back.

"Somebody in this family has to think rationally." He bounded up the stairs.

"There you have it, ladies and gentlemen! Mr. Sensitivity," Brianna said. "I pity the woman he marries."

"He's not so bad," Megan said. "At least with him you know where you stand."

Brianna smiled. "You could say the same thing about a charging rhino."

"Are you going to want to move back in?" Carolyn asked.

"If you'll let me."

"Of course. When do you want to move?"

"Right away," Megan said. "The rent is due tomorrow."

"Bryce and I can help you move tonight," Brianna said.

"You'd better ask Bryce about that," Carolyn suggested. "He's put in a hard day's work already."

"Yeah, right," Megan said. "Like, standing around and telling people where the hammers are is so tough."

When Bryce bounded back down the stairs on his way out for the evening, Brianna confronted him. "Megan's moving back home. We need you to help out tonight getting her moved out of her old place."

"Who made you the boss of this family?"

"C'mon, Bryce, don't be such a grumposaurus rex. We need your strong muscles and weak mind."

He fought back a smile. "Well, if you put it that way, then I'll help."

On the way across town, Megan, Bryce, and Brianna dropped by the freight door of Home Depot and gathered up some empty boxes and then headed for Megan's apartment.

All Megan had to do was throw her things in boxes while Brianna and Bryce carried them out to his pickup truck.

"What's that noise?" Brianna asked on one trip.

"That's talk radio from Mr. Podolsky next door."

"Is it always this loud?"

Megan nodded. "It's worse when he starts yelling at his radio."

"What's his problem?"

"He thinks there's a plot to destroy our way of life. He lies in wait during the day for anyone who'll listen to him. In a way, I feel sorry for him."

Brianna smiled. "I think I'll go make his day."

"What are you going to do?"

"Nothing. I'll be back in a minute."

Megan watched from the hallway as Brianna knocked on Mr. Podolsky's door.

"Excuse me, I was next door visiting my sister, and I couldn't help hearing your radio."

"You want me to turn it down?"

"No, I was wanting to know if what I heard is really true."

"Yes, and they've done it again!"

"Please tell me."

"Do you want to come in?"

"No, not really. Can't you just tell me here at the door?"

91

Megan went inside and continued packing, but she left the door open so she could check on Brianna.

"That is so awful!" Brianna said.

"That's just the beginning of it," Mr. Podolsky said enthusiastically.

"Oh, please tell me more. This is so interesting!"

Bryce came back for another load. "What's Brianna doing?"

"Making some guy's day." She glanced at Bryce. "You're probably thinking, 'It must run in the family.' Right?"

"I didn't say a word, did I?"

"No, you didn't."

"If you'd just talked to me." He banged the counter with his hand. "People come to me all the time. They're building this or they're fixing that. And I tell them how to do it, and they take my advice and things work out for them."

"Living a life is not exactly like remodeling a kitchen."

"I know that." He turned to face her, his hands out like he just needed the proper tool to make all their problems go away. "I could've helped if you'd asked. I know about guys. I know everything about guys."

"I know."

"You want me to pay this guy a visit and help him reorder his priorities?"

"I don't want you to beat him up."

"It's no problem, you know. I'd be happy to do it."

"He's not worth you getting in trouble."

"What do you want me to do then?" he asked.

"Just be around when I need you. And don't remind me what a fool I've been. Oh, and go easy on Brianna. This is hard for her, too."

"That's all you want from me?"

"Yes."

"I'd rather bang some heads together."

"It wouldn't do him or me or you any good."

"I just wish I could do more, that's all."

"I know." She put her arms around him and kissed him on the cheek. "You know what? You're my favorite big brother."

It was an old joke. He smiled.

She said, "If you want to help, here's another box to take out."

"That I can do." He took the box and left.

Megan could hear Brianna in the hall, trying to wrap up her conversation with Mr. Podolsky. "I'm *so* happy I got a chance to talk to you, and I just want to say, keep telling everyone about this! I'm just surprised more people don't know about it, that's all."

"Tell your friends!" Mr. Podolsky called out, his voice more excited and happy than Megan had ever heard.

"Great idea! Well, look, Mr. Podolsky, I've got to run now, but thanks for the pamphlets and for giving me the name of the radio station. Thanks again. I'll see you. I'm going now. Good-bye."

She ran inside Megan's apartment and closed the door. She had a big grin on her face. "The world as we know it is doomed. Isn't that great?"

"You're evil," Megan said with a smile.

"Well, maybe so . . . except I do feel sorry for him."

"I wonder what's keeping Bryce. It wasn't that heavy of a box." Megan looked out the window and saw Bryce standing by his pickup talking on his cell phone.

There wasn't much left to do. A few things in the bathroom, some groceries in the kitchen. The apartment was furnished, so they didn't have to move the furniture.

Bryce returned. "I've got to go back to the store. They've got a problem. It'll take about ten minutes to fix and then I'll come back."

"Okay, we'll finish up while you're gone."

"You stud, fixing the problems of the store single-handed," Brianna called out.

He knew she was teasing him but smiled anyway at the veiled compliment. "See you later."

They went in the bedroom and started to put Megan's clothes into boxes.

"So, this is where you got pregnant, right?" Brianna asked, looking at the beat-up bed frame with its lumpy, stained mattress, now visible because they'd removed the sheets.

Megan shook her head. "Let's not go there, okay?"

"You're right. Sorry." Brianna quit working. "What do I tell my friends when they come up and go, 'So your sister got herself pregnant?' What do I tell them?"

"I guess you tell them the truth."

"All my friends know I'm Mormon. What kind of great impression is this going to make with them about the Church? And what do I say to make it better? 'Yeah, she's pregnant, but it's not what she was taught all her life.' I'm sure that'll smooth things over in a big way."

"I'm sorry."

Brianna sat cross-legged on the bed with her elbows on her knees, her hands propping up her head. "And then there's the other thing."

"What other thing?"

"Bryce was active when he was little, but now he doesn't go to church anymore. You're pregnant and not married. So am I next?"

"No, you're more like Heather."

Brianna shook her head. "Nobody's like Heather. She's, like, perfect. Always has been. She sort of wills herself to not mess up. I mean it's like she's never even tempted. She just has this tremendous willpower."

"She does. She's amazing."

"But the thing is, she's never needed us. I mean the family. She always lived above whatever the family was doing."

94

Brianna shook her head. "I'm not like that. I like people too much. Got to be around them all the time. I'm more like you."

"You're way better than me," Megan said.

"Maybe that's just because I'm younger. Maybe I'll follow in your footsteps."

"I hope you don't."

"Me, too. At least that's the way I feel now. But who can say what's going to happen?"

"What would take you away?" Megan asked.

"That's easy. My friends. My friends mean a lot to me. The only trouble is none of them are in the Church. I don't particularly like the kids my age in the ward. They're all right, I guess, but none of them are people I like to hang with."

Megan finished packing her clothes in boxes in the bedroom. She grabbed another box to gather her belongings from the bathroom. Brianna followed.

"You had interviews with the bishop, though, right?" Brianna asked.

"I did. I lied."

Brianna shook her head. "Why?"

"I didn't want him to know."

"But if he'd known, he could have helped you. And then maybe you wouldn't have got pregnant. I always tell the bishop everything. Sometimes I wonder if he wishes I didn't talk so much, but he never says anything."

When Bryce returned, they carried the rest of her things to his pickup. Just as they were about to leave, Megan took one last chance to look out the kitchen window. "Before we go, there's something I want to tell you guys. A few weeks ago something happened. It was raining, and I was doing the dishes and I looked out and there were all these lights, like a million beacons coming from everywhere I looked. It was the most beautiful thing I'd ever seen. I don't know. It was like it was a sign from God that he loved me. It brought tears to my eyes. I prayed for the first time in I don't know how long."

"You were looking through the screen?" Bryce asked.

"Yes, why?"

"I can tell you why that happened. The screen broke the light up. It's the same thing that happens when you look at a CD. All you need is small lines, and they'll break the light up. That's not God. That's just optics."

"Okay, so there's a reason, but I can't deny the way it made me feel."

"That's just because you didn't know what was causing it. It's not a miracle."

"How can you say that?" Brianna said.

"Because I can explain it. Anything that has an explanation can't be a miracle."

"So what would be a miracle?"

Bryce shook his head. "I haven't seen any. Let's go."

◆　　◆　　◆

Megan moved her things into Brianna's room, the same room they'd shared before she'd moved out. Before, it had been Megan's room that Brianna was sharing. Now, it was Brianna's room that Megan was sharing.

After unpacking most of her things, Megan went downstairs to the kitchen for her favorite snack since childhood, graham crackers and milk.

Brianna was watching TV and talking on the phone. Bryce was gone to a friend's place.

Her mother joined Megan at the kitchen table. "You all moved in?"

"Yeah, pretty much."

Her mother nodded. "I think we need to call your father and see if he can come home tomorrow, so you can tell him your news."

"That's going to be hard," Megan said.

"I know, but he has to hear this from you, in person, and

it has to be done right away. If we put it off, he might hear it from someone else, and that would be very bad."

"Can you call him and see if he can come home tomorrow?"

"Yes." Her mother looked at the clock on the wall. "He should be in his motel room by now." She asked Brianna to get off the phone.

Ten minutes later Brianna came into the kitchen with the phone. "Why do you need the phone?"

"We're going to call your father."

Brianna cringed. "I'll be upstairs. If anyone beeps in, tell 'em to call back. It could be important." She ran up the stairs, then yelled down, "One point two seconds, a new world's record!" She made a hissing sound to imitate the roar of the crowd, then slammed the door to her room. And then it was quiet again.

Her mother punched in the phone number.

Walter answered it on the first ring.

A little small talk and then Carolyn said, "Something's come up . . . in the family. I was wondering if you could come home tomorrow, instead of waiting until the end of the week."

Megan could only imagine what her father was saying.

"No, nothing like that. Everyone is healthy."

A pause, followed by, "It's not something we can handle over the phone."

Megan's head was beginning to throb.

"I understand that you're two hundred miles from home, and that you have appointments set up in the morning, but you really need to come home. I'm sure you can reschedule your appointments."

Carolyn was tapping her fingernails on the kitchen table. "I can't tell you what it is over the phone. You'll have to come home for us to tell you." A long pause. "Why are you arguing with me? Why can't you just take my word that you need to be here? It won't take long. Maybe a couple of hours, and then you can go back and see your people."

A pause and then, "No, I can't even give you a hint. Just come home."

Megan couldn't stand it any longer. She reached over and asked for the phone.

Carolyn shrugged her shoulders and handed it to her.

"Daddy, hi, it's me, Megan. I moved back home today. . . . Why? Well, I lost my job, so I couldn't afford to stay in my apartment. . . . No, that isn't all. There is something else . . ."

"Don't tell him over the phone," her mother said. "He can come home and hear it from your own lips. This is not something that should be discussed over the phone."

Megan held her hand over the mouthpiece. "I don't want to put him out any."

Carolyn shook her head. "Don't do it. He is the father of this family. He can rearrange his schedule when there's a crisis."

"It's okay, Mom."

"It's not okay," she said with tears in her eyes as she left the room.

"Daddy, are you still there? I'm fine . . . except there is one thing . . ."

Megan dabbed at her eyes with a napkin. "You remember Kurt, don't you?"

"Is he getting baptized?" her dad asked excitedly. "Is that your big news?"

Megan covered her eyes with her hand. "No, that's not it."

"What is it then? He hasn't been in an accident, has he?"

"No, he's fine. It's something else."

"Why don't you just tell me? It doesn't look like it's something I'm going to be able to guess."

"Probably not."

*Just get it over with,* she thought.

"I'm pregnant, Daddy."

There was a long pause.

"I see," her father said quietly.

"I'm real sorry."

"I don't understand. We talked about chastity every month in our interview, and every month you said there was no problem. So did this just happen since our last interview?"

Tears were streaming down her face. "No, it's been going on since a little after I started seeing Kurt."

"But, how can that be?"

"I didn't tell you the truth like I should have."

"Just a minute. I need to turn the TV off."

He came back a few seconds later. "Why did you conceal the truth from me?"

"I guess I didn't want you to worry about me."

"I would have rather worried about you then than have this to deal with. Are you and Kurt going to get married?"

"No, Daddy, we're not."

"Maybe if I talked to him."

"I'd rather you didn't talk to him. It's over between us. I don't respect him anymore. I would never marry him now."

"So what are you going to do?"

"I'm not sure, except I know that I'm not going to have an abortion."

"I just don't understand why this is happening to us. They said for us to have family home evening, so we started doing that. They said for me to interview my children once a month, so I started doing that. They said for me to talk about our courtship and what it was like for your mother and me to get married in the temple, so we did that. We have family prayer. We go to church every Sunday. We pay our tithing. We go to the temple at least once a month. So what did we do wrong, that this should be happening to us?"

"It's a choice I made, Daddy."

"Sometimes . . ." Megan knew what caused him to stop in the middle of a sentence. It was something he did when his emotions got the best of him. Where her mother would just cry and let it out, her father would stop and wait for it to pass.

" . . . sometimes . . . I just don't know . . . how this could have happened to us."

There was nothing more from him for what seemed like an eternity, and then he said, "Could you put your mother on?"

Megan went upstairs to her parents' bedroom. The door was closed. Megan knocked.

"Come in."

Her mother was just sitting on the bed.

"Daddy wants to talk to you."

"I'll take it up here, if that's all right."

Megan went downstairs and hung up the phone, then went back upstairs and sat outside her parents' bedroom so she could at least hear what her mother was saying.

"No, I suppose there isn't any reason for you to come home now," she said, her voice sounding hollow.

Brianna came out of her room. "Did you tell Daddy?"

Megan nodded.

"What'd he say?"

Megan shook her head. "I don't want to talk about it now."

"Sure. I'm going to make myself a grilled cheese sandwich. You want one?"

"No."

"They're very good."

"No thanks."

Brianna clomped down the stairs.

Megan was about to leave the hallway and go to her room and finish unpacking her things when she heard her mother say, "No, Walter, I did not know you had a Scout Jamborall this weekend. But I'm quite sure that you can get some of the dads to fill in for you."

An icy silence followed.

"Yes, I understand there will be competitions for the boys, and I'm happy they've worked so hard, but I'm sure there are others in the ward who are perfectly capable of being with the boys and cheering them on to victory."

The seconds passed.

Her mother said quite coldly, "I see. Yes, good-bye."

Megan waited a minute before going in to see her mother. She was sitting on the bed, her head down, her eyes closed.

"You okay, Mom?"

She looked up and smiled thinly. "Yes, of course. I'm fine." She stood up. "Do you have any laundry that needs to be done tonight?"

"No, I'm okay."

"I need to turn on the dishwasher." Carolyn started out the door, then stopped. "Your father has a Scout Jamborall this weekend, so he won't be around all that much."

"It's okay, Mom."

"Yes, of course, everything is okay," she said bitterly. "That's the way it is around here. Everything is always fine."

◆　◆　◆

Walter came home a little early on Friday but mainly to pack up for the Scout Jamborall. Megan was the only one home. She was in the living room watching *Wheel of Fortune*.

Her father came into the living room. "Well, I'm home."

"Did you have a good week?"

It was the question the family usually asked when he came home from a week on the road, but this time it had a warped, almost surreal quality to it.

"I mean as far as placing orders," she added.

"Pretty good week."

"Good. I'm glad."

"You doing okay?" he asked.

"I'm fine, Daddy."

Ordinarily, he would have given her a big hug, but this time he held back. "I'm glad to hear you're doing well."

101

"Thank you. I went to Doctor Sullivan today. He'll be the one who delivers the baby."

"I see. What did he say?"

"Everything seems normal so far."

"Good. Normal is good." He looked at his watch. "Well, I hate to run off, but I really need to get ready for the Scout Jamborall. It's the biggest they've ever had around here. I'm very hopeful that our troop will be recognized as one of the best."

"Well, good luck, Daddy. I know your Scouts will make you proud, just like they always do."

"Thanks. Scouts always do their best to do their duty."

"Yes, I know."

It was an awkward moment for both of them. Megan felt that she would never match up to her dad's Scouts.

"Well, I'd better get my gear packed."

"Can I help?"

"No, it's better if I do it. That way I know where everything is."

"Of course."

Her father went into the garage.

A few minutes later Carolyn came home from work. She went into the garage to talk to Walter.

Seated at the kitchen table, Megan could hear everything they said.

"Did you even ask anyone to take your place this weekend?" she asked.

"No, I did not."

"Your family needs you. Megan needs you."

"Why? She's already pregnant. So what would my staying home this weekend accomplish?"

"This isn't going to be easy for her. She needs us to support her."

"She lied to me, month after month. Maybe I'm old fashioned, but to me, when someone lies to you again and again and again, that shows a lack of respect. So if she doesn't respect me, and if she has no interest in my opinions, and if she won't follow my counsel, then what on earth am I going to accomplish this weekend by being here instead of where I've been called to serve? At least the boys listen to what I say. That's more than I can say for anyone in this family."

"I don't want to have to carry this all by myself. Sometimes I get tired of being the one everyone else depends on. I have my limits, too."

"You'll do fine. You always have."

"I don't know how to say this any clearer, Walter. If you won't stay home for Megan, stay home for me. I need you to be here."

"Do you have any idea how much the boys have worked to prepare themselves for this weekend? If I'm not there, they'll have a tough time achieving all the goals they've set for themselves."

"I see. Well, I guess I know where I stand in your list of priorities then, don't I?"

"There will be other weekends that I'll be home. Besides, I'll be back tomorrow night."

"Yes, of course. And we'll both be tied up all day Sunday in meetings, and then you'll leave first thing on Monday. Maybe if I gave out little patches you could sew on your shirt, like they do, you'd be around more when I need you."

"What do you want me to do?"

"I've already told you what I want you to do, but you won't do it. Good-bye, Walter."

Her mother came through the side door, walked past Megan, went upstairs to her room, and closed the door.

Her father made a couple more trips inside and then backed the car out of the driveway and drove away.

The house was silent again, except for some nameless contestant on *Wheel of Fortune*, asking for the letter R.

103

# 6

Megan arranged to meet with Bishop Oldham on Saturday afternoon at one-thirty. When she arrived, his ward clerk was in the office next door working on the computer.

"Thank you for being willing to see me on such short notice," Megan said as she sat down in the bishop's office.

"No problem."

Megan closed her eyes. *I've got to start and just trust that things will go okay.*

She gave him an embarrassed smile. "I guess you're wondering why I wanted to talk to you today instead of waiting until tomorrow."

He nodded. "I'm sure you'll tell me."

She took a deep breath. "Well, yes, I will. Let me just spit it out. I'm pregnant."

He nodded. "I see."

As she talked she felt as if the room was tipping to the left and that she needed to hold on to her chair to keep from falling out. She spoke fast in a strained, high-pitched voice.

"The father's name is Kurt. He's not a member of the Church. I started sleeping with him a few months ago."

Megan cleared her throat. *At least it's out in the open now, so that's good.* "It was a dumb thing for me to do, I know, but I did it."

"Have you told your parents?"

"Yes."

"How did they react?"

"They were very disappointed."

"You understand why, don't you?"

"It goes against everything they've taught me."

The bishop nodded, then asked, "Did you start sleeping with your boyfriend before we had our last interview?"

She waited for a long time before saying, just above a whisper, "Yes."

"I see. So that means you weren't completely honest with me?"

"No. I wasn't."

He rested his elbows on the desk and covered his eyes with his hand.

"I'm real sorry," she said. "I should have told you, but I was too embarrassed."

He looked as though he had more to say but stopped and took a deep breath. "Have you thought about what you're going to do?"

"Kurt wants me to get an abortion. I thought about it, but then I decided I can't do that because it's not the baby's fault how it came to be conceived. So I'm not going to get an abortion."

"Good for you."

She was surprised he could say anything positive about this. "Thank you."

"What about you and Kurt?" he asked. "Is there any possibility you two could get married?"

She shook her head. "He's not ready to settle down. He

pretty much just wants to continue his life the way it is now. He likes the freedom to do whatever he wants. He likes to sail and backpack and be with his friends. I don't think I'd want to marry him, even if he asked me."

"Has he asked you?"

"No." She paused. "He offered to pay for the abortion, and that's the last I've heard from him." She cleared her throat. "What do I need to tell you about Kurt and me?"

"I'm not sure I understand what you're asking."

"Do I need to tell you how many times we . . . were together?"

He shook his head. "No, that's not necessary."

"Are there any details about what we did that you need me to tell you about?"

"No."

She sighed. "Good. I was worrying about that."

"Yes, of course."

The bishop didn't say anything for a few moments, then he said, "Megan, why have you come here today?"

"I needed to talk to you. You know, to confess."

"Is there something you hope to gain from that?"

"It's just something I've always heard. When you mess up, you're supposed to go talk to the bishop."

"Why?"

"I don't know. You just do."

"Megan, let me ask you something. How do you feel about what's happened to you?"

"I feel awful. I mean, I'm pregnant and I'm not married. It's embarrassing."

"Is that all it is? Embarrassing?"

"No. It's not easy. I'm going to have a baby. That really scares me."

"I'm sure it does. But I want you to think about something else. You have been taught that immorality is a major sin, haven't you?"

106

She panicked. "Are you going to excommunicate me?"

"Does the Church mean that much to you, that you'd care if you were excommunicated?"

She was shocked by the question. "I've always been active in the Church."

"Yes, that's true. You could often be found within the walls of this building. You were in the Church, but was the Church and its teachings in you?"

He took his scriptures from a shelf behind the desk. "Have the teachings of the Church entered your heart and mind? Or have you just gone through the motions?"

It was a painful question, one she was not willing to answer.

He continued. "Megan, I don't mean to be unkind, but what you have done is very serious. Let's read something together."

He thumbed through his scriptures, then turned the book so Megan could see it.

"This is Alma talking to his son Corianton about sexual sin. Please read verse five."

Megan read: "'Know ye not, my son, that these things are an abomination in the sight of the Lord; yea, most abominable above all sins save it be the shedding of innocent blood.'"

"What that means, Megan, is that the sin of immorality is second only to murder."

Megan didn't know what to say. She looked down at her hands.

Bishop Oldham continued, "If that was all we know, you would be in a hopeless situation, but the Lord is merciful and kind. Let's look at something else he has said."

He thumbed the pages again and pointed to a passage he had marked in red. "Read this," he said.

Megan cleared her throat and read the passage: "'Behold,

he who has repented of his sins, the same is forgiven, and I, the Lord, remember them no more.'"

"I know that is true, Megan. Because of the Atonement, the Savior is able not only to forgive but forget our sins. The question you need to ask yourself is if you're willing to make major changes in your life, so that you can be forgiven of the sin you've committed."

"Is that still a possibility?"

He nodded his head. "It's always possible."

"Are you saying that as far as God is concerned, it could be like it never happened?"

"That's exactly what I'm saying."

"I'm not sure I believe that."

"Why not?"

"It doesn't seem fair."

"In what way?"

"Well, take a girl who's always lived the way the Church teaches. Like Alexis, for example. So, basically, she's never done anything wrong. How can it be that I could be forgiven of all the things I've done wrong, and have all my sins forgiven, so that as far as God is concerned, we're both the same in his eyes?"

"I'm not saying you won't have regrets. I'm not saying you'll forget what's happened. I'm not saying there will be no natural consequences of your misdeeds, such as sexually transmitted diseases or things of that nature. There will be regrets, there will be heartache. But in time even that pain can be wiped away. The beauty of the gospel of Jesus Christ is that we can be totally forgiven of our sins, so that as far as Father in Heaven is concerned, you can start over again, clean, completely forgiven, and approved of by him and our Savior."

That was something Megan hadn't even dared hope for. She sat in stunned silence for a few moments. Then she asked, "What do I have to do?"

"It's going to take some time and some hard work on your

part. We can talk about it over the course of the next few weeks. I'll start by giving you some reading assignments. Then we'll need to get together, every week, to check on your progress."

"Do you want me to come to church?" she asked.

"Yes, of course, but there is one thing I would ask of you."

"What's that?"

"That you refrain from taking the sacrament until I give you permission."

"Why?"

"Before you partake of the sacrament again, I want you to understand its significance and what it has to do with being forgiven."

She was worried what people would think if she didn't take the sacrament, but she didn't say anything about it.

The bishop closed his scriptures and set them aside. "Megan, I'm so sorry for what's happened. I can't even imagine what you've been going through. But I want you to know that I'm here for you and that there is a way back."

She looked at him but was too emotional to respond.

"Now, what else should we talk about?" he asked.

She cleared her throat. "Well, I'm not sure if I should keep the baby or put it up for adoption."

"I'm sure that will be a difficult decision. I'd like to put you in touch with LDS Family Services. They really specialize in these kinds of issues. They won't pressure you either way, but they will help you see more clearly the consequences of the decision you make, both for you and your baby. If you want, I can call and make an appointment for you."

Megan thought about that for a moment, then said, "I'd like that. Thank you."

"Sure. Is there anything else you'd like to talk about?"

She closed her eyes. The fear she had felt in coming had been forgotten. Even though she was still pregnant and her troubles hadn't gone away, she felt calm, even a little hopeful.

She opened her eyes. Bishop Oldham was sitting patiently, looking at her, a look of kindly concern on his face. She shook her head. "No," she said. "Thank you."

◆　　◆　　◆

After Megan got home, while she and Brianna were sitting at the kitchen table, her father returned home from the Boy Scout Jamborall. Although his face had a smudge of charcoal on it and his Scout shirt looked like he'd slept in it, which he had, he was excited and talkative.

"Well, we did it! We really cleaned up! Four first place awards, the troop medallion, and a good sportsmanship award. Not bad for one troop, right?"

"I'm like 'Whoa, Nellie!' Way to go, Scout Daddy!" Brianna called out.

"Good job," Megan said, much more constrained.

"I'm very proud of the boys. They're the ones who did it."

"Yeah, but you're the one who taught 'em," Brianna said.

Carolyn came in from working in the tiny flower garden they had in their abbreviated backyard.

"If you ask me, those boys are lucky to have you," Brianna continued.

Walter and Carolyn exchanged painful and awkward glances. "I see you're home," she said with little enthusiasm.

"Daddy's troop won almost everything! Isn't that amazing?" Brianna said.

"Yes, I'm sure it is," Carolyn said in a dull monotone. "I need to finish up my work. Walter, you don't know where the pruning shears are, do you? You didn't take them with you to Scout camp, did you? I can't find them anywhere."

"I don't know where they are."

"We shouldn't have to buy pruning shears twice a year. It's a needless waste of money."

"Do you have some of the medals with you, Daddy?" Brianna asked.

"Yes, they're in the car. Would you like to see them?"

"I would! How about the rest of you?"

Carolyn hesitated and then said quietly, "I need to finish up outside. It looks like it might rain."

Brianna practically did cheers as Walter showed her each ribbon and award his troop had earned at the jamborall. Megan was less enthusiastic, not because she didn't value his work with the boys in the ward, but because she shared her mother's feeling of disappointment that he had not arranged for someone else to take the boys so they could face their biggest family crisis together.

Brianna left a few minutes later. Walter unpacked his own and the troop's camp equipment and stored it back in the garage.

Megan knew that her parents were going to have what could be an argument, or at least a tension-filled discussion. She didn't want to be in the house when it happened, so she decided to take a walk.

It was a hot, sunny day with few clouds, except there was still a fog bank to the west over the bay.

Because it was Saturday, people were mowing their lawns or working in their gardens. She passed a young married couple putting up a swing set for their little boy. Except for being frustrated trying to read the instructions, they looked happy. She wondered what her baby would look like at three years old, and if she'd even know. She wondered if in an adoption she would be able to even see her son or daughter.

She was just heading back when a car slowed down and stopped. Megan looked over. It was Kurt's mother. They'd met once.

She pulled over and stopped and rolled down the window on the right side of the car.

"Hello, Megan. Taking a walk?"

"Yes. It's a beautiful day."

"It is. I stopped by the house and your mother said you were out. I'm fortunate I found you. I'd like to talk to you, if that's all right."

"Okay."

"Why don't you come sit in the car?" Megan got in the car and shut the door.

Even wearing slacks and a blouse, Kurt's mother looked elegant, as usual. "You're looking good, Megan. How do you feel?"

"All right . . . so far."

"Wonderful." She cleared her throat. "This is awkward, isn't it?"

"Yeah, it is."

"Kurt told his father about you being pregnant."

"Why?"

"I'm not sure. I guess he was worried about legal and financial issues."

"That sounds like Kurt, always looking out for himself."

"I'm hoping that you and Kurt will get married."

"That would make things simpler, that's for sure."

"Of course it would. Then there would be no question about what to do."

"No, there wouldn't."

"Kurt does love you, I think."

"Does he?"

"Of course he does."

"Is that why he offered to pay for my abortion and hasn't contacted me since? Because he loves me?"

"He just panicked, that's all."

"Actually, he didn't offer to pay for the abortion. He offered to pay what the insurance wouldn't cover. And if my insurance wouldn't cover abortion, he said there were doctors he'd heard about who charge for something the insurance will cover and then will go ahead and do an abortion. So, yes, I can see why you'd say he loves me. That's easy to see, now that I think about it."

"He's very concerned about you."

"Really? Is he home right now? Let's both go talk to him and have him tell us how concerned he is about me."

"Well, he's not home now. He's gone scuba diving with some friends."

She nodded her head. "I see. Well, that sounds like fun. Kurt really knows how to have a good time." Even as she said it, she began to blush, hoping Kurt's mother would not take her comment wrong. "What I meant is, he has some outdoor adventure planned nearly every weekend."

"I understood what you meant. And I quite agree."

The two women endured a painful silence.

"I'm not going to get an abortion."

"I'm happy to hear that. I'm very hopeful that his father and I can talk him into marrying you."

"How would you do that?" Megan asked.

"I would tell him he has a responsibility to do the right thing by you."

"And that would be enough, just you telling him that?"

There was a long pause. "I'm not sure."

"Well, you could always threaten to cut off his allowance."

Kurt's mother cringed. "He doesn't get an allowance."

"I'm sorry. That was a cheap shot. I shouldn't have said it. How would you get him to marry me?"

"Why do you want to know?"

Megan shrugged. "I don't know. Just curious. When a boy has everything, what do you do to get him to do what you want?"

Kurt's mother smiled. "I wish I knew the answer to that. We don't give him money. He works for what he gets."

"He doesn't seem to work very hard though."

"Well, that's because he's very good at what he does. He's always been good with computers."

113

"He's perfectly happy with the way his life is now. I'm sure he doesn't want a wife and a baby to get in the way of his good times."

"He's very good with children, though."

"Yes, of course, he's a real charmer," Megan said.

"How can I be of help to you?"

"I'm not sure you can."

"Please let me know."

"I will."

"What will happen to my grandchild?"

"I can't tell you that yet. Except I've decided to have the baby. After that, I'm not sure. I'll either keep the baby, or else I'll put him or her up for adoption."

"The way things are going with Kurt, I may never have a grandchild."

"That's possible. I don't see him settling down anytime soon."

"Life is too easy for him."

"It's just the way he wants it to be."

"Do you need money? I can give you whatever you want, for doctor's expenses and to pay for your stay in the hospital. Whatever you need. Just let me know."

"I will," Megan said, knowing full well that she would never ask for money.

"Would you like me to drop you off some place?"

"No, I'll just continue my walk. Thank you for coming. That means a lot to me."

"We're not enemies, you and I."

"No, not at all."

They said good-bye one more time, then Megan got out of the car and watched her drive off.

The house was quiet by the time Megan returned home. Her father was airing out the tents and his sleeping bag and cleaning up all the cooking equipment they'd used on the camp out.

"Where's Mom?" she asked.

"She's gone grocery shopping," her dad said quietly.

*They've been arguing,* she thought. *I can always tell.*

She went to her room and lay down and took a nap.

She slept through supper, not waking up until seven-thirty that night. The house was quiet, except she could hear her mother and father in the next room talking.

"I think you're being totally unreasonable," Walter said. "You want me to ask to be released from being Scoutmaster because I wasn't around here last night?"

"It's not just last night. You're always gone. I don't see why the only man in the ward who's gone all week should be taking a group of boys out camping on the weekends. You've been Scoutmaster long enough. They can get someone else."

"You know what the troop was like when I took over."

"Your number one priority should be your family, not some Scout troop. Your family needs you now."

"Needs me? What for? They don't need me. You think Bryce needs me? I don't. Megan? What can I do for her now? It seems to me like the damage has already been done. And Brianna? I can't even understand half the things she says."

"I want you to ask to be released, Walter. That's what I want. I can't face all this by myself. Do you want to talk to the bishop about having you released or do you want me to?"

"I really think you're overreacting. The Scouts don't have any more weekend activities planned for a month. I'll see if I can cut down on the days I'm out of town. I'll get an assistant Scoutmaster called who can help out. All I'm saying is give me a little time to rearrange my life. And then, if you're still not satisfied, I'll ask to be released."

After a long pause, Carolyn said, "All right, we'll give it a month."

"I will spend more time at home. You'll see. But . . ."

"What?"

"Well, because I was gone all day, tonight I need to go to

my office and get caught up on my sales reports and get ready for next week. Is that okay with you?"

"You do what you think best," she said.

That night Brianna had some friends over to watch movies, and Megan avoided them by going upstairs and reading until they left, just after midnight.

Brianna knocked quietly on the door then opened it a crack. With a Swedish accent, she said, "Room service. You want I should fluff up your pillow?"

Megan laughed. "Yes, come in."

Brianna, true to her word, fluffed up Megan's pillow. "Fluffy pillows help you sleep, yah?"

They talked for half an hour, and then Brianna got ready for bed and soon returned, talked Megan into having a prayer with her, then climbed into bed and fell asleep within a few minutes.

Megan couldn't sleep and so half an hour later she got up and went downstairs and watched an old movie on TV.

Bryce came home at two-thirty. He grabbed something to eat, then came into the living room and sat down. "You're up kind of late, aren't you?" he asked.

"I couldn't sleep."

"Got a lot on your mind?" he asked.

"Yeah."

He took a bite of the sandwich he'd made. "You want me to make you one of these?"

"No, I'm fine."

"You still thinking about keeping the baby?" he asked.

"I am."

"What would you live on?"

"I could get a job."

"You have no skills."

"I have . . . " she paused, "eight months to get some."

"What are you going to learn in that time that'll give you a decent living? All I'm saying is give this kid a chance by letting a family adopt it."

"Why is everything so black-and-white to you?"

"That's just the way it is. Sometimes you got to use logic and reason. This is one of those times. Think about it."

"I will."

"Be right back." He went into the kitchen.

She was bored with the movie, so she went in to talk while he made himself another sandwich. "Are you going to keep going to church through all this?" he asked.

"Yes."

"What for? People at church won't want to have anything to do with you. So why go back? You're the exact opposite of what they want their girls to become. If they're nice to you, then it takes away from the threat they use to keep other girls in line. They can't be good to you, because if they are, the whole thing will start to unravel and fall apart."

"I'm going to try it anyway."

He shrugged his shoulders. "Suit yourself."

"I'm going to bed," she said.

"Whatever."

Megan went to bed and thought about what it was going to be like going back to church.

She sighed. *This is too hard. Everything now is so painful. Sometimes I wish I were dead.*

She opened her eyes. *I can't die though. Not now. Because of the baby.*

The next day was Sunday. Megan had told Brianna she would be going to church but felt sick when she got up, so she went back to bed.

Brianna got up, took a shower, then came back to the room they shared. "You going to church today?"

"I feel sick."

"Yeah, right. I've used that excuse, too, when I didn't want to go."

"I want to go."

"Then get up and at least try to get ready."

"I'm not making this up. I don't feel well."

"Will you ever feel good enough to go?" Brianna asked sarcastically.

"Just go away and leave me alone, okay?"

"Fine, whatever you say."

By then Megan was too mad to go to sleep. *I'll show her,* she thought, standing up, fully expecting she'd throw up. But nothing came. She walked gingerly into the bathroom and looked into the mirror. *I look awful. How can I go to church looking this way?*

And then a new thought came into her mind that brought her to tears. *It doesn't matter anymore how I look. I'm pregnant and I'm single. That makes me of no interest to anyone. Not to any guy and not to the girls my age. I am on my way to becoming invisible. So there's no reason to go to church except if I want to worship God because nobody cares what I look like anymore.*

She was about to go back to bed when another thought came to her. *Except the bishop. He'll notice if I'm not at church. And if I go, he'll come over and say hello to me. He'll be my support, even if nobody else in the ward is.*

She began to wash her face. *I'll go to church today for the bishop. In time I may have other reasons to go, but for now it will be for him.*

She still felt sick to her stomach but thought that if she had something to eat, the nausea would go away. So after getting ready, she went downstairs and had half of a banana on some cold cereal. The phone rang. Brianna answered it. It was for Walter.

"Thank you. Yes, I am proud of the boys. What they did is quite an achievement. . . . Well, I'd say Derek Adams and Jonathan would be the ones to ask to talk. . . . Well, yes, I'd be willing to say a few words, too."

118

An hour later Megan, Brianna, and their parents walked into church twenty minutes early. It wasn't until then that Megan realized that Brianna wouldn't be sitting with her because she was singing in a Young Women's choir and would be sitting on the stand. Her mother was the chorister and wouldn't join her until after the sacrament. Her father would also be sitting on the stand with his Scouts.

*I'll be all alone,* she thought.

Brianna went to practice with the chorus, her mother left to find some sheet music for a missionary farewell scheduled in two weeks, and her dad was busy shaking hands with some of his friends.

Megan stood alone near the door of the chapel. *How many know about me?* she thought. *Some must know. Brianna must have told some people. I never said she shouldn't. It's all going to come out anyway.*

She looked around to see if people were staring at her. They didn't seem to be, but there weren't that many people in the chapel yet. Megan felt a dull ache in her stomach. *When they find out about me, what will they say? Will they say, I'm not surprised. Will they say, I could see it coming. Will they say, Why is she even coming to church?*

Her face was flushed, and she felt sick to her stomach. *I can't go through this. I've got to get away from here. I never should have come in the first place. This is all a terrible mistake. Bryce was right. I don't belong here anymore.*

She left and walked quickly to the restroom, planning to throw water on her face and then walk home, never again to return.

She looked at herself in the mirror, something she'd been doing in that room for as long as she could remember. She had a sudden rush of memories of growing up as a member of the Church in that building. She knew every room in that building. Rooms where she'd been taught in Primary. Rooms for Sunday School and Young Women. It all came back to her.

All the lessons, all the treats, all the activities, all the times she'd felt the love of her teachers and leaders.

*And now look at me,* she thought.

Tears began to stream down her face. She couldn't stop herself.

Sister Amundson walked in. Her husband was in the stake presidency and hardly ever attended church in his own ward. She had a boy who was seven and a girl who was four. Sister Amundson had come in to assist her daughter.

Megan wiped her eyes and glanced at Sister Amundson in the reflection in the mirror. *I've got to go now.*

"Tiffany, you go ahead and go potty. I'll be right here if you need me."

Tiffany entered the stall and closed the door.

Sister Amundson touched Megan's arm lightly. "You okay?"

Megan nodded. "Yes, I'm fine."

"Are you at peace?"

It was such an odd question, one that nobody had ever asked her before. Megan glanced quickly at Sister Amundson to see if it was just a question she asked mindlessly, or if she actually meant it.

They made eye contact. The sincerity in Sister Amundson's expression was evident.

"I'm having kind of a rough time today," Megan whispered through the rush of tears.

Tiffany, in the stall, was singing a Primary song.

"What can I do to help you?"

"Nothing," Megan said barely above a whisper. "There's nothing anyone can do for me now." She covered her eyes with her hand and began sobbing.

Sister Amundson at first just put her hand on Megan's back but then drew her into a hug. "I'm pregnant," Megan blurted out.

"It's okay, Megan. We're still here for you. All of us."

"I don't think I can go to church anymore. It's too hard."

"But you're here, Megan. You've already done the hard part, just getting here."

"My mom and my dad and Brianna are all on the program today. I'm afraid I'll have to be all by myself."

"Sit with us."

"I'm afraid people are going to look down on me."

Sister Amundson smiled. "If they're going to look down on you, well then, they can just look down on me, too."

Megan bit her lip, fighting back the tears. "Are you sure?"

"Absolutely. You belong in church. No matter how bad things are, the gospel will make it better." She turned to the stall. "Tiffany, please, hurry up."

When she entered the chapel, her father came up to her. "I was looking for you."

"Sorry. You're speaking today, right? Shouldn't you sit on the stand? Sister Amundson said I could sit with her and her kids."

He thought about it for a minute. "You don't mind?"

"No, I'm okay."

"All right then. It might be better if the boys and I sit together on the stand, especially after they pass the sacrament."

"Sure, go ahead."

Megan sat near the front with Sister Amundson and her two children. "Thank you so much," Megan whispered, just as the bishop stood up to begin the meeting.

Sister Amundson squeezed Megan's hand. "You're going to be fine," she said.

Megan nodded, afraid to say anything for fear she'd lose the small amount of composure she was struggling to maintain.

When it came time for the sacrament, she tensed up, wondering if anyone would notice her not taking the bread or the water.

She was sitting on the end of the row. When the tray of

bread came to her, she passed it to Sister Amundson, who took it and held it while her son, Mark, took a piece and put it in his mouth. Then Sister Amundson held the tray for Tiffany to take a piece.

"Why didn't Megan take any?" Mark whispered.

"Sometimes people don't," his mother said.

"Why?"

Megan quit breathing, wondering what Sister Amundson would say.

*Because they're not worthy*, she thought. *Because they've messed up big-time. Because the bishop told them not to. Because they went against all they were taught. Is that what she'll say?*

"It helps them remember what the sacrament is all about, so that when they take it, it means so much more to them."

That seemed to satisfy Mark.

Megan's face was red, wondering who else had noticed she hadn't taken the sacrament. She glanced around. Everyone seemed lost in their own thoughts.

After the sacrament, Megan's mother came and sat with her in the same row with Sister Amundson and her two kids.

After the meeting was over, Bishop Oldham came down from the stand and shook her hand. "Good morning, Megan. I'm so pleased you came today." He smiled at Sister Amundson. "And that you were looked after so well."

"Thank you," Megan said.

"Could we get together after the block? Just for a few minutes."

"Yes, of course."

"It will be right after, if you could just have a seat outside my office and relax. I promise not to take too long."

Megan nodded, and the bishop moved away to catch someone else he needed to see.

Megan's mother thanked Sister Amundson, or Peggy, as she called her, for "looking after Megan."

"Oh, she was a big help to me. She kept Tiffany occupied, going through one of her books with her."

"Well, let's go to Sunday School, Megan," her mother said.

Megan was glad the Gospel Doctrine class was full of adults anxious to answer all the questions.

"How many of you did the reading for today's lesson?" Brother Halverson, the teacher, asked. Less than a fourth of the class raised their hands.

"Thanks to those of you who did. That is so helpful to a teacher to have people in the class who've read the lesson. For those of you who haven't, please read the lesson for next time. Let me ask you a question. You don't have to raise your hands, but I wonder if there is anyone here who's never read the Book of Mormon from cover to cover?"

Megan had never read it all the way through, so she was glad he didn't call for a show of hands.

"I just want to say that you will never have a sufficiently strong testimony of this work until you've read the Book of Mormon. And for those who have read it, some of you many times I'm sure, please read it again this year."

After Sunday School, Megan went with her mother to Relief Society. The lesson would have had no interest to her ordinarily, but because it was about rearing children to follow the teachings of the Church, and because she still wasn't certain what would become of the child she would have, she paid more attention.

"I need to see the bishop," Megan said to her mother after Relief Society was over and the women were filing out of the room.

"How long will you be?"

"The bishop said not very long."

"Should I take Brianna home and then come back for you?"

"I think I'll just be a few minutes."

"Okay, we'll be in the car then."

Megan sat down on a couch outside the bishop's office.

The executive secretary saw her sitting there and came over. "I don't have you scheduled to see the bishop," he said, looking down at the calendar where he kept track of the bishop's appointments.

"He said to come right after the block."

"I see. What for?"

Megan looked at the executive secretary, wondering why he would ask that.

"He didn't say," she said.

He nodded. "Sure, no problem. He should be here any minute now." He hesitated, then said, "When I asked what for, I didn't mean I needed to know. The reason I asked is because the bishop has a number of other people who have appointments, and I just need to know how long you'll be. That's all I meant."

She wasn't sure how to respond, so she just smiled and said, "Okay."

He moved on. Megan relaxed.

The bishop showed up a few minutes later, looked at those waiting for him, then said, "Megan, you're first."

She went with the bishop into his office.

He shook her hand warmly, and they sat down. "I was very pleased to see you in church today. Was it okay for you?"

"Yeah, it was. It was good."

"Maybe the Gospel Essentials class would be better for you. It's a smaller class, and the people who attend are either new converts or just starting back, like you. I go there whenever I can. Why don't you try that next week and tell me what you think."

"Okay."

"What shall we talk about today?" he asked.

"I'm not sure. I'll probably have more to talk about after I meet with LDS Family Services on Wednesday."

"Good. I'd like to know how that goes for you. If it's okay,

I'd like to see you every Sunday about this time. We won't take long. Now let me give you some more scriptures I'd like you to read before we meet next week."

A few minutes later Megan said good-bye to the bishop and went to find her mother and Brianna. She felt good, hopeful that she could change, at peace with herself, looking forward to a good week. She felt good about her decision to have the baby.

The only question now was what to do with the baby after it was born. She was hoping LDS Family Services could help her with that.

# 7

Megan dreaded keeping her appointment with LDS Family Services. She was scheduled to meet with a Sister Gardner. She didn't know her and wasn't sure what to expect. *I don't like having to open up details of my personal life with complete strangers, wondering what they think of me. It isn't fair for me to have to face this all by myself.*

But there was no other choice.

A few minutes later, Megan sat down across the desk from Sister Gardner. She was in her early thirties and single. Megan appreciated her friendly smile and approved of the warm and casual way she'd decorated her office with American Indian artwork.

"Did the bishop tell you why I'm here?" Megan asked.

"A little bit, but why don't you fill me in?"

She took a deep breath. "Well, I'm pregnant, and I'm not married."

"And the father?"

"He's out of the picture. He has no interest in me or the

baby. He suggested I have an abortion, but I'm not going to do that."

"Good for you."

"I want to keep my baby, but my brother thinks I should put it up for adoption. That's why I'm here."

"Well, fine, you've come to the right place. That is what we do here, explain the options that are available."

"I've been thinking that I'd really like to keep the baby."

"Of course. Many of our clients do that." She reached for a piece of paper. "Where will you be living after the child is born?"

"Well, I'll be at home right after. That's where I'm staying."

"So will you stay there after the baby is born?"

"For a while I guess, but then I'll get an apartment."

"Will you be working then or would you be a stay-at-home mom?"

"Well, I guess eventually I'll have to get a job."

"How about child care? Have you thought about that?"

"My mom can help me. She works during the day, so like if I got a night job I could have her take care of the baby while I'm at work. And my younger sister, Brianna, is willing to help, too. She likes kids and is really good with them."

"So you'll be looking for a job you can do at night."

"Yes, that's right."

"Very good. Well, we've got a worksheet here that will help you as you make your plans. What would you think about working on it at home and then bringing it back when you're done? We can look it over together as you plan for your and your baby's future. It's always better to have a plan, don't you agree?"

Sister Gardner was easier to talk to than Megan had expected, but, still, she had her doubts. "Can I ask you a question?"

"Yes, of course."

"You're supposed to try and talk me into giving my baby

away, aren't you? I mean, that's the purpose of the worksheet, isn't it? To get me to realize that it would be better to give my baby away."

"We prefer to call it placing the baby for adoption."

"You can call it what you will, but it's the same thing, isn't it?"

"The term *giving away a baby* implies a lack of concern for the child, but the term *placing the baby for adoption,* in my mind at least, implies a different image. But that's just because I work with this every day. The thing is, Megan, I'm happy to work with you, whatever you decide to do."

"You're sure about that?"

"I am."

"Okay. Well, I just had to ask."

"And I'm glad you did. Fill out the planning form, then we can go through it together. If you'd care to, that is."

"I guess it couldn't hurt anything."

"I don't see how."

As Megan worked on her plans over the next two days, she began to see some difficulties, which Bryce, peering over her shoulder when he came home from work the next evening, immediately seized upon.

"What are you doing?" he asked.

"Nothing. Go away."

"Don't say 'nothing.' You are doing something. Just tell me what it is."

"It's none of your business."

"Just tell me, and I'll go away."

"I'm working on plans for what I'm going to do once I have the baby."

"What's there to plan? You have the baby, you give it to the adoption agency, and you come home."

She hated his know-it-all attitude. "Gosh, Bryce, why don't I have you plan out my entire life?"

"You're not still thinking of keeping the baby, are you?"

"Why shouldn't I keep it? I'm going to be its mom."

"How are you going to support a kid all by yourself?"

"I'll get a job."

"And who will be taking care of your kid while you're working?"

"I'll get a night job, so Mom can take care of it while I'm working."

"Have you talked to her about it?"

"Not yet, but I will."

"Are you going to live here the rest of your life?"

"No, I'll get an apartment."

"How much do you think you're going to be making with just a high school degree?"

"Enough to get by."

"Barely enough."

"It will be enough, Bryce. Now go away and quit bothering me."

"Let me crank out some numbers for you, okay?"

She threw up her hands. "Why can't you just leave me alone?"

Bryce went into the kitchen and started rummaging through a kitchen drawer. "We used to have a calculator in here. Whatever happened to it?"

"I don't know, Bryce."

"I've got one in my car. I'll go get it."

"I don't need your help."

"No, that's just it. You do need my help. Desperately." He went outside.

A short time later he returned.

"How much was your rent in your old place?"

"I'm not moving back there."

"I know. I just need a number."

She told him what her rent had been.

"Okay, even if you get a good job and make what I make at Home Depot, by the time you pay your rent and car insurance and buy groceries there will be less than fifty dollars a month left over. You'll spend well over that on things for the baby."

"I'll go to college then, so I can get a good job."

"Good idea, Megan. And who's going to pay for college? Mom? Dad? Way to show your independence."

"I'll take classes before I go to work each day."

"Okay, well, you could do that, same as me. One class a semester. At that rate you'll be done with college by the time your child is . . ." He stopped to do some figuring. " . . . ten years old."

"It won't take that long, Bryce. I'll take summer classes."

"I put that in my estimate."

"Why are you so negative all the time?"

"Why can't you face the facts?"

"It's not for the rest of my life. I'll probably get married in a couple of years. Then things will be better."

"Who are you going to marry?"

"How should I know?"

"Hey, it should be no problem," he said sarcastically. "Every day at work guys come up to me and say, 'Where can I find a single woman with a kid, so I can get married and take on some responsibilities and debt?' And I say, 'Man, I wish I knew. I'd snap her up in a minute.'"

"I hate it when you're this way," she said.

"You mean when I'm logical? I bet you do. Sorry to burst your bubble, Megan. You can go on living in that imaginary world of yours, but don't drag some kid into it. Put the kid up for adoption. You can't feed a kid on love. You can't send him to college. You can't give him piano lessons. You can't send him to camp. You can't be there for him when he comes home from school."

She threw a couch pillow at him. "Don't tell me what I can or can't do! I'll make it just fine. You'll see!"

"What if you don't? Who's going to be the worse off? A kid

only has one chance to grow up. Why not give him the best that life has to offer?"

"Who are you to tell me how to live my life, Bryce? You're twenty-one and still living at home. And, while we're at it, why don't you show me your college degree? I must have missed it when you brought it home. And how many classes have you taken the past year? How dare you lecture me about how to live my life when you're not doing that great yourself."

He glared at her. She wasn't sure if he was going to swear at her or walk out.

When he began speaking, he spoke quietly. "Okay, maybe I could be doing better than I am right now. And maybe I have wasted my time, but the thing is, Megan, it's my life to waste. I'm not dragging anyone else down. I don't have a kid depending on me to give him or her a chance to make it."

"Some people make it in spite of their circumstances," Megan said.

"I know, some do. More power to them. Do you want to take that risk for this kid you're going to bring into the world? Because it's the one who will ultimately pay the price for your bad decisions."

In a rare display of affection, he put his hand on her shoulder. "Okay, look, maybe I have been too rough on you. And if I have, I'm sorry. All I'm saying is, why not think of what's best for the kid, okay? That's all I'm saying." And then he left.

She did think about it.

In fact, that's all she thought about.

◆　　◆　　◆

That night Thomas came over to see her. She was surprised to see him.

"Thomas?" she stammered at the door.

"Can I come in?" he asked.

"Sure, I guess so."

She wondered if he'd heard she was pregnant. And if he had, why he was coming around.

"Sit down," she said. "Can I get you something to drink?"

"No, I'm fine. I was just wondering how you're doing."

She wasn't sure how to answer, not knowing how much he'd heard about her. She sat down next to him on the couch.

"Good, and you?"

"Good, too."

"I'm glad."

There was a long awkward silence.

*He's come here as a friend because he knows,* she thought.

She looked down, took a deep breath, and then said softly, "I'm pregnant."

"That's what I heard, but I wasn't sure if it was true or not."

"It's true. Pretty dumb, right?"

He shrugged. "It happens. How is Kurt handling it?"

"I guess he's pretending it didn't happen. I'm not sure though. I haven't talked to him for a while."

"Is there any chance you two will get married?"

"No, no chance at all."

"How come?"

"He's not ready for that." She paused. "He did offer to pay for an abortion though. The guy is a real prince, right?"

"Are you going to take him up on the offer?"

"No."

"How come?"

"Because I think abortion is wrong."

"So what are you going to do?" he asked.

"I'm not sure. Either keep the baby and raise her myself, or . . ." She was going to say, "give her away," but she couldn't say it. It sounded so heartless. She decided to talk about it in the terms Sister Gardner had used. " . . . place her for adoption. Some couples can't have children, you know."

132

"It's not something I've ever thought about."

"Me, either. I've thought about a lot of things lately that I've never thought about before."

"You said place *her* for adoption. So, you know for sure it's a girl, then, right?"

"No. I just think of her as a girl."

"It could be a boy."

"I know."

He smiled. "So you're not going to decide on a name yet, right?"

"Right."

"Well . . ." He cleared his throat and fidgeted. "I could marry you, if that'd help you out any." He said it in the same tone of voice he'd use if he were offering to loan her his car.

His remark left her stunned. She studied his face to see if he was joking. He wasn't even smiling. *He's serious. I can't believe it.* "Thomas, why would you want to do that?" she asked softly.

"So you could keep your baby."

"You'd do that for me?"

He shrugged his shoulders. "I'm going to get married someday. So it might as well be now . . . to you."

She felt her eyes begin to sting, and she put her hand to her mouth. "I . . . I don't know what to say."

"I've got next Monday off. We could get married on Saturday and have ourselves a three-day weekend together. What do you say?"

She dabbed away the tears. "That is so . . ." She struggled for the right word. *Kind? Sweet? Thoughtful? Generous?*

"Dumb of me to even suggest?" he asked.

"No. No, it's heroic. That's what you are. That's what you've always been in my life."

"I think we could be reasonably happy, Megan."

"But we're just friends."

"I know, but sometimes friends get married. And if we got married, then for sure you could keep the baby."

"Would you love this baby, or would it remind you of Kurt and me?"

He paused. "I've thought about that. I love kids. I don't actually care where they come from. I mean, up to last year, I thought they came from a stork. So compared to a stork, Kurt's a big improvement."

She smiled through her tears. "You'd be the best daddy in the world, Thomas. I'm sure of that."

He stood up from the couch. "So it's decided, right? I'll take care of everything . . . the cake, the place. I can do the invitations on my computer, print 'em out and have 'em in the mail by tomorrow morning. Now if this is too fast for you, we could postpone it a week and even have a reception. If we do have a reception, what would you think about having chocolate cake with chocolate frosting? That's your favorite, right? And we'll have pizza, too. Lots of it. You know what? I bet I could get a really good deal on pizza. In fact, we could even have our reception at Leo's. Wouldn't that be great? It'll be the best wedding in history. And we'll have a drawing every fifteen minutes for a free pizza. And . . ."

She was laughing. "Stop, will you? I'm not going to marry you this weekend . . . or any weekend in the near future." As she said it, she could tell she'd hurt his feelings. And that surprised her.

He went to the window and looked out, then turned and, with a smile, said, "Of course. What was I thinking?"

"You're my best friend, though."

"You're mine, too. That will never change."

"Thanks, Thomas. For everything. I didn't think you'd want to have anything to do with me once you heard about me being pregnant."

"It'd take more than that."

She stood up, walked over to him, and put her arms

around his neck and kissed him on the cheek. "You're the best."

"Sure I am."

"Would you have really married me?"

He smiled. "I guess we'll never know, will we?"

"I guess not."

He stepped back from her. "I'd better go."

"Sure. Thanks for coming."

"Come by Leo's sometime around closing."

"Well, I'm not real comfortable being with people."

"It'll just be you and me," he said.

"How come?"

"My boss said no more parties after closing. But you can come by . . . if you want, that is."

"I'd like that. I don't get out much anymore."

"I'm working tomorrow night if you want to come by."

"I might do that."

"I'll let you make me a pizza while I clean up."

"Just like old times, right?"

"Sure, why not?" He started for the door.

"Thomas?"

"Yes."

"Thanks . . . for everything."

He nodded, then left.

The next night at nine o'clock Megan went up to her room to change. She had decided to go visit Thomas, and she wanted to wear something nice for him. Also, she wanted to decide which of her clothes she'd be able to wear for at least part of her pregnancy.

A few minutes later, she had two piles of clothes on her bed. In the larger pile were clothes she wouldn't be wearing anymore. She'd either give them to Brianna or take them to the Salvation Army.

She picked up the one tank top she owned. She remembered where and when she'd bought it, how she liked it

135

because it showed off her body, and how nervous and excited she'd been to wear it for Kurt the first night at Leo's.

But now she viewed it much differently, almost as if it had betrayed her. She had also been wearing it the night she and Kurt had first been intimate.

She picked up the tank top and held it out to get a good look at it. *What was I thinking of? What was I trying to prove? Was I so desperate I'd do anything to get some guy's attention? Why couldn't I just follow what I'd been taught all my life? Why did I think I had a better way?*

She remembered when she was fourteen, and her mother had told her not to wear clothes she wouldn't be able to wear after she'd gone through the temple. At that time she thought the advice was stupid because she was years away from going to the temple.

She picked up each item from the pile. With each one she remembered when and where she'd bought it and some of the times she'd worn it. And she remembered the effect some of the clothes had had on Kurt.

*I can't give these to Brianna. I don't want the same thing happening to her that happened to me.*

*I'll take them to the Salvation Army.*

She was putting the clothes into a box to take to the Salvation Army when she pictured in her mind some fourteen-year-old girl buying them and wearing them and ending up abandoned and pregnant, like herself.

She carried them outside and dumped the box of clothes into the dumpster.

On her way back into the house, she thought, *I'm paying a huge price to have this baby. So why not keep my baby and do my best to give her all she needs in life? To give her away would be the easy way out. Up to now I've always taken the easy way out.*

She nodded her head and smiled. *That's it. Now I know for sure. I'm definitely going to keep my baby.*

# 8

Megan arrived at Leo's Pizza at eleven-fifteen. Since it was after closing, the front door was locked. She knocked for a few minutes, decided Thomas must be in the back, walked around to the back door, and knocked.

Thomas opened the door and let her in. He seemed surprised to see her. "You came?"

"Sure, why not?"

"What can I get you to drink?"

"Water would be great."

"Is that all?"

"Yeah, just water."

"You want to watch me mop the floor?" he asked.

"Really? You'd let me do that? My life would have meaning if I could do that."

He pulled a bar stool into the middle of the room for her, then got her a glass of water.

"Anything else I can do for you?"

"Dazzle me with your floor cleaning skills."

He smiled at her. "It's good to have you back."

"Thanks. It's good to be back. Thanks for . . . still being my friend."

"I will always be your friend."

"I know that now."

He began to mop. "I didn't think you'd come."

"How come?"

"I thought me asking you to marry me would freak you out."

"You did it because you wanted to make it easier for me."

"That's what friends do, isn't it?" he asked.

"Not usually. You're a special category of friend. You're the best." She paused. "Friends . . . all I ever wanted in high school was to have friends."

Thomas noticed her getting emotional. "Hey, don't get upset just because I missed a spot, okay?"

She smiled. "You're doing great." She looked around. "Remember the good times we had here with all our friends? What's happened to everybody? Where have they all gone?"

"Most of 'em went to college. Did you know that Brad Parkinson is at NYU studying film arts?"

"No, I didn't know that."

"And Mike Young is at Cal Tech, studying aerospace engineering."

"Gosh, I could see that coming back in ninth grade when we were in the same math class."

"And Andy Kukendall is back East, playing basketball at Marquette."

"He was big enough and good enough to play college ball when he was a sophomore."

"You're right." Thomas sighed. "So, you know, people move on."

She caught the melancholy in his eyes. "You're moving on, too."

He smiled faintly. "Sure I am. You don't have to move away from home to go to college."

"No."

"My sister, Elizabeth, is in her second year at Cal Poly, so she's doing good."

"That's great."

"Have you heard anything from Kurt?" Thomas asked.

"No. His mom came to see me, though."

"What'd she want?"

"She was hoping she could get Kurt and me together, and that we'd get married, so the baby would stay in the family."

"What did you tell her?"

"I told her I have no interest in marrying Kurt."

Thomas smiled. "That's fairly direct."

She shrugged her shoulders. "He has no interest in marrying me, either."

"Does that surprise you?" Thomas asked.

"In a way it does. I mean when you're in the middle of a relationship, you're sure that this is the ultimate expression of love and affection and trust. I mean, at least I felt that way . . . at first. But then you find out that for the guy you're with, it's just a game. And if it's a game, well, anyone can walk away from a game. There are always other games, and other people to play them with."

"I'm sorry things didn't work out."

"Thanks. You know what? I'm glad I came. Maybe I should help you, so you can finish up."

He shook his head. "No, while I clean up in front, make me a pizza, like old times. With a personalized message to boost my ego."

"You got it. What message do you want?"

"That we're still friends. That's the most amazing thing about all this." He said it again. "That we're still friends."

On his way to the front, as he passed her, he paused. "You want a hug?"

"I would love a hug."

139

He seemed a little wary. "I won't break anything, will I? I mean, you know, inside, where the baby is."

"The baby probably needs a hug, too."

When he held her in his arms, she had the feeling she'd come home, and it brought tears to her eyes.

◆　　◆　　◆

In the next two weeks, Megan met twice more with Sister Gardner at LDS Family Services. They went over Megan's plan of how she was going to manage as a single mom. Sister Gardner was a good listener and occasionally made a few suggestions or brought up things she hadn't thought about. She began to think of Sister Gardner being on her side.

Megan's waistline was beginning to grow. If she pressed her stomach, she could feel a bulge, which she learned by asking her mother was her enlarged uterus, now about the size of a grapefruit.

She and Bryce could hardly stand to be around each other anymore. Whenever they were together, he tried to talk her out of keeping the baby. Once he told her she was being selfish.

"How can you say it's selfish for me to take care of my baby?" she countered.

"Because you're only thinking about what *you* want. You're not thinking about the baby."

"Who could take care of my baby better than me?"

"Almost anyone who's married."

"You don't know what you're talking about. There are plenty of families where the parents don't get along, where the kids would be better off if they were raised by just one parent."

"I know that, but they're not likely to want to adopt a kid. And even if they did, the adoption agency would know they weren't suitable parents. Adoption is the only way to get born where the parents are carefully chosen. Every other way is pure chance."

"I'll be a good mother. You'll see."

"The baby will be better off with a happily married couple than with you."

"Why should I believe anything you tell me? You sell plywood and screwdrivers, so what makes you such an authority about this?"

"Logic and reason. Something you've never been any good at."

"That is such a sexist attitude."

"Maybe so, but in this case it happens to be true."

"I don't care what you say. I'm not giving my baby away."

She continued to meet with Bishop Oldham once a week. He asked her to read the book *The Miracle of Forgiveness*. He warned her that it would be painful reading but encouraged her to read it all the way through. He was right. She didn't like having to face how far she'd strayed from the teachings of the Church. Even so, to try to do what the bishop asked, she forced herself to read a few pages each day.

With her mother at work, Brianna busy with friends, Bryce working at Home Depot, and her father gone during the week, Megan was home alone most of the time. At first it seemed strange not to be going to a job or to school. Many of her friends had summer jobs, so she had little contact with anyone. Sometimes she desperately missed Alexis, but pride prevented her from calling her at BYU or writing her a letter.

She could finish the reading assignments the bishop had given her in half an hour. The rest of her time she spent watching soaps on TV. The only reason she could think of to read more was to impress someone in the ward. But then she realized that being pregnant and single put her in the category of a person who's not going to impress very many people in the ward, no matter how diligently she reads the scriptures. Whether she read or not, she would not be asked to give a talk in sacrament meeting or to work with the Young Women in the ward.

In spite of her situation and the fact that she was beginning to show, she was becoming more comfortable attending Relief Society. She had to admit that she felt warmth and concern from many of the sisters in the ward. She did not understand why, but it was there.

Except for one woman. The bishop's wife.

♦    ♦    ♦

Diane Oldham had lived her entire life being true and faithful to the teachings of the Church. And now here she was at the top of what would be recognized as success for a woman her age in the Church—her husband serving as bishop, with them living in a new home, with money enough that they didn't have to worry, and with four beautiful children. Her oldest, twelve-year-old Rebecca, was especially talented in music and an exemplary young woman.

It was a matter of pride for Diane that she had always lived the way her leaders had taught, had kept the Word of Wisdom from her youth, had avoided watching R-rated movies, and had filled her life with activity in the Church. She was tall and had played basketball in high school, an activity that had taken up most of her time and kept her from dating much.

She had met her husband at BYU, where as freshman students they were in the same ward. When he left on his mission, she wrote to him faithfully. Then, two months before he came home, she left on a mission, and it was his turn to be supportive as a friend.

He attended her homecoming in San Mateo, driving from Provo most of Friday night to be there. They talked at her house over lunch. He had planned to leave later that day, so he would be back in Provo for his classes on Monday, but they enjoyed their time together so much that she asked him to stay another day.

That night he asked her to marry him, and she said yes.

They were married the Wednesday before Thanksgiving, just a couple of months after Diane got home from her mission. She was proud of the fact that the first time they kissed was across the altar in the temple on their wedding day.

Diane had very little sympathy for those who gave in to physical passion. It had not been a temptation for her. Looking back at her life, she was grateful she'd been chaste and, as the Mia Maid adviser in Young Women, she wished the same for all the girls under her charge.

She kept a well-organized house with everything in its place, with a beautiful flower garden, which she tended herself and took great pride in. She liked things neat and tidy and under control.

Maybe that's why the presence of Megan each week in church bothered Diane. The more apparent it became that Megan was pregnant, the more troubling it was for Diane.

All the time Megan had been growing up, she'd been the one that others looked up to for leadership. Part of it came from her appearance—her flashing, brooding, dancing eyes, and her expressive mouth, and animated laugh.

Diane had an image in her mind, that of Megan bringing her baby to church, showing it off proudly to the girls in Young Women, and all of them, the Mia Maids she taught as well as her own precious twelve-year-old Rebecca, fawning over what would no doubt be an adorable baby. *What if the girls see no bad consequences for Megan? Who will they believe? Megan, with her natural charisma? Or their leaders, older and maybe a little out of touch with the way things are now? Who will they believe?*

She worried about the way Megan was being fussed over by some women in the ward, and she resented the time Megan took up with her husband—valuable time that could be better spent at home helping with the children or working around the house or in their yard and garden.

Diane knew it wasn't any of her business and that she shouldn't say anything, but she couldn't help herself.

"I worry that the girls in our ward will see how much fuss is being made over Megan and that they'll decide it's okay for them to get pregnant before they're married, too." It was a Saturday, and she and the bishop were working together in their backyard.

"How are we making a big fuss over her?" her husband asked.

"She's the center of attention. People go out of their way to make her feel welcome."

"And that's bad?"

"It could be."

"As members of the Church, isn't that what we're supposed to do?"

"How can I talk about temple marriage when my girls see this girl suffering no consequences because of her actions?"

"There are consequences."

"Is she going to keep the baby?"

"She hasn't made her mind up yet."

"If she keeps the baby, and if she brings the baby to church, then what's going to stop some girl from thinking she wants a baby, too, so people can fuss over her."

"I think the girls in our ward can see the difference between having a child out of wedlock and having one who has been born into a family that has been sealed together for time and eternity."

"Why is she still a member of the Church?"

He turned to her and shook his head. "Diane, I can't believe you'd ask me that question."

"I'm sure others are asking it to themselves. I'm the only one who has the courage to ask you."

"You want me to excommunicate her, so you can use her as an example in Young Women? I'm sure you don't mean it."

"She takes a lot of your time, too, doesn't she?"

"I see her once a week."

"I imagine it's the highlight of her week. I mean, you're always very optimistic and upbeat. Why does she get singled out to receive such special treatment? It's almost like she's being rewarded for bad behavior."

"This is not easy for her. She has some difficult decisions to make about whether or not she's going to keep the baby."

"Oh, she'll keep the baby. I'm sure of it."

"How can you say that?"

"So she can continue to be the center of attention in the ward."

"Diane, I don't discuss these things even with my counselors. It's not an appropriate topic."

"I will not bring it up again. I just wanted you to know how some people in the ward feel about you bending over backwards for this girl."

"You've made your point very well then," he said. "Excuse me, I need to mow the lawn."

*Why can't he see my point?* she thought. *Why can't he see that he's only encouraging other girls to do the same thing?*

She wondered how it would be between them now that she'd criticized him for what he was doing as the bishop. This was the first time she'd done it. In fact, it was the first time she'd found fault with any of her bishops. It was hard for her to separate their personal relationship and her role as a ward member who needed to sustain her bishop.

*In other calls he's had, he's always asked me for my advice, but in this one he hasn't. I hope I haven't upset him too much. I never meant to do that. I just don't want him to make a mistake.*

*I'm just trying to help out, that's all.*

♦  ♦  ♦

After several days of watching game shows and soaps, Megan had had enough and decided to try to go an entire day with no TV.

It was a Thursday, and she had a reading assignment from the bishop. He had asked her to read fifty pages in the Book of Mormon by the time she met with him Sunday after church. He had also asked her to read two more chapters of *The Miracle of Forgiveness*. But she hadn't even begun.

*I should get started. But I don't want to. I should though. What am I so afraid of?*

She went into the tiny backyard of the condo and sat down at their picnic table. *This is my world now,* she thought. *An empty house, with no job. No friends except Thomas. Do people make fun of me now? Do they tell each other what a fool I was to get pregnant? And what do the people in my ward say about me? Do they wonder why I'm even bothering to go to church? Do they call me a tramp behind my back?*

*Why am I so afraid of reading what the bishop asked me to read? What am I afraid of?*

She was no gardener, but looking at the rosebushes she saw roses that had been beautiful days earlier but were now dying. She'd spent enough time with Mr. Podolsky in his flower garden to learn that if the bush is to produce more roses, the dead and dying blossoms need to be cut off. She went into the garage and got her mother's pruning shears and returned to the rosebush. It produced American Sweetheart roses. She sat down and began to cut away.

She became absorbed in her work, concentrating on caring for the rosebush. *If a rosebush needs to be pruned to get rid of what isn't working, why shouldn't the same be true of people, too? We get rid of what isn't working for us, and then we can go on. This rosebush is a growing thing, not doomed because of the past.*

146

She felt tears coming into her eyes. She hadn't expected to learn anything of value about her life by tending a rosebush. And yet she did feel comfort.

*Father in Heaven, how can you still care about me when I've messed up so many times? Why do you comfort me? Why do I feel like you care about me when I've gone against everything I was taught?*

She went into the condo and picked up her triple combination from the coffee table in the living room. She held it in her hands, without opening it.

*What am I afraid of?*

It was painful to admit, even to herself. *I'm afraid that the more I read the more awful I'll feel. Or that I'll realize that if I'd read the Book of Mormon earlier, then it would have been enough to keep me from making the mistakes I made. I'm worried that the closer I get to God, the more condemned I'll feel. And that I'll end up feeling worse than I do now.*

She closed her eyes and began to pray. *Oh, dear Heavenly Father, please don't make me suffer this alone. Please don't make my trying to get closer to you make me feel so awful that I can't stand to go on. Please don't make me bear this burden alone. It's too much for me to carry.*

*If I am a damned soul as far as you are concerned, with no hope for the future, tell me now. Don't let me go on thinking I can have my sins forgiven, only to yank the hope away from me at the last minute.*

*Am I damned forever because of my sins? Please let me know now. Right now. Today. So at least I'll know.*

She sat for a time, waiting for some impression, but nothing came. Finally, she opened her eyes, wiped her eyes and cheeks with a tissue, and set the triple combination back on the coffee table. She sat staring at it. The book had been a gift from her parents. They'd given it to her on the day she was baptized, and it had her name embossed on the leather cover.

*I could at least look in the index,* she thought, reaching

for the book. She found the word *Damnation* and scanned the entries: *Men bring damnation to their souls except they humble themselves; . . . if men have been evil, they shall reap damnation of their souls.* She continued reading the entries, stopping at: *Alma was wracked with pains of damned soul.*

*That's like me,* she thought. She turned to chapter 36 in Alma and began to read:

"And it came to pass that as I was thus racked with torment, while I was harrowed up by the memory of my many sins, behold, I remembered also to have heard my father prophesy unto the people concerning the coming of one Jesus Christ, a Son of God, to atone for the sins of the world.

"Now, as my mind caught hold upon this thought, I cried within my heart: O Jesus, thou Son of God, have mercy on me, who am in the gall of bitterness, and am encircled about by the everlasting chains of death.

"And now, behold, when I thought this, I could remember my pains no more; yea, I was harrowed up by the memory of my sins no more.

"And oh, what joy, and what marvelous light I did behold; yea, my soul was filled with joy as exceeding as was my pain!

"Yea, I say unto you, my son, that there could be nothing so exquisite and so bitter as were my pains. Yea, and again I say unto you, my son, that on the other hand, there can be nothing so exquisite and sweet as was my joy."

She was crying again, but these weren't tears of despair. *God still loves me,* she thought. *I am not cast off.* She fell to her knees by the couch and poured out her heart in thanksgiving for what she was feeling.

She spent the rest of the day reading everything she could find about Alma's life and about the testimony he bore throughout his life of the great gift he had been given at the worst time of his life.

*Tomorrow,* she thought, *I will start from the beginning and read the Book of Mormon from cover to cover.*

By the time she met with the bishop on Sunday, she was in Mosiah.

"Well, you have been busy," Bishop Oldham said with a broad smile.

"It's making sense to me, too. It's so great, Bishop. I feel happier now, and I'm more positive about the future."

"Good for you. What about your reading in *The Miracle of Forgiveness?*"

"It's good, but . . . it's also kind of depressing. I mean, I can see myself and what I was so clearly now. It makes me wish I'd done better."

"You're doing well now, though. That's the important thing."

"I think so, but I'm having trouble knowing how I should feel about myself."

"How do you mean?"

"I worry about what the people in the ward think about me."

"I understand what you're saying. But that shouldn't be a concern. The bigger question is, what does the Savior think about you?"

"The Savior still loves me," she said softly.

"How do you know that?"

"I've felt it when I've been reading the Book of Mormon, and when I pray. But that doesn't keep people from talking about me."

Megan looked down at her hands and then asked, "What does your wife think about me?"

He cleared his throat. "I'm curious why you'd ask that question."

"No reason. It's just the way she looks at me."

"How does she look at you?"

"Like I have no business being in church. Do you know what the word *tramp* means, Bishop?"

"Yes."

"I think that's what she thinks I am." Megan sighed. "That's what I was, I guess . . . or am. Maybe once a tramp, always a tramp."

The bishop opened his Bible and thumbed the pages, looking for a passage, then he began to read:

"'And the scribes and Pharisees brought unto him a woman taken in adultery; and when they had set her in the midst, They say unto him, Master, this woman was taken in adultery, in the very act. Now Moses in the law commanded us, that such should be stoned: but what sayest thou?

"'This they said, tempting him, that they might have to accuse him. But Jesus stooped down, and with his finger wrote on the ground, as though he heard them not.

"'So when they continued asking him, he lifted up himself, and said unto them, He that is without sin among you, let him first cast a stone at her.

"'And again he stooped down, and wrote on the ground.

"'And they which heard it, being convicted by their own conscience, went out one by one, beginning at the eldest, even unto the last: and Jesus was left alone, and the woman standing in the midst.

"'When Jesus had lifted up himself, and saw none but the woman, he said unto her, Woman, where are those thine accusers? hath no man condemned thee?

"'She said, No man, Lord. And Jesus said unto her, Neither do I condemn thee: go, and sin no more.'"

Bishop Oldham set his Bible aside and looked up. "What do you learn from this?"

"The Savior didn't condemn her."

"That's right, he didn't. What counsel did he give her?"

"To go and sin no more."

"Was he sinless?"

"Yes."

"Did he understand the seriousness of adultery?"

"Of course."

"That's right. Better than anyone else. He was the one who gave the Ten Commandments to Moses. So if this woman had no reason to hope for her future, he'd be the one who would know, and, most likely, he would have told her so."

"I guess that's true. I've never thought about it like that."

"What is interesting to me," the bishop continued, "is that this woman was dragged forcefully out of her house to the Savior by a mob. And yet, after they had all left, the woman stayed there in his presence. As soon as her accusers left, she could have run away, but she stayed there. Why do you suppose she did?"

"I'm not sure."

"Well, was she terrified of him? Was she afraid he might pick up a stone and throw it at her?"

"I don't think so."

"Why do you suppose that is?"

"Because she could feel he meant her no harm."

"I think that's true."

"I don't know how to act anymore."

"How do you mean?"

"I used to be so self-confident in social settings. But now I'm not so sure of myself. Like at church. I think about answering questions in Sunday School class, but I don't because I'm afraid people would think, 'If she's so smart, and if she knows so much about the gospel, then how come she went out and got herself pregnant?'"

"How would you answer that question?"

"I'm learning things I didn't know then."

"I can see that. I encourage you to participate in Sunday School class discussions."

"I feel like I have to go through this long explanation. 'Excuse me for raising my hand. And, yes, I am pregnant. And, no, I'm not married. And, yes, the bishop does know everything. And, no, I'm not excommunicated, even though some of you think I should be. Now can I answer the question?'"

The bishop smiled. "I don't think you need to explain a thing."

"Could you make an announcement, so we can get this all out, once and for all?"

"Should I make a similar announcement for everyone in the ward who has committed a sin recently? Would it be good to post a list of sinners on the bulletin board? The thing is, Megan, everyone I know is working on something. And if they're not, they should be. This is a church where we're all trying to do better. You're not the only one."

"But I'm starting to show that I'm pregnant."

"So?"

"Well, I mean it's pretty obvious, isn't it, what's been going on."

"You're carrying the baby. You're thinking about the welfare of the baby. You could have had an abortion, but you didn't. You decided to give life to your baby. In many people's minds that makes you a little bit of a hero."

"I wish I'd lived the standards of the Church."

"I know you do."

"The thing is, now when I read the Book of Mormon, I get so excited. It's such a wonderful book. And to think it was there for me all along if I had just picked it up and started reading."

"Heavenly Father sent us to earth so we could learn from our mistakes. I'm sure that he's pleased that you're learning from yours."

"I am. I really am. If I could just talk to the girls in Young Women. If I could just tell them what I've learned."

The bishop cleared his throat and nodded politely.

"Can I do that, Bishop?"

He glanced away. "I'm not sure that would be for the best."

She knew what he meant. He couldn't risk her influenc-
ing the younger girls in a negative way.

"I understand."

"I hope you do."

# 9

At a school dance after a football game, Brianna worked the crowd as only she could. With her out-going personality and sense of humor, she was on good terms with almost everyone in school. Every group—the preppies, the druggies, the gay-prides, the cowboys—they all loved her.

On her way to the girls restroom she passed a girl and a guy in the hall making out. They seemed nearly out of control.

It made her feel sick. *Don't go there, girl, or you'll end up like my sister.*

She thought about stopping to say something, but she didn't because she didn't know what to say. And she knew it wouldn't make any difference.

A few minutes later, in the restroom, she looked at herself in the mirror.

*It's not going to happen to me.*

She'd had a dream the night before that she was pregnant but couldn't remember how she'd gotten pregnant. In her dream she was trying to talk to her mother about it.

Her mother handled it well. "Well, I'm not surprised. I knew it was only a matter of time."

"How can you say that? I'm not a bit like Megan."

"You are, though. You're just like her."

No matter how hard she tried, she couldn't make her mother feel otherwise.

When she first woke up from the dream, she felt great relief that it wasn't real, but at the same time she worried that it might just be a matter of time.

The dream had ended with her saying over and over again, "I'm a good girl."

On the way back to the dance, the girl and the boy were still there.

Brianna stopped. "Not here."

The boy glanced up, looking like he was in some kind of a trance. "What?"

"Are you picking up what I'm putting down? Is the sprinkler hitting the grass? I said, not here."

"What's it to you what we do?"

"I don't care to watch what you're doing. So either quit or do it some place where people walking by can't see it."

The guy looked like he wanted to beat up Brianna, but the girl didn't want any trouble. She pulled her boyfriend by the hand. "She's right."

They were turning to leave, but Brianna locked eyes with the girl. "Be careful, okay?"

She nodded, and they left the dance.

*I'm hurting,* she thought. *I don't show it, but I'm hurting. Real bad.*

She hurried back to the dance where she could put on a happy face once again.

As she approached her group of friends, she called out, "Peace out, my homeys!"

Walter and Carolyn were seeing the bishop to renew their temple recommends. Bishop Oldham visited first with Carolyn. An interview that usually took five minutes ended up lasting half an hour.

And then it was Walter's turn.

The temple recommend interview took only a few minutes. And then Bishop Oldham leaned back in his chair and asked, "How long have you been a Scoutmaster?"

"It's been five years."

"You've done a magnificent job with the boys. How many Eagle Scouts did we have last year?"

"Seven."

"That's just amazing."

"Especially when you consider there hadn't been any for years before I took over the troop."

"You've done a great job. We'll always be grateful to you for showing us how a Scout program should be run."

"We've got some good boys coming along. The way I look at it, Bishop, it's just the beginning."

"Well, perhaps, but I think it might be time to extend a release to you and let someone else continue on."

Walter was shocked. "Did Carolyn say something to you?"

"Well, yes, she did. She thinks you need to be home more for your children. Especially now, with Megan going through her difficult time. She told me that with your traveling each week and then taking the boys camping, that you're not around much."

"I think Megan is okay now. She's back on track. And Bryce is never around anyway. And Brianna, well, she's doing okay. So I don't see how going camping one weekend a month is taking me away from my family."

"Carolyn is concerned."

"Don't release me from Scouting, Bishop. It's taken me a

long time to get it to where it is now. I can cut down on week-end activities for the boys for the next few months."

"Let me talk with my counselors about it, and then we'll get back to you. Believe me, trying to find a new Scoutmaster is not something I look forward to."

The next Sunday Walter was released as Scoutmaster and called to be the Gospel Doctrine Sunday School teacher.

He was devastated and resentful of Carolyn. When he accused her of engineering his release, she said, "All I did was tell the bishop our situation. I didn't ask him to release you. He made that decision himself. Don't get mad at him or me. If you believe the Lord called you to be the Scoutmaster, then you should also believe he released you. That's what happens in the Church, Walter. We serve, and then we get released. Except as parents. From that we never get released. Your family needs you now more than ever."

"They don't need me."

"They do, but you've always been gone so much that it's going to take some time before your children feel comfortable enough to come to you."

Walter spent the next Saturday cleaning out the garage, gathering all the Scout equipment in one place for his replace-ment, a twenty-eight-year-old novice in Scouting, to come and pick up.

*This is a mistake*, he thought. *This is a big mistake. The bishop should never have released me.*

*It's going to be tough to watch the program I worked so hard on crumble away to nothing. And for what? So I can be home? Well I'm home today. And what good has it done? Brianna's gone all day. Megan avoids me, and Bryce is always gone. And even when he's around, he doesn't want any advice from me on how to live his life.*

*This is a big mistake, that's all there is to it.*

After he'd been working in the garage for two hours,

Carolyn came out to see him. She brought him a glass of lemonade. "How's it going?"

"I'm almost done."

"We're going to have a lot more room around here."

"Everything I worked so hard to achieve is all going to fall apart. The new Scoutmaster doesn't know a thing about Scouting."

"He'll learn, just like you did."

"I care about the boys."

"I know you do, Walter, but someone else also cares about them, even more than you do."

"Who?"

"The Lord. Why don't you just assume that he knows what's best for you, and for your family, and for the boys in our ward? Give it up, Walter. It's not your responsibility anymore."

She turned and walked back inside.

His immediate response was to dismiss what she'd said because she'd never shared his enthusiasm for Scouting. But a short time later a new thought came into his mind.

*What if she's right?*

♦　　♦　　♦

On her mission in Montana, Heather read over again the letters she'd received from home in the past month. She was troubled, not by what was in the letters but because of what was missing.

The first odd letter came four weeks before. Her mother wrote: "Megan lost her job, and so she's moved back home. But she's doing really well."

Since then, in subsequent letters, there had never been any mention of Megan getting another job.

*What is she doing home if she's not working?* Heather

thought. *And why isn't she at least taking night classes? I don't understand.*

And then came the cryptic letter from her father, which read: "I've been released as Scoutmaster and called to be a Sunday School teacher."

She knew how much he loved Scouting. In many of his previous letters, he'd gone on and on talking about the progress the boys were making toward Eagle. For him to just state he had been released, with no explanation, seemed to her very strange.

Megan had written once since returning home. She wrote: "You've always been such a good example to the family. I wish we'd been closer when you were home. I could have learned a lot from you."

*Something's wrong. There are no details. I still don't know what Megan is doing at home with no job and not going to college. And why would they release Daddy when he was probably the best Scoutmaster the ward's ever had?*

*What is going on? And why aren't they telling me?*

She hated it that she'd always been put on a pedestal by the family. What it did was distance her from everyone else, so nobody brought their problems to her. Because Megan and Brianna and Bryce didn't believe she'd even understand being tempted to do something wrong, they never approached her with what they were facing. And so she had always felt isolated from everyone else in the family.

*They're still doing that to me*, she thought. *All I get is good news from them. Do they think I'm so fragile that I'd cave in with the truth? Well, I'm not. I've had enough bad news on my mission, faced the same problems my investigators face, helped them struggle with the repentance they need in their lives, that I can take any truth and any bad news and any disappointments my family can give me.*

*If only they'd trust me. If only they'd let me in and not keep me out the way they've been doing all my life.*

*I'll write and ask them to let me in on all the family secrets.*

◆　　◆　　◆

Once a month, on a Sunday afternoon, Thomas's family got together for a huge spaghetti dinner at his grandparents' house. His three uncles and his father stayed in the living room and argued politics or sports while the women worked in the kitchen preparing food. The custom was that none of the men did anything in the way of food preparation—in the Marconi family, that was women's work.

Thomas sat with the men for fifteen minutes. They were talking politics. Typically, the conversation was loud and animated. He'd heard it all before.

Finally, he went into the kitchen. "Can I help?"

"You wouldn't even know what to do."

"Are you kidding? I work in a pizza place, okay? I know my way around a kitchen."

"He wants to help? Let him help," his Aunt Beth said in a somewhat sarcastic manner.

They let him put a glass of ice water beside every plate.

On his second trip to the dining room with a tray of glasses, his Uncle Al called out, "You need an apron there, missy?"

The men all laughed. Thomas smiled. *This is how we keep everyone in their place. Men aren't supposed to help out.*

His Uncle Bill gestured. "Sit down and talk with us. The women can see to that."

"Soon as I finish up with the water."

"Such a nice girl. She'll make someone a wonderful wife," Uncle Al continued.

"She'll need to do something about that figure of hers, though."

"Someone will come along who won't mind."

160

Uncle Al burst out laughing. "That's what worries me."

*I can't let them get to me,* Thomas thought. He finished setting out the water glasses and returned to the kitchen. "What else can I do?" he asked.

His sister, Elizabeth, who'd heard the men teasing Thomas, came into the kitchen. She was easily the most gifted one in the family, a classical pianist, in her junior year in college, majoring in music. She had long, straight, dark brown hair and thick eyelashes and eyebrows that imbued the simplest sentence with drama and intrigue.

She put her hand on Thomas's back and said confidentially, "Don't let them get to you, Thomas, okay?"

"It's okay. They don't bother me."

They made eye contact. *She understands how oppressed I feel when I'm here.* "Can we talk?" he asked.

"I'd like that."

*How come I feel that Elizabeth is a stranger, even though we grew up together? It's like we've never really talked. When we come here, it's like being in a play, and everyone acts their part. And everyone asks the same questions, like how's school going? And we obediently give the expected answers.*

"Let's go in back and swing on the porch swing, like we used to when we were kids," Elizabeth said.

They walked through the kitchen and out the back door, away from the view of anyone inside the house, and sat down together in the swing.

"You okay?" she asked.

"I guess so. You know what's amazing about our family get-togethers?"

"What?"

"How many don't come. Amanda never comes. Josh, Ryan, Zach, Isaac—they all quit coming years ago. You know why they don't come anymore?"

"Why?"

"Because they don't fit in. The only ones welcome are the

161

ones who haven't stepped out of line." He turned to her. "How come we never talk about the ones we've driven away? How come it's either 'Be the same as us or stay away'? How come?"

"I don't know, Thomas."

"Me, either. I'm not what they think I am. I just play the part they've given me while I'm here. They don't know what I'm really like. And they don't even want to know."

"I feel the same way," she said.

"How about you and I agree to talk honestly about ourselves?"

She leaned her head on his shoulder. "I'd like that very much."

"Good. How are things going for you? I mean, really."

"Well, I'm very happy in my classes."

"Good."

"And I keep busy. I'm accompanying the college choir. I love doing that."

"Great."

"Although, to be perfectly honest, I'd have to say that there's something missing in my life," she said.

"What?"

In a nervous gesture, she brushed back the hair from her forehead. "Oh, gosh, this is going to seem so dumb to you."

"No, it's okay, go ahead."

"Well, the truth is, I've had such bad luck with guys."

"In what way?"

"Well, like last week, this guy in one of my classes asks me to a movie. On the way out of the theater, he suggests we sleep together. One movie and a bag of popcorn, and he's asking me that? Where did that come from? And then last month I was dating a guy. Two or three times. He treated me with respect, but then some friends of mine told me he actually prefers guys and that he was just dating me so his parents wouldn't catch on. Well, of course, I ended that. So now I'm wondering where I can find just an ordinary nice guy." She smiled faintly. "Like you, for instance."

"Good luck," he said with a silly grin. "I'm one of a kind."

"Oh, man, I hope not. There's got to be more out there somewhere. But where?"

"I'll look around for you and see what I can come up with."

Aunt Beth opened the door. "Hey, you two, it's time to eat."

They returned to the house.

◆　　◆　　◆

Megan's mother, Carolyn, worked at city hall in the accounting department. Her two closest associates were both women.

Dottie had worked there the longest. Her body was starting to sag and fall apart, but her brassy, red-tinted hair stayed the same color and style. She'd long ago dropped the idea of giving her all for the job, and now the only things she looked forward to at work were coffee breaks, lunch hours, and holidays. She was the most knowledgeable one in the office, the one the bosses came to when they wanted to know something.

The other woman was Mary. Because city hall had many iron-fisted administrators, the place needed someone like Mary, who served as the heart and soul and conscience of city government. She was the one who knew when someone was having a birthday. She was the one who sent cards when someone had been sick or had problems in their family. Even so, she was undervalued by her superiors and consistently overlooked for promotions.

Although these women appeared to be very different from each other, they had one thing in common: they both had grandchildren whom they adored.

They were always showing Carolyn photographs of their

grandkids and bragging about the children's superior intelligence and wonderful accomplishments.

"Isn't she the most adorable child you've ever seen in your entire life?" Mary or Dottie would ask.

"She is. No doubt about it."

"Grandchildren are great. You've got to get yourself some."

"I will. Someday."

And now that *someday* was coming sooner than she'd ever expected. Carolyn wasn't sure, though, what Megan would decide to do—keep the baby or place it for adoption. Although Carolyn was trying to be impartial, her mind said one thing, but her heart said another. She yearned for a grandbaby. One she could fuss over and buy cute outfits for and hold in her arms and rock to sleep. She had kept the rocking chair she had used when her own children were small, and she looked forward to using it again, this time as a loving grandma.

*I know I need to let Megan make this decision,* she thought. *If I jump in and try to talk her into keeping the child, it might not be the best thing, either for the baby or for my relationship with Megan.*

Even so, when she went shopping alone, she often found herself diverted to the racks filled with baby clothes. She would have bought several but didn't know where she could hide them at home where nobody would find them.

With Megan pregnant, Carolyn began to fantasize about having a grandchild to love and being able to bring her own pictures to work to show off. She tried to resist the idea, but it was always there. She knew it would be emotionally difficult for her if her first grandchild were given to another couple to raise.

She did not tell Dottie or Mary that Megan was expecting a baby. She knew they would have strong opinions about what was the right thing to do, and that they would do their

164

best to convince her they were right, and might even get her to try to talk "some sense" into Megan.

*This is a decision Megan needs to make for herself. I will support her in whatever she decides to do. If I jump in too quickly, then she will feel alienated from me if she chooses to do something else.*

Even though she was trying to be neutral, she did break down and buy a few things for the baby. She hid them in her bottom dresser drawer, where she hoped nobody would find them.

*This is very hard for me, too, because, more than anything now in my life, I want a grandchild to call my own.*

*I just have to be patient, though. Be supportive and patient.*

◆　　◆　　◆

Ann Marie woke up at two-thirty in the morning and couldn't get back to sleep. Weston was in the guest bedroom. Or at least that's what they called it now. It had at one time been known as the baby's room, but that had been a long time ago.

They had argued just before going to bed, and Ann Marie, in tears, had suggested he sleep somewhere else that night. And before she could call her words back, he had taken his pillow and left. She couldn't call him back because her own feelings were hurt.

He had hurt her by what he'd said, and at first she didn't think she could ever forgive him.

"All I'm saying," he had said, "is that we both need to face the fact that we're not going to have kids by ourselves. If we want to have kids, then we'll have to adopt."

"I don't want somebody else's mistake. I want a child of my own."

"It's not going to happen, Ann Marie. Why can't you see that? Everyone else can."

In the beginning her failure to get pregnant had been *their* problem, but their doctor had told them long ago that it was primarily Ann Marie who was responsible.

Because it was too much to bear, too oppressive a burden, she had pulled in and grown silent and moody and depressed.

And that's why she'd lashed out at Weston.

She turned on a light next to the bed and sat up. *It's strange to have his side of the bed empty. We've never slept apart since we were married. And tonight I drove him away.*

*I could lose him if I'm not careful. There are so many women out there who'd do whatever it takes to make him a part of their life.*

She got up and padded down the hall to the guest bed-room, opened the door, and without a word, crawled into bed next to him.

"I hope that's my wife," he said quietly.

"It is."

"Are you lost?"

"I was, but I'm not anymore."

He put his arm around her and drew her in close to him.

"You're probably sleepy, right?" she asked.

"Not really."

"Me, either. Do you want to talk?"

"Might as well," he said.

"Let's go in the kitchen and have some hot chocolate and cookies," she suggested.

"Okay."

In the kitchen she fussed with making the hot chocolate and getting out a plate for the cookies, then sat down across from him and handed him the plate of cookies—chocolate chip for her and Fig Newtons for him.

"I'm sorry for getting so emotional earlier," she said.

"I should have been more understanding," he said,

looking down at the floor, as if he were a little boy who'd been caught doing something wrong. It was a look she had grown to cherish, one of a few left over from his childhood.

He finished his Fig Newton, then reached across the table and held her hands. "There was something I should have said . . . that I didn't."

"What?"

"I will love you with all my heart whether we have kids or not. Our love isn't at risk here, no matter what happens."

She pursed her lips and nodded. "I should have said that, too." She dabbed at her eyes with a napkin. "I've always been able to solve my own problems, but I can't solve this one. That's been really hard for me to accept."

"It's been hard for me, too."

She lowered her gaze and let the tears come, tired of being strong, exhausted by having to always be in control, to always be the one that others could depend on.

He held her hands and let her cry. He'd run out of encouraging words. He, too, was on empty.

A few minutes later, she looked up and said, quite simply, "I think we should look into adopting a baby of our own."

He nodded his head and squeezed her hand.

They didn't go to sleep right away, which meant they were up way too late. They slept in the next morning, waking up too late to be on time for work. But neither of them cared.

# 10

Megan went back to spending time with Thomas at Leo's Pizza after closing time. She usually showed up between ten and ten-thirty at night. She'd go around to the back and knock, and he'd let her in.

Sometimes, when she was feeling good, she'd help Thomas clean up. At other times, she just sat near where he was working, and they would talk.

"You seem kind of quiet," he said one night.

"Sorry. I've been doing a lot of thinking lately."

"What about?" he asked as he wiped tables.

"My life."

"What about it?"

"I've pretty much made a mess of things, haven't I?"

"Nobody's perfect."

"I should've done better."

"Why? What makes you so special?"

"You don't even know, do you?"

"Know what?"

"Nothing."

"It must be something."

"You wouldn't understand."

"Try me."

"I'm a Mormon."

"So?"

"I shouldn't have messed up."

"What are you saying, that you're the first Mormon who messed up?"

"No."

"Then let it go. You'll drive yourself crazy trying to relive the past. It's gone. There's nothing you can do to change what happened."

"I know that, Thomas."

"Good."

"I've been reading the Book of Mormon lately. It's really helped me. I think if I'd been reading it all along, I wouldn't have made so many bad decisions."

"Books don't have the power to change people's lives."

"This one does," she said.

"That's hard to believe."

"I'll bring you a copy. You can read it and see for yourself."

He shrugged his shoulders. "Sure, whatever. I'll read it."

The next night she dropped by and gave him a copy.

A couple of days later, he called her at home. He told her he'd been reading the Book of Mormon and had some questions. She wasn't sure how to answer them, so she asked if he'd be willing to listen to the missionaries sometime at her house.

He said yes.

She got off the phone and called the ward mission leader and asked him to send her some missionaries on Sunday night. Once her mother heard about the arrangements, she called and invited the missionaries to come for supper that evening.

On Sunday there was a knock on the door at 5:30 P.M.

169

Megan's mother answered it and let the missionaries in, then called upstairs for Megan to come down. Brianna was at the home of one of her church friends.

"This is my daughter Megan."

The senior companion shook her hand. "I'm Elder Spaulding," he said with an easy smile. "I'm please t' meetcha." He had dark brown hair with, at least on that day, the cowlick of the century, a patch of hair sticking up from the back of his head, which he kept trying to smooth down with his hand.

He was three inches taller than his companion. Megan imagined that his height, along with his friendliness and a resonant voice, gave him an advantage over his peers. He had the easy manner of someone who had always been looked to for leadership. *I bet he was a student body president in high school. You can always tell.* Even so, she didn't resent his assumption of being in charge.

She was intrigued by his voice. It was, when he was in control, lower and more modulated than when he was excited. She wondered where he'd learned that—if it was from his mother or from a speech teacher or just because he was vain and wanted to sound like Arnold Schwarzenegger. But unlike Arnold, Elder Spaulding had a Southern accent.

"This is my companion, Elder Anderson," he said.

*I'm sure Elder Anderson is perfectly capable of introducing himself,* she thought.

Elder Anderson was shorter, had a round face, wore glasses, and appeared to be well on his way to going bald. He shook her hand briefly, smiled without enthusiasm, looked her in the eye for perhaps half a second and then looked down at the floor, as if greeting people was an ordeal to be endured. He glanced at the clock on the wall and then, almost as an accusation, glared at his companion.

*Whoa! These two don't get along,* Megan thought.

"What time is your friend coming?" Elder Anderson asked.

"Seven."

"Dinner appointments are only supposed to be an hour," he said to Elder Spaulding.

"It'll be okay, Elder. We're havin' a cottage meetin'."

"But the cottage meeting isn't until seven. We'll have half an hour unbudgeted time. We could go tracting."

"No, we'll just stay here, Elder. Relax, it's okay, all right?"

"Maybe so, but we'll be wasting half an hour," he said quietly.

"I'll take full responsibility for that half hour," Elder Spaulding said.

Elder Anderson gave up and sat down.

Megan had been worried about meeting the elders, not only because they were about the same age as she was, but also because she wasn't sure if they knew about her condition. It was one thing to tell her bishop, a man much older than she was, but it would be much more embarrassing to tell two guys her age, who had probably always been active in the Church.

"Where are you from?" she asked, trying to put them and herself at ease.

"Biloxi, Mississippi," Elder Spaulding said with a big smile. He pronounced it "Missipee." "Home of the Crawdad Festival."

"The Crawdad Festival?" she asked.

He smiled. "Yes. I can tell you've never heard of it."

"Do they crown a Miss Crawdad?" she asked.

"Yes, they do, as a matter-a-fact."

"That must be a coveted title. I mean, you know, the responsibility to represent all the crawdads in the state of Mississippi."

He broke into a big grin. "Yes, ma'am, it's not somethin' we take lightly."

"I can see that."

"I'm from Detroit, Michigan," Elder Anderson said.

171

"Home of what?" Megan asked.

"I don't know. Cars, I guess."

"No, no," Elder Spaulding teased. "Home of the driveby shootin'."

Elder Anderson's feelings were hurt. "You know what? I get that all the time, and, really, it's so unfair of people to say things like that."

"I was just jokin', Elder," Elder Spaulding said.

"Instead of just wasting our time talking, how about if we read the Book of Mormon together?" Elder Anderson suggested.

Elder Spaulding frowned.

"Mom, when will supper be ready?" Megan called out.

"Five minutes."

"Not 'nuff time to get much read," Elder Spaulding said.

Megan's dad came in, shook hands with the elders, and sat down. "Well, I understand we're having a missionary lesson here tonight."

"That's right," Elder Spaulding said enthusiastically. "We're very grateful to you and your family for takin' an interest in missionary work."

"Oh, it's not me. It's Megan. I'm very proud of her. The way I see it, some good is coming from this, after all."

Megan cringed and started to blush.

There was a long pause.

"Some good is coming from what?" Elder Anderson asked.

Walter glanced at Megan, then stammered, "Well, oh . . . I thought you both knew."

"Knew what?" Elder Anderson asked.

Megan could feel her face turning red.

"I'm sorry, Megan," her dad said. "I thought they knew."

She nodded. "It's okay. It has to come up sometime."

"Do you want me to tell them?" her dad asked.

"Yes," she said softly. "You'd better."

Her dad wiped his perspiring forehead. "I don't want you to get the wrong idea. Megan is a good girl. She always has been, but a little while ago she made a few bad decisions, and now she's having to live with that."

Megan's hand went to her face. *Don't let them see me cry,* she thought.

Her father cleared his throat. "Maybe if I'd been around more, things would be different. It's hard for me to admit that, but I've been doing a lot of thinking lately."

There was a long, uncomfortable pause. Elder Anderson was staring at Megan. Elder Spaulding was embarrassed and kept his head down. Megan was dabbing at her eyes, and her father, the man who prided himself on never showing emotion, was having trouble finishing a sentence without having to stop to gain better control of himself.

"We can't dwell on what could have been, though, can we?" Walter said. "We have to take things the way they are and try to make the best of them."

"You know what? I still don't know what you're talking about," Elder Anderson said.

"Oh, good grief," Elder Spaulding muttered. "Let it go."

"My daughter Megan is expecting a baby."

It didn't phase Elder Anderson. "So, is the father the one we're teaching tonight?"

"No."

"So how does the guy we're teaching fit into the picture?"

"He's just a friend," Megan said.

"Well, that's a relief," Elder Anderson said.

"Elder, don't talk anymore, okay?" Elder Spaulding said, shaking his head.

Megan had had it with Elder Anderson. "I'm going in the kitchen to see if I can help out."

Her mother put her to work putting salad on some plates. "How are things going in there?" her mother asked.

"It's unbelievably awkward. Elder Anderson has the social skills of a rhinoceros."

"Elder Spaulding seems nice, though, doesn't he?"

Megan shook her head. "I suppose. Except he's from the South."

"Why's that a problem?"

"When anyone talks with a Southern accent, I tend to think they're not very smart."

"I'm sure he's plenty smart."

"He comes from a town that has a crawdad festival. How smart can he be?"

"I'm sure he didn't have much choice about where he was raised."

"Maybe not, but if I came from a town with a crawdad festival, I wouldn't go around telling people about it."

Her mother smiled. "You think you might be a little unfair?"

"No, not at all."

Megan was carrying the salad plates to the dining room table when Brianna burst into the house, crying out in her cheerleader's voice, "Oh, my gosh, I've got to go to the bathroom *so* bad!" She stopped in her tracks when she saw the elders in the living room. "Good thing I didn't say that in front of the missionaries, right?" she called out, bounding up the stairs.

"That's my sister Brianna," Megan said.

"Oh, we know her," Elder Spaulding said. "They asked us t' substitute teach early morning seminary last week. Brianna answered most of the questions. She knows a lot about the gospel. We were both impressed. Weren't we, Elder?"

"Yes, we were," Elder Anderson said mechanically. "She's a lot smarter than she looks."

A short time later, Brianna came down the stairs. She had been to a planning meeting and was still wearing her Sunday clothes. "Hey, Elders, whatsup?" She high-fived both of them.

"Doin' good!" Elder Spaulding answered with a big grin. "How 'bout you?"

"Hey, today was journal writing material, you know what I'm saying?"

Elder Anderson smiled faintly.

Bryce was the next to show up. He came in through the garage into the kitchen. He'd spent his Sunday helping his boss and his wife sheetrock a family room.

"Bryce, I'm glad you're here for supper," his mother said. "How did it go?"

"Well, except for the fact that my boss is a complete idiot, it went all right. But if the man would just listen to me, we'd have been done three hours ago. But, no, he has to do it his way 'cause he's the boss."

Megan came into the kitchen.

"The elders are here," Megan said, trying to warn Bryce so he wouldn't say anything he'd regret.

Bryce swore. "What for?"

"They're going to give my friend Thomas the missionary lessons."

"Oh, great, that's all I need," he muttered. "Go ahead without me. I'll grab something after I take a shower."

Bryce walked through the living room and went upstairs without saying anything to the missionaries.

"And that was my brother, Bryce," Megan said.

"He's not active in the Church, is he?" Elder Anderson said.

"No."

"I could tell."

Elder Spaulding shook his head. "I understan' you're a cheerleader, Brianna, is that right?"

"For sure," she said. "You want to see a new cheer I just worked up?"

Before he could answer, she was standing in the living

room doing a cheer, which ended with her jumping into the air, kicking her legs, throwing up her hands, and shouting.

Elder Anderson lowered his gaze during Brianna's performance.

"That was amazin'!" Elder Spaulding called out excitedly when she was done.

"Well, it's better with a short dress."

Elder Anderson shook his head. "For some maybe, but not for me," he muttered.

"Is the sprinkler hitting the grass, Elder Anderson?" Brianna asked.

Elder Anderson's eyebrows raised. "What?" he asked.

"Are you picking up what I'm putting down?"

Elder Anderson turned to Megan. "I don't know what she's saying," he said privately.

"What'd you think I meant when I said it was better with a short dress?" Brianna asked.

"Well, I . . . thought . . . that . . . you meant it would . . . well . . . show more."

"How could you think that? What kind of a girl do you think I am? What I meant was I can jump higher and kick out my legs more with a short dress. That's what I meant."

"I understood that's what you meant," Elder Spaulding said.

Megan, totally embarrassed, put her hand to her forehead. *How could this possibly go any worse?*

Conversation during supper was subdued. Trying to be considerate, Elder Spaulding ate sparingly. Unfortunately, he didn't pay enough attention to Elder Anderson, who finished one pork chop, then grabbed another and started eating it.

"Isn't that pork chop supposed to be for Bryce?" Brianna asked.

"Well . . ." her mother stammered, not wishing to embarrass Elder Anderson.

Still chewing, Elder Anderson looked up to see the

disapproving eyes of everyone at the table. The pork chop was halfway eaten.

"You go ahead and finish, Elder Anderson."

"How was that pork chop, Elder?" Brianna asked, playing with Elder Anderson like a cat playing with a mouse it's caught.

"It was good," Elder Anderson said.

"Great, we'll tell Bryce that when he comes down and wants to eat. I'm sure he'll want to know what he missed."

"Sorry," Elder Anderson said. "I didn't know."

Brianna had a big grin on her face and turned to her mother. "Mom, we need to invite the missionaries over more often. I'm having a great time."

Twenty minutes later Thomas showed up. Bryce grabbed a sandwich and escaped as fast as he could because he knew that if he listened in on the discussion he'd end up arguing with the missionaries. Not that he wouldn't have enjoyed the experience, but he didn't want to hurt Megan's feelings.

The missionary discussion with Thomas went well. He agreed to read the Book of Mormon and to attend church on Sunday.

"We need to go now," Elder Anderson said, looking at his watch.

"No, stay," Megan said. "My mom baked a pie. She'll be disappointed if you guys don't have some."

"We really need to go," Elder Anderson said.

"What for?" Elder Spaulding asked. "We don't have any other appointments tonight. What kind of pie did your mom bake?" He pronounced it "pah."

"Apple. And she's got some ice cream to put on it."

"Well, bless my soul," Elder Spaulding said. "I think we'd better stay, Elder. We don't want to disappoint Megan's mom, do we?"

"All right, but then we really need to go."

They ate their pie, then visited for a while. As the elders

were leaving, Elder Spaulding sat down at the piano and began playing a hymn. They ended up singing some hymns, and before they knew it, it was nine-thirty.

"We really need to go now," Elder Anderson spoke privately to his companion.

Elder Spaulding broke into a big grin. "Oh, my gosh, you're right. Why'd you let us stay here so long, Elder? I'm surprised at you."

Elder Anderson saw little humor in the remark.

Thomas and Megan watched them go. "This was very interesting tonight," Thomas said.

"I'm glad you liked it. I'm proud of you for taking the discussions, Thomas. I'll read the Book of Mormon right along with you so we can talk about what you're reading."

"That'd be great. Well, I'd better be going." He gave her a quick hug and kissed her on the cheek and then left.

*Even though there were some rough times, all in all this has been a good day,* she thought. *I shouldn't be so happy, but I am.*

*I wonder why?*

♦　　♦　　♦

Megan had heard people talk about the missionaries bringing a special spirit into a home, and now she could see it for herself. She looked forward to each discussion. She could see the changes in Thomas, not so much in his actions but in his countenance. He smiled more, and when he prayed at the end of each discussion, it was from his heart.

Although Elder Anderson and Elder Spaulding still had their disagreements, there were times when they got along and worked effectively together.

In order to be as much help as she could to Thomas, Megan spent at least two hours a day reading the Book of Mormon. When she had a question or an insight about a particular passage, she'd write it down, then she and her mother and Brianna would talk about it during or after supper. When Walter wasn't on the road, he would join in. If Bryce was there when they started talking religion, he would usually excuse himself, although sometimes he'd stay and listen, hoping to find a weak argument he could pounce on.

Bryce got involved with the missionaries, too, but not in the way anyone could have predicted.

The elders dropped by unannounced one afternoon when Bryce wasn't working.

"Nobody's here except Megan, and she's upstairs taking a shower."

"We were just out tractin' and we're kind of thirsty. Suppose we could beg a glass of water from you?" Elder Spaulding asked.

"Yeah, sure, come on in," Bryce said.

They sat down in the living room while Bryce fixed them some ice water and a plate of cookies.

Suddenly, water began pouring through the chandelier above the kitchen table.

"Is that supposed to be happening?" Elder Anderson asked politely.

Bryce swore, ran up the stairs, and started banging on the bathroom door. "Megan, get out! Turn off the water!"

"Just ten more minutes!"

"No, now! Water's pouring through the ceiling!"

"What?"

"I said water's pouring through the ceiling! Turn off the shower and get out!"

She turned off the shower.

Bryce ran downstairs and out to the garage, bringing back a saw and a drill.

"You need any help?" Elder Spaulding asked.

"I do," Bryce answered.

The three of them ran upstairs. "You out of there yet, Megan?" Bryce shouted.

"I've still got shampoo in my hair!"

"We need to get in there."

"I'm hurrying as fast as I can."

"Well, it's not fast enough."

Seeing that Megan might take too long, Bryce led the elders into the adjoining master bedroom. "Okay, start pulling everything out of the closet. What we're going to do is cut a hole in the wall to see if there's a broken pipe."

The elders grabbed everything and piled it on the bed while Bryce drilled a hole big enough to get his saw started.

Hearing the saw, Megan quickly put on a robe and ran to her room.

Ten minutes later they peered into the ragged hole in the closet wall. No pipes were broken.

"Let's go downstairs and see what we can find out," Bryce said.

Downstairs, Bryce stood on the kitchen table and cut a hole in the ceiling by the chandelier to investigate further. They found no broken pipes.

"Megan, I need to talk to you! Right now!" Bryce shouted.

By this time she'd gotten dressed. She came out wearing slacks and a sweatshirt. Her hair, still not rinsed, was wrapped in a towel.

"All right, what did you do?" Bryce asked.

"Nothing. I just took a shower."

"You must have done something. What were you doing, right before I started yelling?"

"Well, I was shampooing my hair."

"And?"

"Nothing. . . . Well, I turned the nozzle up."

"You turned the nozzle up? How could you do that?"

"I always do it."

Bryce ran upstairs and into the bathroom. "That's it!"

180

He appeared at the top of the stairs. "Don't ever point the nozzle up again, you hear me?"

"What's wrong with that?"

"You want to come up here and see what's wrong with that?"

Megan shrugged. "Not particularly."

"This was all your fault!"

Megan's dark eyes flashed. "Don't you get after me, Bryce! I've been doing my shampoos the same way for years."

"Well, something happened today. The caulking around the shower has come loose, so the water got between the shower and the wall."

Megan shrugged. "Caulking is not my responsibility."

"Caulking is everybody's responsibility," Bryce answered with great solemnity.

"Don't mind him," she said. "He works at Home Depot."

Elder Spaulding nodded his head. "That, of course, explains everything."

Bryce came down the stairs. "We've got to get this cleaned up before Mom comes home. I'm going to Home Depot and get some sheetrock and popcorn spray for the ceiling."

"You need any help?" Elder Spaulding asked.

"No, it'll be quicker if I go by myself."

"We'll start cleanin' up while you're gone," Elder Spaulding said.

Half an hour later, Bryce returned. The first thing he did was cut out and replace the sheetrock in the upstairs closet wall, and then they all put Walter and Carolyn's clothes back in the closet.

Downstairs, Bryce refused help. The elders and Megan sat on the sofa and watched.

Bryce was in his glory. For him this was the perfect opportunity to show off his skills and great knowledge of home repairs. He lectured as he worked.

Finally it was time to apply the popcorn ceiling spray to

the ceiling. Bryce again stood on the table, shook the can, and sprayed. Only a few specks of the ceiling texture material actually landed on the ceiling. The rest landed on him, coating his face, clothes, arms, shoes, table, and wall.

Megan tried her best not to say anything, and perhaps she'd have succeeded if Elder Spaulding hadn't whispered to her, "Do my eyes deceive me, or is that truly the Pillsbury Dough Boy come to visit us today?"

Like a leaking balloon at first, and then, full bore, Megan broke out laughing.

"It's not funny!" Bryce shouted.

"No, of course not," Megan said, forcing her mouth to turn down. "It's not a bit funny."

Bryce slowly raised his arm to see the coating of white popcorn. "I'm going to change."

As soon as Bryce left the room, Megan and Elder Spaulding broke up, laughing in spasms, laughing so hard that tears were streaming down their cheeks. Elder Spaulding fell off the couch and grabbed his sides. For his part, Elder Anderson gave a five-second laugh and then just smiled a bit after that.

By the time Bryce returned wearing clean clothes, he had a plan. "The reason it didn't work the first time is because I held it too close to the ceiling. Now when you do that, then the air pressure bounces off the ceiling and sends the spray back down again. The first thing you should do before you try it on the ceiling is try it outside. And then you'll know better how it works."

"Good advice, Bryce," Megan said, biting her lip to keep from losing it all over again.

Because they were hoping for another disaster, they all followed Bryce outside. He tried it out, but it came out faster than he expected, so it ended up covering the tree, the fence, grass, rocks, and a flower or two.

Megan sank to the grass and held her sides. "That's a lot better."

Bryce, his pride hurt, headed back inside. "We'll clean that up later."

They followed him inside. "I love home repair projects," Megan said quietly, then started laughing again.

Bryce gave the second in his home repair lecture series, sprayed again, and, amazingly, had the same results as before.

Megan might have laughed but caught in Bryce's eyes his disappointment at failing once again.

"It's okay, Bryce."

He nodded and excused himself once again to get cleaned up before making another trip to Home Depot.

Ten minutes later Carolyn got out of her car after a hard day at work and started up the walk. She was puzzled by what looked like snow on part of the yard.

She entered the house. The chandelier was still on the floor, and it looked like a blizzard had attacked the kitchen.

"What on earth?"

"We can explain," Megan said.

The seconds passed. "Yes?"

"Actually, Bryce can explain it better than I can," Megan said.

"Where's Bryce?"

"Upstairs. Cleaning up."

Carolyn looked at the white-coated bowl of fruit and shook her head. "Maybe you'd better explain."

"Well, we'd better get goin," Elder Spaulding said, wanting to escape before anyone started yelling. "Nice t' visit with you and Bryce."

As the elders left, Megan heard Elder Spaulding say softly to his companion, "I've never wanted to go tractin' so much in my life."

Carolyn tried to stay mad, but as Megan explained what had happened, she ended up laughing about it, too.

183

Bryce left the ceiling the way it was. He had no heart to go back for round three.

◆　　◆　　◆

"This is so amazing!" Megan said to her family one night at supper. "I can actually understand the Book of Mormon. It makes sense to me. Sometimes I feel the Spirit so strong when I'm reading."

"I'm so happy to hear that," her mother said.

"Totally," Brianna said with a smile.

"You say you feel the Spirit?" Bryce asked. "So what good is that? What does it change? You're still pregnant. You're still planning to keep the baby."

"So?"

"So it's the wrong decision. How many times do I have to tell you that?"

"Well, I'm sorry you feel that way, but it is my life. Or are you taking that over, too, Bryce?"

"Why not give your baby to a couple who will devote their life to it? Your kid is going to spend his life being dropped off here while you go to work or to be with your friends."

"Bryce, cut her some slack," Brianna said. "She's doing the best she can right now."

"But it's all a sham. Megan, do you really think God wants you to raise this kid by yourself?"

"Yes, I do."

"With all due respect, how could you possibly know what God wants?" he said.

Brianna came right back at him. "Like you'd know anything about what God thinks, Bryce."

With that stinger, Bryce walked out.

Brianna and Carolyn looked at Megan, wondering how she'd react to what Bryce had said.

"Bryce didn't mean to hurt your feelings," Carolyn said.

"Of course not. That's because to him feelings don't matter."

"Don't listen to him," Brianna called out. "Keep the baby. We'll take care of it. I'll even quit school if I need to."

"Mom, what do you think I should do after the baby is born?"

The answer was a long time in coming. "Well, I think that's a decision you need to make. I'll support whatever you decide."

"I keep changing my mind from day to day, and it's driving me crazy. I've got to decide once and for all. Excuse me, I need to be by myself for a while."

Megan went to her room, closed the door, and knelt down by her bed. *I've got to decide what to do. I've got to do the right thing for my baby. Whatever that is, I've got to do the right thing.*

"Heavenly Father . . ." she began.

# 11

It was fast Sunday, and Megan had planned on fasting, hoping to come to a decision whether to keep her baby or to place it for adoption. But her doctor had told her it wasn't wise for a pregnant woman to go without eating, so instead of fasting she was praying to know what to do. She had thought she'd made up her mind to keep it, but Bryce's insistence that it was a bad idea kept bothering her. She didn't agree with Bryce on most things; but she respected him. He was one of the smartest people she knew. She didn't want to make a mistake on this. It was too important.

From his place on the stand, Bishop Oldham saw her enter the chapel and smiled at her. As a result of their interviews, she had come to appreciate his kindness and concern. She smiled back.

She sat on the third row of the chapel with Brianna and their father. Their mother was on the stand leading the music.

*Heavenly Father, please help me to know what to do*, she thought, offering a silent prayer.

She tried to pay attention to every testimony, hoping for

what could be a personal message from God to her. But there wasn't anything she could point to that would help her know what to do about her baby. By the end of the meeting, she was still undecided and discouraged and just wanted to go home.

"Will you be coming to my class?" her dad asked. "I could really use some suggestions on how I can improve."

She hated to turn him down. "All right, but please don't ask me any questions. I'm not ready for that yet."

As she sat in her dad's Sunday School class, she was impressed with all the work he'd done to prepare the lesson. It's what he did at night in motel rooms, instead of watching TV. On Saturday he had spent two hours downloading additional information from the Internet, and he gave everyone two handouts that were very informative.

Even with all his preparation, Megan noticed the members of the class seemed uninvolved in the lesson. People sat with their shoulders slumped and their heads lowered. Some were even sleeping.

Because there was so much material to cover, it was almost like a lecture. Walter asked very few questions, and most of the questions could only be answered by gospel scholars. Even so, several people stopped after class and thanked him for the excellent lesson.

"Good job," she said enthusiastically, moving up to the front.

"Really?"

"Sure, there was so much new information. You really worked hard on that lesson, didn't you?"

"I did. I learned a lot."

"I'm sure everyone else did, too."

Women were starting to come in for Relief Society. Megan wanted to get out of the room before anyone could ask her to stay to the meeting. Keeping her head down to avoid the gaze of the sisters, she said good-bye to her dad and slipped out the door.

Three hundred miles away, Ann Marie Slater stood at the pulpit to bear her testimony. "I would like to bear my testimony that I know that God lives and that Jesus is the Christ and that we have a living prophet on the earth today." She paused, pulled a tissue from the box next to the pulpit, and held it in her hand.

"I'm here today to also ask your forgiveness."

She dabbed at her cheek with the tissue.

"I've been having a hard time lately. I've felt angry at God and had uncharitable feelings toward members of this ward. I know that's not right, but that's the way I've felt. I'm trying to work on that. I know I'm the one at fault. Please, if I've seemed unfriendly, I'm sorry."

She closed her testimony and sat down.

After sacrament meeting Colleen Butler, the Young Women president, cornered Ann Marie. "Let's go talk, okay?"

"I'd like that."

They ended up sitting in Colleen's car in the parking lot.

"Have I offended you?" Colleen asked.

"No, not at all."

"You want to talk about it?"

Ann Marie nodded but hesitated. "This is so embarrassing." She took a deep breath and then said, "It's about me not being able to get pregnant. We've tried so hard, and nothing has worked. It's always been frustrating, but we've recently been told there's not much chance we'll ever be able to have a baby. Then when someone like Melissa Partridge gets pregnant, without even trying . . . it seems so unfair!"

She put her hand over her eyes but was unable to control the flood of tears. Colleen fished a tissue out of her bag and handed it to her.

Ann Marie pinched her nose with the tissue and wiped at the tears on her cheeks. "When I was growing up, all I ever wanted to be was a wife and mother. But sometimes we don't get what we want, do we? No matter how hard we pray about it."

"I'm sorry I haven't been more of a support to you."

"What's hard is what this has been doing to Weston and me." She shook her head. "We both want the same thing, but sometimes it's like we're competing or something."

She went on. "Things have always come easy to me, but I've had to face the fact that I can't do everything, that some things aren't just a matter of trying hard, or having a good attitude, or never giving up. I can't do the one thing that most women take for granted will happen to them. I've had to concede that it's not going to happen to me." She took a deep breath. "That's been hard for me to accept."

She wiped her eyes. "Do you have another tissue?"

She took it and wiped her nose. "I'm so grateful to Weston for being so patient with me. We've decided to look into adopting a baby. Of course, we have no idea how long that will take."

She sighed and shook her head. "What I said in church must have seemed strange to people, but I felt like I needed to apologize to the ward."

She smiled through her tears and looked at Colleen. "I'm sorry to unload on you, but just talking has helped. I'll be all right."

Ann Marie took a deep breath and pulled down the visor to look at herself in the mirror. "I'm a mess."

Colleen reached across the seat and put her hand on Ann Marie's. "Any time you need to talk, just give me a call."

"Thanks. I will." Ann Marie looked at her watch. "Well, let's go get ready for Young Women."

◆  ◆  ◆

Megan was on her way out of the Relief Society room when Kristin saw her. She was two years older than Megan, but they'd been friends in high school. Kristin had fallen in love and gotten married her first year at BYU—had married a returned missionary and was now pregnant with her first baby. She and her husband, Justin, were temporarily living in an apartment in Kristin's parents' basement.

"You want to sit with me in Relief Society?" Kristin asked.

"Well, I don't know . . . I wasn't going to stay."

"C'mon. If the lesson gets boring, we can compare notes about our pregnancies."

Megan hesitated, then nodded her head and followed Kristin to Relief Society.

During the opening song, Megan's mind wandered.

*What am I doing here? Kristin and I have a few things in common, but not the most important things. She's married and I'm not. When she found out she was pregnant, she was happy. She has a husband who will support her when she's down. I don't have anyone. Her family is proud of her. Mine is ashamed of me.*

The teacher began the lesson. "I have a copy of the 'Proclamation to the World' that I'll pass out to everyone. I thought I'd just have everyone take a turn reading one sentence and then we'll talk about it afterwards."

As one of the women in the ward read the part that said that the powers of procreation are only to be used by a husband and wife, Megan wondered if other women were curious what she thought about that. *What do they think, that I'm going to argue against that? I should get up and leave. The only trouble is that if I leave, I'll have to crawl over Kristin to get to the aisle.*

*What am I doing here? Why do I come here each week? Why don't I just quit and give up and stay home?*

*I'll wait until the next person starts to read, and then I'll go.*

Another woman began to read: "'The family is ordained of God. Marriage between man and woman is essential to His

190

eternal plan. Children are entitled to birth within the bonds of matrimony, and to be reared by a father and a mother who honor marital vows with complete fidelity.'"

Megan, her mouth wide open in astonishment, reached for Kristin's copy of "The Family: A Proclamation to the World" and quickly found the paragraph that had just been read.

She read it again. *Children are entitled to birth within the bonds of matrimony, and to be reared by a father and a mother who honor marital vows with complete fidelity.*

Tears began to well up in her eyes. *That's it. That's my answer. I have to do what's best for my baby. I will place my baby for adoption.*

In tears of relief, she leaned over and gave Kristin a big hug. "Thank you for getting me to Relief Society," she whispered.

◆　　◆　　◆

On nights when a missionary discussion was scheduled, Megan's mother invited the missionaries and Thomas to have supper with the family. Sometimes Thomas wasn't able to come for supper because he was either working or in class, but the missionaries were usually able to make it.

Having the elders to supper gave Megan and her family a chance to get to know the missionaries better. In time they learned that Elder Spaulding had a girl waiting for him. She was someone he'd met his first year at BYU.

"Do you have a picture of her?" Megan's mother asked.

"Well, yes, I do, as a matter-a-fact," Elder Spaulding said with a big grin. "I carry it in my wallet, next to my heart." He smiled. "Of course, I also carry a picture of the car I left behind, too." He pulled out his wallet and passed the picture of a pretty blonde. "Ain't she a beauty?"

Elder Anderson fidgeted.

"What's her name?"

"Melissa."

"How did you meet her?" Megan asked.

"Craziest thing. We met in a Laundromat. She stole my detergent. I set it down one minute, and then the next thing I know, she's carryin' it out of the place. I'm not talkin' a small box here. I'm talkin' a 'conomy-sized box, enough for like an entire semester. Well, I couldn't let her get away with that, so I went after her. I caught up with her jus' before she was goin' into her dorm. I called after her, so she stopped.

"So she looks at me and says, 'Yes?' So I go, 'You have my Cheer.' And she's all, 'What is up with this guy anyway?' I point to the box and say, 'That's mine.' And she goes, 'No, it isn't. I bought this yesterday.' So I go, 'You may have bought a box of Cheer yesterday, but it wasn't that box. Maybe you left your box in your apartment.' And she goes, 'Well, I can check, but I'm sure I didn't.' So she goes inside and comes back about a minute later with a second box of Cheer, and she's all, 'I'm so sorry.' And I'm all, 'Hey, don't worry about it.' So she invites me for supper the next day, and I meet her roommates and everythin', and she and I get along really good after that. So I started hangin' around and lovin' every minute I could spend with her." He chuckled. "I tell people, I've had Cheer ever since the day I met her."

"Elder," Elder Anderson warned.

"I'm almos' done. Anyway, the point is, 'fore long we were talkin' about gettin' married after my mission. So that's where it stands now. She bakes me cookies about once a month."

"Well, that must be a treat," Megan's mother said.

"Not really. To tell you the truth, they're pretty awful. Seems she's on a molasses kick. Claims it will keep me from gettin' sick. So she makes all her cookies with molasses instead of sugar. Each one weighs about ten pounds. Elder Anderson likes 'em though, don't you, Elder?"

Elder Anderson nodded.

"Course you'd expect that. He likes anythin' that's hard."

Elder Anderson was about to speak, but Elder Spaulding cut him off. "Not me, though. I like things easy. 'Easy does it.' That's my motto. Do the easy things first, and then maybe you'll never have to do the hard things. You know what I mean? Like what we're doin' here tonight. Teachin' Thomas, that's easy. Goin' tractin' in a rainstorm? That's hard . . ." With a sideways glance at his companion, he continued, " . . . hard and not all that productive."

Elder Anderson protested. "We had an hour left. I wasn't ready to just close up shop."

Elder Spaulding suddenly looked over at Megan, Brianna, Bryce, and their mother. "I'm sorry. We shouldn't be havin' this discussion in front of you, should we? We'll talk about this later, Elder."

Elder Anderson nodded his head. "You're right. I'm sorry for bringing it up here."

"Remind me never to serve a mission," Bryce said.

"It's the greatest two years of a person's life," Elder Spaulding said enthusiastically.

Bryce laughed. "Right," he said sarcastically. "I can see that, hearing you two argue."

"I love my companion," Elder Spaulding said. "He knows that, don't you, Elder?"

Elder Anderson gave the expected answer. "I suppose."

"This is good preparation for marriage," Elder Spaulding said.

"How's that?" Bryce asked.

"It teaches you how to work out problems with someone who doesn't think 'xactly like you do. Elder Anderson an' me, well, we're not the same. We both look at things differently. But I respect him. I'm learnin' to work with him, and he's learnin' to work with me, so that's good."

"You want to know who you two remind me of?" Megan asked.

193

"I'm not sure we do," Elder Spaulding said with a smile.

"Tigger and Eeyore. Elder Spaulding, you're Tigger. You're bouncing all over the place all the time. Elder Anderson, you're more mellow and thoughtful, and you always try very hard to live the mission rules. So that's good, too. I think you make a good team."

Elder Spaulding locked his arm around Elder Anderson's shoulder and pulled him into a momentary hug. "We *are* a good team," Elder Spaulding pronounced. Elder Anderson just looked uncomfortable.

After that it was hard for Megan not to want to call Elder Spaulding Tigger, which he constantly lived up to, as, for example, after supper, when he jumped up and started clearing off the plates. "What can I do? You want me to stack the plates in the kitchen? I can do that. Whatever you want. You cooked this wonderful meal for us. The least we can do is help clean up."

"Brianna can take care of that."

"No need. No need at all. Let me do it. Brianna, you've had a hard day."

"Okay, thanks."

"You should help him," her mother said.

"Why? He's doing okay by himself."

"It's your job."

"I know, but he wants to do it."

They heard a loud crash in the kitchen.

"Don't worry! It's not a plate or anythin'!" Elder Spaulding called out.

"What is it?"

"Jus' the fish bowl. But don't you worry none. I got all but one of the little buggers. He's under the 'frigerator, but I'm movin' the 'frigerator, and I'll have him in water 'fore you know it."

Elder Anderson shook his head.

"I got it!" Elder Spaulding called out. "They're okay."

194

He came out of the kitchen, carrying a Tupperware bowl with the fish in it. His pant legs were wet from the fish bowl breaking on the floor.

Brianna ran to him. "I love my goldfish! To me, they're part of the family," she said, choking with emotion.

Megan looked on in amazement because she knew Brianna hated the goldfish.

"Which one went behind the fridge? Tina or Buffy?" Brianna asked, peering into the plastic container.

"I don't know."

"Buffy has a little red mark on her side. I got her from my best friend just before she moved away. It was her last gift to me. She said, 'When you look at this goldfish, you'll remember the good times we had together.' I don't know what I'd do if anything happened to Buffy."

"I don't think she got hurt none when she hit the floor 'cause she jus' kept wrigglin', like she wasn't even stunned."

Brianna faked heartache. "First the fall and then not being able to breathe. She must have been *so* scared. And then being behind the refrigerator, wondering if anyone would even know she was back there. Poor Buffy." Brianna covered her eyes and pretended to cry.

"I feel real bad."

"And then there's Tina. She's had a hard life. One time the cat knocked her bowl off the counter and had her cornered. She even took a swat at her. I came home just in time. She didn't eat for days after that. That's when I first started calling her Tina. Before that she was a two-pound trout. And now look at her."

Elder Spaulding, his gaze on the floor to indicate his great sorrow, looked up to see Brianna's cheesy smile. "You've been funnin' me all this time?" he asked.

Brianna laughed. "Yeah, pretty much."

"I'll get you for this. I was feelin' worse and worse, the more you talked."

"I got you, didn't I?"

"I'll get you back."

"I don't think so. You're a missionary. You have to be good."

"No, I *will* get you. You just wait and see. Sometime when you're least expectin' it."

"But if you do that, then I'll have to get you back, so there'll be no end to it."

"And that'll be my fault?"

"Yes, you should just accept the fact that you can't win."

Megan watched with amusement the feuding between Elder Spaulding and Brianna. It was like a brother and a sister at each other, like the way Megan and Bryce had been when they were growing up.

A few minutes later, Thomas showed up for his weekly lesson.

After the opening prayer, Elder Spaulding asked, "Were you able to get any readin' done since the last time?"

"Well, I read some. Not everything, though."

"What did you read?"

"I read the pamphlet you gave me, and I read a few pages in the Book of Mormon."

"That's real good," Elder Spaulding said.

"Really good," Elder Anderson agreed.

"What did you think of what you read?" Elder Spaulding asked.

"It was okay. It kind of made sense. It's all new of course."

"Be sure and write down any questions you might have as you're reading, and then we can talk about them," Elder Anderson said.

As the discussion proceeded, Megan was surprised what an effective teacher Elder Anderson was. She'd always thought of him as the weaker of the two missionaries, the one who'd rather be doing something else than what they were doing.

196

*He's not a bad guy,* she thought. *He just wants to make the best use of his time. There's nothing wrong with that.*

At the end of the discussion, Elder Anderson asked if Thomas had any questions.

"Just one. These lessons, they're about me joining your church, aren't they? I mean, it's not just me learning more about it. It's about me becoming a Mormon, isn't it?"

"If you knew it was true, wouldn't you want to be a part of it?" Elder Spaulding asked.

"I'm not sure I could live up to all that's expected of a member of your church."

"You could do it, Thomas," Megan said.

"You didn't though, did you?"

Megan felt devastated. "That's true. I didn't, but I'm trying to change. People can change, Thomas. Even you and even me."

"Why do I have to change? I'm already living the way Mormons are supposed to live."

Megan felt once again the sting of regret that she hadn't been a better example to Thomas.

"Isn't knowing the truth important to you?" Elder Anderson asked.

"All churches think they have the truth."

"That's right. They do. But there is a way to find out if what we're tellin' you is the truth," Elder Spaulding said.

"How's that?"

"By continuin' to learn what we believe and then prayin' to ask God if it's true."

"And you think he'll answer me?"

"We know he will."

"What if he doesn't?"

"Then you're off the hook."

Thomas nodded. "Sounds fair."

Megan, for the first time in her life, ached to talk about her growing testimony—about the truths she had discovered in reading the Book of Mormon. But she kept silent because she didn't feel that what she would say would have much impact with Thomas because he'd seen her at her worst. And so she sat there quietly, silently praying that Thomas would someday feel the way she did now about the Church.

Thomas agreed to continue with the discussions, and he even set a date for baptism, although he kept saying that he hadn't made up his mind about it yet.

After the discussion the elders stayed and had dessert and sang a few songs, with Elder Spaulding again at the piano.

After the elders left, as Megan helped clean up in the kitchen, her mother asked, "What do you think of Elder Spaulding?"

"He's okay, I guess."

"I agree. You and he seem to get along well together."

"Mom, he's a missionary, and I'm not married and pregnant. It's not exactly the best timing for either one of us. Someday he'll go back home and marry Melissa, the Cheer girl."

"You don't know that for sure."

"I don't want to talk about this anymore, ever, okay?"

"Of course, whatever you say."

They didn't talk about it anymore. But that is not to say that Megan didn't think about it. She did almost every day. And felt guilty doing it.

*It's because I have nothing else to think about,* she thought, lying in her bed that night. *My life is so isolated now. I stay in the house by myself alone all day, and I don't go out much because I'm beginning to show and it's too awkward to have friends from high school come up and start asking questions, and so I stay in the house, and the only guys I see all week are Thomas and the missionaries. Elder Spaulding is a good missionary, but he's nice, too, and easy to talk with and has a good sense of humor.*

*I guess it's possible I might be falling for Elder Spaulding, but that's because he's such a good example of a worthy priesthood holder. And because he's on a mission and dedicating his life to God. I'm not sure I'd like him that much if he wasn't on a mission.*

*Maybe it's not that I'm falling in love with him. Maybe it's just because he's nice to me and doesn't seem to be judging me harshly because of my past. Maybe that's it. Or maybe it's because he acts like he's got all the time in the world for us when he's here.*

*I'm sure that's it. It's not that I'm falling for him. It's that I respect Elder Spaulding for putting people first. That's what it is.*

*I wonder what his Melissa is like? I hope she's wonderful. I hope she waits for him his whole mission. I hope they get married a few weeks after he gets home from his mission.*

*I hope I come to my senses soon.*

*I can't let Elder Spaulding suspect anything because that would ruin everything. I have to keep telling myself that I'm not thinking clearly now and that I have to be strong and not cave in to some silly fantasy that would ruin everything for Thomas and his chances to become a member. I have to keep my feelings to myself.*

*There, that's taken care of. I've got things under control.*

*I wonder if I could get a picture of Elder Spaulding. That would be great.*

She smiled and closed her eyes and soon fell asleep.

# 12

Megan had gained seven pounds. It was obvious to her family that she was expecting, but her mother said she didn't think most people would notice.

On the day the elders were to give Thomas his last discussion before his baptism, they showed up before anyone else except Megan was home.

She seemed surprised to see them but let them in and then excused herself and went upstairs to change clothes.

"We shouldn't be here with just Megan," Elder Anderson said as they sat down in the living room.

"Brianna will be showing up soon."

"We'll be here until ten again, won't we?" Elder Anderson asked.

"Probably."

"The president said—" Elder Anderson began.

"I know what the president said, okay? You don't have to remind me every five minutes."

"You don't even care what the rules are, do you?"

Elder Spaulding, red-faced, barely under control, turned

200

to confront his companion, "And that's all you do care about, isn't it? You didn't come out here to baptize, did you? You came out here to harass your companions. Well, Elder, if that's your goal, let me congratulate you because you're a big success."

The elders quit arguing when Brianna showed up.

An hour and a half later, Brianna, Bryce, Megan, and Carolyn sat down with the elders to supper.

Elder Anderson didn't say much at all, but Elder Spaulding tried to make up for it by being even more talkative and charming than usual. Even Bryce was enjoying himself.

After finishing supper they waited another half an hour, but Thomas didn't show up. After forty-five minutes, Megan telephoned his house. Thomas answered. It was a short conversation.

Megan hung up. She turned to the others, feeling as though she'd been kicked in the stomach. "Thomas says he's decided to quit taking the discussions."

"Why?"

"He says his entire family has always been Catholic. It's been good enough for them, so it's good enough for him."

"We need to talk to him," Elder Spaulding said.

"He said he doesn't want to talk to you guys anymore. He just wants to go back to the way things used to be."

They sat in silence for a few moments.

"I can't believe it," Megan said. "Why would he quit taking the lessons when he was so close to being baptized?"

"Maybe if he'd had a better example," Elder Anderson said softly.

Megan, painfully, took a deep breath. "You mean if I hadn't been sleeping around before he started taking the discussions?"

"No, no," Elder Anderson stammered. "You don't understand. I didn't mean it like that. I was talking about Elder

Spaulding and me, if we were getting along better. That's what I meant."

Tears burning her eyes, Megan got up to leave.

"Please, don't go," Elder Anderson pleaded. "I was talking about Elder Spaulding and me. Not about you. I would never say that about you."

"Don't worry about it. But it is true. I should have been a better example. Thomas is the best friend I've ever had, and if he doesn't join the Church because of me, well, I don't know what I'll do."

Megan went to her room. A few minutes later she heard the elders leave and watched through the window as they drove away.

She stayed in her room the rest of the night, listening to music and agonizing over Thomas's decision. Brianna came in and tried to cheer her up, even inviting her to go to a movie with her.

"Thanks, but I think I'll just stay here. I don't want to go where any of my old friends will see me."

"How about I put a pillow under my sweatshirt? Then people won't notice you so much."

Megan couldn't help but smile. "Sure, that would solve all our problems."

"For sure. Come be with me and my friends then. They won't care."

"No, I'll just stay here. I'm fine, really."

Brianna bent down and wrapped her arms around Megan. "I love you."

"I love you, too. I'm fine here, really."

"Well, then, I'll be going."

A while later Carolyn opened the door a crack. "You okay?"

"Yeah, I'm okay."

"Can I get you anything?"

"No, but thanks anyway."

Megan was sitting up in her bed with a comforter wrapped around her. Carolyn came and sat on the bed and reached for her daughter's hand. "Sometimes people decide not to join the Church—not because of something a member said or did, but just because it's such a big step in a person's life. Sometimes people aren't ready to take that step." She sighed. "So I don't think you should blame yourself because Thomas decided to stay with his own church."

She nodded. "I know. It's just such a big disappointment, that's all."

"Of course it is."

"It's everything coming at me all at once. Like, I worry so much about what's going to happen. When you were pregnant the first time, were you ever afraid of what could happen in the delivery room?"

"Yes, of course, it's only natural to worry about that."

"Like, what if the baby is born deformed or stillborn or dies right after it's born? And I'm not sure I can take all the physical pain that goes with having a baby. I mean, there's all these things. And if I was married, I'd have a husband who could be with me and support me and help me get through whatever happened, but I don't have anybody."

"You have a family who will be there for you."

"Mom, why doesn't Kurt ever call me? Why doesn't he care about this life that he's helped to create? How can he just walk away like it never happened? Did I mean so little to him that he won't even call and ask how I'm doing? Why was I so stupid to think he cared about me? And how can he go on like everything's the same? Well, for me nothing's the same. And it never will be."

"I can't answer any of those questions. He's the only one who can."

Megan shook her head. "It's not that I want to see him or have him in my life. I don't. I just can't understand someone who would walk away from this and pretend it never happened. I was so wrong about him."

They talked for another hour, sometimes as mother and daughter, but sometimes, when talking about having a baby, they talked as friends, two women, who shared a common bond.

Carolyn excused herself at nine-fifteen. She usually talked to Walter every night at that time. At nine-twenty the phone rang.

Five minutes later Carolyn returned.

"Your father is coming back tonight."

"What for?"

"I told him about our talk. He was wondering if you might like a priesthood blessing—tonight or tomorrow."

"But . . . he never comes back before Friday."

"I know, but he is this week. It'll take him about three hours to get here. You think you'll still be up?"

"I'll be up for him if he's coming all that way just for me."

"Good. He'll be pleased."

She wanted to prepare herself as much as she could for the priesthood blessing from her father. And so she took a bath, put on Sunday clothes, and sat down and read in her Book of Mormon.

Brianna came home just after ten o'clock. She noticed Megan's Sunday clothes.

"Whatsup?" she asked.

"Dad's going to give me a priesthood blessing."

"Is he home?"

"Not yet. But he's coming."

Brianna thought about that for a minute. "That is so cool," she said. "Can I listen?"

"Sure. But it'll be a while. He's driving back."

Her dad arrived at twelve-thirty, found Megan sitting in the living room, and asked if she would like a father's blessing. Then he changed into his Sunday clothes.

To keep Bryce from barging in when he came home, they put a note on the front door telling him what they were doing and asking him to be quiet until the blessing was completed.

They gathered in the living room, with Brianna and Carolyn sitting on the couch and Megan seated on a dining room chair her father had brought into the room. He asked Carolyn to say a prayer, and when she was finished, he placed his hands lightly on Megan's head. He closed his eyes and, calling her by name, began. " . . . by the authority of the Melchizedek Priesthood, I lay my hands on your head . . . "

By the time he finished, they were all in tears.

But this time they were happy tears.

◆　　◆　　◆

A few days later, Megan showed up at Leo's Pizza after hours. Thomas seemed surprised to see her.

"Can I come in?" she asked.

"Please do."

Thomas was mopping the floor in the dining area.

"What can I do to help out?" she asked.

"Actually, I've pretty much got things under control," he said.

"Sure."

He worked for several minutes without either one of them saying a word.

"We're both kind of quiet tonight, aren't we?" she finally said.

"Yeah, we are."

Another unbearable silence followed.

"Would you rather I just go home and let you get your work done?"

"No, don't go," he said quickly.

She gave a sigh of relief. "Good. I don't want to go home."

"What *do* you want?"

"I want it to be like it used to be between us."

He nodded his head. "Me, too."

"It's okay if you don't join the Church, Thomas. I can understand that."

He shook his head. "It just got to be too much, that's all. My family especially."

"Sure, I understand."

He quit working and stared at her for the longest time.

"What?" she asked.

"Can a guy ask a girl for a hug?" he asked.

"Oh, yeah! I'd love that."

He draped his long arms around her but didn't hold her tight like he used to. She knew it was because he was afraid he'd hurt the baby inside her.

"This feels so good, Thomas."

"I know. It really does."

"Do I feel different now?"

"A little."

"I've missed not having you come around," she said.

"I've missed it, too." He pulled away enough to make eye contact. "But it's for the best, as far as my family goes."

"Okay."

"Besides, all churches do good."

"That's true. They do."

He caught the look in her eye. "But what?"

"Just give me five minutes, and then I'll never bring it up again."

"Okay."

"Let's sit down for this, okay?" she asked.

She sat down across from him, and she held his hand in hers, not out of any kind of romantic feelings, but more because she wanted him to somehow sense how strong her testimony was.

"You know me better than anyone else in the whole world. I've told you things I've never told my parents or Brianna or anybody. You know the worst about me. But, Thomas, I also want you to know the best about me, too. I have to tell you how much I've changed in the past few months. I know for myself that the Book of Mormon is true and that Jesus Christ is my Savior and that he loves me. And I know that Joseph Smith was a prophet of God. I know it by the influence of the Holy Ghost. Can't you feel something while I'm talking to you?"

He didn't say anything for a moment, then said, "I do feel something."

"What do you feel?"

He smiled. "That you're squeezing my hand really hard."

She blushed and pulled away. "Well, that's it then, isn't it? I gave it my best shot."

"You did."

She grabbed a napkin and wiped her eyes. "Sorry to get so emotional."

"It's okay."

She stayed a few more minutes and then left.

◆    ◆    ◆

On Sunday Thomas went to mass with his Grandmother Marconi. She was by far the strongest in her faith of anyone else in the family. His parents never went to church. His three uncles also never attended, though they were the first to defend it.

It had been his Uncle Al who had talked him into not meeting anymore with the Mormons. "Our family already has a church. It would break your grandmother's heart if you threw away all you've been taught your whole life. We're a family, and we got to stick together. If you put as much time and study into your own religion as you have the Mormons, you'll see it's just as good and, I'm sure, a whole lot better."

It was an argument that was hard to refute. Family had

always been a big thing, and Thomas knew his grandmother would never understand his willingness to give up their traditional religion. To keep peace he agreed to stop meeting with the missionaries. Everyone in the family was relieved. He got phone calls of support from his extended family all that week.

And so when Sunday came around, he envisioned the entire family at church with him—his mom and dad, his uncles and aunts, and all his cousins. He started phoning Saturday morning, inviting members of his extended family to go to church. But everyone was busy, what with work and needing time to rest up from a hard week, and doing some shopping.

And so he went to church with his grandmother. The sermon that day was entitled, "New Wine in Old Bottles."

At first Thomas didn't pay much attention to the sermon. But then a question rang out from the pulpit: "What did our Lord mean when he said that we cannot put new wine in old bottles? Did our Lord form a task force suggesting small changes that might be made? No, he had to start over with completely new ideas. We must also take stock of ourselves and throw out those things in our patterns of thinking which are not in keeping with God's will for us." The sermon went on to other themes, but Thomas felt like the message he'd heard was a message from God.

As he and his grandmother left the church, Thomas shook the priest's hand. "Your sermon today was inspired."

The priest smiled. "Thank you very much. We hope to see more of you from now on. Your uncle told me you've recently made a wise decision. I'm very pleased."

Thomas smiled, but only halfheartedly. "I find myself changing in ways I never dreamed. It's almost like God is leading me in a certain direction."

"I'm sure he is," the priest said with a broad smile.

That afternoon the family got together for their traditional Sunday spaghetti dinner.

As Thomas entered the living room, Uncle Al grinned and asked, "So tell us about the Mormons. How many wives did they promise you if you'd join up with 'em?"

"None."

"No wives? Right now that sounds good to me! I've got one I'd like to get rid of! So how do I join?" Uncle Al laughed until it brought up phlegm, and he started coughing out of control.

"Seriously, what could they possibly say to you that would cause you to even think about leaving the church our family has been in for hundreds of years?"

"They say that just like in Bible times, God called a modern-day prophet named Joseph Smith."

"Yeah, right, like God couldn't come up with a better name for a prophet than Joe Smith."

"I knew a Joe Smith once . . . ran a pawn shop in Cleveland."

Thomas let the comments continue, deciding that nobody wanted a serious discussion. He glanced at Elizabeth. Her head was down, as if she were in a storm trying to stay upright while facing a stiff wind.

"I have a question for you all to consider," Thomas said. "What's worse, to give allegiance to a church you don't attend and beliefs you don't try to live, or to try to find a set of beliefs that has the power to make you a better person?"

Everyone stared at him, stunned. Family members didn't ask questions like that at occasions like this.

"Well, you can look all you want but not where you been looking," Uncle Bill said. "The way I heard it, the gal who got you studying with the Mormons got herself pregnant with some guy she met at a bar. She don't exactly sound like Mother Teresa there, right? I'm not sure she's the one you should go to for spiritual guidance."

Elizabeth came to him, put her arm around him, and

asked, "Thomas, while we're here, could you look at my car? I can't get the oil light to go out."

Still in a combative mood, Thomas nodded his head and followed Elizabeth out to her car in the driveway.

They sat in her car. "What about your oil light?"

She shrugged. "Looks like you fixed it. Thanks."

"No problem."

"Don't let them get to you," she said.

"I won't."

"You think you might become a Mormon?"

He shrugged his shoulders. "I'm not sure. But I do think I'll go back and meet with the missionaries again. Megan talked to me the other night and told me how much the teachings of her church mean to her. She asked me if I felt anything."

"I don't understand. What did she think you'd feel?"

"She thought God would let me know that what she was telling me is true."

"Did that happen?"

Thomas sighed, "Yeah, I think so, but I didn't admit it."

"How come?"

"Afraid of change I guess." He sighed. "But now that I've had a chance to think about it, I've decided to give it another try."

"Let me know how it goes."

"I will."

Elizabeth pursed her lips. It was something she'd been doing all her life when she couldn't decide whether or not to say what was on her mind.

"Go ahead and say it," Thomas said.

Instead of looking directly at him, she stared at the steering wheel of her car. "This is embarrassing to talk about, but, the fact is, I feel lonely so much of the time. Not so much in the daytime, you know, with classes and accompanying the choir, getting ready for concerts. Mainly at night, when it's late and there's nobody to talk to. I can't find anyone for me. Well, I could, I guess, but not what I'm looking for."

"What do you want me to do about that?"

"That's such a guy response." She smiled and shook her head. "I don't need you to *do* anything, except maybe to listen to me whine."

He started chuckling. "New whine in old bottles."

She looked at him with a puzzled expression.

"It's a play on words. It's funnier on paper. You know, w-h-i-n-e, as opposed to w-i-n-e."

"Give it up, okay? Tell me something. What are Mormon guys like?"

"Well, you'd probably like Elder Spaulding, except you can't like him."

"I can't like him? Why's that?"

"Not for two years. Well, less now. What I'm trying to say is he's a missionary. They don't date for two years."

"Two years, huh?"

"That's right."

She nodded her head. "I guess I'm a missionary, too, then. It's been about that long for me."

"But they have other guys who aren't on missions."

"How could I check out the ones who aren't on missions?"

"You could come to my next discussion with the missionaries and then go to church with me."

She broke into a wide grin.

♦  ♦  ♦

On Thursday Elizabeth went to Thomas's next discussion and met Elder Spaulding and Elder Anderson, who were delighted to have Thomas back and to have him bring his sister along.

On Sunday Elizabeth and Thomas entered the chapel and

sat down. Because they weren't members, they'd made the mistake of coming early.

Elder Spaulding and Elder Anderson, on their way to correlate with the ward mission leader, stepped into the chapel and welcomed Thomas and Elizabeth to church and then left for their meeting.

"Elder Spaulding seems like a nice guy," she said.

"He is. Very nice."

"Did I ever tell you that for the past little while I've been trying to decide if I should switch?" she asked.

"Switch to what?"

"That I might give up on men and turn my attention to women."

He raised an eyebrow. "No, you didn't mention that."

"Well, I was thinking about it. I've had such rotten experiences with guys. After a while, you start to wonder." She paused. "Do you want to know why I was thinking about it?"

He cleared his throat. "You know what? I'm not sure I do."

"It was because I started to think all guys were scum."

"I'm a guy."

"Not you, of course. Just everyone else. It's not that I had any great attraction for those of my own gender. It's sort of like if you're answering a multiple-choice question and there's only two choices and you're pretty sure the answer isn't A. So then you start to think that maybe B is the right answer. So, I was thinking B because A had worked out so badly for me." She smiled. "But now I'm thinking A might not be that bad of a choice."

"What happened to change your mind?"

"Meeting Elder Spaulding."

Thomas cocked his eye at her.

She said, "I suppose there are others just as nice as him. But I guess it's kind of like the first time you see a PT Cruiser. You always remember the first one you see. And then, before you know it, you see them all over the place. It's very encouraging."

"I suppose."

"Thomas, I've got a confession to make."

He faked a scowl. "You know what? I wish we'd come late like everyone else."

"My confession is that I checked out the website for BYU. They have a men's chorus . . . full of really decent looking guys."

"That's sort of what you'd expect for a men's chorus."

"But these look like nice guys." She smiled. "I have a whole new mission in life."

"What?"

"To go to BYU and accompany the men's chorus."

"I wish you and the men's chorus every happiness."

"See that young couple with the baby?" she asked.

Thomas turned to look at them. "What about them?"

"They seem nice, don't they? Happy in a domestic kind of way. I guess what I'm trying to say is I want to be like these people. I want to marry a member of the BYU Men's Chorus and have children and come to church with four diaper bags. What do you want?"

He sighed. "I'm thinking about getting baptized."

She nodded her head. "Me, too."

"You have to actually know something about the Church first."

"Okay then, after that, I'll get baptized."

"Why?"

"I think the BYU Men's Chorus would expect that of me."

"We'll have to tell the family then."

"We will someday," Elizabeth said.

"I mean, before we're baptized."

"That seems like a bad idea. Why don't we just, every Sunday, say we're going to Wal-Mart. Who would know the difference?"

"No, we have to tell them."

She shook her head. "Here comes World War Three."

◆   ◆   ◆

When the ward mission leader learned that Elizabeth wanted to learn about the Church and that she had a crush on Elder Spaulding, he made arrangements for the sister missionaries to teach her at his home.

Elizabeth received two lessons a week, which helped her catch up with Thomas.

Three weeks later they were both ready to be baptized.

Thomas and Elizabeth agreed to tell their family about their decision to get baptized. They were prepared to do so at the next Sunday family dinner.

"When do we tell them?" she asked.

"After dessert."

"Why after dessert?"

He flashed her a grin. "It's pecan pie. I want to get some before they throw us out."

"Is that what you think will happen?" she asked.

"I'm not sure what will happen."

They waited until they had finished their dessert and then Thomas stood up.

"Elizabeth and I have an announcement to make. We're going to become Mormons."

The announcement had the effect of freezing everyone in time.

"So what's the punch line?" their uncle asked.

"It's not a joke. We're going to become Mormons. We're getting baptized next Saturday. You're all invited."

"What's he talking about?" Grandmother Marconi asked.

"They're changing churches."

"We're Catholic," she said. "We've always been Catholic. We will always be Catholic."

"That's good . . . for you . . . but not so good for us," Elizabeth said.

"Mormons? Who are they?"

"They're the ones with the choir," Elizabeth answered.

"We have choirs."

"They're in Salt Lake City . . . in Utah."

"You're moving to Utah?"

"Well, maybe," Elizabeth said. "You see, BYU has a men's . . ."

"Not now," Thomas said to her privately. "One family crisis at a time, that's my motto."

"Our family has been Catholic for hundreds of years."

"True, but we think we'll like this better," Elizabeth said.

"You can't go around changing religions like you do a shirt. You have to have a reason."

"We have a reason."

"What's your reason?"

"They have a prophet."

"You're joining their church because they make a profit? We make a profit, too."

"Not that kind of profit. A prophet like Moses."

"What about Moses?"

"Is Moses a Mormon?"

"No, he's dead. They have a prophet just like Moses."

"Can he walk across the Red Sea on dry ground?"

"I don't know. It hasn't come up yet. Besides, he lives in Utah."

"Then he's not just like Moses. Can he send a plague of frogs?"

"No."

"If you ask me, you're not getting your money's worth."

Their grandfather stood up. "You're not joining the Mormon Church, so just forget about it."

The conversation quickly changed to sports for the men and to children for the women.

215

Thomas and Elizabeth walked outside.

"They don't believe we'll do it."

"But we will, won't we?" she asked.

"Yes, I think we'd better."

"It's going to change a lot of things," she said.

"I know."

"I want to become better friends with Megan."

◆　　◆　　◆

On Monday, during the day, Elizabeth dropped by the house to visit with Megan.

They sat in the living room. At first it was a little awkward.

"How are you doing?" Elizabeth asked.

"Okay, so far."

"Good. Expecting a baby is a big deal, isn't it?"

"It is. It's the hardest thing I've ever done."

"Have you been sick a lot?" Elizabeth asked.

"Not too much. It's other things."

"Sure. Thomas and I are getting baptized."

"You are? When?"

"Next Saturday. Can you come to it?"

"Of course!"

Elizabeth paused. "I wanted to thank you for getting Thomas interested in the Church."

"I wasn't the best example. He's been great, though. He's helped me get through this."

Elizabeth smiled. "He's like that, all right." She cleared her throat. "What can you tell me about Elder Spaulding?"

"Elder Spaulding? Well, he's from Biloxi, Mississippi. Home of the Crawdad Festival."

"The Crawdad Festival?"

"That's what I said. Anyway, he's got just a few months left of his mission. Oh, there's a girl waiting for him. Of course,

216

it's been two years since they've seen each other, so who knows how that will go."

"And you, what about you? Are you hoping this girl doesn't wait?"

"Well, I've fantasized about it from time to time. But there's no reason to expect we'll ever be more than just friends after he goes home."

"I'm not sure how this works with missionaries."

"Basically, it's best to back off until they go home."

"And then?"

"He'll go back to his friends and family and then pretty much forget all about us, except maybe he'll tell about teaching Thomas when he gives his homecoming talk in church." Megan nodded her head. "Basically, that's how it works."

"Okay. I had to ask. I didn't know."

"Sure, I understand."

"Do you love him?" Elizabeth asked.

She hated it that she was blushing. "I respect him. I guess you could say we're friends. But that's all."

Elizabeth pulled a video out of her backpack. "Well, if he's not in the picture, I have here a video of the BYU Men's Chorus that I think you might be interested in. I don't have all their names yet, but I'm working on it. It's one of the wonders of the Internet. BYU has a stalker-net that has been very helpful."

They watched the video, laughing hilariously as they singled out the ones they liked. "Oh, baby, sing that Bach!" Elizabeth cried out.

Megan soon caught the spirit of it. "Oh, yeah, Mr. Bass Man! I'm yours, baby, yes, sir!"

Brianna came home in time to join in the silly frenzy. "Uuuuh, baby, I'm your biggest fan! Sing the tenor like a man!" she shouted.

The three of them ended up on the floor in pain because they were laughing so hard.

217

"So, when are you going to go to BYU with me?" Elizabeth asked Megan. "We'll room together."

"That would be great." She patted her tummy. "I've got a few things I need to take care of first."

"Okay, you take care of business, girl, and then we're out of here. Just the two of us."

"That sounds so fun."

Elizabeth stood up, extended her arms, and, mimicking Buzz Lightyear from the movie *Toy Story*, called out, "To the BYU Men's Chorus . . . and beyond!"

♦   ♦   ♦

The day before Thomas and Elizabeth were scheduled to be baptized, Elder Spaulding and Elder Anderson dropped by to see Megan.

"I just wanted to make sure you'd be at the baptism Saturday," Elder Spaulding said.

"I'll be there."

"Good. I'll be leavin' right after the baptism. I'm being transferred."

She was stunned. "Transferred? Where?"

"The president said he needs me in the mission home. One of the elders in the office got sick and had to be sent home. So I'll work there until I go home."

She felt awful. "Oh, I see. I know you can't write to me on your mission, but I hope you will after you get home."

"You know I will."

"No, I don't know that, but I hope you will."

"Well, anyway, thanks for sharin' the gospel with Thomas."

"I enjoyed having him taught here. You did a good job."

"It wasn't me."

"No, of course not, but you know what I mean." She wanted to say something but wasn't sure what to say. *Some*

218

*days just knowing I was going to see you kept me going.* A dozen other thoughts ran through her mind. But, in the end, she said nothing.

"I'll always remember you," Elder Spaulding said, extending his hand.

Elder Anderson quickly interjected, "Elder, we need to go. We have an appointment in ten minutes."

Elder Spaulding nodded. "Well, I'll see you at the baptism, and then we can say good-bye."

"I'll be staying," Elder Anderson said.

She didn't care if Elder Anderson stayed or left, but she didn't want to hurt his feelings. "Okay, good."

Elder Anderson cleared his throat. "I've said some things I regret. I hope you won't hold it against me. I'm trying to do better. I wanted you to know that now I can see some good things about Elder Spaulding, and I'm going to try to be a little bit more like him."

She was surprised to hear that from Elder Anderson. For just an instant, she saw him in a new light. *He's like me in some ways. Trying to change, trying to be better. I'll try not to be so judgmental about him from now on.*

She walked them to the door and said good-bye.

◆　　◆　　◆

On Saturday she got up early so she could do her hair in time for the baptism. It had been scheduled in the morning to allow Elder Spaulding to catch his Greyhound bus to the mission office.

She was up early enough to get in Bryce's way as he got ready for work. "What are you doing up so early?" he asked.

"Thomas and his sister, Elizabeth, are getting baptized. I wanted to look nice for that. Also, Elder Spaulding is being transferred today."

"You fixing up for Elder Spaulding?"

"No."

"I bet you are, aren't you?"

She hated it that he knew her so well.

"Can I give you a little advice? I think washing your hair is not going to make that much of a difference to Elder Spaulding. Why should he pay any attention to you after his mission when he'll have his pick at any of the Church schools?"

"You're such a total jerk sometimes, Bryce."

"Maybe so, but I'm right, and you know it."

She breezed past him and went to her room and closed the door and crawled back in bed. She cried herself to sleep.

She would not have gone to the baptism at all were it not for Brianna, who got up an hour later and got ready to go, coming into their room every few minutes to tell Megan to get up and get dressed.

"You got to get up now, or you'll miss the baptism."

"I'm not going," Megan muttered.

Brianna grabbed the covers and ripped them off the bed. "You gotta go! I don't care how tired you are! You got to do this for Thomas and his sister!"

"Leave me alone."

"What is your *problem?*"

"Elder Spaulding is being transferred today."

"Do you want me to get a tissue so we can cry about it? So what? Elders get transferred all the time. That's not the point. The point is Thomas and Elizabeth need you to be there for their baptism."

"Don't you understand?"

"Understand what?"

"I'm in love with Elder Spaulding."

Brianna scowled. "Oh, good grief. That's not supposed to happen."

"I know that. I couldn't help it."

"So because you love him, you're going to miss your last

220

chance to see him before he leaves town? Sure, that makes perfect sense."

"Just leave me alone."

"It's not going to happen. You're going to the baptism, one way or another. I'd suggest you put on some church clothes, but, hey, I'll take you in a blanket if I have to."

Brianna prodded and poked and finally got Megan to a standing position.

"Look at me, I look pregnant."

"That's not exactly news to anyone. Put on something and let's go. You can do your hair on the way."

"Don't boss me around!"

"I will boss you around until you get your senses back."

Megan stood in front of her closet and picked out a loose skirt and an overblouse.

"Yes! We're on the move now! You da mama!"

Megan turned around and scowled at her.

"It was a compliment, okay?"

Ten minutes later they left the house for the baptism.

◆    ◆    ◆

It was like most baptismal services, with all the right people in attendance: the bishop, the ward mission leader, the man and his son who would be Thomas and Elizabeth's home teachers, Walter and Carolyn, and all of the missionaries in the district.

Megan and Brianna sat in the back.

"Isn't this great?" Brianna whispered.

Megan nodded. Even though she couldn't stand the thought of Elder Spaulding leaving, she was thrilled that her best friend and his sister were getting baptized.

"You made it happen," Brianna whispered.

"I wasn't a good example for him."

"Maybe not at first, but now you are."

221

After the opening song and prayer, Brianna gave a talk about the importance of being baptized. In her talk she almost entirely avoided jargon. For her it was like speaking a foreign language. Sometimes she would stop, as if she were searching for the way to say things in plain English.

And then it was time for the baptisms. They gathered by the font as Elder Spaulding and Thomas entered the water together.

And then Elder Spaulding baptized Thomas. After Thomas surfaced he threw his arms around Elder Spaulding, and they hugged each other.

And then as Thomas went up one set of stairs, Elder Spaulding turned to escort Elizabeth into the font. Dressed in white, with her long, dark brown hair hanging down to her waist, she looked like an angel.

Elder Spaulding took her hand and began, "Elizabeth Marconi, having been commissioned of Jesus Christ . . ."

And then he baptized her.

She came out of the water with the biggest smile anyone had ever seen from her, but she did not hug Elder Spaulding. She had learned the rules.

◆　　◆　　◆

Thomas and Elizabeth were confirmed a week later in sacrament meeting. Elder Spaulding had been transferred, and as the holdover from the original companionship, Elder Anderson confirmed both Thomas and Elizabeth. Megan cried tears of joy as she listened to the blessings they were given.

After the closing hymn and prayer, Elizabeth and Thomas stood up and put their arms around each other.

"I feel so good now," Elizabeth said. "How about you?"

"Me, too."

"It's true, isn't it?"

"It is."

"Isn't that nice that it's true?"

"It is. It's very nice."

They embraced again, brother and sister in a family, and brother and sister in the gospel.

Brianna leaned over and whispered in Megan's ear. "You made this happen."

"No, not me."

"Who then?"

She pointed at her stomach. "This baby made it happen."

Brianna put her face down close to Megan's stomach and called out softly, "Way to go, baby."

# 13

When Weston came home from work, Ann Marie ran to meet him. She excitedly threw her arms around him. "Come see what I've done today!"

Ann Marie had informed her boss she could only work part-time until their baby came and that then she'd be quitting for good. She'd spent the extra time working on the baby's room. She and Weston now stood in the doorway, arms draped around each other, and looked in at what would be the nursery for their baby.

In one week's time, she'd painted the room a color that the paint store called "Georgia Peach," made some cute animal cracker curtains for the window, had new carpet installed, and purchased a crib and a changing table, blankets, a month's supply of diapers, and one of the new glider-type rocking chairs so she could rock her baby to sleep.

Weston shook his head in wonder. "This looks great!"

"It's been so much fun!" She kissed Weston on the cheek. "I'm so excited. It's going to happen, isn't it?"

"Sure it is." Weston paused. "Sooner or later."

"I've got an idea. Let's have family home evening in here tonight."

"We never have family home evening."

"I know, but we need to start, don't you think, so it's a part of our life when the baby comes."

Weston nodded. "Whatever you say." They headed into the kitchen. "What's for supper?" he asked.

She made a guilty face. "I have no idea. I was working so hard on the baby's room."

"But we will eat, right? I mean, I think we should. It'll set a good example for the baby if the parents eat."

Ann Marie laughed. "I'm hearing a desperate man here, aren't I? Okay, okay, I get your point. I've been having way too much fun lately, haven't I?"

"It's fun for me, too. Do you want to call out for pizza?"

"That'd be great. I'll go downstairs and get some ginger ale." She started down the stairs but stopped and said, "I've got an idea! Let's have a picnic in the baby's room."

"You sure you want to do that? I mean, what about the new carpet?"

"It's okay if we spill. I need practice cleaning up the carpet for when the baby comes."

Ann Marie put out a red and white checkered tablecloth on the floor of the nursery. They were careful and didn't spill anything. Ann Marie was almost a little disappointed because she'd bought an arsenal of cleaning products in preparation for the baby.

"Let's have the lesson right here on the floor, okay?" she said.

"I don't know how it is for you, but sitting on the floor isn't as easy as it used to be," Weston said, getting to his feet.

He helped Ann Marie up, too. "You're right, but we'll get used to it. Let's take a break. We'll meet back here in ten minutes."

"Why do we need a break?"

225

"Well, we've got to have refreshments. And you need to work on a story."

"What story?"

Ann Marie started singing the Primary song, "When the family gets together." She added, "See, Daddy tells a story, Mother leads us in a song."

He scowled. "Oh, good grief, we're not really going to sing, are we?"

"We have to."

"I'll go warn the neighbors."

She burst out laughing. "It's not going to be that bad."

"Look, you're talking to a guy who once received a call from the bishop not to be in the youth choir."

"That doesn't matter. You'll get better."

"We're actually going to sing every Monday night?"

"We are. Every Monday night. No exceptions. Okay, you work on your story, and I'll get the refreshments. Do you need to go potty before we start?"

Weston laughed and shook his head. "Potty? You've gone too far this time."

"Sorry, I'm just practicing."

Ten minutes later they were sitting again on the floor in the baby's room.

Weston asked Ann Marie to say the prayer. And then, using a newly purchased copy of the *Children's Songbook,* they sang "Families Can Be Together Forever." By the time they finished, they were fighting back the tears.

And then it was time for a story. Weston read from a book of children's stories Ann Marie had purchased during the week.

" . . . I think I can . . . I think I can . . ."

Ann Marie loved the story. "Tell me another one."

Weston smiled. "You think our child will ever say that?"

"I'm sure of it. You're really very good. Lots of good vocal inflection."

226

He modestly shrugged. "Well, it's better that way." He put his arm around Ann Marie. "I love you, Annie."

Nobody called her Annie, except Weston, and only when they were alone.

"I love you, too."

"We're not setting ourselves up for heartache, are we?" he asked.

"How do you mean?"

"There are so many couples like us, and so few babies. There is no guarantee in this that we'll get a child."

She pursed her lips. "I know."

"I worry about you, that's all." Positioning himself behind her, he wrapped his arms around her waist and kissed her on the back of her neck.

They gazed up at the crib.

"What are you thinking?" she asked after a minute or two.

"How bad my hips are hurting right now."

She leaned back and they fell over. They ended up on their backs laughing.

"You think I should wallpaper the ceiling? I saw a cute pattern at the paint store. Little farm animals."

"Do we really want our kid thinking animals crawl on the ceiling? I don't think so." He stood up, offered his hand, and then pulled Ann Marie up. "Are we done yet?"

"No, we've got to have a lesson."

"Can we do it at the kitchen table? If I spend any more time on the floor, I'll need hip replacement surgery."

"Okay, we'll adjourn to the kitchen."

Before they began the lesson, she set a plate of chocolate chip cookies on the table.

"You made cookies?"

"Yeah."

"How come?"

"That's what moms do."

"Not anymore. Now they buy them."

"My mother made cookies for us. Sometimes she'd have them ready for us when we came home from school."

"Are you going to actually let me have one of these, or are you saving them for when our child is in first grade?"

"You can have as many as you want."

"Thanks." He reached for one.

She put her hand on his. "After the lesson."

A grin spread across his face. "You want me to do the lesson? I've got one that'll take about thirty seconds . . . and then we can get to the cookies."

"No, I'm going to do it."

"How long will it take?" Weston asked.

"Why are you asking?"

"The cookies look very inviting."

"Am I going to have to put these away, so you'll be able to concentrate on the lesson?"

"You're absolutely right. Here, I'll put them in the pantry."

He kept his back turned to her as he opened the pantry door.

"Weston?"

"What?"

"What are you doing?"

"Nuffing."

"Did you have a cookie?"

"Um-uhm," he said.

"How many cookies did you have?"

Without turning around, he held up one finger.

"There's more than one in there."

He held up two fingers.

"You're setting such a bad example."

He looked around.

"For who?" he mumbled, continuing to chew.

"The baby."

"Why don't we wait until the baby shows up?"

"It's just a matter of time," Ann Marie said.

"I hope so."

"Somewhere out there is a girl who is determined to do the best for her baby. She's been to LDS Family Services, and she's thought about her particular situation. Maybe marriage to the biological father isn't the best option for her. So she's wondering what to do. It's not an easy choice. And everybody has an opinion on the subject. But someday she'll learn about us and will sense how much we want a baby in our home, and maybe Heavenly Father will help her decide to trust her baby to us."

"I just don't want you to get hurt by getting your hopes up too high."

She nodded. "I'm going to be all right. Which brings us to our lesson."

She opened her Book of Mormon to Ether, chapter 12, and handed it to Weston. "Will you please read verses 23 through 25?"

Weston began to read:

"'And I said unto him: Lord, the Gentiles will mock at these things, because of our weakness in writing; for Lord thou hast made us mighty in word by faith, but thou hast not made us mighty in writing; for thou hast made all this people that they could speak much, because of the Holy Ghost which thou hast given them;

"'And thou hast made us that we could write but little, because of the awkwardness of our hands. Behold, thou hast not made us mighty in writing like unto the brother of Jared, for thou madest him that the things which he wrote were mighty even as thou art, unto the overpowering of man to read them.

"'Thou hast also made our words powerful and great, even that we cannot write them; wherefore, when we write we behold our weakness, and stumble because of the placing of our words; and I fear lest the Gentiles shall mock at our words."

"Thank you," she said. "That's all for now. Something struck me about this. Moroni was doing what I do sometimes."

"What do you mean?"

"Think about it. There's a thousand years of history contained in what his father had abridged. A thousand years of written documents. And yet Moroni picks out the best writing from that thousand years to compare what he and his father were able to contribute. I do that, too. In fact, I think I've been doing that most of my life."

"Making comparisons?"

She nodded. "I remember in high school wishing I could be as beautiful as Shauna Mortensen, or as gifted a violin player as Judith Carter, or as good at basketball as Jill Dunn. And these were the very best in our school. Well, that's what Moroni is doing here, isn't it? He wishes he could write like the brother of Jared, the best writer over a thousand-year period."

"I see what you mean. I do that, too."

"What's interesting to me is what advice the Savior doesn't give Moroni."

"I can tell you've thought about this a lot."

"It's what you can do when you're not working full-time, and you have time to think. Okay, here are some things the Lord could have told Moroni. He could have said, 'Maybe if you wrote it out on paper first, got your rough draft, then worked it over, made the corrections you need to make, then I think things will work out a little better for you.' That's the 'Just buy a self-help book and work a little on it every day' approach. But that's not what the Savior said."

"You're not saying it's bad to try to learn new skills and get better at something, are you?" he asked.

"No, not at all. But it's not the approach the Savior used with Moroni. Okay, another thing the Savior could have said to Moroni. He could have said, 'It's not that bad, actually. And, in fact, you'd be surprised if you knew how many millions of people are going to have a life-changing experience as they read the Book of Mormon.' But he didn't say that. What did he say? Would you read verses 26 and 27?"

Weston began reading:

"'And when I had said this, the Lord spake unto me, saying: Fools mock, but they shall mourn; and my grace is sufficient for the meek, that they shall take no advantage of your weakness;

"'And if men come unto me I will show unto them their weakness. I give unto men weakness that they may be humble; and my grace is sufficient for all men that humble themselves before me; for if they humble themselves before me, and have faith in me, then will I make weak things become strong unto them.'"

"Thank you," Ann Marie said. "That's what the Lord said. His grace is sufficient for all those who have faith in him. I love that. It brings me such comfort."

"We all need that, don't we?"

"I know I do. There's one more lesson I've picked up. It's found in verse 36, when Moroni prays that the Gentiles will have grace, that they might have charity. Once again, the Lord brings him up short. Will you read verse 37?"

"'And it came to pass that the Lord said unto me: If they have not charity it mattereth not unto thee, thou hast been faithful; wherefore, thy garments shall be made clean. And because thou hast seen thy weakness thou shalt be made strong, even unto the sitting down in the place which I have prepared in the mansions of my Father.'"

"Here's how this applies to me," Ann Marie said. "I've tortured myself, wishing I could be like the women in the ward with a large family. I've gone with the self-help approach. I know as much about how babies are made as any woman I know. I've also tortured myself wondering if the reason why I haven't been able to have children is because of something

I did when I was growing up. I've agonized over every action, every harsh word, every sin I've ever committed, looking for the one sin so serious that in his wrath God would punish me by making me unable to have children."

She used a napkin to dab at her eyes. "But, in the end, I am left with what the Lord said to Moroni. I've been faithful, I've seen my weaknesses, and that's all that counts. My disappointment that my life hasn't turned out exactly the way I envisioned is lifted from me when I realize that all the Lord requires from me is to be faithful. Nothing else matters. Just being faithful."

She reached for Weston's hand. "Whatever happens, it's going to be all right. The Savior has promised us that, and I believe him with all my heart. So don't worry about me, okay?"

Weston leaned across the table and kissed her on the forehead. "Do you have any idea how much I adore you?"

"Actually, I think I do." She got up and went to the pantry. "Who wants cookies?" she asked.

"I do!" Weston said.

"I do!" Weston said, imitating a teenage boy.

"I do!" Weston said, imitating a teenage girl.

"I do!" Weston said, imitating a five-year-old boy.

"I do!" Weston said, imitating a three-year-old girl.

Ann Marie made a worried face. "You know what? I'm not sure I made enough for everyone."

"You didn't," Weston said with a big grin.

And, sure enough, he was right.

# 14

At four months Megan's doctor did an ultrasound test. She was blown away by the images on the screen as he moved the sensor around on her abdomen, pointing out the baby's head, legs, and even the heartbeat. He froze the frame at one point and said, "Well, he's going to be a little man." That reality would ripple through the lives of many people.

♦　♦　♦

Megan's regular clothes were now too snug. She went shopping with her mother for loose fitting and casual outfits to wear around the house and a couple of nice maternity dresses for church.

In previous visits with Sister Gardner of LDS Family Services, Megan had outlined the qualities she wanted in the couple who would be adopting her baby.

In her next visit, Sister Gardner gave her letters from three couples who, in general, met Megan's requirements. Glancing at the way the letters began, Megan saw that the people did not know her name. She assumed it was to protect her privacy. They signed their first names but not their last name. Also, Megan had no idea where they lived. She could understand that was to protect their privacy.

"Can I take these home?" she asked.

"Yes, of course. Take your time. There's no hurry. Take all the time you need."

"Are all these couples active in the Church?"

"Yes."

"What about being sealed? Will they be able to have my baby sealed to them in the temple?"

Sister Gardner nodded. "Yes, that's right. After the adoption is final."

"Can I meet with them first and then decide?"

Sister Gardner paused. "Well, if possible, we'd like you to come to a decision without us bringing them in."

"I'm not sure I can make a decision like this without meeting them."

"I understand. Do your best, and please make this a matter of prayer. Heavenly Father knows which couple would be best for your baby."

"What about later? After my baby goes home with the couple I choose, will I find out how he's doing?"

"Yes. You'll receive a letter each month, along with pictures. They'll send the letters to us, and then we'll forward them to you. The same is true of the letters you send to them."

"How long will that last?"

"For at least six months. After that, when the adoption is final, then the amount of correspondence you have is whatever you and the adoptive parents feel comfortable with."

Megan ran her hand over the folder. "It's a big decision."

"That's right. Maybe the biggest you'll ever make. Be sure to pray about it."

"I will, for sure."

At home, after reading the letters, she offered a prayer, asking for help in making the decision.

After the prayer, she still didn't know.

♦　　♦　　♦

Diane Oldham was primed for war when her husband walked in the door on Sunday afternoon, a full three hours after the block of meetings ended. She was waiting for him at the door.

"I need to talk to you, Bishop," she said with anger in her voice.

"When?"

"Now. Right now."

"Can't I eat first?"

"How many people did you talk to after meetings today?"

"I don't know. Five or six, I guess."

"You didn't eat before you talked to them, did you?"

"No."

"Well, then, I deserve as much. I am a member of your ward, aren't I?"

"Okay, let's talk."

"Not here in front of the children. Let's go some place. We can talk in the car."

He couldn't help but let out a troubled sigh. He had been looking forward to coming home and relaxing.

He put his tie back on. "Yes, of course."

"You don't need to put your tie back on."

"It's no problem."

She felt a tinge of conscience for being one more burden he had to carry, but there was no one else she could go to except her bishop.

They drove to a neighborhood school and parked.

"Today in Relief Society I got a new visiting teaching route. Megan's name is on it. You did this, didn't you?"

"I had nothing to do with it."

"I don't believe that for an instant. You must have said something to someone in the Relief Society presidency."

"I didn't say a word."

"Then how do you explain me being assigned to her?"

"I have no explanation."

"I'm not assigned to her mother, just Megan. It makes no sense. You must have said something."

"I didn't."

"I will not visit teach her."

"Then you should talk to someone in Relief Society, not me."

"Can't you take care of it?"

"No, I'm sorry. I can't. The assignment didn't come from me. You'll have to explain your reasons to Marilyn Mortenson."

"I will. Don't think I won't. I'm not going to back down."

They drove home. As soon as the car stopped, she got out. "We've already eaten, so if you want something, get it out of the fridge. You can warm it up in the microwave just as well as I can."

"Yes, of course."

She turned to confront him. "Don't you be nice to me. I know you're behind this, one way or another."

He got out of the car. She came around to the driver's side, got in, and drove off.

A minute later she was met at the door of the Relief Society president's house by a three-year-old boy. "Is your mother here?"

He nodded and walked away.

She thought he was going to get his mother, but minutes passed. She stepped inside and waited.

And waited.

"Hello?" she said quietly.

No one answered, but she could hear voices. She walked toward the sound of the voices.

"Hello?" she called out again.

The source of the voices was a TV in the living room. The boy who'd let her in was sitting in front of the set, watching a video about Daniel in the lions' den.

"Hello?" she called out.

"Is someone here?" It was Marilyn Mortenson's voice. Diane took a few more timid steps into the hallway, came to a room, and looked in. There on a large couch with blankets draped over them were Marilyn, two of her kids, and her husband. Everyone else was asleep, but Marilyn and Diane made eye contact.

"I'm sorry," Diane said. "Your boy let me in. I didn't mean to just barge in. I'll go now."

"No, that's fine. We were just taking a nap, that's all. Sunday is such a busy day for us that by this time of the afternoon, we're completely wiped out."

Marilyn managed to untangle herself from the arms, legs, and knees of her children and husband. She was wearing a baggy sweatshirt and some yellow sweatpants.

Diane envied the scene that she'd barged in on. *We never do that on Sundays. It looks so good. I wish we spent more time like that.*

"I am sorry," Diane said.

"It's no problem, really. Let's go in the living room."

The living room had newspapers scattered all over the floor. There was also a box of Cheerios turned on its side, with its little round O's scattered everywhere.

"Looks like Adam has been having a good time while we were napping, doesn't it?" she said, getting down to clean up.

"You don't have to clean up for me."

"All right, I won't," she said, getting up again. "If you can overlook our Sunday mess."

"I can."

237

"Fine. Please sit down. Can I get you something? A glass of water? Some lemonade?" She smiled. "Cheerios?"

"No, I'm fine. I won't take much of your time. I just needed to ask you a question about my visiting teaching. I just wanted to know why I was assigned to Megan Cannon."

"We thought it would be better to have someone who can pour some time into Megan."

"Why did you choose me?"

"Well, I'm not sure, except to say we talked about it at a presidency meeting."

"My husband claims he didn't put you up to it."

"Of course not." She paused. "Is there a problem?"

Diane closed her eyes. *Yes, there's a problem. The whole ward is coddling Megan, turning her into some kind of a celebrity. If we paid as much attention to the girls who don't step out of line, then there would be less of this going on.*

That's what she wanted to say to this woman, still warm from the combined heat from her husband and her children, who had been caught in the act of napping on a Sunday afternoon after church while their little boy, totally unsupervised, made a mess of the house.

*She's no better than me, and yet she's the Relief Society president.*

"I'm just curious why you've assigned me to be her visiting teacher?" Diane said.

"I'm not sure what you want me to say. Do you want me to say we fasted and prayed about who should visit teach Megan? Well, I'm sorry. We didn't, but I did feel good about our decision. For one thing, you don't work. And your children are all in school. We were hoping you and Sister Baker could visit her during the day when she's all alone."

*You can't even keep your house under control. Why should I believe God would guide your decisions?*

Adam wandered into the room with a half-gallon of ice cream and a large spoon.

238

"Adam, you're having a real good time, aren't you?" Marilyn asked with an amused smile.

He smiled back.

"You know the rules, Adam. Let me have the ice cream."

He handed over the ice cream. She took it into the kitchen, returned it to the freezer, and came back into the living room.

"You need to clean up the mess you made, Adam."

"It's too hard for me," he whined.

"You start and I'll help."

Adam sat down on the living room floor and picked up a few Cheerios and put them in the box.

Transfixed, Diane watched the scene playing out in front of her. For every Cheerio Adam placed in the box, his mother did a handful.

"He's not much help at this age, is he?" Diane said.

"He's doing as much as he can. When he does as much as he can, then I step in."

Diane watched this for a few minutes and then the thought gradually came. Diane repeated the words: "He's doing as much as he can, and then you step in." Diane pictured Megan on her hands and knees, picking up the consequences of her mistakes. Who would step in and help her?

"Is there a problem with the assignment?" Marilyn asked.

The image in her mind had disarmed Diane. "No, I just wanted to check with you, that's all."

"I see."

"I'd better be going now."

*Have I been wrong all this time?* Diane thought.

As she drove home, she felt the gentle tugging of conscience she associated with the influence of the Holy Ghost. *I have been wrong, but there's still time to change.*

When she arrived at home, she found her husband in the kitchen with a full plate of food but not eating because he was on the phone.

She took his fork and took a small taste of the food. It was room temperature. She put it in the microwave to reheat it, then wrote him a note: "Who is it?"

Still listening, he wrote back: "Brother Snyder."

Brother Snyder was a member of the stake high council. She gently removed the phone from her husband's ear. "Hello, Brother Snyder? How are you? Can I ask you a question? Have you had your dinner?"

"Yes, of course," he said over the phone.

"Well, my husband hasn't. Can you call back in a couple of hours? Yes, thank you. Bye."

The microwave dinged. She removed the food and put it in front of him.

"Eat," she said gently.

"How did your meeting go?"

"Good."

"Who's going to visit teach Megan?"

"Sister Baker and I."

"Really?"

"Yes."

"How come?"

"That's who Father in Heaven wants."

She found a box of Cheerios in the cupboard. "After you finish eating, can we take a nap together?"

"We don't take naps." He seemed confused. "Do we?"

"I think we should start."

He yawned. "I guess I could stand a nap."

She put the box of Cheerios on the kitchen table.

"What's that for?"

"In case anyone gets hungry."

"I'm not sure I understand what's going on."

"I know."

"But I like it."

They had a wonderful Sunday afternoon nap together, joined later by their dog, Blue.

Two days later Diane and Sister Baker visited Megan. Barbara Baker, a woman in her mid-sixties, gave the visiting teaching message for the month, then asked Megan, "How are you doing?"

"Good. I mean, considering my . . . situation. I'm doing all right."

"How do you spend your time? You're not working are you?"

"No. I'm mostly just here at home. With everyone else gone during the day, I have a lot of time by myself. I've had a chance to read quite a bit. I'm on my second time reading the Book of Mormon."

"That's wonderful."

"Yes, it's been very helpful."

"Do you ever get discouraged?" Diane asked.

"Honestly? Yes, I do. When I think about how I've messed up and how complicated my life has become, it's hard. I hate that I've hurt people. Not just my mom, but Brianna and Bryce, and my dad. I'm afraid a lot of the time, too, especially when I think about actually having this baby. And when I think about my baby and how he deserved to be born to a mother who'd lived a better life . . ." She sighed. "When I think about those things, then I get very discouraged."

"It must be hard."

"Also, I know I've disappointed a lot of people in the ward. I'm sure they feel bad for my mom, who did everything she could to teach me how to live my life."

"We have such high hopes for our youth," Diane said.

"Can I be perfectly honest? Sister Oldham, I know you've never said anything to me, but I've gotten the feeling that I've been a great disappointment to you."

"Megan, I will be honest with you, too. I've really struggled with my feelings about your situation."

241

"I can understand that. I went outside the bounds of morality when I truly knew better."

"No, it's not so much that. We all make mistakes. But I've been worried that if we made it too easy on you, or if we made too much of a fuss over you, other girls would think that what had happened to you was no big deal. Or maybe even follow your example—so they could get the same kind of attention."

Megan nodded her head. "I can understand why you'd think that."

"It wasn't anything against you personally."

"Okay. Also, I suppose you were probably aware of how much of your husband's time I was taking."

"Yes. He works very hard at his calling. Sometimes he gives so much there's not much left for him to give our family."

"I'm not meeting with him that often anymore."

"He never tells me who he's meeting with or why."

"That's probably good, that you don't know."

"Yes. I'd rather not know."

"I'm usually okay during the week. As long as I have my morning prayers and read the scriptures, but when I leave the house, then things happen that make me feel bad."

"What kind of things?"

"Like when I meet one of my friends from high school and they ask me what I'm going to do, and I tell them I'm going to place my baby for adoption. And they say, 'I could never do that,' like I'm cold and heartless to even be thinking of letting my baby be adopted."

"Just the opposite is true, though."

"I know. It's because I love him so much that I want him to have more than I can give him. I can't give him a father who will love him. I can't give him a situation where his mother can stay home and be with him all the time. I can't give him any of that."

"I think it's commendable that you're thinking of his welfare more than your own," Sister Baker said.

"That's the way I see it, but my friends from high school don't see it that way." She paused. "And then there are the people who think I'm a fool for not having had an abortion. To them, seeing me getting bigger, knowing I've given up all my social life, to them I'm a fool. That's hard to take, too."

"I'm sure it is," Diane said.

"Sometimes it's hard to go to church, too."

"Is it?"

"Yes. I'm still not allowed to partake of the sacrament. That was one of the things the bishop asked of me while I go through the process of repentance. At first it didn't mean that much to me, except that I was embarrassed to have the deacons wonder about me. But now, after studying the gospel so much, I can see the value of the sacrament, and I want to take it, but I can't."

Sister Baker smiled. "I raised four deacons. Believe me, they don't think about things like that. Heavenly Father was wise to appoint twelve-year-old boys to pass the sacrament."

"That's good to know." Megan focused her gaze on the floor. "Also, at church, I can tell by the way people look at me how they feel about me."

Diane wiped her eyes. "I'm sorry I've been one of those."

"Thanks for admitting that." Megan cleared her throat. "To tell you the truth, when you called and said you'd been asked to be my visiting teacher, I didn't know what to expect. I wondered if you were going to come and tell me what a sinner I've been. The thing is, I know that. I'm not sure you could say anything that I haven't said to myself."

"I've had a change of heart."

Megan smiled. A thin, little smile.

Diane had only intended to pat Megan's arm, but it turned into a hug that left them in tears.

"God sent you both to me, didn't he?" Megan asked.

"Yes, I believe he did."

# 15

Megan was talking to her mother about how they were going to decorate for Christmas when suddenly she stopped talking. With a look of astonishment on her face, she put her hand on her stomach. "Oh, my gosh! I can feel the baby moving. Here. Put your hand here."

Carolyn gently placed her hand on Megan's tummy and felt a tiny movement. "Well, hello, little one. We're glad you've come to say hello."

"This is so amazing!" Megan cried out. "I'm really going to have a baby, aren't I?"

"Looks that way."

"My little baby."

"Yes, what a thrill it is to hold your baby in your arms and count all its fingers and toes. Every birth is such a miracle."

Tears of joy began to run down Megan's cheeks.

Over the next few days, she made sure each member of the family had a chance to feel the fluttering motions of her baby. Brianna put her mouth close to Megan's tummy and sang to it. Bryce was too self-conscious and pulled away after about two seconds. Her father smiled broadly as he felt the motion.

"Too bad we can't tell Heather about this," Megan said.

They still had not told Heather about her pregnancy, using the excuse that they didn't want her to worry or be diverted in any way from missionary work.

Megan tried to get Thomas to feel the motion, but he was too embarrassed to even try. "We're best friends, but I'm not sure you want me doing that."

"C'mon, I'm wearing this heavy sweater. It'll just feel like there's a mouse inside my stomach, that's all."

He felt uneasy. "How about if I just take your word for it?"

Elizabeth wasn't at all bashful. "Wow, there is something in there after all, isn't there?"

"I think so," Megan said happily.

"Have you decided who you want to adopt your baby?" Elizabeth asked.

"Not yet. I'm still working on it."

As Megan read and reread the three letters Sister Gardner had given her, one couple kept coming to the top, the couple whose first names were Weston and Ann Marie. When her mother read over the letters, she also rated them very highly.

And so Megan prayed.

And prayed.

And prayed.

After a week she'd come to a decision. It would be Weston and Ann Marie.

"I'll let them know," Sister Gardner said. "You can be sure, they'll be thrilled."

Arrangements were made to meet the couple in Sister Gardner's office.

Megan wanted this first meeting to be special. She decided to buy a baby outfit and present it to them as a token of what she would be giving to them in a few months.

She went shopping by herself for a baby outfit that her son could be blessed in by his father.

It was the Christmas season and even on a Wednesday morning Wal-Mart was packed with people. Megan went to the racks with baby clothes and slowly looked at each one, excited to be doing something for her baby.

And then it struck her. *This is the only time in my life I'll buy clothes for this baby. I won't ever buy him socks and I won't ever buy him shoes and I won't ever buy him a white shirt for church. This baby, who is stretching and rolling around inside of me, will never call me Mommy. He won't nurse from me or be changed by me or be cuddled at night when he's crying. I'll never read to him. I won't be the one to teach him to ride a bicycle. He'll never come to me in tears with a scratched knee.*

*This is it. All I will ever give to my baby is this one little outfit.*

It was too hard. On the verge of crying, she had to leave the store.

She hurried to her car and drove to a park and sat in her car and mourned the loss that was to come. *How can I do this? How can I give up my child?*

She drove to Home Depot and went to the information desk and asked them to page her brother.

A few minutes later, Bryce showed up.

"What's wrong?"

"I need to talk to you."

"You look terrible."

"Where can we go to talk?"

"Lumber."

They ended up in a cavernous room, stacked to the ceiling with forests' worth of lumber.

"So, what's wrong?"

She told him about shopping for an outfit for her baby.

246

"It's not the only thing you're ever going to give your baby," he said.

"What else am I going to give him?"

"A mom and a dad who've been waiting for years for him to show up. That's better than any set of clothes you could ever buy."

"This is so hard, Bryce."

His first reaction was to discount what she was saying because it involved the emotions, but then, in a rare display of concern, he said tenderly, "I know it is. It's probably the hardest thing you'll ever do. I wish I could make it easier." He bit his lip. "I do that here, you know, for people with projects. But for this project I'm pretty much at a loss to know what to do to make your pain all go away."

"Could you give me a hug?" she asked tentatively.

"On company time?"

"Yes."

He smiled faintly. "Usually they frown on us hugging the customers."

"I'm not a customer."

"Then I guess it'll be all right."

He held her in his arms and then kissed her on the cheek.

"Sometimes it's almost like you're . . . well, a real human being," she said.

He chuckled. "We'd better not let that get around, okay?"

"Okay."

"Can I interest you in a load of plywood while you're here?"

"You know, I just bought some the other day."

"Well, come back when you want some more. I'll give you a good deal."

He walked her to her car and hugged her again before she got in.

He even watched her drive off.

Megan returned to the store and bought an outfit her son could wear when he was blessed in church.

♦   ♦   ♦

Sister Gardner asked Megan to take a seat in a small conference room while waiting for Weston and Ann Marie to arrive. Her heart pounding and feeling more anxious than she ever remembered being, Megan sat alone with her thoughts. *How can I be sure this is right? What if these people are weird? I mean, they're strangers, and here I am thinking of giving them my baby. Just giving him to them?*

The clock on the wall had a minute hand that jumped ahead every sixty seconds. It was now ten minutes after the scheduled meeting time.

*I wonder what they think of me? I don't know what Sister Gardner has told them. They probably think I'm some little tramp, who goes around sleeping with guys and getting pregnant. I'm not though. That's not the way it was.*

In the silence of the room, the minute hand jumped to fifteen minutes after the hour.

"We're so sorry we're late," she heard a woman's voice say. "We got lost."

"It's no problem. We're just glad you arrived. Please come with me, and I'll make the introductions."

Megan stood up as Ann Marie burst into the room, full of apologies.

"We took a wrong turn," Weston added.

The man reminded Megan of someone who could have played the sheriff in a western movie. He was tall, lean, and big-boned, with broad shoulders. He was wearing slacks and a white shirt and tie for the occasion, like he might wear to church, but the cowboy boots gave him away.

His pretty wife was also tall, wore a dress, and had her

blonde hair pulled up, seemingly more to get it out of the way than to show it off.

Sister Gardner introduced them by their first names and then gestured for them all to be seated at the conference table.

"Megan has prepared a list of questions. Megan?"

Ann Marie was smiling but looked nervous. Weston was unable to keep his big hands still on the tabletop.

Megan pulled out a paper and unfolded it in front of her.

She looked at Weston. "You'll be the daddy for my baby. Can I ask you a question? What was your dad like when you were growing up?"

Weston cleared his throat. He smiled as he said, "I grew up on a farm, so my dad always had work for us to do. But he didn't just tell us what to do. He worked alongside my brothers and me."

"Was he good to you?"

"He was. He wasn't the kind to take vacations, but every so often my dad would just take the day off with us, and we'd go fishing or even just float down the river in inner tubes."

Megan looked at her notes. "Were you afraid of him?"

Weston chuckled. "Well, we never talked back to him, but that was because we respected him. But, no. We weren't afraid of him."

"Did you love him?"

"Our family wasn't one to *talk* about love. But I loved him, and I knew he loved me. Because of how much time he spent with me and all the things he tried to teach me—not just about farming, but about other things, like always telling the truth and being honest and working hard . . . things like that."

"Was he religious?"

Weston smiled. "I never think of him like that, but I guess he was. He served as a bishop for six years, so that probably counts as being religious. He didn't preach much, though, if that's what you mean. Right now he and my mom are temple

249

ordinance workers, so they've turned out okay, I guess." He smiled as he said it.

Megan turned to Ann Marie. "How long have you been trying to have a baby?"

"It's going on nine years," she said.

For a moment Megan saw in Ann Marie's expression the pain and anguish that had played out over that time, but then Ann Marie covered it up with a weak smile.

Then she said, "Having a baby has been the most important thing in our lives. But when you're doing everything they say, and nothing happens . . . month after month . . ." She hesitated. "I'm sorry. I'm sure you don't want to know any of that, do you? I'll just say that, eventually, when we couldn't go on the way we'd been going, we talked it over and finally decided to try to adopt." She cleared her throat. "We've been waiting for such a long time. I promise you, we'll give him all the love he deserves."

Weston put his arm around Ann Marie's shoulder. "You'll never find a better mother than this gal."

Megan looked into their hopeful faces. It was a strange situation. Even though she was so much younger than they, she could feel them wanting her to like them, hoping she would be impressed enough to grant them their desire.

Her heart went out to them. They were obviously good people. Sister Gardner had recommended them, and they wanted this so much. It felt right. Her own heart pounding, she folded up her notes and reached down and picked up a gift-wrapped box she had set on the floor next to her chair.

She slid the box across the table to Ann Marie and said, "May I be the first to congratulate you both."

Ann Marie brought her hands to her mouth, then turned to look at her husband, tears springing into her eyes. He put his arms around her and held her without speaking.

They opened their gift to find a baby outfit. Ann Marie

took it out of the box and held it, just looking at it, tears rolling down her cheeks.

After a time Ann Marie said, "Five years ago we bought a tiny pair of cowboy boots in hopes that someday we'd have a little boy to fill them. They've been on our mantle ever since, and now, finally, we're going to have a boy who can wear them."

"Thank you for this . . . outfit," Weston said, fighting to keep from bawling.

"We have a gift for you, too," Ann Marie said. She stepped into the next room and brought back a beautifully wrapped present. Megan opened it. It was a photo album. "This is for you to keep the pictures we'll be sending you of your baby."

Megan felt a rush of emotion, as did Ann Marie, and they met in a big hug.

The thought ran through Megan's mind as she was being held by Ann Marie, *I'm giving my boy far more than I could ever give him by myself. I'm doing the right thing for him. And that's what counts.*

◆  ◆  ◆

Two Sundays before Christmas, Megan attended her dad's Gospel Doctrine class.

It was another masterpiece. Her dad used excerpts from Handel's *Messiah* along with video clips of the General Authorities bearing their testimonies of the Savior's mission.

It was a wonderful presentation and brought many compliments after class.

But like all of his lessons, there was no class participation.

Megan wished there had been time for class members to talk about their testimonies of the Savior, because if there had, she would have told what he now meant to her.

That night her father came to her. "How did you think the lesson went today?"

"It was a wonderful lesson."

"Yes, I've had many compliments. Several people want copies."

"Every week you just get better and better," she said.

"Something's missing though."

"What more could you have done?"

He put his hand on her shoulder. "You know what this reminds me of?"

"What?"

"Our father-daughter interviews when we used to hide the truth from each other. When I pretended that I wanted to know details about your life, and you pretended to tell me the truth. I mean, we have gotten beyond that, haven't we?"

"We should have by now," she said with a sigh. "After all we've gone through."

"So tell me what you really think about my lessons."

"I'm not a teacher. I wouldn't know what to tell you."

"Tell me how you feel."

She let out a deep sigh. "You talk about the Savior each week, and I sit there almost overcome with my gratitude to him for providing me a way to be forgiven of my sins, and I want to bear my testimony, but you don't ask anyone to do that. Sometimes I feel like your lessons are designed to get people to compliment you for being such a great teacher."

She grimaced. It was a harsh thing to say, and she was fearful he would take offense. He didn't seem to, though.

"What should I do differently?"

"I think members of the class need opportunities to bear their testimonies about what the Savior has meant in their lives."

"How can I do that?"

She shrugged her shoulders. "I don't know. I'm not the teacher."

"Let me think about it, and I'll get back to you."

"Sounds good."

He was about to leave when she said, "Dad?"

"Yes?"

"If we're being honest with each other, then why don't we tell Heather I'm expecting a baby?"

"We haven't wanted to distract her from her mission."

"If I were her, I'd be insulted not to be told the truth."

"Let's go talk to your mother about this."

Five minutes later they agreed to tell Heather.

Megan told her on the phone on Christmas Day when Heather called to wish them a merry Christmas.

"I knew something wasn't right," she said. "I'm glad you told me."

"We don't have family secrets anymore," Megan said. "So don't you keep anything from us either, okay?"

"It's a deal," she said.

◆　　◆　　◆

Elizabeth was dead set on going to BYU winter semester. She had a high enough GPA, and her audition tape featuring her on the piano was enthusiastically received by the music department. She phoned often enough that she finally gained provisional acceptance, with the understanding that she'd only take evening classes during her first semester.

After she was accepted, Elizabeth worked on talking Thomas into going with her. Since he was working and only taking one class a semester, she argued he could do the same thing in Provo, where he could enroll at UVSC while waiting to get into BYU.

She eventually wore him down, and he agreed to her plan. Out of respect for their family, they attended one last Sunday family supper. It was the first one they'd attended since joining the Church.

"Where you two been?" Uncle Al asked. "Your grandmother asks about you all the time. You're breaking her heart by never coming around anymore."

"It's good to see you again, too," Elizabeth said.

"So, you got that Mormon thing out of your system yet? I knew it was just a matter of time before you gave up on it."

"Not really. We're moving to Utah."

"No, you're not. You wouldn't be that heartless—to abandon your family."

"You know what, Uncle Al? We'll miss you telling us how to live our lives," Thomas said with a good-natured grin.

"I hope you know you're going to break your grandmother's heart."

"Sometimes I think you say that just so you can control us," Elizabeth said. "We'll talk to Gramma. I think she'll be glad for us. We're going to get a college education."

"You think there's no colleges out here? Is that what you think?"

Elizabeth smiled politely. "Nice to see you again."

On January 3 they left for Utah. All the way there Elizabeth insisted they listen to a CD of the BYU Men's Chorus.

# 16

Megan's baby was growing. Now, when she felt him moving, she could sometimes distinguish between a tiny arm or leg and a head or buttocks. The baby's heartbeat was strong enough to be heard with a stethoscope.

In January life seemed to slow down to a crawl for Megan. No more missionary discussions. No going to Leo's Pizza to talk to Thomas. No friends she'd known in high school to visit with. They'd written her off, either because she was going to have the baby or else because she was going to place it for adoption.

Her due date was May 10. At times it seemed that date would never come. And at other times, she wished it wouldn't; she knew there would be a great sense of loss in giving up her baby, who, by now, seemed to have a personality, communicating to her with his kicking and tapping on the walls of the place that was his home until he would be born.

She spent her days at home, mostly alone. Brianna worked after school, and so she was gone a great deal of the time. Bryce continued to work full-time at Home Depot.

And, of course, her father was always gone, leaving each Monday, returning every Friday, on the road all the time. It was a pattern she'd grown up with.

But near the end of the month, he announced to his family that he'd told his boss he was tired of being gone all the time. The company found him a place in the home office. It paid less but at least he'd be home every night.

On his first day at his new job, he came home happier than Megan had ever seen him. To celebrate they all went out to supper.

Also, in January Elder Spaulding went home from his mission. Megan didn't get to see him off. It would have meant a long drive to the airport. And, besides, she hadn't been asked.

Ann Marie and Weston wrote several letters to Sister Gardner, and she passed them on to Megan. They were excited and making preparations. They sent photographs of the baby's room.

She still met occasionally with Bishop Oldham, but they were running out of issues that needed to be resolved. She had faithfully gone through the process of repentance he had outlined. She'd read the Book of Mormon twice since she started meeting with him. She had also finished reading *The Miracle of Forgiveness,* and they had discussed each chapter in detail.

"Is there anything else we need to do?" he asked after one of their visits.

She thought for a minute. "There is one thing, Bishop. I feel like I've made a lot of progress, but when will I know I have been forgiven?"

He leaned forward across his desk. "I can't give you a time. That is something that only you and the Lord will know. The only thing I can tell you is that if you keep going on the road you're on, the time will come when you will know in your heart that you are forgiven."

He leaned back in his chair and studied her face. "I think it's time for you to begin partaking of the sacrament again."

She closed her eyes and tried to keep from crying. "I would like that very much."

"Do you understand why I asked you not to partake of the sacrament?"

"So that I would appreciate its significance?"

"That's right. The sacrament is a sacred ordinance. If we partake of it, knowing that we are unrepentant, it no longer becomes a blessing to us. I wanted you to be ready."

She grabbed a tissue and wiped her face. "Thank you very much."

"There's something else about the sacrament. Let's look at the prayers."

Bishop Oldham flipped through the pages of the Doctrine and Covenants until he found what he was looking for. He had Megan read the two prayers.

Then he asked, "When we partake of the bread and water, who do we remember?"

"Jesus Christ."

"That's right. And what do we say we are willing to do?"

Megan looked at the prayers again. "Take his name upon us."

"And?"

"Always remember him and keep his commandments."

"You made that same promise when you were what?"

She looked at him without understanding.

"When you were eight years old . . ."

"Baptized?"

"Exactly. So, when you partake of the sacrament, you are really renewing your baptismal covenant. Does that make sense?"

"I never thought of it in that way."

"Now consider this. When you were baptized, it was for what?"

"The remission of my sins."

"Megan, think about that. When you partake of the sacrament worthily, after having truly repented, you can be as clean and acceptable to the Lord as you were when you were baptized. Can you think of anything more wonderful?

"As you take the bread and water, think about what he did for you. Remember the price he paid in Gethsemane and on the cross. If it weren't for the Atonement, none of us would have any hope. But because he has already paid for our sins, he can forgive them. Listen to the words of the sacramental prayers and be grateful for his love and mercy. That's what I want you to do."

"I will. I promise I will."

"Then I'm not sure we need to continue meeting on a regular basis. If you have problems, please let me know, and we can talk, but, otherwise, I think we're done here."

"I'll try not to have to come back."

He smiled. "I'll miss talking to you."

"Maybe out in the hall," she suggested.

"Let's do that."

He stood up and shook her hand and walked her to the door.

"Thank you for all you've done for me," she said.

"If you've been comforted, that's come from the Savior. He's the one you should thank."

"You know what I mean."

"Yes, of course."

She wanted to give him a hug but didn't.

The next Sunday she partook of the sacrament. It was an amazing experience to her.

It was a holy day.

♦    ♦    ♦

## APRIL, NINTH MONTH

For Megan life revolved around her family and the baby she carried.

When she lay in bed at night, she could sometimes see her whole tummy change shape as the baby moved. It was getting harder to move around. Her stomach seemed to be in the way whatever she did, and because she was retaining water and her ankles were swollen, walking became a challenge. Her lower back also sometimes ached.

As general conference approached, Megan began to look forward to watching it. It was the first time in her life she'd ever felt that way—not just because the talks and music promised to be good but because she had heard that if members of the Church will approach the experience prayerfully, and listen carefully, they will receive promptings that will help them answer some of their questions and worries.

It was with that hope that she faithfully listened to each session of conference.

What she wanted to be assured was not so much if God could forgive her for what she'd done, but to know if he would hold it against her in some way, if she would forever be on his list of those who had messed up and had to set their lives back on course.

She wanted some assurance that she could still have all the blessings promised to members of the Church.

And, to her amazement, that was the topic of Elder Richard G. Scott's conference address. She felt as though he were speaking directly to her when he said:

"If you have repented from serious transgression and mistakenly believe that you will always be a second-class citizen in the kingdom of God, learn that is not true. The Savior said:

"'Behold, he who has repented of his sins, the same is forgiven, and I, the Lord, remember them no more.

"'By this ye may know if a man repenteth of his sins—behold, he will confess them and forsake them. . . . ' (D&C 58:42–43).'

"To you who have sincerely repented yet continue to feel the burden of guilt, realize that to continue to suffer for sins when there has been proper repentance and forgiveness of the Lord is prompted by the master of deceit. Lucifer will encourage you to continue to relive the details of past mistakes, knowing that such thoughts can hamper your progress. . . .

"When memory of past mistakes encroaches upon your mind, turn your thoughts to the Redeemer and to the miracle of forgiveness with the renewal that comes through Him. Your depression and suffering will be replaced by peace, joy, and gratitude for His love.

"How difficult it must be for Jesus Christ, our Savior and Redeemer, to see so many needlessly suffer, because His gift of repentance is ignored. It must pain Him deeply to see the pointless agony both in this life and beyond the veil that accompany the unrepentant sinner after all He did so that we need not suffer."

It was the answer she'd been looking for.

♦     ♦     ♦

## MAY 29, PAST DUE

A little after two in the afternoon, Megan's labor pains began. At first she thought it was just false labor, but when the pains became worse, she became concerned.

Since The Home Depot was only five minutes away, compared to where her father and mother worked, Bryce had been designated the one for her to call when she needed to go to the hospital.

As she reached for the phone, Bryce was at that moment talking to the most amazing young woman he'd ever met—a brunette with short hair that bounced when she turned her head, high cheekbones that made him wonder if she was part American Indian, and blue eyes that reminded him of a deep lake. She said she was planning to add a garage to a house she'd just bought, but, unlike so many young women who wandered the aisles of Home Depot, trolling for guys, she didn't seem to need help. That bothered Bryce. Women customers always needed him. But this one didn't seem to.

"I could give you some tips about this if you'd like," he said.

She looked up from the list of supplies she needed.

"No, I'm okay."

"A lot of people forget to cut the top plate so it breaks at the center of a stud."

"I know that, but thanks anyway."

"You sure?"

"Positive. I've been helping my dad build houses since I was twelve."

"Then why did you come here?" he blurted out.

"For supplies."

He felt himself blushing. "Oh, sure."

She went back to studying her list of materials. He just stood there and stared at her.

She looked up. "Don't you have some other customers who actually need help?"

"Look, if you want, I could come out on my day off and help you."

"Why would you want to do that?"

"I'd like to get to know you."

"Is that why you work here, to meet women?"

"I've never done this before."

"Yeah, right," she scoffed.

"Forget about me. Let's talk about your project. Are you telling me you couldn't use a hand?"

"Are you any good?"

"Better than you."

"Now I know you're lying."

"Try me out and see."

"Well—"

"Give me at least a try. If I don't work out, then you can just tell me to get lost."

"Well, okay."

"I'll need to know your name and address and phone number."

She said, "My name is Jordan Taylor" and had just written her phone number on a scrap of paper when one of Bryce's coworkers hurried over to him. "Bryce, your wife called. She's in labor. She needs you to give her a ride to the hospital."

Jordan threw up her hands. "You're getting my address while your wife is about to have a baby?"

"No! You don't understand! I'm not married."

She glared at him. "You are *so* pathetic."

"No, it's not like that. She's my sister. We live just a few blocks from here. That's why she called me. To take her to the hospital."

"Just give it a rest, okay?"

"I've got to go now, but I'll call you." He stuffed the paper with her number on it into his pocket and turned and ran for the door.

Five minutes later Bryce burst into the house. "I'm here! Let's go!"

Megan was sitting on the couch in the living room, her arms wrapped around her sides as she rocked back and forth, writhing with pain.

"Just give me a minute, okay?"

"Sure. Do you need me to get you anything upstairs?"

262

"No, I've got it all here in this bag."

"I'll take it out to the car."

She nodded.

"He carried her suitcase out to the car and then hurried back.

She stood up. "I think I can move now."

He held his arm out for her to hold as they slowly made their way to the car.

He opened the car door for her and helped her in, then raced around to the other side of the car, jumped in, and backed down the driveway.

"How much of a hurry are you in?"

Her eyes were closed. "Just drive the way you usually do. That'll be fast enough."

A few minutes later, when a stoplight changed to green, Bryce gunned it, pushing Megan's head against the headrest. She grimaced with pain.

"Go easy, okay?"

"Oh, sure, sorry."

The admittance process went smoothly, and ten minutes later Megan was lying in a bed in the Women's Center, in the room where she would give birth and also be staying. She paid no attention, but unlike a normal hospital room, it was nicely furnished, with subdued lighting and a bed that had a brass rail headboard.

While the nurse was settling Megan in, Bryce called his parents and told them to come right away.

Then, just when she was so close to delivery, things slowed down dramatically.

"You want to go back to work?" she asked.

"No, I'll stay here with you."

She smiled. "Thanks."

It was quiet, except for the occasional sound of a woman in the next room, who was in the last stage of delivery and cried out in pain whenever she had a contraction.

263

"She sounds like she's having a rough time," Megan said.

"Sounds like it."

"I suppose I'll be just like her before very long."

"I suppose." Bryce paused. "I met this incredible girl today. She's going to build a garage."

"What made her incredible?"

"She didn't need my help. She said she's been building things with her dad since she was twelve."

"What is she like?"

"Well, she knew not to buy the top grade two-by-fours. That's where a lot of people go wrong. You don't need that for a garage."

"I meant what did she look like?"

"She looked real good."

Megan smiled. "You're going to make me pry this out of you, aren't you?"

"I could hardly keep my eyes off her."

"Describe her to me."

"She looks like a girl who'd sell backpacks on the Home Shopping Network."

"So, you like her then, right?"

"Yeah, pretty much." He sighed. "She has kind of a bad impression of me, though. When one of the guys came to tell me you'd called, he said that my wife was having her baby. Naturally that put a damper on our relationship. I tried to explain, but I'm not sure she believed me. I have her number here if you want to call her."

She gave him a wry smile. "Maybe later. I'm kind of busy here now."

Carolyn was the first to arrive. Her face was full of concern. "Megan, how are you doing?"

"The pains slowed down for a while, but they're starting to come back."

"Your father should be here any minute."

"Good. What about Brianna?"

264

"She's working. I haven't tried to get hold of her."

"I think you should."

"She might not be able to get off work."

"Maybe not, but she should be told." Megan paused. "Remember, no secrets, no holding back."

"I'll call her work and see if I can talk to her."

Carolyn left the room, and Bryce came to stand at the side of Megan's bed. She didn't have much energy to carry on a conversation, so he just stood there, keeping her company. Whenever she felt a labor pain, she would take hold of his hand and squeeze.

"Megan, you know what? I'm sorry I chased you through the house with the vacuum cleaner when you were little."

"I can't remember that."

"You were about four years old. You were screaming. I think you really thought I'd vacuum you up."

"Why would I think that?"

"Well, maybe because that's what I said I was going to do."

She smiled weakly. "That would explain why I have an irrational fear of vacuum cleaners."

"There's more," he said.

"Not now, Bryce. Just hold my hand."

A labor pain came. She squeezed.

"That's quite a grip. You been working out?"

"Would you go tell Mom to phone Sister Gardner and tell her I'm in labor? Then she can call Weston and Ann Marie."

Megan, now alone, waited for the next contraction. It was all she could really think about—how bad would it be and how many more of them were yet to come.

After a few minutes, her mother came in to be with her. "I phoned Sister Gardner. She said she'd call the adoptive parents."

"Mom, I'm really scared."

"Of course you are. It is a scary experience, especially the first time."

"Was it for you?"

"It was. Very much. But I got through it, just like you will."

Her dad came in the room.

"Daddy, can I have a priesthood blessing?"

"Yes, of course."

"Ask Bryce to assist you."

"Bryce? He'll never do it."

"Maybe not, but ask him anyway."

Her dad left to go ask Bryce.

Bryce returned. "I can't do that."

"I wish you could."

"I know. Me, too."

"You're one of the most honest guys I've ever known, Bryce. If I can change, anyone can. Even you."

He nodded his head but didn't commit to anything.

Walter returned and, with Carolyn and Bryce in the room, he laid his hands on her head, took a deep breath, and in a quiet voice blessed her that she would get through the birth process safely and have a healthy baby.

Megan kept her eyes closed after the blessing as the tears ran down her face. Carolyn was crying, too.

◆　　◆　　◆

The night dragged on.

Ann Marie and Weston arrived at the hospital a little after three in the morning. Ann Marie knocked on the half-open door and then stepped into the room. She took Megan's hand. "I'm sorry you're in so much pain. I wish I could take some of it."

"I know."

They talked about details for a few minutes, and then Ann Marie left to allow a family member to be with her.

The doctor, an older man who was substituting for Doctor Sullivan, broke her water about three-thirty in the morning. The contractions that followed were intense, about two minutes apart, and lasted about a minute each.

The nurse instructed Megan not to move during contractions, but the next one was so painful she thrashed around a bit until it was over.

"How am I supposed to hold still?" she complained. "It hurts!"

As the pain momentarily subsided, she closed her eyes and said a silent prayer. She asked Father in Heaven to help her get through the ordeal and to bless the baby.

Right after that she was given an epidural, which took away much of the pain.

Later, during hard labor, Megan began shaking uncontrollably due to a reaction to the epidural. Nothing could stop it.

"Would you like another blessing?" her dad asked.

"Yes, please."

As he put his hands on her head and gave her a blessing, the shaking subsided. Her dad promised her she would have control over her body and that her baby would come quickly.

She was in tears when he finished his blessing. "Thank you."

The doctor examined her and said she had some more pushing to do.

She didn't think she could stand any more of this. Even though there were people in the room—the doctor, a nurse, her mother—she closed her eyes and spoke softly, "Father in Heaven, if I ever needed you, I need you now. When it comes time to push, I need you to push this baby out for me."

"What's she doing?" the doctor asked Megan's mother.

"Praying."

The doctor rolled his eyes but made no comment.

Megan opened her eyes.

He explained the process of pushing and had her do three, small, practice pushes just to make sure she understood. And then he turned to the nurse. "I'm going to grab a cup of coffee. Call me when you need me."

The next contraction was beginning.

"Okay, Heavenly Father, I need you to take this baby out," she said softly.

She pushed.

"What's she doing?" the doctor asked.

"Having a baby?" her mother asked.

Megan pushed, and the baby's head came out.

"Good grief!" the doctor said, rushing to get his gloves on. "I can't believe it!"

Megan heard the sound of a baby crying. "Thank you, Father in Heaven."

"My sentiments exactly," the doctor said.

◆　　◆　　◆

After the baby had been bathed and wrapped in a receiving blanket, the nurse laid him in her arms. "Will you be nursing the baby?" she asked.

"No."

The nurse returned with a bottle.

It was, at once, the happiest and saddest day she'd ever known. As tears streamed down her face, she looked at and touched and spoke to her baby. He was the greatest miracle she had ever experienced. She loved him more than she had ever loved anyone before in her life.

# 17

It began with an offhanded comment by one of the nurses. "I know I should admire you for giving up your baby to a married couple, but it's not something I could ever do. I love my children too much to do that."

The remark devastated Megan so much she began to have doubts if she was doing the right thing.

*When they take him away, I will lose everything*, she thought.

Her mom and dad showed up a while later. They had gone home for a few hours of sleep and were just coming back.

"Can we see the baby?" her dad asked.

A few minutes later, Walter picked up his grandson for the first time.

"Oh, he's a fine one, that's for sure. Look how strong he is. Look how he's holding onto my finger."

"He is so adorable," her mother said.

"I wonder if we could get a picture of me holding the baby," her father said.

"I brought my camera," Megan said. "It's in my bag over there."

"I can take the picture," Carolyn said.

"No, you both have to be in it. Let's see if we can get a nurse to do it."

A minute later the picture was taken of Walter and Carolyn proudly showing off the baby. And then they took several pictures of Megan with him.

Then it was her mother's turn to dote on the baby. As Megan watched her mother hold her baby boy and coo, Megan realized she had been the recipient of the love her mother was now showering on this child.

"To tell the truth," Megan said, "I've been thinking about keeping him."

"Really?" her mother said.

"Things were so clear to me before he was born. Now, with him here, it's harder to think clearly. And then this nurse said she loved her kids too much to ever be able to give them away."

"It's because you love him so much that you're doing this. You're thinking of his welfare above your own interests," her mother said.

Sister Gardner of LDS Family Services dropped by an hour later and asked Megan how she was doing.

"I'm having a tough time with this," Megan said. "I'm having second thoughts."

Sister Gardner nodded. "I can understand that."

With tears in her eyes, Megan asked, "Why did I ever agree to give up my baby?"

"Because you based your decision on what would be best for the child."

Megan broke down and sobbed.

Sister Gardner sat by her side and held her hand.

"I love my baby," she sobbed.

"Of course you do, Megan."

There was nothing that could be said. No magic words to make it all better.

"I want to talk to Bryce. Where is he?"

"I'll go ask your mom to get him."

Forty-five minutes later, Bryce showed up. "You wanted to see me?"

"I want you to hold my baby."

"Sure, no problem."

A few minutes later Bryce was holding her baby.

"Isn't he the most wonderful baby in the world?" Megan asked.

"He is, no doubt about it. I think he looks a lot like me when I was a baby."

Megan smiled through her tears. "That's why he's wonderful?"

"Yeah, pretty much," he said with his mischievous grin.

"While you're holding him, you tell me that I should go ahead and give him away."

She'd never seen Bryce emotional. He fought it, but she could tell because he brushed a hand underneath his right eye. "It's best for the kid, Megan. That's what I've always said. It's the truth, and you know it."

She nodded, then asked him to leave, so she could be alone with her baby boy.

After he left, she began to sob. But this time it was not out of desperation or being torn by indecision. She could not doubt the validity of her former decision.

She was going to place her baby. And it cut her to the very core of her existence.

◆    ◆    ◆

A day later, an hour after Megan had been released from the hospital, she placed her baby in Ann Marie's arms. Ann

Marie leaned forward and kissed Megan on the cheek. "Thank you for giving us such a wonderful baby."

Ann Marie smiled through her tears as Weston stepped forward to give Megan a hug. "I promise you, I'll be a good daddy."

"I know you will," she said, barely able to speak.

Ann Marie and Weston turned and left with their new baby.

That night, at two-fifteen in the morning, Megan got out of bed and went downstairs. Her mother must have heard her because she came down to check on her.

Megan was on the patio in the backyard, looking up at the stars.

"He'll see the same stars I will."

"That's true." Her mother put her arm around her. "He'll be all right."

"I know he will. My question is, will I?"

"You did the right thing."

"I did the right thing for him."

"Yes. That's what mothers do."

"My little angel has gone away."

Her mother brought her into her arms just like she'd done when Megan was little. "Oh, Megan, I know it's hard. I wish I could make it easier."

"The baby was the one who got me back on the right track," Megan said.

"Yes, I guess, in a way, that's true."

"And now he's gone. I feel so empty, like there's nothing left, that all the good in me left with him."

"That's not true."

"How do you know that? I'm not sure who I am anymore."

♦   ♦   ♦

## A WEEK LATER

Megan had slept until ten in the morning. She got something to eat but delayed getting into the shower, waiting for the mail to come. She had already received some pictures of Joshua from Ann Marie and Weston and was hoping there would be some more that day.

She heard the sound of mail being shoved through their slot next to the front door and went to see what had come. There was nothing from Ann Marie and Weston, but there was a letter from Elder Spaulding.

She tore the letter open and sat down on the couch. There was a letter and a wedding announcement, with a photograph of him and Melissa, the girl who had waited for him. As Megan began to read his letter, she could just hear his Southern accent.

Dear Megan,

Well, as you can see, I have big news! I wanted you to be one of the first to know. Even though it'd been two years, the moment I saw Melissa when I got off the plane, standing there holding a silly balloon in her teeth with a rose in her hair, I just started laughing. She said she didn't want me to feel any pressure from her, so she decided to make it funny. Well, we started laughing, and we haven't stopped yet.

In many ways she reminds me of you. I think she even looks a little like you. She's been busy while I've been gone. She'll graduate from college this spring, so she'll be able to work some while I'm going to school.

We're getting married right after she graduates.

I know that's not very far away, but, the truth is, we can't wait to be married. It's the right time (after my mission), the right place (the temple), and we're totally in love. We both hope you'll be able to come to our reception.

I sure enjoyed knowing you and appreciated being able to teach the gospel in your home. Those were great times.

Well, I got to run. Melissa and I send our love.

Your favorite elder, James Spaulding.

♦    ♦    ♦

*So, that's it then. No surprise there. I must have been delusional to think that anything would ever come from my friendship with Elder Spaulding.*

*Still, though, he did help me get through a tough time in my life, and for that I'll always be grateful.*

*It's just that I feel like I'm on empty. No hopes. No plans. Nothing to look forward to, except a letter and some pictures once in a while.*

She got up to make herself a cup of peppermint tea. As she was filling the cup with water, she suddenly started to sob. She set the cup on the counter and surrendered to the grief.

When she had finally cried herself out, she took a shower and got dressed and went out to look for a job.

# 18

## LIFE GOES ON

Megan reserved every Saturday night to help her dad with his Sunday School lesson. After reading everything they could about effective teaching, they had agreed that effective teaching involved asking questions that would encourage participation from everyone in the class and, at the same time, bring the influence of the Holy Ghost.

"That's what I need," her father said, "not more research, but good questions."

They began to learn from the scriptures how the Savior used questions in his teaching.

This was their project, and Megan loved it because it gave her time to spend with her father, and, she hoped, to help him.

And, on one Sunday, she herself was blessed by what they'd learned.

"In the last year, how has your testimony of the Savior's atonement increased?" Walter asked in the middle of his lesson.

At first there was no response.

Megan and her dad had talked about what he would do if there was no response.

"Just wait," she had said. "People need time to respond to the prompting of the Holy Ghost."

And so, on that Sunday, her father waited.

Ten seconds went by.

And then thirty.

And then Megan raised her hand.

"Megan?" he said with a smile.

"In the past year, I have learned that Jesus Christ is my Savior, and that he loves me, and that he has forgiven me. He knows me by name, and he thinks about me, and that, more than anything, he wants me to have joy in this life and in the eternities to come. That's how my testimony of the Savior has grown in the past year."

"Thank you, Megan," her dad said.

Five other hands went up.

By the time the class was over, there was not a dry eye in the room.

After the class no one approached Walter to tell him how impressed they were by all his preparation. They were too overcome by the Spirit to do that.

Megan was the only one to come up to him.

They embraced and hugged each other.

"I'm so proud of you," her father said, his voice choked with emotion.

"I'm so proud of you, too, Daddy."

◆　◆　◆

Megan got a job working as a reservation clerk at a motel. It was the perfect job for her because she got to meet new people every day. She enjoyed making them smile and helping them have a pleasant stay.

Sister Gardner passed along pictures and letters from Ann

Marie and Weston. They wrote every week. Little Joshua was healthy and growing fast. Megan cherished every picture and every detail about him.

◆　◆　◆

"That was definitely a smile," Weston said, looking down at Joshua in his mother's arms.

"I don't think so. It's too early for him to be smiling."

"He's very advanced for his age."

Ann Marie shook her head. "It's gas, Weston."

"Okay, there may be a little gas here, but that doesn't account for his smile. He's smiling because he made gas. He thinks it's very funny."

"Oh, right."

"Look, I don't expect you to understand this. It's pretty much a guy thing."

She burst out laughing. "You are pathetic."

"There it is again. Are you saying that's not a smile?"

"Go away."

"No. I'd rather be here with him."

"Me, too."

"You know what? I'm thinking of canceling cable. Nothing can compete with watching your son smile back at you."

She kissed him on the cheek. "I'm so happy."

"I know. Me, too."

"I think a lot about Megan. How much love she showed to this child. I'm very grateful to her, and I always will be. She gave us the gift that nobody else in the world could give us."

"Let's take some more pictures of Joshua and send them to her."

"We just did two days ago."

"But now we have news."

"What's our news?"

"He's smiling now."

Joshua made a tiny sound.

"Wait a minute," Weston said. "Was that a *Ma?* I think it was. Let me go get my camera."

Ann Marie started laughing as Weston went to get the camera. She gazed down at her baby. "Your daddy is so funny! Yes, he is! He is. He's so funny. You're going to have such a fun time with him. Just you wait and see."

◆　◆　◆

One night after her parents had gone to bed, Megan fell asleep on the sofa reading her scriptures. She was awakened by a strange, chattering noise. She looked over at the door and, much to her delight, saw a mother raccoon demonstrating to her three babies how to go through the cat flap, find the kitchen, pull out the bag of cat crunchies and have a good meal.

Megan had to work hard to stifle a giggle as she saw the raccoon babies march in through the flap and then back out, over and over.

She heard a car door slam and Brianna say good-bye to her friends.

The raccoon family made a quick exit through the cat flap.

Brianna opened the door and turned on the light. Megan sat up.

"Brianna?"

"That's me."

"You'll never believe what just happened."

Brianna looked at the mess on the kitchen floor. "Hmmm. You've been nibbling cat candy again, haven't you?"

"No, they were raccoons. A mother and her three babies. They came in through the cat flap."

"No way!"

"I was asleep on the couch when they came. It was so funny! I wish you'd been here to see it."

"Maybe they'll come back. I want to see this."

They turned off all the lights, scrunched down on the sofa, and threw a blanket over themselves.

"It's okay, everyone's asleep," Brianna called out quietly to the raccoons.

Megan poked her in the ribs. "You've got to be quiet."

"Right."

Ten seconds passed. "You ever going to date?"

Megan laughed. "That's not being quiet."

"Just answer my question."

"Yes, I am, when I'm ready."

"I know a guy. His brother just got back from a mission."

"I'm not ready for that."

"Do you miss Elder Spaulding?"

"Not that much, actually. What I liked most about him is that he honored his priesthood." She paused. "You know what? More than anything I miss Thomas."

"Call him then."

"No, he's in Provo, surrounded by thousands of coeds."

"So what? Call him anyway."

"What for? We're just friends."

"But he's the best friend you've ever had. That's got to count for something."

"I'll call him sometime."

"Let's call now." Brianna grabbed the phone and called information.

"Provo, Utah . . . Thomas Marconi . . . Thank you. I just want to say I think you people are doing a great job. I know it's not easy pretending to be a computer twenty-four/seven." She hung up. "Now, that wasn't so hard, was it?"

"Don't call him."

"Why not?"

"It's too late."

"We're up, aren't we?"

Brianna started to punch in the numbers. Megan grabbed for the phone. They started wrestling on the couch and giggling.

Brianna broke free and stood up, shielding the phone. "Resistance is futile."

"Give me the phone."

"Don't get loud and vibrant on me," Brianna said.

"Don't call him."

"I'm calling him." Brianna punched in the first two numbers. Megan lunged at her.

They ended up on the floor, laughing as they wrestled for control of the phone.

And then Bryce walked in, stood at the edge of the living room, and watched.

"What is going on here?" he asked in his sternest voice.

Brianna tried her best to be the well-meaning and sincere victim. "I need to make a phone call, and Megan won't let me."

"That is such a lie. She wants to phone Thomas."

"It's a free country. I can phone anyone I want."

"Give me the phone," Bryce said in his best commanding voice.

"Do what he says," Megan said.

Brianna handed over the phone.

"Frankly, I'm surprised at the two of you," he said.

Brianna mimicked him. "Frankly, I'm surprised at the two of you."

"I will keep the phone in my room for the night," he said.

As he walked off, Brianna whispered in Megan's ear, "Let's get him."

They tackled him on the stairs. "Oh, now, you two be careful! Don't get me riled."

Brianna ran into the garage and came back with two plumber's helpers. "I'm going to suck the brains out of you with this, Bryce."

"Where do you get this stuff?"

"That's what you did to me when I was about five years

280

old," Brianna complained. "You chased me around the room with these."

"She's right. You were such a pest, Bryce," Megan added.

He laid the phone on the stairs. "You know what? I give up. I'm too tired for this. I'm going to bed now. I'll leave the phone here. I just hope you two will show a little maturity and good sense." As he turned to go up the stairs, Megan and Brianna grabbed for the phone.

They tried, but neither one of them could wrest it away from the other.

"Truce?" Megan asked.

"Truce."

They returned to the couch to wait for the raccoons to make another appearance—and fell asleep that way, loosely entangled with each other on the couch.

♦   ♦   ♦

If they had called that night, they would not have reached Thomas. He had a date with a girl in his ward.

Thomas and Elizabeth worked at a pizza place near campus. Thomas was the manager. And so, when the date was over, Thomas dropped by to talk with Elizabeth and help her clean up.

"How'd it go?" she asked.

He grabbed a mop and a bucket. "It was okay, I guess."

"Just okay?"

"We didn't talk much."

"Whose fault is that?"

"I tried. I asked her a lot of questions. She answered them with either a yes or a no. Do you have any idea how many questions you can run through in an hour that way? I actually know how old she was when she got her smallpox vaccine."

"I'm running out of girls in my ward I can line you up with."

281

"I know."

"Why don't you just say it, Thomas?"

"Say what?"

"You miss Megan."

Thomas started mopping. "Megan is just a friend."

"I know that, but as far as I can tell, she's the only friend you've ever had who's a girl. Maybe that's worth pursuing."

He shrugged his shoulders but didn't tell her not to try to get them together.

The next day Megan received an unexpected phone call from Thomas.

"Guess what? I've just been named the manager of a pizza place in Provo. It's brand-new, and you should see the kitchen! It's state-of-the-art! The decor is terrific, and the own-ers insist that the waiters know how to sing in Italian. There's even an artificial waterfall in the middle of the dining room. Oh, and we have great bread sticks that we bring right away when someone shows up to order. It's such a great place, but it's missing one thing."

"What?"

"You. Come and work here with me. You could room with Elizabeth, if you want. They just had a girl move out. It'd be perfect. Whuduya say? It'd be like us at Leo's, except maybe ten times better."

She tried to think of a reason why she couldn't leave town but couldn't come up with any.

"Are you sure you want me?"

"Are you kidding? Of course I want you. It'd be just like old times."

"When would you need me?" she asked.

"Right away. This weekend, if possible. That's when we're the busiest."

"I can't just pack up and move to Utah."

"Why not?"

"Because—"

"Because why?"

"I'm thinking, I'm thinking, okay, don't rush me."

"Look, this is just a business proposition. I mean, I wouldn't want you thinking it was anything but that. Good business . . . and because of our being such good friends. That's all it is."

She could hear Elizabeth in the background. "You're making such a mess out of this, Thomas. Give me the phone."

"I'm not making a mess out of this."

"I said give me the phone."

"Well, all right, but I wasn't making a mess out of it."

Elizabeth came on the line. "Megan, hi, this is Elizabeth. How are you doing?"

"Real good."

"How's your baby?"

"Real good. I get pictures at least once a week. He's growing so fast."

"I can't wait to see those pictures. Look, Thomas and I both really want you to come out here. Thomas is a complete grump without you around to brighten his day."

Megan could hear Thomas grumbling in the background, "That is *so* not true."

"It is true, Thomas, and you know it. Now go away so Megan and I can talk in private."

"Where do you want me to go?"

"Outside or in the hall, I don't care. Just get out of here."

Megan smiled at hearing the two of them carry on.

A few seconds later, Elizabeth resumed their conversation. "Megan, I know Thomas wants you to believe this is just business, but, between you and me, it's way more than that. If you care anything about him, even if just as a friend, please come out here and spend some time with him. And then if nothing comes of it, well, then fine. At least you'll have had some good laughs—and also some excellent pizza."

Megan tried to think of what she should do.

"I need a little time to think about this," she said.

"Of course, take all the time you need," Elizabeth said.

*Just do it,* Megan thought.

*No, I can't just pick up and move.*

*Why not? Thomas will be there, and Elizabeth. It'll be great.*

*If I do it, Thomas might think there's more to it than just friendship.*

*It's because of you being best friends that he asked you. It's not the worst thing in the world, to be Thomas's friend.*

*No, it's not. It's the best thing in the world.*

*Then just do it.*

She could hear Thomas in the background. "Can I come in now?"

"No, I'll tell you when you can come in," Elizabeth said.

"Why are you taking so long?"

"We're talking."

"You're not talking to her. You're talking to me."

"And that's because you're still here. I want you out of here. Go sit in the car."

"I don't see why I have to sit in the car when I'm the one who called Megan."

Megan began to laugh. She decided to end their good-natured bickering.

"Elizabeth, I'm going to do it. I'll be there in two or three days."

"She's going to do it!"

"Let me talk to her!"

Thomas was the next to speak. "You're coming?"

"I'm coming."

"I can't believe it! That is so great! Give me your email address, and I'll send you directions on how to get here."

A few minutes later, she hung up the phone.

She felt very happy and very excited about her future.

And, also, a little hungry for a really good pizza.

284

# LDS Family Services

LDS Family Services is a private, nonprofit corporation that has been established by The Church of Jesus Christ of Latter-day Saints to provide licensed, child placement services and to help Church members and others resolve social or emotional problems. The agency also provides help to LDS Native Americans, refugees, and other members of minority cultures. All services provided are consistent with gospel principles.

**Birth Parent Services**

*Helps birth parents apply gospel principles to their decisions about the child.*

LDS Family Services assists individuals involved in a pregnancy out of wedlock or an unplanned pregnancy. Available help includes counseling, foster care, education and medical assistance, adoptive placement of the child, if desired, and understanding from caring professionals and volunteers. Birth parents are encouraged to use gospel principles to make decisions in the best interests of all concerned. These services are offered confidentially, and referrals are accepted from any source, without concern for clients' religious affiliation.

**Adoption**

*Assures temple sealing of adoptive children to worthy families.*

LDS Family Services provides licensed adoption services to Latter-day Saint families. The agency may also help families identify other resources that can help with adoption. The goal of LDS Family Services is to ensure a successful adoption, including the temple sealing of the child to the adoptive parents.

Natural Law, whether grounded in human reason or divine edict, is an unwritten form of law which encourages people to follow virtue and shun vice. The concept dominated Renaissance thought, where its literary equivalent, poetic justice, underpinned much of the period's creative writing. R. S. White's study examines a wide range of Renaissance texts, by More, Spenser, Sidney, Shakespeare and Milton, in the light of these developing ideas of Natural Law. It shows how writers as radically different as Aquinas and Hobbes formulated versions of Natural Law which served to maintain socially established hierarchies. For Aquinas, Natural Law always resided in the individual's conscience, whereas Hobbes thought individuals had limited access to virtue and therefore needed to be coerced by the state into doing good. White shows how the very flexibility and antiquity of Natural Law enabled its appropriation and application by thinkers of all political persuasions in a debate that raged throughout the Renaissance and which continues in our own time.

# Natural Law in English Renaissance literature

# Natural Law in English Renaissance literature

R. S. White

*Professor of English at the University of Western Australia*

CAMBRIDGE
UNIVERSITY PRESS

Published by the Press Syndicate of the University of Cambridge
The Pitt Building, Trumpington Street, Cambridge CB2 1RP
40 West 20th Street, New York, NY 10011–4211, USA
10 Stamford Road, Oakleigh, Melbourne 3166, Australia

© Cambridge University Press 1996

First published 1996

Printed in Great Britain at the University Press, Cambridge

*A catalogue record for this book is available from the British Library*

*Library of Congress cataloguing in publication data*

White, R. S. (Robert Sommerville), 1948–
Natural Law in English Renaissance literature / R. S. White.
   p.  cm.
Includes bibliographical references and index.
ISBN 0 521 48142 2 (hardback)
1. English literature – Early modern, 1500–1700 – History and criticism.
2. Didactic literature, English – History and criticism.
3. Natural Law – History – 16th century.
4. Natural Law – History – 17th century.
5. Natural Law in literature.
6. Renaissance – England.
PR418.N37W48   1996
820.9′38 – dc20   96–4795   CIP

ISBN 0 521 48142 2 hardback

CE

For John Colmer
In memoriam

# Contents

# Contents

# Preface

> Law rational therefore, which men commonly use to call the Law of Nature, meaning thereby the Law which human Nature knoweth itself in reason universally bound unto, which also for that cause may be termed most fitly the Law of Reason; this Law, say I, comprehendeth all those things which men by the light of their natural understanding evidently know, or at leastwise may know, to be beseeming or unbeseeming, virtuous or vicious, good or evil for them to do.[1]

Natural Law is law which 'authorises' all positive, human laws. According to its classical exponents it is located in the purity of human reason, and, to its Christian theorists, in reason and conscience, motivated by an instinctive need to guarantee human survival. It is a form of knowledge which spurs us to follow virtue and shun vice. The concept dominated Renaissance thought and, through its literary equivalent, later to be called poetic justice, it influenced all English writers of the period in fundamental ways. There was a sceptical and resistant tradition dating from Calvin and summated by Hobbes, suggesting that after the Fall Natural Law existed, not, as Aquinas held, in the human mind and heart, but in God's will and the sovereign's fiat, but even this line of argument necessarily worked within the terms laid down by Aquinas.

Natural Law may be regarded simply as an intellectual 'model', since in the realm of observation it has 'never really existed'.[2] No actual society has ever been built upon its premises. It may be no more than a rational hypothesis, or a useful, even necessary, construction, suggesting what 'ought to be' rather than what 'is'. Other ways of saying the same thing might be, first, that Natural Law has the status of 'reality' only as an 'imaginative projection',[3] or that it is not a finished product but a process, that process being reason itself as it contemplates good and evil. Postmodern theory has, if nothing else, made us wary of anything that smacks of universalism, and there is absolutely nothing to refute the argument that Natural Law is no more and no less than a constructed fiction. 'There is nothing either good or bad, but thinking makes it so', says Hamlet, in richly ambiguous fashion. Even when constructions are elevated into values for living, it is utility rather than truth that guides such priorities. All I claim to do in this book is to prove the existence and importance of the ideas in the English Renaissance, and to demonstrate that these ideas had creative outcomes throughout the literature of the period. Indeed, it could be claimed that the proximity of poetic justice and Natural Law in the English literary Renaissance centrally defines the continuing intellectual and emotional power and vitality of the period's output.

The primary contribution this book is intended to make is to literary history, as a selection of important texts are interpreted in the context of pervasive debates in the English Renaissance on Natural Law. However, given the sheer scope of Natural Law itself, which was an ancient concept going back to pre-Socratic Greek writers and which was given magisterial expression in the writing of the medieval St Thomas Aquinas, and since its implications reach into law, religion, politics, and moral philosophy, a part of the book is devoted to setting up intellectual contexts before moving primarily on to texts. I hope literary readers will find this preparatory attention justified, and, more than this, I hope it will make the book of some interest to students of the history of ideas and to legal historians, as well as to that figure who, however elusive, inspires most writers, 'the general reader', who may start from an interest in the current revival of Natural Law thinking.

It is important to stress that the writers and the particular works I choose to analyse are by no means the only ones showing Natural Law influence. They are exemplary of a pervasive and profound tendency in English Renaissance literature to address the subject in terms established by Aquinas and challenged but not denied by the Reformation. Almost any major work written during the period could have been analysed fruitfully, but, in terms of the texts chosen, I have tried to make my book complementary to those by John S. Wilks (who writes mainly on *Richard III*, *Hamlet*, Marlowe, Webster, Tourneur, and Ford),[4] and George C. Herndl (who concentrates entirely on Jacobean drama),[5] and to cover a range of different literary forms, in prose, poetry, and drama; comedy, tragedy, romance, and polemic. The only real regret I have is omitting *Hamlet*, which is covered especially thoroughly by Wilks from the point of view of conscience. Hamlet could be regarded as the Natural Law hero *par excellence*, the philosophy student from Faustus' university at Wittenberg which was also Luther's place of confrontation, and spending his play brooding on the fundamentals of reason and conscience in action.

My analysis is also incomplete in the sense of not covering all aspects of Natural Law in each work, and not consistently following through the same preoccupations through each work. I try to deal with each text as *sui generis*, raising its own problems, and standing at a unique place along the spectrum from idealism to scepticism. Although I argue that Natural Law provided a constructed model whose basic reference points of 'right reason' and conscience had virtually normative status in the Renaissance, yet I do not pretend that it was universally accepted as an agreed, singular or straightforward concept. It was, on the contrary, a site for considerable argument because of its inherent generality and the undoubted ambiguity of applying it to actual circumstances. Because of its antiquity and ubiquitousness, Natural Law was ripe for appropriation by thinkers of virtually all persuasions, leading to a plethora of descriptions, hazy lines drawn between reason and 'natural' passion, dispute over its jurisdiction and applications, and even to scepticism about whether it can ever operate in a fallen world. For example, Renaissance Natural Law could be, and was, used to justify the freedom of the rich at the expense of the poor, or freedom for the poor at the cost of abolishing private wealth. I hope my analysis of texts reflects the fact that such controversies are inscribed in literature. Such apparently simple dicta as 'trust reason and conscience; follow virtue, shun vice' become surprisingly complex and contentious in particular fictional circumstances, and the fundamental argument over whether Natural Law lies in the human heart, as Aquinas argued, or is almost irretrievable by fallen human beings without the extension of God's grace and the strong political actions of a monarch, is also reflected in the writings. Every writer takes an individual stand on such matters, making each work different, sometimes radically different, from the others. But the simple, overarching idea that the model of Natural Law is a central analogy for notions of 'poetic justice' invariably applies to the anticipated reception by readers and audience, in the fullest, educative function of 'poesy'.

As Herbert Butterfield memorably argued, victors rewrite history. There is a problem of historical retrieval for modern scholars, since between us and the sixteenth century stands the bulky *Leviathan* of Thomas Hobbes. After this book took root in England, the name Aquinas was barely heard again, and Natural Law became a justification for what Aquinas would have regarded as very dubious positions which emphasised individual freedoms often at the expense of community and fellow-beings. I should make it clear from the outset that my highlighting of Hobbes is not done with any suggestion that he was the first to voice a sceptical view of Aquinian Natural Law: far from it, since, as I make clear, his ideas synthesise and extend many others available since the Reformation. But it is, rather, to identify and clear away the 'victor's perspective' which has made it possible, to my mind, to overstress the influence in the Renaissance of Calvinist scepticism, and to minimise the normativeness, sheer flux, and diversity of Natural Law thinking before 1660, which operated, I argue, within a generally Aquinian orthodoxy even while it faced sceptical challenges.

This statement of intention allows me to 'position' myself in relation to books which deal with similar terrain. The few scholars who have written systematically on Natural Law in Renaissance literature, (for example, George C. Herndl, John S. Wilks, and Richard A. McCabe, all cited in the Bibliography), have tended to focus fairly exclusively on drama in the Jacobean period, and to emphasise the Calvinist approach which centralises the fatal corruptions rendered by the Fall, clouding man's access to Natural Law and casting deep suspicion on the view that reason and conscience are innate gifts. This view was certainly powerful and important in a time of rapid political change in England, and in some ways it was the ultimate victor in the argument. As I have mentioned, the sceptical position was to be rationalised so eloquently and powerfully by Hobbes in 1651 (although even he significantly does not question the existence of Natural Law, but relocates its operation) that it was to become the new norm of the 'Enlightenment'. But, as I try to stress, this should not make us read the sceptical tradition into everything in hindsight. Spenser and Sidney were generally more Calvinist than, for example, Shakespeare, More, and Milton, but even they accepted some kind of Natural Law model, accessible to the reader's understanding as a basis for morally judging characters' actions. The evidence points rather to the anti-Calvinist, Hooker, contemporary of Shakespeare, Webster, and Ford, as the spokesman for the 'establishment' view, and for the dominant one before Hobbes, in the quotation at the beginning of this Preface. The English Revolution brought back Natural Law thinking as a basis for argument, and after the Restoration it lived and thrived in the American colonies under the term 'fundamental law'. Rather than agreeing with Herndl that Aquinian concepts of Natural Law were dislodged at the beginning of the seventeenth century, my research confirms Robert Hoopes' argument that the supremacy of 'Right Reason' was not to be undermined until after the Restoration, although obviously the roots of the dislodging forces were evident very much earlier.[6] If anything, it gained fresh force in the English Revolution of the seventeenth century. I try to guide attention back to the seminal work of the gentle, corpulent Saint Thomas Aquinas, and to the classical formulations of Natural Law itself which provided imaginative writers with such a comprehensive and fertile analogy for the kind of justice operating in their own works.

At the same time, it is undoubtedly true that the tensions entered in the

Reformation, and I have tried to build into my argument the very important influence of the sceptical tradition, and to incorporate the findings of Herndl and Wilks. This tradition is especially important for Spenser, Sidney, and a reading of Edmund in *King Lear*. But it is significant that none of these writers actually challenges Natural Law itself. Like Calvin, Luther, and Hobbes, they simply express problems about man's exact relationship to the Natural Law. Rather than engage in direct dialogue with Herndl's and Wilks' accounts, however, or go over the territory of the Jacobean drama, both of which would risk overbalancing my own argument, I hope that the breadth of my chosen period, reaching from More to Milton, will be seen to establish a rather different focus, which allows for the existence of dominant and dissenting views, amalgamated in complex fashion in works of the imagination. At the same time, I readily acknowledge my pervasive debt to these scholars who are among the few to have ploughed the same vast field.

A few caveats need to be entered to define our own, twentieth-century, intellectual distance from earlier Natural Law assumptions. First, Renaissance Natural Law has only a tangential relationship with one phenomenon which seems to be sweeping at least the English-speaking world in the 1990s under the name of Natural Law. The creation of 'New Age' thinkers, this movement has its roots almost entirely in eastern traditions of mysticism rather than Greek philosophy and Roman Law, although it is clear that the two traditions sprang from similar community and personal, human needs. It may be generally characteristic of the two ancient cultures that where the eastern is mystical and amorally sense-based, the western is rooted in reason and morality. I am dealing with the western line, and do not address other versions of Natural Law.

Secondly, and perhaps more worrying, I am acutely aware that the tradition of Natural Law with which I am dealing was fairly implacably patriarchal, and all the commentators in both their language and their narratives tacitly assume its operation to be an exclusively male domain. 'What a piece of work is man', says Hamlet, and, given his treatment of Ophelia, there is no reason to believe that he means the phrase to be interpreted in any way but literally. Constance Jordan, even while arguing for the existence of 'Renaissance feminism', sharply observes 'that there were very few ways to interpret contemporary concepts of natural law that were not prejudicial to women'.[7] This is not to say that the underlying and basic theory cannot for all time be applied in egalitarian and enlightened ways. After all, the abolition of slavery was effected largely with the rhetoric of Natural Law, and the gradual emancipation of women has undoubtedly been influenced by its tradition and logic. On the other hand, the assumption that supremacy of male over female, white over black, are 'natural' is clearly at the heart of profound inequalities. In the interests of pursuing my main theme of the influence of the general theory of Natural Law on literature, I do not pursue these uncomfortable facts beyond occasional statements, since I regard them as lying in the realm of 'positive' applications of the model, and, as such, intrinsically contentious and not a necessary part of the structure of ideas or the Natural Law model itself.

Although the task of the book is historical retrieval, there is also a contemporary dimension. The literary and philosophical material with which I deal may appear to belong to an age which is alien to our own and long gone, but the fundamental questions about good and evil which led to the construction of Natural Law will, to any reader in the late twentieth century, evoke haunting associations. The Nazi extermination of millions of Jews, the destruction of 200,000 innocent civilians in the moment it took to explode an atomic bomb over Hiroshima, the system of *apartheid*, and the policy of 'mutually assured destruction' (MAD) upon which the policy of proliferating nuclear weapons was based, have been our most recent witnesses to the fundamental injustice of consciously not allowing human beings to die as human beings, in the order of nature. Such actions and policies have shown, I believe, not only disregard for the sanctity of human life, but a violation of human reason. As Natural Law gives pre-eminence to reason, to conscience, and to human survival, open debate with its terms in mind might have made such actions unthinkable. What is truly appalling is that none of these policies was the isolated whim of a single madman or criminal. All were the result of policies collectively endorsed, sanctioned in some form of positive law, and carried out by whole populations through elected representatives, as part of their national aspirations.

The contemporary issues are not anachronistic in a book on sixteenth- and seventeenth-century English literature. My version of the Renaissance is not one of antiquarian or safely conservative enclaves of hooded scholars and meretricious poets and playwrights, destined to be swept into oblivion by the sophistications of postmodernism and cultural studies. The thinkers and writers dealt with in this book had the lucidity and courage to raise questions of a fundamental order, which, one could be forgiven for thinking, have been neglected in our own 'progressive' century. May we bequeath our children a sense of urgency in returning to these questions, for now, with the invention of ever more destructive technology and the rapid development of something wrongly called 'communications', and with the growth of an ever greater group of consumers, the stakes are as high as the survival of the human race itself. If the underlying logic of the model of Natural Law was to guarantee such survival, sometimes at the cost of challenging the morality behind positive laws, then it may still have something to teach us.

A few explanations and justifications are necessary. I consistently privilege by capital letters the terms Natural Law and Law of Nature (by which I intend the same thing, in line with most Renaissance theorists), because in certain contexts I wish to distinguish it from natural law or natural philosophy, intended to mean laws governing the physical universe and the animal world, without moral content. Secondly, I must continually assert that, by and large, the central subject of the book is the basic model of Natural Law, not its specific, contested, and confusing application to particular situations. I am looking at 'the thing itself', and such a distinction can easily be justified, given the abstraction and intended universality of the model. As an example, I do not address the objection anticipated above, which feminists will immediately make, that the way Natural Law was used in the Renaissance was systematically in the service of a patriarchal society and against the 'rights of women'. My argument is that this would properly belong in a different book dealing with a particular application. The problem is not *inherent* in the Natural Law model itself, because its terms could easily and obviously be used to argue for women's rights.

There are some other initial qualifications I should make, 'that future strife may be avoided now' as fellow scholars and readers move through the book. A work that addresses legal, historical, theological, and literary issues from pre-Socratic times to the end of the seventeenth century, may be destined to please no specialist in any one of these disciplines, but I would plead for some interdisciplinary tolerance from my readers, and a focusing on the broad ideas in their literary manifestations. More positively, I must thank the many hundreds of scholars in all fields who, in their books, have made my task less impossible by clearing some of the dark spaces. I modernise all quotations, since the emphasis is on ideas rather than linguistic niceties, and I do not wish to distract or alienate readers who are not scholars of the English Renaissance by 'old spelling'. Only in the case of Spenser's poetry is old spelling adopted, since it is customary, and sometimes necessary for metrical scanning. Finally, I have tried to keep footnotes to a necessary minimum, leaving the Bibliography as an indication of the quarry from which the argument, which I hope stands alone as a piece, was made. If I had followed up every qualification and modification that should be made to many of my over-confident generalisations, the footnotes alone would have made another book, or instead, like an academic *Tristram Shandy*, the book would never have advanced further than the first few footnotes.

# Acknowledgments

Like most books, this one has taken many years to write, and has incurred many scholarly debts. In carrying out research for this book I have been helped by many institutions and people, and it is a pleasure to thank them.

The Australian Research Council funded some research assistance, a semester free of teaching and, more crucially, trips to Oxford without which I could never have written the book. The University of Western Australia approved my study leave for one semester. Balliol College gave me the great honour of an invitation to take up their Visiting Research Fellowship for a year. Because of administrative commitments binding me to the University of Western Australia I could not accept this generous offer, but I did have the pleasure of being Academic Visitor to Balliol for six months in 1992, when the bulk of the work was done. This opportunity gave me proximity to the unrivalled collections at the Bodleian Library, the Bodleian Law Library, the English Faculty Library, and Balliol College Library, all of which I offer thanks for resources and human assistance from staff. It is literally true that without such access I could never have contemplated writing this book. It was difficult to consult many essential texts in Western Australia, but the Reid Library, the University's Law Library, and the Alexander State Library of Western Australia were useful starting-points. The librarian at Gray's Inn in London generously answered my questions on Sir Philip Sidney. The Literary and Philosophical Society in Newcastle upon Tyne allowed me to use their beautiful library when writing the book, and the Allegretta Art Studios in Fremantle gave me a private haunt when I needed to escape from the world of obligations, and to write.

No book of this kind can be written without help from individuals, which was always given generously, whether it came in the form of research assistance, information, reading my confused manuscript in embryonic form, scholarly and moral support, encouragement, or the inspiration of human warmth and hospitality at crucial stages. I offer particular thanks for comprehensive help to Desmond Graham, David

Norbrook, Marina White, and Jane Whiteley, and I list some of the other special people in no order other than alphabetical: Alan Brissenden, Jane Brownlow, Ann Chance, Julia Darling (and Scarlet and Florrie), Alan Dodds, Kieran Dolin, Katherine Duncan-Jones, Pina Ford, Hilary Fraser, Cathy Higgins, Ernst Honigmann, Gail Jones, Claire Lamont, Sue Lewis, Susan Hayes, Suzanne Montgomery, Elizabeth Moran, Bernard and Heather O'Donoghue *et famille*, James Paris, Sue Penberthy, Bev Robinson, Trude Schwab, Nigel Smith, Jeannie Sutcliffe, Adam Swift, Joanna Thompson, Helen Vella-Bonavita and Christopher Wortham. As the proofs of *Natural Law* arrived, so did my second daughter, Alana. Hers was a far more joyful arrival. At the Cambridge University Press, Andrew Brown, Kevin Taylor, Josie Dixon, and Gillian Maude were exceptionally agreeable and helpful to work with. Thanks to the two anonymous Cambridge readers (who will remain in my mind as Aquinas and Calvin respectively), whose stern but kindly advice saved me from many an error, and who spurred me to climb a little higher up the hill. That I never quite reached the top is my own failing, and probably the fate of every writer. The late John Colmer, to whom the book is dedicated, showed me the gift of dedicated scholarship, and gave me a love for learning which is lasting a lifetime.

# 1 Natural Law in history and Renaissance literature

I am tempted to think that only a saint could properly write this book, but only a fool would make the attempt. It explores the literary traces of an idea which, in some form or another, has struck every human society from antiquity onwards as fundamental, an idea which is breathtakingly simple and said to be innate to human beings, but at the same time is considered to be ambiguous, variable, and situational in the ways in which it is applied. A modern dictionary of terms used in English Law defines Natural Law as 'rules derived from God, reason or nature, as distinct from man-made law', and Law of Nature as 'certain rules of conduct supposed to be so just that they are binding upon all mankind'.[1] Behind these bland words lies a world of doubt, centuries of dispute, the English Civil War of the seventeenth century and the American Civil War of the eighteenth, the abolition of slavery, the Nuremberg Trials, and other great upheavals of history. At the heart of the concept lies a belief that survival of the species is a fundamental instinct to human beings. The theory has been around for at least 2,500 years, at its zenith in England in the Renaissance, and now, at the end of the twentieth century, it is rising again into ascendancy, generally in a related but significantly different guise of 'natural rights' or 'human rights' (*ius naturale*) rather than 'Natural Law' (*lex naturae*), or appearing in borrowed robes of eastern mysticism (which is another story altogether). We are dealing with the justice of justice, and with something indeed awesome.

Saint Augustine said 'There is no law unless it be just', and Saint Thomas Aquinas glossed 'And if a human law is at variance in any particular with the Natural Law, it is no longer legal, but rather a corruption of law.'[2] Natural Law is essential justice, justice itself, the origin and test of all positive laws, and 'the ultimate measure of right and wrong'.[3] It is above all rational, discoverable through reason, and therefore '*justi*fiable'. It has been said to be known by all people at all times because of the universal human capacities for exercising reason. Although its actual implementation in any one circumstance or society may differ from that in another, it is said to generate all other laws. With its aid humankind can live compatibly in the rational order of nature. Hugo Grotius (1583–1645) linked it with a form of reasoning which is 'of a rational and social nature', the cause of which 'can hardly be anything else than the feeling which is called the common sense of mankind'.[4] Francis Bacon evocatively describes good and evil as having 'colours' which can be observed and apprehended as distinctly through the senses as colours in the physical world.[5] Its most general precept, again according to Aquinas, is 'do good and avoid evil', and the human head and the human heart – reason, later supported in Christianity by conscience – are said to be capable of filling this axiom with meaning in every situation. As George C. Herndl epigrammatically sums up, 'Evil is unnatural, and man's highest virtues profoundly natural to him.'[6] No wonder poets, who take as their province the human mind and heart, have been drawn to the subject, whether or not they know its tangled history, or directly refer to its philosophical roots.

Early theorists of Natural Law, at least up to St Thomas Aquinas and through several centuries of his scholastic followers, maintain that it is an innate form of knowledge, imprinted on the human mind (although this knowledge can, to a greater or lesser extent, be clouded over by experience), and they concede that no single definition can be universally accurate. It sounds somewhat mystical in its origin, and yet no significant western theorist has used the appeal to mysticism, locating Natural Law rather in faculties like reason and knowledge which are presented as practical, not theoretical qualities. Reason itself is the faculty separating humans from animals: 'How noble in reason ... the paragon of animals', is Hamlet's optimistic assessment of humanity. The elegantly argued book by Robert T. Hoopes, *Right Reason in the English Renaissance* most comprehensively recuperates the Renaissance emphasis on reason, and defines the point of view which could effortlessly equate knowledge and virtue through it: 'True knowledge, i.e., knowledge of Truth, involves the perfection of the knower in both thought and deed; the exercise of virtue is itself part of what Whichcote called the "true use of Reason".'[7] While earlier traditions of Natural Law relied solely on reason, Christianity, largely through Aquinas and in England St German, added conscience. The Christian version of the theory maintains that God established a universe governed by reason, and he imprinted conscience on the human mind to enable us actively to choose virtue and reject vice. Even conscience itself is interpreted as based on reason: that which conscience bids is by definition reasonable and that which it forbids is unreasonable. Equally, that which is reasonable will satisfy the conscience. In this formulation we find an explanation for one of the great historical shifts in Natural Law thinking, which happened during the Reformation and deeply influenced the Renaissance world. Classical and early medieval Natural Law theorists built their ideas upon reason alone, while Christianity, afraid that such a reliance might eliminate the need for God (as some, particularly Grotius, deduced by arguing that conscience is no more than reason applied to ethical problems)[8] added conscience, insisting also that both faculties are God-given.

The essence of Natural Law, by definition, lies not in substantive rules, but in precepts which are the basis for rule-making, and which can be exercised even where no positive laws exist. Many descriptions have been attempted: 'incline to virtue, murmur at vice', *bonum faciendum, male vitandum* ('good is to be done, evil to be avoided'), 'do as you would be done by', 'To thine own self be true', and sometimes more specifically 'private interests should be subordinated to the community's good', all areas constantly plumbed by imaginative writers. John Finnis, who has written one of the most comprehensive books in recent times on Natural Law theory from an ahistorical and jurisprudential point of view, formulates it as 'practical reasonableness in relation to the good of human beings who, because they live in community with one another, are confronted with problems of justice and rights, of authority, law and obligation'.[9] Natural Law is what enables us confidently to make, if not always to prove, spontaneous statements like, 'That is not fair' or 'That is unjust', even if the actions we are commenting upon may come within 'the letter of the law' or not be covered by any law. By implication it also informs our very powerful feelings about the moral pressures resolved or conspicuously not resolved at the end of works of fiction, particularly Renaissance ones, backed up as they are by a theory of didacticism, and some kind of 'poetic justice' which is the literary work's analogy of Natural Law.

My intention in this book is to demonstrate that a belief in the classical model of Natural Law had widespread, even normative, popular currency in the English Renaissance, no matter how variable were opinions about its specific applications. Most memorably, it inspired works of literature which have long outlasted the bedrock of jurisprudential ideals upon which the theory was built. These works drew not only upon Natural Law itself, but also on the inherent ambivalence of its worldly manifestations, and at times a more damaging scepticism which led to its eventual demise. To claim More, Spenser, Sidney, Shakespeare, Milton, and many others as writers drawing consciously upon Natural Law is to place in its orbit the most important authors of the whole period in England. Before we can interpret their works from a Natural Law perspective, we need to retrieve in some detail the historical conditions and ideas which prevailed, and so the first part of the book unavoidably deals with legal history, philosophy, political history, and the history of ideas rather than primarily literature. I hope readers will at least be patient, and ideally interested, in the early stages, as we trace classical Natural Law thinking from its source in pre-Socratic times up to its strongest and most comprehensive statement by St Thomas Aquinas; its reception into English legal structures and its pervasive influence on Renaissance literary theory; and then the lengthy path to its eventual dismantling in the late seventeenth century.

## Natural Law in Renaissance thought

Renaissance legal theorists, in England and on the European continent, accepted the existence of two major, mutually compatible and ideally synonymous spheres of justice: God's law (often called either divine or eternal law) and man's law (positive law). Since the former is unknowable to human eyes (God works in mysterious ways) a bridge between the two systems was required in order that man-made law should coincide with God's law. Accordingly, medieval and Renaissance theorists revived from the pre-Christian Aristotle and Cicero (who in turn received it from the pre-Socratic philosophers and Plato) the notion of Natural Law. This decrees that human beings, because they have been given the capacity of reason and, according to the Renaissance Christian, the spark of conscience, know enough of the general precepts of the eternal law to live virtuously and make just laws. Natural Law is assumed to be as un-changing as eternal law, but, since social circumstances and attitudes change, it is a barometer by which people must adapt their worldly laws to come as close as possible in a fallen world to enacting and obeying divine law.

   Doing what is necessary for survival is at the heart of the moral programme, and this priority, for example, invariably manifests itself as ways of forbearing from violence in killing or inflicting bodily harm. It may also require approximate equality between life and life, and group support, since most Natural Law theorists agree that some form of communitarianism is essential to all human conditions for survival. The primacy of mutual survival also implies at least a limited altruism, exercised in forbearance from (or condemnation of) selfish behaviour and some concept of sharing limited resources. In this sense the tyrant, even if he is in his own right a lawfully instituted authority, may be opposed by the community. These axioms might stand as a modern equivalent of doing good and avoiding evil, as the moral bases of positive law which, as a bare minimum, constitute a state of justice and fairness. Without some such basic premises, the survival of human beings in community would be jeopardised, and indeed human beings would cease to be reasonable, conscientious beings, and forfeit their right to share the unique 'nature' of their species. It is tempting to think the retreat from reliance on nuclear weapons in the 1990s, if indeed this trend is not reversed, is an assertion of Natural Law in the interests of survival of the human world, and a revival of the model. Those not sharing minimum premises would, in short, be denying the fundamental 'nature' of human beings. As Hume says, 'Human nature cannot by any means subsist without the association of individuals: and that association never could have place were no regard paid to the laws of equity and justice.'[10] All these preoccupations with essentially collective, sociable, and communitarian values are central, for example, to *King Lear*, even if, like all the imaginative writers, Shakespeare realises that breaches of Natural Law are just as theatrically interesting as observance of it. To the creative writer, a Macbeth, who knowingly violates conscience and must live with the consequences, is more arresting and useful than a Duncan who faces no such crisis of conscience and reason in the play. But for such crises to be dramatically interesting, it is important that the dramatist rely on his audience to discriminate between good and evil actions, without necessarily presenting overt moralisations himself, thereby crediting the audience with prior knowledge of the Natural Law model.

However, there was no unanimity amongst Renaissance thinkers and writers about what Natural Law would dictate when applied to a particular set of circumstances. From Luther to Milton, there were choruses of complaints from those who suspected the portability and contradictoriness of claims to base actions on Natural Law. John Donne, for example, lamented that the term Natural Law is 'so variously and unconstantly deliver'd, as I confess I read it a hundred times before I can understand it once, or can conclude it to signify that which the author should at that time mean'.[11] The fine book by Richard A. McCabe, *Incest, Drama and Nature's Law, 1550–1700*[12] on every page gives examples of the fluctuating interpretations of what exactly constitutes the act of incest, even while its existence is never denied by writers of the time as proscribed by Natural Law. Throughout its history, and particularly during the Renaissance, McCabe argues, 'The very repetition of the word "natural" in so many contexts placed the concept itself under intense strain.'[13] At the same time, I argue that such variations are best seen as belonging to debate within the sphere of positive laws, and they do not undermine the writers' belief in the existence of the model of Natural Law itself. That is, incest is wrong according to the model, but what constitutes an incestuous relationship is subject to cultural definition and has clearly been different from time to time, and place to place. This is why arguments can be conducted for and against the marriage between Claudius and Gertrude. Similarly, Natural Law was invoked to justify male supremacy and racial domination, but it could (and should) be used to justify equality: such are the different positive applications of the idea which different cultures construct. It is the very stuff of drama and romance that writers presuppose some guiding precepts of what is right and what is wrong (enacted through poetic justice), and their interest lies in the sheer multifariousness and ambiguity of actions generated within such a system.

## Natural Law in Renaissance literature

Poets have always taken some version of Natural Law as their province, believing, as Shelley asserted, that their profession confers upon them the mantle of 'unacknowledged legislators of the world'. As authority for their particular legislative jurisdiction, at least in the English Renaissance, poets inserted themselves in a contemporary, legal debate between the claims of Natural Law as an unwritten and intuitive basis for all law, and positive law (man-made 'law of the land'). They firmly asserted the primacy of the former over the latter, although in the truly just state the two would be synonymous. If through Natural Law, according to Aquinas, people 'participate in' eternal law, then literature is treated by theorists and practitioners as a medium through which this participation could be effected. Readers and audiences are encouraged, even required, to make moral judgments which are at least implicit in the narrative and sometimes explicit, and thus confirm that they themselves have the potential to 'do good and avoid evil'. The English Renaissance (in this book, taken to run from More to Milton) was a period in which at least writers felt that the order of imaginative literature was parallel to, and even coterminous with, the order of Natural Law, implicating and testing audiences and readers as much as fictional characters in making moral choices.

Poetic justice is about as close as we can come to an observable enactment or construction of Natural Law, in a kind of dynamic experiment set up by the writer. The connections between legal theory and imaginative literature in the Renaissance are sometimes direct and at other times oblique, but they centre on the shared reliance on the justice that poetry can enact. Both legal and literary theory in the Renaissance insisted that right and wrong exist prior to positive law, can be known by people through reason and conscience, and can finally prevail as a resolution to conflicts. While the fictional characters constructed by a writer can, with a greater or lesser degree of voluntariness, *choose* right or *choose* wrong as a path of action, in hindsight, at the end of the work, the moral nature of their choice will be known to the audience and, more often than not, to the protagonists themselves. Othello commits suicide when he realises he has violated virtue and followed vice in the figure of Iago; the Capulets and Montagues are reconciled after recognising that their feud has had evil consequences in several deaths; Adam and Eve become aware of sin after committing it, and they are destined for suffering. Even the apparent exception proves the rule: however shocking and unexpected is the death of Cordelia, it is the inevitable result not of her own transgressions but of others', compelling audiences and readers to understand the tragedy as the result of prior violations of Natural Law by a host of characters 'Drest in a little brief authority'. That such moral awakenings come after the events does not diminish the operation of Natural Law, because all the conditions for understanding moral choice are present earlier, and audiences recognise violations as they occur, and are not surprised by narrative retribution. Poetic justice is the literary equivalent of Natural Law. This is essentially the basis of the 'defence' of poetry offered by Sidney: it can teach general, moral precepts through enacted fables. It is no exaggeration to say that Natural Law in particular provides the key to understanding the moral patterning, and sometimes the legal and political significance, of important imaginative works in the period. At the very heart of literary theory of the time lies a model which draws upon, and closely mirrors, the basis of Natural Law as it was discussed in legal circles, that people are in some fundamental way attracted to good and repelled by evil, and that they know the moral status of what they are doing or what they have done.

'Poetic justice' (although the term was not coined until later, the concept was clearly available) had a direct line to Natural Law. In the eighteenth century the vestiges of this model attracted the *name* poetic justice, although by this time (following Hobbes' onslaught on the assumption that humans are rational beings endowed with conscience, which he paradoxically couched as a defence of the Law of Nature) Natural Law theory was in eclipse. Consequently, the eighteenth-century literary concept, endorsing rewards for the virtuous and punishment for the evil, was a considerably watered-down and simplified version of its richly complex Renaissance equivalent, as evidenced in the neo-classical rewritings of Renaissance texts to conform with 'rules' of literary decorum. Ironically, this result was directly contrary to the Renaissance belief in the primacy of Natural Law over man-made rules, of intuition over prescription, and it marked a literary equivalent of a Hobbesian sovereign state imposing norms upon recalcitrant literary works as on mankind in general. For Milton and his precursors, fictional works were a test of the reader's own rational capacities.

The Renaissance imaginative writer, in creating fictions, thought of literature as performing the function of God, just as (Aquinas says by way of analogy), God is performing the function of an artist. The writer is controlling deity of a constructed world of human beings who make, obey, and break their own laws within that world, and must stand judged and often condemned by themselves, their fictional peers, readers, and audiences in the universal court of Natural Law. As deity, the writer presupposes a shared moral perspective which enables the reader or audience to exercise the god-like function of discriminating between good and evil. Clearly, writers would, in Faustian fashion, be blasphemous to claim for themselves any comprehensive knowledge of eternal law. What they could claim, however, and what they did claim, is superior insight into the intermediary precepts of Natural Law, its human equivalent, and the capacity to tap into shared knowledge of these in readers. They see themselves, in Shelley's words, as unacknowledged legislators of the world. In their works narrative carries plausibility, a logic based on reason, and there is a compelling appeal to the reader and audience to exercise conscience in understanding and judging the morality of actions carried out by their characters, more or less like a modern jury. This goes even for the so called 'decadent' Jacobean dramatists who, I contend, do not deny the omnipresence of Natural Law, but insist on the complexity and ambivalence of its applications to human behaviour.

There are, I shall argue, certain reasons for the interaction of law and literature in the English Renaissance, both institutional (the existence of the Inns of Court and their practices) and professional (shared reliance on rhetoric and fictions). The specific importation of Natural Law into literature also stems from the fact that the theory's central preoccupations – the survival of humanity effected first through propagation (writers call it love) and secondly through avoidance of killing – immediately raise the central subjects of Renaissance imaginative literature, sexuality (comedy), and murder (tragedy). Both subjects are fertile because of the sheer difficulties and ambiguities inherent in knowing what is 'natural', what is good, and what is evil, although such contentiousness lies not in the structure of Natural Law itself, which is largely presupposed, but rather in its myriad applications. Like ecclesiastics, writers were interested in the fine but immensely important distinction between sexuality as enactment of the logic of human existence on the one hand, and as violation of it on the other. Gloucester and

Edmund may view bastardy as 'natural' from one point of view, while other perspectives in *King Lear* show its existence and consequences to be lawless, anti-communitarian, and analogous to political 'illegitimacy' in the state. Furthermore, works like More's *Utopia*, Spenser's *The Faerie Queene*, and *King Lear* deal with questions which were within the province of Natural Law, such as whether private property can be morally justified, the flaws in human beings which can make the dictum 'follow reason and conscience' so difficult to implement, and the bases and limitations of worldly authority. The natural imperatives dictated by 'need' crop up in pivotal contexts in literature, just as the word is a primary term in Natural Law and, incidentally, in one of Natural Law's modern, political offsprings, the theory of philosophical anarchism.

### Natural Philosophy

If some theorists have derived Natural Law purely from human reason, some from reason and conscience, others have come to the same point through observations of nature in its material sense. 'Laws' which appear to operate in the physical universe (the movement of the heavens, waxing and waning of the moon, gravity, procreation and self-protection in the animal and plant world, the growth and decay of living organisms) in their reliable, predictable, and symmetrical patterns are, it is argued, justification for assuming the existence of comparable moral laws. Reading from what Marvell called 'nature's mystic book'[14] has always been an option for those who believe in some order beyond the humanly constructed, and which can be given a place in the sphere of jurisprudence. A relatively modern exponent of such a philosophy is Prince Kropotkin, the pacifist anarchist, who, from his scientific observations of self-preserving strategies in communities of animals, developed a theory of 'Mutual Aid' amongst human beings, to counter what he regarded as the pernicious assumption behind extreme Darwinists like Huxley, that human community is a matter of 'survival of the fittest' in a state of constant struggle. Properly speaking, this kind of 'natural law' can be distinguished from Natural Law by calling it something like natural philosophy, variously regarded as a contributing proof of the existence of Natural Law rather than the thing itself, or more fundamentally as a kind of prior version of the Law of Nature. According to Natural Law, each animal has its own unique nature, and, since it is in the nature of humankind to have reason, we are the one species which can not only use reason, but can also reflect consciously on our own nature and on those of animals. If the physical world is ordered along rational lines, the argument runs, so is the moral world, and people are the only ones capable of understanding and implementing in their own lives some such order. As Copleston, in his useful book on Aquinas, summarises:

It is sufficiently obvious that the term 'natural law' does not bear the same sense here that is borne by the term 'law of nature' when the law of gravitation, for example, is spoken of as a law of nature or as a natural law. Irrational things do indeed reflect the eternal law in their activities and behaviour; but if we talk about them as obeying a natural law the word 'law', insists Aquinas, is used analogically. For law is defined as an ordinance of reason, and irrational creatures, being irrational, cannot recognise and promulgate to themselves any natural law. Human beings, however, can do so.[15]

Today, we are witnessing a new equation between Natural Law and natural philosophy, as the increasingly horrifying recognition dawns that the survival of the human race is profoundly interconnected with the preservation of the environment, and that only the rationality of human beings can prevent disaster.

It should be said early in this book that natural philosophy comes from a different intellectual tradition based on a host of writers including Pliny and Cato, Theocritus and Virgil, and the *De Rerum Natura* of Lucretius, channelled through Virgil but influential in its own right, and it is to be distinguished from the model of Natural Law deriving from the pre-Socratics, and from Cicero and Aquinas. Natural Law would claim natural philosophy as a sub-branch of itself, a description of the universe emphasising its supreme rationality according to Natural Law, or a physical equivalent of Natural Law. The exhortation to the poet to 'follow nature' was synonymous with 'follow Natural Law' rather than 'follow the laws of flora and fauna', the crucial difference lying in the rationality underpinning human moral choice. Herein lies the key to the flawed reasoning of Edmund in *King Lear* and Faustus. In different ways, both abdicate from the very defining components of Natural Law – reason and conscience – in favour of the amoral and unreflective 'nature' of the material world.

Marlowe in *Doctor Faustus* does not probe the issues deeply, but his play does present the two systems as in some kind of consistent relationship. Faustus offends against Natural Law as reason and conscience, because he attempts through magic to control nature itself, thereby seeking to usurp the power of the creator of nature but without that being's rational and moral supremacy. Even more fundamentally, he turns away from virtue and towards vice, reversing the rule of Natural Law. Other Renaissance writers, in particular Sidney and Spenser, found that nature's laws within men and women, impulses they share in common with animals, such as sexual desire, very often come into conflict with

Natural Law, positive laws, and sometimes with each other, when rationality is abandoned. Such clashes, they realised, made interesting works of art, which could be inconclusive and thus exercise the reader's or audience's moral faculties. In other cases, by following their own passionate feelings, characters may break positive laws, but in doing so follow the Law of Nature, when marriage is their destination. Young lovers, for example, following the natural imperative of mutual desire, come into conflict with worldly authority, but their instincts are finally vindicated and allowed to satisfy reason and conscience in 'happy endings'. Feelings which initially seem to oppose positive law and threaten society become in time the bonds of community and harmony, and can therefore embody enacted Natural Law. Again, an exception is instructive: the 'marriage' of Touchstone and Audrey, legally dubious as it is, will collapse after two months, because it is based solely on the animal drive of sexual desire, without the substantial basis of rational choice exercised through time by Rosalind and Orlando. Sidney builds *Arcadia* around these various kinds of conflict between sexual desire as 'natural' and the Natural Law, just as he exploits problematical distinctions between positive laws and Natural Law. Shakespeare provides comic patterns where feelings may be in line with Natural Law and dictate the terms of 'poetic justice' in the closure, no matter how much they offend patriarchs and laws. The real moral malefactors are the authority figures who attempt to use positive law to control life itself, Egeon in *The Comedy of Errors*, Egeus in *A Midsummer Night's Dream*, the young males in *Love's Labour's Lost*, and so on, are clear examples, and a more complex case of the conflict between life and law will be seen in *Measure for Measure*.

But sexuality provides the most difficult problems for Natural Law: on other social issues writers could be less equivocal. Those who were directly commenting upon social justice and politics of their day could take their stand more unequivocally on reason and conscience. Thomas More, Edmund Spenser, and John Milton all accepted the certainties of natural philosophy but relegated its importance below that of the creation of human, social justice. In all cases, there was agreement on the existence of a supreme and rational moral law, universally binding, but each writer differed profoundly when he came to analyse applications of Natural Law, and each built into his works the inbuilt ambivalence of the concept. A central question, for example, is whether men and women who have fallen from grace in the theological sense are really capable of making decisions based on moral grounds: they may still have an inbuilt perception of good and evil, but so clouded has it become that they cannot utilise it as God intended, and require faith or command as an alternative route to virtue. On this crucial issue, Milton and his contemporary, Hobbes, were to take opposite sides.

## The intervention of Hobbes

The act of historical retrieval of Renaissance Natural Law is not entirely straightforward, because a quite fundamental impasse to our thinking was erected by Thomas Hobbes in the mid-seventeenth century, to be reinforced by succeeding generations of philosophers and rational sceptics through Bentham to Austin and even down to the present day. Hobbes did not invent the notion that virtue is not necessarily 'natural' to man but must be imposed by authority: the seeds of this contention were laid mainly by the medieval nominalists and Calvinists. The Hobbesian line of thought, while not denying Natural Law, draws a sharp, a priori distinction between what law *is* and what law *should be*, saying that these two must be kept strictly apart. The former is the province of law, the latter of morality, and the two should not be confused. This is the basis of legal positivism, as espoused, for example, by Austin in the twentieth century. In essence, Hobbes claims that only God, and his anointed on earth, the ruling sovereign, has the authority to make laws and thereby implement the Natural Law, and that the rest of us are not only hopelessly flawed but may even be 'naturally' opposed to Natural Law, using the argument that the impulse towards disobedience is just as innate as a desire for virtuous action, and that after the Fall the more evil impulses will dominate the good ones. We are said to be lawless, selfish, and in need of strong coercion and punishment: our own reason and conscience, buried beneath layers of sin, are unreliable and even inactive. Natural Law exists, and it is as rational as Aquinas and his followers had claimed, but it is safer to assume that its existence is external to the human mind rather than internal, beyond the capacities of mankind to know, and we have lost our direct access to it. As Rommen states, 'The entire theory of Thomas Hobbes (1588–1679) amounts at bottom to a denial of the natural law',[16] even though Hobbes claims belief in the model and argues from its premises. In drama, the classic Hobbesian stance is adopted by Shakespeare's Edmund: 'human nature' is, it is argued, implacably opposed to a moral order. Other perspectives available in the play do not support this view, but its articulation in the early seventeenth century reminds us that Hobbes was only the latest and most comprehensive Renaissance spokesman for a line of reasoning available much earlier.

The Hobbesian separation of Natural Law and laws governing human nature rendered Natural Law in its classical version virtually impotent.

In classical Natural Law theory a law cannot *be* unless it is what it *ought to be*. *Lex iniusta non est lex* – an unjust law is not a law. Martin Luther King in jail in Alabama was to use precisely these words to justify his actions on behalf of civil rights.[17] A positive law which is inconsistent with Natural Law was considered no law at all. Similarly, what *ought to be* a law *is* such, whether codified in a positive way or left unstated. The other corollary is that positive law, law made by people, is consistent with Natural Law unless proved otherwise, because lawmakers were presumed to construct laws according to reason and conscience. Any rigid separation of law and morality would have made little sense to medieval and Renaissance thinkers of Aquinian persuasion: the two were if not synonymous, at least implicated in each other, by definition. However, this is not to deny that the two areas had different spheres of application. I take it that this is the point which A. P. d'Entrèves is at great pains to make.[18] Natural Law may be 'superior' to positive law, not in being at odds with it, but in being the source of positive law, and positive laws were only law in so far as they effected Natural Law. Morality was considered to be individual in its operation, law was social; morality was an ideal standard of conduct, while law was coercive in forbidding certain conduct; and, d'Entrèves argues, it was politically healthy to maintain the independence of religion and the state as separate spheres. The presumed intersection of morality and law was not bought at the expense of the distinctiveness of each.

But, to Hobbes and later legal positivists, the only relevant issue is whether a law was passed by a legitimate authority with due procedures: if so, it is simply law, and its goodness or badness is completely irrelevant: morality has nothing to do with law, and law need have nothing to do with morality. The shift from synonymy to division between morality and law is the largest conceptual stumbling-block to modern theorists in jurisprudence seeking to understand classical Natural Law, since it governs the very structure of their ideas. We accept readily, even cynically, for example, that laws may be passed for political reasons rather than moral, and we take their rationales with a pinch of salt. As More wittily anticipates, driving a wedge between Natural Law and human nature almost inevitably concedes victory to sceptics, pragmatists, and pessimists over idealists in actual political settings, since morality is so evanescent and debatable. There is, after all, no incontrovertible *proof* of Natural Law, and people daily argue over what is reasonable and conscientious in human action: better, said Hobbes, just to cast ethics adrift and define right and wrong simply by accepting the commands of sovereign bodies which have authority to make law. In building up a Renaissance context we must dismantle the distinction so cherished by the modern mind, accept some understanding of an assumed link between law and morality while respecting their unique spheres of operation, and at the same time acknowledge that the sites of argument were already present in the earlier period.

It is certainly true that before Hobbes there were sceptics who exploited the uncertainty of what constitutes an act based on Natural Law and what does not, but there were few challenges to the edifice itself. The real debate was not over whether Natural Law existed, but over the extent to which human beings could live according to it. Calvin and Luther, for example, had argued that after the Fall humans had lost touch with their innate sources of knowledge, and could not be presumed to be in touch any more with the inner promptings of Natural Law. Montaigne develops this line of challenge further. The Renaissance version of 'scepticism' which has become virtually synonymous with his name, is summed up in the very title of one of his essays: 'That it is madness to judge the true and the false from our own capacities'. For him, pride was the greatest sin,[19] and it was pride which made man claim innate knowledge of truth: 'if you condemn ... anything whatever as definitely false and quite impossible, you are claiming to know the frontiers and bounds of the will of God and the power of Nature our Mother'.[20] As in the world of physical things, so in the moral: any claim to know truth is a 'silly arrogance' which confuses knowledge with opinion. Ironically, however, Montaigne bases this conclusion on reason, saying that 'reason has taught me that', laying himself open to the challenge that he is just as wedded as anybody else in the period to the idea of 'right reason' as an innate faculty which can be either followed or denied. Montaigne posed awkward questions by pointing out the oddity of claiming that there are immutable 'natural' laws when every example given is contradicted by some nation's version of them,[21] but again it is his rationalism which leads him to this observation. He says that it is 'not beyond dispute' that there is 'truly a Law of Nature – that is to say, an instinct which can be seen to be universally and permanently stamped on the beasts and on ourselves', but yet in the same paragraph opines that 'the concern for self-preservation' and 'the love which the begetter feels for the begotten' may well belong to such a law: and he gives to humans 'some slight capacity for discursive reason' to distinguish us from animals, and says 'Reason alone must govern our inclinations.'[22] So it is not true to say that Montaigne denies the Law of Nature altogether. At most, he simply sidesteps it, as he regards its generality as less intrinsically fascinating than the diversity and individuality of human motivation. Rochester, writing after Hobbes, was more deeply sceptical, for he sought to deconstruct reason itself by using reason, and this basic kind of scepticism was to become more deeply entrenched after Hobbes in the European Enlightenment. Ironically, 'the age of reason' was also the age which most systematically questioned reason. But in the sixteenth and seventeenth centuries reason was seen as a less negative faculty, and one shared potentially by all mankind. Even Hobbes did not deny the existence of Natural Law as the product of reason, but instead located its field of operation beyond the individual's reason and conscience, as if these are not inborn gifts but exist as collective agreements or imposed rules. Machiavelli, again, does not deny Natural Law, but chooses instead largely to ignore it, dwelling on the conflicts of temporal *realpolitik* without looking for ultimate moral answers. Thomas More in *Utopia* dramatises the clash between an Aquinas and a Machiavelli, Natural Law theorist and sceptical pragmatist. The most radical denial of Natural Law may, at least according to traditional views, have come from Descartes who, by allegedly arguing for the complete separation between mind and matter, denied the implication of reason in nature, which was the plank of Aquinas' thought.[23] But Descartes' voice, if indeed it has been accurately understood, was not the loudest one in the Renaissance, although it was to become much louder in the scientific rationalism of the eighteenth century.

Where the earlier sceptics and their Renaissance sympathisers became significant for the formulations of Hobbes, was in a decisive redirection of emphasis rather than a dismissal of Natural Law itself. Generally speaking, classical theory places the understanding of Natural Law within the individual human mind, and this emphasis, for example, fuelled Milton's resistance to the vicissitudes of political fortunes and to the decrees of worldly power. Where Hobbes, and predecessors like even the Protestant Spenser, differed in emphasis, was to assert that mankind since the Fall had been cut off from the sources of inner knowledge, and therefore needed to have unambiguous applications of Natural Law imposed on them by a state apparatus controlled by a worldly authority standing next in line from God. Individual reason and conscience were at best unreliable since each person could find a different way: a degree of simple faith in higher authority was required. Similarly, although with very different implications, Roman Catholicism has always upheld the primacy of papal pronouncements over individual opinion, however rationally and conscientiously the latter is expressed, even while insisting, like Hobbes and Spenser, on the prior existence of Natural Law. The radical potential in this formulation lies in a further inference that Hobbes emphatically denies: if people are cut off from their own capacity for exercising reason and conscience, and if they need to be coerced by strong laws and a strong state, what makes Natural Law any different

from positive law? Why, then, is there any need for a belief in Natural
Law? These inferences were certainly drawn later, particularly by legal
practitioners, and they led to the almost total eclipse of Natural Law, but
this story was to lie in the future. All the writers we shall be examining
display neither simple-minded faith in what Natural Law dictates nor
radical scepticism about its very existence, but rather their fascination
lies in the ways in which, differing from writer to writer, human beings
wrestle with their consciences and, while seeking the path of reason, are
misled by baser passions or make choices which are flawed. The one
belief they hold in common is the sanctity of a model of Natural Law
which exists, whether inside or outside the human mind, and allows
human beings consciously to choose either to follow virtue or to shun it.
This is the basis of Renaissance literary theory and literature.

### Natural Law in the modern world

Because of the historical rift signalled by Hobbes' *Leviathan*, the essence
of Natural Law cannot be presupposed these days as it could before
1700. In explaining its content and purposes to a twentieth-century
audience generally inimical to its very existence, all that can be done by
its supporters is to provide a series of definitions and redefinitions that
take account of the sceptical tradition. The terms of the Renaissance
Christian no longer sound convincing, and nor do those of the classical
Greeks and Romans. A modern legal writer, H. L. A. Hart (although
himself a 'positivist' generally accepting Austin's distinction), provides
the kind of argument that may more readily invite modern assent or at
least comprehension.[24] He speaks of Natural Law in terms of morals that
lie behind or underpin those positive laws which are made by humans
and encoded in some sort of legal system. The argument runs that human
laws can be made only if some minimal but central truisms of a moral
nature are agreed upon beforehand, and this 'minimum content' is
Natural Law. Such minimum content may be that laws must be
demonstrably fair in operation to all individuals, must discriminate
against none, and must be passed according to due process. Positive law
is designed to provide a framework within which the behaviour of
citizens in a society may be consistent with what is 'natural' to that
community and to human beings in general, and which guarantees their
survival. Of course, what, precisely, will guarantee community and
survival in particular contexts, is just as hotly contested in our century as
in others. During two world wars there were obviously those who
believed in 'just wars' as there were conscientious objectors who argue
that no war can be just; there have been wars of liberation, mass

demonstrations of civil disobedience, just as there have been popular movements of opposition to government policies such as involvement in the Vietnam conflict and reliance on nuclear power and nuclear weapons. Arguably, all these examples exemplify the continuing tensions between individual conscience and state policy, between Natural Law and positive laws.

Within positive law itself, officially nowadays Natural Law is treated with suspicion, as the province of theorists and philosophers, and the only vestige in English law is the concept, most relevant in administrative law, of natural justice, which dictates that in quasi-judicial circumstances authorities must, for example, be impartial, give reasons for decisions, listen to both sides of an argument, and so on. Full-blown attempts to link this with any version of Natural Law which is deemed above the common law have often been treated with contempt by practitioners:

In so far as the term 'natural justice' means that a result or process should be just, it is harmless though it may be a high-sounding expression; in so far as it attempts to reflect the old *jus naturale* it is a confused and unwarranted transfer into the ethical sphere of a term employed for other distinctions; and, in so far as it is resorted to for other purposes, it is vacuous.[25]

This judgment, given early in the twentieth century, has in one respect been overtaken by judicial events. Since a dictum by Lord Reid in 1963,[26] natural justice has become increasingly strengthened as an assertion of fair play in contexts where 'watchdog' committees have proliferated to oversee such agencies as tribunals, clubs, government departments, employers, and other bodies which hold power over ordinary people's livelihoods.[27] But this movement to clarify and use natural justice has not opened any doors to the acceptance of Natural Law as part of the common law.

In maintaining its attitude of indifference bordering sometimes on hostility to Natural Law, common law has been rather insular, since there are systems of law based on 'Bills of Rights' which implicitly or explicitly assert a form of Natural Law. The American Declaration of Independence (1776) declares that according to 'the Laws of Nature and of Nature's God' all persons are created equal and are endowed with inalienable rights over life, liberty, and the pursuit of happiness, and France's *Déclaration des Droits de l'Homme et du Citoyen* (1789) speaks of 'the preservation of the natural and inalienable rights of man' which are 'simple and indisputable principles'. The Nuremberg trials of Nazi officers (1945–6) and the ongoing trials against Nazi war criminals have been based on a belief in the Natural Law model, or at least in a law which overrides unjust state laws. The United Nations Declaration of

Human Rights (1948), which attempts to preempt what it calls the kind of 'barbarous acts which have outraged the conscience of mankind' in two world wars, grows out of the Natural Law tradition. 'Human rights' is the twentieth century's preferred term for the terrain previously called Natural Law. Activists for 'civil rights' and 'civil liberties' from Martin Luther King Jr to those who oppose the British 'poll tax' because it is a charge against existence rather than property or income, take their stand for civil disobedience largely on the grounds of Natural Law. Whether consciously or unconsciously the women's movement has used the basic reasoning of Natural Law theory to demand equality, and some of the more radical sisters amongst legal theorists now argue that positive law as a total system is a male construct which does not extend full and equal protection to minority cultures as well as majority ones, and which requires dismantling and fundamental critique from what amounts to a Natural Law perspective.

Not that Natural Law is always used in support of 'people's movements' for social reform. Hobbes used it instead to justify a coercive state created in order to preserve peace, bolster individualism within a competitive framework, and protect property interests. Since Hobbes' time, and taking legitimacy from him, a western movement of thought has defended the right of one person or group to oppress others on what are framed as appeals to Natural Law assumptions concerning the sanctity of individual liberty. Those who support a 'free-market' economy regard Hobbes as influential, and they cite Natural Law in defence of 'deregulation' even as they substitute one kind of sovereign control for another.[28] Laws to prevent racial vilification have been attacked on the curious ground that they violate freedom of speech, an example of the modern tendency to equate Natural Law with individual rights rather than community values.

The general debate over Natural Law is once again alive amongst theorists respectively espousing communitarian or individualistic points of view.[29] Dressed in modern clothing, the debate has percolated down to the popular consciousness and to some extent even to the ballot box in western democracies.[30] It is not surprising that legislating bodies and the legal profession have an aversion to any appeal to a universal moral law, a justice beyond human laws. First, there would be no agreement on the content of such a law,[31] and secondly the legal mind is hesitant about admitting anything that smacks of moral judgment which seems subjective in its operation. However, the classical line of jurists dealing with Natural Law anticipates such objections. They answer that Natural Law does not require subjective, moral opinions but can be derived entirely from human reason, compelling assent from all rational human beings.

They answer also that it is not a list of rights, obligations, proscriptions, or duties that can ever be specified or written down, but rather general, unarguable, overarching guidelines which in themselves generate positive laws. Natural Law might be seen as a prerequisite for the enactment of positive law, or a form of 'meta-law' within which positive law can take place, or as a court of appeal against any man-made laws which violate human rights. Furthermore, it is assumed that law made by a valid authority will be consistent with Natural Law, or flow from it, in that such a body by definition serves the community's interests, until proved otherwise. The actual laws made by human societies will differ from community to community according to local conditions, conventions, and customs. Some form of Natural Law (whether or not the term is used) has been said to operate where positive law has proved itself inadequate to deal with manifest injustices, or is transparently unjust in its own operation: where, in short, it can be seen to have failed its community's interests. One can point to revolutions throughout history as occasions preceded by conditions, legally sanctioned, which worked against the community's welfare and which invited political change by appeal to a moral or legal order beyond the 'law of the land'.[32] Those who argue that manifest corruption, exploitation, or even atrocities, are in some way acceptable because 'authorised' by properly constituted, legislatively sanctioned bodies or individuals, and that the first duty of functionaries in such a situation is to carry out the law, are considered beyond both a moral and a legal pale. The point will be relevant to our analysis of *Measure for Measure* and *King Lear*. Most legal systems have come to build in some safeguards to achieve relative fairness within a community. In English law, at least historically, equity was preserved to correct injustices caused by strict application of common law, and the royal prerogative has existed for related reasons. In the USA the Fifth Amendment has been used since 1868 to draw limits around legislating capacity in order to safeguard fundamental freedoms of citizens particularly against economic laws, although exactly where the lines are drawn has been constantly disputed. We are dealing with a concept which is elusive, to some vague and unacceptable, and always disputable in particular applications, but self-evidently powerful and central to human, social existence and to all legal systems. It has equivalents in cultures as diverse as Japanese (*kejime*) and Australian Aboriginal ('law of the land'), as well as in those taking guidance from some 'divine book' such as the Christian Bible or the Moslem Koran.

There is a larger story to be told, beyond the scope of this book, tracing the fortunes of Natural Law thinking as it has informed historical, political events. Even if classical theorists such as Plato,

Cicero, and St Augustine ranked as subsidiary to other concerns the maxim *lex injusta non est lex*, it has always been the issue that attracts most attention to Natural Law. It has constantly been invoked in justification of political action, from the English Civil War, through the American War of Independence down to its revival in twentieth-century debates centring on 'Natural Rights' (rights established by the natural fact of existence rather than material means). Condemnation of war crimes, genocide, and assertion of human rights, environmental ('natural') constraints on human laws, efforts to restore customary laws and lands to indigenous, aboriginal peoples have all been conducted with reference to some aspects of the Natural Law model, and we may now in the 1990s be seeing a full-blooded resurgence of the general theory. If this seems an enormous terrain, it is, and we might keep in mind the words of George W. Keeton:

Over the whole history of Christian thought, no other single idea has influenced Western thinking upon the nature of law and the State so profoundly as the Law of Nature, for it is concerned with the problem of abstract justice and with the standards which should be applied not only to human law making but human conduct generally.[33]

The only word we can quibble with here as unduly restrictive is 'Christian' since Natural Law was first articulated by the pagan, classical world, and it is equally a *credo* of some modern 'pagans'.

# 2    The heritage of classical Natural Law

One way to grasp something of the essence of Natural Law is to consider its history. Like most leading ideas in western thought, the first systematic presentation of Natural Law can be traced back to Plato and his star student, Aristotle. The latter is the more significant in this tradition, but it was Plato in *The Republic* who posited a moral order which embodies eternal laws, existing beyond the temporal world but binding upon this world.

However, the story begins even before these two thinkers, since they themselves drew, often in a spirit of opposition, from the work of the first and probably most remarkable group of philosophers, Heraclitus and the Sophists. Now known as the pre-Socratics, these men date back to 585 BC – a curiously precise and therefore nominal date handed down by tradition – and they built upon each others' ideas up until Plato's time. None of their own writings exist, and their ideas are known entirely through fragmentary quotations and descriptions by later figures. In many ways they can be seen as the most original thinkers in the entire western philosophy, and a link with the eastern. Heraclitus, known as 'the Obscure', was the most seminal of them all, and it is no exaggeration to say that he initiated many of the fundamental questions which have preoccupied Western philosophy down through the centuries. The radical nature of his thinking is best illustrated by two, apparently contradictory, paradoxes: 'beginning and end are common'[1] and 'it is not possible to step twice into the same river ... nor to touch mortal substance twice in any condition' (p. 117). The first posits an unchanging and immortal universe, the second a world of flux. That both exist simultaneously is summed up in the further paradoxes: 'We step and do not step into the same rivers, we are and we are not' and 'changing, it rests' (*ibid.*). In essence, this is the basis of Natural Law. Two realms operate at the same time, the metaphysical and the physical. The one is defined by unalterable, binding, and immutable laws, while the other is characterised by an infinity of unique and unrepeatable applications of the universals which can be observed in nature or constructed by mankind. What links the two realms is human reason itself, a faculty which discovered, or constructed, or at least hypothesised, such a distinction, and in doing so intuited the fundamental principle of universal reason itself in the metaphysical law. Heraclitus' faith lies entirely in the capacity of reason to supply understandings of Natural (divine) Law and positive laws. By proposing this clue, he anticipates many of the positions adopted by St Thomas Aquinas, including the observation that the diversity of species disguises the fact that each has its own unique *raison d'être*, its own 'nature' to which it must by law be 'true': 'It seems that each animal has its own pleasure ... The pleasures of horses, dogs, and men are different' (p. 116).

Already, at its very birth, the ambivalence of Natural Law is revealed. Even if everybody were to agree about its existence, they would inevitably disagree about its content or what it means in application. As Heinrich A. Rommen in his classic work *The Natural Law: A Study in Legal and Social History and Philosophy*[2] notes, the very completeness of Heraclitus' paradoxical concept allowed for political appropriation by opposing tendencies. 'Conservatives' such as Plato, drew from it the inference that the law of the state could be brought into exact equivalence with Natural Law, and thus could be all-binding and immutable; whereas 'revolutionaries', the first of whom were the Sophists, strangers to Greece and therefore with no vested interest in the Athenian state, concentrated on the temporality of all human laws, their very impossibility of being universal and therefore inviolable: 'Socrates, despite his distinction between what is naturally right and legally right, pronounced the laws of Athens to be right' without qualification, but 'To the Sophists the laws were not venerable because of tradition or by reason of having stood the actual test of life in the city-state: they were artificial constructs and served the interests of the powerful (Thrasymachus)'.[3] Rommen notes 'the remarkable fact' that from its very inception Natural Law has been seized upon equally by political conservatives who wish to maintain the status quo, and by revolutionaries who maintain the artificiality of human society and laws, and who seek radical change. Neither 'faction' wishes or needs to ditch the idea of Natural Law itself, although they differ so markedly in their interpretations of its application. Precisely the same distinction runs through the Renaissance: the model of Natural Law based on reason as virtue is agreed upon by all, but very few if any worldly applications need to be agreed upon for this to be so. A figure like Shakespeare, who, like most of his contemporaries, loved paradox,[4] seized upon such a dramatically fertile construction, while the political philosophy of Sir Thomas More searches its implications for human organization. Meanwhile, towards the end of our period, we find Milton and Hobbes agreeing on the existence of Natural Law, but disagreeing implacably and fundamentally on what this means for the state and its need to construct positive laws.

### Aristotle

Aristotle is a pivotal figure in this book, partly because his revival in, and influence over, sixteenth-century thought was incalculably wide, and partly because he linked up law, rhetoric, and poetry indissolubly through his various writings. However, his contribution to Natural Law thinking is contributory rather than seminal, since his real emphasis lies on the internal dynamics of positive law, and his attitude to Natural Law is revealed only through occasional *obiter dicta*. Human justice rather than divine law is his chosen field. Aristotle's general ideas on law and justice are recorded in *Nicomachean Ethics (Ethica Nicomachea)*, Book V.[5] His guiding principle in all areas was the *via media*, a 'mean' between extremes, and words like 'geometrical' and 'arithmetical' pepper his theory of justice as 'distributive' and 'retributive' ('rectificatory' might be more accurate for the second). Justice is something which, in his terms, can be measured. Law aims, he argues, to 'tend to produce and preserve happiness and its components for the political society' (1129a). It is 'complete virtue, but not absolutely, but in relation to our neighbour' (1129b): 'For this same reason justice, alone of the virtues, is thought to be "another's good", because it is related to our neighbour; for it does what is advantageous to another, either a ruler or co-partner' (*ibid.*).

Aristotle can then argue for a kind of mathematical model by defining justice as involving two things (the self and others) and claiming that for its perfection these two things must be in equal relation. Justice can be seen as a 'distribution' according to merit. Injustice is the opposite: inequality, where one man gains something at the expense of another.

This, then, is what the just is – the proportional; the unjust is what violates the proportion. Hence one term becomes too great, the other too small, as indeed happens in practice; for the man who acts unjustly has too much, and the man who is unjustly treated too little, of what is good. (1131a)

The judge, whose nature is 'to be a sort of animate justice' exists to restore equality (1132a) and proportion, so each party has a fair portion.

So far, this conception of law and justice has a formal application to Elizabethan literature, but not an especially dynamic one related to ethical complexities. Its influence can be seen, for example, in the title of *Measure for Measure* (although the words themselves are biblical) but the play of that name so qualifies the concept of distributive justice that it amounts to a questioning of it. We find that in endings to those works which culminate in a court case, such as Sidney's *Arcadia*, *The Merchant of Venice*, or a quasi-judicial ceremony, as in several works by Jonson and Middleton, Aristotelian justice is an implicit model by which wrongs are righted, equilibrium and equality restored.

A more interesting strain underlies the *Nicomachean Ethics*, surfacing at times. Aristotle admits that his model of justice applies centrally in 'measurable' areas and particularly in areas where property and money are involved. Where there is no commercial loss, there is no injustice, although there may be other culpable states. He gives an example which, incidentally, has telling significance for *Measure for Measure*:

if one man commits adultery for the sake of gain and makes money by it, while another does so at the bidding of appetite though he lose money and is penalized for it, the latter would be held to be self-indulgent rather than grasping but the former is unjust, but not self-indulgent; evidently, therefore, he is unjust by reason of his making gain by his act. (1130a)

This is the kind of distinction that might in *Measure for Measure* have exonerated Claudio (who does not even commit 'adultery'), while incriminating the inmates of the brothel, which presumably was the 'spirit' behind Vienna's law. Aristotle admits, however, that 'There is more than one kind of justice' (*ibid.*) and that the form which deals with tangible objects is by no means the only one. Later in Book V he makes a crucial distinction in the area of what he calls 'political justice':

Of political justice part is natural, part legal, – natural, that which everywhere has the same force and does not exist by people's thinking this or that; legal, that which is originally indifferent, but when it has been laid down is not indifferent. (1134b)

He emphasises that 'a thing is unjust by nature or by enactment', and that the latter 'are not everywhere the same', thus introducing the classic distinction between things *mala in se* (evil in themselves) and *mala prohibita* (evil by enacted law), between Natural Law and positive law, unwritten and written laws. Under both systems, Aristotle places centrally the fact of voluntariness. A person may 'be' unjust (or make a 'mistake') but not 'act' unjustly if he does not voluntarily choose the action, for example if he or she acts through ignorance or under compulsion. This question of motivation is addressed by all later theorists, but, as Kathy Eden has demonstrated, for Aristotle it is important to his theory of tragedy as of law.[6] Intention, for Aristotle, is central to justice and to drama alike.

At the very end of Book V of the *Nicomachean Ethics* there is a kind of lacuna typical of Aristotelian texts whose transmission from oral lecture form to mediated written texts was so imperfect. Aristotle turns to 'equity and the equitable' (1137a) and its relation to 'justice and the just'. The gap in reasoning is that he provides no context for defining 'equity'. By deduction, however, it is reasonable to infer that the relation is the same as that lying between Natural and enacted law. Whereas 'justice is essentially something human' (*ibid.*), 'the equitable is superior' to the just, and therefore beyond the human world. Aristotle says that equity and human justice are not opposed to one another and that they may be simultaneously present, but he emphasises that equity is 'better than one kind [enacted or positive law?] of justice'. His need of a concept of equity stems from the fact that laws enacted by men are necessarily couched in abstract or 'universal' language designed to cover unforeseen occurrences, which may in practice cause a manifest 'injustice'. Those who make a law may not foresee some particular act which is *mala in se* so that, for example, a self-evidently evil man may be acquitted on a technicality. Or a law in its operation, technically and narrowly construed, may call somebody guilty whom we do not think has done anything wrong. Antonio, judged on the narrow grounds of law of contract, is to lose a pound of flesh, but in the 'superior court' it is Shylock who is on trial. 'And this is the nature of the equitable, a correction of law where it is defective owing to its universality' (1137b) (a better translation might be 'generality'). Aristotle concludes: 'It is plain, then, what the equitable is, and that it is just and is better than one kind of justice' (*ibid.*). His added comment that equity 'is a sort of justice' in itself supports the inference that its relation to the other 'kind of justice' is the same as that later drawn between Natural Law and positive law.

Aristotle's account of Natural Law is sketchy, ill-defined, and question-begging. But the distinction between unwritten and positive laws, is significant in the Natural Law tradition, as well as for the English legal system in the sixteenth century. It implies that there is a legal dimension beyond man-made law, a more eternal form of justice than that which is meted out by the state. And in English law it led to the uneasy coexistence of two legal systems, common law (augmented by parliamentary enactments) and equity, the latter administered by the king's 'court of conscience', Chancery. In the sixteenth and early seventeenth centuries the two systems were at loggerheads, as we shall see. Fundamentally, the clash was based on the theoretical distinction between Natural Law and positive law, a debate which Aristotle helped to initiate. From our point of view it is significant that Aristotle was just as influential for Renaissance literary theory as for jurisprudence, intimating the close links between Natural Law and poetic justice.

## Cicero

Aristotle had considerable influence over Roman Law. This system, while influential during the middle ages after the discovery of Justinian's *Codes*, suddenly took off in revived form and swept Europe in the sixteenth century, leading to radical reforms in the legal systems, and even causing a flurry in England. Roman Law firmly acknowledged a concept of Natural Law, although its operation was always disputed. Cicero, another who can be seen as a father of Elizabethan rhetoric and of law equally, gives classic statements in his *De Re Publica* and *De Legibus*, for example:

Well then, the most learned men have determined to begin with Law, and it would seem that they are right, if, according to their definition, Law is the highest reason, implanted in Nature [*lex est ratio summa insita in natura*], which commands what ought to be done and forbids the opposite. This reason, when firmly fixed and fully developed in the human mind, is Law. And so they believe that Law is intelligence, whose natural function [*vis*] it is to command right conduct and forbid wrongdoing ... Now if this is correct, as I think it to be in general, then the origin of Justice is to be found in Law, for Law is a natural force [*naturae vis*]; it is the mind and reason of the intelligent man, the standard by which Justice and Injustice are measured.[7]

Cicero carefully explains that in this context Law is not 'the crowd's definition' of man-made law, but a 'Supreme Law which had its origin ages before any written law existed or any State had been established' (319). The definition of Law as a 'natural force' which is 'the highest reason, implanted in Nature' sets the terms for later debate in the context of medieval Christianity. Even more eloquently, Cicero expands on the subject in *De Re Publica*:

True law is right reason in agreement with nature; it is of universal application, unchanging and everlasting; it summons to duty by its commands, and averts from wrongdoing by its prohibitions. And it does not lay its commands or prohibitions upon good men in vain, though neither have any effect on the wicked. It is a sin to try to alter this law, nor is it allowable to attempt to repeal any part of it, and it is impossible to abolish it entirely. We cannot be freed from its obligations by senate or people, and we need not look outside ourselves for an expounder or interpreter of it. And there will not be different laws at Rome and at Athens, or different laws now and in the future, but one eternal and unchangeable law will be valid for all nations and all times, and there will be one master and ruler, that is, God [*omnium deus*] over us all, for he is the author of this law, its promulgator, and its enforcing judge. Whoever is disobedient is fleeing from himself and denying his human nature, and by reason of this very fact he will suffer the worst penalties, even if he escapes what is commonly called punishment.[8]

The terms used by Cicero in his pagan setting make the idea directly portable into Christian thought. *Omnium deus* becomes the Christian God, and the phrase 'we need not look outside ourselves for an expounder or interpreter of it' equates with Christian conscience, as does the spiritual penalty accorded to one with a guilty conscience who 'escapes what is commonly called punishment'.

Cicero also opens up here a distinction which is ripe for disputation of a political kind, and which came to be highly significant to More and Milton. He argues that any laws made by men (senate or people) which go against the Law of Nature are simply not valid laws. Natural Law is altogether above human law, and it is a measure of the validity of human laws. Cicero goes on to talk of tyrants, those who attempt to pass laws which conflict with the supreme moral obligations of reason. We should not be too worried by the lack of precision of the word 'nature' in any of our theorists' writings. It is close to a circularity: that which is eternal is natural, therefore that which is natural is eternal. The word connotes ideas of unchanging order in the moral world as an analogue of the predictable physical laws of the natural world. The one thing nature does not mean in this context is what the post-Romantic world calls nature – observable, transient phenomena such as trees and flowers – except in so far as these obey 'laws' of growth.[9]

Natural Law came to be incorporated in Roman Law as an orthodoxy in its classical period. Our sources are the writings of the jurist Gaius, and the later compilation and rationalization of law, the *Corpus Iuris Civilis* commissioned by the Emperor Justinian. It was issued as a Digest and known as Justinian's *Institutes*, taking force from 30 December AD 533.[10] The earlier *Institutes* of Gaius, a textbook for students, was discovered as late as 1816, and it clearly formed the basis of Justinian's *Institutes*.[11] It opens with these words:

Every people that is governed by statutes and customs applies partly its own peculiar law and partly law which is common to all mankind. For the law which each people establishes for itself is peculiar to it and is called *ius civile* as being the special law of the state (*civitas*); but the law which natural reason establishes among all mankind is observed equally by every people and is called *ius gentium* as being the law applied by all nations (*gentes*). And so the Roman people applies partly its own peculiar law and partly that which is common to all mankind.[12]

Like Cicero, Gaius assumes the oneness of *ius naturale* and *ius gentium*, but Justinian's *Institutes* separate them. The primal motive behind all law is, the work says, the law of nature itself:

The law of nature is the law which nature has taught all animals. This law is not peculiar to the human race, but belongs to all living creatures, birds, beasts and fishes. This is the source of the union of male and female, which we called matrimony, as well as of the procreation and rearing of children; which things are characteristic of the whole animal creation.[13]

He also distinguishes the civil law, what I am calling positive law of the state, from 'the law which natural reason has prescribed for all mankind ... held in observance amongst all peoples and is thus called universal law, as being the law which all peoples use'.[14] He emphasises that the civil law can change with communities, but Natural Law is fixed and immutable and is 'common to the whole human race'.

The other term of Roman Law which at first sight looks very similar to Natural Law, *ius gentium* or Law of Nations, has been open to much scholarly debate, but it does seem clear that Justinian distinguished it sharply from Natural Law. It was a pragmatic way of resolving differences between different legal systems, given the international scope of the Roman Empire, the equivalent of modern international law. For example, since Roman Law was based on a strictly defined set of classes of people (free men, slaves, each with various sub-divisions between 'born' and 'made', depending on birth and circumstances), *ius gentium* was a means of classifying non-Romans according to the Roman system, thus allowing justice to be done to them. It was, properly speaking, a fiction, asserting that under certain circumstances non-Roman citizens were to be treated as if they were Roman citizens, in order to achieve consistent solutions to legal problems. The existence of such differences appears to contradict Cicero's and Gaius' merging of Natural Law and *ius gentium*. However, even these two writers, like all other theorists, assert that though in essence it is unchanging, the *application* of Natural Law may be different in different places at different times, and social customs may change. Even they implicitly distinguish between the source of all law (Law of Nature) and derivations from it, which can include the laws of one community (civil law) or a law which functions to bring consistency between different communities (*ius gentium*).

In practice, as one modern writer says, both *ius naturale* and *ius gentium* may have played little more part in classical law than rhetorical adornment,[15] but this is a lawyer's rather than a philosopher's view, and the truth is that the existence of the theory was to exert comprehensive influence on succeeding movements of thought. In the early seventeenth century, for example, the Dutchman known as Grotius (Hugo de Groot, 1583–1645) used principles from Roman *ius gentium* to generate the basis of modern international law, as well as commenting significantly on *ius naturale*. It might also be possible to argue, as does Barry Nicholas,[16] that the distinctions are hopelessly vague in that they confuse what 'ought' to be law and what 'is' law,[17] but again, this is a limited view in

the light of the long history, both before and after Justinian, of the
theory of Law of Nature. It is the distinction to be seized upon by
Hobbes as a way of undermining Natural Law viewed as a basis for
practical problem-solving or political organization. Nicholas admits that,
at least in the sphere of literature, which will come to be our subject here,
the idea is potent, and he mentions, for example, the conflict between
positive law and conscience in Sophocles' *Antigone*, which seems to mark
the inception in drama of Natural Law. Antigone asserts the primacy of
higher law over positive law as she condemns the mortal Creon for
decreeing that her brother should not be buried. She refers to unwritten
and unshakable laws of the gods overriding human laws:

> Because it was not Zeus who ordered it,
> Nor Justice, dweller with the Nether Gods,
> Gave such a law to man; nor did I deem
> Your ordinance of so much binding force,
> The unchangeable unwritten code of Heaven;
> This is not of today and yesterday,
> But lives forever, having origin
> Whence no man knows: whose sanctions I were loath
> In Heaven's sight to provoke, fearing the will
> Of any man.[18]

### Aquinas

Between classical and medieval times there lies something of a hiatus in
the story, although Saint Augustine made his contribution in importing
classical ideas into Christianity. But Natural Law was given a triumphant
revival in the thirteenth century by St Thomas Aquinas in his *Summa
Theologica*, the greatest and most challenging statement of the concept.
The way for him had been paved by the rise of scholastic dialectic as an
intellectual method in the preceding two centuries. A Bolognese monk,
Gratian, for example, in about 1140 wrote a monumental work called,
rather unpromisingly, *A Concordance of Discordant Canons* which was,
in the words of Harold J. Berman, 'the first comprehensive and
systematic legal treatise in the history of the West, and perhaps in the
history of mankind',[19] and which firmly endorsed Natural Law. In his
synthesis, Gratian categorized different forms of justice and placed them
in a hierarchy overarched respectively by divine law and Natural Law.
Berman emphasizes the revolutionary potential of Gratian's analysis,
which argued that both princes and custom must yield to Natural Law,
and which distinguished between *ius* [*naturale*] and *lex* on the basis that
*ius* is the genus, *lex* a species of it.[20] This statement paved the way for

plural legal systems in which 'victims of unjust laws could run from one jurisdiction to another for relief in the name of reason and conscience',[21] which is precisely what happened in sixteenth-century England. The great achievement of Gratian and his fellow canonists was to link up and organise ideas from Greek philosophers and from Roman lawyers. It remained for Aquinas a century later to write the classic work on Natural Law itself.

Aquinas' *Summa*, a work 'designed to cover every part of a given field of inquiry' (1, xxii) written sometime between 1265 and his death in 1274, was designed to fight 'on two fronts, against an anti-rationalism and an ultra-rationalism' (1, xxiii) in theology. So tightly argued is the analysis, and so comprehensively integrated is the theory, that summary can do no more than give an impression of its complex unity. Human reason lies at the heart of his thinking, and it is envisaged as the gift which places people above instinctual animals and enables them to understand something of God's moral universe: 'the rule and measure of human action is reason, which is the first principle of human action' (II. Qu. 90, Art. 1). Three sets of order exist in man, he argues, the Natural, the Divine and the Political:

The first is that which derives from the rule of reason: in so far as all our actions and experiences should be commensurate with the guidance of reason. The second arises from comparison with the rule of divine law, which should be our guide in all things. And if man were actually a solitary animal, this double order would suffice: but because man is naturally a social and political animal ... it is necessary that there should be a third order, regulating the conduct of man to his fellows with whom he has to live. (II. Qu. 72, Art. 4)

At the top of the hierarchy is the eternal law which is no more and no less than 'divine reason ... the rational guidance of created things on the part of God' (II. Qu. 91, Art. 1). This 'has the quality of law' which measures and regulates all things. 'All things participate to some degree in the eternal law in so far as they derive from it certain inclinations to those actions and aims which are proper to them' (*ibid.*). Each living creature has its particular, appropriate inclinations, aims, and tendencies. In animals these *raisons d'être* are instinctive, but people 'have a certain share in the divine reason itself, deriving therefrom a natural inclination to such actions and ends as are fitting' (*ibid.*). Polonius' 'precept', no matter how platitudinous it seems to us, takes on added significance in the context of Natural Law: 'This above all: to thine own self be true, And it must follow, as the night the day, Thou canst not then be false to any man' (*Hamlet* 1. iii. 78–80). Rationality and consciousness, Aquinas argues, are unique gifts, and their exercise allows man to understand and follow eternal law and his own 'nature', but not directly. The process is mediated through an earthly analogue to eternal law, namely Natural Law:

This participation in the eternal law by rational creatures is called the natural law ... As though the light of natural reason, by which we discern good from evil, and which is the natural law, were nothing else than the impression of the divine light in us. So it is clear that the natural law is nothing else than the participation of the eternal law in rational creatures. (*ibid.*)

We should pause a while over terms. 'Participation' seems to indicate similarity and causality between eternal law and Natural Law.[22] More substantially, it is clear that Aquinas is using words like reason and nature in ways that need to be explained. Reason is not simply the faculty which allows us to be logical or deductive. Its flavour, if not its force, is akin to that of modern law's fictional, unfortunately gendered, character, 'the reasonable man', a person incapable of knowingly doing anything wicked or stupid, a person with a knowledge of right and wrong and a predisposition, through rationality, to follow right and shun wrong. Although Aquinas emphasises reason above all, and it was left to later thinkers to give equal prominence to conscience, yet conscience, or *synderesis*,[23] identified by St Jerome who was the first to use the actual term *synderesis* in AD 415, is fundamentally implied as a component of reason itself. For Aquinas, one could almost say that conscience *is* reason, or at least a necessary component of it: if one is reasonable one will act conscientiously, and if one has a conscience one will be reasonable. Our common phrase 'Please be reasonable' usually implies in context the exercise of such morally based qualities as fairness, tolerance, and an awareness of others' needs, rather than simply being grounded in 'logical' or 'rational' thought.[24] Similarly Aquinas' 'nature' can be obliquely evoked through such statements as 'It is the nature of birds to fly, of fish to swim, of people to think.' The nature of a thing is its own unique, inescapable quality whose perfecting, or at least survival, is the central tendency of the creature's life. It can refer in humans to moral qualities: 'It is the nature of X to be courageous, of Y to be compassionate.' A literary example: Berowne in *Love's Labour's Lost* argues against the decree not to speak to women basically on grounds of the Law of Nature. He says, in short, that it is a decree which may be appropriate (natural) to old age, but it is not natural for youth: 'Young blood doth not obey an old decree' (IV. 3. 217). The action of Shakespeare's play demonstrates this as a central tenet of all romance and romantic comedy. It is not only a biological compulsion, but also a process with its own rational drive, that men and women will fall in love, and that no amount of coercion, parental opposition, or will power can prevent this. Aquinas agrees, in less heady language than Berowne's: 'every substance seeks its own preservation ... In virtue of this inclination there pertains to the natural law all those instincts "which nature has taught all animals" such as sexual relationship, the rearing of offspring, and the like' (II. Qu. 94, Art. 2). Although sexual coupling is that part of the Law of Nature which is common to people and animals, what separates them is the former's capacity to exercise reason itself – to reflect rationally – in the service of virtuous actions. People may be held responsible for the wisdom or folly, virtue or vice of their actions, in a way animals cannot, and ultimately the basis of such a responsibility rests on Aquinas' primary principle that human life is a good to be sustained, and what threatens it must be prevented.[25] Human judgment may be uncertain in a fallen world, but Aquinas considers it the highest aspiration or inclination in people according to the law of nature to *seek* what is good and avoid what is evil. In the search, Aquinas himself stresses the primacy of human and humane reasoning, 'menaced in its clarity by the passions',[26] while later writers were to stress conscience or *synderesis*. This faculty 'incites' to the good and 'murmurs' at evil (I. Qu. 79 Art. 12) and is a human capacity which can become a habit. Good is 'naturally' attractive to the reason, evil is abhorrent, although again it is quite possible for the clouded mind of fallen man to ignore its own knowledge of the distinction. This in itself was to become a corner-stone of Elizabethan theories of poetic fictions, although again the later age stressed conscience alongside reason while Aquinas required only reason, defined broadly enough to include moral judgment, to reach the same conclusions.

As in Heraclitus, we look in vain in Aquinas for lists of what is good and what is evil in practice. The *content* of Natural Law, its worldly applications, are relative and situational and may be different for each person in each particular circumstance: 'It is true that justice must always be observed, but the determination, by human or divine ordinance, of what is just must needs vary according to the different states of man' (*Summa*, 1a 2ae, 104, 3, 1). Again like Heraclitus, by his concentration on the inner logic of Natural Law and only occasionally on what it might mean in individual cases, Aquinas' theory lays itself open to hijacking by opposing groups, conservative and radical, idealistic and sceptical, and such appropriations were exactly what happened in later ages. Aquinas does not offer Natural Law as a set of rules which give us prescriptive solutions to our problems. Rather, his notion of Natural Law is offered as an explanation of why and how we are capable of dealing with moral problems by reference to forms which are embodied in human thoughts and feelings, and which bring us into contact with 'an external order of morality accessible to reason. Natural law is unwritten, its existence is eternal, but its principles are not immutable' (II. Qu. 94, Art. 5), and its application is infinitely various according to the particular person and circumstances. As Aquinas' most learned commentator says 'justice itself is constant, but, like any other analogical perfection, is variously modulated in its concrete realizations'.[27] It is knowable by individuals only through reason. This faculty can be clouded, for example, by passion (II. Qu. 94, Art. 4), but Aquinas is said to maintain that 'Human nature remains sound at its depths despite original sin, and its stream towards goodness, though partially choked up, is still to be relied on.'[28] The force of the word 'partially' was to be addressed by Protestants, and particularly Calvin. Positive laws are rules 'derived from natural law like conclusions deduced from general principles ... like implementations of general directives',[29] on the analogy of an architect constructing a particular house with its own specifications from a general idea of 'houseness'. In this sense, at the core of Natural Law is a Christian model linking theories of form and analogy, descending from Plato.[30]

Aquinas uses a metaphor which will come to be of fundamental importance for the practice of Renaissance writers, and which I shall have cause to repeat:

Just as in the mind of every artist there already exists the idea of what he will create by his art, so in the mind of every ruler there must already exist an ideal of order with respect to what shall be done by those subject to his rule [law] ... Now God, in His wisdom, is the creator of all things, and may be compared to them as the artist is compared to the produce of his art. (Article 1, Question 93. Also see 1a 2ae, 91. 1 and 91. 3)

Aquinas is dignifying the artist/writer with god-like powers, and some Renaissance literary theorists, pre-eminently Sidney, leapt on this opportunity to advance their claims to importance by naming themselves 'makers', following the etymology of the word 'poets'. The quotation emphasises the constructed nature of Natural Law and of art, the one shaped by God beyond our immediate understanding, the other by the artist, who hopes and trusts that his constructions will be in conformity with God's laws.

Below eternal law in Aquinas' hierarchy is natural law, and below that is human law, namely positive law made within human states and enforceable on earth. Aquinas believed (unlike Hobbes later) that 'there is in man a natural aptitude to virtuous action' (II. Qu. 95, Art. 1), but that 'discipline' is required to fulfil this aptitude. Here is where positive law is required to protect those who live virtuously from those who are 'of evil disposition and prone to vice', those whose aptitude for virtue has been habitually perverted or suppressed. Human Law is what makes it possible for people to live peacefully and virtuously together in communities. It is, however, distinctly subsidiary to Natural Law, or at least in the best communities the two are synonymous:

Saint Augustine says (I *De Lib. Arbitrio*, 5): 'There is no law unless it be just.' So the validity of law depends upon its justice. But in human affairs a thing is said to be just when it accords aright with the rule of reason: and, as we have already seen, the first rule of reason is the natural law. Thus all humanly enacted laws are in accord with reason to the extent that they derive from the natural law. And if a human law is at variance in any particular with the natural law, it is no longer legal, but rather a corruption of law. (II. Qu. 95, Art. 2)

This is Aquinas' cryptic pronouncement on the most contentious area in modern Natural Law theory: can a man-made law be 'unjust' in ways that authorise resisting or breaking it? The question is no arid or speculative one, but one with practical import not only in times of war but in times of peace when laws are made by ideologically motivated governments. On this point, Aquinas' own opinion is that unjust civil laws should be observed in order to preserve civil peace, but he seems uneasy:

A tyrannical law is not according to reason, and therefore is not straightforwardly a law, but rather a sort of crooked law. All the same it possesses some quality of law in wanting the citizens to be good. This it does as being the decree of a presiding authority set on rendering its subjects amenable, which is for them to be good from the point of view of a government, not thoroughly good in themselves. (1a 2ae, 92, 1)

This sounds like a classic description of what would now be called 'false consciousness', an ideology or set of attitudes accepted by the populace, even though it does not serve its community interests, but rather the self-interests of the ruler or ruling body which has exercised a kind of deceit based on propaganda. It is unlikely that Aquinas foresaw or intended any radical implication behind his advice, but rather he is being consistent to his model. His point is that human law is expected to be a derivation from Natural Law and therefore in accord with it, and that if laws are passed with due procedure by one in authority, it should be presumed consistent with Natural Law. Redress is for God not man. Where Natural Law is general, positive law is specific, and Aquinas illustrates this by saying that 'Do not murder' is one of many, particular, enacted human laws which are derived from the more general and abstract 'precept', 'Do harm to no person' (*ibid.*). Positive laws are 'particular applications' of Natural Law precepts, and their basic purpose is to order and maintain 'the common welfare of the city' (II. Qu. 95, Art. 4) and are adapted to the particular requirements of the city. Such laws will change from time to time, as circumstances change and as man's reason develops into deeper understanding of Natural Law.

The drama of salvation is acted by real persons each in the uniqueness of [their] own knowing and loving, of [their] own responsibility and choices, not as one playing a role or exemplifying a type or discharging the duties of an office.[31]

An essential characteristic of human law is that it should be promulgated by 'the ruler of the civil community' (*ibid*.) which may be embodied in a monarch, or aristocracy, or oligarchy (government by the rich and powerful) or democracy (*democratia*, 'government by the entire people') or 'mixed government'. Whatever kind of government is adopted, it must have constitutional power to make law. This aspect of Aquinas' theory became highly relevant in sixteenth- and seventeenth-century England, when monarchy, parliament, and common law all fought over the question of which bloc had the authority to make law. It is also relevant in those works of literature where authority is a central issue (*Macbeth* and *King Lear*, for example) or where existing rulers who have the power to change laws which appear to be against the Law of Nature conceived as a survival mechanism, choose not to do so, as in *The Comedy of Errors*, *A Midsummer Night's Dream*, and *Measure for Measure*.

St Thomas Aquinas, himself drawing on Aristotle, Cicero, and St Augustine, had an enormous influence on medieval and Renaissance thought, to the extent that we can speak of a school of Thomists (schoolmen, scholastics, scholiasts). Undoubtedly this is because of the integrated elegance of his thinking, the logical power of his writing, and the gentle beauty of his vision of the world. Of course there were differences among his followers, and in the field of Natural Law not all medieval writers meant the same thing as he. Among other commentators, Francis Oakley, for example, has argued for an influential difference between those like Aquinas, the 'realists' who said Natural Law is not a command from God but a discovery by human reason, and the 'nominalists' or 'voluntarists' like William of Occam and Duns Scotus who regarded Natural Law as a series of divine commands which happen, secondarily, to be rational.[32] McCabe may overstate the importance of the nominalists' position in the Renaissance,[33] for it seems to me that at most the two systems were in contention and at least the Aquinian position was in ascendancy in this debate until about 1650, if only because opponents took the Natural Law model as their point of departure. That was the year when Thomas Hobbes, drawing on the scepticism of those who had argued that Natural Law was a command rather than being within human nature, turned Aquinas' theory on its head by using its terms, if not its concepts, to justify a rigorous 'command theory' apparently more or less killing off the Thomist influence, much to the delight and relief of all succeeding, authoritarian governments.

There were also, of course, differences of emphasis among Aquinas' followers. He himself, for example, writes primarily as a theologian expounding religious truth, while his Spanish commentators such as Vitoria, Dominic de Soto, Medina, and Suarez write more as 'law-minded philosophers and lawyer-statesmen'[34] in a more worldly and pragmatic way. A third important difference among 'schoolmen' hung on whether or not Natural Law necessitated God. Aquinas clearly thought it did, but Grotius, writing at the end of the fifteenth century, argued that, in the words of a modern commentator, 'some acts would be enjoined and some forbidden by human nature and human reason, even supposing that there were no God or that he did not concern himself with human affairs'.[35] John Finnis puts Grotius' point of view differently and more precisely in saying that what is right and wrong can be discerned with the reason alone since it stems from the nature of things, but that the *obligation* to follow right and avoid wrong depends upon a decree given by God.[36] In the more secular climate of the twentieth century, the difference of opinion between those who equate the law of nature with God and those who separate the two has led to radically different theories. While the pope, for example, proscribes birth control because it is opposed to the 'Natural Law' of procreative sexuality as both a God-given function to all animals and as a command from God, libertarians implicitly appeal to Natural Law as a system which necessarily excludes God from human affairs, relies on human reason alone, and in the particular instance gives free choice to a woman as to whether she will practise birth control or not. The inescapable fact is that, throughout its history, Natural Law has been used in the service of mutually incompatible positions. This is not to deny its profound significance, but indeed to highlight it, as diverse thinkers saw it as important to gain support from Natural Law and sought to work under its aegis towards their particular ends. It is important, however, to keep separate, consideration of the concept itself and of its applications.

### Luther and Calvin

Catholic writers did not have a monopoly on Natural Law, for the Reformation also respected it, and used it for different ends. Luther was to write 'The law of nature is the law of God, and the prophets teach that one person owes love to the other.'[37]

For when you judge according to love, you will easily decide and adjust matters without any law books. But when you ignore love and natural law, you will never succeed in pleasing God, though you have devoured all the law-books and jurists; they will only cause you to err, the more you depend on them. A good and just decision must not and cannot be given out of books, but must come from a free mind, as though there were not a single book. Such a free decision, however, is given by love and the law of nature, of which the reason is full; but out of the books come rigid and vague judgments.[38]

Luther's own emphasis, in equating the Law of Nature with the law of love, itself derived from Aquinas, points towards the equity of mercy, and stresses the social, communitarian aspect of Natural Law. However, because of the Reformation insistence on salvation of the elect (who do not know whether or not they are elect), Luther needs to stress that we can never really know whether or not we are acting in accordance with Natural Law. He is sardonically aware that this fact generates a whole array of equally confident but discrepant opinions:

At present people are beginning to praise natural law and natural reason as the source from which all written law has come and issued. This is true, of course, and the praise is well placed. But the trouble is, everyone likes to think that the natural law is encased in his head ... therefore it is also a fact that among those who presume to have natural reason or natural law, and boast of it, there are very many great and efficient natural fools. The noble gem called natural law and reason is a rare thing among the children of men.[39]

His emphasis tends towards Calvin's, that Natural Law, if it is intrinsic to humans, is obscured by sin. On the two issues that were to become the most disputed, Luther creates the neat, if somewhat easy, distinction between true Christians, who hold Natural Law 'in the heart, in faith, and love' and whose authority therefore cannot be resisted, and non-Christians or 'the unrighteous' who have no such innate knowledge of Natural Law, or who have lost touch with it, and who must be ruled coercively by the righteous.[40] The latter group, comprising the vast majority, have, after the Fall, been cut off permanently from true reason. Luther's general assumption about worldly power was that the faithful would eventually inherit government and control the wickedness of the faithless, and so he advocated co-operation with authorities, failing to realize that this policy would contribute to nationalism and separatism, and the fragmentation of Protestant energies. By contrast, Protestants who came to shape England's Civil War, at least the more radical amongst them, argued that Natural Law places individual conscience above state authority, and enables the conscientious to resist positive law. Milton, while still believing like Luther that the good would prevail, took every opportunity to condemn what he regarded as false authority.

Luther's framing of Natural Law seems to give it less than universal existence, which is a dilution of the concept. Other Reformation writers argued not that it is confined just to the elect but that Natural Law exists in all, however impaired it may be after the Fall. The Protestant view of the Fall will also come to cause some confusion for imaginative writers. While Aquinas had 'emphasized the goodness inherent in mankind and asserted that the freedom of the will was not seriously impaired by man's first disobedience',[41] the Protestantism of Luther and Calvin was a creed stressing man's wickedness since the Fall. Sidney, Spenser, and Milton alike are problematical in dealing, for example, with human sexuality. While they can accept it as 'natural' and instinctive, their Protestantism commits them to seeing it in some circumstances as a betrayal of Natural Law's primary priority, reason, and an act inherently flawed since the Fall. In the writers' hands, this ambivalence led to some richly complex narratives at the cost of a degree of moral uncertainty, although, as we shall see in *Love's Labour's Lost*, *Measure for Measure*, and Milton's tracts on divorce, the debate may sidestep the issue of the Fall and concentrate rather on the question of whether or not positive law can police sexuality, or whether the only law that should apply is Natural.

John Calvin is often taken to be the chief antagonist against Aquinas' view of Natural Law, as if he intended to dismantle it and replace it with God's sovereign will. However, while the influence of Calvin's scepticism about man's ability to be innately good, came eventually to chip away and finally dislodge crucial parts of Natural Law thinking, his own attitude does not do so. The crucial passage in his *Institutes* (published in its first English translation in 1561)[42] on this matter is the following:

Now that inward law, which we have above described as written, even engraved, upon the hearts of all, in a sense asserts the very same things that are to be learned from the two Tables. For our conscience does not allow us to sleep a perpetual insensible sleep without being an inner witness and monitor of what we owe God, without holding before us the difference between good and evil and thus accusing us when we fail in our duty. But man is so shrouded in the darkness of errors that he hardly begins to grasp through this natural law what worship is acceptable to God ... Accordingly (because it is necessary both for our dullness and our arrogance), the Lord has provided us with a written law to give us a clearer witness of what was too obscure in the natural law, shake off our listlessness, and strike more vigorously our mind and memory.[43]

He does not deny the existence of the inward Natural Law, nor of the individual conscience, which in fact he stresses, and the real difference from Aquinas is one of degree: after the Fall man needs help in discovering the inward law. Aquinas did not entirely deny this conclusion, so that both ways the thinkers are using the same basic model and are not so far apart as schematic treatments often suggest. (Also, one finds in reading Calvin that he has a tendency to change his mind on some issues, unlike Aquinas, who is nothing if not consistent.) At one point, Calvin asserts that even the elect are reprobate, and the fact that they 'are not carried to utter and even desperate impiety is not due to any innate goodness' but to God's watchful eye (iii, xxiv, 10). Calvin admittedly trusted less in the power of human reason. He summarises that 'We see among all mankind that reason is proper to our nature', but then distinguishes between 'born fools' and the rest of us. At his most pessimistic, he asserts that reason, 'neither approaches, nor strives toward, nor even takes a straight aim at, this truth: to understand who the true God is or what sort of God he wishes to be toward us'.[44] He also placed greater emphasis than Aquinas on conscience, but he sees it more as a punitive and corrective faculty than an active instrument choosing between good and evil in actual situations. Lady Macbeth and Claudius would be typical examples in his scheme: those who do wrong and are pursued by their guilty consciences. Calvin wrote that 'God wished men to retain some ability to discriminate between justice and injustice' after the Fall[45] and acknowledged that Natural Law was the instrument of such knowledge.

We must take our definition from the etymology of the word. When men grasp the conception of things with the mind and the understanding they are said 'to know', from which the word 'knowledge' is derived. In like manner, when men have an awareness of divine judgment adjoined to them as a witness which does not let them hide their sins but arraigns them as guilty before the judgment seat – this awareness is called 'conscience'. It is a certain mean between God and man, for it does not allow man to suppress within himself what he knows, but pursues him to the point of making him acknowledge his guilt.[46]

More poetically, he used a favourite metaphor: 'While the whole world was shrouded in the densest darkness of ignorance, this tiny little spark of light remained, that men recognised man's conscience to be higher than all judgments.'[47] As Richard A. McCabe points out, there is a paradox in that Calvin 'preserves natural shame while disabling natural law',[48] but the overall difference between Aquinas and Calvin is not over the existence or otherwise of Natural Law, but the way that man is to know it, and the precise point of his knowledge. There is a distinction to be made between Macbeth and Claudius, for example, on this matter, since the former decisively knows he is doing wrong before the event, whereas Claudius arguably knows afterwards (or at least we cannot tell either way). While Aquinas is optimistic and trusts human reason, Calvin is pessimistic and sceptical, and as a consequence his model requires more trust in corrective conscience and divine grace.

Calvin's version of Natural Law stemmed from the regularity and observable phenomena in the world of nature, such as the movement of the stars, what we have described above as natural philosophy or laws of nature. Transferring such observations into the moral sphere, he argued that 'pagans have a law without [written] law' and 'are by no means lacking in the knowledge of right and equity',[49] a proof that he believed in 'the universality of an innate law of nature'.[50] Milton, for one, was to echo his words. Calvin in his *Institutes* places the emphasis on individual conscience, saying that 'the distinction between good and evil is engraven on [people's] consciences' and is 'inscribed in the hearts of all'.[51] But if the source of choosing between good and evil is individual, its exercise is social in consequence, and therefore subject to codification in positive law:

Since man is by nature a social animal, he tends through natural instinct to foster and preserve society. Consequently ... there exist in all [people's] minds universal impressions of a certain civic fair dealing and order. Hence no [person] is to be found who does not understand that every sort of human organization must be regulated by laws ... Hence arises that unvarying consent of all nations and of individual mortals with regard to laws. For their seeds have without teacher or lawgiver, been implanted in all [people].[52]

Calvin is invoking *ius gentium* in mentioning 'the unvarying consent of all nations', but fundamentally he builds on Natural Law foundations, which he sees as an ideal and a guide to the faithful as they build up a holy community. However, he does not place positive law above Natural Law: 'human laws ... still do not of themselves bind the conscience'.[53] On the other hand, as both John S. Wilks in *The Idea of Conscience in Renaissance Tragedy* and George C. Herndl in *The High Design: English Renaissance Tragedy and the Natural Law* emphasise, Calvin is profoundly pessimistic about man's ability to follow consistently his conscience. Wilks writes: 'Calvin is still further [than Luther] from scholasticism in his wholesale depreciation of nature; Adam not only deteriorated his race by his fall, but "perverted the whole order of nature in heaven and earth".'[54]

I would argue that it is possible Calvin's pessimism has been over-emphasised in analyses of Jacobean tragedy like Herndl's. Although, with the medieval nominalists, he tended to place the existence of Natural Law in the will of God rather than the free choice of humans, yet Calvin did not deny at least the potential for reason and conscience within people, and the more positive aspects of his theology show that he believed depravity could be overcome. Parts of his argument, if not the whole, were deployed by radical writers and political figures in the seventeenth century such as Winstanley, Lilburne, Walwyn, and Milton, all of whom quote Natural Law to justify radical, revolutionary policies. Earlier in 1556 John Poynet (or Ponet) who wrote the first Renaissance treatise discussing 'whether it be lawful to depose an evil governor, and kill a tyrant', and who advocates resisting unjust laws, does so in the name of reason and by reference to Psalm 118: 'it is better to trust in the Lord than to trust in Princes' (used as the epigraph to his book). His *A Short Treatise of politik power and of the true Obedience which subjects owe to kings and other ciuil Gouernors* is subtitled *with an Exhortation to all true natural English men*, a clear signal that before the Norman invasion in a kind of Protestant English myth of the Golden Age, people were 'natural' without formal authority, and obeyed the Natural Law based on reason and conscience. Moreover, it is not self-evident that *Macbeth*, for example, is irredeemably pessimistic in Calvin's sense. After all, Macbeth does come to a point of crisis when contemplating regicide, and both conscience and reasoning are powerfully enough evoked by him to make the audience realise he has a genuine choice.

> This even-handed justice
> Commends th'ingredience of our poisoned chalice
> To our own lips. He's here in double trust:
> First, as I am his kinsman and his subject,
> Strong both against the deed; then, as his host,
> Who should against his murderer shut the door,
> Not bear the knife himself. Besides, this Duncan
> Hath borne his faculties so meek, hath been
> So clear in his great office, that his virtues
> Will plead like angels. (1. 7. 10–19)

If there were ever a man wrestling with his conscience, pulled by good and evil, this is he, and we find similar crises in *Faustus*, *Hamlet*, Ford's *'Tis Pity She's a Whore*, and Webster's *The Duchess of Malfi*, as well as all Milton's epic poems. That individuals choose to turn away from the righteous path does not mean they do so without struggle involving reason and conscience. In fact the audience's own grasp of the nature of the moral decision which Macbeth is making, our realisation that he has chosen wrongly, supported also by the retributory design of the play as it unfolds, demonstrates his aberrancy rather than his representativeness, and the fact that audience response can extend to making moral decisions. Although I have decided not to look at non-Shakespearian Jacobean tragedy in a book which is already rather large, I believe an argument can be mounted that plays such as Webster's *The Duchess of Malfi* and Ford's *'Tis Pity She's a Whore* both presuppose active and positive audience implication in making moral decisions, and although they may portray corrupt characters they also contain countervailing statements based on virtue and show characters wrestling with their consciences. They do not simply abandon men and women to ignorant and blind courses of evil action in a fallen world, but instead show people making moral decisions within social worlds that are themselves unsympathetic, prescriptive, and prejudiced. Like *Macbeth*, they can be analysed as neither optimistic nor pessimistic about human capacity to follow conscience and reason, but simply as sharply observant of the difficulties when people, demonstrably capable of exercising reason and conscience, apply Natural Law in their own lives, when the political world around them is so corrupted. That not all choose to do so (Faustus, Macbeth, Giovanni in *'Tis Pity She's a Whore*) makes the drama didactic and educative rather than irredeemably mimetic. Aquinas had never pretended it is easy to implement Natural Law in a fallen world, and Calvin had never claimed it is impossible; and it is quite characteristic of creative dramatists and writers to represent moral struggles at their most complex and ambivalent without drawing simple conclusions. For these reasons I am not yet persuaded by Herndl that between the relative simplicity of Marlowe's *Doctor Faustus* and the complexity of Jacobean tragedies lies a Calvin-inspired disintegration and a 'withering' of the basic model of Natural Law underpinned by reason and conscience.[55] Such a disintegration did, I argue, occur later, when Hobbes's *Leviathan* was absorbed into mainstream thought, but if anything the Jacobean and Commonwealth writers, while showing awareness of the kind of scepticism which led to Hobbes, tended to locate evil as present in society, the potential for good lying in a fragile but real state within corrigible but vulnerable protagonists. *King Lear*, in my reading, is a more exemplary text of its time, depicting both Natural Law and scepticism in conflict. At the very least the case is more ambiguous than the one Herndl puts.

It is clear that, although the Catholic Aquinas provided the most sustained account of Natural Law in medieval times and was the most influential figure in Natural Law theory even in the Renaissance, the Reformation Protestants were to be equally insistent on its existence. The latter, however, drew very different conclusions about the possibility of agreeing in any detailed way on the content of Natural Law. John Donne's complaint, echoed by Luther and Calvin, applies only to the applications of Natural Law, not to its essence. The theory itself has an elegant simplicity, but certainly it was (and is) used to justify a range of mutually incompatible positions. However, lawyers were in broad agreement about its essential features, and imaginative writers from More to Milton found it a useful moral basis for their art. This was primarily because the ethical stance of the imaginative writer, in Aquinas' words, could be seen to be directly comparable to that of the Natural Law theorist. Both were comfortable with the notion that what ought to be done is at least as 'real' as what is actually done, if not more so, and is a branch of knowledge rather than speculation. By the sixteenth century in Europe, Natural Law held a central and tenacious place in legal, theological, and political thought, and the fact that its terms 'reason and conscience' were so elastic that it could stretch in many different directions and be used by opposing political factions, made it all the more fertile a field for writers.

# 3    The reception of Natural Law in Renaissance England

Until the end of the seventeenth century the model of Natural Law was debated and contested in England throughout the system of law and politics. So radically ambivalent was the theory itself that it did not escape attention it held political implications, and could be appropriated by those of many different persuasions. The issue that was to become more and more crucial was whether reason and conscience are God-given faculties that lie within the human head and heart, able to be exercised in particular circumstances, or whether fallen man has lost touch with these faculties and needs to be coerced into obedience to the laws of the state, which were assumed axiomatically to be consistent with Natural Law if passed by the properly constituted authority. Those who believed in the political necessity of strong monarchy would argue for the latter, those who believed in the sanctity of individual or collective choice would rely on the former. Within this overarching conflict lay another political contestation over the credentials of 'properly constituted authority', which partly explains Shakespeare's giant family saga of history plays, where the right to succession is the crucial struggle. In the English Renaissance, this struggle was acted out not only politically, but also within legal institutions themselves, as conflicts between rival legal systems. All systems, however, made claims by appealing in greater or lesser degree to Natural Law. This was so even of the positive law system, an uneasy triumvirate of common law, equity, and parliamentary statute.

The most comprehensive legal system in England, the common law, very early in its history absorbed central precepts from Natural Law. Henry of Bracton, a contemporary of Aquinas in the mid thirteenth century and one of the great luminaries of the law, not only described his book, *On the Laws and Customs of England* as a *summa*, but he also showed direct knowledge of Aquinas' thought. He gives the widest definition of Natural Law, and includes it as part of English concepts of law:

It may first be said to denote a certain instinctive impulse arising out of animate nature by which individual living things are led to act in certain ways. Hence it is

44

thus defined: Natural Law is that which nature, that is, God himself, taught all living things ... [or] Natural Law is that taught all living things by nature, that is, by natural instinct.[1]

By roundly declaring that 'the King is under God and the law' he implicitly repeats the tripartite division of law affirmed not only on the continent but by some Englishmen as well, most famously Stillington who, in a speech to Parliament in 1467–8, claimed that all the laws in the world can be divided into three: 'that is to say, the Law of God, Law of nature and positive Law'.[2] Natural Law's potential for political appropriation was already in place. Thomas More went to his death avowing that the law of treason under which he was condemned was contrary to the law of God, the law of reason, and the law of the land. Sir John Fortescue, a Chief Justice and another great authority on the common law, writing in his book *De Natura Legis Naturae* (1661–3), defined Natural Law as 'law of kind, which is doom [judgement] of reason and moral philosophy'. He classed Natural Law as the law of God, 'according to which every man is commanded to do unto another what he would have done unto himself, and is forbidden to inflict what he would not have done unto himself ... Love is the fulfilling of the law.'[3] Fortescue's own aim in writing the book was to comment on the thorny and contentious issue of authority, 'concerning the right of succession in supreme kingdoms' (p. 187), which was to be a central concern of Shakespeare's history plays and *King Lear*. On the general issue, he more or less quotes Aquinas: 'A true circle proves its centre, but yet more truly the centre indicates the truth of its orbit; so also right reason reveals the law of nature, but yet more surely that law displays the certainty of reason' (p. 225). One quite specific area in which the common law with its Christian guiding principles moved ahead of Roman Law and of Aquinas as well, was in affirming that slavery was contrary to Natural Law.[4] However, by 1500 it seems true that Natural Law content was not playing a significant part in the precedent-bound, pragmatic system of common law, and that indeed common law came to be in some points in conflict with Natural Law. The basic reason for this was common law's claim to consistency, and its exclusion of discretion according to reason and conscience, beyond precedents and deductive logic. Reason and conscience, however, were the rationales for the other English system of law, equity.

The sixteenth century witnessed some of the most momentous struggles and transformations that have ever occurred in legal systems throughout Europe. Country by country adopted reforms based on Roman Law which centrally included some Natural Law content. There was a strong push for the same to happen in England, but the outcome was rather different. The common law which had been entrenched in the twelfth century and is said to have been in existence since 'time immemorial' (dated with odd precision in 1189) proved strong enough to prevent wholesale change. From one point of view the system may still appear quaintly antiquarian. For all its supporters' claims to its consistency and rigour, common law could appear to be based on obscure precedents and customs which lay down principles which, it is said, can be brought to bear on new circumstances. Inevitably there is something *ad hoc*, potentially arbitrary, and dependent on an artificial, deductive logic, nowhere more obvious than in the sixteenth-century's reliance on fictions and forms of words, the legacy of which has always made it mysterious to lay people. On the other hand, in the sixteenth century the common lawyers were a tightly knit group of professionals who would not willingly concede any power to state legislatures or ecclesiastical bodies, or surrender their mystique to the laity. It had been centralised and reformed much earlier than legal systems in other countries, which made it at the time more stable and modern than its continental counterparts, and thus more impermeable to the Roman Law revival.[5] It also had the strength of custom, a dotty sense of local Englishness, which made it into a kind of national institution not easily dislodged. At the same time, the existence in England of another, equally time-honoured but more limited law-dispensing machinery alongside common law led to direct conflicts. The Court of Chancery, presided over by the Lord Chancellor, had since the fourteenth century stood as an alternative route to justice for plaintiffs. The Chancellor was 'the keeper of the King's Conscience' and his discretion became ever wider, as Selden put it, under 'the law of conscience, which is law executed in the Court for default of remedy by Courts of the Common Law'. The system centrally included notions of Natural Law derived from Aquinas: 'The Chancellor, in brief, was guided by a simple principle of jurisprudence drawn from the Canon Law in the application to each individual case of the test of reason and conscience.'[6]

The kind of law dispensed by Chancery was equity, a word which became closely associated with 'mercy', and owed something to Aristotle's idea of law as rectificatory equity, as well as bearing ecclesiastical backing from the concept of God's mercy. This double system held all the seeds for conflict, because it was based on opposite versions of reasoning (strict adherence to precedent on the one hand, appeal to abstract reason and conscience in particular cases on the other), and because the struggle had acute political implications. Henry VIII almost inadvertently strengthened common law, not least by instating as his

Chancellor after Cardinal Wolsey Thomas More, a lawyer rather than an ecclesiastic (although the distinction meant less then than now). Henry encouraged the drift to centralisation of the common law, as of power in general. On the other hand, by partly 'secularising' the office of chancellor, he equally strengthened its moral authority over the common law.[7] In the see-sawing struggle throughout the century, both systems claimed 'popular' support. Equity was a system ideally suited to the poor and to women because they could come directly and freely to the Court of Chancery,[8] whereas common law was prohibitively expensive, lengthy, rigid, and obscure. On the other hand, the great advocates of common law, like Coke in the early years of the seventeenth century, saw the common law as the 'popular' restraint on the monarch's prerogative which could lead to tyranny and also, by this time, as a restraint on parliament which could be seen as changeable and representative of vested interests. (Coke was not, however, the enemy to parliament that some have seen, according to the patient research of Stephen D. White.[9]) Ironically, in the overall battle for the power to make laws, it was parliament which finally 'won' over common law and equity in the three-way battle to claim a popular mandate, but that victory lay in the future.

As the differences between common law and equity became unavoidably intractable, the boundaries of the respective jurisdictions became more contested and hazy. The hierarchy of courts was in dispute. Coke championed the cause of common law above all other systems; Bacon asserted that Chancery was pre-eminent because the Chancellor's office was higher than a common law judge's;[10] and increasingly in the seventeenth century puritans scorned Chancery as a monarchical invention, common law as a product of the Norman Conquest, and instead argued that parliament was the most important body in the law. The claim of equity was to be a kind of court of appeal in cases where common law, through its adherence to deduction and literalism, could not achieve a 'just' result. The common law, on the other hand, could not accept that its decisions might be unjust, nor could it abide the existence of two systems which in particular cases might produce mutually incompatible decisions. Therefore, common law defined equity's orbit as quite distinct and separate. Plaintiffs could approach one system or other, but not both. In the 1590s common law judges intensified the pressure by issuing 'a constant stream of prohibitions'[11] preventing decisions of equity made in Chancery from taking effect. In order to survive, equity was forced more and more to confine itself to areas where common law was manifestly incomplete or imperfect, particularly in the area of fraud, which led to the body of substantive law (however apparently marginal and ossified) which nowadays goes by the name of equity, and which ironically is administered in as inflexible a manner as any legal system could be, and is notorious in literature as the system parodied by Dickens in *Bleak House*. S. F. C. Milsom quotes (without reference) the caution of a late sixteenth-century note by Chancery: 'this Court forbeareth directly to examine any judgment given at common law'.[12]

Just as both systems claimed 'popular' roots, so they both appealed either directly or indirectly to the rhetoric and theories of Natural Law, and it is a measure of the power of the Natural Law tradition that existing English systems had more or less to appropriate it rather than allow the sweeping reforms of Roman and canon law. Lord Ellesmere as Lord Chancellor roundly declared that 'The common law of England is grounded upon the law of God, and extends itself to the original Law of Nature, and the universal law of nations.'[13] His contemporary Coke, who angered King James by his implacable defence of the common law and who was finally dismissed from office, was not so sure, arguing that common law was not the rigid body of rules that some attacked it for being, but rather a system of reasoning designed to reveal just solutions:

*Nihil quod est contra rationem est licitum;* for reason is the life of the law, nay the common law itself is nothing else but reason; which is to be understood of an artificial perfection of reason, gotten by long study, observation, and experience, and not of every man's natural reason.[14]

The first part of this formulation sounds like that of Natural Law, but by then drawing back from reliance upon 'every man's natural reason', and basing his definition on the 'experience' of precedent and custom, Coke is covertly attacking Natural Law as described by Aquinas. He is, however, claiming the older theory for his own uses rather than refuting it since, by his insistence on reason, he is invoking Aquinas' model and also a very Aristotelian version of law as a process of reasoning. Elsewhere he derived common law from 'the law of God, the Law of Reason, and the Law of Nature, not mutable'.[15] On the other hand, equity, probably with more justification, made no bones about its unequivocal reliance on the main principles of Natural Law: reason and conscience. Common law haughtily retorted: 'Conscience is a thing of great uncertainty ... and so, diverse men, diverse consciences.'[16] Again, Coke, anticipating *The Merchant of Venice*, says that, at least in the field of commercial transactions, morality has little place and the law must above all be 'certain': 'causes which concern the life or inheritance or goods or fortunes of subjects are not to be decided by natural reason, but by the artificial reason and judgment of law'.[17] One might wryly observe that over the centuries the common law has been popularly perceived to have quite a wide latitude and lack of 'certainty' when particular precedents have been used to draw opposite conclusions, when many decisions are overturned on appeal, when 'minority' reports by judges seem just as convincing as 'majority' and where the power of advocacy sometimes dominates a case. Even at the time, Francis Bacon wrote that 'the incertainty of law ... is the principal and most just challenge that is made to the laws of our nation at this time'.[18] None the less, Coke is arguing that the actual system of reasoning and procedures used in making legal decisions are fixed, predictable, and not subject to whimsical opinion of one person presented under the guise of conscience. In retaliation, equity could unashamedly claim the high moral ground of Natural Law because the king (as long as he was not a tyrant) was said to have quasi-divine knowledge of right and wrong which could place his grasp of reason and conscience in the realms of the 'natural', beyond the vagaries of man-made law. No matter that he delegated this function to his Chancellor. Natural Law and a conscientious attitude 'tempered with the sweetness of mercy'[19] were claimed as the province of equity. This distinction was to be of importance in both Shakespeare's and Spenser's schemes of justice.

Incidentally, it may come as something of a surprise that Natural Law rarely seems to have been invoked to justify the English institution of trial by jury, at least until the mid seventeeth century. Earlier, in fact, the jury was seen by many, including Thomas More and St German, as an obstacle to the application of reason in the judicial process.[20] The apparent reluctance to refer to juries as a collective application of human reason and conscience, is why a writer such as Ben Jonson, who often invokes jury procedure in his drama, sometimes addressing the audience as a jury, does not figure prominently in this book. Trial by jury was instituted after 1220, more or less as an administrative expediency to replace trial by ordeal and other forms of proto-jury, and throughout its colourful history it has been marked most obviously by institutional conflict between court authority of judges and jury recalcitrance, each trying to nullify the other, rather than systematic appeals to fundamental principles except those implicit in the concept of trial by peers. There is no agreement among legal historians about some basic facts of the development of juries, especially during the period 1550 to 1650, but a cautious commentator suggests that by about the 1590s the judge-controlled jury prevailed, and that 'a modern era of greater sharing of power between judge and jury emerged fairly suddenly' during the interregnum, just before the Restoration.[21] There was only one brief, troubled age when jury trial was at least advocated by some as an arbiter of lawfinding through conscience, and that was, not surprisingly, during the commonwealth period, when the Levellers and Fifth Monarchists in particular attacked the common law as elitist, as favouring property owners, and as over-centralised.[22] Indeed, the call from radicals such as Lilburne and Walwyn, unheeded by parliaments, for law to be made by juries along the lines of 'equity, justice, and mercy' shows that they considered jury trial to be the people's equivalent of the royalists' equity system and the king's prerogative. All in all, during the Renaissance in England, the existence of rival machineries of justice, each making some appeal or challenge to Natural Law, inevitably confused and made contentious the concept itself, despite the widespread adherence to the rhetoric of reason and conscience.

### Saint German and others

The struggle in England between Natural Law and positive law fought between courts of equity and common law, king and parliament, was institutional in its nature, but there were some individuals who contributed to the debate. The most celebrated was St German, a contemporary of Thomas More, with whom he publicly disputed. In political terms, he began like More as a Catholic conservative supporting the rule of Rome, but moved much further than More ever did towards upholding parliament as England's decision-making body, rather than the pope. His book of Dialogues between *Doctor and Student*[23] was published first in Latin in 1523 and then again in 1530. It became so controversial that its first Book was translated into English (somewhat abridged) and was reprinted many times during the sixteenth century. It became an important statement of the issues at stake in the dialogue between common law and Chancery. The book seems to have been intended for a readership of non-lawyers. Unlike Aquinas' *Summa*, Christopher St German's *Doctor and Student* is not a book which deserves resurrection for its style. However controversial in its day, it is now laborious to read, and its details have little more than historical interest. However, the book was enormously influential, and, from my point of view, it is a crucial document, since it introduces into England in at least relatively palatable form the fundamental ideas of Natural Law. His main sources were Aquinas and Gerson, and there is little originality in St German's work, but in itself this was an important factor in injecting a 'faithful', scholastic account of Natural Law into the English life-blood. It is also important because it directly links equity and Natural Law, and attempts some compromise with common law.

St German sets up categories of law which are very close to those of Aquinas. 'Law eternal' is 'that supreme reason in God for governing things ... to a good and due end' (p. 9), and all other laws are derived from it. Doctor Faustus, he argues, violated this first 'legal obligation'. From this level are generated three different systems, since eternal law cannot directly be known, except through certain channels. First, it can be seen by 'creatures reasonable', 'by the light of natural reason' or 'natural understanding'. This St German calls 'the law of reason', but it is very clearly the same as Aquinas' Law of Nature, and indeed chunks of Aquinas are reproduced. 'This law stirs and inclines a man to good and abhorring evil. This law is immutable' (p. 15). The crucial phrase for the Law of Reason or Nature is 'reason will that such a thing be done' (p. 33). It teaches us to love good, flee evil, not to do to another what we would not have done to us; to do nothing against truth, to live peacefully with others, to ensure that justice is done to every man equally, and so on. The Law of Reason is written in the heart of every person, but it has been blinded by evil customs and original sin, which makes it necessary to have external laws made by princes or governors (positive law) since not everybody is in touch with the inner promptings of the Law of Reason. St German also mentions another channel for eternal law, namely divine revelation, but he does not expand on this except to refer to the laws revealed in the Bible. He more or less sets up this category in order to emphasise the discreteness of the Law of Reason which, he emphasises, is *not* based on revelation. To those who have followed the internal struggles over Natural Law given above, it will be clear that St German's watchword is *toujours la politesse*, as he refuses to be dogmatic about the problematical, political applications. His views came to be used in defence of different systems, ensuring, once again, some component of Natural Law in each.

St German, like Aquinas, says that the various forms of law are quite consistent with each other, although they exist on different levels of generality. This allows him, when he comes in the dialogue to describe the laws of England, to present equity and common law as complementary and mutual:

For like as makers of laws take heed to such things as may oft fall, and do most hurt among the people rather than to particular cases so in like wise the general grounds of the law of England, heed more what is good for many, than what is good for one singular person only ... and if such default happen in any one person, whereby he is without remedy at the common law; yet he may be holpen *in equity* by a sub pena, and so he may in other cases where conscience [is] for him, that were too long to rehearse now. (p. 79)

Equity is said to follow 'the intent of the law, rather than the words of the law' (p. 98). Unlike common law it considers the unique particularity of each case rather than its similarity to others, and it 'also is tempered with the sweetness of mercy' (p. 95). Because laws are necessarily general in their scope they can lead to decisions 'both against Justice and the common wealth' (p. 97) and here 'equity is ordained, that is to say to temper and mitigate the rigour of the law' (*ibid.*). The point about intention is an important distinction between equity and common law. Common law was based on a literal reading of older laws and was a judgment upon whether procedural forms of action had been correctly followed; equity could look behind both, seeking the spirit behind a law rather than the letter, and implementing the Sermon on the Mount's direction that sinful intentions are just as culpable as actions. It might be roughly accurate to say that St German's account presupposes that common law is based on Natural Law at the very source, in its basic laws, whereas in equity Natural Law is applied to the particular circumstances. English law, while it has never accepted that there can be a crime without an action, moved gradually towards a scrutiny of *mens rea*, the state of mind of the alleged criminal, seeking to know whether the intention in sound mind was to commit the crime or whether the actions were carried out negligently, ignorantly, accidentally, recklessly, or in self-defence.[24] In such ways common law could build into its basic framework some element of equity's principles.

In St German's account, the double springs of equity are reason and conscience, and he is perhaps most original in stressing conscience rather than reason. Whereas reason, although the noblest faculty which is capable of discriminating truth from falsehood and which, more importantly, indicates what should be done 'and *wants* it to be done' (85), yet it can be led astray by passion, imperfect knowledge, or an evil disposition. Conscience, however, derived etymologically from *scientia* and therefore a knowledge, is superior to reason because it cannot be led astray and it 'inclines the soul to pursue good and eschew evil' (p. 87). He defines the related concept of *synderesis* as a 'natural power or motive force of the rational soul set always in the highest part thereof, moving and stirring it to good, and abhorring evil [p. 81] ... And therefore synderesis is called by some men the law of reason, the which be in every man by nature in that he is a reasonable creature [p. 83] ... Again synderesis is sometimes called a spark of reason, and aptly so; for just as a spark is a mere fragment flying out of the fire, so this virtue is but a fragmentary participation in intelligence' (*ibid.*). On the other hand, the examples St German compiles indicate that he regards conscience itself as no ground for *enforcing* action on another person. Shylock cannot be compelled to change the terms of his contract with Antonio and take money instead of flesh, because, as St German would agree, such action must be left up to his own conscience: 'in the tribunal of conscience he certainly ought to

do so, if he would preserve a clear and healthy Conscience, even although
he cannot be compelled' (109) writes St German some seventy years
before *The Merchant of Venice*. The general drift of St German's
discussion is that decisions in equity are more morally compelling
(because they directly address morality) than those of common law, but
in practice they can be less effective as binding law. This is why common
law could place prohibitions on judgments at equity.

If anybody, then, created the opportunity for the reception of Natural
Law principles into England, it was St German. He may not have tipped
the balance inexorably towards equity, but his influential statement
ensured respect for Chancery, and also forced common law to accommodate some Natural Law content. For example, the fiction of the
'reasonable man', now enshrined in common law, was a direct consequence.[25] St German is said to have 'linked the medieval world and the
modern'.[26] Moreover, *Doctor and Student* ensured that in all forms of
law (common law, equity, parliamentary legislation) the rhetoric and
some substance of Natural Law reasoning were preserved. Francis
Bacon in the famous *Calvin's Case* (1608) couched his statement on the
underlying basis of law in these broad terms containing a touch of
complacency:

Is it not a common principle, that the law favoureth three things, life, liberty and
dower? And what is the reason of this favour? This, because our law is grounded
upon the law of nature, and these three things do flow from the law of nature;
preservation of life, natural; liberty, which every beast or bird seeketh and
affecteth, natural; the society of man and wife, whereof dower is the reward,
natural. It is well.[27]

More succinctly, John Doddridge in *The Lawyers Light* (1629), an
instructional manual for would-be lawyers, writes: 'A Ground, Rule, or
Principle, of the Law of England is a conclusion either of the Law of
Nature, or derived from some generall Custome used within the Realme'
(p. 6). William Lambarde is another humanist of the 1590s,[28] whose
work *Archeion or, a Discourse upon The High Courts of Justice in England*
(1591) was written for legal novitiates and those unlearned in the law. It
has been argued that his book and his person were known by Shakespeare and that they influenced the dramatist.[29] Lambarde clearly wished
to find some compromise between common law and equity:

For *written Laws* must needs be made in a generality, and be grounded upon that
which happeneth for the most part, because no wisdom of man can fore-see every
thing in particularity, which Experience and Time doth beget.
...
And therefore, although the *written Law* be generally good, and just; yet in
special case, it may have need of Correction ... And hereof this *Equity* ... doth

not only weigh what is generally meet for the most part, but doth also consider, the person, time, place, and other circumstances in every singular case that commeth in question, and doth thereof frame such judgement as is convenient and agreeable to the same ... (p. 43)

Lambarde's description of written law as 'like to a stiff rule of *Steel* or *Iron*' in contrast to the flexibility of equity, is likely to have influenced Spenser's creation in The Book of Justice in *The Faerie Queene* of the iron man, Talus, and the bearer of equity, Britomart. Lambarde, however, who himself worked in Chancery, is keen to conciliate common lawyers, and he describes the kind of 'good *Chancellour*' who will not make a 'violent irruption' upon the borders of common law and 'will so moderate his power, and provide, that the Gate of *Mercy* may be opened in all Calamity of Suit; to the end, (where need shall be) the Rigour of *Law* may be amended, and the short measure thereof extended by the true consideration of *Justice* and *Equity*' (p. 45). *Toujours la politesse* once again.

Central concepts from Natural Law, then, survived in sixteenth-century England partly through their incorporation into the system of equity which, while under siege, continued to be important. Common law may have been opposed to the central principle of justice lying within individuals, as Coke asserted, but this sceptical reasoning had not gone as far as Hobbes was to take it, and it was generally expected that the laws themselves would be consistent with Natural Law. Natural Law still provided the dominant model, and had to be favourably addressed, and preferably appropriated, by all those law-making systems which claimed secular authority.

### Hooker

By far the most important late sixteenth-century English text preserving and transmitting Natural Law principles was Richard Hooker's *Of The Laws of Ecclesiastical Polity*.[30] This work has been described as 'primarily the revision of St Thomas Aquinas in the light of medieval English law, Roman law, and the philosophy of Aristotle's *Politics*'.[31] Because *Ecclesiastical Polity* had clearly a political intent in seeking to influence the organisation of the Anglican Church (and in consequence state policy and the law), controversy has raged up to the present day about its significance. By adopting the medieval and Thomist form of the *Summa*, Hooker's strategy was to claim an olympian position above the fray of political infighting, but friends and foes alike would acknowledge that the book was a political intervention to consolidate Elizabeth's religious settlement, placate Rome, and to attack the Calvinists.[32] Where friend parts from foe in the critical debate is over the issue of Hooker's political stance on the issues of the day. Those sympathetic to radical Protestant opinion (and, as research is continually showing, there were more of these than traditional history records) would be alienated by Hooker's virulent attacks on Calvinists and more generally on Puritans as a group, whom he sees as next to atheists. Another negative view of Hooker is that he is unprincipled, a 'trimmer' or a man who for expedient reasons alone shifts and slides his attitudes. Puritans called him 'Jack Newter' implying that his various compromises cancel each other out and fill his work with contradictions. On the other hand, supporters of Hooker turn his capacity for compromise into a positive strength and he has been placed (with Shakespeare, Aristotle, and Aquinas) among those who are 'neither radicals nor conservatives, neither Papists nor Calvinists, neither entirely for the new movements nor opposed to the old movements'.[33] On the very English philosophy (ostensibly following Aristotle's *via media*)[34] that the world is made up of stark antitheses which we must reject in favour of a middle ground, Hooker has been praised for his judiciousness, his balance, his search for reconciliation, and his broad insight. He has also been condemned for complacency and conservatism at a time when necessary, radical change in English government seemed possible without bloodshed.

Whatever our attitude to Hooker's politics, his work is important in this context for reaffirming Natural Law as a presence in English justice available also for writers. It has been disputed whether his ethics follow more closely those of Aristotle or St Thomas Aquinas, whom he called 'the greatest amongst the School-divines' (III. ix. 2)[35] but his belief in reason as central to 'human Nature' and to moral choice is indisputable:

the nature of Goodness being thus ample, a Law is properly that which Reason in such sort defineth to be good that it must be done. And the Law of Reason or human Nature is that which men by discourse of natural Reason have rightly found out themselves to be all for ever bound unto in their action ... the works of Nature are all behoveful, beautiful, without superfluity or defect; even so theirs, if they be framed according to that which the Law of Reason teacheth. (I. viii. 9)

Hooker has so much confidence in reason as an instrument that, in comparison with Aquinas and St German, he tends to minimise the role of conscience. The desire to do good and shun evil, in his account, emerges not as a mysterious, god-given *synderesis*, but as a rational conclusion deduced from the Law of Nature. For example, he writes as follows: 'My desire to be loved of my equals in Nature as much as possible may be, imposeth upon me a natural duty of bearing to themward fully the like affection' (I. viii. 7). The appeal here is to reason, or what Hooker sometimes calls 'common sense', rather than to any mysteries of conscience, faith, or revelation. There is even an element of Benthamite utilitarianism in his linking of charity and self-interest. Hooker argues that the two broadest commandments – love God and love others – can be discovered in 'axioms and laws natural', through reason rather than revelation.

Hooker accepts as axiomatic Hippocrates' statement that 'each thing both in small and in great fulfilleth the task which destiny hath set down' (I. iii. 4), and in a series of eloquent examples he refers to a law for the rain, another for the sea, and others for 'those principal and mother elements of the world' (I. iii. 2), namely the physical world which would 'loosen and dissolve itself' if these laws are not obeyed. For man, creature of rationality, 'the task which destiny hath set down' is 'to know truth from falsehood, and good from evil' (I. viii. 3) and the instrument for such knowledge is 'the light of Reason'. The Law of Reason is created by God and is consistent with eternal law, but it is investigable by human reason itself, without the help of revelation. The law also takes permanent validity from its connection with eternal law:

the knowledge of them is general, the world hath always been acquainted with them ... It is not agreed upon by one, or two, or few, but by all ... this Law is such that being proposed no man can reject it as unreasonable and unjust. (I. viii. 9)

In orthodox fashion, Hooker distinguishes 'positive laws which men impose upon themselves' from Natural Law. 'In laws, that which is natural bindeth universally, that which is positive not so' (I. ix. 7). Like most of the theorists before and after him, Hooker follows St Paul [Romans ii. 13–15] in affirming that not only Christians can understand and obey Natural Law:

Under the name of the Law we must comprehend not only that which God hath written in tables and leaves, but that which nature also hath engraven in the hearts of men. Else how shall those heathen which never had books but heaven and earth to look upon be convicted of perverseness? But the Gentiles which had not the law in books, had, saith the Apostle, the effect of the law written in their hearts.[36]

Hooker sums up the 'common' nature of the Law which is variously called that of Nature and of Reason:

Law rational therefore, which men commonly use to call the Law of Nature, meaning thereby the Law which human Nature knoweth itself in reason universally bound unto, which also for the cause may be termed most fitly the

Law of Reason; this Law, I say, comprehendeth all those things which men by the light of their natural understanding evidently know, or at leastwise may know, to be beseeming or unbeseeming, virtuous or vicious, good or evil for them to do. (I. viii. 9)

Hooker's ringing words here will, we shall find, be directly echoed in Renaissance literary theory which makes imaginative literature into something akin to an enactment of Natural Law. His is a crucial restatement in the volatile decade of the 1590s of the powerful under-current of theory carried from Aristotle and Cicero through Aquinas and St German, an intervention of Natural Law on behalf of the Elizabethan settlement. Hooker not only kept Natural Law alive, but gave it new breath in the 1590s, when Shakespeare and Spenser were writing.

## Bacon

Francis Bacon, in his theology as in his politics, was often studiously equivocal. In *The Advancement of Learning* (1605) he discusses the concept of Natural Law, without using the term itself. At first he declares himself a nominalist: 'sacred theology ... is grounded only upon the word and oracle of God, and not upon the light of nature'.[37] This truth, he says, holds not only for points of faith like the creation and redemption, 'but likewise those which concern the law moral truly interpreted'. But, as the father of empirical science in England, Bacon is using the word nature in his own way, signifying the natural world which is external to the human mind, the observable phenomena of God's creation. Therefore, when he affirms that the moral law 'is a voice beyond the light of nature', he does not necessarily mean it is entirely beyond the capacities of the human mind to comprehend:

So it must be confessed, that a great part of the law moral is of that perfection, whereunto the light of nature cannot aspire: how then is it that man is said to have, by the light and law of nature, some notions and conceits of virtue and vice, justice and wrong, good and evil? thus, because the light of nature is used in several senses; the one, that which springeth from reason, sense, induction, argument, according to the laws of heaven and earth; the other, that which is imprinted upon the spirit of man by an inward instinct, according to the law of conscience, which is a sparkle of the purity of his first estate; in which latter sense only he is participant of some light and discerning touching the perfection of the moral law: but how? sufficient to check the vice, but not to inform the duty. So then the doctrine of religion, as well moral as mystical, is not to be attained but by inspiration and revelation from God. (p. 201)

Bacon does, and does not, affirm Natural Law. On the one hand, conscience is 'imprinted upon the spirit of man by an inward instinct', a 'sparkle' and 'light' which can make us recognise vice, but, on the other, reason is a more earth-bound faculty, given by heaven but limited by the physical reality in which people live and of which they are a part. We know what *not* to do, but it is harder to know what we *should* do, except by revelation. He does, however, give a 'very great and general' latitude to the operation of reason so long as it is guided by belief and faith rather than becoming an end in itself. Human reason is capable of unravelling 'the conception and apprehension of the mysteries of God' (p. 202), but 'by way of illustration, and not by way of argument'. Both human observation and divine revelation are equally essential to the operation of reason properly used. Bacon likens reason in this sense to the key to a lock. To make things even more complicated, he makes a further distinction between this 'original and absolute' reason and a 'secondary and respective' reason which enables us to make derivations and inferences through analogy, about things which are not directly observable, 'exempted from examination of reason'. Thinking again through images, he draws the comparison with a game like chess, where there are a priori ground-rules which cannot be examinable by reason, but in directing the play reason is quite sufficient. So we must simply accept God's 'absolute' maxims but our own human, positive laws can be constructed by using reason and analogy. Bacon finally tends to duck away from explaining the basis of God's prior laws, not surprisingly if they are beyond inspection by reason 'but what is most just, not absolutely but relatively, and according to those maxims, that affordeth a long field of disputation' (p. 203).

Bacon's need to make apparently supersubtle distinctions within nature and reason, lies in his overall programme of the advancement of learning, which both empowers and delimits the scope of human reason. If God has given the world as a mystery which can be understood in its particularity by humans, then the extraordinary, 'great and blessed' capacity which man uses is reason. But reason cannot be used 'to search and mine into that which is not revealed' like a kind of 'divine dialectic'. Those thinkers who seek to give reason a wider latitude, in Bacon's view, fall into the error of 'demanding to have things made more sensible than it pleaseth God to reveal them'.

On the questions of law and justice themselves, Bacon is just as finely balanced. He condemns philosophers who, like More's Raphael Hythlodaeus and perhaps Natural Lawyers in general, create 'imaginary laws for imaginary commonwealths' (p. 198) since 'their discourses are as the stars, which give little light because they are so high'. He equally condemns positive lawyers who 'write according to the states where they live what is received law, and not what ought to be law'. On the other hand, he does go on to say that 'there are in nature certain fountains of justice, whence all civil laws are derived but as streams', and he asserts that laws in different societies, while differing from each other all ultimately proceed from the same fountain. It is the job of the statesman (neither philosopher nor lawyer) to ascertain the appropriateness of law in particular circumstances, and to make judgments like 'how they are to be pressed, rigorously or tenderly; how they are to be mitigated by equity and good conscience, and whether discretion and strict law are to be mingled in the same courts'. (Bacon at this stage of his career was King's Counsel, a common lawyer, and much later in 1618 he was to be made Lord Chancellor and head of equity.) But, as in his discussion of reason, Bacon seems to be ultimately agnostic on the issue of Natural Law itself, not trying to explain how the 'fountain' of absolute justice found its way into men's dealings. The general intention of his *The Advancement of Learning* is to locate defects and matters for investigation rather than give firm answers, and this is his justification for some calculated obscurity.

## Spenser's Book of Justice[38]

In order to demonstrate the relevance of legal concepts to Renaissance literature, we may turn to *The Faerie Queene* Book 5, Edmund Spenser's Book of Justice. Artegall, a kind of travelling assizes in the common-law system,[39] pursues endlessly the quest of imposing law and order on a society which reflects largely the chaotic state of a resistant Ireland in which the author worked. Later Artegall is assisted and even rescued by Britomart who, in this Book, plays the role of equity. Spenser gives us in characteristically allegorical fashion his own brief history of the reception of Natural Law into positive law, and his own account of the relationship between common law and equity.

Spenser's initial fable of the inception of justice makes it clear that Natural Law in its purest form is the basis and measure of all human law. In the Proem to Book 5 he harks back to a perfect, prelapsarian (and even pre-Christian) time:

> For during *Saturnes* ancient raigne it's sayd,
> That all the world with goodnesse did abound:
> All loued vertue, no man was affrayd
> Of force, ne fraud in wight was to be found:
> No warre was knowne, no dreadfull trompets sound,
> Peace vniuersall rayn'd mongst men and beasts,
> And all things freely grew out of the ground:
> Iustice sate high ador'd with solemn feasts,
> And to all people did diuide her dred beheasts.                (V. proem. 9)

This is the vision of original innocence which lies at the heart of Natural Law thinking. People are innately aware of good and evil, and equally innately they tend towards virtue, peace, and living in harmony with beasts and the natural world. 'All things freely grow out of the ground', and mankind takes guidance from them. This is the natural state in which Natural Law prevails unchallenged. In the next canto, Spenser Christianises the idea, saying that justice itself is 'Most sacred vertue she of all the rest, Resembling God in his imperiall might.' It is consistent with Aquinas to say that Natural Law 'resembles' God but is not the same as eternal law which God alone can know. In terms of the narrative, Artegall is presented as 'the instrument' of justice in the fallen world. He takes over from Astraea who, when the world began to abound with sin, departed to heaven to preside over 'euerlasting' justice (V. i. 11). It is Astraea, the embodiment of perfect justice, a mover between heaven and earth, who is the personification of Natural Law, while Artegall must implement her decrees through positive law. The link between the human world and divine law is now a fragile one, for Astraea has withdrawn and Artegall is part of the fallen world himself, with human fallibilities such as anger and inappropriate pity, particularly for women.[40]

Spenser places himself on the conservative side in the sixteenth- and seventeenth-centuries' debate about the monarch's authority, for, like Fortescue, he transfers directly to 'Princes' the capacity to understand, embody and instinctively administer true justice. This inevitably leads to a Spenserian eulogy to 'Dread Souerayne Goddesse, that doest highest sit / In seate of iudgement, in th'Almighties place' who is simultaneously Astraea, the Faerie Queene and Elizabeth. There is, however, a warning to rulers that they must not become tyrants. Readers have met Artegall earlier in the work (III. 2. 17ff., III. 3. 26ff., IV. vi. 42–6), mainly as the future lover of Britomart, but it is significant that Spenser recalls him as a scourge of tyranny, and links him with Hercules who 'monstrous tyrants with this club subdewed' (V. i. 2).[41] In Book 5 also, Artegall is engaged in campaigns against tyranny of one sort or another, sometimes aimed at him personally and sometimes at others. This is Spenser's quiet hint to princes and rulers that if they neglect abstract justice and Natural Law, they will be punished as tyrants. The overall quest upon which Artegall is sent is to free Irena from a tyrant Grantorto, a thinly disguised reflection of Spenser's own minor role in the major task, as he explained it in the *View*, of restoring Ireland to a state of antique virtue, and freeing it from the evil of Rome. Public justice, not individual conscience, is the bulwark against tyranny.

Artegall was brought up in the ways of Natural Law. Chosen in his infancy by Astraea, he is persuaded to accompany her, 'Into a caue from companie exilde', and there he is instructed in justice: 'In which she noursled him, till years he raught, And all the discipline of iustice there him taught' (V. i. 6). He is taught both Aristotelian distributive justice and also equity, and Astraea's pedagogical method is to encourage him to observe and practise on wild animals.

> There she him taught to weigh both right and wrong
> In equall ballance with due recompence,
> And equitie to measure out along,
> According to the line of conscience,
> When so it needs with rigour to dispence.
> Of all the which, for want there of mankind,
> She caused him to make experience
> Vpon wyld beasts, which she in woods did find,
> With wrongfull powre oppressing others of their kind. (V. i. 7)

At this stage Artegall does not represent the limited jurisdiction of common law, but all human law which is in accordance with Natural Law, and at this time there is no need for further distinctions. We are reminded that Artegall earlier had appeared in the guise of the Savage Knight, savagery here meaning something like Rousseau's primitive nobleman who is instinctively moral rather than consciously so, and 'salvageable' to polite society. He is linked, then, with the order of nature, implying not only that he is an instrument of Natural Law but also that justice itself, in Spenser's view as in that of other writers of the time, is the most fundamentally natural faculty of all, even if many have lost touch with it.[42] This is an important admission in a work which presents the world as a dichotomy between layers of illusion placed upon natural truth.

But, even if justice is natural, in Spenser's view, as in Calvin's, fallen mankind needs strong positive laws to compensate for the dimming light of instinct. Even Artegall's innate tendency needs to be 'trayned' and 'taught' by Astraea, until animals and men fear and admire him. He represents the most effective form of positive law available in the fallen world, although the very fact of the Fall means he has human flaws. What the people he encounters in his travels fear is 'the horror of his wreakfull hand, When so he list in wrath lift vp his steely brand' (V. i. 8), for Astraea had given Artegall a sword with a mighty history 'to make him dreaded more' (V. i. 9). This is the first of many references to his righteous anger, and can be linked with his other characteristic emotion, compassion for the weak. He is no inhuman force, and his capacity to be fair and impartial in his judgements springs as much from his emotions as his mind: a sense of injustice moves him emotionally to anger and pity. However, his emotiveness also gets him into trouble, for it leads him to overreact to situations, and leads him into compromising positions such as his entrapment by Radigund. To be driven by feelings is not entirely out of line with classic Natural Law thinking, although reason is the necessary brake which Artegall does not always practise. Because of his flaws and limitations, another kind of justice will be required. The alternative conception of justice as a blind figure, without feelings, and detached from emotion to the point of indifference, belongs within the function of what we now call the police-force, public executioner (in more barbaric, recent times), and prison officers. Such professionals are involved in the administration of justice rather than in issues of justice itself, and they are expected to be competent, consistent, and not to exceed their limited briefs by exercising discretion. Spenser does give us such a figure in Talus.

Talus is the executor of justice. He is appointed by Astraea to serve Artegall, just before she parts from the earth and retires to heaven. To most modern readers he is a truly gruesome figure and at one stage his 'cruell deed' horrifies even Artegall who 'commaunde[s] him from slaughter to recoyle' (V. xi. 65). This effect is partly intended, for punishment should be such a terrifying spectacle that wrongdoing is deterred, in a world where natural virtue does not automatically prevail. Like all law enforcers, Talus simply does what he is told and he does it with relentless efficiency. 'His name was *Talus*, made of yron mould, Immoueable, resistlesse, without end' (V. i. 12). The very name recalls public revenge for wrongdoing, *talionis*. His weapon is an iron 'flayle', perhaps the agricultural tool used to beat grain in order to separate the wheat from the chaff, with which he sets about scourging enemies of the peace, separating good from bad. He acts so mechanically that the initial horror he evokes in readers turns, surely without Spenser intending it, into something comic. His main function is to separate legal judgment from actual punishment, a distinction which becomes problematical in Shakespeare's *Measure for Measure* in a way that Spenser avoids.

Artegall and Talus set out on their mission to liberate Irena from Grantorto. On the way they encounter various situations which call for the exercise and administration of justice. Spenser's characteristically episodic technique dominates. In the first five books, most of the 'cases' (in the legal sense) illustrate some aspect of Natural Law as it has been positively codified within what could be broadly called common-law offences, and the most recurrent are those relating to property and violence to the person. In the next three books, Spenser introduces equity, and the final books move into the realm of international law and England's foreign policy, as well as depicting allegorically the trial of Mary Stuart. As Michael O'Connell summarises, 'The thematic movement of the book, then, is outward from the common operations of English law to the place of England in establishing justice among nations.'[43]

The other major figure in Book 5 is Britomart, the Amazonian champion of chastity and friendship. Britomart, of course, has appeared before Book 5, but her function now changes in partnership with Artegall. Whereas in Books 3 and 4 her role was knight of Chastity, involved in interpersonal emotional relationships as she herself prepares for marriage, now she becomes an aspect of justice itself, complementary to Artegall in a legal sense. To be precise, she represents 'That part of Iustice, which is Equity' (V. vii. 3), which in the sixteenth century was seen as 'woman's law', particularly when administered under Queen Elizabeth.[44] We are primed for her taking on this mantle when we realise that it is she who must come to rescue Artegall when he is imprisoned through his own fault by Radigund. Equity must come to the aid of common law when the latter fails or is insufficient. Her close identification with Artegall as judiciar, shown in her first vision of him in Merlin's mirror, is stressed through the fact that she is mistaken for him by Dolon, 'a man of subtill wit and wicked minde' (V. vi. 32), whose son had been slain by Artegall for treason. The mistaken identity is caused by 'many tokens', but especially by the presence of Talus who is travelling with Britomart, another sign that she is at this stage undertaking a quest on behalf of justice. Her version, however, excludes anger and includes mercy.

Britomart's education into her legal function is completed in Isis Church, in an episode which is a centrepiece of Book 5. Canto vii begins with a celebration of 'true iustice' as the highest virtue. The pagan myth of Osyris is recalled, 'the iustest man aliue, and truest did appeare' (V. vii. 2) who came to signify the sun. Isis, portending the moon, is his wife:

> His wife was *Isis*, whom they likewise made
> A Goddesse of great powre and soueraity,
> And in her person cunningly did shade
> That part of Iustice, which is Equity,
> Whereof I haue to treat here presently.
> Vnto whose temple when as *Britomart*
> Arriued, shee with great humility
> Did enter in, ne would that night depart;
> But *Talus* mote not be admitted to her part.          (V. vii. 3)

Osyris and Isis are, like Artegall and Britomart, complementary systems of justice. The fact that Talus cannot enter has twofold significance. As a man of force he cannot enter this place of peace, and as executive of justice he must be once again distanced from the source of judgment.

Furthermore, in equity mercy can overrule strict legal judgment. Even Artegall would not be allowed in, for it is Britomart's domain. The presiding figure is an idol of a crowned female, married to Osyris who is a mythological equivalent of Artegall. Inevitably implying a prechristian anticipation of Elizabeth I, Isis has one foot on a crocodile and the other on the ground, 'So meaning' the poetry tells us 'to suppresse both forged guile, And open force' (V. vii. 7). Her priests did not sleep on beds, 'But on their mother Earths deare lap did lie' (V. vii. 9), as mortification of the flesh but also, it might be argued, because equity was the legal system closest to the Law of Nature. Britomart sleeps 'Vnder the wings of *Isis* all that night' (V. vii. 12), and in a dream vision she has her future revealed. In the vision she sees her linen stole transformed into a robe of red scarlet and her crescent mitre changed to a gold crown, clearly the trappings of regal control of equity through the Court of Chancery. A tempest below her whips up the embers of the fire and threatens to burn the temple. This may be Spenser's allegory for the religious struggle between Rome and England, with the legal analogy of the attacks made by Roman civil law on English law during Spenser's century (although, ironically, equity through its ecclesiastical connection, had roots in civil law: a kind of 'false equity' may be figured in Radigund). The sleeping crocodile wakes and devours the flames and tempest, threatening to eat her also (as common law threatened to swallow up the work of equity), until she beats him back with a rod into humility, just as Britomart must restrain and temper the anger of Artegall, and equity must add mercy to common-law justice. They fall in love and produce a lion that subdues all other beasts: England in its national glory. When she awakens, Britomart is told that the vision is a prophecy; the crocodile, transformed into a 'righteous Knight, that is thy faithfull louer' (V. vii. 22) is Artegall to her, just as Osyris is to Isis. It is said that Isis/Britomart through 'clemence oft in things amis' will restrain 'those sterne behests, and cruell doomes' of Osyris/Artegall. This is precisely the relationship between common law and equity in the sixteenth century, at least in theory, and Spenser hints that equity is feminine in its nature, common law masculine. As W. Nicholas Knight points out, equity in the Book of Justice is firmly associated with women: 'Spenser employs four female figures connected with or representing equity: Astraea teaches equity to Artegall; Isis signifies that part of Justice which is equity and educates Britomart in its principles; Britomart in turn conveys her knowledge to Artegall; and Mercilla presides over cases of equity.'[45] This accords with the social reality that equity was the court sought by women and poorer people.[46] Equity is based on 'clemency' whereas common law insisted on the letter of the law in strict application. After this episode, Britomart's future function is clear, and she moves on boldly and confidently to liberate her lover.

At this stage I should express some doubts about the place of equity in Spenser's overall view of law, lest the analysis misrepresent the treatment in *The Faerie Queene* by oversimplification. While we can see exactly how the allegory works in this sequence, it does not have the seamless unity of vision that other Spenserian set-pieces exhibit. There are uneasy notes in the shifting attitude to the crocodile (although, as Donald Cheney warns, 'in the shifting sands of Spenser's allegory syllogisms are often treacherous'),[47] and in the light of the Protestant Spenser's aversion to 'idols' of any kind, Isis is perhaps a little too idol-like for comfort. Given his ideology of the 'naturalness' of male domination, there is also something false about the apparent dominance of equity in this vision, and questions are raised about whether its legislation extends far outside Isis' church, in Spenser's version of 'the real world'. These tensions and ambivalences may have their explanations in the present reality for Spenser. Equity and common law were not reconciled in England, and in the particular case of Ireland at least, and probably more broadly, he rarely shows clemency playing much part in his vision of justice. The allegory may pay lip-service to a message which Spenser does not entirely endorse, although he can hardly express doubts too loudly, particularly since he himself was for a time a clerk for the Court of Chancery in Ireland. (We cannot make too much of this fact, for his position, unlike More's, appears to have been the very lowly one of merely issuing licences, and the experience may even have persuaded him of the relative inefficacy or at most supplementary nature of equity, beside common law and statute law.) It is significant that equity plays little or no part in the discussion of law in *A View of the Present State of Ireland*, and even in *The Faerie Queene* he seems to restrict its operation to rare cases.

These kinds of doubts make me finally unconvinced by the central argument of W. Nicholas Knight that Book 5 is dominated by issues of equity. Spenser seems to me a fairly consistent legal positivist, despite his tracing of all law back to Natural Law, and his schematic presentation of equity. Knight's article is fine and detailed, not incompatible with the approach adopted here, and we agree on many points of detail, but Knight seems to give a wider jurisdiction to equity than Spenser. It is misleading if not wrong, for example, to stress as he does legal possession of property as the arena where equity exclusively prevails, since property law was exactly the terrain the two systems were contending over. The emphasis I have understood from Book 5 is that justice in the sixteenth century (as now) in England is *all* dispensed under the name of the monarch and Artegall, in the sense that Justice itself constitutes the whole. Within this, the overwhelming jurisdiction belongs to common law. It is only occasionally that common law needs 'rescuing' by the residual jurisdiction of equity, the area under the Queen's personal control, either through royal prerogative or equity. Each of the different branches of the law, in theory, was consistent with the other and with Natural Law, however in certain cases the dominant system of common law needs supplementation from equity alone in order to achieve 'true' justice, particularly when a woman has caused the problem. We have seen that Artegall was taught the principles of judging equitably (which initially means simply 'fairly' in the world before distinctive legal jurisdictions) by his training in Natural Law under Astraea, but, at the same time, in some cases harsh justice must be tempered. The book, like Spenser's *View of Ireland*, leaves no doubt that common law is primary in his account of justice.

Artegall's imprisonment by Radigund shows common law's strict enforcement of the letter of a contract paradoxically trapping itself into an inflexible position, from which it needs to be released by equity: *The Merchant of Venice*, if it had been set in England, would have given a precise comparison. Such is a case where the figure of Britomart is required, and where equity operates in *The Faerie Queene*. Britomart is ashamed and embarrassed to find her heroic lover entrapped by a woman and even dressed in female clothes. The case is rather complex because Radigund is presented ambiguously. She is a natural rival to Britomart (like Mary Queen of Scots) but she seems also to have kinship in having the ability, as did the Church of Rome, to make law (for example, in her judgment over Sir Terpine, which Artegall reverses). Spenser's usual way of showing kinship within antagonism is to confuse the pronouns when they are in battle, and this happens in the fight between Britomart and Radigund. Radigund seems to represent some rival, quasi-equitable, but ultimately false, legal system. Since Radigund is an Amazon, it seems to represent an overbalance of the kind of law Britomart dispenses, and it certainly reverses what Spenser regards as the 'natural' order of male domination (except, of course, in the case of Queen Elizabeth). After Britomart releases Artegall from his captivity, she is herself put back into her place as subsidiary to him, in the male-dominated view of Spenser who, after using her as agent for Artegall's release, then requires her to change the form of the Amazonian 'common weale' to restore male dominance:

> The liberty of women did repeale,
> Which they had long vsurpt; and then restoring
> To mens subiection, did true Iustice deale:     (V. vii. 42)

This action is said to bring Britomart the admiration and adoration of
the formerly free women, in what we might sceptically see as a spectacular manifestation of false consciousness: 'true Iustice' is clearly male.
Duessa is the other arch-villainess of the whole *Faerie Queene*, and we
notice that in this book all the wicked men are sustained and urged on by
wicked wives and daughters. Behind the lawless violence of the Souldan
lies his sinister wife, Adicia, 'Injustice'. As in his defence of the economic
status quo, Spenser uses a form of Natural Law to rationalise his
questionable attitude to women:

> Such is the crueltie of womenkynd,
> When they have shaken off the shamefast band,
> With which wise Nature did them strongly bynd,
> T'obay the heasts of mans well ruling hand,
> That then all rule and reason they withstand,
> To purchase a licentious libertie.
> But vertuous women wisely vnderstand,
> That they were borne to base humilitie,
> Vnlesse the heauens them lift to lawfull soueraintie.          (V. v. 25)

Once again, we find the adaptibility of Natural Law to rationalise quite
diverse and opposite positions, and the part of equity is further
restricted.[48]

Artegall is released and reconciled with Britomart – common law and
equity are symbolically if not literally wedded – and Artegall, back on his
quest, joins up with Arthur, symbol of magnanimity. Together, Artegall
and Arthur defeat the fundamental threats to justice, the Souldan who
represents 'lawlesse power and tortious wrong' (V. ix. 51) and Malengin
('Evil Nature', 'Guile'), apparently a figure deriving from nature but only
the nature of wild beasts. Malengin is nature without reason or conscience, an oily and plausible trickster who can continually change his
shape into aspects of nature, a fox, a bush, a stone, a hedgehog, in order
to escape justice. He spends his days fishing for fools (V. ix. 11). Just as
there are images of false justice, false law, and false equity, so Malengin
is an image of false nature, a precursor of Shakespeare's Edmond. Whilst
he lives in nature he exploits it rather than being a part of it in the
natural order of things. In Spenser's characteristic allegorical strategy,
evil shadows good with dangerously alluring but false equivalents, and
the ultimate touchstone is Natural Law.

The full English legal system and its methods of doing justice are laid
out in the heraldic episode in Mercilla's palace in canto ix. All the
conditions are ready for such a comprehensive overview. This court is
the full bench of justice, representing common law, statute law, and
equity sitting together, as happened in the trial of Mary Stuart, Queen

of Scots (1587). Mercilla is, of course, the sovereign Queen Elizabeth, but she is also the system of justice in its entirety, including, as her name indicates, mercy and conscience, neither of which is institutionally available within common law alone, which needs the help of equity. Artegall and Arthur are guided through her palace, which is described in terms of a court of law. A figure resembling a giant called Awe sits outside 'To keepe out guyle, and malice, and despight.' The first hall is full of 'people making troublous din' and the picture presented is similar to contemporary descriptions of the Court of Chancery with many plaintiffs clamouring for justice. Through the press comes Order who commands peace and guides them further. They now see the peaceful workings of those 'dealing iust iudgements' that cannot be broken with bribes or threats. Finally, they reach the presence of the Queen on her golden throne, the lion of England firmly controlled under her feet. She holds the sceptre of justice 'The sacred pledge of peace and clemencie' (V. ix. 30).

Artegall and Arthur then witness a trial in process. It is not just any trial, but the one which was most traumatic to England and Elizabeth, that of Mary Stuart for treason, figured in Duessa, the allegorical figure who is behind much of the evil in *The Faerie Queene*. The prosecuting barrister is Zele who pursues his case on strictly legal grounds, using Authority, 'the law of *Nations*', Religion, and Justice. Mary's trial was unusual in that, because of its perceived seriousness, it involved both common law and equity. The defence is able to bring forward only advocates who more or less admit guilt by appealing beyond law to mercy: Pity, Regard of womanhead, Danger, Nobility of birth, and Grief. Zele returns with his eponymous zealousness to the attack, bringing forward Ate, Murder, Sedition, Incontinence, Adultery, and Impiety as aspects of Duessa's treasonable crimes: all outlawed by common law or statute. The respective responses of Arthur and Artegall are significant. Arthur, the more regal figure, is at first struck with pity and inclined towards mercy but is persuaded out of his feelings, while Artegall, legalistic and not at this stage in need of equitable assistance, agrees with Zele 'with constant firme intent' (V. ix. 49). When Mercilla comes to give judgement, Spenser is at his most opaquely non-commital. Mercilla's 'princely breast' is filled with 'piteous ruth' so her feelings are inclined to the clemency of equity, but she can see that the verdict is overwhelmingly guilty. Equity is theoretically available, but Spenser rules out its operation here. It is curious, given the fact that Elizabeth did eventually order the execution of her sister after apparently agonising for some time, that Spenser does not quite give this resolution.

Yet would not let iust vengeance on her light;
But rather let in stead thereof to fall
Few perling drops from her faire lampes of light;
The which she couering with her purple pall
Would haue the passion hid, and vp arose withall.                    (V. ix. 50)

Spenser is obviously engaged in some enormous feat of political reticence
and diplomacy in order to avoid the fate of the poet accused of bad faith,
but just why he does not simply represent the historical fact is unclear.
Nor does the reference in canto x, verse 4 help, since, although it refers to
the 'wretched corse' of Duessa and speaks of a 'strong constraint' which
enforced Mercilla to action, yet there is still no frank mention of the
death sentence, and the stress is again on Mercilla's 'more then needfull
naturall remorse' ('natural' here because of her kinship with the accused).
There is a hint that equity and common law are at odds and Elizabeth
does not exercise her equitable prerogative.[49] 'Conscience' cuts two ways
here, for the 'naturall' law would take account of relationship by kin –
'bands of nature, that wilde beastes restraine' (V. xii. 1) – as well as
public interest, just as in Sidney's *Arcadia*, where Basilius discovers that
he is presiding over the trial of his nephews, and must overrule his
human feelings in the interests of public justice. Given Elizabeth's well-
known reluctance to bring judgment against her sister, Spenser's allegory
may suggest that for the good of the nation she should relinquish
personal responsibility and simply let law itself dictate the result. This
indeed would be a tactful and cautious gloss for a poet to make when
representing one of the most volatile issues in the period. It is one of the
ironies of history that it was the very law of kind which got him into
trouble with King James, who objected to Spenser's treatment. But
despite the velleities of the allegory, the overall intention is clear: Mercilla
is the new Astraea, exercising 'a subtle mingling of strict justice with the
restraining powers of prudence and mercy'.[50] In this case, since Duessa
poses a threat to Mercilla's authority, mercy cannot be invoked.

Although Spenser presupposes an 'ur-text' of Natural Law lying
behind positive law, existing in a lost, golden world, and gives equity a
limited jurisdiction alongside common law and statute law in his scheme
of justice, he is, on the evidence of Book 5, predominantly an advocate of
common law and positive law strictly enforced. His general view is the
Calvinist one, that fallen man has lost touch with innate knowledge of
Natural Law. Artegall's wrath and the remorselessness of Talus dominate the spirit of the Book, despite the countervailing influence of
Britomart, Isis, and Mercilla. Certainly Spenser's attitude to policies in
Ireland, and his generally jaundiced view of the English court, could well

have led him to a harsher view of justice than the existing institutions quite allowed, and his final image in the book allegorises Lord Grey as a deeply misunderstood hero who could not finish his task in bringing Ireland under legal submission to common law. Politically, Spenser seems to embrace what was to become the Hobbesian position that strong social control is necessary because people left to their own devices no longer have the resources of reason and conscience even to know, let alone to act, in accord with the Law of Nature. Only in the Golden Age of Saturn was this harmony possible, and the Iron Age was far removed from the contemporary state. As Donald Cheney points out, Spenser makes it clear that there is no return in Spenser's vision to Astraea's state of peace, and that the theological division inexorably applies: *ante legem* (Astraea and Natural Law), *sub lege* (Artegall's administration), and *sub gratia* (the need for Christian redemption).[51] Book 5 is the one Book of *The Faerie Queene* where it could legitimately be argued that Spenser was too professionally implicated in the politics of his day, with their conflicting ideologies, factional struggle, obdurate historical facts, and changing alliances, to maintain a consistent line of vision. None the less, he offers in poetry a colourful, allegorical account of the whole legal picture as we have seen it historically evolve in England: Natural Law in paradise is received into the fallen world as Artegall's common law, which in turn is complemented and supplemented by Britomart's equity as an extension of her role as Knight of Chastity, and Mercilla's royal prerogative. Still, however, the reservation must be registered that Spenser is much more of a legal positivist than an advocate of classical Natural Law, as an inner resource available to individual human beings.

Even if a range of different attitudes towards Natural Law was generated in the English Renaissance, the model itself was alive and thriving. In the early part of the period, its main institutional context was the Court of Chancery, court of the king's conscience, equity; while, during the Commonwealth, Natural Law was openly debated by some as a preferred basis for parliamentary legislation and the rectification of injustices. The chequered but not inglorious history of Natural Law thinking after Shakespeare's time is continued in the last two chapters of my study. It may have had a resurgence in Milton's works, and been eclipsed after 1660, just as equity and poetic justice themselves hardened into more or less forms of positive laws, but from beyond many apparent graves the concept has periodically been revived in the particular circumstances of different historical and political contexts. In the meantime, the main purposes of these early chapters are to establish the pervasiveness and importance of the theory in the sixteenth century, and to indicate its key precepts, potential contradictions, and debating points. Not only was it impossible for imaginative writers alert to burning contemporary issues to be ignorant of Natural Law, but also the doctrine supplied them with a perfect model for effecting their own primary, poetic objectives, to teach and delight. Liberated from factuality by the medium of fiction, they could claim to themselves the territory of a moral law, governed by reason, mercy, and conscience, beyond arid technicalities analogous to English common-law procedure. They could then create fictions in exactly the way lawyers did, to find just solutions to problems where two systems of law clashed, positive law and Natural Law, or at least to highlight problems and exploit their dramatic significance, in such cases. The period can justifiably be seen as one of the few epochs when poets could confidently claim to wear the mantle of unacknowledged legislators of the world.

# 4 Law and literature in sixteenth-century England

Poets were not reticent about claiming for themselves, in George Puttenham's words, the roles of 'the first priests, the first prophets, the first legislators and politicians in the world'.

And for that they were aged and grave men, and of much wisdom and experience in th'affairs of the world, they were the first lawmakers to the people, and the first politicians, devising all expedient means for the establishment of Common wealth, to hold and contain the people in order and duty by force and virtue of good and wholesome laws, made for the persuasion of the public peace and tranquillity.[1]

Puttenham was no stranger to the law, a fact which might give added emphasis to his point. He was related to distinguished lawyers, and was a lawyer himself, having attended the Middle Temple in the late 1550s.[2] His own career as lawyer and apologist for poetry epitomises the closeness of these pursuits in the Renaissance. Not only did he rub shoulders at the Inns of Court with poets and poets-to-be, not only did he share the common aim of rhetoric employed in a forensic oratory and poetry ('persuasion of the public peace and tranquillity'), not only would he have understood the nature of legal fictions and poetic fictions, but he also sees the deeper theoretical issues, later plumbed by Sidney, implicit in his statement that poets 'were the first lawmakers to the people'. Each of these aspects of the close relationship in the Renaissance between law and poetry deserves attention, and by a circuitous route we shall find ourselves back to the Law of Nature. For if a belief prevailed that law and justice are innate to human beings as part of their very nature, stemming from a transcendent reason informed by conscience, then writers who had always been credited with superior capacity to reflect upon human potential were ideally placed to draw upon this source of knowledge. However, the fact that they knew enough about law to make such claims is based on a community between lawyers and poets in Elizabethan England.

### Inns of Court

Ben Jonson dedicated the printed version of *Every Man out of his Humour* (1616) 'To the Noblest Nurseries of Humanity, and Liberty, in the Kingdom: the Inns of Court' Even after admitting that many of his drinking companions at the Mermaid Tavern were lawyers, that he was a friend of the great legal thinker John Selden, and that there were many occasions on which he needed expert legal advice himself, the very fact that one of the foremost dramatists of the day could pay so fulsome a homage to an ostensibly legal institution is telling evidence of the closeness of literature and the law. Jonson himself in his plays alludes many times to legal practices, but, since his imagery is entirely from the common law rather than Natural Law, he must await another chronicler.

Since some informative books have been written on the Inns of Court, including Wilfrid Prest's *The Inns of Court under Elizabeth 1 and The Early Stuarts*,[3] S. F. Johnson's *Early Elizabethan Tragedies of the Inns of Court*,[4] and Philip Finkelpearl's *John Marston of the Middle Temple*,[5] we need not tarry too long but simply restate some salient facts. The Inns of Court as a group were called by Sir George Buck in 1612 'The third University of England'. By Elizabeth's time there were four Inns – Inner Temple, Lincoln's Inn, Middle Temple, and Gray's Inn. To each was attached one or more Inns of Chancery (eight in all) which were considerably less prestigious. They were so-called not because they taught equity or Roman civil law (which was the preserve of Oxford and Cambridge) but because clerks of the Chancery traditionally resided there. So did Shakespeare's Justice Shallow in his youth, and perhaps Sir John Falstaff: 'I was once of Clement's Inn, where I think they will talk of mad Shallow yet' (*2 Henry IV*, III. ii. 14). Shallow's lively misrememberings of his escapades do catch an aspect of the life of the Inns in general. There were also, according to Stow in his *Survey of London* (1598), fourteen 'houses of students in the common law' and two Serjeants' Inns.[6] The key to these institutions lies in the fact that they were not solely, nor even primarily, organised to teach law, but rather they were societies or guilds, existing not only with the authority to call to the bar, but also to instil a sense of community amongst men who might or might not become lawyers or influential figures at Elizabeth's court. Those who seriously intended to pursue a legal career entered an Inn in the status of an apprentice rather than a student in the modern sense. It is not at all surprising, then, to find the future luminaries of the law such as Bacon, Hooker, and Coke rubbing shoulders with hundreds of nonentities whose respective commitment to a career in common law varied considerably each to each. Others, such as Sir Philip Sidney (who entered Gray's Inn at the age of thirteen), no doubt were expected to form relationships of influence in preparation for a life in the public sphere. For many, the Inns provided congenial accommodation and company in London. It is not surprising, then, to find Finkelpearl describing the Inns as 'the largest single group of literate and cultured men in London' (p. 5). In many ways this aspect of the Inns was their *raison d'être*. The formal teaching of law did not have high priority. Lawyers in practice had chambers there and offered advice, students were expected (if they were serious) to engage in moots (practice trials), there were available some manuals, elementary and advanced, but, generally speaking, instruction was haphazard, unsystematic, and voluntarily undertaken.

Amongst the literate and cultured men were, of course, writers. Droves of them. Some might have entered with sincere intentions of following 'learned Littleton' but went the way of George Gascoigne: 'in the end, he proved but a daw / For law was dark and he had quickly done'.[7] Thomas Campion, after a longer time than Gascoigne, also saw the light of poetry, and Thomas Lodge gave up his studies in Lincoln's Inn. Others seem to have pursued both law and literature seriously. In their different ways, Bacon and Sir John Davies did so, while still others such as Donne, Raleigh, and Sidney may have picked up a smattering of law, but probably used the Inn as a hall of residence. At least one, John Marston, followed the not uncommon practice of sharing chambers with his father in Middle Temple. The writing of imaginative prose does not seem to have been a preference among lawyers, but even this is represented by John Grange's romance, *The Golden Aphroditis* (1577). Up until the emergence in the 1590s of professional writers such as Shakespeare and Spenser, the Inns housed, at one time or another, all the significant writers of the second half of the sixteenth century.[8] The numbers of poet-lawyers remained constant in the 1590s and after, but the gentlemanly assumption that one does not write for money or publication inevitably reduced the prominence of the group as public writers.

There must have been at the Inns many a young Shallow and Falstaff whose preference was for 'Shakespeare's plays instead of my Lord Coke'.[9] Even if they were not themselves poets or dramatists, members provided essential patronage for the book trade (booksellers operated within the precincts of the inns), and for the multifarious occupations in the theatre. Donne was not alone in being 'a great frequenter of Playes'.[10] Budding lawyers and their associates went to plays in public and private theatres, and they also invited companies to perform in the Inns. Shakespeare's *Twelfth Night* was performed in the Middle Temple Hall, and *The Comedy of Errors* in Gray's Inn, the latter as a suitable occasion for misrule in the *Gesta Grayorum*, the famous Christmas revels of 1594–5. As we shall see in a later chapter, *Love's Labour's Lost* could easily have been written for an Inn of Court. Original plays were written and acted within the Inns. The fifteenth-century play *Wisdom*, a 'Dickensian' evocation of legal corruption[11] is reputed to have been originally presented in an Inns of Court setting.[12] Some plays have been critically hailed, whether rightly or wrongly, as innovative and seminal. Gascoigne's *Jocasta* (1566) has been claimed as the earliest English tragedy in blank verse, his *Supposes* (1566) as the earliest extant comedy in English prose, while Sackville's and Norton's *Gorboduc* (1562) is often seen as the first true, vernacular tragedy. All these happen to be plays attributable to particular writers, but there were also masques and entertainments which were collaborative in their nature and laid the foundations for the golden age of the masque at the Stuart court. *Misfortunes of Arthur* was one such collaborative effort, on which Francis Bacon is reputed to have worked. The *Gesta Grayorum* Revels seem to have had as their main author Francis Davison, but many others contributed (including Campion, and again, by repute, Bacon), and in the actual production of this enormously elaborate event, virtually all the 150-odd inmates of Gray's Inn over Christmas had some function (Finkelpearl, *John Marston*, pp. 35–44).

Three men who were products of the Inns of Court system came to wield great power in the state. Nowadays Thomas More, Francis Bacon and Richard Hooker are regarded as great writers, an assessment which would have surprised them because their real commitment was to law and, respectively, state government and ecclesiastical government. Writing happened to be a medium, alongside oratory, for political persuasion. This glaring discrepancy between sixteenth-century and twentieth-century perceptions is in itself evidence that our culture and our public life have lost the equal valuing of literature, law, politics and religion in the tight knit which could be fostered in the environment of the Inns of Court. Nor was it a self-absorbed or insular ethos, for men would move on, like Sidney, to the court or, like Justice Shallow, to Gloucestershire and Windsor, or anywhere in Britain, either to practise law or perform other duties. The cultural influence of the Inns, then, was widespread, continuing, and self-generating. The three examples mentioned above are especially significant for this book, since in their different ways they contributed to Natural Law Theory. Bacon, as chancellor, had to make the system of equity work at the time of the common law's fiercest onslaught. More had also been chancellor, and as we shall see he debated in *Utopia* one of Natural Law's most perennial questions – is the existence of private property against Natural Law? As we have seen, Hooker (who was a reluctant Master of the Temple, the church serving both Inner and Middle Temple) drew on Aquinas and Natural Law theory in his own version of a *Summa* which was to guide the governance of the Anglican Church. If these men saw themselves as 'poets' then it was in Puttenham's full sense, as among 'the first law-makers'. Furthermore, the ferment of ideas generated at the Inns of Court amongst lawyers, literati, and future statesmen evidently included Natural Law, even in the very heartlands of the common law. This was because many came from Oxford or Cambridge, with civil-law training. It is easy to see how writers such as Sidney, Spenser, Jonson, and Shakespeare could not avoid coming into contact with the current debates and legal questions, including the dominant ones concerning Natural Law and equity.

One book, more than any other symptom, testifies to the close amalgam of poetry, law, and statecraft which typifies the way in which the Inns of Court saw their own nature and function. *The Mirror for Magistrates*[13] is, like Sidney's *Arcadia*, nowadays one of the most respected and yet least read books of the sixteenth century, and it can be seen as a production of the Inns. Most of the writers who contributed historical poems to this monumental collection were attached to an Inn of Court in the capacity of professional lawyers. They were equally well known for some literary activity. Sackville collaborated on at least one play, *Gorboduc*, Thomas Phaer, George Ferrers, and John Dolman were translators of repute, while William Baldwin, the chief editor of the volume, was what we might now call an arts administrator. Since the massive volume is entirely in poetry (admittedly, of variable quality) it goes without saying that all the contributors were practising poets. Principally, however, all those mentioned above were trained lawyers, and it is indicative of the twentieth-century blind spot that Lily B. Campbell, the editor of the modern edition, ignores this fact, choosing to describe Baldwin as 'philosopher, poet, printer, playwright'. Campbell also, in her zeal to find the orthodox, Tudor political doctrine which she pursues in her own books, cleanses and anaesthetises some of the radical material which she acknowledges but does not emphasise.

The whole project of dealing with kings, queens, and leading historical figures in an often critical way was fraught with dangers, and the writers made life even more risky for themselves by dealing entirely with those in public life who fell rather than those who succeeded, following the model of Lydgate's *Fall of Princes*. Even trickier, many of the figures were tyrants, and, as a comment by Ben Jonson in the Induction to *Bartholomew Fair* (line 55) makes clear, readers and audiences were alert to the possibility of veiled contemporary reference in literature. It is not surprising that the mouthpiece of 'The Poet Collingbourne' who 'was cruelly executed for making a foolish rime' (p. 347) counsels caution:

> Beware, take heed, take heed, beware, beware
> You Poets you, that purpose to rehearse
> By any art what Tyrants doings are,
> Erinnis rage is grown so fell and fierce
> That vicious acts may not be touched in verse:
> The Muses freedom, granted them of eld,
> Is bard, sly reasons treasons high are held.

He advises poets to 'Touch covertly in terms' and thereby remain safe, while being ready to 'gallop there to keep his carcass safe'. This poem, significantly, is placed before the one on the tyrant, Richard, Duke of Gloucester. However, the Poet concludes by confirming Baldwin's stated purpose which is to advise and warn 'the nobility and all other in office', including monarchy, of the dangers of tyranny and injustice: 'And therefore Baldwin boldly to the good Rebuke thou vice' (p. 358). Lily B. Campbell reads *The Mirror for Magistrates* as an exemplification of 'divine right of kings' in the sense that monarchs are acountable to God but not to their subjects. This cannot be entirely so, since we sometimes find advice, for example, that none should take office under a faulty prince, 'Save he that can for right his prince forsake' (p. 202), and that 'who reckless rules, right soon may hap to rue' (p. 345). Equally, it cannot be the whole truth to see 'the wheel of Fortune' as a guiding philosophical theme, since writer after writer demonstrates that those who 'Fortune oft doth blame' (p. 317) are in fact the architects of their own fates.

Here we have a set of very important men, many of them lawyers, writing in verse explicit and covert criticism of monarchs. All survived, and political adroitness helped them sail so closely to the wind. But the sheer ambition and even audacity of the project as a whole places the self-images of these Inns of Court men in the category of 'the first lawmakers to the people, and the first politicians', as well as lawyers and poets by profession.

### Rhetoric

Rhetoric: 'the art of using language so as to persuade or influence others'. (Oxford English Dictionary)

Inns of Court gave opportunities to lawyers to read poetry, write poetry, attend plays, and participate in dramatic events. Likewise, they allowed poets to fraternise with lawyers on a daily basis. No wonder, then, that

Elizabethan imaginative writing reveals full awareness of the significant debates in law. Moreover, there is a doctrinal reason for linking the two areas. Lawyers and poets, together with preachers, shared the common heritage of classical rhetoric, and, since the sixteenth century saw a great revival of classical rhetoric in England, the common links were reinforced.

'Rhetoric' nowadays occurs most frequently in the phrase 'mere rhetoric', implying redundant verbiage, flowery excess, hollow sound without substance, arcane and pedantic figures of speech. Scholars who write on rhetoric are ridiculed as hopelessly antiquarian and out of touch even with modern, let alone postmodern, thought. Some of them, of course, may be just this, but the subject itself, properly understood, underpins many of the central tenets of the postmodern movement, one of whose *credos* was memorably anticipated and encapsulated by Marshall McLuhan in the 1960s: 'the medium is the message'. The vehicle is inextricable from its content, and indeed, it *is* the meaning. It is a modern application of the ancient principles of rhetoric that leads semioticians to discover linguistic and visual signs which carry meaning in every medium, and it is the same understanding of the persuasive tool of rhetoric that leads advertisers, television programme-makers and newspaper editors to seek to manipulate through conventions their often willing audiences. It is an understanding of rhetoric that allows feminists, Marxists, and deconstructionists, in their very different ways, to sharpen our awareness that language and art inevitably carry unacknowledged, unaccountable, and manipulative value assumptions. It is at least arguable that we are, at the end of the twentieth century, living through a revival of rhetoric as important as the Renaissance's. Even if the actual terms and forms of rhetoric may change, the underlying rationale does not, and this is being rediscovered.

Deborah K. Shuger, in one of the best books on the subject, *Sacred Rhetoric: The Christian Grand Style in the English Renaissance*,[14] helps to recuperate the fundamental ends of rhetoric by focusing on the 'Christian grand style', the dominant rhetorical medium from 1560 to 1620, but with its roots in Aristotle and his followers. This rhetorical mode in particular, she argues, was essentially passionate and affective in intention:

The grand style moves the emotions, whether the harsher forensic impulses of pity and fear or the numinous feelings of wonder and mystery. Its language is not necessarily periodic and copious but often brief, dense, and jaggedly asymmetrical. It is neither playful nor subrational. Rather, the grand style expresses a passionate seriousness about the most important issues of human life; it is thus the style of Plato and the Bible as well as Cicero and Demosthenes. (p. 7)

At its heart lay the ancient impulse common to lawyers and poets and, later, preachers, to persuade listeners or readers by engaging their feelings, while presenting an argument which is the product of reason, and finally to move their consciences to moral action. 'Therefore', Shuger writes, 'emotion is not hostile to reason, but passionate volition and reason together carry man to his highest end' (p. 243). The terms are not so different from those of Natural Law, and we shall see close and important connections.

Books of rhetoric, that is, manuals offering principles governing the invention, arrangement, and expression of ideas and feelings through persuasive language, were a growth industry in the sixteenth century.[15] Even a cursory glance at the hundreds of titles (many of which are commentaries on Aristotle and Cicero) reveals the centrality of rhetoric to fields as diverse as politics, ethics, theology, sermons, grammar, oratory, teaching, poetry, law, and letter-writing. Acceptance was international, and its importance in everyday life was understood. Most of the manuals, however, were aimed particularly at either lawyers or poets. Both groups, after all, the one through oratory and the other through writing, shared a professional, vested interest in the classical strategy of rhetoric to move hearts and minds in a certain direction through language. What we discover through the rhetoric books, and what brings the two groups even closer together, is that lawyers had a far greater investment than we would assume in moving the emotions (seen today as the poet's domain) to sway judges and juries, and that poets had a far more acute sensitivity to narrative logic and rationality (normally seen as the lawyer's *forte*) than we might expect. These facts, taken together, give lawyers and poets nearly identical goals and methods. As in Natural Law, reason and a passionate conscience are compatible, mutually supportive, and equally necessary to moral judgment and action. Similarly, in both legal advocacy and written poetry, mastery of rhetoric was equated with values such as reason, virtue, and justice.

Thomas Wilson ends his extremely readable and influential *The Arte of Rhetorique* (1553) with the bold statement that 'the good will not speak evil: and the wicked can not speak well' (p. 249, G, g iii r). Stephen Hawes in his long poem *The Pastime of Pleasure* writes that before law there was no order, 'Till rhetoricians / found Justice doubtless ... The barge to steer / with law and Justice Over the waves of this life transitory'.[16] On the path towards the sixteenth-century manuals of rhetoric, Aristotle, Cicero, and Aquinas are once again our guides. Aristotle in particular is enormously important, first because his *Rhetoric* is the oldest textbook that we have on the subject, and secondly because his *Poetics* was the first in the long line of Defences of Poetry which continue down to the present day in some form or another. The basic principles underlying both works are fundamentally related, as fully demonstrated in Kathy Eden's scholarly book *Poetic and Legal Fiction in the Aristotelian Tradition*.[17] This, Eden argues, is no accident, since the law courts of fifth- and sixth-century Athens were in close league with tragic drama, sharing a common preoccupation with justice, and both arising more or less contemporaneously and in the same place. Legal process in Athens in Aristotle's time, seen in the light of the concerns of my argument, has many things in common with Elizabethan law. Robert Potter independently points out that 'judicial processes are inherently dramatic' and that 'dramas are in some senses implicitly judicial': 'It is worth remembering, for example, that the Ancient Greeks used their theatres for assemblies and courts of law; their rhetorical tradition of education, directed towards litigating in the public courts, clearly had a shaping hand in determining the form and character of their drama'.[18] In some ways the connections between the two works by Aristotle are somewhat obscured, but with the help of Eden (who draws also on the *Nicomachean Ethics*) the links can be clearly spelt out. Aristotle is speaking of poetry as dramatic tragedy, but the process is equally applicable to other narrative literary forms. Both forensic oratory and poetry have the common task of presenting a series of related events leading up to a significant event, for example, a murder, or an *anagnorisis*, a revelation of truth. They both present a narrative moving towards a dénouement. In these narratives they must show their respective audiences in the courtroom and the theatre first *what* happened, and secondly *why* it happened, and the narrative must be arranged in a comprehensible and plausible fashion. The '*why*' implies some scrutiny of motivation and intention in the protagonists, especially because Aristotle, in common with the practice of modern criminal law, stresses guilty intention as the heart of a wrongdoing. (In the sixteenth century, common law was moving towards this position, but rather slowly.[19]) Such preoccupation with intention is the concern with tragic awareness and 'characterisation' that is the stuff of drama. The lawyer and poet alike must, then, not only show that the events and motivations presented are a logical and reasonable fit with a plausible 'reality', but also, just as importantly, they must arouse appropriate feelings in the audience. They must make the audience/judge (or jury) feel as though they have been actual witnesses to a living event, and steer them towards adopting a particular emotional attitude. Technically, the word 'pathos' refers to the emotional state which the orator (from his own 'ethos') seeks to stir in his audience. This in turn leads on to a *judgment* made by the judge/audience on the significance of the train of events. Just as the defendant must be found guilty or not guilty, so, in a less specified but still powerful way, audiences in the theatre (or for that matter readers of novels and romances) are impelled to judge whether the central protagonist is worthy of praise or blame. At every stage, rhetoric, techniques of presenting information so as to persuade, is crucial, and equally applicable in law and imaginative literature.

In the English Renaissance, if there was one figure considered more important than Aristotle it was Cicero, who significantly was the other classical writer who adverted to Natural Law. His interest in rhetoric is more practical and less theoretical than Aristotle's, and so his *De Ratione Dicendi* (*On the Theory of Public Speaking*) and his *De Oratore* are manuals of effective ways of composing and delivering speeches. The main purpose of rhetoric as used in oratory is persuasion: 'The task of the public speaker is to discuss capably those matters which law and custom have fixed for the uses of citizenship, and to secure as far as possible the agreement of his hearers.'[20] The main areas in which he envisages oratory being used lie in the threefold classification of praise/ censure, discussion of policy, and judicial or legal settings. In this sense, rhetoric is primarily a part of political philosophy. However, when he comes to speak in detail about style in Book IV of *De Ratione Dicendi*, he openly states that he will give examples 'from a reputable orator or poet' (p. 229). Thereafter, he mentions indiscriminately 'the orators or poets of highest reputation' (p. 231) and he sometimes affirms that he regards the poet as the rival of the orator and almost the equal. He regards the study of rhetoric as giving an analytical tool to listeners and readers, as much as being a weapon for the advocate: 'Laymen, reading good orations and poems, approve the orators and poets, but without comprehending what has called forth their approval, because they cannot know where that which especially delights them resides, or what it is, or how it was produced' (p. 239). Cicero then goes on to list and illustrate all the figures of style (diction and thought) in teaching the 'technical skill' in oratory. It is clear from sixteenth-century manuals of rhetoric in law and poetry that unimaginative writers (for example, Henry Peacham in *The Garden of Eloquence* (1577)) take from Cicero a slavish tabulation and exemplification of rhetorical and grammatical terms. It is this habit that has in later times given a bad name and a pedantic ring to the phrase 'mere rhetoric'. The more individual writers, however, like Wilson and Sidney, clearly understand that Ciceronian rhetoric hinges on effectively persuasive expression used not for sensational but for moral purposes, and which can be either spoken (legal oratory) or written (poetry).

Quintilian, a lesser but still significant influence on the sixteenth century, sees rhetoric as fundamental to the education of anybody destined to play a part in public life. He calls it an 'art',[21] and like Aristotle he stresses rhetoric's capacity to work on the emotions of the judges, whether they are in a courtroom or otherwise, by heightening pathos, ethos, emotional appeal, and sometimes using laughter, wit, and humour (Book IV, chs. 2 and 3). He also goes a long way to equating rhetoric with truth – good speaking and good living – answering the charge against rhetoric 'that orators speak indifferently on either side of a case' (I, 339) by saying that rhetoric 'teaches what ought *not* to be said' (*ibid.*, my italics) as well as what ought to be said. Therefore, a good person will not or cannot, use rhetoric to defend what ought not to be done. Only a bad orator, a bad person, will attempt to do so.[22] Close analysis of the rhetoric of Elizabethan heroic 'villains' such as Marlowe's Faustus, Shakespeare's Iago, and Milton's Satan show the writers building into the arguments rational flaws or 'wrong reason', which are designed to alert us to their morally dubious character. On the other hand, the existence of these characters, and of Spenser's more eloquent villains, indicates that rhetoric is a double-edged sword. By equating 'proper' rhetoric with morality, and later (Book XII) with both nature (in Aristotle's sense) and justice itself, Quintilian left an important legacy for Renaissance theorists of law and poetry, which they enthusiastically took up. Rhetoric, like Natural Law itself, was seen as something which in its own right could make listeners follow virtue and murmur at vice.

In medieval times classical learning was kept alive by the Church Fathers and their successors, and it was Saint Thomas Aquinas who ensured the survival of pagan material, by initiating an ambitious scheme of translation, often from intermediary, Arabic texts. Aristotle's *Rhetorica* was one such text, translated by William of Moerbeke.[23] Aquinas himself draws copiously on Cicero in quotation. Once again, as in the case of Natural Law, so with rhetoric, it was Aquinas who laid the basis for the Renaissance revival of the classics. However, in the particular area of rhetoric, Saint Augustine in the fourth century was a champion. The fourth book of *De Doctrina Christiana* has been called 'the first manual of Christian rhetoric'.[24] Augustine, like many early Christian authorities, was tormented by the problem of what, if anything, Christianity could conscientiously adopt from Roman culture. He decided that, in the case of rhetoric, *eloquentia* can be reconciled with Christianity, as it can help preachers deliver effective sermons. Since, as we have seen, the central purposes of rhetoric are to convince audiences of the truth (teach) and to move them through emotions towards virtuous action and away from evil-doing, it could then be regarded as a tool rather than an end in itself. Augustine shrewdly realised that, pagan as it was in origin, rhetoric could be the most powerful weapon at the disposal of the early church. Sermons, therefore, took their place beside law and poetry, as areas in which rhetoric was a suitable basis, and the links between rhetoric, theology, and Natural Law were tightened.

The development in sixteenth-century England of manuals of rhetoric was a further link between law and literature. The earliest ones were aimed at lawyers, and they in turn generated instructional textbooks of law for students. They were also, however, written to be used by orators and writers in other fields, including poetry and preaching, and by the end of the century more specialised manuals existed for poets.

We have very little documentary evidence about the formalities of legal education in Tudor times. There is little if any reference to the teaching of rhetoric at the Inns of Court, although the study was compulsory at Oxford and Cambridge for those pursuing Roman civil law. Sir Thomas Elyot in *The Governour* (1531) advocates as the basis of a truly civilised country an education in philosophy for youths up to twenty-one years, and then in the laws of the realm (I, 141). But he repeats several times that the language of law needs to be reformed. He says many lawyers have good 'reason' but lack 'doctrine', and he says this can be remedied by the study of 'eloquence' (I, 145). He deplores

the great fardels and trusses of the most barbarous authors, stuffed with innumerable glosses, whereby the most necessary doctrines of law and physic be minced into fragments, and in all with men's opinions, do perceive no less in the said learnings than they which never knew eloquence, or never tasted other but the faeces or dregs of the said noble doctrines. (I, 146–7)

After this colourful exercise in rhetoric, Elyot provides a section on 'ancient rhetoric', noting that it is used in moot trials, if not perfectly. Rhetoric, he argues, lies behind all good oratory, and will aid 'the sharp wits of logicians, the grave sentences of philosophers, the elegancy of poets, the memory of civilians [civil lawyers]' (I, 155). In addition to moots, common lawyers at the Inns of Court would have encountered rhetoric in the revels and academic drama. *Gorboduc*, for example, is steeped in rhetorical practice, as is *The Mirror for Magistrates*.

Elyot may implicitly be making reference to a small book that had been published in 1524, Leonard Cox's *The Art or Craft of Rhetoric*.[25] This appears to be the first book of rhetoric in the English language. It seems to be aimed at a 'general readership' and it is broadly summary in its approach rather than detailed or specialised. But there appears to be an expectation that lawyers in particular will use the book. As an example of a rhetorical oration, Cox presents an argument about justice. He, like Elyot, also laments the decline of rhetoric in the law. He says that judicial orations 'in old time' were used by judges and men of law, 'but now for the more part it is neglect of them, though there be nothing more necessary to quicken them in crafty and wise handling of their matters' (D 5 r).

Thomas Wilson's *The Art of Rhetoric*, written 'for the use of all such as are studious of Eloquence' (1553),[26] deserves more analysis. It was enormously influential, being reprinted eight times before 1600, and it is a book that genuinely appeals not only to lawyers, but also to writers. It is possible, as we shall see, that Wilson's greatest protégé was Sir Philip Sidney. Other books of the time tended to aim at either lawyers (John Doddridge, William Fulbecke, Abraham Fraunce), or poets (Richard Sherry, Henry Peacham, George Puttenham) and John Rainolds' *Oratio in Laudem Artis Poeticae*. Wilson, above all, stresses the necessity of orators and writers to be able to move the emotions, and his comments on this matter should be of great interest for literary scholars. Wilson was a civil lawyer, but he expresses great respect for the common law, as for law in general, saying that it is the safeguard of civilised life. However, his background in civil law is all-important for it colours his account of justice in a way that links up with later literature through Natural Law. He also wrote a book significantly called *Rule of Reason*.

Wilson defines the requirements of an orator basically in the Horatian terms so much repeated by poets, namely, to teach, to delight, and to persuade. He goes on to provide classical kinds and divisions of rhetoric. Like Cox, he provides a set-piece oration on justice, but the terms he uses are purely from the world of Natural Law. He writes that 'Justice naturally [is] in every one of us', 'seeing God poured first this law of nature into man's heart, and granted it as a mean whereby we might know his wit ... God hath lightened man with knowledge, that in all things he may see what is right, and what is wrong, and upon good advisement deal justly with all men' (D 3 v–D 3 r *passim*). Reason and conscience are these god-given lights that enable people to have knowledge of God's law. More explicitly, Wilson writes of fulfilling 'the law of nature' (D 3 v) and asks 'Even among brute beasts nature hath appointed a law, and shall we men live without a law?' (*ibid.*). Natural Law is fulfilled, he says, by people helping one another in 'just dealing': 'Then if we do not justice (wherein law doth consist) we do neither love man, nor yet love God.' He goes on to argue that where there is a conflict between laws, man's law must give way to God's law. It is this kind of content which makes Wilson's treatise as much a subtle intervention in the debate between Chancery and common law as an apparently innocent textbook on rhetoric.

It is also Wilson's continued references to the Law of Nature, which all humanity is expected to know and share, which make his account of rhetoric's power to move the emotions, to 'delight' and 'persuade', so important. At its most superficial, Wilson says that humour and wit are necessary even in sermons, for otherwise audiences would listen more diligently to a 'merry play' (A 3 v). When he comes to analyse in detail how mirth is created, Wilson's explanation is in part pure, classical literary theory. We laugh as a corrective at 'the fondness, the filthiness, the deformity, and all such evil behaviour, as we see to be in each other'. More profoundly, Wilson writes of rhetoric moving emotions to stir the conscience or to spur others to moral action. His words are, like Aristotle's, equally pertinent to lawyers and tragic dramatists: 'In moving affections, and stirring the judges to be grieved, the weight of the matter must be so set forth, as though they saw it plain before their eyes' (T 1 v) ... 'Now in moving pity, and stirring men to mercy, the wrong done must first be plainly told: or if the Judges have sustained the like extremity, the best were to will them to remember their own state' (T 1 r). There is very little difficulty in seeing this as the most profound intention behind closure to drama of both classical and Elizabethan tragedy, a kind of transferred *admiratio*. S. F. Johnson, who wrote on drama in the Inns of Court, shows that such works as *Gorboduc* and *Arthur* produced in the Inns can be analysed along the lines of rhetoric laid down by Wilson.[27] Wilson makes the affective part of rhetoric all-important, and we can now see why. For one who believes in Natural Law, reason and conscience must be activated by the emotional appeal to shared human experiences and feelings. He makes it very clear, as does John Rainolds for poetry in *Oratio in Laudem Artis Poeticae* (1572), that the true end of rhetoric is not only to persuade audiences, but to stir them to moral action.

The classic case of stirring emotions to inspire action is again relevant to both law and literature. In describing a crime (or, adds Wilson, acts of tyranny) the focus may be on the innocent victims rather than on the malefactor: 'Likewise we may exhort men to take pity of the fatherless, the widow, and the oppressed innocent, if we set before their eyes the lamentable afflictions, the tyrannous wrongs, and the miserable calamities, which these poor wretches do sustain' (I 4 v). Wilson appeals to the argument of nature, that 'flesh and blood' moves us towards a common empathy with suffering human beings. Following this theory through into literature, the deaths of Ophelia and Cordelia should stir our feelings to recognise the state of tyranny under which they were forced to live and suffer, and the death of Desdemona should shock us into analysing the male stereotyping that caused it.[28] It means that even Shylock can strike a common chord of human sympathy. In legal terms, by becoming keenly aware of the victim's suffering, we are impelled to examine with cool reason the circumstances that caused it, and to make judgment accordingly. 'If a wicked wretch have his deserts, we are all glad to hear of it, but if an innocent should be cast away, we think much of it, and in stomach repine against wrong judgement.' This could stand as a cryptic description of an audience's feelings, towards on the one hand Macbeth's death, and on the other the deaths of Lady Macduff and her children, and the principle of moralising from empathetic suffering is enormously important to the moral patterning of Shakespearian tragedy. The basis of such effects is Natural Law presupposed as being within the consciousness of members of the audience, an inbuilt desire to follow virtue and 'murmur at' vice.

Behind Wilson's account of 'Affections ... (called Passions)' lies another of Natural Law's essential tenets, that we 'naturally' love virtue and detest vice. The only thing that the art of rhetoric adds to nature is a consciously moral intensity:

Affections therefore (called Passions) are none other thing, but a stirring, or forcing of the mind, either to desire, or else to detest, and loath any thing, more vehemently than by nature we are commonly wont to do. We desire those things, we love them, and like them earnestly, that appear in our judgement to be goodly, we hate and abhor those things, that seem naught, ungodly, or harmful unto us. (S 4 v)

By this stage it should be clear that Wilson is presenting a system which, although called rhetoric, in fact tightly links the common concerns of Renaissance law and literature, pre-eminently persuasion towards moral action, through the theory of Natural Law, 'grounded wholly upon natural reason'.[29]

If Wilson writes primarily for lawyers, John Rainolds' undergraduate exercise, *Oration in Praise of the Art of Poetry* (1569–72) is wholly a celebration of the power of poetry, underpinned by rhetorical theory. For Rainolds, poetry was, above all else, a form of persuasion whose end was to stir the emotions not for the sake of it but to move readers to virtuous action. 'Nothing else can more violently arouse the emotions of mankind' (pp. 34–5) he writes. Poetry is 'that famous Persuasion towards appropriate action' (p. 39) and he gives the example of courage. Poetry is a moral force, leading men 'from gross ignorance to learning, from civil discord to friendship, from thorough wickedness to honesty, and from barbaric wildness to gentle manners' (p. 45). It brings justice to a savage world 'after confining violence'. For Rainolds, 'the very parent of poetry' is God, and although it 'is aroused by the forces of the mind' it is just as much 'instilled by a divine afflatus'. This places the poetic mind right at the source of Natural Law, and, sure enough, Rainolds claims that 'it is not produced by assiduous practices, but is apprehended by excellency of nature'. It is evolved 'not by endless labor, but by a certain impact of a superior nature' (p. 35). The short book is at times absurdly hyperbolic in its claims for poetry, but its existence is important as a precursor of Sidney's great *Defence of Poetry*, and it demonstrates that poets were borrowing from civil lawyers the convenient theory of Natural Law.

## Legal Fictions

What you have been doing by the fiction – could you, or could you not, have done it without the fiction? If not, your fiction is a wicked lie: if yes, a foolish one.
    Such is the dilemma. Lawyer! escape from it if you can.[30]

One link between law and literature takes law right into the realms of poetry. Both disciplines share a reliance on fictions. In a profession which prides itself on dealing in logic and with facts, this has been an uncomfortable realisation for some lawyers throughout the ages. The objections to fictions are that they are an untidy and disorderly way of solving problems, that they upset the stable consistency of law based on precedent, that they enable law to usurp the functions of legislation by doing something which is not openly possible within existing law, and that there is an arbitrariness about their application. These charges should ring bells, for they are more or less those levelled by the common lawyers against equity in the Court of Chancery. Indeed, a legal maxim unites the two: *in fictione juris semper equitas existit* (in a fiction of law, equity always exists).[31] Just as Chancery argued that it was 'correcting' inadequacies in the common law in order to achieve a state of equitable justice, so the defenders of legal fictions argued that fictions are created to resolve in a just manner problems which otherwise would be insoluble, or where the law strictly applied would cause manifest injustice.

Despite the high hopes of academic lawyers to drive out reliance on fictions,[32] it is difficult to see how this can be done, so widespread, overt, and covert are their existence. Terms such as 'constructive intention' (killing A when intending to kill B can still be murder, even though murder is defined as the intention to kill a specific person), 'presumptive knowledge', 'implied in law', 'notional', 'a reasonable construction', and so on, in effect, say something like 'No matter what the true facts are, this is what the law will deem them to be.' A woman did not know something, and yet the law says it is reasonable that she should have, and therefore, for its purposes, she *did* know it. A corollary is the maxim that runs 'Equity [fairness] looks on that as done which ought to be done.' A concept like 'the fictitious person', that is a company, corporation, or institution which may be legally responsible and liable like an individual, has entered both the law and the popular consciousness so deeply that it is regarded as a 'reality' rather than the fiction which it properly is. Furthermore, there are some very large fictions underlying law which in fact constitute its foundation. Law based on precedent is said to be reliable because it never changes but is merely applied to new situations. But the history of English common law shows that it has always changed and will continue to do so because old precedents in new situations can be interpreted in new ways. J. Walter Jones observes that some writers argue, in short, that all that goes by the name of legal science, if not the whole of the law itself, is no more than a mass of fictions.[33]

Today, as in the sixteenth century, fiction is defined in a more technical sense. Lon Fuller says a fiction 'is either (1) a statement propounded with a complete or partial consciousness of its falsity, or (2) a false statement recognized as having utility'.[34] A very simple example is the colourful one of the 'fertile octogenarian'. For purposes of inheritance law it sometimes needs to be assumed that a woman over eighty can bear children. No argument to the contrary can be mounted, and statistics and biology are irrelevant. Equally fictitious is the axiom that a person missing for seven years is deemed to be dead. A minute's thought will show why such fictions are adopted: although they are known to be not necessarily or even plausibly true, they are required to solve a problem of who inherits property. Another example is what is called 'British Summer Time' which fixes legal time an hour in advance of Greenwich Mean Time in the summer months. For that matter, Greenwich Mean Time itself is an agreed quasi-legal fiction that imposes a pattern on the natural rhythms of the rising and the setting of the sun, a construct which solves many problems but which is, none the less, purely fictional.

In this specific sense, a legal fiction is 'a rule of law which assumes as true, and will not allow to be disproved, something which is false'.[35] Fictions are 'statements or suppositions which are known to be untrue, but which are not allowed to be denied, in order that some difficulty may be overcome, and substantial justice secured'.[36] This definition shows how close they can be in function to Elizabethan equity and the Law of Nature. Once again it was Roman civil law that instituted the *fictio*. Indeed, it can be argued that the early progress of Roman Law from its seminal 'Twelve Tables' demonstrates 'a development of the law by legal fictions, that is, contrivances by which a legal rule or institution is diverted from its original purpose to accomplish indirectly some other object'.[37] For example, under the *ius gentium* a foreigner, although not owing allegiance to Roman Law, was deemed 'as if' a Roman in order to give the courts jurisdiction, and this assumption could not be traversed.

Gaius, a great academic lawyer, made the distinction which becomes crucial when we come to observe poetic fictions. He reasoned that there is an implicit 'as if' lying behind a valid fiction. The law cannot turn a man who is not a thief into one who is, however, 'What the law can indeed do is to make a man liable to the same penalty *just as if* he had committed theft or adultery or murder, even though in fact he has committed none of these.'[38] As Touchstone says 'If is the only peacemaker', able to turn a 'Lie direct' into a truth by creating a fictional context.[39]

As in almost every area of legal activity, the sixteenth century was the heyday of the legal fiction, for the familiar reason that different institutions – common law (and branches within it), Chancery and parliament – were competing for jurisdictional power and engaged in various unsubtle poaching exercises. In theory, one type of court was barred from intruding into an area of law unique to another, but often a fiction could be created which would allow a plaintiff to approach a different type of court. This clearly is a more murky or political motivation than the principle espoused by classical jurists, that fictions are solely designed to create a state of justice.

Another explanation is that common law evolved from a limited and inflexible set of 'forms of action', and claimants had to adapt the circumstances of their case to a specific procedural form.[40] Rather than flexibly allow new circumstances and social conditions to generate new forms, the law (in exercising its basic fiction that it never changes) chose to allow fictional wrenching of facts to fit a form. One very common Elizabethan fiction was that raised as a case of 'ejectment'. The story is tangled and tortuous, and in this context a misleadingly bald summary will suffice as an example of how fictions worked. Before the nineteenth century, there was, incredibly enough, no straightforward way to test one person's claim to land against another's, without placing one party or the other in jeopardy of some sort. The appropriate court to approach was assizes set up by Henry II, but the procedure was slow and expensive. The most direct way was for the rival claimant to make use of the action of ejectment which was tried by a different court and was simpler and cheaper. He would 'eject' forcibly the sitting claimant and in turn face a legal challenge which would sort out the title. Since this procedure had obvious social disadvantages, physical dangers, and further legal problems if the rival lost the case of ejection brought against him, a set of fictions was evolved. The ritual involved the rival giving a leasehold title to a non-existent character called Richard Roe, who, on the basis of this lease 'ejected' an equally fictitious tenant called John Doe. John Doe then brought a case of *ejectio firmae* against Richard Roe, and the court had to decide who, of the two real people who claimed to be landlord, had title to the land and could therefore legally lease it. By the middle of the seventeenth century this extraordinary procedure was the commonest way to ascertain contested ownership of freehold land. There were similar, and equally arcane fictions created, whereby a host of charges (such as debt) could be settled quickly by the King's Bench without a lengthy writ of Chancery or an expensive approach to the Court of Common Pleas, simply by the filing of a fictitious claim of 'trespass'. As a criminal offence, originally designed to cover cases involving 'force and arms', this brought the debtor under the King's Bench jurisdiction, which meant he was automatically imprisoned for the felony without bail, pending the trial. The magic phrase was simply to add either *'cum'* (whereas) or *'ac etiam'* (and also) to the charge of trespass with force and arms: trespass (fictitious) *and also* debt (the real cause of action). Legal historians are by no means certain why such fictions were developed,[41] but the most likely reasons are competition between courts and the convenience (if that is the word) offered to clients who could get quick, cheap judgments in particular courts by the use of fictions. Bentham, himself critical of legal fictions, mentions another use of the hapless Roe and Doe. If a defendant were allowed bail, two names were entered on the record to stand as sureties either to pay the money owed by the defendant or to return him to prison. Poor Roe and Doe were customarily the names entered. Another fiction which took root in the fifteenth century and flourished in the sixteenth goes under the name *trover*. A person lends an object to another, who refuses to give it back. Since there is no evidence of an agreement on either side, the plaintiff must say the defendant 'found' the object, and then all he needs to do is prove his own ownership. Even then the object may not be handed back, but instead a sum of money is assigned which the jury places as its value.[42] Bentham sharply blames the existence of fictions on 'jurisdiction-stealing' competition between courts: 'King's Bench stole business from Common Pleas; Common Pleas stole it back again from King's Bench. Falsehood, avowed falsehood, was their common instrument. B.R. let off one lie; C.B. answered it by another. The battle is in all the books' (p. 145).

Bentham piles up example after example of legal fictions in an Appendix to his *Theory of Fictions*, calling them simply 'lies', with the same derisive confidence that Plato exhibited in branding poets liars. Lawyers and poets found themselves sharing the same boat because of their mutual, staunch reliance on fictions or 'lies'. Whatever the reasons, such fictions abounded in the sixteenth century to a point where many people must have regarded the law itself as a kind of self-sufficient, artificial fiction, not so very different from *The Faerie Queene*. Just as

Spenser's work reveals its allegorical meanings to those willing to surrender themselves to its fictional assumptions, so the law could be used effectively and successfully only by those able and willing to suspend disbelief and accept some basic fictions in the interests of achieving substantial justice. Some such subterranean connection must lie behind the perennial interest in 'pure' works of the imagination which deal with the bizarre fictionality of law, from *The Merchant of Venice* and *Measure for Measure* to *Bleak House*.

Bentham asserts that 'on the other side of the Tweed ... no such lies are told' (p. 149). This is a reference to the fact that in Scotland the law was based on Roman civil law and evolved along different lines from common law. He would appear at first sight to be mistaken, since fictions are adopted in Roman Law, such as that already mentioned concerning *ius gentium*. But there is a substantial correctness in what Bentham says, for, believe it or not, there are in logic true fictions and false fictions, or more succinctly the difference between a fiction and a lie. It is a distinction which gives an advantage surprisingly shared by Roman Law and by poetry over common law of Tudor times. It lies in what has been called the 'Philosophy of As-If',[43] and it lies at the centre of Bentham's own theory of fictions. Hans Vaihinger, who coined the phrase, argues that fictions are essential to human thought because they facilitate abstract conceptualisation. Gaius, the Roman jurist already mentioned, says the law may make a person liable to the same penalty as a person who has committed a crime *as if* he had committed it himself. A modern commentator provides a simple example: 'You cannot say that red is green, but you can declare your intention to proceed as though red were green. This is the line between falsehood and fiction.'[44] Roman Law, tidied up by the orderly mind of Gaius, does contain fictions of the 'as-if' kind which are consistent with avoiding outright falsehood. This is a consequence of the essentially rational and logical foundation of Roman Law, underpinned by Natural Law's reliance on reason and by its own necessary status as a 'true fiction' existing in an 'as-if' realm. This, as we shall see, is the underpinning logic of the poetic fiction.

No such logic marks Renaissance English law because, as we have partially seen, it evolved under pressures from competing jurisdictions of which only one (equity) had any basis in Roman Law. The foundation of common law itself could not be said to be rational, but rather experiential or evolutionary, based as it is on the authority of precedent. Where Roman Law stressed what is 'true' and rational, common law stressed what is *useful* about fictions. To put the matter charitably, it is more useful for a client to get justice quickly and cheaply from one kind of court, even if it involves a 'false fiction', in order to avoid the slower, more expensive, but technically appropriate, court. As a consequence, English law was littered with 'false' fictions where no attempt was made to avoid the falsehood.

The overriding rationale was to achieve justice, to reward goodness and flush out wrongdoing, in short to achieve precisely what equity set out to do more explicitly in taking to itself the power to override in the name of justice other forms of law. In a broad sense, Natural Law itself is based on a premise of 'as-if': what *happens* may be 'fact', but what *should happen* may be equally 'factual', if we insert a predicate that justice operates *as if* reason and conscience are manifested with perfect consistency. What is equally significant for us is that such a rationale underpins also the didactic aim of literature, according to Renaissance theorists. Paradoxically, fictions could achieve a state of Natural Law where 'reality' or truth hindered its emergence. This is the basis upon which Sidney, for example, was to defend the fictions and figurativeness of imaginative poetry, and it is an argument that he, like many other poets, could have picked up from English law of the time.

### Poetic fictions

We need not be so judgmental and critical as Bentham of the fictions employed by the law in the sixteenth century. My intention here is simply to show that, in a very crucial legal concept, lawyers and judges could readily accept the centrality in their profession of the poet's *sine qua non*, fictions. It is, of course, easy to compile unashamed and forthright defences of fictions by poets themselves, since literature is, in its relation to reality, an 'as-if' construction. By its very nature poetry is figurative and metaphorical rather than literal.[45] Ever since Plato's famous attack on poets as liars in *The Republic,* Book X, and the classic response in Aristotle's *Poetics*, poets have been driven to justify their practices in 'defences' of poetry. Invariably, these are based on some version of the 'as-if' philosophy, which links them with civil law, legal fictions, and ultimately Natural Law.

Thomas Lodge's *Defence of Poetry* (1579) is a splenetic and *ad hominem* attack on Stephen Gosson whose *School of Abuse* (1579) was an equally querulous attack on 'Poets, Pipers, Players, Jesters and such like Caterpillars of a Commonwealth' (title-page), and dedicated to Sir Philip Sidney. It may have come as a surprise to Gosson and other Puritans that Sidney, staunch Protestant though he was, chose to defend poets in the mid 1580s. There is a kernel of important doctrine in Lodge's outburst, for he sees imaginative literature as a 'decipherment' for moral purposes: 'Did you never read (my over witty friend) that under the persons of beasts many abuses were deciphered? ... The vanity of tales is wonderful; yet if we advisedly look into them they will seem and prove wise.'[46] Lodge wittily comments that it is no wonder Gosson should attack poetry when he cannot understand its hidden meanings, and he piles up example after example where classical writers use fables and fictions to advance some moral point. Lodge's theory of moral allegory recalls Rainolds' *Oration*, in which 'the complicated shades of obscurity and the shadowy coverings of myths' are justified 'in order that the beauty of the poems should draw good men to solve the riddle, and the obscurity should deter evil men from touching it'.[47] Once again, the fundamental basis of Natural Law raises its head. Like Rainolds, Lodge eulogises the poet as superior to the orator, and as inspired by God directly: 'It is a pretty sentence, yet not so pretty as pithy, *Poeta nascitur, Orator fit*: as who should say, Poetry cometh from above, from a heavenly seat of a glorious God, unto an excellent creature man; an Orator is but made by exercise' (p. 71). To substantiate his point, Lodge quotes Horace's words and translates them, beginning with the description of the poet as 'The holy spokesman of the Gods' (p. 74). He also contributes to the long line of writers who equate the poet and lawmaker: 'Poets were the first razors of cities, prescribers of good laws ... inventors of laws' (p. 75).

The significance of this equation, in tandem with the idea that 'poetry is a heavenly gift', God-given, is that they place poetry firmly in the same relation to God and humanity as Natural Law is to God and positive law. That Lodge distinguished 'prescribers of good laws' from 'inventors of laws' as two separate functionaries, implies that he is making precisely the point that the poet can not only discriminate between good and bad positive laws, but can also divine the Natural Law from which all positive law flows, and convey it to readers. He admits, however, that we find few poets 'if it were exactly weighed, what they ought to be' (*ibid.*). Lodge's view of the 'as-if' world of poetic fictions is that through 'decipherments' of fictional tales the poet, plugged into a law superior to man's which he links with nature, conveys wisdom and truth. The classical advice to writers to 'follow nature' does not, then, refer to an art mimetic of physical nature, but one based on the moral purpose of Natural Law.

Puttenham, although he works from a more literal meaning of 'nature', argues the same case. He takes one meaning of art (the artificial) to build up his argument. Artifice-making is, he claims, just as healthy an activity from the poet as from the physician or the gardener. Artifice is simply good workmanship in these occupations, and, just as the physician can make defective bodies well again and the gardener can improve the soil to produce better plants, so the artist can similarly aid nature. All three can also alter nature, for the physician may prolong life, the gardener can create new hybrids, and the artist can do such 'things nature could not do without mans help and art' (p. 304). Furthermore, art can imitate or 'counterfeit' the actions and effects of nature, and this is the area where painting, carving, lapidary and so on are a 'participation' in the operations of nature itself (p. 304), producing out of the stuff of nature forms that are strange and diverse. Through this argument Puttenham breaks down the conventional distinction between the natural and the artificial, saying they can in poetic fictions be one and the same thing, or, if not, at least mutually enhancing. The poet, for example, needs both 'natural instinct' and 'art and precepts' (p. 305). Artifice can be a perfecter of nature. The crescendo of Puttenham's argument is that the poet, when 'he speaks figuratively' through fictions is superior to all other artificers in uniquely participating in nature itself, producing 'effects utterly unlike [nature's], but even as nature her self working by her own peculiar virtue and proper instinct and not by example or meditation or exercise as all other artificers do' (p. 307). The paradox is that the poet will be most admired when he is 'most natural and least artificial', and yet in order to seem 'natural' in the 'feats of his language and utterance, his discourse and persuasion', the poet must 'dissemble' and disguise the substantial artifice: 'we do allow our Courtly Poet to be a dissembler only in the subtleties of his art: that is, when he is most artificially, so to disguise and cloak it as it may not appear, nor seem to proceed from his by any study or trade of rules, but to be his natural' (p. 302). By specialising in 'Art and cunning concurring with nature, antiquity and universality' (p. 23), the poet, Puttenham boldly asserts (with a parenthesis to avoid blasphemy), is no less a figure than God: 'Such as (by way of resemblance and reverently) we may say of God: who without any travel to his divine imagination, made all the world of nought. Even so the very Poet makes and contrives out of his own brain' (p. 3). As Aquinas had likened God to the poet making laws in his little jurisdiction, now poets could be seen as capable of reversing the equation.

Sidney's *Defence of Poetry*[48] is another triumphant claim for the poet as legislator, and as one able to 'make' a second nature just as God created primary nature. So intertextually loaded is the work that scholars sometimes imply, as they do when considering More's *Utopia*, that everything in it had been said before by writers from Aristotle up to Puttenham. However, in the synthesis of Sidney's treatment lies the stamp of a powerful unity and originality of vision. Sidney, like Puttenham, argues that the writer is a god of his own created universe, and that in this activity he is imitating God. As God is Creator of the world we live in, the writer is the creator of a new world. This is to provide an ambitious gloss on Aquinas' metaphor. More specifically, Sidney locates the writer in precisely the terrain occupied by Natural Law in Aquinas, as mediator between eternal and human law, going 'hand in hand' with the creativity and moral patterning of nature itself. In his *Arcadia*, which we shall look at later, Sidney provides his own exemplification of such a daring conception of art in practice, as well as providing a playful critique on different versions of 'natural law', and a sardonic theme that fallen man may not be able to live up to the precepts of Natural Law itself.

Judging from the many references in his works, Sidney must have had at least a smattering of legal knowledge, and possibly a more intensive knowledge of contemporary debates going on in legal circles. On 2 February 1567/8 he was admitted as a member of Gray's Inn at the age of thirteen.[49] This was not uniquely young for the time, and quite appropriate for one who at the age of eleven was fluent in French and Latin and could write on the moral conduct of life.[50] Both his father Henry and his younger brother Robert are also listed as having been members of Gray's Inn. A record of a journey costing a conspicuously expensive £49 from his school at Shrewsbury to London at the time,[51] suggests that he at least travelled with serious intentions to London, although the family connections and the expectation of serving at court may have been the main reasons for his entry. He would have met important people at Gray's during his year: Francis Bacon, Francis Walsingham, and William Camden were contemporaries, and he was under the care and tutelage of the all-powerful William Cecil, whose daughter Sidney might, if he had gained the father's consent, have married.[52] He also quarrelled over a game of tennis with another member of Gray's Inn, Lord Oxford, who did in fact marry Anne Cecil. Fulke Greville, his closest friend, lived close to Gray's Inn, and was some twenty years later to join the Society himself. We know also that Sidney had lawyer-friends such as Henry Fisch. However, we have no hard facts about Sidney's time at Gray's Inn, and all we know is that he spent a year under its aegis. Depending on his commitment, and on the amount of time and attention he devoted to the Inn's activities, a year may have been long enough to initiate him into some of the knowledge and ideas in the field of law which were later to enter the *Defence* and *Arcadia*.

Sidney is recorded as matriculating at Christ Church, Oxford, in February of the next year. Perhaps more significantly, in his trip from London to Oxford he was accompanied by an old family friend (under the patronage first of the Dudleys and later of Sidney's uncle, Leicester), none other than Thomas Wilson, Doctor of Laws, whom we have already met in this chapter. We recall that Wilson's *Art of Rhetoric* (1551) anticipated the *Defence* in its concentration on the capacity of rhetoric to move audiences to moral action and in many other respects. Wilson's book was aimed at lawyers and law students. It has set-pieces on justice, and it is guided by an explicit belief in Natural Law. Moreover, the influence of the long section which Wilson enthusiastically wrote about comedy can be traced in the comic touches in the *Defence* and the sustained comedy of much of *Arcadia*. It is fanciful but enticing to imagine Wilson tutoring the young Sidney on law and rhetoric, on that trip to Oxford.

The whole enterprise and structuring of *A Defence of Poetry* is at least related through the common ground of rhetoric to the defence at law. Poetry is on trial, prosecuted not only by minnows like Gosson, who may have stirred Sidney's ire by dedicating to Sidney his waspish attack on the stage and poetry, but also by a whale like Plato. Sidney is drawn by the slanderous attacks into making 'a pitiful defence of poor poetry' (pp. 73–4). The deployment of the argument follows the rhetorical pattern of forensic advocacy in its organisation. It proceeds through Exordium, Narration (evidence, or a laying out of the facts of what poetry is), Proposition (a definition of poesy or poetry), Divisions (akin to legal distinctions, kinds of poetry), to the heart of the defence in Examinations I and II (akin to our 'cross-examinations'). There follow Refutation (of charges against poetry), Digression (about the current state of poetry in England), and Peroration (a stirring summing-up of the case for poetry). Many specific phrases and references further reveal the legal substratum of the work: 'And for the lawyer, though *Ius* be the daughter of Justice, and justice the chief of virtues, yet because he seeketh to make men good rather *formidine poenae* [in the form of punishment] than *virtutis amore* [from love of virtue]; or, to say righter, doth not endeavour to make men good, but that their evil hurt not others' (p. 84). This passage, incidentally, indicates a central attitude that poetry complements law in promoting justice: law punishes vice while poetry incites to virtue and deters us from vice. It also highlights the central distinction between positive law, which coerces people out of wrongdoing, and Natural Law, which incites people to be virtuous.[53] Sidney also shows acquaintance with the fictional characters so beloved of lawyers of the sixteenth century, John Doe and Richard Roe, although he uses other names equally familiar in the context of legal fictions: 'And doth the lawyer lie then, when under the names of *John-a-stiles* and *John-a-nokes* he puts his case?' (p. 103).

Sidney's starting-point, and his fundamental ontological assumption, launches us straight into conceptions of the 'natural' in human behaviour, morality, and law:

There is no art delivered to mankind that hath not the works of nature for his principal object, without which they could not consist, and on which they so depend, as they become actors and players, as it were, of what nature will have set forth ... The natural philosopher thereon hath his name, and the moral philosopher standeth upon the natural virtues, vices, or passions of man; and follow nature (saith he) therein, and thou shalt not err. The lawyer saith what men have determined; the historian what men have done. (p. 78)

Like Puttenham, he quite clearly adverts to Natural Law as the domain of the moral philosopher who 'standeth upon natural virtues, vices, or passions of man' and advises 'follow nature ... therein, and thou shalt not err'. By working from the physical universe towards the moral, he is simply drawing attention to something assumed and not often elaborated by thinkers in the Natural Law tradition, that the fundamental fact from which we derive morality and law is ultimately the physical universe of God-given nature in all its rationality. The next step in his logic is that the poet creates forms which take their place among those already pre-existing in the natural world. The difference is that his creations may be 'better' (more polished, complete, perfect, satisfying) than those already existing, or even things 'quite anew' never seen before:

Only the poet, disdaining to be tied to any such subjection, lifted up with the vigour of his own invention, doth grow in effect another nature, in making things either better than nature bringeth forth, or quite anew, forms such as never were in nature, as the Heroes, Demigods, Cyclops, Chimeras, Furies, and such like: so as he goeth hand in hand with nature, not enclosed within the narrow warrant of her gifts, but freely ranging only within the zodiac of his own wit. Nature never set forth the earth in so rich tapestry as divers poets have done; neither with so pleasant rivers, fruitful trees, sweet-smelling flowers, nor whatsoever else may make the too much loved earth more lovely. Her world is brazen, the poets only deliver a golden. (p. 78)

The phrase 'so as he goeth hand in hand with nature' locates the poet in Aquinas' terms as a very part of Natural Law itself, which is an earthly 'participation in' the eternal. Sidney is not blaspheming in asserting that poets can out-do nature in producing the natural, since, in Aquinas' view, nature is in man's stewardship and so can legitimately be improved. Besides, poets inevitably come after the Fall and can be seen as correcting some of the postlapsarian blemishes in nature. However, Sidney sails a little close to the wind in following the Greeks in naming the poet as 'maker', gesturing towards the divine Creator by noting 'how high and incomparable a title it is' (p. 77). He discreetly covers himself by saying that his intention in using such an ambitious word is rather to limit the scope of other sciences than to make any 'partial allegation' that the poet is equal to God. Having made and deferentially retracted the comparison, he goes on rather slyly to pursue the analogy while claiming not to make it:

Neither let it be deemed too saucy a comparison to balance the highest point of man's wit with the efficacy of nature; but rather give right honour to the heavenly maker of that maker, who having made man to His own likeness, set him beyond and over all the works of that second nature: which in nothing he showeth so much as in poetry, when with the force of a divine breath he bringeth things forth surpassing her doings – with no small arguments to the credulous of that first accursed fall of Adam, since our erected wit maketh us know what perfection is, and yet our infected will keepeth us from reaching unto it. But these arguments will by few be understood, and by fewer granted. This much (I hope) will be given me, that the Greeks with some probability of reason gave him the name [maker] above all names of learning. (p. 79)[54]

The argument is that human beings constitute a kind of primary nature superior to the physical world of 'that second nature' over which they preside, and that poetry is a vehicle for perceiving 'what perfection is' even though we cannot, because of the fall of Adam, in actuality ever emulate it. He must, however, still distinguish between the 'essential' creations given by God and the fictive or imitative forms of poetry, novel and self-sufficient as these may be:

Neither let this be jestingly conceived, because the works of the one be essential, the other in imitation or fiction; for any understanding knoweth the skill of each artificer standeth in that *idea* or fore-conceit of the work, and not in the work itself. And that the poet hath that *idea* is manifest, by delivering them forth in such excellency as he had imagined them. Which delivering forth also is not wholly imaginative, as we are wont to say by them that build castles in the air; but so far substantially it worketh, not only to make a Cyrus, which had been but a particular excellency as nature might have done, but to bestow a Cyrus upon the world to make many Cyruses, if they will learn aright why and how that maker made him.

The crucial phrase is 'as nature might have done', and here we find invoked the admirable evasion of Touchstone's 'if' and the whole 'philosophy of as-if', the lie that is a truth because it claims no more than figurative existence rather than literal. The poet does not simply make a series of 'new things': he is in control of the creative blueprint itself, capable in effect of creating new Platonic forms which can in turn generate an infinity of particular manifestations. This Gaius-like reasoning about the 'true fiction' is a cornerstone of Sidney's defence against the charge that 'poetry is the mother of lies': 'for the poet, he nothing affirms, and therefore never lieth' (p. 102). In this context we need not pursue the paradox, except to repeat its connection with the legal fiction.[55]

What deserves reflection here is the closeness of Sidney's phraseology and concept of the '*idea* or fore-conceit of the work' to Aquinas' analogy between the artist and God, and the similarity seems more than coincidental in the light of the fact that Sidney shows awareness of the writings of the 'schoolmen' who were followers of Aquinas. Undoubtedly, Aristotle was the ancestor of both. I quote Aquinas again, this time in the translation by J. G. Dawson, since it captures the tone of Aquinas more sharply than the rather stodgy Blackfriars edition:

Just as in the mind of every artist there already exists the idea of what he will create by his art, so in the mind of every ruler there must already exist an ideal of order with respect to what shall be done by those subject to his rule. And just as the ideal of those things that have yet to be produced by any art is known as the exemplar, or actual art of the things so to be produced, the ideal in the mind of the ruler who governs the actions of those subject to him has the quality of law – provided that the conditions we have already mentioned above are also present. Now God, in His wisdom, is the creator of all things, and may be compared to them as the artist is compared to the product of his art; as we have shown. Moreover he governs all actions and movements of each individual creature, as we also pointed out. So, as the ideal of divine wisdom, in so far as all things are created by it, has the quality of an exemplar or art or idea, so also the ideal of divine wisdom considered as moving all things to their appropriate end has the quality of law. Accordingly, the eternal law is nothing other than the ideal of divine wisdom considered as directing all actions and movements.[56]

Aquinas compares the Creator to the poet while Sidney compares the poet to the Creator. Their basic idea is the same, and even the phrases are similar. 'Our world is God's poem, said Augustine, and Landino after him', says S. K. Heninger,[57] reminding us that the idea is not unique to Aquinas. In a creator's mind there lies an 'ideal' or 'exemplar' even before the artefact is made, and this ideal 'has the quality of law' in its intrinsic pattern and driving morality. This law is Natural Law, the inner compulsion guiding the product into existence, the very cause of its existence. The secret of 'why and how' it is produced, when it exists, may be inspected by the reason of others.

What the analogy between poet as creator and the divine Creator enables Sidney to do is to move into discussion of the morality of poetry, its status and operation, using now the analogy of Natural Law based on reason and conscience. He does so by making a series of comparisons with other disciplines which claim truth and moral efficacy as their province. Now, in terms of the argument, he realises that he need not rely on the ambitious definition of poet as creator authorised by 'the etymology of his names' (p. 79), and he withdraws to the more conventional assumption ('more ordinary opening') that the poet is an imitator of nature. However, the god-like metaphor still guides the argument and the contexts of law and Natural Law in particular remain relevant, not least because he immediately reasserts that poets of antiquity 'did imitate the inconceivable excellencies of God' (p. 80). Throughout the work, one may detect a further analogy between Natural Law on the one hand and common law and civil law on the other: the former being equivalent to the 'should be' province of poetry, the latter of the accidental events of history.

Sidney opens this section of the argument by asserting that poetry as imitation is a 'counterfeiting, or figuring forth – to speak metaphorically, a speaking picture – with this end, to teach and delight' (p. 80). This is the classic, Horatian position, but Sidney, given confidence by Wilson, Rainolds (if he read him), and Puttenham, takes the Aristotelian line of concentrating his analysis almost exclusively on 'teaching', while taking the 'delight' for granted as the primary reason for poetry being such an effective didactic agency. Again, the means and the end of poetic teaching are uncannily close to the terms of Natural Law. Poetry, like Natural Law, is what leads people 'into the divine consideration of what may and should be' rather than what it is. The efficacy of poetry in this direction lies in the stress placed by Aristotle when dealing with rhetoric – its capacity to move the emotions: 'to move men to take that goodness in hand ... and teach, to make them know that goodness whereunto they are moved' (p. 81). The seriousness of Sidney's claims is reinforced when he says that this aim is 'the noblest scope to which any learning was directed'. Like the operation of reason and conscience in Natural Law, poetry's effect is 'well-doing and not of well-knowing only ... So that, the ending end of all earthly learning being virtuous action, those skills that most serve to bring forth that have a more just title to be princes over all the rest' (p. 83). Poetry incites and moves readers along the lines of the golden rule of Natural Law, to desire virtue and shun evil. In order to confirm this point, Sidney draws his famous comparisons between the poet on the one hand and the philosopher and historian on the other. The one gives the 'precept', the 'bare rule', in a such a dry and 'sullen gravity' that nobody will be moved to follow it; while the other gives the 'example', the 'bare was', what happened in the past not what *should* happen, tied 'not to what should be but what is, to the particular truth of things and not to the general reason of things' (p. 85). The poet alone gives the general precepts of good and evil, guidance as to what 'should be', 'instructing parables' that allow us not just to hear but 'clearly to see through them ... the general reason of things'. In the 'universal consideration of doctrine the poet prevaileth' (p. 88) because he shows particular instances which, since they are feigned and claim no historical truth may provide a 'conjectured likelihood, and so go by reason', framing his example 'to that which is most reasonable', according to reasonable likelihoods rather than either the ideal perfection taught by the philosopher or the wayward arbitrariness of what actually happened in history. And the main advantage the poet has is to stir the passions through rhetoric. The 'feigned example' or fiction 'may be tuned to the highest key of passion' (p. 89), so that its narratives may '[move] to well-doing', proving on the pulses why virtue should be exalted and vice punished. The element of emotiveness adds conscience to reason in the operation of poetry for 'where once reason hath so much overmastered passion as that the mind hath a free desire to do well, the inward light each mind hath in itself is as good as a philosopher's book'; '*since in nature we know it is well to do well, and what is well, and what is evil*' (p. 91, my italics). Poetry, then, has all the attributes of Natural Law, 'the most conveniency to nature of all other', the 'inward reason' and the 'inward light' or scintilla of conscience, all activated through 'heart-ravishing' language to move readers towards an enactment of Natural Law's decrees. Pretending no more than a delightful tale presented enticingly, the poet 'doth intend the winning of the mind from wickedness to virtue' (p. 92), which is precisely the operation of Natural Law. For something which Sidney with mock-modesty disclaims as 'this ink-wasting toy of mine', his claims for educative functions of poetry could not be larger.

Sidney's contemporary, Edmund Spenser, knew full well the risks of using poetic fictions to advise courtiers and monarchs through the medium of poetry. Significantly in the Book of Justice, Book 5, he offers a dire warning to poets who adopt this mantle without being careful to present 'true' fictions:

> There as they entred at the Scriene, they saw
> Some one, whose tongue was for his trespasse vyle
> Nayld to a post, adiudged so by law:
> For that therewith he falsely did reuyle,
> And foule blaspheme that Queene for forged guyle,
> Both with bold speaches, which he blazed had,
> And with lewd poems, which he did compyle;
> For the bold title of a Poet bad
> He on himselfe had ta'en, and rayling rymes had sprad.
>
> Thus there he stood, whylest high ouer his head,
> There written was the purport of his sin,
> In cyphers strange, that few could rightly read,
> BON FON: but *bon* that once had written bin,
> Was raced out, and *Mal* was now put in.

So now *Malfont* was plainely to be red;
Eyther for th'euill which he did therein,
Or that he likened was to a welhed
Of euill words, and wicked sclaunders by him shed.          (V. ix. 25–6)

Punishing a poet by cutting off the hand with which he wrote seditious lines was the practice of monarchs who were offended by receiving advice they did not wish to hear,[58] and Spenser makes the point even more symbolically clear by silencing the poet by cutting out his tongue. The power of poets to influence opinion is not so much acknowledged by western governments nowadays, but the death sentence imposed by Iran in the 1980s on Salman Rushdie shows that some countries do take it seriously. Spenser himself sailed very close to the wind from his early poem *The Shepheardes Calender*[59] through to the later parts of *The Faerie Queene*.[60] For example, again in Book 5, he equates the wicked Duessa with Mary Queen of Scots and directly allegorises her trial under her sister Elizabeth. This certainly offended Mary's son, James VI of Scotland who was to succeed Elizabeth to the throne of England (V. ix. 38–50). The poem as a whole deals with contemporary legal and political realities, and also contains material which was dangerous from a legal point of view, especially in the light of Spenser's general cynicism about corruption and duplicity at court. Spenser seems adroitly to have escaped censure and censorship alike, and he did so partly by exercising innate political caution expressed through sycophantic obeisance to his own 'faerie queene', Elizabeth, and more pertinently by implicitly relying on Sidney's clever use of the quasi-legal fiction, arguing that one who writes a fiction affirms nothing and therefore cannot lie. His defence against the charge of representing Mary in an evil light, would be that the character is not a historical personage at all but the fictional Duessa. Of course the argument is disingenuous since Spenser would also claim the contemporary 'truth' of his poem in a different sense. His most powerful defence against charges of sedition, however, is that he could claim that he is standing by the principle of rule by law and hence supporting the reigning authority. Duessa is, after all, given a 'fair' trial under both jurisdictions of common law and equity.

Shakespeare was a dramatist, not a theorist, but there is evidence in his plays that he had thought about the nature of fictions and the 'as-if' worlds he gives us. The attitude that emerges is one much more worldly-wise than Sidney's, and more playful in its double-edged praise of the medium of poetry. In a play dealing with fortune and flattery, it is significant that he opens *Timon of Athens* with a poet and a painter making observations on their respective arts. The poet points out that many allegorical paintings deal with the change that overcomes sycophants' attitudes to a wealthy man. When his fortune changes they desert him. This is exactly what happens in the play, as the Poet's forecast establishes that the fictions of representational art can be truth-seeing mediums. At the same time, poetry can be misused in the service of flattery, and the misanthrope Apemantus, in saying this, reiterates Plato's charge against poets, poetry and fictions in general:

APEM     ... How now, poet!
POET     How now, philosopher!
APEM     Thou liest.
POET     Art not one?
APEM     Yes.
POET     Then I lie not.
APEM     Art not a poet?
POET     Yes.
APEM     Then thou liest. Look in thy last work, where thou hast feign'd
         him a worthy fellow.
POET     That's not feign'd – he is so.                    (I. i. 216–26)

Ironically, in a metadramatic sense, both characters are 'feign'd' by Shakespeare and yet, in the actors' bodies, 'are so'. By Act V we discover that both Poet and Painter are as self-serving and hypocritical as the rest of those eager to benefit from Timon's hoarded gold, but the implication is not that fictions in themselves are necessarily lies, but that they may be used to tell lies just as adroitly as truths. Which is which, true fiction or false, becomes a moral problem rather than one of representation. Timon at least acknowledges the difficulty by echoing Lodge's words:

TIMON    ... And for thy fiction,
         Why, thy verse swells with stuff so fine and smooth
         That thou art even natural in thine art.          (V. i. 81–3)

The best art is the most artful, that which paradoxically uses art to conceal its art, and appears as nature itself. 'The truest poetry is the most feigning' as Touchstone quips (*As You Like It*, III. iii. 16). But how to discriminate between what is true and what is false in poetry remains a problem which was to exercise especially Protestant poets such as Spenser, Herbert, Milton, and Marvell.

Shakespeare is constantly aware of the ambivalent relationship between fictions and nature, rhetoric and 'reality'. In the 'as-if' world of a play or a poem, the medium may tell deeper truths of nature's law than any other; or it may be a skilfully constructed lie:

VIOLA    Alas, I took great pains to study it, and 'tis poetical.
OLIVIA   It is the more likely to be feigned ...

                                             (*Twelfth Night*, I. v. 182–3)

The context of Touchstone's comment in *As You Like It* on the truest poetry being the most feigning, establishes that he is quite capable of telling lies. Shakespeare maintains the ambivalence, constantly leaving open questions about the moral status of poetry, whether it comes from a seer or from one who shares the 'shaping fantasies' of the lunatic and the lover. He challenges audiences to dismiss the fiction, but at the same time by doing so he confirms the fiction's truth to the imagination and the senses: 'FABIAN If this were play'd upon a stage now, I could condemn it as an improbable fiction' (*Twelfth Night*, III. iv. 130).

> PUCK   If we shadows have offended,
> Think but this, and all is mended,
> That you have but slumber'd here
> While these visions did appear.
> And this weak and idle theme,
> No more yielding but a dream,
> Gentles, do not reprehend.      (*Dream*, V. i. 412–18)

A spirit of bold challenge informs Shakespeare's use of the word 'fiction', since words like 'feign' and their derivatives are in his lines used mainly pejoratively to denote deception, or else they are undercut by context. However, there is a constant sense that his fictions are 'natural' in Lodge's sense of the word, a convincing replica of our world, or in Sidney's sense, a plausible construction of an equally substantial existence. The overall moral is that, like poets such as Spenser, Herbert, and Milton, Shakespeare cautions readers and audiences to be constantly vigilant, and to be aware that poetry may be a false emanation from a wicked magician like Spenser's Archimago, or the prophetic truth-telling of one in touch with Natural Law itself. He can create with apparently equal ease a convincing rogue such as Iago and an omniscient seer like Prospero, leaving it to us to discriminate morally between the two.

Apart from *The Faerie Queene*, the most self-consciously 'as-if' work in the period is the aptly named *As You Like It*. Critics have repeatedly drawn attention to the world of hypothesis that the play inhabits, the repeated syntactical dependence on 'if', and the running debates on nature and nurture, nature and artifice. The familiar Shakespearian ambivalence flickers over the fiction. On the one hand, the forest encourages 'feigning' in the sense of pretending, playing, disguising, making-believe, all as a distraction from the painful realities and responsibilities of the life from which the characters have fled, and which is emblematised in the wrestling match. On the other hand, the forest can be interpreted as the realm of moral responsibility, a domain where Natural Law prevails without the curse of Adam, in a prelapsarian way, and where people become one with nature, whether in the form of the churlish chiding of the winter's wind or the sunlit days of summer. Natural processes such as romantic matchmaking can occur without the constraints of the court, and the guilty, such as Oliver and Duke Frederick, can acquire consciences and be reformed. Shakespeare even explicitly draws attention to the aspects held in common between legal fiction and poetic fiction. According to Touchstone, the legal fiction is one step beyond 'a lie seven times removed' (V. iv. 65). He tells the tale of how he became involved in a quarrel which threatened to lead to a duel. In detailing the steps in this quarrel, he builds up through the 'lie with circumstance' (upon conditions) to the most dangerous 'Lie Direct' which can be neutralised by what is essentially a legal fiction:

All these you may avoid but the Lie Direct; and you may avoid that too with an If. I knew when seven justices could not take up a quarrel; but when the parties were met themselves, one of them thought but of an If, as: 'If you said so, then I said so'. And they shook hands, and swore brothers. Your If is the only peacemaker; much virtue in If. (V. iv. 90–7)

Touchstone's words, parodying the common use of legal fictions and anticipating Vaihinger's 'as if' philosophy, recall Quintilian's definition of 'fictitious arguments' in oratory: 'The proposition of something which, if true, would either solve a problem or contribute to its solution.'[61] In this sense, legal fictions and poetic fictions alike, based on an implied 'as-if' formulation, are properly used as problem solvers in order to achieve a state of equity and 'natural' peace. *In fictione juris [et poeticae] semper aequitas existit.* In the fiction lies the power to implement or represent a moral state which satisfies reason and conscience, based on charity which in Shakespearian comedy means human love and the community values, both celebrated by Hymen at the end of *As You Like It*, and canonised in twentieth-century criticism as the 'festive ending' by C. L. Barber and Northrop Frye. The playful ambivalence which Shakespeare builds into his own implicit theory of fictions is that, unfortunately, they can also be 'lies direct' in themselves. The act of believing a poet's fictions may constitute as much an act of faith as belief in God, or it might be one of misplaced and foolhardy trust. Whereas other theorists of the time tried to claim that only the virtuous speak rhetoric, and (in Protestant eyes) only truth-telling shepherds write genuine poetry, Shakespeare wryly observes that the very tools of rhetoric and poetry are double-edged and ambiguous, and that their truth value is at best relative, yoked to the moral vision of the

literary work and its audience. The only way to resolve such ambivalences is by assuming some ethical dimension beyond man-made
systems and positive laws, to a dimension said by Elizabethan theorists
to be shared by all readers as by all humanity: to reason, conscience,
and community 'needs': in short, to Natural Law.

# 5 More's *Utopia*[1]

The inscrutable economy of Thomas More's *Utopia* is capable of telling us more about its readers' views than its author's. For a book written with such clarity, it is remarkable for the number of conflicting interpretations it has generated. Even what kind of book it is has been disputed. For one set of readers it is a straightforward Renaissance imitation of Plato's *Republic*, a vehicle for ideas never intended for practical application. For one set it is a satire on Plato's form, while for another it has only the most superficial connections with *The Republic*.[2] It has been read as a purely 'literary' work, playing wittily with ideas, a youthful *jeu d'esprit* written by More for his fellow-humanist Erasmus in a period of enforced idleness. Connected with this reading is the approach through role-playing, the notion that *Utopia* is an exercise in exemplifying and exploring Renaissance political decorum, fitting one's conduct flexibly to the context of the moment.[3] For still others who fundamentally believe the book is 'literary' in its kind, it becomes an analogue to *The Tempest* or a contribution to literature drawing on and satirising contemporary travel documents such as Vespucci's in More's time.

Opposed to the 'literary' readers are those who see More as a political theorist, an adviser to kings.[4] *Utopia* then becomes a powerful example of rhetoric and fiction, as analysed in the previous chapter, persuading readers through reason, controlled language, and an appeal to common humanity to adopt and enact a political programme. But here the fun really starts. What political programme More is advocating is bitterly contested by a set of views ranging apparently across the whole political spectrum from one extreme to the other. Alistair Fox attempts to mediate the vast discrepancies by arguing that, while some contemporaries were delighted by the iconoclastic radicalism of *Utopia* which they took seriously, More himself shows signs even within the work itself of distancing himself from its programme, since he was writing it at the very moment his career was changing from obscure insignificance into a position of political power.[5] Rather than rehearsing the galaxy of arguments that have been mounted, I shall simply sketch two dominant viewpoints, the conservative and the radical. Conservative commentators focus on the pragmatic figure 'More' in the book, a man who can see defects in his own society, and some merit in utopian morality, but finds its political system inappropriate and impossible to realise in his own world. 'Utopia' we are constantly reminded, means 'No-place' and Hythlodaeus means 'Nonsense'. We are invited by conservative readers to look very critically in the utopian scheme at contradictions and denials whose existence makes it inconceivable that the writer could endorse it. Slavery, an anathema to the modern world, exists. The utopians claim to despise war and to have no concept of private property, and yet they will go to war 'to protect their own land' (p. 87). All religions are tolerated, but the person with no religion is not. The utopian political system respects no authority except that of collective decision-making, and yet it does have its own social and sexual hierarchy which is seen at its most rigid in prescribed behaviour in church (p. 105). Having located those other contradictions in Utopia, such readers then find also severe restrictions on personal freedom and dignity, including the freedom to be different, to be personally ambitious, to 'better oneself'. All these factors add up to a reading which, taken to an extreme, is capable of making *Utopia* sound like *1984*, a satire on a totalitarian state which practises thought-control on its subjects. A milder version of this approach would suggest that the writer has deliberately made *Utopia* into a flawed commonwealth so that we should not assume its perfection, and that its function is as a touchstone by which the existing political institutions may be judged and improved with a dose of Christian humanism.

The radical reading of *Utopia* sees the description of the organisation of the state as an early communist manifesto. Indeed, Karl Marx himself placed the book in this line of thought, connecting it with the views of the Levellers in the seventeenth century.[6] One commentator, probably the best, J. H. Hexter, sees the book as even more radically communist than any actual twentieth-century system, carrying through with rigorous logic the axiom that 'Equality is justice' (p. cxxiii). In the utopian system all labour and assets are equal, no profits or losses are ever made, there is no poverty, everybody has employment and is provided by the state with handsome houses, medical care, and enlightened education. Another radical pedigree is the only truly utopian form of communism – anarchy – and More has been claimed by philosophical anarchists as their precursor.[7] Political decisions are made collectively, there is no concept whatever of private ownership, and the Kropotkinite message is clear in 'The Utopians think it is hardly right to take what they don't need away from people who do need it.' Indeed, of all modern political philosophies, that of non-violent anarchism is closest in spirit and detail to the utopian vision. What links all these radical readings are commonly held assumptions that Thomas More meant utopianism to be taken seriously rather than just entertained intellectually, that 'More' in the book is not an authorial mouthpiece, but something of a stooge apologist for the corrupt European system, and that Hythlodaeus is much closer to what More, at least in this book, really believed. Moreover, radical readings take equally seriously the blistering attacks on contemporary injustice, poverty, and enclosures in England, arguing that no amount of tinkering with a system which is fundamentally flawed and unfair will ever improve things.

There can be few books which are open to such opposite readings, each held with equal conviction and even vehemence. Attempts at compromise can invariably be shepherded into tacit collusion with either the conservative or radical fold. It is a book which, willy-nilly, forces readers to disclose their own fundamental political ideologies, since the differences are over assumptions and world-views rather than interpretation. What is it about the book's deployment of the art of persuasion that allows it cogently to persuade in opposite directions? The first and obvious point is the formal one that it is presented in dialogue form, and that adoption of one or other interlocutor as either the writer's mouthpiece or as 'neutral' is perilous. 'More' and Hythlodaeus represent respectively the two opposed world-views on offer, and no internal reason for preferring one over the other can be logically sustained. At a more abstract level, the two debate in ways that reveal minds that can never meet. Raphael is committed by his personal experience to imaginative construction and reconstruction of quite different systems (he is, after all, remembering), while 'More' is rooted in the Eurocentric present, unable or unwilling to imagine that there can be other systems available, or even possible, in what he would call 'the real world'. The debate really takes us right to the heart of the clash between Natural Law and positive law in the sixteenth century, and some of the inherent ambiguities surrounding the application of Natural Law.

Thomas More was not only ideally placed to comment on the rift between the legal systems, but he was also, at least later in his life, to become personally compromised by it. His education began at Oxford in 1492–4, so, unlike the common lawyers at the Inns of Court, he would have been thoroughly trained in rhetoric. He read classics and divinity under Linacre and Grocyn, and if he was exposed to law, it would have been canon law and Roman civil law, both of which incorporate Natural Law thinking. In preparation for a career in law, he went in 1494 to New Inn, significantly an Inn of Chancery whose master belonged to the

Chancery Court, but then in 1496 to Lincoln's Inn, a common-law institution. By 1516 when he wrote *Utopia,* More was a very busy common lawyer and had distinguished himself enough to be appointed an undersheriff of London, which meant that he would be a judge for perhaps a day each week. His first biographer, Roper, says that throughout his professional life one of More's particular hobby-horses was that equity should influence common law, for he regularly urged judges to mitigate the rigour of the letter of the law 'by their own discretions (as they were, as he thought, in conscience bound)'.[8] This is what Raphael urges in the presence of Morton, before he reveals a more radical approach. His insistence on equity was rewarded in 1529 when he was appointed Lord Chancellor, head of the Chancery Court. As one of the rare non-ecclesiastic appointments to the post, his claim to the position lay precisely in his equal experience as common lawyer and his insistence on equitable principles,[9] stemming from canon law and ultimately Natural Law. Tragically, he became to Henry VIII like a Hythlodaeus to the court – an intransigent advocate of principle, standing out against the expedience and compromises of his powerful rival, Cardinal Wolsey. It is a poignant touch that he went to his death proclaiming to the end that the law under which he was being executed was contrary to reason and conscience, and thus to Natural Law.

Even without reading the book with the benefit of hindsight, it is clear that the two systems, utopian and European, which are juxtaposed in *Utopia,* are Natural Law and positive law (based on custom and expedience), and the fundamental question is whether Natural Law, however fine in theory, can ever be systematically followed. The reason the book is so ambivalent and its readers so divided between the systems, lies surely in the fact that More himself could equally appreciate the nature of each, and, given the nature of his rigorous mode of argument, he could also appreciate their mutual incompatibility. Following reason and conscience as strictly as Raphael Hythlodaeus does, leads to an impasse with existing legal systems which are based on more political considerations. From one point of view the shoddy corruption and inequities of English positive law are exposed as being irrational and against conscience, and in their place is proposed Aquinas' optimism about a new system. But from another point of view the question is raised whether man is actually capable of being strictly rational anyway; whether, as Calvinists argued, in the fallen state, Natural Law is clouded over in the human heart. The argument for Natural Law is pursued so passionately and patiently that I would say that More, at this stage of his career and in correspondence with the iconoclastic Erasmus, favours the Aquinian view that it can be retrieved if people can simply think clearly and comprehensively about justice without preconceptions based on the status quo. The very fact of the book itself is evidence for this optimistic message. But I cannot in honesty deny the implicit strain of pessimism of the other belief, since Raphael's interlocutors, while they have been entertained and cajoled into new thinking, have not radically changed their positions by the end of the book. *Utopia* could be a celebratory manifesto or it could be a despairing tract on the intransigency of human thought in being unable to move beyond existing assumptions. There is, then, a surprisingly modern, even postmodern, emphasis on the relativity of ideologies.

### Ideology as fiction

Book 1, amongst other functions, dramatically demonstrates the failure of the European minds of 'More' and Peter Giles to meet the utopian's mind. The two Books are rather different in kind. While the first is dramatic dialogue the second is a formal discourse, presupposing the context offered in Book 1 and confirmed by 'More's' peroration. They both 'work' perfectly well in their different aims and in their sequence, and we do not need to know of Erasmus' remark that More 'had written the second part because he was at leisure, and the first part he afterwards dashed off as opportunity offered. Hence there is some inequality in the style.'[10] The 'inequality' lies not primarily in style but in the book's rhetorical intention, from which appropriate styles follow. To put it briefly, Book 1 is a debate about fundamental assumptions, and a clear demonstration that anybody who adopts the stance of 'More' and Giles will never comprehend the true ideological purpose of Book 2. Book 1 amounts to an invitation to the reader to abandon European assumptions, and to yield imaginatively to the utopian fiction which will follow. At the same time, a deeply sceptical strain runs through the Book, implying that such a suspension of ingrained assumptions will prove as impossible to the European reader as it does to 'More' and Giles.

It could be said that Book 1 is 'about' the nature of ideology, as that word is understood by recent literary theorists. On the one hand ideology is a construction, a fiction, whose relationship to 'reality' is analogical rather than inevitable. On the other hand, ideology can find so profound and unconscious an agreement in a person or a culture that it is uncritically accepted as axiomatically 'the truth' about the world. It can be difficult, perhaps impossible, to inspect with critical circumspection one's own ideology, so tenacious is its hold on the set of assumptions one maintains about the world we live in. It can also be hurtful and even devastating to be told that one's most cherished assumptions about the world are fictions with no more and no less 'truth' than another person's fictions. This is precisely the area being quarried by Book 1 of *Utopia*.

The book appears to open on the firm ground of autobiography. The narrator says he is on a diplomatic mission for Henry VI to Flanders, to settle a commercial dispute between the two nations. His main adversary in negotiations is the Provost of Castile, a lawyer. They cannot agree, adjourn the meeting, and in the lull 'More' goes to visit his friend Peter Giles, an agreeable companion. All of this appears to fit the facts of More's own activities in 1515, so it seems that at this stage 'More' is More. Moreover, this context of an intractable difference over money affairs between two political entities crucially anticipates the main debate to be sustained in the rest of Book 1, concerning ideological misunderstandings and mutual incomprehension.

At this point enters Raphael, a man held up for curiosity value, full of travellers' yarns, given to quaint philosophical sayings adapted from Seneca and Cicero like 'The man who has no grave is covered by the sky' and 'the road to heaven is equally short from all places' (p. 10). The conversational context is important. 'More' is taking time off from lofty state business, Giles is a most trusted friend, and Raphael is an outsider. Tensions build up, for 'More' and Giles amiably patronise Raphael, which generates some heat in Raphael's tone and his content. He knows that people like 'More' and Giles, like other statesmen he has met such as Cardinal Morton, Lord Chancellor of England, can never understand what he is really talking about, and after an eddy of energetic hope, he despairingly admits this, and confronts them with the perception. As elsewhere, 'More' and Giles are complacently unaware even of the problem let alone attempting to find a solution. In a displaced way and on different issues, Thomas More himself on his diplomatic mission may have found himself becoming as frustrated as Raphael, and *Utopia* may be his attempt to understand this frustration.

The sticking point comes when Giles, genuinely impressed by Raphael's knowledge and shrewdness, exclaims 'My dear Raphael ... I'm surprised that you don't enter some king's service' (p. 13). Raphael's presence at the 'counsel board' would, he says, be wanted by any prince, and he hints that Raphael's 'relatives and friends' would benefit in pecuniary ways. Raphael picks up what he may see as the most insulting suggestion, and says he has already distributed all his money and possessions to relatives and friends, and that they should be content with this. He regards as a kind of blackmail the suggestion 'that for their sake I should enslave myself to any king whatever'. Giles mildly remonstrates that he did not mean servitude to a king but 'service' and Raphael

sardonically replies 'the difference is only a matter of one syllable'. Giles
plods on, saying that Raphael could be 'useful' and this would make him
'happier', a reasonable enough assumption to a Eurocentric administrator but not to the uncompromising Raphael. Such service, he sharply
says, would be 'repellent' to his spirit and would make him unhappy. To
anticipate my argument a little, Raphael is here staking his place as one
who believes wholly in Natural Law. He simply will not do anything
against his own nature. 'More' now enters the debate, appealing to the
altruism involved in advising a king, inciting him 'to just and noble
actions' (p. 14) even if it goes against the grain of his temperament.
Raphael sharply insists first that he does not have the capacity ascribed
to him and secondly that nobody would be better off if he 'bartered [his]
peace of mind for some ruler's convenience'. Rulers, he says, are more
interested in war and empire-building than peace, courts are crippled by
flattery, envy, time-serving, and an inertia rationalised as 'custom'. He
recalls his brief experience at the English court, when he ventured to
criticise a system of justice which favours the drone-like rich and bleeds
the poor. Speaking in the presence of the cardinal, Raphael had warmed
to his task and, in memorable and powerful fashion, attacked the system
of enclosure which was gathering speed in Thomas More's own England.
The cardinal interrupted and tried to silence Raphael (unsuccessfully,
since he persists). His diatribe was ignored by those around the cardinal,
one rather peripheral point was appropriated by the cardinal, whereupon
it was hailed by the listeners as his own great thought, and the discussion
trickled into foolery. Raphael sums up his 'long tale' by telling 'More'
and Giles that his experience showed the futility of offering advice which
is ignored or misused, to a court which is hierarchical and riven with
sycophancy.

Still unable to grasp Raphael's point, 'More' persists in his glib advice:
'I think if you could overcome your aversion to court life, your advice to
a prince would be of the greatest advantage to mankind' (p. 28), not
realising that Raphael's position is not 'aversion' but rational objection
at a fundamental level. At this point it must be clear that 'More' cannot
be More, since a person so crassly unaware of what Raphael is saying
could not conceivably write Raphael's very lucid and definitive dismissal
of political life. Only a person ideologically at one with the system
Raphael is condemning could possibly misunderstand. When 'More'
invokes Plato's advice that 'commonwealths will be happy only when
philosophers become kings or kings become philosophers' (double-edged
advice, because Plato added that either case would be virtually impossible), Raphael identifies very clearly what has been going on in this
cross-purposes conversation:

Plato was right in foreseeing that unless kings become philosophical themselves, the advice of real philosophers would never influence them, *immersed as they are and infected with false values from boyhood on.* (p. 28, my italics)

The real problem he faces in his attempts to persuade 'More', or at least enlighten him, is that 'More' and Giles are victims of this ideological blinkering, through an upbringing which immerses and infects them so thoroughly with certain values, that they take these to be truth itself and can see no further outside their constructs.

Raphael with surprising patience continues to give examples of the impotence of philosophy (and truth) at court, concluding,

'Now, don't you suppose if I set these ideas and others like them before men strongly inclined to the contrary, they would 'turn deaf ears' to me?' (p. 35)

Inadvertently, 'More' reveals that he too has been turning 'deaf ears' on Raphael:

'Stone deaf, indeed, there's no doubt about it', I said, 'and no wonder! To tell you the truth, I don't think you should offer advice or thrust forward ideas of this sort that you know will not be listened to. What good will it do? When your listeners are already prepossessed against you and firmly convinced of opposite opinions, what can you accomplish with your out-of-the-way notions? This academic philosophy is pleasant enough in the private conversation of close friends, but in the councils of kings, where grave matters are being authoritatively decided, there is no room for it.'
    'That is just what I was saying', Raphael replied. 'There is no place for philosophy in the councils of kings.'
    'Yes, there is,' I said, 'but not for this school philosophy which supposes that every topic is suitable for every occasion.' (p. 68)

This exchange brings to a crescendo the debate as exemplification of ideological misunderstanding, the impossibility of a meeting of minds. The acrimonious confrontation lies between one ideology that equates pure reason with truth, and the other that assumes truth is relative to an occasion, that philosophy should be 'adapt[ed] to the drama in hand', playing its part with decorum rather than breaking the decorum of the occasion with 'inappropriate' references to facts, principle and logic. 'More' depicts himself as a compromiser, not realising that compromise, in Raphael's eyes, will never solve problems:

If you cannot pluck up bad ideas by the root, or cure long-standing evils to your heart's content, you must not therefore abandon the commonwealth. Don't give up the ship in a storm because you cannot direct the winds. And don't force strange and untested ideas on people who you know are firmly persuaded the other way. (p. 40)

Raphael proclaims himself the absolutist, well aware that he has been fruitlessly engaged in trying to persuade the unpersuadable. He says he cannot cure others of madness by raving himself, and that he sees it as the business of a philosopher not to tell expedient lies. Now broaching some of his apparently crazier ideas (to 'More's' ears) such as the possibility of running a commonwealth on grounds of utopian equality and communion, he more or less finally dismisses 'More's' point of view as one which fails to imagine, and which cannot hypothesise a fiction which is antithetical to his own ingrained fiction:

'I'm not surprised that you think of it this way,' said Raphael, 'since you have no idea or only a false idea of such a commonwealth'. (p. 40)

There is, however, a shrewd hint dropped, that Raphael may be little better in this respect at least, for it was only by 'seeing' Utopia and living in it, rather than constructing the ideas for himself, that he was persuaded of the possibility of alternative modes of government. This may be the most depressing insight by the writer, Thomas More, into the universality of what Blake came to call 'mind-forged manacles'. Until we witness them with our own eyes, we cannot imagine, let alone create, better worlds.

I have spelt out the strategy of the conversation in such detail because it is crucial to the book's effect on readers. Book 2 which follows dispenses with the resistant interlocutor, by being a straightforward account of utopian life, not even set in quotation marks, as if it is a philosophical discourse without a context. However, it *does* have a context, made up of readers who are either resistant (having aligned themselves with 'More' and Giles) or credulous (having aligned themselves with Raphael), time-serving on the one hand or strictly rational on the other. The multiplicity of conflicting readers, conservative and radical, is neatly explained within Book 1 itself as its primary purpose: the nature of political ideology as fiction, and the apparent impossibility of persuading a person who regards his own fiction as truth and cannot concede to its contrary any plausibility.

### Natural Law and equity

What, then, are the principles guiding the actual content of Raphael's fiction, his ideology? In answering this question, the book itself guides us first to look at what Utopia is *not*.

Utopia is emphatically not Europe, at least as organised and governed in More's time. Much of Book 1 consists of Raphael's anatomy of European deficiencies. The first instance links injustice and poverty, historically placed. Raphael had been close to Cardinal Morton at the time of the Cornish uprising when, in 1497, Cornishmen marched on London to complain of Henry VIII's taxes, only to be slaughtered. A layman, speaking like Angelo in *Measure for Measure*, praises 'the rigid execution of justice then being practised on thieves' (p. 15) who are being hanged in their thousands. Raphael speaks freely, condemning the system, arguing that the penalty is too harsh, and it is not an effective deterrent against theft. His attack is very closely based on the argument of equity as a legal system. The subordination of human life to property is wrong in conscience,[11] and the strict application of the law in practice creates inequities according to reason. This result, Raphael says, is because many are through poverty 'driven to the awful necessity of stealing and then dying for it' (p. 16). He parries the argument that there is always gainful employment by saying that many men crippled in wars 'are too shattered to follow their old trades and too old to learn new ones'; and that meanwhile noblemen 'who live idly like drones off the labour of others' bleed their tenants by rack-renting. Meanwhile, jobs disappear and men are forced to become vagabonds and to steal to survive.

Raphael now, in one of the best-known passages in the book, pungently pinpoints the causes and effects of enclosures, whereby throughout the sixteenth century private landlords could buy up common lands in order to graze sheep. This was one of the many changes taking place in agriculture that disrupted the old society, and a particularly controversial one. Sheep-farming being economical of labour, requiring only a shepherd (and, moreover, being one that erodes the land), the result was that farm-labourers simultaneously lost their employment, lost access to common lands for subsistence farming, and lost their tied cottages, and the land itself symbolically lost its fertility. All they could do was wander and beg, while food prices soared beyond reach. Raphael indignantly points out the deep injustice of then punishing these victims as vagabonds or thieves. 'Hideous poverty' exists beside 'wanton luxury' caused ultimately by 'the crass avarice of a few' (p. 20).

If you don't try to cure these evils, it is futile to boast of your severity in punishing theft. Your policy may look superficially like justice, but in reality it is neither just nor practical. (p. 21)

At this stage Raphael suggests reform rather than overthrow and, like Sir Thomas Smith (to be praised by Milton later as a Protestant writer) in *A Discourse of the Commonweal of This Realm of England* (1549), suggests a package of changes which would restore agriculture. Raphael also contrasts another state he has seen, that of the Polylerites

(Much Nonsense), where theft is a matter for restitution rather than punishment.

The issue of enclosures was a controversial one throughout the sixteenth century, and by way of contrast to More's attitude we can quote Edmund Spenser eighty years later. While in Utopia there is no strong opposition to Hythlodaeus' condemnation of enclosures, Spenser's thinly disguised persona, Irenius, in *A View of the Present State of Ireland* is quite unambiguously in favour of them:

EUDOXIUS   For what reasonable man will not think that the tenement shall be made much the better for the lord's behoof, if the tenant may by such means be drawn to build himself some handsome habitation thereon, to ditch and enclose his ground, to manure and husband it as good farmers use ... and to all these other commodities he shall in short time find a greater added, that is his own wealth and riches increased and wonderfully enlarged by keeping his cattle in enclosures, where they shall always have fresh pasture, that now is all trampled and overrun, warm cover, that now lieth open to all weather, safe being, that now are continually filched and stolen.

IRENIUS   Ye have well, Eudoxius, accounted the commodities of this one good ordinance amongst which this that ye named last is not the least; for all the other being most beneficial both to the landlord and the tenant, this chiefly redowndeth to the good of the commonwealth, to have the land thus enclosed and well fenced. For it is both a principal bar and impeachment unto thieves from stealing of cattle in the night, and also a gall against all rebels and outlaws that shall rise up in any numbers against government.[12]

There is no resistance to this view offered in the book, and it is clear that Spenser would not countenance the analysis of Hythlodaeus which highlights the adverse social consequences of enclosures.

So far the debate between Raphael and the lawyer seems to be the traditional kind of *exemplum* on justice which opens manuals of rhetoric such as Wilson's and Cox's, with the significant difference that Raphael focuses on *in*justice and its social and political consequences. At Cardinal Morton's court, Raphael poises himself ominously on the edge of the savage attack on private property which he will unleash later in conversation with 'More' and Giles.

Scattered throughout Book 1 are hints and declarations that Raphael does have an overall legal *schema* which he is using as the basis for his argument against the lawyer. Drawing a contrast between the crimes of murder and theft of a coin, he says 'If equity means anything, there is no proportion or relation at all between these two' (p. 22). It is necessary to quote at length what he says next:

If mutual consent to human laws entitles men by special decree to exempt their agents from divine law and allows them to kill where he has given us no example, what is this but preferring the law of man to the law of God? The result will be that in every situation men will decide for themselves how far it suits them to observe the laws of God. The law of Moses is harsh and severe, as for an enslaved and stubborn people, but it punishes theft with a fine, not death. Let us not think that in his new law of mercy, where he rules us as a father rules his children, God has given us greater license to be cruel to one another. (p. 22)

The rhetoric and the substance here appeal to Natural Law and the English system of equity, as well as to Mosaic law which was considered later by Puritans like Milton to be the closest to God's law available to man. Implicitly there is an attack on common law and parliamentary enactment – all forms of positive law – since they can so easily move out of line from divine law and be made for the convenience of rich people rather than from humble submission to God and motives of equity. They are based on custom rather than equitable distribution or reason, or conscience. The reference to Mosaic law, in tandem with the 'new law of mercy' established by Christ is to demonstrate that both agree that theft does not deserve hanging as a punishment. Observably, positive law has violated divine law, as known by man through reason and conscience. References to equity, the laws of God and the new law of mercy, in sixteenth-century terms, place Raphael squarely within the line of equity and Natural Law.

There are later references which confirm this point. Raphael is the Natural Lawyer, arguing throughout from the point of view of reason and rational analysis alone, refusing doggedly to allow any considerations of expediency or compromise to enter his train of thought. His crescendos of anger and indignation are not abdications from reason but the result of its exercise: if rational thought leads to the conclusion that an injustice exists, then conscience takes over, as the passionate faculty stirring people's hearts into action to right a wrong. Following Aristotelian rhetorical strategies, Raphael first seeks to convince his audience by narrative logic and telling examples, and then to stir their emotions, touch their consciences, and incite them to moral action. Here, I believe, lies the true heart of *Utopia* as a book, allowing us to bypass arid arguments about whether it is conservative or radical (the futility of which the writer anticipates, as we have seen). Raphael is the 'natural' man, in all Tudor senses. He can live as he pleases, avoid what is repellent to his spirit (p. 13), be utterly and uncompromisingly honest; living, in short, in a natural state. He also argues from an acceptance of Natural Law precepts, using them throughout as a touchstone for true law in contrast to man's positive laws. He can also, in the other sense of the word, be dismissed as a 'natural', a fool, a nonsense, as his name suggests. The outcome of this is that Book 2, an apparently factual presentation of utopian life, is the imaginative projection of the natural man. It is a state existing entirely by reason and conscience, according to Natural Law. It has no need to compromise with European positive law or custom. It can also, like Raphael, be dismissed (at our peril, admittedly) as a projection of a fool, a no-place based on nonsense.

Like Raphael, the inhabitants of Utopia all live by nature. Most sons 'feel a natural inclination' (p. 50) to 'train for their father's crafts', but if they are attracted by their nature to another trade they are at liberty to follow it. The utopians can declare war on those in their community who will not live by its distributive and egalitarian laws:

The Utopians say it's perfectly justifiable to make war on people who leave their land idle and waste yet forbid the use and possession of it to others who, by the law of nature, ought to be supported from it. (p. 56)

They produce no more than 'those commodities that nature really requires' (p. 53). Utopians have not apparently contemplated vegetarianism, but they will not themselves slaughter animals because it 'gradually destroys the sense of compassion, the finest sentiment of which our human nature is capable' (p. 57). Utopians are allowed to indulge any kind of human pleasure 'as long as it's true and natural pleasure' (p. 53), and so long as harm does not come of it (p. 60). Their moral philosophy dwells on the subjects considered central in Natural Law: 'the nature of the good', having as their chief concern 'human happiness' (p. 67). Indeed, like Aquinas and other Natural Law exponents, utopians believe 'that all or the most important human happiness consists of pleasure'. (Raphael distances himself from this 'comfortable' opinion.) Their philosophical method is precisely that of medieval, Christian Natural Law, although the book does not specify Christianity.

they never discuss happiness without joining to their philosophic rationalism certain principles of religion. Without these religious principles, they think that reason is bound to prove weak and defective in its efforts to investigate true happiness. (p. 68)

The 'religious principles' are roughly analogous to conscience as the knowledge of good and evil in pursuing pleasures. People are born for happiness, and their immortal souls will after death be rewarded for virtues and punished for sins. There is the careful statement that 'Though these are indeed religious beliefs, they think that reason leads men to believe and accept them' (p. 68). The dictates of conscience are as rational as reason itself. Their motto is 'According to nature' and 'with good reason' as the text says because 'By simply following his senses and his right reason a man may discover what is pleasant by nature' (p. 71).

'Human reason' (p. 77) guides all their contemplations of virtue and pleasure and their admiration of the physical pleasures of sound, sight and smell 'recognising that nature intended them to be the particular province of man' (p. 76).

One long paragraph (pp. 69–71) sums up all these moral considerations, and places Utopia firmly in a state of 'right reason' and Natural Law.

They define virtue as living according to nature; and God, they say, created us to that end. When a man obeys the dictates of reason in choosing one thing and avoiding another, he is following nature. (p. 69)

'The first rule of reason' is to venerate the creator. 'The second rule of nature is to lead a life as free of anxiety and as full of joy as possible, and to help all one's fellow men towards that end.'

Nothing is more humane (and humanity is the virtue most proper [i.e. natural] to human beings] than to relieve the misery of others, assuage their griefs, and by removing all sadness from their lives, to restore them to enjoyment, that is, pleasure. (p. 70)

There is nothing self-sacrificial about such altruism, since nature, prescribing for us 'a joyous life', in other words, pleasure, as the goal of our actions condones through reason the living of as 'cheerful' a life as possible. No one person's welfare is nature's sole concern: 'she cherishes alike all those living beings to whom she has granted the same form' (p. 70). This account of utopian morality is the most specific, eloquent, and detailed statement of Natural Law since Aquinas wrote his *Summa*, and its spirit and details underpin everything in Books 1 and 2 of *Utopia*. It is the touchstone by which the corruptions of Europe are judged, and it is the basis of the alternative political, economic and social system of *Utopia*. At the book's centre lies a celebration of rationality, equity and Natural Law.

More's credentials were hardly those of a radical, although as evidence that More could countenance unorthodox ideas, one may point to his friendship with Erasmus, against whose subversiveness More was warned by a 'friendly' monk and to his own *History of King Richard the Third*, written just before *Utopia* and warning monarchs against tyrannical tendencies. Whether or not he was by temperament a radical or conservative, More's hypothetical speculations on posing the question 'What would a state be like if it were based solely on Natural Law?' lead him to propose in his fiction the most radical idea possible in the world of political thought: abolition of private property.

### Utopian communism

Most modern writers call the economic basis of More's Utopia, communism, and J. H. Hexter, more precisely calls it utopian communism. This is rather misleading, not because it implies too radical a stance but that it is not radical enough. What is today known as communism, broadly speaking an economy run along lines advocated by Karl Marx, is not the system that prevails in Utopia. No state in modern times has been run on the total abolition of private ownership of property, and no state has done away with a money-exchange economy. There are precedents for such a system, such as that lived by Australian aboriginals up until white settlement, but state Communism (let us capitalise it to distinguish from other sorts) in the twentieth century retains money as the mode of exchange, and institutionalises common ownership only of the means of production and manufacture, accommodation (often), and health and education services. Beyond these, a citizen may privately own books, for example, cars, clothes, and so on. Utopian economics (or more precisely abolition of economics) is more thoroughgoing, since 'all things are held in common' (p. 37) and 'everything is shared equally, and all men live in plenty' (p. 38). A straightforward example is what happens in the market-place. Everything produced, both manufactured and farmed, is simply brought to a warehouse or a food market and displayed, and people take only what they 'need', an important word in Natural Law:

Here the head of every household looks for what he or his family needs and carries off what he wants without any sort of payment or compensation. Why shall anything be refused him? There is plenty of everything, and no reason to fear that anyone will claim more than he needs. (p. 56)

Before we come to examine the utopian system, it is useful to recall that political systems based on common ownership (communism) have had a long and illustrious history of advocates, before and after More wrote. Raphael is not radical in the sense of breaking new ground, only in the rational thoroughness of his application of the principle. Plato admittedly confined communism in *The Republic* to an elite of guardians of the people, not extending it further, but this in itself implies that he saw it as the highest system which could be aspired to.

In the first place, none must possess any private property save the indispensable. Secondly, none must have any habitation or treasure-house which is not open for all to enter at will.[13]

Food is given to them as the wages of their guardianship, 'so measured that there shall be neither superfluity at the end of the year nor lack.

They have no need of gold and silver, and it is not lawful for them to touch it.' Because Plato confines communism to a small, elite group, his system is not based on equality as More's is, but rather on removing the grounds for self-interest amongst those required to be disinterested. Later in the *Laws*[14] Plato reluctantly renounced the programme, not because it was a bad idea, but because it was too good for human beings, in the sense that he argues such a system can work only where people are as perfect as gods. Aristotle, with his emphasis on proportionate rather than equal rights, rejected the whole idea except in the sphere of ethics where he quotes the proverb 'what friends have is common property ... for friendship depends on community' (*Amicorum communia omnia*). He also gives a glimmer of support for the idea of communalism by saying that 'property ought to be common in a sense', but he adds that this 'sense' is that 'private property should be privately owned, but common in use'.[15] On the other hand, utopians regard the perfect state as one where private property is abolished and everything is common. Virgil, in an evocation of the Golden Age of Saturn, used words that would be echoed down through the fifteenth century to the Industrial Revolution in Europe:

> No fences parted fields, nor marks nor bounds
> Divided acres of litigious grounds,
> But all was common.                              (*Georgics* I, lines 125–7)

And Seneca wrote of earlier times: 'To all the way was open: the use of all things was a common right.'[16] Lactantius was another pre-Christian who, in the reign of Diocletian, condemned private property.[17] With the coming of Christianity, communism was given a powerful model. The style of living adopted by Christ, and some of his actions such as the scourging of the tax-gatherers from the temple, at least imply a rejection of worldly property and an angry contempt for the system of money. The disciples read his actions in this light:

And all that believed were together, and had all things common And sold their possessions and goods, and parted them to all men, as every man had need. (Acts of the Apostles 2: 44–5; 1611 edn.)

And the multitude of them that believed, were of one heart, and of one soul: Neither said any of them, that ought of the things which he possessed, was his own, but they had all things common. (*Ibid.* 4: 32)

And distribution was made unto every man according as he had need. (*Ibid.* 4: 35)

Once again, it is 'need' that motivates people's attitude to property, and this concept, central to Natural Law, is used by Shakespeare. Raphael himself points out that 'Christ encouraged his disciples to practise community of goods' and he says 'that among the truest groups of Christians, the practice still prevails' (p. 96).

In the development of Christianity, there have always been monastic communities, following the example of the Apostles and the teachings of Saint Jerome, which have run along the lines of ascetic communism. Indeed, it was this group that More would have had in front of him to prove the viability of the utopian ideal, and their existence must have powerfully sustained his confidence in its reasonableness. Saint Gregory says 'the soil is common to all men', and restoring it to the poor is 'an act of justice [rather] than compassion'.[18] Erasmus, who self-evidently communicated his views to More, supports the adage quoted from Aristotle, 'what friends have is common property'. Although later in life, like Plato, he accepted property as necessary but corrupting, earlier he had repeated that 'the perfect state is one where there is no mine and thine but instead all is held in common'.[19] Another friend of More, John Colet, agreed, as Martin Fleisher points out:

They agree with him that the institution of private property is a corruption. Colet associates the law of property with the law of nations. And this, in turn, is identified with the law of corrupt nature in direct contrast with the community of all things which Colet defines as the law of grace.[20]

More himself follows up Colet's linkage of the abolition of private property with the *ius gentium*, for in his *Correspondence* he argues that individualism threatens the common cause of communities.[21] In *Utopia*, as we shall see, he argues not on the grounds of law of nations, but on grounds of reason and conscience, that is, from the Law of Nature.

In this he had support from a significant minority of Englishmen throughout the fifteenth, sixteenth, and seventeenth centuries. In popular uprisings, such as the Peasants' Revolt (1381), the Kentish Rebellion led by Jack Cade in 1450, the Cornish Uprising (1497), and Robert Kett's Rebellion in Norwich (1549), the institution of private property was presented as a cause of basic social inequities and of civil unrest. The appeal was invariably made to natural rights in some form:

> When Adam delved and Eve span
> Who was then the gentleman?                    (Anon, 1381)

In *The Life and Death of Jack Straw*, an anonymous play published in 1593 and based on the events of the Peasants' Revolt in 1381, the Kentish rebels, Straw, John Ball, and Wat Tyler, rail against authority and the rich. Ball, while he does not suggest abolishing private property, certainly preaches equality of status and wealth:

> But I am able by good scripture before you to prove,
> That God doth not this dealing allow nor love.
> But when *Adam* delved and *Eve* span,
> Who was then a Gentleman.
> Brethren, brethren, it were better to have this community,
> Than to have this difference in degrees:
> But follow the counsel of *John Ball*,
> I promise you I love yee all:
> And make division equally,
> Of each mans goods indifferently          (lines 80–5 and 104–7)

For these rousing words of communist sentiment, Parson Ball is hailed by the leader of the rebels, Jack Straw, as the future Archbishop of Canterbury and Chancellor of England. The rebellion was crushed, but its historical occasion, and the later play based on it, are witnesses to its popular message.

The Anabaptists were a group that used scriptural and Natural Law theory to reach the same conclusion.[22] Spenser places its existence back in the Golden Age rather than the present, and he also acknowledges a Natural Law argument:

> For why should he that is at libertie
> Make himselfe bond? sith then we are free borne,
> Let vs all seruile base subiection scorne;
> And as we bee sonnes of the world so wide,
> Let vs our fathers heritage diuide,
> And chalenge to our selues our portions dew
> Of all the patriminie, which a few
> Now hold in hugger mugger in their hand,
> And all the rest doo rob of good and land.
> For now a few haue all and all haue nought,
> Yet all be brethren ylike dearly bought:
> There is no right in this partition,
> Ne was it so by institution
> Ordained first, ne by the law of Nature,
> But that she gaue like blessing to each creture
> As well of worldly liuelode as of life.
> ('Mother Hubbard's Tale', lines 132–47)

As we shall see, in *The Faerie Queene* Spenser does not believe in the communist argument, and significantly the words quoted above from 'Prosopopoeia or Mother Hubbard's Tale' are put in the mouth of a rebellious villain, the Ape. This fact reflects Spenser's fear of rebellion, while at the same time representing the argument from Natural Law mounted by egalitarians at the time.

The English Commonwealth from 1642 to 1660 was, of course, the period when calls for equality and for the abolition of private property were at their loudest, from such groups as the Levellers under John Lilburne and the Diggers under Gerard Winstanley. Their argument was based equally on Natural Law and history, for they saw 'The Norman Yoke' placed upon them after 1066 as marking the destruction of Anglo-Saxon institutions based on equality rather than property rights. The Diggers took up spades against the unproductive use of land, marched up to St Georges Hill in Surrey and began to till the soil which they regarded as common and theirs by Natural Law. They argued that no man should own or hold more land than he could work with his own hands, and their leader, Winstanley, traced all evil to private property (as does Raphael) since it gives rise to the cardinal sin of covetousness,[23] and ultimately to wars (*Law of Freedom*, p. 90). Throughout his writings and recorded speeches we find a peppering of the phrase 'in the light of reason and equity' (e.g. pp. 133, 111).

> The law is righteous, just and good
> When reason is the rule                              (Poem, *ibid.*, p. 138)

In *Poor Oppressed People of England* he summed up an honourable and vociferous tradition to which Raphael Hythlodaeus belongs:

And to prevent all your scrupulous objections, know this, that we must neither buy nor sell; money must not any longer (after our work of the earth's community is advanced) be the great god that hedges in some, and hedges out others. For money is but part of the earth: and surely, the righteous creator who is King, did never ordain that unless some of mankind do bring that mineral (silver and gold) in their hands to others of their own kind, that they should neither be fed, nor be clothed. (p. 100)

Aquinas, whose work was known and cited by More, has been cited by commentators as condoning private property. In fact his treatment is far more equivocal.[24] In a nutshell, he places within Natural Law the right to *use in common* property, as being 'according to the order of natural inclinations' and 'a means of preserving human life and of warding off its obstacles' [*Summa*, I–II, Qu. 94, Art. 2]; but he concedes that agreements about individual ownership may be made for exactly the same reasons. He asks first 'Whether the possession of external things is natural to man?' (*Summa*, 29–29e, lxvi). In answer to this, rather deftly, he distinguishes between an exterior thing considered in its nature and in its utilisation. In its nature it cannot belong to man because it originates from God who can presumably recall it. But man was given exterior things for a purpose, human benefit. He argues, then, that in its utilisation man may have possession or even 'natural ownership' because, directed by natural reason and intelligence he holds 'the power of using them'. In more familiar terms, man is but the steward of God's gifts, not the owner of them. Now, because Aquinas has limited this question to the issue of 'mankind's' ownership, his statement can easily be taken to justify common possession and communism. He is more specific in his next question: 'Whether it is lawful for a man to possess a thing as his own?' (*Summa*, 29–29e, lxvi. 2), and once again his answer turns on the ability to administer and 'enjoy' (utilise) the thing:

Here man ought to possess them, not as his own, but as common, to the extent of being ready to communicate them to others in their need. Hence St Paul says: *Charge the rich of this world to give easily, to communicate to others, &c.* (1 Timothy vi. 17–18)

Overall, Aquinas' argument is that the right to own private property is an addition to Natural Law, a kind of positive law, but not a contradiction of Natural Law. Because of its subsidiary status, Aquinas need not arbitrate between systems. While not mandating private property, Natural Law can happily accommodate it; and equally, while not mandating communalism, it can happily accommodate it, just as on the political level Natural Law can accommodate rival political systems like monarchy and democracy. The notion of stewardship enables him to invoke the more communitarian values of charity, responding to need, and right use of property.[25]

Community of goods is attributed to the natural law, not in the sense that natural law dictates that all possessions should be common and that nothing should be possessed as one's own, but in the sense that the division of possessions is not made by natural law but by human agreement, which belongs to positive law. (*Ibid.*)

Exactly, utopians would say, and they, unlike western states, have chosen *not* to make this human agreement, and not to make a positive law condoning private property. Aquinas' conclusion, 'that private ownership is not contrary to natural law, but is an addition to it devised by human reason' seems judicious enough to satisfy supporters of both sides of the question, except that Raphael might argue that the 'human reason' in this context is not 'right reason'.

As in the case of enclosures, so with the notion of communal ownership of property, Edmund Spenser in *The Faerie Queene* gives the conservative view which contrasts sharply with Raphael's. Artegall and Talus encounter a charismatic Giant surrounded by an assembly of 'many nations met' (V. ii. 30). He is not quite so radical as Raphael, as he argues not for the abolition of money and property but for their redistribution. Spenser views the principles he advocates as the most pernicious of all, simply because they appeal to spurious models of reason and conscience. Dangerously seductive, the Giant sets himself up like Raphael as a figure representing social justice as an enactment of Natural Law. He guilefully uses as his symbol the set of balances identified with justice itself, but which are seen here ironically as 'levelling' rather than bringing justice. The Giant's mission is to restore surplus to its source wherever he finds it, and he beguilingly draws upon the laws he observes in nature:

> For why, he sayd, they all vnequall were,
> And had encroched vppon others share,
> Like as the sea (which plaine he shewed there)
> Had worne the earth, so did others parts empaire.
> And so were realms and nations run awry.
> All which he vndertooke for to repaire,
> In sort as they were formed aunciently;
> And all things would reduce vnto equality. (V. ii. 32)

The Giant is undoubtedly representative of the Anabaptist view (somewhat simplified by Spenser for polemical reasons) and those others in the sixteenth century who urged social revolution, whom we have already met in dealing with More's *Utopia*. Spenser is scathing about this populist demagogue and his adoring followers:

> Therefore the vulgar did about him flocke,
> And cluster thicke vnto his leasings vaine,
> Like foolish flies about an hony crocke,
> In hope by him great benefite to gaine,
> And vncontrolled freedome to obtaine. (V. ii. 33)

Artegall, seeing how the Giant 'mis-led the simple peoples traine' argues with him, using the same kind of appeal to nature and to reason employed by his adversary. He points out that God created everything in equal poise from the beginning, so that water, earth and air are perfectly balanced. 'Such heauenly justice' is tampered with only at our peril. To 'equalise' or level mountains with the lowest plains would jeopardise the delicate balance. Spenser's conservatism is evident behind Artegall's: 'All change is perillous, and all chaunce vnsound' (V. ii. 36), but he claims to derive his conclusion, as does the Giant, from natural reasoning: a salutary reminder of the portability of Natural Law. The Giant, like Raphael, argues that things are so bad in the present that God cannot have intended what seem manifest social inequalities, and he draws a conclusion which again appeals directly to reason and conscience:

> Were it not good that wrong were then surceast,
> And from the most, that some were giuen to the least? (V. ii. 37)

Disarmingly, he says he will overthrow tyrants (which is also Artegall's mission), curb lords, 'and all the wealth of rich men to the poore will draw'. Artegall continues to reason, the Giant refuses to give way, Artegall becomes angry, and the situation is resolved (if that is the word) by Talus abruptly shouldering the Giant off the cliff into the sea, thus drowning him. Spenser provides a neat epitaph: 'So was the high aspyring with huge ruine humbled.' The people rise up in civil war, and yet again Talus is called in to lay about them with his flail, dispersing them 'like a swarme of flyes'. Although it is impossible to find any glimpse of self-doubt on Spenser's part in this episode, it leaves an uneasy feeling that the only way Artegall can really defeat the appeal to social equality and democracy is through sovereign force, after he has been driven through his form of reasoning from conclusions into something of a *reductio ad absurdum* of the conservative view. Perhaps the real threat from the Giant's quarter is not that he refuses to listen to 'reason' but that his own brand of reason is at least superficially just as powerful as Artegall's and has a more direct appeal to conscience. I do not know if there is evidence that Spenser read *Utopia*, but this episode stands as a strong, conservative answer to Hythlodaeus.

However, before leaving the populist Giant, we should notice that Spenser is equally opposed to his opposite, the monopolistic landowner. Artegall as Knight of Justice must run a gauntlet of two figures who represent different aspects of money and property, oligarchy and anarchy respectively. Pollente ('powerful') comes before the Giant, to set up a contrast. He is a powerful landowner who has accumulated great lordships and land and extorts money from others 'through strong oppression' (V. ii. 5), and by demanding payment from travellers who cross his bridge. His own version of Talus beats back all who will not pay (the rich) and those who cannot afford to pay (the poor). Pollente himself tyrannises over the rich, giving all their money to his daughter, Munera ('gift') who hoards it. Without pausing to discuss or reflect, Talus slays his opposing counterpart, and Artegall wins a lengthy fight with Pollente. Talus then enters the castle and 'withouten pitty of her goodly hew' (V. ii. 25) chops off the hands and feet of Munera and throws her torso in the river. Rather than redistributing the money, he burns it and throws it also in the brook, thus ending the monopoly of wealth. The head of Pollente is displayed on a pole for many years,

> To be a mirrour to all mighty men,
> In whose right hands great power is conteyned,
> That none of them the feeble ouerren,
> But alwaies doe their powre within iust compasse pen.          (V. ii. 19)

If we take Pollente to be a landowner, demanding gifts from his inferiors and money for passage through rights of way, then Spenser's attitude is in this case comparable with Raphael's in condemning the practice. If, picking up the pun on 'poll', the sarazin represents a government agency imposing a poll tax, then Spenser would be underlining the terms of Magna Carta that a charge made simply on the basis of a person's existence is contrary to Natural Law. However, the allegory can be read in other ways as well. It may be a condemnation of the Vatican's demand of tithes from England before Henry VIII, and thus part of the virulent, anti-Catholic propaganda so common in *The Faerie Queene*. It could figure the growing practice of private monopolies in Elizabethan England. It could attack the practices of the Anglo-Irish, whom Spenser condemns in his *View of Ireland*. Or it could be a condemnation of government taxes in general the intention behind which, however unsystematically, represented some attempt at redistribution of wealth by curbing the power of the wealthy to become richer. If the last explanation is present as part of the poem's ideology, then Spenser would be once again set apart from the radical Raphael.

Raphael's revelation about the absence of private property and money in Utopia comes at the end of Book 1, when he is deeply exasperated at the failure of More and Giles to understand that the gulf separating Utopia from Europe is a profound one that cannot be bridged by compromises and palliatives. It also comes as part of a logical, sequential argument, opening up at this point the most radical foundation of the utopian value system which makes it so different from the European. Raphael has piled high his devastating indictments of European practices: injustice within the law, exploitation by the rich and by arrogant and complacent authority, enclosures which cause poverty, theft and vagabondage, and so on. He constantly stresses *superbia*, pride, and greed, as the root moral causes of these manifest ills. Now he homes in on the material cause of pride and greed.

> wherever you have private property, and money is the measure of all things, it is hardly possible for a commonwealth to be governed justly or happily – unless you think justice can exist where all the best things in life are held by the worst citizens, or suppose happiness can be found where property is limited to a few – where even those few are always uneasy, and where the many are utterly wretched. (p. 38)

Wealth creates poverty; inequality creates sin. In Utopia the converse holds: 'virtue has its reward, yet everything is shared equally, and all men live in plenty' (*ibid.*). Raphael then formally opens the debate on this alternative system by making the conventional reference to its starting-point, Plato:

When I consider all these things, I become more sympathetic to Plato, and wonder the less that he refused to make laws for any people who would not share their goods equally. Wisest of men, he saw easily that the one and only path to the welfare of all lies through equality of possessions. I doubt whether such equality can ever be achieved where property belongs to individual men ... Thus I am wholly convinced that unless private property is entirely abolished, there can be no fair or just distribution of goods, nor can mankind be happily governed.

The imagery of the healthy and sick body now used by Raphael guides us towards Natural Law as the basis of his argument. Speaking of short-term, European compromises, he says:

Laws of this sort, I agree, may have as much effect as good and careful nursing has on persons who are chronically sick. The social evils I mentioned may be alleviated and their effects mitigated for a while, but so long as private property remains, there is no hope at all of effecting a cure and restoring society to good health. While you try to cure one part, you aggravate the disease in other parts. Suppressing one symptom causes another to break out, since you cannot give something to one man without taking it away from someone else. (pp. 38–40 *passim*)

Obstinate to the end, 'More' interjects and answers these statements with 'But I don't see it that way' (p. 40) and, anticipating Spenser's defence of enclosures which we shall quote later in this chapter, he repeats Aquinas' flawed anecdote that people are too lazy to work under an egalitarian, common system. But by this stage of the argument, 'More's' value system, based on custom and positive, coercive law, has been rationally opposed. Giles can do nothing but point to the 'long experience' Europe has had in governing (exhibiting precisely the complacency condemned by Raphael of those who say 'The way we're doing it is the way we've always done it, this custom was good enough for our fathers, and I only hope we're as wise as they were') (p. 14). The way has been cleared of doubts, negations, and objections to the Natural Lawyer's argument from the basis of reason and conscience (property causes vice, utopian communism leads to virtue). Raphael looks forward over 300 years to Piérre-Joseph Proudhon's answer to the question *What is Property?* (1840), 'Property is theft.' From now on in the narrative, Hythlodaeus adopts a less argumentative and more calm manner in simply describing how the utopians arrange their life. Reason and conscience are the rudders that guide Book 2.

The attitude to money in Utopia runs along the same lines as that to private property. Utopia is literally flowing in gold and silver, but they are considered useless, except for forging chamber pots, slaves' fetters, and earrings to mark criminals. 'Thus they hold up gold and silver to scorn in every conceivable way.' In other countries, says Raphael,

Human folly has made them precious because they are rare. But in fact nature, like a most indulgent mother, has placed her best gifts out in the open, like air, water and the earth itself; vain and unprofitable things she has hidden away in remote places. (p. 62)

Similarly, 'precious' stones like diamonds and garnets are given to children as toys. Without a concept of private property and without a money exchange system, the argument runs, the central vices of pride, greed, envy, luxury, competitiveness, and all 'false ideas of pleasure' (p. 71) are eliminated at a stroke. In a republic 'where everything belongs to everybody', people are not distracted into antisocial practices of individualism, and they are free, materially and spiritually, to pursue Natural Law's *summum bonum*, pleasure which harms nobody and fulfils every person's nature. Indeed, the legal system itself is akin to Natural Law, being made up of very few laws which appear to be general precepts rather than specific directives. If one were to eliminate from any European system all the laws related directly or indirectly to property (even murder may be motivated by greed of some sort), there would be very few left. Raphael is as tantalisingly unspecific as all Natural Law theorists in telling us what these laws are. The closest he comes is in phrases like 'plain dealing' and 'fairness', with one guiding precept, which is a recording of Natural Law's incitement to follow good and shun evil:

As they see things, all laws are promulgated for the single purpose of advising every man of his duty. (p. 85)

It is hinted that, unlike Natural Law's reliance on the individual's exercise of reason and conscience to steer towards a particular 'duty' in each circumstance, the utopians need a few clear guidelines, for 'simple-minded men (and most men are of this sort ... )' need to be told where their duty lies (p. 85). In Hexter's words, the utopians 'brace conscience with legal sanctions' rather than leaving it to Natural Law which may be 'a small voice so often still' (p. cxi). At the level of what we would call international law, the same spirit of Natural Law prevails, holding that words are irrelevant beside 'good faith' and reason:

If nature, they say, doesn't bind man adequately to his fellow man, will an alliance do so? If a man scorns nature herself, is there any reason to think he will care about mere words? (p. 86)

'The kinship of nature is as good as a treaty', and 'men are united more firmly by good will than by pacts, by their hearts than by their words' (p. 87).

The ending of *Utopia* returns to the strategies of contrast, invective, and dialectic which were set up in the framing narrative. Raphael perceptively acknowledges that in the European system of private wealth, 'bitter necessity' drives everybody to be individualistic and in this they are 'right' because they have no alternative to survive within the system. Equally, utopians are 'right' to co-operate and shun wealth because their system itself would disadvantage individualists. To this extent, he again asserts that compromise is impossible between implacably opposed value systems. However, he clearly favours the utopian world, and he returns to the injustices, parasitism, exploitation of labour, and starvation of the European. The utopian Republic 'has abolished not only money but with it greed!'

What a mass of trouble was cut away by that one step! What a thicket of crimes was uprooted. Everyone knows that if money were abolished, fraud, theft, robbery, quarrels, brawls, seditions, murders, treasons, poisonings and a whole set of crimes which are avenged but not prevented by the hangman would at once die out. If money disappeared, so would fear, anxiety, worry, toil and sleepless nights. Even poverty, which seems to need money more than anything else, would vanish if money were entirely done away with. (p. 109)

It is clear by now that Raphael is attacking not just an economic system, but a whole structure of apparent justice which is exposed as unjust by comparison with Natural Law. Pride is the central problem, since it 'measures her advantages not by what she has but by what other people lack'. The disagreement between Raphael and 'More' (unrepentantly European to the end) lies in the basic problem of defining 'human nature'. To the Natural Lawyer, pride is not 'natural' but it is the consequence of an ingrained ideology resulting from customary ownership, a fiction so firmly fixed that it seems a 'truth'. Raphael knows that 'Pride is too deeply fixed in human nature to be easily plucked out' (p. 11), but he believes it can be. 'More' cannot countenance such a radical change in people's convictions, and so he sees in Utopia at best only 'many features that in our societies I would like rather than expect to see'.

Undoubtedly the most appropriate way to describe *Utopia* is as a debate or dialogue, whose function in the Renaissance, Roger Deakins argues, was to pit one truth against another, not expecting or even wishing the reader to agree with one spokesman or the other.[26] This is quite consistent in itself with the principles of Natural Law, which invites a free response based on circumstances rather than rigid rules. At the very least, however, we may see in Raphael's argument the deployment of reason and conscience as central touchstones for social and political organisation. Whether postlapsarian humankind can ever be capable of such consistency is the other story, expressed through More's *persona*. It is clear from the tribe of correspondents whose letters appeared as prefatory materials in the 1516 edition (and particularly that from Jerome Busleyden), that early readers (that is, if the letters are not another spoof and fiction), were capable of being as cautiously optimistic as Raphael, but there are built into the work the stresses and strains of a more sceptical view, anticipated by Calvin, which was to be triumphantly systematised by Hobbes almost 150 years later. On one reading, man's reason and conscience are internal faculties, confused only by the existence of institutions which work against the implementation of a state based on Natural Law. On the other reading, men made these very institutions *because* their understandings were corrupted by the Fall, and only God or a holy fool like Hythlodaeus can see this. *Utopia* remains a work built upon implacably opposed positions which are both explicitly referred to the existence of a Natural Law whose application in the fallen world becomes as problematical as the author's stance in this enigmatic work.

# 6 'Love is the fulfilling of the law': *Arcadia* and *Love's Labour's Lost*

> The order of the precepts of the natural law corresponds to the order of our natural inclinations. For there is in man a natural and initial inclination to good which he has in common with all substances; in so far as every substance seeks its own preservation according to its own nature. Corresponding to this inclination, the natural law contains all that makes for the preservation of human life, and all that is opposed to its dissolution. Secondly, there is to be found in man a further inclination to certain more specific ends, according to the nature which man shares with other animals. In virtue of this inclination there pertains to the natural law all those instincts 'which nature has taught all animals' [Ulpian], such as sexual relationship, the rearing of offspring, and the like. (Aquinas, *Summa* Qu. 94. Art. 2)

Aquinas' apparently unproblematical words on the 'naturalness' of sexual relationship open up a thorny area for the Renaissance and conceal yawning gulfs and treacherous debates within Natural Law theory. Indeed, the difference of degree between Aquinas and Calvin over the issue of the inwardness or otherwise of Natural Law becomes a fundamental one, which was to exercise Milton in particular, when it is focused on sexuality, with its negative and positive concomitants, shame, companionship, and procreation. To make a very sweeping generalisation, English Renaissance writers were beneficiaries of two quite contradictory approaches to love and sexuality, which could have been a crippling legacy, but which in fact contributed to the creation of a complex view of the subject. One approach was the Augustinian, which took sexual desire to be, however compulsive and animalistically 'natural', by definition irrational in human beings, degrading, trivial, and sinful, even in marriage. His preferred options were continence or sex without desire, carried out perfunctorily in order to guarantee propagation of the species. Courtly-love conventions seem to be a consequence of this embargo: if, despite all repressive attempts, desire will out, then it will be guilty, furtive, clandestine, and ultimately unrequited. Aquinas and his followers, on the other hand, assumed sexual desire to be natural, and, if fulfilled within marriage, and governed by reason and temperance, it could be enjoyed as an unadulterated pleasure. Richard Rolle eloquently expresses this attitude:

There is a certain natural love of a man for a woman and of a woman for a man which no one lacks ... following the nature instituted by God from the beginning. Through this love existing together and in harmony with one another, they rejoice companionably by natural instinct.[1]

The 'sage And serious doctrine of Virginity' expounded by the Lady in Milton's *Comus*, confirmed by her philosophically inclined, rational Elder Brother, restates a distinction between natural and unnatural (lustful) sexuality. Spenser's Britomart must be educated into such a distinction by observing others in love and feeling the sacred fire of desire herself.

Meanwhile, it will be the theme of this chapter, and in the analysis of *Measure for Measure* in the next, that in the relaxed and relatively uninhibited modes of romance and comedy, writers like Sidney and Shakespeare did not need to take a dogmatic stand on such issues, but rather they exploited and relished the problems, internal contradictions, and even absurdities that ensue when positive law seeks to judge or suppress 'natural' sexuality. As a consequence of the very modes themselves, they lighten, transfer, and detonate in laughter the over-solemn ways in which legal problems raised by passion were being publicly debated.

There was never much doubt that positive law could legitimately take sexual behaviour within its purview, but, throughout the period, debate swung to and fro concerning the issues on which law (common or ecclesiastical) was to adjudicate, and to what extent human law could judge sexual behaviour. Overarching these debates was a general sense, which might be imputed to Aquinas, that sexual desire is so innate and 'instinctive' that apart from notable transgressions damaging to society, the rest should be left entirely to reason, individual conscience, and to God. The fact that laws concerning sex were, up until 1650, restricted to the sphere of ecclesiastical law (through a monopoly on marriage and betrothal laws, but not divorce and inheritance), indicated some tacit acknowledgment of Aquinas' implication that only God can judge, and that it was for the church rather than the state to decide difficult cases, more or less on behalf of God. But within this broad agreement lay radical differences of opinion. An extreme Natural Law position (although few expressed it so boldly in the Renaissance) might be that sanctions on sexual morality are exclusively a private matter for the individual's reason and conscience: the real questions underlining the disputes about who is and who is not married in *Measure for Measure* relate to which liaisons are sanctioned 'in the eye of God' rather than law of church or state, and the Princess in *Love's Labour's Lost* makes her *handfast* contract with the duke of Navarre conditional not on man's law at all, but on whether they will or will not, at the end of a year, be 'entitled in the other's heart'. The more orthodox line was that law had some more or less coercive or prohibitive role to play in certain specified areas, but not beyond. It was generally agreed, for example, that incest needed to be banned by positive law (although, clearly, debate could rage over what constitutes incest).[2] This would have been regarded as simply spelling out in positive law what Natural Law itself decreed. Homosexuality, while not at the time a particular preoccupation of law, was seen as being against Natural Law, as in Sidney's *Arcadia,* where Philoclea's desire for Pyrocles whom she thinks a woman, is branded unnatural, and as evidenced by the notoriety of those like Marlowe reputed to be homosexual. Beyond such cases were grey areas and black holes galore. Adultery and sex outside marriage were constant subjects of controversy and eventually legislation, and the begetting of bastards was given legal implications for inheritance, as we see in the case of Edmund in *King Lear*, but not as part of ecclesiastical purview of sexual offences. Late twentieth-century *mores*, at least in liberal circles, may be very different from Renaissance ones, witnessing again to the problematical nature of the application of the Natural Law model itself, but this should not restrain us from recognising the genuine reticence of the Elizabethan church and state to intervene in matters which they saw as so personal that they seek as witness God alone and personal conscience. The fundamental nature of the debate over sexual morality has always hinged on the actual competence or jurisdiction of positive law to legislate over what, at any one time, could arguably be considered to lie within the province of individual reason and conscience. Shakespeare in particular makes comedy out of just this debate.

The debate between the two positions – on the one hand, that sexuality is beyond legal control, and on the other that it is validly subject to positive law – is inscribed in Sidney's *Arcadia* and Shakespeare's comedies, where the actual terms and subtleties of Natural Law are less significant than acknowledgment of its existence as something which licences the possibility that positive laws may be challenged. In this chapter we examine works where positive law (whether imposed by the state or ecclesiastical authority is irrelevant) is set up to override or punish, or judge, or in some way police, forms of sexual conduct. Our concentration here, then, falls on the problematical nature of positive laws intended to govern 'natural' impulses. There will in the examination be some inevitable blurring of definition between the use of 'Natural

Law' as the innate exercise of reason and conscience, and 'natural law' as the force of sexual desire, since this is intrinsic to the subject. Indeed, Aquinas' statement itself makes such a blurring inevitable, and, as Richard McCabe's book on incest in the Renaissance shows, sexuality was the site for considerable dispute about what is reasonable, conscientious, and 'natural' in particular circumstances. The set-piece debates of reason *versus* passion, which we find all through Elizabethan literature, show that on the subject of sexual desire, reason and conscience may either support or be in conflict with nature, although the resolutions of comedies and romances invariably fuse the two in the state of marriage.

(i)     The Countess of Pembroke's Arcadia[3]

Sidney's seminal romance which exists in two versions and a textual hybrid,[4] is known as *Arcadia*, a title as boldly simple and archetypal as *Utopia*, itself a book which Sidney refers to by name in the *Defence of Poetry* describing it as a 'determination of goodness' that can direct 'a whole commonwealth' (p. 86). His title signals Sidney's definition of his genre. Arcadia is as much an 'as-if' place as Utopia, its associations equally charged, conjuring up memories of Theocritus and Virgil, images of green landscape and contemplative shepherds tending their flocks. Although Arcadia at the beginning of the book is a whole country including city, court, and country, the name becomes increasingly associated with proximity to nature, distance from the city and court, and their restrictions such as law, and these are its literary and cultural connections as well. Relationship with nature is Arcadia's *raison d'être*, its setting, its human significance, and its way of measuring how far humanity has strayed. If the Law of Nature exists anywhere, it should be in Arcadia.

And so it does, in a sense. But Sidney's *Arcadia* is also like More's *Utopia* in its playful wittiness, which has never properly been critically addressed. At the centre of its wit lies Sidney's realisation that there is not just one single Law of Nature, but also another set of laws of nature that impel us,[5] and that the two systems may well be in conflict with each other. As Bottom sagely comments, love and reason keep little company. Accordingly, questions are raised concerning the extent to which man-made law can either legitimately or realistically seek to legislate over activity which is 'natural' in the most physical and animal sense, and which may not be governed by reason and conscience in any meaningful way. Sidney also realises that in practice, in a fallen world of women and men, there is conflict rather than harmony between 'natural' love and Natural Law, a tendency explained by the 'dangerous division of men's minds' (p. 305), driving them in different directions both with and against the Law of Nature. Ultimately, the warring models of nature are no more and no less than fictions or constructions reflecting the warring impulses within people. In acknowledging the various tensions within the concept of the Law of Nature, Sidney stands somewhere between Aquinas and Calvin or Hobbes, More and Shakespeare, classical literature and Romanticism. His moment in the history of ideas may have been the only one when such a work could have been written, and it is further arguable that without Sidney there could have been no Shakespeare, at least in the radical ambivalence by which we know him.

Judging from the first, leisurely sentence of the *Arcadia*, we might well anticipate a fable of the Law of Nature as we have observed it in philosophical writers:

Arcadia among all the provinces of Greece was ever had in singular reputation, partly for the sweetness of the air and other natural benefits, but principally for the moderate and well tempered minds of the people who (*finding how true a contentation is gotten by following the course of nature*, and how the shining title of glory, so much affected by other nations, doth indeed help little to the happiness of life) were the only people which, as by their justice and providence gave neither cause nor hope to their neighbours to annoy them. (p. 4: my italics)

This perfect and even utopian state of natural serenity reigns until the ruler makes a fateful decision. At first, however, as we are introduced to the characters, they seem to personify aspects of the moral law. Duke Basilius is a skilful prince, governing a country 'where the good minds of former princes had set down good laws'; his wife Gynecia is, we are told, a woman who will come to exercise 'conscience'; and their daughters Pamela and Philoclea are as gifted as one could imagine 'reasonable creatures' to be, 'in whom nature promiseth nothing but goodness' (p. 7). The two 'foreign' princes, Musidorus and Pyrocles, are introduced as young men intent on perfecting 'the divine part of man', and they practise 'true laws of friendship' which are as tight in their bonding as laws of kind. We could be forgiven for expecting a work showing people living by the Law of Nature, acting by reason and conscience to effect justice in their world, another Utopia, in fact.

Immediately, the waters are muddied by the titular head, Basilius, who out of a curiosity that almost immediately seems futile and hubristic, seeks from the oracle to know more than he should about the future. He gets gnomic answers which turn out to be virtually self-fulfilling prophecies when Basilius wilfully attempts to evade the predictions. By trying to rise above his station of human humility, Basilius like Faustus shapes his own destiny and those of others around him, in first a comic and then increasingly tragic sequence of events. Furthermore, impelled to try to avoid the oracle's doom-laden prophecies, fleeing to a secluded rural existence with his family, Basilius transports into the most 'natural' and at least potentially Edenic part of his dukedom the human reality of original sin which threatens to destroy the pastoral haven of the Arcadian countryside, just as Sir Calidore, Spenser's knight of Courtesy, imports into the perfect world the germs of imperfections. Amongst other things, Basilius introduces into the organic and harmonious pastoral context a rigidly ordered social model that is intended to restrict his daughters' affections as much as their movements. Philanax, who at this stage of the narrative is a wise counsellor, questions Basilius' 'dukely sophistry to deceive himself', pointing to the central law of nature that each creature must act like itself, fulfil its own destiny: 'the rocks stand still and are rocks' (p. 8), and just so a duke should not be as yielding as the reeds. Basilius insists, however, on cloistering his family in the countryside in an attempt to avert the apparently courtly disasters predicted. The real lesson we shall see enacted is that man is neither rock nor reed, but flesh and blood, a fact that 'nature, the most noble commandment that mankind can have over themselves (as indeed both learning teacheth and inward feeling assureth)' (p. 193) needs somehow to accommodate.

Coincidentally, two young princes from Thessalia arrive at the same grove in Arcadia. Both are committed to perfecting virtue and heroism, but each in turn falls in love with the beauty of Basilius' daughters. Pyrocles dotes on a picture of Philoclea and disguises as a woman to thwart the restriction on her speaking to courtly men, and thereby gain her company. Musidorus his cousin is appalled by this transformation, and he delivers a long lecture. The place, he says, is natural perfection and should be lived in with an equal perfection of the mind which 'should best know his own good or evil by practice' (p. 15). He cannot understand how one 'formed by nature and framed by education to the true exercise of virtue', who has been guided by 'the reasonable part of our soul' which is 'to have absolute commandment' can be overthrown by 'so unnatural rebellion'. 'If reason direct it', he says, 'we must do it; and if we must do it, we will do it', but he recognises that in Pyrocles, passion 'subverts the course of nature in making reason give place to sense'. In orthodox Natural Law fashion, Musidorus equates reason and nature. In response, Pyrocles puts an equally 'natural' set of points. He first reprimands Musidorus for misogyny and then points out (and at least one Natural Law thinker, More's Hythlodaeus, would agree in general terms) that 'enjoying' is the end and measure allotted to us by nature. While the head gives direction the heart gives life, and such life is as natural as reason itself. Even Aquinas concedes the naturalness of

sexual attraction, and, although Musidorus sees his friend's transformation as one of 'poor reason's overthrow' and as an emblem of 'what a
deformity a passion can bring a man unto when it is not governed by
reason' (p. 30), yet Pyrocles/Cleophila is satisfied that 'conscience' has
not been violated (p. 32). Sidney is systematically building up a complex
situation in which it is by no means clear what are natural, reasonable,
and conscientious actions, when sexuality is involved.

One by one all the central characters succumb to passion. Basilius and
his wife Gynecia both fall in love with 'Cleophila' as does their daughter
Philoclea. Hers is the 'uncouth love, which nature hateth most' (p. 5)
predicted by the oracle, not unnatural to the Renaissance mind only
because it is lesbian, but also because in this case it is based on a
'counterfeit', a deception. Musidorus eats his words as he falls in love
with the other daughter, Pamela. He disguises as a shepherd, and
eventually abducts Pamela (acquiescently in her case, though against her
better judgment) and attempts something like rape, although he is
prevented at the last minute. The erotic confusions and predicaments
need not be rehearsed, but it is important to note that Sidney, like many
a dramatist after him, milks the situations for purely comic effects.[6] Even
the coy prurience of tone cannot be condemned as authorial, for Sidney
is comically tracing the sometimes ridiculous and sometimes morally
degrading antics and behaviour of his characters, using a narratorial
*persona* who is enjoying rather than judging. The switch of narrative
voice in Book 4 confirms this. As the creator of his work, like God
presiding over his creation, the poet has licence to move his characters'
feelings in whatever direction he likes, always ready to rein them back
when the time comes to assert the moral law of poetic, and legal justice in
closure. The characters are at this stage driven on by some kind of
natural law, human desire, and passion which are as instinctive and
compulsive as the forces that drive the lioness and her cub and the bear
to erupt on the scene and chase the humans (p. 42). The censorious
perspective of the narrative implies that the 'laws of love' are 'contrary to
all general laws of reason' (p. 172), but they cannot be avoided by
hapless human beings. *Arcadia* places at centre-stage exactly what *Utopia*
excluded, the 'violent desire' (p. 89) of passion, and questions just how it
fits into a moral universe which should be governed by reason.

Much of the book demonstrates the 'naturalness' of human desire
while also showing its often disastrous and ridiculous consequences.
'What marvel if in youth such faults be done?' (p. 69) asks Mastix the
shepherd in the First Eclogues, and Cleophila laments in verse 'None can
speak of a wound with skill, if he have not a wound felt' (p. 75). It has
force 'to conquer the strongest hearts' (p. 105), with devastating effects

on people endowed with 'natural wisdom' (p. 93) and brought up 'according as the natural course of each thing required' (p. 95). Much of the imagery of love is of 'extreme and unresistable violence' in the natural world, of rushing rivers, fire, and wild animals, and the natural perversion of 'infection' and festering sores. The running debate between Reason and Passion is altogether weighted towards Passion up until the beginning of Book 4. Reason seems incapable of resistance to 'the laws of love' (p. 172).

A qualification should be entered before we move on to the reassertion of reason and public justice. The real error against nature committed by all the characters, is not falling in love, because this does seem natural in itself, but rather deceit, and the biggest deceiver of all, the one who compromises other characters, is Basilius himself. A distinction as insistent as reason and passion in *Arcadia* is that drawn between the natural and the counterfeit, and Basilius is the most hypocritical of all. After Basilius, Pyrocles is the main offender, since his disguise as an Amazon is represented from the start as a 'deformity' (p. 30). Gynecia and Philoclea also practise deception and hypocrisy, however much we see their actions as responses to importunate, male-created circumstances. It is the distinction between the natural and the counterfeit that will enable Sidney eventually to square up the laws of love with the Law of Nature: what is counterfeit cannot be natural. Love practised without deception, compulsive passion followed without resort to false images and counterfeits, are as 'natural' as nature itself. In a telling counterpoint, shepherds and shepherdesses woo, guilelessly garlanded by the natural delights of trees and spring flowers:

Lalus, not with many painted words, nor false-hearted promises, had won the consent of his beloved Kala, but with a true and simple making her know he loved her; not forcing himself beyond his reach to buy her affection. (Eclogues 3, 212)

'Let mother earth now deck herself in flowers' (p. 213) begins the prothalamion, a song which celebrates the kind of family and social integration of marriage which Basilius' camp has abdicated.

For Sidney the writer of *A Defence of Poetry*, all this has considerable resonance. A fiction, if it is in accordance with reason and conscience, and rhetorically presented not just to delight but to teach with compelling images of the attractiveness of virtue and the repulsiveness of vice, may be a creation on the same level of reality as nature itself, an addition to nature which is equivalent to Natural Law itself. On the other hand, a fiction which is no more than a 'counterfeit' from nature, designed either to mislead morally or not to demonstrate morality at all, is something

'Which breeds naught else but glosses of deceits' (p. 58). As in love, so in poetry, the heart and the head must work together for their effects to be as 'natural' and as admirable as God's creations.

Up until the end of the third Book, Sidney's moral pattern is not revealed, and if anything the narrator relishes images of deception and dubious ethics which seem superficially to be condoned by an inner law of human sexual attractiveness. From the 'delight' of sexual comedy, Sidney turns to the enacted 'precepts' of moral judgment, and the opening words of 'The Fourth Book or Act' dolefully signal the change of tack: 'The everlasting justice' (p. 230). Basilius, it seems, is dead, poisoned by liquor bought by Gynecia in the belief that it is an aphrodisiac with which she planned to seduce the disguised Pyrocles. Both Basilius and Gynecia have been outwitted by 'Cleophila' who has tricked them into bed with each other rather than with 'her'. Basilius voluntarily takes the drink, but the consequences embroil all the main characters in some form of judicial prosecution and punishment. Of course, in good romance fashion, Basilius is not dead, and he awakens after sentences have been meted out, but it should be said that this is not entirely a glib exercise of a *deus ex machina* simply to arrive at a happy ending. The real punishment has taken effect already, for the fourth Book could aptly be called 'The Book of Conscience'. Ever-lasting justice is said to use 'ourselves to be the punishers of our chastisement, that our shame may be the more manifest, and our repentance follow the sooner' (p. 230), and indeed all the characters undergo such pangs of conscience in prison as they contemplate suicide. This is the real punishment adduced by Calvin for those who break Natural Law. The most moving depiction of conscience is that of Gynecia, the older woman who, in clear-eyed fashion, has seen through Pyrocles' disguise, fallen in love with him as a man, felt jealousy for her daughter, and been unrequited in love. She also blames herself entirely for the death of her husband. The misery and despair to which her conscience and sense of shame reduce her are worse than any public punishment could bring.

Pyrocles, who has been even more centrally responsible for the disastrous chain of events, is also wracked. His redemption, however, is signalled by his concern that Philoclea must not suffer, and his reasoning shows that he is now back in touch with the reason and conscience-driven imperatives of Natural Law:

It is the right I owe to the general nature that (though against private nature) makes me seek the preservation of all that she hath done in this age. Let me, let me die! There is no way to save your life, most worthy to be conserved, than that my death be your clearing. (p. 254)

He is willing to make the supreme sacrifice of his life to save that of his beloved. By this time he is still driven by 'love's force' which he 'neither can nor will leave' (p. 256), but his decision is as one made by 'a man that run not unto it by a sudden qualm of passion, but by a true use of reason' (p. 260). It seems that love and reason can in fact exist together as natural forces not incompatible with each other, and at least Pyrocles can now honestly reveal and state his feelings, but for him the lesson seems to have come too late. Similarly chastened, Musidorus, Pamela, and Philoclea also reassess their conduct and adjust their feelings to penitence and self-recrimination. The conditions for full redemption, and a return to a state of Natural Law in the dukedom, are in place, but there is still the uncomfortable fact of the corpse which requires the exercise of public justice. It must be admitted that my reading of these characters' penitence can be challenged as sentimental and over-solemn, since their self-lacerating remorse appears to be excessive and their offers of self-sacrifice might be seen as hollow bravado, coolly calculated to win sympathy. But to say this is a markedly modern exercise of scepticism where the context seems without irony. Such a cynical resolution, an argument that right to the end the characters remain hypocritical and calculating, is not in keeping with the sober tone of the last two Books, nor the genre of romance, although as we shall see, there is certainly a different kind of unease in the actual closure.

Euarchus ('good ruler'), king of Macedon, who coincidentally enters now, dominates the last Book, which we may call 'The Book of Justice'. Philanax, as temporary ruler of Arcadia, realises that it would be 'not only unjust and against the law of nations not well to receive a prince whom goodwill had brought among them' (p. 305), and invites him to adjudicate the trial. Euarchus is, moreover, remembered for 'the excellent trials of his equity which made him more famous than his victories' and 'his equity such as no man need to fear him' (p. 307), and so he is welcomed as the person best fitted to preside over the legal trial which follows discovery of Basilius' 'death'. It is repeated yet again that he is a man of 'equity' (p. 312) and this in Elizabethan terms places him close to the Chancellor, one able to override positive laws with either mercy or a superior justice, 'a right knowledge when correction is necessary, when grace doth more avail'.

in the end, wisdom being an essential and not an opinionate thing, made him rather bend to what was in itself good than what by evil minds might be judged not good. (p. 312)

He sees his own duty clearly: 'nature required nothing more of him than that he should be a help to them of like creation' (p. 312). His 'unpassionate nature' (p. 313), 'natural imperiousness' (p. 314), and circumspection immediately impress the Arcadians, as does his refusal to countenance 'hearsay' as evidence (p. 313). He reminds his audience that he is 'a man; that is to say, a creature whose reason is often darkened with error' (p. 315), but he vows to carry out justice as he sees it:

I will promise and protest unto you that to the uttermost of my skill, both in the general laws of nature, especially of Greece, and particularly of Arcadia (wherein I must confess I am not unacquainted), I will ... see the past evils duly punished. (p. 315)

This, surely, a man 'whom the strange and secret working of justice had brought to be the judge over them' (p. 333), is the paragon of a judge with expertise in every jurisdiction and the ability to make reference to 'eternal justice' (p. 331). He even has a grasp of the Roman *ius gentium*:

Arcadia laws were to have their force upon any were found in Arcadia, since strangers have scope to know the customs of a country before they put themselves in it ... Therefore, if they had offended (which now by the plaintiff and their defence was to be judged) against the laws of nations, by the laws of nations they were to be chastised; if against the peculiar ordinances of the province, those peculiar ordinances were to lay hold of them. (p. 333)

This statement, however, amounts to a potentially fatal limitation on Euarchus' exercise of justice. In the final analysis, he admits he is circumscribed by positive laws and unable to exercise fully the discretion which is the basis of Natural Law. That is, he feels compelled to acknowledge that some crime has been committed, rather than simply refuse to apply flawed, human reason to an area of human experience such as love and sexuality which, it could be argued, is the domain of God alone.

Philanax, motivated by love of Basilius and hatred of Pyrocles, laces his accusations with appeals to Natural Law, condemning 'corrupted reason of mankind', 'unnatural desires', and violations of 'the justice of nature, the right of hospitality' (p. 337), but we are primed to suspect his testimony because of his 'malice' (p. 338). However, even the defendants condemn in themselves their manifest violations of nature and reason. Like Aristotle, Euarchus makes some effort to judge not only actions, but also intentions (*mens rea* in the legal parlance), however inadequate is the evidence in this emotional area, but he is forced more or less to abandon the search for truth. He is spared some anguish, for in court even the accused confess themselves guilty.[7] Gynecia demonstrates her conscience-driven penitence, while Pyrocles and Musidorus appeal to reason and nature in pleading that their respective loved ones should not suffer for their own indiscretions. The crowd, represented by the significantly named Sympathus, records through its responses the Aristotelian effectiveness of this rhetoric, which at last is free of deception, and is, in Musidorus' words, full of 'love of justice that would brook no wrong to myself nor other' (p. 341).

Euarchus' judgment is at last handed down, and true to expectation he ignores 'the flowers of rhetoric', while concentrating on laws which are 'the bonds of all human society' and on 'universal civility, the law of nations (all mankind being as it were coinhabiters or world citizens together)' (p. 349). In choosing this communitarian ground for his judgment, he must of necessity legislate against the individualistic and uncontrollable spirit of sexual love. Pamela for one is found guiltless, but Philoclea is found 'not altogether faultless' and is to be imprisoned among nuns to curb her sexual desire. Gynecia, fully confessing, is sentenced to a living death incarcerated with Basilius, since she has broken the marriage vows and thus has jeopardised the people's welfare. There is thought to be no 'overbalancing' in this set of judgments. Euarchus concludes that 'by all laws of nature and nations' (p. 350) the young men are 'accidental, if not principal, causes of the duke's death' (p. 350) as well as of other intended crimes. According to 'the neverchanging justice' they must be executed. Euarchus rules out the solution of marrying off the couples, saying that 'love may have no such privilege' (p. 352), and that the law must be enforced strictly rather than 'by a show of conveniency'. Up to this point, Euarchus has acted like Spenser's Artegall, more or less like a common lawyer in implementing Arcadian laws (which seem very restrictive in themselves) to the facts of the matter, and these facts include confessions from the accused. He has not been able with any finesse to inquire into underlying motives, let alone the culpability of Basilius, as equity would do, and as the fictional narrative requires us as readers to do. From our point of view the judgments are frankly against generic expectations which anticipate the 'natural' marriage of the two sets of young lovers, and therefore against what we intuit to be Natural Law in operation. As Constance Jordan, who argues that the romance as a whole demonstrates Sidney's 'concern for equity as the feminine complement to justice', says, 'Euarchus actually suppresses the virtue of equity that he was credited with earlier.'[8] But the important point is that at this stage of the narrative the reader knows far more about the feelings and intentions of the characters than does Euarchus. If there is a discrepancy between 'poetic justice' and the actual result, then the fault lies not in Euarchus' judgment, but in the ramshackle nature of positive law itself as it seeks to control through law human sexuality.

To test his rectitude, the narrative introduces another twist, for it is revealed that the young princes are Euarchus' son and nephew respectively. This personal quandary between legalism and feelings of kinship is a symptom of the juridical division between Natural Law and positive law which compromises the judge presiding over affairs of love. Stoically and with private sorrow, Euarchus refuses to change a judgment made according to 'what justice itself and your just laws require' by the exercise of his 'most unpartial and furthest reach of reason'. 'But, alas, shall justice halt, or shall she wink in one's cause which had lynx's eyes in another's?' (p. 355). 'No, no, Pyrocles and Musidorus, I prefer you much before my life, but I prefer justice as far before you' (p. 356). The future writer of *The Merchant of Venice* must have paid particular attention at this point of maximum suspense hanging on the exercise of positive law. In *Arcadia*, Pyrocles completes his redemptive course by agreeing with the strict application of law, and by altruistically pleading for Musidorus' life. Likewise, Musidorus pleads for Pyrocles'.

It would appear by now that passion, love, and such 'natural' affections have been thoroughly controlled by positive law. We look at the least for mitigation, and, since all the protagonists are punished already by their consciences, redeemed by their generous and self-sacrificing gestures, it is time for equity to raise its head and, by grace and mercy, effect a happy ending, as Sympathus and Kerxenes have advocated.[9] We look at the least for a Portia to find a legal loophole. In a sense, these things do indeed happen, for the shroud stirs, Basilius is alive, and, since he has the power to suspend the operation of law, the prisoners are freed. Besides, on the legal maxim of *corpus delicti*, since there is no corpse there can be no murder and therefore no crime. Of course this miraculous event, so close to the 'grace' or mercy which is God's equity, is explained plausibly within the narrative, but admittedly it is a romance ending rather than a realistic one. Given all the twists and turns of a complex overlaying of various conflicting systems of justice, from the physical laws of nature to the more philosophical Natural Law, from Arcadian positive laws to the law of nations, from the strict letter of common law to the mercy of equity, Sidney has manœuvred his tale to a conclusion which does not entirely conclude. Less like the ending of *The Merchant of Venice* and more like the ending of *Measure for Measure*, *Arcadia* closes with questions rather than certainty, and an uneasy sense that although positive laws are inappropriate in the field of human, sexual relations, and that they are ineffectual and ignorant of human feelings, yet without them the damage to the social fabric is perceptible. Reason cannot control passion, and yet passion may under certain circumstances be reasonable, all of which makes human judgment dangerous if not impossible. As in Natural Law itself, the morality of unique situations cannot be the subject of positive legislation.

The full moral pattern of the ending of *Arcadia* is complex and subtle, demonstrating unavoidable conflict between positive laws and Natural Law. Although I argue that the implicit model on which characters have been throughout judged is Natural Law, Sidney leaves it largely unsaid, but surely central, that the breaches committed by the male lovers in particular, driven in desire and lust by natural laws of another kind, may be forgiven but not forgotten. The sardonic ironies of the last movement are purposeful. Neither Euarchus nor the attending crowd knows as much about the characters' private feelings, moral deviations, and true remorse as the readers of the book. Characters must judge each other simply according to their inevitably limited knowledge: 'so uncertain are mortal judgements, the same person most infamous and most famous, and neither justly' (p. 360). What the fiction demonstrates is that any kind of man-made, positive law is too blunt an instrument ever to reach or contain the fluctuating dynamics of human intentions and feelings. No matter how exemplary a judge is Euarchus, and no matter how hard he tries to represent Natural Law, in the end he is controlled by Arcadian laws, which he enforces strictly. He is forced, for example, to ignore the central fact of the narrative, that it was Basilius who set in motion the whole set of catastrophes by performing a set of 'unnatural' acts. The judgments handed down by Euarchus are recognised by the reader, if not by Arcadians, to be deeply flawed. However, these disturbing elements are not in the book to divert us from the level of Natural Law but to confirm its operation. The fiction as a whole depends on the reader making reference beyond Euarchus to a superior Law of Nature embedded in the narrative itself, and realising consciously that, as S. K. Heninger pithily says, 'behind the quintessential human fact, original sin, lies prideful disobedience, and active choice'.[10] The real concentration is first on the fallibility of human judgment in deciding the truth where there is misleading, insufficient, and self-interested presentation of evidence, and secondly on the inadequacies and even injustices that follow from strict enforcement of positive laws in sexual matters. On both issues the reader is perfectly aware of the total pattern. Euarchus cannot judge the case in Natural Law, but the reader, guided by knowledge of the action as a whole and accorded at the end the godlike perspective conferred by the poet, can begin to do so. In that court, reason and conscience far outweigh the letter of any man-made law. This is why there can be a celebratory 'happy ending' leaving paradoxically a disturbing note: there is some providential order at work, and although it may not be effected from within the characters' moral choices, it does lie in the structure of romance, and to that extent it lies in readers' expectations of a Natural Law working itself out. Punishment goes on internally within those who carry the memory of their deeds, and Gynecia's continuing and conscientious remorse stands at odds with the 'mortal judgments' of her as 'the example and glory of Greece'. In these mortal judgments, the narrator wryly comments, the same person may be cursed or praised as 'most infamous and most famous, and neither justly' (p. 360). Sidney's final verdict is still true to Natural Law in giving priority to conscience, which cannot be externally enforced, over fallible human laws, which can.

As God created people and planted within them Natural Law's tools of reason and conscience, so the writer has created his little 'golden' world of people whose complex motivations, actions, and their consequences have been rigorously tested according to the natural laws of sexual desire, man-made positive law, and Natural Law. More significantly, he has placed readers in the same godlike relationship to the work, inviting them to pass ultimate judgment and to put into practice in their own lives the lessons taught by the representation of breaches of Natural Law realised in his narrative. There is a general similarity to one conclusion of More's *Utopia*: although Natural Law is available to humans as an innate model of conduct, we are either unwilling or unable consistently to follow its precepts in practice. If, as Sidney's theory suggests, fictions can instruct, then in his own case the fiction teaches us not a dogma but the danger of judging dogmatically, where human emotions of love and lust are active.

## (ii)    Love's Labour's Lost[11]

We do not need knowledge of Aquinas to realise that the clash between law and some kind of 'life force' is central to many of Shakespeare's comedies. One of Northrop Frye's comments refers us to what he regards as the basic structural dynamic of Shakespearian comedy:

This structure, then, normally begins with an anticomic society, a social organisation blocking and opposed to the comic drive, which the action of the comedy evades or overcomes. It often takes the form of a harsh or irrational law, like the law of killing Syracusans in *A Comedy of Errors*, the law disposing of rebellious daughters in *A Midsummer Night's Dream*, the law that confirms Shylock's bond and justifies his actions, the law that Angelo invokes to make Vienna virtuous, and so on. Most of these irrational laws are preoccupied with trying to regulate the sexual drive, and so work counter to the wishes of the hero and heroine, which form the main impetus of the comic action.[12]

Frye was too busy developing a theory about the reception of classical New Comedy into Renaissance comedy to follow up, or tidy up, his comment about laws, and his interest really lies in the endings and in the romance elements of the comedies, rather than beginnings. Furthermore, his cryptic and sweeping statements open him up to the criticism levelled by Ralph Berry,[13] who concludes that in some plays there are no such laws, and that those mentioned by Frye are, for the most part, neither self-evidently harsh nor unreasonable, especially given the unrealistic conventions of Shakespearian comedy. However, Berry should not be allowed to have the last word on this, and his strictures should not go unchallenged. Once we are made aware of the kinds of resistance to positive laws not in conformity with reason, which were available in the Renaissance, Frye's comment opens up fertile ground.

We must first draw a subtle difference of emphasis. Frye, with his eye on the ending of a play, tends to assume the initial 'laws' are simply *data*, by definition irrational and harsh, to get the plots moving. Berry is right in arguing that the laws (or edicts or customs), however repressive, are not always self-evidently irrational. What makes them appear irrational is what happens *during* the plays. The action can be interpreted as not only anticipating a happy ending but also, and perhaps more importantly, reflecting back on the beginning, providing evolving evidence that the opening circumstances, based on a form of authoritarian status quo embodied in a law or quasi-law such as a decree, are contrary to some inbuilt Natural Law. Two plays, taken as examples in which this pattern drives the narratives, are *Love's Labour's Lost* and *Measure for Measure*, unlikely partners as they may seem.

Although we have no concrete evidence that *Love's Labour's Lost* was a play written for an Inn of Court, the suggestion has occasionally been made, especially by legal writers themselves. There are many reasons why this hypothesis is an attractive one, and since we know virtually nothing about when and where the play was first presented, or about its sources (if any), speculation is not out of place. It has been suggested, for example, that the mock embassy of Muscovites accompanied by black-amoors with music is a reference to the 'Negro Tartars' and to the Sixth Entertainment of the 1595 Gray's Inn festivities where the Emperor of Russia and Muscovy enters to the sound of trumpets.[14] More generally, the preparations for the entertainment in the 'posteriors of this day' (v. i. 79) involving 'some delightful ostentation, or show, or pageant, or antic, or firework' (v. i. 100–1) has the air of the planning towards the *Gesta Grayorum* and their equivalents at other Inns. The *Gesta Grayorum* themselves are full of the kind of undergraduatish wit that marks *Love's Labour's Lost*, as well as dwelling on the aspiration towards 'Renown and Fame' that begins Shakespeare's play. The published script makes some bawdy puns upon the various distinctions between bucks, does, and prickets, it has various elaborate edicts couched in the legal terms of 'Items' that we find in *Love's Labour's Lost*, and it even ends, in the spirit of the Songs at the end of the play, with a gesture towards the Christmas, heralding Lent, 'a time most apt, and wholly dedicated to Repentance'[15] a word which might encapsulate the 'married men' whom the cuckoo mocks, and also invoke the harshness of Mercury's message after the revels of Apollo. From the other direction, there are many technical, legal references in *Love's Labour's Lost*, ranging from the set formulas of the oath and the 'manner and form' in which Costard is apprehended (I. i. 199ff.) to stray topicalities like 'statute-caps' (V. ii. 281). There are also sententious phrases such as 'Full of dear guiltiness' (V. ii. 779) and 'justice always whirls in equal measure' (V. i. 359). As we shall see, the crucial narrative event turns on the legal definition of perjury. Further-more, the running debate about the 'sweet smoke of rhetoric' pitched against 'honest plain words' recalls the admonitions against legal jargon made by Sir Thomas Elyot, and could be Shakespeare's own advice to advocates to use rhetoric only in the service of clear meaning with situational decorum. A kind of extra-curricular link is that at the Inns dancing and masquing were central and even compulsory activities[16] and *Love's Labour's Lost* uses these, although in frustrated form, at impor-tant points. Since there is definite evidence that at least *The Comedy of Errors* and *Twelfth Night* were performed before the Gray's Inn audience in these Christmas entertainments, Shakespeare may even from first-hand observation be parodying the ribaldry that reigned amongst the young lawyers watching serious actors doing their best to present a play like *The Nine Worthies*. After all, it seems that 'upon *Innocents-Day* at Night' *The Comedy of Errors* was played in an atmosphere of such 'Confusion and Errors' that 'it was ever afterwards called, *The Night of Errors*' (p. 32), and Hibbard recalls the occasion in annotating the lines:

> Here was our consent,
> Knowing aforehand of our merriment,
> To dash it like a Christmas comedy.                    (V. ii. 460–2)

The little society of courtiers in Navarre resembles not some cabbalistic 'school of night' magicians so beloved of older literary critics such as Frances Yates, but rather the enclosed, male society of a university college or, even more appropriately, an Inn of Court. These institutions exist for cloistered study, and many a father, it was said, sent his sons to an Inn 'to preserve them from the contagion of vice',[17] and in the hope of achieving fame. We do not hear how the courtiers intend to win fame except through 'study' which could, as in the Inns, involve not only legal training but other time-stopping pursuits such as translating the classics, one way of 'living art'. Another way was practised by Baldwin, whose *Mirror for Magistrates* was declared by Jasper Heywood to 'proclaim eternal fame' in the manner coveted by Navarre.[18] Even the Inns' architecture mirrors the imagined spaces of *Love's Labour's Lost*. An exterior is designed to be forbidding to all strangers, and presumably females in particular. Buildings have the air of a 'silent court' leading to an inner 'curious knotted garden' and quadrangle. Beyond, open fields are set over to nature's purposes. The analogy to something like Magdalen College, Oxford or sixteenth-century Gray's Inn does not hold entirely, for it would appear that the princess and her retinue approach not through an awesome front door but through the open fields at the back, but even the symbolism of them entering through the 'back door' of nature is appropriate to the play's pattern. They have, in Biron's phrase, climbed over the house to unlock the little gate (I. i. 109), since they would have been denied entrance by some Cerberus-like porter or misogynist, growling bursar at the front lodge. Inner and Middle Temple Inns backed not onto open fields but onto the Thames at the Embankment, as some Cambridge colleges are on the watery 'Backs', and entrance along a river would have the same effect. There was contemporary evidence that the single-sex Inns were not worlds apart from the 'academe' of *Love's Labour's Lost*. An Inner Temple regulation of the day reads:

Item, that no woman shall have recourse to the gentlemen's chambers for any cause, except to be as suitors to 'experyensors' in term times, openly, without evil suspect, upon pain of forfeiture of 3s.4d. for every time any such woman shall have resort, the same to be paid by the gentleman that lieth in the chamber whereunto any such resort shall be found or perceived.[19]

Although 1598 is far later than any critic has dared to date *Love's Labour's Lost,* that year saw what appears to be a sober reiteration of Navarre's proclamation by no less a figure than Queen Elizabeth, when she made new statutes for Gray's Inn which repeated those from its sister institution, Inner Temple. It seems that female distractions were considered a problem in the Inns as they are in the court of Navarre.

If the Inn of Court analogy is taken, then the initial 'law' or edict renouncing the company of women is not at the outset obviously irrational, at least in Elizabethan terms. The whole context enforces 'study' on young men who were expected to resist their own sexual desires, most decisively done, it would appear, by abstention from the company of women. It is part of the play's strategy to *prove*, in the legal sense and perhaps to the satisfaction of an audience of law students, the unreasonableness and unnaturalness of an edict which will prove to be a breach of Natural Law. Shakespeare's success in this scheme may reflect the bemusement of one observing the closed, academic institution, and its relinquishment of 'common sense' (I. i. 57). His position is clearly on the side of the students in the Inns of Court against parietal laws, since they would, of course, have been delighted to admit women.

The plot turns on the very simple fulcrum of a positive law being passed which will prove to clash with that aspect of Natural Law which covers sexual relations as briefly described by Aquinas in the quotation at the beginning of this chapter. The king of Navarre, whose position undoubtedly gives him authority to make law, passes an 'edict', and his subjects (those of them whom we see) confirm their agreement by swearing an oath. The 'deep oaths' are initially taken seriously, and even the sceptic, Biron, emphasises their legal force:[20]

> So to the laws at large I write my name;
> And he that breaks them in the least degree
> Stands in attainder of eternal shame.                    (I. i. 154–6)

Biron is convinced the oath will soon be broken, but his language mimics the serious intent of his more grimly determined friends. 'Eternal shame' is the spiritual punishment for perjury, and 'attainder' introduces implications of outlawry and forfeiture of property rights as a consequence of treason. Shakespeare is making a contemporary legal point of some significance. Traditionally the 'law of words' was considered as at most a matter between a person and his or her conscience. A case of blasphemy, for example, would be business for the ecclesiastical courts rather than the common law. This situation was changing in Elizabeth's time, as Selden was later to report:

Perjury has only to do with an Assertory Oath, and no man was punished for perjury by man's Law till Queen Eliz: time, 'twas left to God as a Sin against him, the reason was because 'twas so hard a thing to prove a man perjur'd; I might [mis]understand him and yet he swear as he thought.[21]

The punishment of 'shame' may have been the only one effectively available under ecclesiastical jurisdiction, but, as Selden implies, it is a dangerous precedent for man to legislate at all over sins which only God can judge. This is precisely the point to be made by Shakespeare in *Measure for Measure*, and by Milton later, in the sphere of sexual relations.

The oath sworn by Navarre and his court does not directly regulate sexuality since its primary aim is to commit the men to singleminded study, but, as Biron points out, by necessary inference it governs both hospitality and relations between men and women. No woman is allowed within a mile of the court, on pain of the grotesquely unfair penalty of losing her tongue (a distant reference to Spenser's hapless poet in *The Faerie Queene* V. ix. 25–6). In Shakespearian romantic comedy, which deals centrally with love, such a law is made to be broken, but the point to be made here is not the banal one that love conquers all, since it does *not* triumph by the end of the play, but that the action and discussions are very much based on whether Natural Law should take priority over a positive law when there is a discrepancy between the systems.

Biron's various attacks on the king's edict are justly famous as expressions of the power of love first learned in a woman's eyes, but his appeals are consistently to 'reason' and to what is natural. He is sceptical of the idea that book-learning can be a route to wisdom:

> Small have continual plodders won,
> Save base authority from others' books.                    (I. i. 85–6)

This draws the king's dry comment 'How well he's read, to reason against reading' (I. i. 94). Biron champions instinct and personal experience as paths to 'the light of truth' (I. i. 75), and these seem also to be the touchstones employed by the Princess in her social and emotional dealings. Biron sees the edict as 'A dangerous law against gentility' (I. i. 127) since it prohibits the social decencies of hospitality. When the king is reminded that the French king's daughter is about to arrive, he concedes that they 'must of force dispense with this decree. She must lie here on mere necessity' (I. i. 146–7). Biron logically points out that if 'necessity', the compulsion of a more pressing priority, is to overrule the positive law, then it will be invoked over and over again since the law itself is against 'necessity':

> Necessity will make us all forsworn
> Three thousand times within this three years' space;
> For every man with his affects is born,
> Not by might mastered, but by special grace.                    (I. i. 148–51)

Worldly 'might' of man-made law cannot, without denying Natural Law, legislate effectively over feelings ('affects') or over God's 'special grace'. It is important to note that 'necessity' is loaded with legal content, both positive and natural. Necessity was, and still is, deemed to be a valid defence against the charge of criminal liability. It is available where a power or force is so great that it admits no choice of conduct even where it results in a criminal act. Self-defence is the most obvious example, where it may be deemed necessary for an innocent person under assault to inflict bodily harm on the assailant if there is no alternative way of protecting life and limb. It is related to Natural Law in its inner logic of survival. Biron, of course, is demonstrating a recognition of the king's legalistic use of the word to cover the imperatives of state diplomacy and simple hospitality, while referring himself to a more 'natural' drive, the instinctive and social 'necessity' of women and men meeting each other. To deny this need would, in extremity, be to consign the human race to extinction, and would therefore be against its 'natural' interests.

Almost immediately we have proof of this, as Costard, the 'natural man' if ever there were one, is the first to 'fall'. He justifies his meeting with Jaquenetta by referring to natural feelings: 'it is the manner of a man to speak to a woman (I. i. 208) ... Such is the simplicity of man to hearken after the flesh' (I. i. 213) (the Quarto text has the inspired misprint 'sinplicity'). Even the ascetic Aquinas had placed sexuality in the realms of Natural Law, making people answerable to God directly rather than to secular authority. Costard's prosecutor or informer, Armado, equally, cannot restrain his desire for Jaquenetta, and during the course of the action he makes her pregnant. The next 'necessity' is for the king to compromise his oath by hosting the Princess and her three women attendants, in order to avoid the 'deadly sin' (II. i. 104) of neglecting 'housekeeping'. His solution is no answer at all, for he accommodates the women in the fields rather than in the court, presumably not a mile away, and he and his courtiers speak freely to the women. They have already effectively broken the oath. In encountering these 'necessities', however lighthearted they may seem, the men are learning the essence of Natural Law, that it is other-centred rather than self-centred, based upon charity and love rather than the individual ego.

The next stage of their conversion might be called the natural law of romantic comedy: if there are four men and four women, it is as inevitable as spring following winter that they will fall in love. Shakespeare employs no suspense and reveals the sets of mutual attraction immediately. The only element of suspense lies in how the hypocrites will be unmasked, and the only surprise is the spectacular change of direction away from the expected world-without-end bargain of marriage at the end. Shakespeare, as in other romantic comedies in different ways, presupposes love as the most natural force of all and thereafter demonstrates the man-made obstacles that must be cleared away before the conditions for fulfilling the Natural Law can prevail. In this play the obstacles lie not externally in the figures of obstructive parents as in *A Midsummer Night's Dream, As You Like It*, (and for that matter in *Romeo and Juliet* and *Othello*), nor are they created by 'errors' or misunderstandings as in Shakespeare's other comedies, but rather they are erected by the male protagonists themselves. Since they have created the positive law which is against the comic version of Natural Law, and then broken their vows, they cannot reasonably be rewarded within the play with fulfilled love in marriage. Even in play, they must be punished, make atonement, and, if successful in this, then their sport may become a comedy and Jack may eventually have Jill. In a twelvemonth and a day they may have their happy endings, but 'That's too long for a play' (V. ii. 860). Shakespeare's simple way of resolving the various narrative drives is to postpone or defer the true fulfilment in love, leaving open the possibility that it will never occur.

To return to Biron's line of argument which has clear authorial support, he asserts another of Aquinas' central assumptions, that Natural Law is contextual. What is natural and right in one context may be unnatural and wrong in another:

| | |
|---|---|
| BIRON | The spring is near when green geese are a-breeding. |
| DUMAINE | How follows that? |
| BIRON | Fit in his place and time. |
| DUMAINE | In reason nothing. |
| BIRON | Something then in rhyme. |
| KING | Biron is like an envious sneaping frost, |
| | That bites the first-born infants of the spring. |
| BIRON | Well, say I am. Why should proud summer boast |
| | Before the birds have any cause to sing? |
| | Why should I joy in an abortive birth? |
| | At Christmas I no more desire a rose |
| | Than wish a snow in May's new-fangled shows, |
| | But like of each thing that in season grows.    (I. i. 95–107) |

Biron's argument that each thing must be 'Fit in his place and time' is not only orthodox Natural Law thinking, but it also anticipates the gnomic songs at the end of the play, where the winter and the spring are juxtaposed without judgments being made, except that activities appropriate in May are not so in December. The reasoning from contextual tolerance allows Biron later to justify love on behalf of the men in defiance of their oaths:

> Sweet lords, sweet lovers, O let us embrace!
> As true we are as flesh and blood can be.
> The sea will ebb and flow, heaven show his face;
> Young blood doth not obey an old decree.
> We cannot cross the cause why we are born,
> Therefore of all hands must we be forsworn.                    (IV. iii. 211–16)

This statement builds into itself several Natural Law precepts, and the truism taken from nature, 'The sea will ebb and flow', indicates that the reference is conscious on Shakespeare's part. 'Young blood doth not obey an old decree' spells out Biron's prediction that a monastic and ascetic oath is simply not appropriate for young men, and Biron later asserts that 'To fast, to study, and to see no woman' is 'Flat treason 'gainst the kingly state of youth' (IV. iii. 290–1). 'We cannot cross the cause why we are born' presupposes the notion of individuated destiny which makes some actions 'natural' and impulsive rather than forced or coerced, and it reminds us that without sexuality we would not have been born. It lies behind Aquinas' thinking, and the same sentiment fuels Biron's 'Let us once lose our oaths to find ourselves, Or else we lose ourselves to keep our oaths' (IV. iii. 336–7). He even says it is 'religion to be thus forsworn' (*ibid*. 338), and the gist of the young men's sonnets is that the 'heavenly rhetoric' (IV. iii. 58) of the women's beauty has taught them self-knowledge. The phrase 'heaven show his face' encapsulates the religious, even religiose, grid of references to the earthly analogue or participation in divine law, namely Natural Law.

Not that the women will accept such a conversion at face value. The men have still broken another ecclesiastically backed law in breaking their oaths, and the Princess has no intentions of letting them off this hook. 'Nor God nor I delights in perjured men', she says, and when the king tries to shift responsibility for their perjury to the beauty of the 'virtue' of women's eyes she sharply retorts:

> You nickname virtue; 'vice' you should have spoke;
> For virtue's office never breaks men's troth.
> . . .
> So much I hate a breaking cause to be
> Of heavenly oaths, vowed with integrity.          (V. ii. 348–56 *passim*)

That her words are seriously meant is demonstrated by the women's relentless refusal to co-operate with the courtship rituals of masque and dance initiated by the courtiers. Indeed, the men have still not learned fully the lesson of fitness in place and time, for they do not realise that the scene begins to cloud with Mercade's message that the Princess' father has died, and that grief and mourning rather than the bombast and lining to the time of courtship are now appropriate. Marriage is deferred, at least for one year and possibly indefinitely, pending the courtiers' successful completion of tasks which will force them to enter a far more 'natural' world than that of the cloistered court. Biron, for example, is directed by Rosaline to use his wit in cheering up hospitalised people in pain, a brief he considers 'impossible' but will undertake:

> To move wild laughter in the throat of death?
> It cannot be, it is impossible.
> Mirth cannot move a soul in agony.          (V. ii. 837–9)

Rosaline's reasonable suggestion is that Biron should try, and if he finds shallow laughter and 'idle scorn' cannot help the dying, then he should

give up these traits forever and stop joking about serious matters. The
final lines from the courtiers show them on the verge of leaving the make-
believe of play for a world where Natural Law, with its requirement of
exercising reason and conscience means something much more serious:

> KING    Come, sir, it wants a twelvemonth an' a day,
>           And then 'twill end.
> BIRON   That's too long for a play.                      (V. ii. 859–60)

Somewhat curiously, even the Princess has her moment of apparently
breaking Natural Law. It is not explained why she agrees to the hunt in
which she kills a pricket, since she clearly shares the humanists' distaste
for the activity. As 'mercy goes to kill' the natural feeling in her is 'pity',
and she realises that it is 'more for praise than purpose' that people kill
animals in sport.

> And out of question so it is sometimes,
> Glory grows guilty of detested crimes,
> When, for fame's sake, for praise, an outward part,
> We bend to that the working of the heart.              (IV. i. 31–4)

Nathaniel's opinion that the hunt was 'Very reverend sport, truly, and
done in the testimony of a good conscience' (IV. ii. 1) seems contradicted
by the Princess's apparently conscience-stricken speech. Her collaboration in the hunt is probably best interpreted not as characteristic of her,
but as offering an occasion for the dramatist to emphasise his 'moral',
since the terms of this speech sum up precisely what the men have done
in the name of 'fame'. The speech can be given only to the Princess since,
if, for argument's sake, one of the men had said it, the charge of
hypocrisy would undermine the message, as it does all their moralistic
statements, even Biron's, after they have broken their vows.

It is no part of my intention to turn a delicate and deft comedy into a
solemn tract, but the very genuine delight given by *Love's Labour's Lost*
in the theatre is built upon a substantial, conceptual foundation concerning rival forms of justice. An Inn of Court audience of lawyers would
have been well able to appreciate Shakespeare's subtle deployment of
legal concepts. If the various debates between positive law and Natural
Law, between proscriptions and desires, public legislation and private
morality are perennially alive and just as unresolved as Shakespeare left
them, then we may have located one of the sources of Shakespeare's
durability with audiences and readers. It enables us to locate also a
dramatic strategy which he was to use later in another play about law

and sex, *Measure for Measure*, a self-evidently 'serious' comedy. We shall return to this play in the next chapter.

Despite the apparently definitive formality of closure in romance and comedy (marriage solves all), the works we have looked at give us conclusions that do not conclude. This is true in an obvious sense for *Love's Labour's Lost*, but it holds true for the others in different ways. Sidney exhibits anxiety about sexual morality, feeling that somehow its transgressions *should* be punishable on earth, yet his overall deployment of the narrative insists that humans alone, flawed and complicit as they are, cannot ever know enough about the individual subtlety of particular situations to judge. Judge not lest ye be judged seems an insistent warning from both him and Shakespeare. In comparison, Shakespeare takes this tolerance a stage further, and his vision is weighted towards indulgence and trust in the internal rationality of desire, leaving the rest for God to judge. But, if this seems to drive the argument too far, at the very least both writers can be said to make into entertaining fictions the problems themselves, making sport of the absurdities law can propagate when it strays into the sexual arena, and the equal absurdities people can manifest when under the influence of a force of love which is simultaneously rational and irrational, ordinary and extraordinary, natural and unnatural. In the final analysis, in keeping with the elusiveness of the subject itself, writers of comedy and romance really do not need to be pinned down to particular conclusions on the nature of love: instead, they create their works out of a recognition that there are no conclusions possible on earth: but this, in itself, tends to align them with Natural Law, and against legal positivists such as Angelo.

# 7 'Hot temper leaps o'er a cold decree': *The Merchant of Venice* and *Measure for Measure*

While *Love's Labour's Lost* has a quasi-judicial sub-structure and may have been written with an Inn of Court audience in mind, it has never ranked as a 'legal' play in the same sense as *The Merchant of Venice* and *Measure for Measure*. The latter have always attracted attention from lawyers themselves for their primary concentration on legal issues, which are immediately seen to be crucial to their respective plots. My concentration here does not lie in the niceties of sixteenth-century contract or marriage laws, but in the overaching conflict between Natural Law and positive law. This framework was seen to be important to *Love's Labour's Lost*, as Natural Law's innate impulses comically overrule the letter of laws which are made by men, and, as we shall see, it informs the tragic world of *King Lear*. Indeed, the overall direction of my argument leads to the conclusion that this is *par excellence* the Shakespearian theme when he bases a drama on the contemplation of issues of justice.

## The Merchant of Venice[1]

It has become a commonplace, at least amongst legal historians who write on Shakespeare, that the central trial scene in *The Merchant of Venice*, despite its Mediterranean setting, dramatises and turns upon the distinctive differences between English common law and equity. Up to a point I agree with this, but only in so far as equity was England's court of Natural Law, and not a specific jurisdiction. In another sense, Shakespeare's courtroom makes no reference to the procedures of common law or English equity, and the real opposition, or rather relationship, is not between these historical systems, but more conceptually between positive law and Natural Law. This virtually archetypal kind of clash forms a structure which Shakespeare uses several times and which he inherited from Sidney.

As the most famous trial scene in imaginative literature, Act Four, Scene 1 of *The Merchant of Venice* has drawn many legal writers to comment on it. Unfortunately, they are by no means unanimous in their explanations of what, legally speaking, is being depicted. Early in the twentieth century German jurists virtually made the scene their own, disagreeing with each other on points of detail, but generally concurring that the contract made between Antonio and Shylock was void *ab initio* and the case should never have come to court. The English legal historian, Sir Frederick Pollock, agreed, while other legal writers have said that the scene turns on a mere quibble in sophistry which would have no place in a court of law anyway. Owen Hood Philips[2] raises the question whether or not Shylock received justice, by summarising problems about the exact status of Portia in this scene: whether she is an advocate for the defence, or a judge in her own right. George W. Keeton says that Antonio had several practical avenues open to him: borrowing the money offered by Portia before the due date rather than waiting; urging that the bond was void as contrary to public policy; and (more weakly) pleading fraudulent misrepresentation since Shylock strongly hinted that 'this merry bond' (II. i. 166) would not be legally enforced but was a joke and was, ironically, urged by Shylock as an act of 'friendship' (II. i. 161). Keeton also argues that the turning-point in Portia's courtroom presentation marks a shift 'from the realm of the Common Law into Equity'.[3] Maxine MacKay[4] turns this argument on its head and says that Portia, knowing that in Elizabethan law a person could not be tried under both common law and equity, or even appeal from one to the other, *first* suggests equity as appropriate in her initial reference to mercy, but, since her plea fails, *then* she turns to trying the case strictly according to a common-law rigour in standing by the letter of the law (flesh, but not blood, is mentioned in the bond). W. Nicholas Knight[5] returned to the argument that Shakespeare is giving pre-eminence to principles of equity, and he quotes from William Lambarde's *Archaionomia* to support him. Knight points out that a copy of this book has Shakespeare's autograph (which does not appear to have been authenticated or disproved by experts), and that Lambarde was a high-ranking chancery official who would have been involved in, and certainly wrote a note on, Shakespeare's own litigation over land (*Shakespeare v. Lambert*, 1597–9). His reading of the scene in *The Merchant of Venice* is that Shakespeare is upholding the jurisdiction of Chancery as 'a superior court with its accompanying appellate function and humane spirit' (p. 95). Mark Edwin Andrews in a whole book devoted to this scene alone,[6] not only supports the view that the scene first follows King's Bench (common-law) procedure, acting *in rem* on property grounds alone, and then 'demonstrates the superiority of equity' which allows considerations *in personam,* but goes further in arguing that Shakespeare in this scene dramatically influenced the contemporary battle between

Coke, representing common law, against Ellesmere, supported by Bacon, who represented Chancery. B. J. Sokol argues that the scene does not reflect common law and particularly avoids doctrines from equity, maintaining rather that the point of reference is mercantile law. The Law of the Merchant, reflected also in Jonson's *Bartholomew Fair*, tended in the sixteenth century to rely on 'good faith' which would normally have meant 'strict compliance with accepted custom',[7] since 'A great mercantile city such as Venice, or latterly London, could not afford to allow its reputation for 'policy of right' to appear to be compromised, especially in disputes involving the international trading community', a point agreed on by both Antonio and Shylock. But 'good faith', while never meaning what a philosopher understands by the phrase, could allow some flexibility of interpretation and Shylock can be accused of not being in good faith. For some, like Donald Cheney, *The Merchant of Venice* as a whole turns on the contrast between an Old Testament, Judaic emphasis on Law and a New Testament, Christian emphasis on Love.[8] John D. Euce,[9] although writing for lawyers in the *Virginia Law Review*, suggests that we should not probe too deeply into legal minutiae in interpreting Shakespeare's play, and he tends to present a 'soft' Christian reading that makes Portia a 'heavenly' agent of salvation. Beyond occasional bare suggestions, nobody appears to have argued systematically that Shakespeare is faithfully representing the Roman civil law which would have prevailed in Venice at the time, an oversight which is surprising in the plethora of conflicting opinions, and which I do not intend to pursue here, except in passing.

Since these commentators offer so many, often mutually contradictory explanations, we are free to pursue our own, and it is refreshing and revealing to hack away at the specific jurisdictional problems and examine the dramatic realities. In some ways students of literature are able to be more flexible than legal writers, since we can more easily accept fluid interplay between literary convention, imaginative creation, and Elizabethan legal practice, without striving for a single, literal level on which to remain. For example, a point which worries lawyers concerning the Duke's role may not trouble the student of drama. Is he, as in Venetian law of the time, presiding over a group of judges, and if so where are the others? Does he have any power of adjudication himself? Likewise, what exactly is the status of Portia or rather, Doctor Balthazar? Those working in the medium of drama intuitively know that economy amongst *dramatis personae* is essential and that one character may play several roles and functions as appropriate in dramatic contexts, even from moment to moment. The Duke cannot unilaterally pass judgment without the full process of a court trial, but, when the legal rights and wrongs are made clear through due procedure of argument and counter-argument, then he can, and he does, take on the authority to pass judgment. He thus fills the roles of presider, panel of judges, and sentencer, a conflation which makes dramatic sense even if it could not operate in a court of law. Portia, likewise, fills several roles. One can be taken as a convention in the same category as her masculine disguise, not to be examined too closely: she has been 'sent' fully briefed as a proxy for the 'learned doctor' from Padua, Bellario, who is 'sick'. 'Balthazar' acts in several ways: first as *amicus curiae*, an expert legal adviser to the Duke;[10] secondly as a 'judge', as both Christians and Jew call him/her; and thirdly as an advocate, first acting for Shylock prosecuting, and then in defence of Antonio. Again, even if it might not make full legal sense, it makes perfect dramatic sense to give these multiple functions to Portia, since by doing so Shakespeare has used one actor to play, effectively, five roles: Bellario; a kind of ombudsman; an impartial judge (or indeed a panel of judges); and two advocates, one on each side. As the disguised wife of Bassanio, she is also for the audience playing a sixth, all-important role which will give her power and information that she uses later in the marital situation. The precise legal status of the Duke and Portia respectively is therefore shifting through time but specific at any one time, reflecting a brilliant economy in Shakespeare's design. The strategy may worry lawyers who want the functions separated, but it does not worry audiences, and it allows us to bypass many problems of legal procedure.

The Duke has done his best to avoid the whole panoply of a trial by attempting to have the case 'settled out of court' in our modern term, but Shylock has intransigently refused to compromise. The terms in which a compromise is offered and rejected come back again later in the trial. The Duke asks Shylock to mollify 'His rigorous course' by exercising 'pity' and 'mercy'. This does not address his *legal* rights, but appeals to his human feelings and invokes the moral territory of Natural Law, with specific hints of equity . Shylock, 'Uncapable of pity, void and empty From any dram of mercy' (lines 5–6), rejects the appeal and, as is his right, demands a narrowly 'legal' judgment of the case. More and more, as the scene goes on, he equates himself with the 'law' itself: 'I would have my bond' (line 86); 'What judgement shall I dread, doing no wrong' (line 89); 'I stand for judgement' (line 103); 'I stand here for law' (line 142); 'I crave the law' (line 202). Addressing Balthazar as 'a worthy judge' he requires legal rigour:

> You know the law, your exposition
> Hath been most sound. I charge you by the law,

> Whereof you are a well-deserving pillar,
> Proceed to judgment.

The particular ground Shylock stands upon is the law of contract, in Shakespeare's Venice as in his England, which enforces strictly the terms of a properly made bargain. At this stage he represents simple reliance on positive law, rather than a characterised human being. Marx argued that Shylock alienates his humanity to commerce, and we could say the same thing about his use of the law. Positive law, whether common law or statutory or otherwise, in any legal system, is by definition rigorous, consistent, unambiguous, and often appears harsh to one or both parties. Feelings and personality are beyond its consideration, except in ascertaining whether the parties intended to make a legally binding contract. This is the point behind the symbol of justice as being blind and holding scales and a sword. On several occasions the reasons for rigorous enforcement in this play are offered very clearly. Especially in Venice, the undoubted centre of trade in the Renaissance world, law must above all be consistent and reliable in its operations, in order to command the trust of all parties. Antonio himself, as 'the merchant of Venice' recognises this:

> The Duke cannot deny the course of law;
> For the commodity that strangers have
> With us in Venice, if it be denied,
> Will much impeach the justice of the state,
> Since that the trade and profit of the city
> Consisteth of all nations.

Any exception will introduce a precedent that immediately makes the law unreliable in future, as 'Bellario' maintains:

> there is no power in Venice
> Can alter a decree established.
> 'Twill be recorded for a precedent,
> And many an error by the same example
> Will rush into the state: it cannot be.

She is here invoking the legal maxim 'hard cases make bad law': hardship caused by strict application of law is irrelevant to the process of judgment. Therefore, any ire that we may feel about the 'cruelty' of the law's operation can be directed not at Shylock but at the law itself, which is unqualified in its terms and which is capable of creating further injustices. Balthazar very clearly articulates the important distinction between consistent law and 'human nature':

> Of a strange nature is the suit you follow,
> Yet in such rule that the Venetian law
> Cannot impugn you as you do proceed.

At this stage of the trial the 'strange nature' of Shylock's individual actions is not in issue. Just as on many occasions in our own daily lives we hear petty officials saying, with Angelo in *Measure for Measure*, 'It is the law, not I', so feelings of sympathy and antipathy alike are rendered completely irrelevant. Even today, for example, certain kinds of honest mistake, and ignorance of the law, are not admitted as defences to actions at law. It is significant that Shylock offers no explanation for relying so totally on the law in his case: 'So can I give no reason, nor will I not ... Are you answered?' (lines 59, 62). 'A lodged hate and a certain loathing' makes him relentless against Antonio, but this is simply an explanation for his refusing to exercise mercy, not for his standing by the law. 'This is no answer' retorts Bassanio, but in essence this is the position upholding positive law itself. Once enacted, the 'reason' behind it no longer matters beside the 'letter' of a law, and personal intentions are not just distracting, but may also fog the issues of justice and destroy the concept of law itself. Not Shylock, but positive law itself, is the impediment to Antonio's life and freedom.

At this stage many legal commentators, treating the word 'mercy' as a talisman, invoke the concept of English equity, saying that some such system must exist in this fictional world of Venice, providing a court of appeal beyond injustices caused by strict application of common law. However, the one thing made quite clear in the text is that here English equity as such does *not* exist. Portia's stirring speech about 'The quality of mercy' is not the basis for a judgment, as it may be in equity, but an appeal to Shylock's own feelings. As Shylock points out, there is no 'compulsion' (line 179) upon him as there would be if a legal system based upon mercy were in operation. Indeed, if such a system were in place it would not be Shylock's choice, but a judge's decree that enforced it. Shakespeare *could* easily have allowed Portia to couch her argument in equitable terms: 'mercy' in equity is not simply clemency (as she encourages), but the overruling of a strict law which in its application offends against reason and conscience. If the play had been set in England he could even have had the court bring down a judgment in equity, however dubious its enforceability might be. Portia conspicuously does not argue in any of these ways, and Shakespeare has chosen a legal setting in which there is no appeal to Chancery, implying that Shakespeare has calculatedly excluded the equitable option. Shylock simply brushes aside the appeal, returning again to the 'law' as his ground. We should also be clear that, when Portia catches out Shylock later by ruling that he can take flesh but no blood, she is not relying on a system of equity but simply invoking another, equally rigorous 'law' of Venice which happens to conflict with the law of contract in this case, just as in

England the law against 'grievous bodily harm' would conflict with such a contractual bargain which of necessity will cause bloodshed. There is obviously a hierarchy of laws in operation here, to which we shall return, but for the time being it is enough to be clear that Shakespeare is unequivocally ruling out the possibility of a system of equity in this context.

However, this is not to say that because the system of equity is not legally applicable in Venice the concept itself is also not imaginatively available in this scene. The overall point made by the outcome of the trial is the more subtle one that equity is not needed to resolve such a problem within the law but that it would be *easier* if there were such a system available. It should be clear by now that the argument turns really on Natural Law and its relationship with positive law, perhaps mediated through Roman civil law which historically operated in Venice in Shakespeare's time. We must recall that in general terms it is expected that properly authorised positive law will always be in accord with Natural Law and that the two systems coexist alongside one another without conflict. If the positive law offends against reason and conscience, against Natural Law, then it is no law at all. Recall also that the essence of Natural Law is that it is flexible and situational, accepting that what is just in one case may not be in another. Clearly Shakespeare has given us a case where there is an acute problem in these terms. The positive law claimed by Shylock is perfectly acceptable and even necessary in the context of contractual obligations, and, given the need for law to be certain, one need not, or cannot, look behind it for 'reasons': 'No reason' as Shylock says, but strict application of the letter of the law. In itself the strict enforcement of contracts satisfies both reason and conscience. The other 'law' produced by Portia is equally available in the legal system of Shakespeare's Venice as it would have been in the historical Venice itself, but its philosophical and legal basis is of a different, more general kind, which makes it recognisable as the appeal to Natural Law. We should not quibble about the distinction between flesh and blood, since to the law of contract 'flesh' does not mean life itself but a commodity – equivalent to a bag of nails or a dozen apples – while in Natural Law flesh and blood are synonymous, representing life itself. The one precept agreed on by all Natural Law theorists is that preservation of life, based on a notion of 'charity' (line 257) as much as on reason and conscience, is a pre-eminent moral and legal touchstone. 'Do harm to no person' is its most universal precept. If in the particular case this is violated even by a positive law, then the law is no law, and is void and unenforceable. Shylock is threatening life. In the circumstances of this particular case the positive law of contract which he stands by, being in conflict with the Natural Law of preserving life, is no law at all. Or, putting it another way, the positive law is appropriately adapted to fit the circumstances of the case by accusing Shylock of attempt to murder which is such a serious offence that it diminishes Antonio's breach of contract. This is the basis of Portia's final advice.

All this, Shakespeare is assuming, can be deduced without transcendental appeal, and without recourse to a specific system of law such as equity. This is why the trial scene seems to 'work' in any community, irrespective of its legal framework. It is not clear from the text whether he knows about Roman civil law, but, even if we assume he does not, the point still stands. The grounds for the decision already lie within the unified system of law itself as it is represented by a Natural Law understanding. However, we can acknowledge that Shakespeare, especially if he is not making reference to Roman civil law, is obliquely commenting on the existing system of equity in England by implying that the problem could have been circumvented and more expeditiously solved without anxiety *if* equity existed. That it does not, is explained by the fact that Venice does not have a monarchy or its equivalent to embody a 'court of the king's conscience' and exercise prerogative in overruling common law. Unlike the English system, in the Venetian the limitations on the powers of the Duke who is not a king become legally functional, since, as we have seen, he has no power unilaterally to intervene until arguments based on reason and conscience have produced an irrefutable verdict. It is absolutely crucial that Portia's speech on mercy does not invoke equity, but yet does turn on the precise *kind* of 'mercy' at work in the English court of Chancery and which is not available in Venice:

> [Mercy is] mightiest in the mightiest, it becomes
> The throned monarch better than his crown.
> His sceptre shows the force of temporal power,
> The attribute to awe and majesty,
> Wherein doth sit the dread and fear of kings.

At the same time, Portia goes on to emphasise that if mercy is a form of law in itself which may be delivered on earth by monarchs alone, its ultimate source of moral authority lies beyond these worldly figures who exercise it only as delegates of God on earth. In theory it can operate without monarchs, since, according to one formulation, such a law is engraven in people's hearts, but there is in Venice no legal authority for it. Shakespeare is simultaneously praising the English system and criticising any attempt to base decisions of justice on positive law alone, which is precisely the point on which *Measure for Measure* turns, as we shall see. Things are simpler and more just with the absolute authority of monarchs in existence:

> But mercy is above this sceptred sway.
> It is enthroned in the hearts of kings,
> It is an attribute to God himself,
> And earthly power doth then show likest God's
> When mercy seasons justice.

*Whenever* mercy seasons justice, whether in the actions of a king or a commoner, the attribute of God is in operation. Natural Law is given supremacy and can resolve conflicts between positive laws. Only when the tide is turned against Shylock, and he is reminded that in pursuing the letter of the law he will himself end up being executed, does he fully understand the nature of the conflict beween Natural Law and the positive law he is invoking. Calvin would see this as an example of the loss of innate understanding of Natural Law in mankind, and a reason for punitive measures, but such a conclusion would lead back into Shakespeare's trap that *any* reliance on what amounts to coercive, positive law will lead to injustices. However, this may be, he does not show special interest in the theological aspects of his argument, and Shylock's enlightenment leads to a neat resolution of the plot.

Shakespeare is not, then, showing in *The Merchant of Venice* the *operation* of English equity or royal prerogative, but rather arguing for its underlying *rationale* which still holds even in a republic, whether or not a separate system exists, and which could equally support a form of law based directly on Natural Law such as Roman civil law. While not denying the universality of Natural Law, Shakespeare's inbuilt flattery of the English monarchical system of equity, may well reveal ulterior motives at a time when he was attempting to pursue through Chancery a case involving his own property interest, where common law would have found against him on the letter of the law.[11]

We may have just about exhausted the Natural Law element in Act Four, Scene 1, but not in *The Merchant of Venice* as a whole. On at least two other occasions in the play there are comparable situations, where the letter of positive law is modified in the light of its apparent conflict with another law which might be described as the law of life, Natural Law. They can be briefly asserted rather than argued at length. Portia feels trapped at the outset by the equivalent of a positive law, made by her father when he was alive, that she cannot marry anybody except a man who chooses the correct casket out of three. Her words summarise the opening situations in *Love's Labour's Lost* and *Measure for Measure*: '... the brain may devise laws for the blood, but a hot temper leaps o'er a cold decree' (I. ii. 20). When 'the will of a living daughter [is] curbed by the will of a dead father', we are faced with another case of the 'dead letter' of the law inhibiting the 'living' situation in which a young woman finds herself, and although Portia self-deprecatingly sees her feelings as 'madness', yet she is restless for some Law beyond the law which will effect her 'natural' desires. Nerissa sagely points out that her father was 'ever virtuous' and that 'holy men at their death have good inspirations' (I. ii. 23–4). She turns out to be correct, and, in practice, there is no conflict because Bassanio, with whom Portia falls in love, chooses 'rightly' and proves his ability to 'rightly love' (I. ii. 28). Bassanio chooses (we might think, somewhat against his commercial and fortune-hunting personality, but motivated now by love) on moral rather than mercenary grounds, choosing lead and rejecting gold and silver. His argument turns on both reason and conscience, that the first represents solid substance rather than the false glitter and ornamented show of gold and silver. Jessica's elopement with Lorenzo can be seen as a parallel, more typically comic situation in which the 'law' of the *senex* is resisted in order to achieve a 'natural' marriage. Even Lancelot Gobbo breaks the contract with his master, leaving Shylock on grounds of 'conscience'. As in the case which we might style *Shylock v. Antonio*, so throughout the play positive laws which are restrictive can be reinterpreted, or broken, when set alongside the operation of a Natural Law based on moral considerations which, as in Shakespeare's other comedies, is drawn from the 'natural' impera- tive behind romantic love and desire, to preserve and continue human life.

The other occasion when some kind of Natural Law resolves a problem in the administration of a positive law comes at the end, and is much lighter in dramatic effect. After the trial, Bassanio and Gratiano both give their rings to the disguised Portia and Nerissa respectively, against the contractual conditions of the bond of marriage. Portia and Nerissa use this fact to establish power over the men at the end, but it is as clear to the audience as to the characters themselves that the men's motives (which, the court scene has established, are relevant to Natural Law if not to the law of contract) were based on the pillars of reason, conscience, and charity. The rings were given in 'charity' to recompense those who had been agents for the preservation of Antonio's life. Cleverly, Shakespeare has also built in the point that there has been no true breach of the marriage bond anyway, since the rings, acting as symbol rather than as commodities, are inadvertently given by husbands to their wives, as they first came from wives to husbands. But the exchanges and their consequences amount to a minor misdemeanour against positive law which brings its own little punishment, just as the courtiers in *Love's Labour's Lost* are punished for breaking their words.

Finally, but in some ways most importantly, we find Natural Law present at the most famous or notorious level, its treatment of the issue of race. Even Morocco, otherwise a figure of fun, is given a line which is a plea for tolerance based on no more and no less than the equality of existence of human beings: 'Mislike me not for my complexion' (II. i. 1). This aspect of what Hart described as the 'minimal content' of Natural Law, the touchstone of what cannot be denied a human being simply *as* human being, is driven home by Shakespeare with unforgettable power and precision in the words of Shylock:

I am a Jew. Hath not a Jew eyes? Hath not a Jew hands, organs, dimensions, senses, affections, passions? Fed with the same food, hurt with the same weapons, subject to the same diseases, healed by the same means, warmed and cooled by the same winter and summer as a Christian is? If you prick us, do we not bleed? If we tickle us, do we not laugh? If you poison us, do we not die?

Shylock may perhaps take a dubious turning in his argument, vowing revenge, but up to this point his statement is an eloquent and central justification for a single and universal Natural Law existing simply on the basis of shared humanity. This aspect of the moral pattern of the play is reinforced in action by its opposite, not only when Shylock hides his humanity behind the law, but when Antonio demonstrates the very act of dehumanisation which provoked Shylock. He swears to call Shylock a dog again, and to spit on him (I. iii. 102–28), hiding his own shared humanity behind the existence of a contract for 'barren metal' which could, as Shylock claims, as much be made with a 'stranger cur' as a man at least in Antonio's eyes.

Shakespeare has therefore built *The Merchant of Venice* on the point made most clearly in the scene of the trial. Positive laws are made by people, but these laws must reflect Natural Law, that which is common to all humanity on the basis of their human status, and if they do not then 'an unjust law is no law'. Such positive laws must be adapted in particular circumstances to conform with Natural Law, or they cease to be law. When the letter of the law kills the spirit of the occasion, then it is valid to return to the source of all human law in the Renaissance, Natural Law, and to adapt accordingly, or commit manifest injustice. As a secondary inference, Shakespeare has, quite deliberately in his oblique reference to the system of English equity in the 1590s, reflected the reasoning that lay behind its existence and therefore has tacitly lent his support to the chancellor in a timely and topical play.

## Measure for Measure[12]

The fantastical Spaniard Don Adriano de Armado may be a strange partner to team with the sombre and sinister lawman from Vienna, Angelo, but in one respect the comparison is apt. Armado informs on Costard for breaking the edict in speaking to Jaquenetta and subsequently falls in love himself. Angelo purports to execute a law against fornication which he himself plans to break after he meets Isabella. The world of difference between the characters points to a profound difference in tone between *Love's Labour's Lost* and *Measure for Measure*, and yet the comparison reveals also a similitude between the plays. Shakespeare returns to the theme of a positive, man-made law which seeks legal control over sexuality. The second play is altogether more problematical and disturbing. It is possible that Shakespeare realised by 1604, a decade or so after *Love's Labour's Lost,* that his own preferred Law of Nature, operating at least in romantic stage comedy, was coming under real threat from the state. The impetus which had been alive at least for half a century for legislation against 'fornication', adultery, and other sexual 'offences', was becoming more earnest. The law which initiates the action of *Measure for Measure* is no self-imposed, idealistic decree appropriate to a youthful, closed Inn of Court, but a law with all the backing of the state and of custom. As in Shakespeare's Vienna, so in contemporary England, at the beginning of the Stuart regime, sexual crime was a genuinely topical issue rather than a dramatist's hypothesis, and its threat was too serious to be laughed away in a lighthearted comedy. The underlying rationales behind the debate needed to be addressed, when a play drew on such material in a more abrasive, legal context.

The historian, Keith Thomas, has conveniently and succinctly summarised the long train of events leading up to an Act of Parliament in 1650 'for suppressing the detestable sins of incest, adultery and fornication', whose terms were analogous to the law against fornication in *Measure for Measure*.[13] The 1650 law has often been seen as a typical Puritan aberration (despite the fact that some Puritan sects endorsed free love), but Thomas shows that it cannot be dismissed in such a crudely propagandist way. It followed pressure over more than a century across a spectrum of political and religious motivations to tighten up such laws as already existed. Adultery and fornication had always been offences in England, under the jurisdiction of the ecclesiastical courts. Lay courts had some power, and as Thomas points out, for example, 'constables could arrest would-be fornicators and ... J.P.s might bind them over to good behaviour' (p. 266). Because corporal punishment was not used after the Reformation, the perception of the sterner-minded was that the modes of punishment, public penance, a fine, or in extreme cases excommunication, were too lenient. There were voices asserting that adultery especially should be a capital offence or at least punishable by life imprisonment. Even orthodox churchmen were of this opinion, but gradually the issue became a political one in that Puritans cited the example as a central charge against the bishops, whom they were seeking to disestablish. By the late 1590s and early 1600s the specific complaint against ecclesiastical law in the area of sexual misdemeanours was exactly that levelled against Duke Vincentio: laxness in implementing with full rigour a law which had been in existence in some form or other since before 1066. In the situation, the call became more persistent to remove sexual offences from the ecclesiastical courts and give them to the common-law courts which prided themselves on having the qualities of Angelo, rigour and consistency. Even the relatively moderate William Lambarde, a lawyer whom Shakespeare evidently knew through his own attempts at litigation, compared the present lenity in 1596 unfavourably with the practices of King Cnut under whom adulteresses lost their goods and their noses, and he blamed the ecclesiastical courts which, in the Protestant reading of history, had wrested power from lay authority:

the bishops had not wholly gotten into their hands the correction of adultery and fornication, which of latter times they have challenged from the laity with such pertinacity, that not only the Prince's commodity is thereby greatly decreased, but also incontinency in his subjects intolerably augmented.[14]

To set the context for *Measure for Measure* we should acknowledge that the call for an Angelo to administer a stern law strictly, was not universally echoed, and that as pressure mounted, so a counter-argument developed that sexual matters (apart from offences obviously criminal such as rape) should not be dealt with by institutional law, whether ecclesiastical or secular, on the essentially Natural Law argument that punishment should be left to God and conscience. After 1600 the debate became increasingly polarised. Those advocating laws against adultery and fornication (sex between unmarried people) used as justification the social and economic problems of unwanted bastards, and the erosion of marriage at a time when its rationale was becoming companionship rather than simply the need to procreate. Puritans pointed to the Mosaic law as authority (Leviticus 20.10; Deuteronomy 22.22). Nowadays feminists would argue that the desire for social control over women lay behind such demands. On the other hand, not just self-proclaimed moderates but some staunch Protestants took their lead from Christ's forgiveness of the adulteress, arguing (just as Isabella does in *Measure for Measure*) that the maxim 'judge not lest ye be judged' should apply. Sexual matters are, and should be, conducted so privately that only God can legitimately make a judgment. After all, the whole area of dispute amongst critics about the legitimacy of the various liaisons in *Measure for Measure* lies in whether words and deeds alone, enacted in private and without a public, legal contract or ceremony, constitutes marriage. There was some self-evident justification to the position that only God can judge sexual matters, in that the 1650 Act in all its severity proved impotent when consenting parties to adultery simply denied the charge and no other proof could be brought. Besides, it was not unusual, as in Shakespeare's own case, for the woman to be pregnant before marriage, perhaps to ensure the economic asset of fertility. There were other folk arguments against legislating on sexual matters, for example, that a woman did not commit adultery if her husband was asleep. Even if the husband did not know it was happening, then God would, and vengeance should be his, if only through punishment by the parties' guilty consciences, as in *Arcadia*. Milton, as we shall see later, pointed out the apparently hypocritical discrepancy between one law which made adultery an offence and another which made it a valid ground for achieving the 'freedom' given by divorce. Following his own chain of Natural Law reasoning, he strongly objected to any state legislation or surveillance of sexual conduct, which he argued was exclusively a matter between the Maker and his subject. Even the law itself recognised the inconsistency, since we find the terms of Natural Law being introduced in defence,

at a time when men and women were pleading conscience to justify adultery, divorce, and bigamy; when the very concept of prohibited degrees had been attacked as unscriptual; and when sectarian religion had become notorious as a cover for unscrupulous sexual adventures. (Thomas, *Puritans and Revolutionaries*, p. 278)

Some even argued unashamedly that there was no immorality at all, in the eyes of God or man, in sex before or outside marriage. Groups emerging in the 1640s such as the Ranters more or less preached that polygamy and free love could be valid if pursued with a clear conscience, and their attitudes and policies were simply extensions of others' who for a century or more had referred all moral, legal and political problems to individual conscience and a version of Natural Law:

Instead of legal rights and the laws and customs of this nation, the sectaries talk of, and plead for natural rights and liberties such as men have from Adam by birth, and in many of their pamphlets they still speak of being governed by right reason.[15]

It may seem invalid to quote sources from the 1640s when *Measure for*

*Measure* is dated 1604. However, it was only under the later, civil jurisdiction that people were forced seriously to argue on grounds of Natural Law or else face extremely harsh penalties. That does not mean the arguments were not available or not mounted long before in the face of mounting pressure for law reform. Even *Love's Labour's Lost*, as we have seen, however light in tone, asserts some kind of Natural Law to justify breaking a positive law which, among other sanctions, would lead to women having their tongues cut out and men facing public shame and pillory. What does seem to have happened since that play (about 1594) was that the pace for 'reforming' (making harsher) the laws governing sexual conduct was quickening (relevant bills were passed in 1601 and again in the very year of *Measure for Measure*), and the voices demanding strict enforcement of the laws were becoming more strident. In other words, at this crucial time when a new monarch took the throne, against strengthening Puritan opposition, the scene was set for the appearance of a 'precise' (the word has connotations of Puritanism) Angelo deputising for a Duke, whose trappings become ecclesiastical in the garb of a monk, and who has let the law inadvertently slip into disuse. At the same time, voices had always been raised on the opposite side, condemning laws that could not or should not be enforced, and significantly Lord Ellesmere the Lord Chancellor, head of the equity system, addressing parliament in 1597, argued in just this fashion:

And whereas the number of laws already made are very great, some also of them being obsolete and worn out of use; others idle and vain, serving to no purpose; some again over heavy and too severe for the offence; others too loose and slack for the faults they are to punish, and many of them so full of difficulties to be understood that they cause many controversies; you are therefore to enter into a due consideration of the said laws, and where you find superfluity to prune, where defect to supply, and where ambiguity to explain, that they be not burdensome but profitable to the Commonwealth.[16]

As a dramatist rather than a religious or legal thinker, Shakespeare exploits for its intrinsic human conflict the situation he creates, but unavoidably also he steers the moral pattern in one direction rather than the other. Pompey, the equivalent of Costard, is under no illusions in his understanding of this great legal debate:

POMPEY     Truly, sir, I am a poor fellow that would live.
ESCALUS    How would you live, Pompey? By being a bawd? What do
           you think of the trade, Pompey? Is it a lawful trade?
POMPEY             If the law would allow it, sir.          (II. i. 192–4)

Pompey ironically has a much keener awareness of the sanctions underpinning man-made laws than those deputed to enforce them. Positive laws are made to be broken if they conflict with the natural right 'to live', an argument based, like Biron's, on 'necessity'.

*Measure for Measure* is a play that has attracted much attention of a legal kind. In particular, analysis has dwelt on the terms of Elizabethan marital law in discussing whether Claudio and Juliet, Angelo and Mariana are 'married' or not.[17] Beyond saying that the very dispute demonstrates the existence of a view that such matters lie within Natural Law and only contentiously in positive law, I shall be begging this question. It will become clear that there are reasons why Shakespeare leaves the matter ambiguous, in order to give himself the latitude of having it either way in different parts of the narrative. The centre of attention here will be the initial law against fornication which drives the whole plot and which oddly enough has not received close attention. After *Love's Labour's Lost*, it is the play which best exemplifies Northrop Frye's argument that Shakespearian comedy (and *Measure for Measure* is formally a comedy, whatever its 'problems') begins with an 'irrational law', or at least an unreasonable and vague one. Once again, however, the force of 'irrational' must be spelt out in the context of Natural Law doctrine, and the law's irrationality is not presupposed but demonstrated by the play's action as a whole.

The terms of the law against 'fornication' are never clearly spelt out, but they do seem to cover the field of the laws envisaged by reformers in England. As in *The Merchant of Venice*, Shakespeare in his use of poetic fiction transposes the problem to a 'foreign' country in order the better to examine its moral status, just as legal fictions could transfer a case from common law to equity in order to achieve a more just result, or create an 'as if' situation in order to inspect a problem. 'Fornication' was used to distinguish pre-marital sex from adultery, but the fact that the Viennese law seeks to eliminate brothels, indicates that its scope is as wide as possible and amounts to imposing the death penalty for all extra-marital sex. The specific 'proclamation' (I. ii. 86) is that the brothels of Vienna be plucked down. Ironically, city brothels have been exempted through the intervention of a 'wise burgher' who has 'put in for them' (line 92), ostensibly so that the buildings can become granaries, but with the dark implication that the lucrative trade will continue.[18] In a play seething with corruption and hypocrisy it is significant that only brothels in the suburbs (and therefore symbolically more marginal) are to go. 'Here's a change indeed in the commonwealth!' (I. ii. 96) exclaims Mistress Overdone. The 'change' is not a change in the law but its application, as in England in the period 1600 to 1650. Former rulers, and certainly the present Duke Vincentio, failed to enforce an old statute, and Angelo takes as his brief the strict, impartial enforcement of all laws.

The continuing attempts to legislate in Shakespeare's time against crimes of venery, are exactly analogous, since customary laws already existed but, through custom itself, had fallen into disuse.

The broader purview of the law in proscribing all pre- and extra-marital sex, is prefigured in the case of Claudio. He is arrested 'for getting Madam Julietta with child' (I. ii. 66). The law is inescapably wider in its scope than one only aimed at brothels, and in the general spirit of Angelo's implementation any house in which extra-marital fornication is committed is a brothel by definition. While more modern legislatures have objected to the payment for sex in money, and feminists have attacked the degradation of women represented by the existence of brothels, these issues are not raised in the play. Whether or not Julietta is a prostitute is never made clear, but since she and Claudio are 'cousins' we presume they have developed a genuine relationship over a long period rather than indulged in the casual sex available in a brothel. Claudio and Julietta are manifestly in love, and Claudio's defence is that he considers himself 'married' to her:

> Thus stands it with me: upon a true contract
> I got possession of Julietta's bed.
> You know the lady; she is fast my wife,
> Save that we do the denunciation lack
> Of outward order. This we came not to
> Only for propagation of a dower
> Remaining in the coffer of her friends,
> From whom we thought it meet to hide our love
> Till time had made them for us. But it chances
> The stealth of our most mutual entertainment
> With character too gross is writ on Juliet.
> LUCIO          With child, perhaps?
> CLAUDIO                    Unhappily, even so.          (I. ii. 134–45)

In short, Claudio and Julietta consider themselves already in a marriage contract (and there is enough evidence that Elizabethan audiences would share their assumption), but they are not 'tying the knot' in the formal sense of 'outward order' until those holding the dower in trust can be persuaded to approve of the match. This is why they had to keep their relationship secret, a ploy that could be regarded (by a legalistic Angelo?) as a kind of deception for monetary gain, although again, this rationalisation is not made. The law of marriage in England at the time, like that in Shakespeare's Vienna, had internal contradictions, and a different interpretation from Claudio's (characteristically one held by Angelo) is that 'outward order' alone defines marriage and therefore sex without prior ceremony is simply illegal.

The ambiguities (or, rather unambiguous contradictions) are another form of legal hypocrisy. For one set of reasons the two are married, for another they are not. The reason Shakespeare leaves both options active is surely purposeful. It is not the first of many occasions where he points to law itself, rather than human behaviour, as the 'problem'. Secondly, if Claudio's and Isabella's relationship at worst lies in a grey area of marriage law, then what Angelo is doing, by not enquiring into this question, is simply making illegal the sexual act itself between certain partners, according to a definition based on a formal and legalistic construal of ceremony. It is tempting today to say that this is so patently absurd that we must take it for granted as a 'stage convention' justified only in that it leads to an interesting plot. Before we do so, however, we cannot dismiss as a stage convention a law which, in the play itself, is so deeply and sharply questioned and tested.

It is time to return to Saint Thomas for authority and to quote his words again to refresh our memory. Celibate as he was, Aquinas had no illusions about the 'naturalness' of sexual desire, and its 'reasonableness' when the product or intention is procreation, as it clearly is in Julietta's case. Indeed, it is first among the very few primary precepts of the Natural Law that he cites. By making Julietta conspicuously pregnant by Claudio, and by giving every indication that they intend bringing up the child within marriage, Shakespeare removes all ambiguity from their act as judged by Natural Law, however problematical it may be in the fictional state law. Claudio and Julietta stand acquitted in the court of Aquinas, while those in the brothel at worst may be condemned in God's universal law but cannot without presumptuousness be so indicted in human law by erring man. As in *Arcadia* the law is too blunt an instrument, men are too unreliable, to judge the intimacies and complexities of sexual conduct, and, as in Milton's attitude to divorce law (to be examined later in this book), only God can make judgment on the morality or otherwise of sex with consent. The inference to be drawn is that any positive laws in this area will inevitably catch the wrong culprits. As in Natural Law, sex should be *ipso facto* beyond the jurisdiction of positive law, and a matter for conscience alone.

'Does your worship mean to geld and splay all the youth of the city?' (II. i. 229), Pompey asks, and, although Escalus replies simply 'No, Pompey', it is a pertinent question. Pompey predicts that a law designed to curb illicit sexual desire is unenforceable:

If this law hold in Vienna ten year, I'll rent the fairest house in it after three pence a bay. If you live to see this come to pass, say Pompey told you so. (II. i. 238–40)

He puts his finger on the central problem in his statement that being a bawd would be 'lawful', 'if the law would allow it' (line 224). This particular law, he is saying, is a man-made, positive law, which man can change. Lucio points out 'What a ruthless thing is this in him, for the rebellion of a codpiece to take away the life of a man!' (III. ii. 106). In the language of Ciceronian jurisprudence, sexual desire is not *mala in se* but rather *mala prohibita*. Furthermore, Pompey implies that the law is not consistent with 'natural' urges, and is therefore against natural philosophy (observable patterns) if not Natural Law. He helps to make his prediction a self-fulfilling prophecy by deciding to open another brothel. One would think that if there were any tangible justification for the law, then Pompey's and Mistress Overdone's 'trade' of prostitution would be the most certain of its targets. However, even this view is undermined by their unswerving determination to set up more brothels, showing that the law is still not effective either as punishment or deterrent, and that attempts to subvert it are as irrepressible as sex itself. Moreover, the dramatist's instinct is that characters such as Pompey's retinue who, like Falstaff, can make us laugh, can circumvent moral reproach from an audience more dexterously than those like Angelo and Malvolio, who are humourless.

From Pompey, the arguments might be dismissed as the desperate sophistry of one who is losing his 'trade', but the point of view is put in various ways in the play and by characters who do not seem to have anything to lose or gain from the law. We need not say that the play's overall moral perspective either condones or condemns sexuality. What it does is accept the 'natural' necessity of it for fallen man, even, we discover, for an Angelo. The one argument used by the saintly Isabella in dealing with Angelo that works, is an appeal to the universality of the 'natural guiltiness' of sexual feelings:

> Go to your bosom,
> Knock there, and ask your heart what it doth know
> That's like my brother's fault. If it confers
> A natural guiltiness, such as is his,
> Let it not sound a thought upon your tongue
> Against my brother's life.
> ANGELO [Aside]                  She speaks, and 'tis such sense
> That my sense breeds with it ...                  (II. ii. 138–45)

Of course, this is the moment of inception of Angelo's lust for Isabella, as he 'desire[s] her foully for those things that make her good' (II. ii. 174–5) and his description of the feeling leaves no doubt that it is compulsive and irresistible, and to this extent 'natural', however morally dubious in the circumstances. We are to find murky secrets in this 'severe' man's life later in the play, and the fact that even the sternest judge is susceptible is persuasive evidence that other mortals are just as prone, and that none can judge. 'We are all frail' (II. iv. 121) even Angelo admits, just as Euarchus, with different intent, had in *Arcadia*. Isabella, the other character who lives by 'strict restraint' (I. iv .3) does 'abhor' sexual licence and desires that it 'should meet the blow of justice' (II. iii. 30), but like Portia she argues that in particular cases, such as her brother's, conditions exist that call for the exercise of 'mercy' and an appeal to general notions of equity. She also evidently later condones (as does the Duke) the midnight meeting between Angelo and Mariana, which is in essence indistinguishable, and surely more fraudulently culpable, than the situation between Claudio and Isabella. The ending of the play, with the Duke's imperious proposal of marriage to Isabella, may be difficult for us to accept, but in the scheme of the play it emphasises that at least the Duke, who had earlier sworn he could not be pierced by 'the dribbling dart of love' (I. iii. 2), and perhaps also Isabella, whose final response is not verbalised and can only be guessed at or constructed in performance, are just as susceptible to desire as anybody else. Claudio, in a weak but revealing moment, says of 'affections', 'sure, it is no sin; Or of the deadly seven it is the least' (III. i. 107–9). Escalus exclaims 'killed for a fault?' The 'natural' imperative is cryptically summed up by Lucio as 'the rebellion of a codpiece' (III. ii. 111). It seems that in the fallen world of men and women nobody is exempt from desire, and the only solution for a woman who does not wish to be implicated in sexuality, is to leave the world for a convent and never speak to men, as Isabella wished at the beginning (and in a modern production, might wish for at the end).

The law which is the crux of *Measure for Measure*, then, is one which is not in accord with nature, and this view is put so many times by so many characters, and implied so often in their actions that it cannot be dismissed. The 'unnaturalness' of Angelo's public front is vehemently noted by Lucio: 'This ungenitur'd agent will unpeople the province with continency; sparrows must not build in his house-eaves because they are lecherous' (III. ii. 163–5). If Shakespearian comedy teaches anything, it is that sexual desire is a powerful drive or inclination, and when mutually felt between two people can override parental opposition, social constraints, restrictive moral dogma, and even laws strictly enforced. 'It is the simplicity of man to hearken after the flesh', and presumably of woman too. For those like Claudio, Angelo, Pompey, and the others who are temporarily impaled on the law, the consequences are potentially fatal. Claudio literally faces death for an urge to create life. But even those like Isabella and the Duke, who do not question the law's rectitude, are constantly compromised into trickery and deception in their attempts to get around the law and save the life of a 'malefactor' Claudio. It does seem part of the play's point that a man-made law, not subject to critical review, which is opposed to Natural Law, will force individuals into impossible predicaments, and, whether it is Shakespeare's satire on the legal reformists' zeal or just an 'as if' hypothesis, the message certainly had contemporary significance.

Those deputed to enforce such a law face an even starker set of contradictions and problems than the victims. There are three characters in this position, and each exemplifies a different policy. These three options are probably the only ones theoretically open to one who feels obliged to put into practice a law which is not in accord with Natural Law. Duke Vincentio's practice has been simply to 'let slip' (I. iii. 21) the administration of the law, so that it has become 'more mock'd than fear'd' (line 27). More positively, he is leaving the matter for God to judge. His flight from office, otherwise so puzzling and hazily motivated, makes dramatic sense as an emblem of what he has been doing for 'fourteen years' (line 21), (and in Elizabethan Puritans' eyes, what ecclesiastical law had been doing since the Norman Conquest), namely running away from what he none the less regards as his duties, more or less as Prospero did. He does feel genuinely at fault, and he does not question whether or not the law should be changed. He also acknowledges that if he were now to become strict after giving so much 'scope' to his people, then

> 'Twould be tyranny to strike and gall them
> For what I bid them do: for we bid this done,
> When evil deeds have their permissive pass,
> And not the punishment.                    (I. iii. 35–9)

The first option for the authority-figure, then, is to avoid the problem by running away, while none the less reasserting the need for the law's existence.

The second option is to apply the letter of the law consistently, severely, and without compromise. Whatever the Duke's private motives for instating Angelo in his stead, he expects that Angelo will be this kind of stern judge who will rule without personal feelings:

> Lord Angelo is precise;
> Stands at a guard with Envy; scarce confesses
> That his blood flows; or that his appetite
> Is more to bread than stone.                    (I. iii. 30–3)

The curious 'test' of Angelo is to see 'If power change purpose' (line 54). In a sense it does, because Angelo is manifestly corrupted, but in another sense power confirms his purpose, because in the public, legal sphere, he is 'precise' and unbending. As his personal rectitude becomes more shady, his public rectitude hardens. Angelo can maintain this consistency because of a belief that 'recorded law' is separate from the administrator. He loftily proclaim s, 'It is the law, not I, condemns your brother' (II. ii. 81). He is also, as a recent literary theorist and philosopher has described him, 'a rigid reader, incapable at first of filling with life the schemata of legal speech'.[19] He ignores the word 'mercy' in the Duke's advice: 'Mortality and mercy in Vienna / Live in thy tongue and heart'. Such narrow legalism is a fault shared with Angelo by many a petty, literal-minded bureaucrat throughout human history down to the present day. The direction in which his policy leads Angelo in dealing with this law blends hypocrisy and tyranny, for it denies any 'natural reason' or reference to individual conscience. He simply follows the letter of a law in which 'sterility of sense meaning is confronted by the fertility of social and political phenomena' and thus compounds the chaotic consequences of a law 'from which the life of psychological needs and social appetites have been excised'.[20] There was biblical sanction behind the view taken by equity that the spirit outweighs the letter: 'the letter killeth, but the Spirit giveth life' (Corinthians, 3.6). The combination of a law without self-evident reason and at least capable of violating conscience in individual cases (Claudio and Julietta *should* in conscience be able to marry and rear their expected child) with an enforcer who is punctiliously devoid of imagination, mercy, fellow-feeling with other human beings, and even conscience if we judge him by his reactions when his former affair with Mariana is revealed, leads to a disastrous miscarriage of justice and a slide into personal corruption by the judge.

Isabella points out the danger:

> ... O, it is excellent
> To have a giant's strength, but it is tyrannous
> To use it like a giant.                                      (II. ii. 108–10)

and Claudio muses:

> Whether the tyranny be in his place,
> Or in his eminence that fills it up,
> I stagger in – ...
>            'tis surely for a name.                        (I. ii. 160–3)

Angelo himself is aware that the application of the law can never be entirely consistent, because even under the strictest judge many crimes must go undetected (II. i. 17–31). He is reminded by both the Provost and Isabella that he himself may have 'Err'd in this point, which now you censure him' (II. i. 15) and should be lenient as an exercise in humility. Isabella and the Duke gain knowledge of just such discrepancies between

Angelo's stern exterior and his errant emotions, which are expressed not only in his lust for Isabella, but also in his previous affiancement to Mariana. When the revelation comes, Angelo speaks to the Duke as if some form of justice higher than man's law has found his guilty secret, although he is simply referring to being found out, rather than asserting any pangs of conscience or Law of Nature:

> O my dread lord,
> I should be guiltier than my guiltiness
> To think I can be undiscernible,
> When I perceive your Grace, like power divine
> Hath looked upon my passes.                    (V. i. 364–8)

It would be a mistake to build upon this quotation an argument, as some have done, that the Duke is a divine figure within the plot.[21] Shakespeare carefully builds flaws into the Duke's character and actions: he is evasive ('duke of dark corners'), he gets things wrong (for example, predicting that Angelo's pardon will come), and most damagingly he continues almost to the end to lie to Isabella about the 'death' of Claudio. His own final disbursement of justice might appear completely arbitrary, and leaves nobody actually happy by his decisions. He is just as vulnerable as Angelo to charges of tyranny and duplicity. We need not condemn him for this, but equally he cannot be sanctified. On the other hand, Isabella's comment throws weight behind the general Natural Law position that only God can know, and therefore judge, sexual behaviour. The Duke's role in the play is bifold. As a 'function' of the plot he has greater knowledge and power than others, and can present himself and be seen by others in the play as a *deus in machina*, but as a 'person' he is as flawed as the others. This is the real point of the play: *all* are fallen and culpable, and should not presume to judge others in matters of 'natural' sexual conduct. The existence of Natural Law is not embodied in any character, since it cannot be. Rather, it operates through the action itself, the interrelationships, secrets and revelations, and by the end the only ones aware of the operation of a higher ethical perspective, more complex than any one character's, are readers and audiences. As in *Arcadia* they, too, are like the characters in their own flawed beings, and so even they (we) cannot judge without risking tyranny. Positive, man-made law is inappropriate in the area of sexual relations.

The third option is exemplified by the approach of Escalus, the Provost, and by the Duke at the very end of the play when he resumes his duties. It reflects the English, double-tiered legal framework of common law and equity. This allows the ruler formally to pronounce sentence on the Aristotelian basis of 'measure for measure', but then soften and exercise 'mercy' or equity at the eleventh hour.[22] Many commentators have seen the policy of strict justice followed by mercy to be the play's advised *via media*, its 'lesson' or moral centre. Equity steps in to 'correct' the inflexible legal code, or to overturn an unjust decision arrived at by common law. However, there still remains an intractable problem with its application in enforcing this particular law, since it would seem difficult, if the law is against natural drives and Natural Law, not to exercise mercy in every single instance, since every sexual act could be mitigated by reference to the fallen nature of man, the privacy of sex between consenting partners, and the applicability of conscience and God's judgment rather than public law's. In the case of Claudio, at least, his actions have been entirely reasonable and beyond reproach from conscience, and so it would be just as arrogant for a ruler to exercise mercy as to 'convict' him. It is also significant that, apart from Claudio and Julietta and perhaps Mariana, nobody at the end is left happy with the actual 'mercy' dispensed – certainly not the most guilty, Angelo and Lucio, who are profoundly dissatisfied. If their consciences are untouched then 'mercy' is neither here nor there, it has no meaning, and ironically both prefer strict punishment to the actual edict. In short, all judgments by rulers, whether on grounds of strict, positive law, or a discretionary form of equity, on this law are capricious and irrelevant, since they can never find universal assent. The existence of equity as a legal system in the area of sexual mores does no more than aggrandise the pomp of 'man, proud man, Dressed in a little brief authority' to assert his power, without actually doing consistent justice in any real sense.

Here lies the clue to the inevitable conclusion that the law itself in *Measure for Measure* should be challenged, before its enforcers or its casualties. Like the edict in *Love's Labour's Lost*, its enforcement by mortals upsets both reason and conscience, the twin pillars of Natural Law, interferes with an individual's relation with God, and places people in impossible dilemmas. It encourages mortals to usurp God's omniscience and sphere of ruling. In claiming to legislate over natural drives, the lawmakers are making the kind of judgment that only the Christian deity is entitled to make, as Isabella eloquently affirms:

> Why, all the souls that were, were forfeit once,
> And he that might the vantage best have took
> Found out the remedy. How would we be
> If He, which is the top of judgement, should
> But judge you as you are?                    (II. ii. 73–7)

The state may compel and coerce actions, but it cannot ultimately bind the individual conscience, which exists in relation to God alone.[23] The Renaissance assumption is that positive law should be consistent with Natural Law. However, Natural Law is so much broader and more universal than positive laws, their jurisdictions are different, and some areas are simply not appropriate arenas for man's law to operate. When Angelo makes reference to nature, Isabella firmly retorts "Tis set down so in heaven, but not in earth' (II. iv. 50). The point is central to sixteenth-century notions of Natural Law. Meanwhile, it is sufficient to say that in *Measure for Measure* the presiding deity over the 'as if' world of the play, the dramatist, through the action, finally endorses the conclusion which marks *Arcadia* and *Love's Labour's Lost*, that laws governing love are not ones that men can make or enforce. Only God may do so if he chooses.[24]

The play's ethical system is not, however, all critical and negative. Exactly as in the Elizabethan doctrine of Natural Law, people are given capacities which are shown to compensate for their fallen nature: conscience and reason. Conscience, which Elizabethan equity counted as crucial but also said was not enforceable in courts of law, is directly in issue throughout the play, and its exercise is central. Claudio has a clear conscience, even if he has violated a law: yet more evidence that the law itself is unjust. Angelo has a guilty conscience with respect to his lust for Isabella but not apparently for his cruel abandonment of Mariana. Isabella's all-important conscience is left inviolate. Furthermore, reason becomes insistently an issue in the final scene, when Isabella makes her plea for 'Justice! Justice! Justice! Justice! Justice!'.

> DUKE                          By mine honesty,
> If she be mad, as I believe no other,
> Her madness hath the oddest frame of sense,
> Such a dependency of thing on thing,
> As e'er I heard in madness.
> ISABELLA                    O gracious Duke,
> Harp not on that; nor do not banish reason
> For inequality; but let your reason serve
> To make the truth appear where it seems hid,
> And hide the false seems true.
> DUKE                          Many that are not mad
> Have, sure, more lack of reason ...          (V. i. 62–72)

The irony, as the audience knows, is that the Duke himself, by pretending to reject Isabella's accusations against Angelo, is hiding the truth. Even Isabella herself is driven into lying that she has slept with Angelo (lines 95–105). The sequence of events, guided by the Duke like a (rather incompetent) dramatist, unfolds to corroborate Isabella's 'reason', and clinches the overall point that a law against both nature and reason and, in particular cases such as Claudio's, against conscience, must by definition be inconsistent with Natural Law. The radical solution, which occurs to nobody within the play but is clearly implicit and inescapable, is just, as in *Love's Labour's Lost*, to revoke, or at least rewrite the law. Bad laws may make a good play, but not a good state, and this law, it has been shown, is at the very least inconsistent in its operation and potentially capable of doing injustice, perpetrating obvious absurdities, and interfering with the most delicate and private matters. That Vienna's ruler does not, apparently, see this at the end, means that the real crux remains unresolved, and that, as at the end of *Love's Labour's Lost*, it is for audiences and readers to make their preferred closures. Given the characteristic pattern of Shakespeare's romantic comedies, there is little doubt which way we are being steered. The world must be peopled.

# 8    Shakespeare's *The History of King Lear*[1]

In the plays by Shakespeare which we have looked at, a running debate is sustained between the rival claims of Natural Law and positive law in effecting 'poetic justice'. So insistent is this debate that it is virtually a Shakespearian signature, and in *King Lear* we find no exception. In this play, moreover, Shakespeare sets in opposition particularly naked forms of the two legal systems, searches more profoundly the nature of their differences, and reveals in the ending an unsettling ambivalence which is a source of tragedy for the protagonists. The play is one of struggle and dialectic, dramatising, amongst other polarities, an archetypal clash between Natural Law and positive law, trust and mistrust in human beings, Aquinas' idealism about people and the scepticism of Calvin and Hobbes. That the struggle is inconclusive, as it is in *Love's Labour's Lost* and *Measure for Measure* does not diminish the play's power, and gives evidence of Shakespeare's preference for incomplete closure, leaving the audience scope for exercising judgment.

In one sense, as many critics have observed, *King Lear* gives us a very simple view of good and evil. In the terms of Natural Law, good is humanitarian, communitarian, and is driven by compassion, reason, and conscience. This rough generalisation applies not only to Kent, Cordelia, Albany, the King of France, and Edgar, but also to a host of 'little people', and it is a lesson eventually learned and acknowledged by the old men, Lear and Gloucester, through the recognition of their own violations of these principles. Evil is represented as an equation between power and positive law, without reference to conscience or any 'higher' morality, and it is fundamentally individualistic, corrupt, and self-seeking: a rerun of Angelo, and a forecast of Hobbes. Cornwall, Gonoril, Regan, and Edmund stand on this darker side of the division. Both Cordelia and Kent promise exemplary poetic justice along the lines of Natural Law, enabling us to admire and follow virtue, murmur at vice:

CORDELIA    Time shall unfold what pleated cunning hides.
Who covers faults, at last shame them derides.

And so it does. But so it does not, at the same time, for although evil is unmasked, good cannot be said to triumph.

Where the play becomes problematical is in the failure of Natural Law to prevail in any *but* a moral sense. Cordelia, the agent most closely equated with Aquinas' maxim that one should follow reason and conscience, lies dead at the end. So, for that matter, do those who conspicuously and unrepentantly (unless we exempt Edmund's final 'good' deed done 'Despite of [his] own nature') violate Natural Law, but somehow the morally satisfying appropriateness of their demise pales into insignificance beside the failure of Natural Law to prevail. The deaths of Cornwall, Gonoril and Regan, and Edmund, have 'poetic justice', but the death of Cordelia makes victory to the virtuous less than Pyrrhic. Meanwhile, even the natural world is deeply ambivalent, at times presented as the pitiless storm which assaults the fragile human community, at others aligned with the healing herbs that gently bring new life and nurture the human world. At the heart of *King Lear* lies a dialectic that underpins More's *Utopia*. Natural Law, based on the dictates of reason and conscience, is entirely vindicated and upheld in a moral sense, but its worldly failure raises disturbing questions about whether those who wield power in the state will ever allow it to be enacted in the world as it is.

The most significant, recent development in the study of *King Lear* is a reassessment of the relationship between the two printed versions. This appears at first sight to be of interest only to textual scholars, but the ramifications are very important for all branches of *Lear* criticism. The editors of The Oxford Shakespeare *Complete Works*, Stanley Wells and Gary Taylor,[2] succinctly state the basis of the 'revision theory', as a prelude to printing not one but two texts, *The History of King Lear* and *The Tragedy of King Lear*:

King Lear first appeared in print in a quarto of 1608. A substantially different text appeared in the 1623 Folio. Until now, editors, assuming that each of these early texts imperfectly represented a single play, have conflated them. But research conducted mainly during the 1970s and 1980s confirms an earlier view that the 1608 quarto represents the play as Shakespeare orginally wrote it, and the 1623 Folio as he substantially revised it.

Some of the evidence for this view, together with consideration of the implications for criticism and stage history, are collected in essays in *The Division of the Kingdoms: Shakespeare's Two Versions of 'King Lear'*,[3] where the date of revision is proposed as 1608, contemporary with the writing of *Cymbeline*, whereas the Quarto was evidently written in 1605, and performed in 1606. Another, even more persuasive view put by Christopher Wortham, is that the Folio represents the play as Shakespeare originally wrote it (in line with the editors' stated principles), and the Quarto is as he substantially revised it for performance before the king, as the title-page announces.[4]

The differences between the texts for the purposes of the present book can be summarised in this way. Both Quarto and Folio texts constitute plays with significant Natural Law content, and this subject can be seen as an identifiable and central 'theme' of each. But there is an important difference in that where the Quarto presents *explicitly* issues of Natural Law, the Folio does so largely *implicitly*, so that in reading the latter we can either presuppose supportive knowledge acquired from the former, or presuppose a more hardworking reader or audience. Whichever tack we take, many of the episodes and characters who appear in the Quarto carrying the Natural Law refrain do not even appear in the Folio, and yet the action in the Folio still invites a Natural Law interpretation. This study is primarily based on the Quarto – what the Oxford editors call *The History of King Lear* – quoting many passages which simply do not appear in the Folio, and accordingly I supply references from the Quarto's Scenes (Acts are not used).

### Trials and justice

There are many trials and quasi-trials in *King Lear*, and these reveal different forms in which justice and law are defined and executed in the play. In the tumultuous middle of the play, two scenes (in conflated texts, Act III, Scenes 6 and 7; Scenes 13 and 14 in the Oxford text of the *History*), are starkly juxtaposed on the issue of law itself. Both scenes are set indoors, but in very different rooms – 13 (III. 6) in the hovel standing against the wind and the rain on the open heath, 14 (III. 7) in Gloucester's castle. The one is a fantasy while the other is grimly 'real', but both in different senses parody the machinery of justice. In the former, Lear in his madness orchestrates an imagined, even hallucinatory trial of Gonoril and Regan. Fictional and fantastic as the situation is played out only in Lear's fevered consciousness, Lear follows strict legal procedure, anachronistically since he imports Elizabethan practice into Celtic England. He declares 'I will arraign them straight' (13. 16, III. 6. 20). Arraign means 'To call a prisoner to the bar of the court by name, to read to him the substance of the indictment, and to ask him whether he pleads guilty or not guilty'.[5] He nominates Edgar, impersonating Poor Tom, as the judge: 'Come, sit thou here, most learned justicer' (line 17). 'Thou robed man of justice, take thy place' (line 32). The Fool represents primarily the Elizabethan system of equity and secondarily the driving spirit of simple fairness behind law in general: 'And thou, his yokefellow of equity, Bench by his side.' That a fool should represent fairness is a comment on the explosive first scene which precipitated the action of the play. The presence of Lear, still thinking of himself as king, establishes that the court of equity, the king's court, is one presiding jurisdiction, while the 'robed man of justice' evokes a common-law setting. It was only under unusual circumstances that common law and equity sat down together in a 'commission', as, for example, in the trial of Mary Queen of Scots which continued to be controversial many years later, as we have seen in Spenser's case. Kent, disguised as servant to Lear, is also declared 'o'the commission' (line 39). Edgar intones 'Let us deal justly' before breaking off into apparent irrelevance. Addressing a joint-stool, Lear states the charge: 'Arraign her first. 'Tis Gonoril. I here take my oath before this honourable assembly she kicked the poor King her father' (lines 41–2). This is the formal indictment, basically a charge of cruelty and a metaphor for the ill-treatment Lear believes he has received from his daughters, which in his obsessive mind appears to be treasonous. There is no time to read the charge against the other defendant, presumably Regan, since she 'escapes' much to Lear's annoyance: 'False justicer, why hast thou let her scape?' (line 51). Both Kent and Edgar, for a moment moved by their feelings of pity for the mad king, step out of their 'counterfeitings', dismayed by Lear's state.

Lear now asks a very central question, and it is one that, in some form or another, the play keeps returning to: 'Then let them anatomize Regan, see what breeds about her heart. Is there any cause in nature that makes this hardness?' (lines 75–6). In the Folio the last phrase is 'these hard-hearts' which is perhaps more useful for our analysis of Natural Law content. Anatomy was a favoured study in the early seventeenth century[6] regarded as if it could reveal nature's secrets about human beings, and even generating its own literary form, the 'Anatomy'. Are the 'hard-hearts' in the play, Gonoril and Regan, Cornwall and Edmund, obeying some law of their own natures, or even nature in general, or are they violating their links with humanity in general? The unnervingly funda-mental question radiates out into others. Are there any equally 'natural' impulses for good? Is a person's nature actively opposed to Natural Law (as an extreme Calvinist might argue), or can evil, indeed, be a product of nature at all? Are the hard-hearts after the Fall closed to reason and conscience, or are they wilfully denying the innate impulses 'natural' to people, and thus betraying their own place in nature? In the event, the 'trial' does not proceed, although, as a legal writer argues,[7] the scene achieves a double effect of providing 'a mocking of the forms of normal human justice' and also a cathartic process for Lear of dealing formal justice, after which he can sleep. But the question about human nature's capacity for knowing and obeying Natural Law remains, and it is one that the whole play interrogates.

Just as the play as a whole oscillates between hope and despair, good and evil, the scene in a quieter way unfolds another image of action which is of something equally basic, the exercise of compassion and fellow-feeling, for Edgar, Kent, and the Fool (by his continued presence, if not by his words) exhibit loyalty, sympathy, and the desire to protect Lear. It is one of many answers offered to the overriding question: in this case human beings *are* capable of knowing and implementing Natural Law, and 'hard' hearts are therefore not natural. It is a vision of community huddling in mutual protection against the elements. Gloucester adds one to the company when he enters and, having heard of an assassination plot, arranges for Lear, by now sleeping, to be conveyed to Dover to meet the French army with Cordelia. Edgar ends the scene by extolling the values of community and support to one who suffers. The mind, he says, can avoid much sufferance 'When grief hath mates, and bearing fellowship' (line 105), reflecting a favouring of community values over individualism. It appears that the machinery of poetic justice, the proof of Natural Law within the play's universe, is being wheeled onto the stage in preparation for the ending.

An immediate and brutal challenge to this expectation comes after the 'mad' cameo of justice. The following scene, III. 7 (line 14), may show a trial, and even some perverse version of fellowship among mates, but these are of a very different order, a dark parody of the hovel, where human nature itself is seen as 'hard'. Cornwall, Gonoril, and Regan have arrived at Gloucester's castle, full of fury that he has intervened to allow Lear to escape. Cornwall, who has now emerged as the decisive ruler and has taken prime authority upon himself, sends Edmund away, since the interrogation and punishment of Gloucester, he says, is not fit for the 'beholding' of a son's eyes, a somewhat uncharacteristic gesture towards the law of filial kind, in the light of these characters' treatment of Lear. He instructs Edmund to accompany Gonoril, so she also is absent from the rest of the scene. Cornwall and Regan, a married couple surpassing even the Macbeths in ruthlessness, now conduct an interrogation and 'arraignment' of Gloucester which is just as fanciful as Lear's, but far more nightmarish, in that these two as monarchs wield full, legal authority to carry out their sadistic and vindictive wishes. Cornwall is quite precise on this point, saying that although they must observe some due procedure of law, yet, even if the form is questioned, opponents will be silenced by their naked power:

Though we may not pass upon his life
Without the form of justice, yet our power
Shall do a curtsy [courtesy?] to our wrath, which men
May blame but not control.                                    (lines 23–6)

Here is one for whom Natural Law either does not exist, or cannot be known by mankind, or simply does not matter. 'The form of justice', positive laws made by worldly authorities, are the only ones that operate. This is legal positivism with a vengeance. Cornwall and Regan bind Gloucester, and, against his repeated appeals to the same conventions of hospitality that haunted Macbeth before the murder of Duncan ('You are my guests', 'I am your host'), proceed to charge him formally with treason and interrogate him about letters he has received from France and about why he has arranged to convey Lear to Dover. Gloucester is as stubborn as Cordelia and Kent had been formerly, in refusing to compromise conscience simply because authority demands – another competing sign of human comprehension of Natural Law – and Cornwall and Regan proceed to their 'punishment', the horrifying act of blinding Gloucester. The narrow legalism of the procedure may accord with Cornwall's 'form of justice', but its sickening inhumanity is thrown into sudden relief by the impetuous act of Cornwall's servant, who relinquishes one duty of 'service' in favour of a duty of conscience:

Hold your hand, my lord!
I have served you ever since I was a child;
But better service have I never done you
Than now to bid you hold.                                    (lines 70–4)

In his 'anger' (line 77), a further sign that moral virtue is based on instinctive knowledge and impulsive acts, he wounds Cornwall, mortally as it transpires, only to be stabbed in the back by Regan and later thrown upon the dunghill. His dying words beg Gloucester to witness the murder with his remaining eye, which provokes Cornwall to remove Gloucester's other eye. In extremity Gloucester calls upon his absent son to 'enkindle all the sparks of nature To quite [requite] this horrid act' (lines 84–5), but, as Regan gloatingly points out, his son Edmund in hatred had been the informant against his father. Immediately Gloucester in remorse realises 'Then Edgar was abused' (line 89), and prays for his own 'forgiveness' and his son's 'protection'. In this sense alone, the 'trial' has succeeded in repeating Lear's anguished question about 'nature', providing contrary and equally poised answers. The scene of legally sanctioned cruelty is ended with discussion between two more servants, like a jury passing a judgment which must by now be shared by the audience in either version of *King Lear*, even though the Folio does not have the words:

SECOND SERVANT    I'll never care what wickedness I do
                     If this man [Cornwall] come to good.
THIRD SERVANT      If she [Regan] live long,
                     And in the end meet the old cause of death,
                     Women will all turn monsters.
THIRD SERVANT      Go thou. I'll fetch some flax and whites of eggs
                     To apply to his bleeding face. Now heaven help
                     him!                               (97–105 *passim*)

In these two scenes, the one painful for its pathos and the other for its cruelty, we see enacted several 'formal' trials and judgments: the first imaginary and inconclusive, ending with a question rather than a sentence, the second relentlessly moving through to sentence and punishment, a third the Servant's judgment on his master, a fourth the adjudication by Gloucester between his two sons, a fifth the common-sense judgment passed by the two Servants on Cornwall and Regan, and so on, reaching out to the audience's judgment about what has happened. Neither of the former sequences is any less 'mad' than the other in a play which questions the boundaries between imagined and real in, for example and in particular, the 'Dover Cliff' scene. The point is that *law and authority*, their officers alienated to roles, can themselves act with insane cruelty, but that *human beings* acting impulsively and from their own 'natures' can be kind and virtuous, ineffectual in the immediate situation but, if the Servant's case is taken into account, finally effective, since the Servant does kill Cornwall. To the question 'Is there any cause in nature that makes these hard-hearts?' we are directed, at least provisionally, to answer 'no' by witnessing the overwhelming evidence of other 'natural' and spontaneous responses to evil, such as anger, indignation, horror, self-sacrifice, fellowship, protection, and simple kindness. As in Aristotle's conception of justice, the audience's assessment may be based on the emotional grounds of pathos, but it carries weight.

One possible argument is that the 'cause' of evil lies not in nature or the human heart, but potentially in 'office' or institutional authority. Not nature, but vested power, creates these hard hearts. Like Angelo, once a person acquires power, he or she may change. Lear only fitfully realises that his own history, as one who ignored virtue and became hardened when in office, softened only when out of office, darkly exemplifies this conclusion. In allowing this judgment to surface, Shakespeare has placed the audience in the position of a jury, and has arranged the action along the lines of Thomas Wilson's advocate who, we recall, stirs the hearts of judges or a jury to pity the plight of the victims and arouse indignation against their oppressors, in order to find justice: 'In moving the affections, and stirring the judges to be grieved, the weight of the matter must

be so set forth, as though they saw it plain before their eyes.' The
Servants act as moral guides in our assessment of justice in the Quarto,
but their absence from the Folio does not exclude the same conclusion,
since the action itself *ipso facto*, stirs the 'affections' against those who
blind Gloucester. However, the sardonic conclusion of the play, as of
More's *Utopia*, is that on earth the positivists and the sceptics have one
trump card, power itself, and this renders those who seek to live by
Natural Law deeply vulnerable. The rest of this chapter will trace the
challenges they face, to the dismaying conclusion where poetic justice
itself is swept aside in the sight of the limp, dead body of Cordelia in her
father's arms. In the terms of this book, *King Lear* affirms the existence
of Natural Law located in the human heart, and the hope that it can be
implemented through poetic justice, but equally fundamentally questions
the likelihood that it can survive more 'unnatural', institutionalised uses
(or misuses) of positive law. Shakespeare, while agreeing with Hobbes
about the jungle-like savagery of human struggles for power, opposes the
Hobbesian assumption that only the state can deliver justice. Indeed, he
tends to locate the true source of injustice in the state itself, and the only
resistance to injustice lies within human reason and conscience.

The 'trials' in scenes 13 and 14 may be cruel parodies of justice, but
they clearly tell us much about the relationship between positive law and
Natural Law in the play. They are also perverse images for the most
important trial of all, the one which opens the play when Lear tests his
daughters' fitness to rule in his stead. The first scene presents a series of
trials within trials. Each of them carries both senses of 'trial', as 'test' and
also as quasi-judicial proceeding. First, King Lear puts his daughters on
trial. If, in this absolute monarchy, his will is law, then he is making
positive law in proposing to divide the kingdom into three parts, and to
distribute them on 'merit'. His particular procedure is to promise
disposal of the largest bounty 'Where nature doth with merit challenge'
(I. i. 53), on the face of it an appropriate task for the machinery of
justice. He puts to each of his three daughters in turn a question designed
to test 'merit' by simultaneously testing 'nature' according to a version of
the law of kind which is expected to operate in Renaissance family
relations: 'Which of you shall we say doth love us most' (line 51). It is
clear, however, that this is a 'show-trial' since his decision has already
been made, and as each sister answers he will offer a predetermined
moiety. His decision has been kept from his courtiers, Gloucester and
Kent, since at the beginning they were discussing which of Albany
(Gonoril's husband) and Cornwall (Regan's) is to gain the larger portion
(emphasising in passing that although the women are tested the men are
the ones who will financially benefit) but Lear has already made his

decision and the public occasion is a ritual affirmation. He has reserved
'a third more opulent' than her sisters' for Cordelia. Gonoril and Regan,
playing their part in the royal ceremony, treat Lear's question as a
positive law and royal command. They trot out speeches that sound just
as pre-scripted as Lear's, and they successfully meet the test. The asides
heard by the audience from Cordelia generate the fundamental clash of
legal and moral values which will throw the state into civil war and send
Lear mad: 'What shall Cordelia speak? Love, and be silent' (line 62).

> Then poor Cordelia!
> And yet not so, since I am sure my love's
> More ponderous than my tongue.                    (76–8)

Appropriately enough for one whose name incorporates the word 'heart'
(*cor*) she is speaking from the heart rather than from political expediency,
from felt duty to conscience rather than hollow 'obedience' (line 278).
None the less, when she speaks, her words have legal substance. To the
question put by Lear she merely says 'nothing' – equivalent to a refusal
to enter a plea of guilty or not guilty, and she redefines the nature of the
trial. If, she says, Lear is proposing a contractual bargain (words in
return for riches) then she cautions him in language of pure reason and
law that such a contract is compromising other contracts:

> Good my lord,
> You have begot me, bred me, loved me.
> I return those duties back as are right fit,
> Obey you, love you, and most honour you.
> Why have my sisters husbands, if they say
> They love you all? Haply when I shall wed,
> That lord whose hand must take my plight shall carry
> Half my love with him, half my care and duty.
> Sure I shall never marry like my sisters,
> To love my father all.
> LEAR              But goes thy heart with this?
> CORDELIA                    Ay, my good lord.          (Scene 1, 87–98)

Cordelia is invoking the terms of Natural Law. Her 'heart' (conscience)
informs an argument which is more soundly based on reason, conscience, and the law of kind than Lear's own command. She points out
with legalistic precision that it is impossible for her sisters to claim to
love a father 'all' when each is married and 'owes' love to her husband.
Cordelia is not married, but she has been told by Lear that her future
husband will be either the King of France or the Duke of Burgundy. At
this stage, in a new sense, Lear himself is on trial, for his decree based
on authority stands unexpectedly questioned in an impromptu court of

Natural Law. Characteristically, he refuses to move his position, and equally true to character Cordelia remains consistent, so that there can be no meeting of minds. By disinheriting Cordelia, Lear is using his royal power in the fashion of Cornwall, to make another decree, directly opposing Natural Law with his authority to make positive law, and ironically displaying the 'hardness' of heart which he later recriminates. His own barely perceived recognition of the fragile basis of his judgment is, no doubt, one of the contributory causes, together with a sense of personal rejection, of his near-hysteria: reason and conscience may be working, but Lear suppresses them, and covers up any doubts he may hold.

The set of trials-within-trials is immediately followed by two others, where the same opposition between Natural Law and positive law is in issue. Kent accuses Lear of madness, folly, and bad judgment in giving his trust and power to the two eldest daughters over his youngest, and by doing so he aligns himself with Cordelia's Natural Law of reason and feelings, claiming to be Lear's 'physician' (line 153). Once again, Lear bases his judgment (if that is not too cool a word for his rage) on the felony of disobedience in trying to make a king break his vow (line 158), of attempting 'To come betwixt [his] sentence and [his] power' (line 160), and he banishes Kent. When he stands on his 'nature' and his 'place' (line 161) he is in reality simply asserting his power over a subject in the manner of positive law. The next trial is between France and Burgundy, over who will choose Cordelia. Burgundy takes his lead from Lear, equating Cordelia with material wealth and since 'her price is fallen' (line 187) he does not feel contractually bound. France, preferring to follow the reasoning of Cordelia and Kent in declaring that 'Love's not love When it is mingled with regards that stands Aloof from the entire point' and that 'She is herself a dowry' (lines 233ff.), takes her in marriage. France takes her 'virtues' as the dowry and discovers that his love has kindled to 'inflamed respect' (line 255). We might add that after this succession of trials in the first scene, another immediately follows in the second, when Gloucester's claim to love equally his sons Edmund and Edgar is tested. Admittedly, this is precipitated by Edmund's trickery but Gloucester, who prefers astrology, superstition and the state's laws of 'legitimacy' to either reason or the feelings he claims to find within him, is an easy dupe. Effectively he is no better than Lear who arbitrarily disinherited his best loved daughter, since Gloucester first accepts society's prohibition against any rights for bastards, irrespective of his own 'natural' affections, and secondly he does not question allegations of Edgar's disloyalty. The results are just as calamitous for the Gloucester family as those stemming from Lear's mistake for his family, since both families are by the end of the play literally destroyed, except for the one survivor, Edgar.

Positive law, at least in this play, is simply the extension of the will of a sovereign ruler, while Natural Law has its source in the human mind and heart working independently of worldly authority. Lear has set up the situation where these systems are in direct conflict, and the titanic struggles which follow are as much in his own mind as in the state, and they are certainly his responsibility. His madness and his mental break-down reflect the fundamentalist nature of the clash, and the play relentlessly follows the course of the dispute.

### Positive law, authority, and evil

Cordelia, Kent, to some extent Edgar and the Fool, together with a procession of kindly servants, gentlemen (at least in the Quarto) and a doctor, all stand out against positive law on behalf of the Law of Nature in acts which the legal theorist John Rawls[8] would call conscientious resistance . Positive law, vested in worldly authority, however, is seen as immensely effective and destructive, even over Natural Law itself, and to understand its power we must examine its claims to legitimacy. Set against the essentially equitable and Natural Law appeal to feelings that lie behind conscience, charity and reason (in the sense of reasonableness rather than strict logic), lies Cornwall's appeal to authoritarian 'form of justice' as the basis for law. His argument is harder to parry in theory than in practice, for there is behind Cornwall's words a firm, if debatable, understanding of law itself. Law for him is positive law, without appeal beyond itself, and positive law is whatever a properly constituted authority deems it to be. Gonoril later makes the same point to Albany: 'the laws are mine, not thine, Who can arraign me for't?' (Scene 24, lines 154–5), and Lear, although now he lacks authority himself, knows that a king cannot be taken for coining since he is the king himself, owning or even 'being' both currency and law. In the general context of jurisprudence Roger Cotterell makes the point by quoting Emil Brunner:

The Protestant theologian Emil Brunner wrote: 'The totalitarian state is simply and solely legal positivism in political practice ... the inevitable result of the slow disintegration of the idea of justice'. And he adds: 'If there is no justice transcending the state, then the state can declare anything it likes to be law; there is no limit set to its arbitrariness save its actual power to give force to its will'.[9]

As many divine-right theorists argued, the monarch is the law, and is at the same time above the law, and one whom only God may judge. Whether or not Natural Law exists is virtually an unnecessary question in this formulation of authority, since not even the monarch needs to be credited with any understanding of it. The situation in the play's kingdom may be messy, with four rather than one in the position of monarchs, but the theory still remains. The only qualification is that authority must be backed up not by morality but by the brute power to enforce law, and it is clear that effectively power now lies with Cornwall, Gonoril, and Regan, Albany being marginalised. Within such an understanding, there is no room for appeals to Natural Law, nor are there *legal* checks against tyranny, arbitrariness, or corruption. Such sanctions as may exist are political (or military), the counter assertion of superior 'power'. The latter half of the twentieth century must be haunted by Hitler's apparent declaration after a massacre of his party members in 1934, ratified by *ex post facto* legislation: 'the supreme court of the German people consisted of myself'.[10] At every level in the system of authority which applies, justice is no more nor less than the will of the person wielding power, and such a will may be implicated in the very corruption which it seeks to judge:

> An the creature run from the cur, there thou might'st behold the great
>     image of authority. A dog's obeyed in office.
> Thou rascal beadle, hold thy bloody hand.
> Why dost thou lash that whore? Strip thine own back.
> Thy blood as hotly lusts to use her in that kind
> For which thou whip'st her. The usurer hangs the cozener.
> Through tattered rags small vices do appear;
> Robes and furred gowns hides all.          (Scene 20, lines 151–9 )

Shakespeare is returning to the terrain of *Measure for Measure*, the corrupting potential of power, its hypocrisy, and its self-referential ability to enforce unreasonable laws. It is ironic that Lear should be the one who comments thus, since it was he who initiated the new, tyrannical regime by royal fiat, more or less as Sidney's Duke Basilius did in the *Arcadia* (a work which the play draws upon), or like Shakespeare's Duke Vincentio, who delegates rather than transfers authority but still effectively abdicates. Gonoril diagnoses Lear's own confusion: 'Idle old man, That still would manage those authorities That he hath given away' (Scene 3, lines 16–17), but it is perhaps a person who has once held, and then relinquished ultimate authority, who can best perceive the misuses and abuses of power exercised by others, and in recollection of himself in his former station, though he may not so readily admit the latter. Cornwall, Gonoril, and Regan think and act as if authority gives the holder free licence unconstrained by moral considerations or any notion beyond their own wills. The legal maxim, posed as a question, *Quis custodiet ipsos custodes?* is consistently and bleakly answered in this play by 'superior force'. Righteousness alone, however true it may be to reason and conscience, is impotent when rulers are not constrained by moral considerations. On the other hand, as we shall see in examining the virtuous side of the question, the final agents of what we might call rectificatory justice do not work directly, or even fully consciously, but they do oppose force: the Servant, Albany's conscience, even the apparently 'natural' tendency of evil characters to quarrel and destroy one another, are all ultimately effective in some way. Natural Law, like God, may act in mysterious and indirect ways, and apparent defeat can lead to ultimate victory. Milton was to place his trust in such a creed, and as we shall see in the next chapter, on issues such as the accountability of rulers and divorce, three hundred years passed before he was vindicated. For the virtuous forces in *King Lear*, to invoke a phrase in *Love's Labour's Lost*, 'That's too long for a play.'

In the context of a play, the positivist logic can be exposed as dangerous if not quite provably fallacious, but it is sobering to remember that the arguments of Hobbes and legal positivists alike, and the modern system of rule by law itself are, in essence, based on just such a logic. If this were not so, where would a properly elected government gain the authority to reverse law made by its predecessor, and why should common law generate new precedents that so qualify earlier ones that they appear to overturn them? Such checks as we have, lie respectively in the political process for passing statutes and in what the prevailing climate of opinion finds acceptable, not in the substance or procedures of law itself. *King Lear* may show positive law in the ascendancy and at its worst, but the train of events also presents at least 'pathetically' to the feelings of the judging audience in Wilson's sense, why some kind of Natural Law is necessary in a world where positive law rules. Authoritarian, positivist versions of law prevail, but audiences and readers are made aware of a coexisting, more benign and morally-based, form of judgment. That such legitimated injustice prevails over Natural Law in the political world of *King Lear* does not mean that the latter does not exist and operate in the play's moral scheme.

### Edmund's law of nature

Before turning more fully to Natural Law in *King Lear*, we must address a different use of the word 'nature'. This second form of 'law of nature' (what in this book has been named natural philosophy as it links all the natural world) is the one under which Edmund at least claims to operate, and it is the driving force behind the other 'evil' characters as well. They obey what is popularly called by neo-Darwinians 'the law of the jungle' (incidentally slighting the peaceable kingdom of animals and plants, where in truth 'necessity' rather than competition is the basic driving force, and also misrepresenting Darwin). Without exception, all critics have interpreted Edmund's famous speech on 'Nature' at face value,[11] but it must be clear on close reading that he is *not* in fact invoking any recognisable version of 'nature'. Rather, he is perversely making himself the slave of the very social 'custom' that he reviles:

> Thou, nature, art my goddess. To thy law
> My services are bound. Wherefore should I
> Stand in the plague of custom and permit
> The curiosity of nations to deprive me,
> For that I am some twelve or fourteen moonshines
> Lag of a brother? Why 'bastard'? Wherefore 'base',
> When my dimensions are as well-compact,
> My mind as generous, and my shape as true
> As honest madam's issue?
> Why brand they us with 'base'? with 'base, base bastardy'?
> Who in the lusty stealth of nature take
> More composition and fierce quality
> Than doth within a stale, dull-eyed bed go
> To the creating a whole tribe of fops
> Got 'tween a sleep and wake? Well then,
> Legitimate Edgar, I must have your land.
> Our father's love is to the bastard Edmund
> As to the legitimate. Well, my legitimate, if
> This letter speed and my invention thrive,
> Edmund the base shall to th' legitimate.
> I grow, I prosper. Now gods, stand up for bastards!     (Scene 2, lines 1–21)

The sense in which Edmund is appropriating 'nature' is semantic rather than substantive, deriving from the term 'natural child' for a bastard who is conceived, as he sees it, outside wedlock in animal passion, rather than within the dull habit of marriage. He also uses nature as antagonistic to society, in the same sense that during the storm scene several characters see the elements of nature as opposing mankind. Like Shylock, Edgar has a point, in so far as legitimate and illegitimate alike are 'natural' in the biological sense and there should be no basis for inequality. However, in his argument he is not appealing to anything beyond human institutions, and in so far as he is relying on a moral order it is merely as a challenge to positive law. He is showing up and railing against the contradictions in laws of inheritance. Renaissance law, for example, based rights to inheritance law on the issue of marriage, and Edmund's complaint is that 'legitimacy' is defined simply through this artificial construction, rather than parentage or even affection. A daughter born before a male heir, even 'legitimately', would have the same grievance. He is not appealing to a transcendent scheme of natural justice, but rather is condemning an existing, hypocritical system and asking for his proper inheritance rights as a 'natural' son, within society's own rules. In his spirit of acquisitiveness he wants not equality and morality as human values in themselves, nor even some form of fair, distributive justice, but rather property and money all to himself. He is no Raphael Hythlodaeus, challenging the basis of property from a 'Natural' point of view. Just as Gonoril and Regan feigned filial love to gain inheritance, so Edmund's plot to turn his father against the 'legitimate' Edgar is a stratagem to get land, not an action based on any kind of law observable in the world of nature. Like Cornwall's group, he basically wants power. Edmund's spurious reference to nature as a goddess is no more than a rationalisation of human greed. It carries no more weight than Lear's description of Cordelia as 'a wretch whom nature is ashamed Almost to acknowledge hers' (Scene 1, lines 202–3).

Obviously, later thinkers such as Hobbes and some followers of Darwin have elevated greed into a 'natural' law by calling it 'human nature', but such a conclusion is not necessitated by Shakespeare's words, nor is it for that matter necessitated by a reading of human history. We may be attracted to the energy and charisma of an actor who plays Edmund, but there are few signs in the text that such admiration should extend to his morality or his actions. They are certainly implacably opposed to the tenets of Aquinas and classical Natural Law.

For every power-hungry tyrant there have been thousands at least silently opposing him; for every greedy person there are many generous ones; for every militarist there have been many who prefer peace, and so on, and all these contrasting types are depicted in Shakespeare's play. Edmund's 'nature' in *King Lear* is something of a red herring, and our reading of More's *Utopia* might invite us simply to replace his 'nature' with 'private property'. This is not to argue that Edmund does not have a just complaint against a society which allows his father to boast about the lust in which his son was conceived, while depriving that son of a share of the father's inheritance. Such a society is neither just nor fair in our terms. As a concession, Shakespeare mollifies the 'poetic justice' which kills Edmund at the end by giving him one last repentance, perhaps even a conscience, when in his dying moments he sends the order to reprieve Lear and Cordelia, an order that comes too late for Cordelia.

Where Edmund departs radically from classical Natural Law is in defining nature as a vindictive force and directly opposed to human society. He is merely employing the forms of social injustice and power-manipulations that he has learned from others, and the kind of positive law implementation that we have observed in Cornwall. The ruthless sexual acquisitiveness with which he throws Gonoril and Regan into competition against each other is evidence that even in intimate situations he follows these rules of power. Natural Law requires quite the reverse, centralising charity and the placing of social good above personal ends, co-operation above competition, drawing on the physical universe, if at all, only as a metaphor for 'laws' which are regular and consistent. Kent's 'The tyranny of the open night's too rough For nature to endure' (Scene 11, line 2) makes clear the reading of 'nature' as human and communitarian in essence, pitted metaphorically against the 'tyranny' of outward storms. The clearest contrast in the play lies between Edmund and Cordelia. Where his actions are motivated by the desire for individual power and status, and where his thoughts reveal little concern for conscience until his final gesture, Cordelia is willing to forfeit power and status when they are offered, before she will compromise on conscience. What we may be witnessing in the creation of Edmund is the birth of a modern myth of nature as red in tooth and claw, and an equally post-Hobbesian, Darwinian, assumption that human nature is the same.

Gonoril and Regan, and later Cornwall, also follow no 'natural' imperative. They simply want power, wealth and property, and given their chance the first two use unashamed flattery and unfelt sycophancy to achieve their ends. Once they have power, as we have seen, they equate law with their own wills, without reference even to the 'gods' that many others call upon, let alone to a system of morality or social justice. Gonoril and Regan, significantly, kill each other: dog may not eat dog in the world of nature (although it may eat, for example, rabbit for necessary food), but human may kill human when they enter the lists of power-play and competition, abandoning the Law of Nature written in their hearts. Cornwall is killed by what can be interpreted as a rival moral system, more literally by a servant acting on behalf of an altruistic set of values, even if the Servant is himself slain. When we wish to answer 'no' to Lear's question 'is there any cause in nature that makes these hard-hearts?' we need not be sidetracked by Edmund's call to 'Nature' as his goddess.

## Necessity, charity, and Natural Law

In our analysis of *King Lear* we may now move to a consideration of most of the major issues raised in this book. The play gives a representation of an absolutist political system where rulers seem rarely if ever constrained by moral considerations (the 'moral' man, Albany, loses power *because* he has qualms, and even when offered power at the end he refuses it) or by anything beyond military power itself. Might is considered, at least by the mighty, to be right, in a treatment by Shakespeare which could be read as a merciless satire on perversions of power. Despite many characters' calls upon gods, there are no *dei ex machina* and no evidence of manipulative gods.[12] The most virtuous character, Cordelia, ends up not only unrewarded but dead, and the two who might, as suffering indexes of good and evil, be said to have learned something, Lear and Gloucester, both also die. We should recall that Shakespeare has gone out of his way to create such an unrelieved and negative picture of the consequences of tyranny, since he has decisively altered most of his sources in giving us these deaths. If, as I have argued, Renaissance literature is, according to rhetorical theory, supposed to be morally educative, Rymer's question of *Othello* could be directed to *King Lear*: 'what learn you by that?', when all vestiges of poetic justice are violated, at least by Cordelia's death.

At the same time, this play above all others has been seen, especially in the twentieth century, as the most morally educative of all those by Shakespeare or any other writer. The contradiction – absence of an effective, implemented moral code within the play-world may paradoxically lead to the construction of a supremely moral experience for the audience – is resolved by the omnipresence of Natural Law in all its facets, and by the crucial 'participation' in Aquinas' sense, of readers and audiences in completing the circle. The resonant line 'Thou, Nature, art my goddess' could be appropriated from the reprehensible Edmund and redistributed in a different sense, certainly to Cordelia and also to each reader and each member of an audience. It is unseen Nature working its Laws of reason and conscience through virtuous characters, which dictates our capacity to make moral judgments on the action, and to distinguish between good and evil even where evil prevails in the worldly sense. The play is far from utopian, and indeed is despairing of social improvement until power itself is eradicated, but it does consistently endorse a code of values based on Natural Law which leads virtuous characters to oppose authority's version of positive law. In turn, Cordelia, Kent, and others are driven by conscience and reason into positions of civil disobedience based on their beliefs in communitarianism, loyalty, and human sympathy. In a play which is backgrounded with the English adversities of common life, 'Poor pelting villages, sheep-cotes, and mills' (Scene 7, line 184), where the mere sight of beggars enforces 'charity' (line 186), a set of local communities with 'wakes and fairs and market towns' (Scene 13, lines 68–9), ranging in its *dramatis personae* from monarchs to a naked

Bedlam beggar, it is significantly those who do *not* hold power who emerge as the most virtuous. They are driven by simple 'need', by 'necessity', and they are solicitous of others in need, only because they know what it is to suffer. In his unregenerate state, threatened with the disbanding of his personal followers, Lear had fulminated 'O, reason not the need! Our basest beggars Are in the poorest thing superfluous': 'Allow not nature more than nature needs, Man's life is cheap as beast's' (Scene 7, lines 423–6), but he speaks without the experience of true need. He is rationalising 'superfluities'. In the next scene but one, cold in the storm and seeking shelter, he recants, musing 'The art of our necessities is strange, that can make vile things precious' (Scene 9, lines 71–2). As the Fool reminds him, and as he altruistically realises, in a storm rain is wet, shelter is welcome. Lear finds that need does exist amongst humans, and furthermore that there is human responsiveness, and the impulse to help others. He has entered a new ethical arena, where 'need' *must* be 'reasoned', and where it is the imperative to charity, Luther's prime nutrient of Natural Law. The lesson is one that can be learned by Lear only in extreme adversity, divested of his pomp and ceremony. It is one of the play's starkest ironies that tenants, paupers, and beggars, all of whom have little means and many basic needs, are able to understand the basis of mutual aid in hardship, while kings, with all the resources at their disposal to eliminate poverty, cannot; that only need can recognise need, and, spurred by reason and conscience, try to meet it.

We have already noted the actions and words of servants who are more moral than their masters and mistresses, and to them we could add other characters who appear at least in the Quarto, such as Gloucester's tenant, the Old Man who offers to help him, the messenger who describes so eloquently Cordelia's grief (Scene 17, lines 17–24), the patient, understanding Doctor who helps Lear, and others. It seems no accident that the dramatic design puts Cordelia in the position of a disinherited child, Edgar into the disguise of a beggar, and Kent that of a Servant, and makes a Fool the trusted companion and political adviser to the fallen king, for it appears that virtuous action is the exclusive prerogative of the marginalised, the powerless, and the insignificant. While the great and lofty in power (including Lear as king) pursue self-interested motives, Machiavellian tactics for holding power, and a Hobbesian sense that human life is expendable, those at the other end of the social spectrum (including Lear himself when he is no longer king), demonstrate sympathetic charity. The 'intense imagining' of Edgar in his construction of the dizzying heights of Dover Cliff has not only a poetic and rhetorical but also a moral basis, and it is significant that his stage-managing of his father's 'fall' is, at least in Edgar's eyes, justified: 'Why I do trifle thus with his despair Is done to cure it' (Scene 20, lines 32–3). Cordelia's responses are consistently based on reason as the moral faculty and conscience as the stimulus to action. Her 'Nothing', simultaneously so disastrous in its results and so glorious in its courage, is based not on obstinacy, but a moral principle, in the face of a statement couched as a request but in reality a command:

> LEAR       But now, our joy,
> Although the last, no least to our dear love:
> What can you say to win a third more opulent
> Than your sisters?
> CORDELIA   Nothing, my lord.
> LEAR       Nothing?
> CORDELIA       Nothing.         (Scene 1, lines 77–83)

Her earlier asides confirm her love for her father and her refusal to be drawn into a public declaration of it for personal gain. Love is silent in a context of power, her 'love's more richer than [her] tongue', to be proved by actions and not by words. Her reasoned response to Lear's demand is to assert some tenets of Natural Law: one loves according to some 'bond' of nature and inclination rather than to prescribed forms of words. Forced to 'heave' her heart into her mouth and use words when she would prefer to be silent, Cordelia must couch her response in terms that sound at first like positive law based on contractual obligations, but this implication is a coercion of Lear in setting up the situation. She is forced to answer authority with law. When we recall that axiomatically positive law is supposed to be in line with Natural Law, we can recognise that Cordelia is not standing upon a positive law – indeed, she is refuting Lear's positive 'law' – but instead explaining rationally the moral basis for the 'law of love' in the very terms introduced by Lear. 'Nothing', her answer to Lear's indecorous question supplemented by her explanations, carries the full weight of reason and conscience. When reluctantly talking, she cannot avoid altogether Lear's linguistic circuit, and, as he asserts an authoritarian version of law (rewards will be distributed according to royal whim), so she asserts a Natural Law (rewards and punishments are irrelevant beside the overwhelming compulsion of reason and conscience). Like most examples of conscientious resistance and refusal to obey authority's demands, Cordelia's gesture precipitates as much if not more anger and destruction than would outright opposition, for she is refusing to accept the basis for authority at all when it conflicts with conscience. The events of the play, dismaying as they are, unravel from this exchange. Responsibility, however, lies not with

Cordelia but with Lear who, again like Basilius, attempts to assert positive law over Natural Law.

Kent's outburst, claiming the privilege of spontaneous and 'natural' anger at witnessing an injustice, is a different kind of political action. He implicitly accepts the absolute authority of Lear, but directly opposes his judgment and justice in the immediate case of appointing royal successors. Like Cordelia, Kent takes inspiration from the 'region' of his heart, but, in accusing Lear of madness, of folly, 'hideous rashness' and of bowing to flattery in misjudging his daughters, he is not questioning Lear's authority. He begs the king to reserve his state and apply 'best consideration' by reversing the decision, thus bringing positive law into line with manifest justice based on true deserts. He claims the position of a physician trying to cure a disease (lines 154–5), a metaphor which points to the 'naturalness' of his advice. Lear, speaking in Angelo's terms of alienated authority based on 'our sentence and our power' (an anticipation of Cornwall) asserts that neither his 'nature' nor his 'place' nor (more to the point) his 'potency' can accept such opposition, and he banishes Kent. Thereafter, Kent is completely and loyally consistent to his own self-defined 'bond', for, disguised as Caius, servant to Lear, he acts in willing servitude to his master. He refuses to accept the legitimacy of the new regime of rulers since, in his view, it is not based on a judgment consistent with reason and conscience. While Cordelia tacitly repudiates Lear's authority to act as he does, Kent accepts his authority but opposes his judgment (in both senses of the word, judicial and psychological), but they both agree that Natural Law is here opposed to positive law. Kent's touching farewell to Cordelia says as much:

> The gods to their protection take thee, maid,
> That rightly think'st, and hast most justly said.    (Scene 1, lines 172–3)

In the 'mini-trial' that follows, Burgundy refuses Cordelia in marriage, revealing that he sees her simply as property, as a dower, whereas France bases his decision to marry her on the basis of love and 'inflamed respect' ('She is herself a dowry'), and on 'reason without miracle' (Scene 1, line 213). Burgundy is establishing himself incidentally as a legal positivist in looking no further than immediate contractual circumstances of a dowry, France as a Natural Lawyer, looking beyond present authority to more ultimate values.

As the action unfolds, Cordelia becomes more and more equated with benevolent and healing natural forces. To her all natural things in distress are equally deserving of pity:

> Mine injurer's mean'st dog,
> Though he had bit me, should have stood that night
> Against my fire. And wast thou fain, poor father,
> To hovel thee with swine and rogues forlorn,
> In short and musty straw? Alack, alack!　　　　(Scene 21, lines 34-8)

Tears of sympathy and grief are her emblem, and virtually a whole scene (17) is devoted to them:

> GENTLEMAN ...
> 　　　　And now and then an ample tear trilled down
> 　　　　Her delicate cheek ...
> KENT　　　　　　　O, then it moved her?
> GENTLEMAN
> 　　　　Not to a rage. Patience and sorrow strove
> 　　　　Who should express her goodliest. You have seen
> 　　　　Sunshine and rain at once; her smiles and tears
> 　　　　Were like, a better way ...　　(Scene 17, lines 13-20 *passim*)

> 　　　　'What, i'th' storm? i'th' night?
> 　　　　Let piety not be believed!' There she shook
> 　　　　The holy water from her heavenly eyes,
> 　　　　And clamour mastered, then away she started
> 　　　　To deal with grief alone.　　　　(Scene 17, lines 29-33)

Kent's comment in response that 'The stars above us govern our conditions' strikes us as glib in the manner of the superstitious Gloucester, when seen in the light of the constant equation drawn in the latter stage of the play between Cordelia and natural forces. It is she who brings the description of Lear,

> As mad as the racked sea, singing aloud,
> Crowned with rank fumitor and furrow-weeds,
> With burdocks, hemlock, nettles, cuckoo-flowers,
> Darnel, and all the idle weeds that grow
> In our sustaining corn.　　　　　　(Scene 18, lines 2-5)

She collaborates with the doctor who uses not drugs but nature and its 'simples operative', perhaps the 'idle weeds' some of which had curative functions, as Culpepper testifies, to induce sleep, and even, in the case of 'sweet marjoram' later mentioned by Lear, to allay madness:

> Our foster-nurse of nature is repose,
> The which he lacks. That to provoke in him
> Are many simples operative, whose power
> Will close the eye of anguish.　　　　(Scene 18, lines 13-16)

Cordelia calls on nature itself to heal:

> All blest secrets,
> All you unpublished virtues of the earth,
> Spring with my tears, be aidant and remediate
> In the good man's distress!                    (Scene 18, lines 16–19)

Cordelia's earlier, stubborn insistence on conscience is now linked with nature itself, as benevolent and as a moral force, to construct an emblem of Natural Law, brought into consistency with natural philosophy. Her nature is poles apart from Edmund's, which is closer to Hobbes's model of acquisitive 'human nature'. The victimisation and execution of her define more clearly than anything else could, that her enemies are also the enemies of both nature and Natural Law. The unutterable pathos (in Thomas Wilson's sense) of her death is generated from the echo of her natural imagery in Lear's anguished 'Why should a dog, a horse, a rat have life, And thou no breath at all?' (Scene 24, lines 301–4). Nature's companion has now become no more precious and unique than any of nature's beings. The image of her lifeless body makes a mockery of Albany's obtusely simple minded distribution of poetic justice:

> All friends shall taste
> The wages of their virtue, and all foes
> The cup of their deservings.                    (Scene 24, lines 297–9)

If this 'friend' is dead, then there is a sense in which virtue itself, far from being rewarded, has ceased to be.

If the audience and readers are in the position of a jury, then the ending of this play requires us to give our verdict by referring to our reasoning powers and activating our consciences, and in this case to feel outrage at the deeds of those who opposed Natural Law, while acknowledging the worldly destructiveness of evil. The educative function of the play, then, lies not in apportionment of rewards and punishments as Nahum Tate's eighteenth-century rewriting attempted to represent, but in making us 'feelingly', through witnessing victimisation, extend and implement the lessons of Natural Law, charity, and sympathy. An unfortunate inference is that outside Thomas More's state of Utopia, no such ideal world is available as a refuge, just as in *Utopia* itself the world of Europe remains incorrigible. Even Lear's comforting vision of prison as a place of observing gilded butterflies and acquiring the mystery of things is a whistle in the darkness.

The ambiguity discovered by critics in the line 'And my poor fool is hanged' (Scene 24, line 300), whether intended by the dramatist or not, points us towards another equation, that between Cordelia and the Fool.[13] The Fool also speaks from a basis in Natural Law, although he is more retributory and reproachful than Cordelia, losing no opportunity to bait Lear with the king's folly and injustice. He is the truly anti-authoritarian man, professionally licensed to challenge and undermine the power of those above him in the social hierarchy, and particularly the monarch at the top, and to disrupt even linguistic and conversational expectations. He taunts Lear, sometimes harshly, for dividing the kingdom so inequitably and for banishing his youngest daughter, but any cruelty in his attacks stems from loyalty towards Lear, love of Cordelia, and respect for a sense of collective good. He is more angrily subversive towards Gonoril when she holds power: 'I am a fool, thou art nothing' (I. iv. 192). In calculated puns, misdirections, underminings, he is directly threatening not only the authority of speakers, but that of language itself, at least in its assumed status as a stable signifier of 'meaning'. Unlike Kent and Cordelia, the Fool has no capacity to influence events. He even 'pines away' after Cordelia goes to France, and eventually out of the play altogether. His role is largely that of gnomic commentator on folly, injustice and breaches of Natural Law. His is the one lonely voice that refers, however sceptically and strangely, to a utopia of justice, equality, and freedom from exploitation, and his mysterious 'prophecy' dwells on how natural these states are – as easy as walking, in fact – and yet how unlikely they seem to be for mankind to achieve, at least in the 'confusion' prevalent in this play's Albion:

> When every case in law is right;
> No squire in debt, nor no poor knight;
> When slanders do not live in tongues,
> Nor cutpurses come not to throngs;
> When usurers tell their gold i'th'field,
> And bawds and whores do churches build,
> Then comes the time, who lives to see't,
> That going shall be us'd with feet. (Folio only, *Tragedy* 3. 2. 87–94)

In other words, when the world is honest, then living will be as easily natural as walking. The weird comment that follows, sounding more the note of postmodern novels than a Jacobean play, 'This prophecy Merlin shall make; for I live before his time', throws the time of utopia outside the play and outside history itself, defining it as the kind of timeless state of Natural Law which is eternally present as a moral touchstone, but which the Fool, in his pessimism, sees as absent from the dealings of people in his world.

Lear himself is disingenuous in claiming to be 'more sinned against than sinning' (Scene 9, line 60) for it was he who precipitated all the disasters depicted as a consequence of the 'division of the kingdoms'.[14] The play can be rather reductively read as a punishment of Lear and the kingdom as a whole for his violation of Natural Law at the beginning of the play, not only a breach of the 'law of kind' in rejecting his best loved daughter, but also an injustice in rewarding the unworthy daughters and punishing the virtuous one. The consequences of these 'sins' are to drive Lear into a direct confrontation with the very forces of nature which he has opposed. The storm scene can be read as allegorical in Spenser's sense, as the forces that Lear has gone against now humble and educate him. From this archetypal encounter Lear may learn some things, but too late for remedy. One thing he does learn about is 'the art of our necessities' (Scene 9, line 71), a concept legally and emotionally defined, which we have seen to be important in *Love's Labour's Lost*. 'Necessities' or needs are infinitely various, and depending on the situation 'can make vile things precious' (*ibid.*). But in this context they take us back to the notion of a minimal content of Natural Law. In order to survive in a violent storm when threatened with assassination, the text reveals, necessities are shelter and protection, literal and psychological, both of which require a form of human bonding which must be 'natural' in all senses, instinctive, and fuelled by reason and conscience. Mutual aid and charity in its fullest sense take the place of self-defence in the struggle for survival, when the antagonist is the natural world of wind and rain rather than a human adversary.

The play gives an array of circumstances in which discrimination between what is a true need and what is not is raised as a problem. It is his daughters' dismissal of his 100 men that drives Lear to contemplate the issue. Gonoril and Regan clearly act politically rather than from their avowed distaste for the retinue's lack of house-training. To tolerate the existence of what amounts to a standing army loyal to the former king would, to these political pragmatists who believe that might is right, be courting the possibility of a reactionary coup. Regan questions Lear's 'need' of even one man in attendance, which unleashes his rather confused but enraged response:

> O, reason not the need! Our basest beggars
> Are in the poorest thing superfluous.
> Allow not nature more than nature needs,
> Man's life is cheap as beast's. Thou art a lady;
> If only to go warm were gorgeous,
> Why, nature needs not what thou, gorgeous, wearest,
> Which scarcely keeps thee warm. But for true need –
> You heavens, give me that patience, patience I need!
>
> (Scene 7, lines 423–30)

Unregenerate as yet, Lear is simultaneously glimpsing and resisting the idea of 'need' as something that applies only in a world of deprivation, and not in that of a privileged 'lady' or a king. Even the poorest beggar wears what is superfluous to his needs, and once we 'reason' about whether something is needed, then we reduce man's life to the level of a beast's and strip it of all dignity. Ironically, a minute or so before, he had been speaking of 'Necessity's sharp pinch', and it is this he is about to encounter in the storm on the heath. Within a scene or two, Lear is to reassess his views, when he meets a 'philosopher' who wears virtually no clothes in a storm.

Lear is forced to test his analysis of 'need' by experiencing a situation offering little more than an animal's comfort in the wild (an analogy drawn by Cordelia), unprotected, 'bare-headed' (Scene 9, line 61) in the storm, 'minded like the weather, most unquietly' (Scene 8, line 2). Here, as he 'Strives in his little world of man to out-storm The to-and-fro conflicting wind and rain' (Scene 8, line 10) on a night when even the bear, lion, and wolf keep their fur dry, Lear learns a fundamental law that 'true need' provides a model for existing within nature and its laws. Increasingly, his perceptions embrace the lesson that previously, kept ignorant in the mantles of authority, he could not have understood. He sees the storm as a judicial scourge, finding out 'undivulged crimes Unwhipped of justice' (Scene 9, lines 52–3) crimes committed by the very people who claim to hold authority in the human world. Reduced to 'necessity' he sees that the true need for humanity is not a troop of men or gorgeous robes, but simple justice. Lear learns that in a storm his companion the Fool 'needs' shelter, the glimmerings of a moral sense which previously had been denied him. Extended to the social and political sphere, the logic leads towards *Utopia*'s:

> Poor naked wretches, whereso'er you are,
> That bide the pelting of this pitiless night,
> How shall your houseless heads and unfed sides,
> Your looped and windowed raggedness, defend you
> From seasons such as these? O, I have ta'en
> Too little care of this. Take physic, pomp,
> Expose thyself to feel what wretches feel,
> That thou mayst shake the superflux to them
> And show the heavens more just.            (Scene 11, lines 25–33)

This marks a reversal of his outburst to Regan. Instead of saying even a beggar has more than he 'needs' to survive, and thus more than animals, he is saying that the beggar has *less* than is necessary, and he perceives that the injustice is directly caused by the superfluity appropriated by the rich and powerful. Gloucester, later reduced to similar need, discovers an equally communalistic, utopian-like basis of social justice, when in severe need himself he finds the compassion to give his purse to a presumed beggar:

> Heavens deal so still.
> Let the superfluous and lust-dieted man
> That stands your ordinance, that will not see
> Because he does not feel, feel your power quickly,
> So distribution should undo excess,
> And each man have enough.     (Scene 15, lines 64–9)

'Enough' for all is the maxim of Natural Law, 'distribution' is its basis for material justice, and the logic of 'feeling' is awakened by the Aristotelian advocate deploying the rhetoric of pathos. The sardonic point silently made by the play is that it seems impossible for anybody in authority to learn this lesson and improve things, simply because they are blinkered by the very fact of holding authority. They have too much to lose personally by instituting such a state of Natural Law.

Lear even finds his natural 'noble philosopher' (Scene 11, lines 141 and 159), his 'learned Theban' (line 144) of Natural Law, in Poor Tom who literally has 'nothing', and who is 'the thing itself! Unaccommodated man', a 'poor, bare, forked animal', and he removes his clothes in fellow-feeling (lines 98–9). Edgar's gibberish in his role as Poor Tom associates him with unpleasant facets of nature, eating cowdung, old rats, and ditch-dogs, like the beggars described by Raphael Hythlodaeus who are 'whipped from tithing to tithing, and stock-punished, and imprisoned' (lines 122–3) simply for existing.[15] He becomes for Lear the walking evidence of man's inhumanity to man, breaches of Natural Law, of injustice, and of the 'need' for conscience in making a human society. As well as being, with the Fool, the focus for Lear's new-found compassion, Edgar's condition also becomes in Lear's eyes the model of an ecologically non-exploitative existence, owing nothing to the silkworm for silk, to cattle for leather, to sheep for wool, and to cats for perfume. In the role of Poor Tom, one of his many quick changes, Edgar is less a 'character' than a functional catalyst, an agency for change and moral awakening.

Lear's sentiments in this part of the play are as communitarian, anti-individualistic, and anti-authoritarian as More's in his fictional version of Utopia. Once again, consistent with the Fool's despairing prophecy, neither Lear nor the play survives to see a state of justice according to Natural Law implemented in human society. Nor are there many signs that such a state will exist, without fundamental change in the world. It is for audiences and readers, as the judge and jury presiding over an 'as-if' scenario, to pass judgment and take the lessons into their own societies. That, as in *Love's Labour's Lost*, is too long for a play and can occur only afterwards.

The parallel, interlocking plot of the Gloucester family, follows the course of Lear's. A father commits an injustice against his progeny, a sin against Natural Law, and not only does he suffer from his choice to follow vice and shun virtue, but so in different ways do the sons. In this case responsibility is shared (as it is between Lear, Gonoril and Regan and Cornwall) because the plot is hatched and perpetrated by Edmund for his own, self-seeking reasons. At the same time, as I have suggested, it was Gloucester (like Lear or, again, like Basilius) who set in motion the train of events by his ambiguous attitude to Edmund, at once admiring him as a reflection of the father's amoral virility and yet disinheriting him according to society's laws on bastardy. In strictly narrative terms we might exonerate Gloucester by saying he is duped, but that would mean we could exonerate Lear also, on the grounds that he was deceived by Gonoril's and Regan's speeches in the first Act. Like Lear, Gloucester acts impetuously, without consulting the evidence of his own eyes and his experience about Edgar's filial affection. He superstitiously blames the 'stars' in the astrological sense instead of his own actions which were indifferent to human reason and conscience. As Lear begins sumptuously dressed, surrounded by troops, and learns by being naked and alone, so Gloucester begins metaphorically with sight which he neglects to use, and learns through blindness. When he is led to 'see' the scene of Dover Cliff through Edgar's poetic construction, he is doing no more and no less than when he had 'seen' Edgar distorted through Edmund's eyes. He too has allowed positive law, the rules concerning 'legitimacy', to blind him to more important, human values. In this sense Edmund does have a grievance, and, although the play does not condone his actions, it does explain them, and in doing so places primary responsibility for the family fortunes squarely with Gloucester himself.

### Power and injustice

Right through his writing career, from the debates on the use and misuse of power centring on Henry VI and Richard III to Gonzalo's vision of a political utopia in *The Tempest*, Shakespeare worried away at problems concerning the nature of justice and authority in political worlds. He encompassed a dizzying kaleidoscope of models of justice, but the central distinction from which his plays derive much of their dramatic, moral, and intellectual energy is between man-made decrees, and something more 'natural' and eternal in its origin, beyond a world where people make mistakes of family justice and where humanity must perforce prey on itself. This is precisely the distinction between positive law and Natural Law. And if the dialectic pervades all Shakespeare's plays, nowhere is it more central, more problematic, and more pressing than in

*King Lear*. This is somewhat ironic, since it is a play, like *Love's Labour's Lost*, which itself flouts all conventions of the form of 'poetic justice' as classically defined. Virtue, far from being rewarded, lies dead. Expectations are unfulfilled at every turn. To suggest that Shakespeare is systematically requiring audiences and readers to act as jury in a case raising Natural Law issues of reason and conscience is, as the evidence of this book testifies, not anachronistic in the Renaissance, but fairly standard practice. Milton's *Areopagitica* is the greatest theoretical exposition of the obligation upon readers to form their own moral judgments, and his *Paradise Lost* is no less insistent a practice of this theory than is *King Lear*. We have constantly discovered through our exploration of Natural Law that, at least in its classical version, its main assumption is that people do not need to be *told* the difference between right and wrong, but that within each individual is the innate capacity to discriminate through the faculties of reason and conscience. Even one like Spenser showing Calvinist influence can, in the medium of poetry, draw upon such a belief. Furthermore, according to the model, a person in tune with Natural Law by a kind of instinct inclines towards virtue and away from vice. In this sense *King Lear* becomes a clear example of a work in which the dramatist appeals to audiences to activate exactly these faculties. The plays of the period themselves bear witness to the fact that audiences were more imaginatively and morally active than those witnessing our post-Victorian stage practices. Brecht was one of the few who sought to tap the same active, judgment-forming faculties in his audiences, but it is arguable that entrenched, modern conventions were against him. Edward Bond follows in his footsteps, and it may be no accident that his most powerful plays are the adaptation called *Lear* and the play in which he represents Shakespeare writing *King Lear*, *Bingo*. Bond, like Shakespeare, gives no pat or easy solutions based on simple poetic justice, but rather he requires each member of his audience to search and construct a set of personal moral values out of the experience of the plays.

The most conspicuous point of both Shakespeare's versions of *King Lear* is the absence of a schematic 'poetic justice' which could easily have been applied by simply following sources, allowing Cordelia to live on, and take up the throne, or even to have allowed Lear to live on with his beloved daughter in autumnal reconciliation, as in Tate's version. Shakespeare has gone out of his way to reject his sources (whether legendary or historical), by killing off Cordelia and leaving a hiatus in the ruling of Britain. No self-respecting dramatist would expect his audience to accept this state of affairs as morally right, no matter what we think of the play's aesthetic qualities. The alternative 'happy ending' such as Tate's simply leaves the reader and audience in a state of cosy complacency, omitting the 'supplement' of manifest injustice chosen by Shakespeare.

An important but sadly overlooked book published in 1949 by Edmond N. Cahn, *The Sense of Injustice*,[16] posits that human beings may well be more 'naturally' able to recognise injustice than justice, as a prelude to the awakening of a desire for justice itself. Aristotle's emphasis on pathos in adjudicating a trial at law could be said to work on the same principle. The moral 'work' required of an audience by such a scheme clearly continues after the play is over, with an invitation to the reader and audience to transfer a largely tacit and emotionally pitched analysis and exemplification of good and evil into their own lives, as, in a very real sense, the capacity to judge came initially from their own experiences. It is in the nature of rhetoric, after all, to convince us 'feelingly' of injustice, without needing to spell out what justice itself compels. Once again, in lighter mode, *Love's Labour's Lost* emerges as the work, in terms of moral structure, oddly closest to *King Lear*, like a playful 'first run' for the immense tragic passion of the *Lear* plays. The crucial difference is that the courtiers in the earlier comedy 'deserve' the deferment and uncertainty of marriage they face at the close of the play, since they have overridden Natural Law by agreeing to obey a misguided edict, whereas Cordelia does not deserve death because she has, if anything, embodied Natural Law by instinctively following reason and conscience and by inclining to virtue. Here we might locate a more general 'law' of Shakespearian drama which has been overlooked in all the hundreds of accounts of 'the nature of comedy' and 'the nature of tragedy'. Shakespeare's comedies, at their heart, become a contemplation of the effecting of justice according to their own internal Natural Law of sexual attraction, while his tragedies become a contemplation of injustice, violations of Natural Law precepts. This is so even in plays with a more 'villainous' titular hero than Lear himself: nobody at the end of *Macbeth* can bring back Lady Macduff and her children, the innocent victims of tyranny, and at the end of *Coriolanus* there is no force that can resurrect all those civilians killed in war by the military machine. The main offenders may be dead, and to this extent some version of poetic justice applies, but the profound injustices perpetrated by them cannot be rectified, and must instead remain as permanent witnesses to injustice. The lesson may be starker in *Lear* since the good and the evil alike are destroyed in a travesty of poetic justice, emphasising that injustice itself is intransigent when there are those around who do not follow innately the tenets of Natural Law.

Here lies an answer to the problems raised by the existence of 'two versions' of *Lear*. Whereas it is becoming common to describe the

Quarto as compassionate and the Folio as harsh, we can equally argue that there is no fundamental moral difference between the two, and that if anything the Folio is more rigorously consistent to the underlying moral schema present in both. The Quarto gives more spoken guidance by offering choric voices and examples of human charity and Natural Law in operation which we may hang onto and identify with. The Folio, by shaving these away, leaves us more morally isolated, so that we must make up our own minds about good and evil without prompting, more or less like Milton's Adam and Eve at the end of *Paradise Lost*. It tests the reader and audience more starkly by requiring us to choose by reference to faculties which come from within us rather than being asserted by the play. This parallels exactly the morally active *practicum* of reading and interpreting advocated by Sidney, Milton in *Areopagitica*, and the Aristotelian theory of rhetoric described by Wilson. Cordelia, in this sense, has acted in lonely integrity, and the audience and reader are encouraged to do likewise.

The actual conclusions drawn by an audience from the Folio cannot be different in kind from those generated by the Quarto. For example, it would be considered frankly impossible for any audience not to be repulsed by the blinding of Gloucester, whether or not we have two Gentlemen moralising directly about it at the end of the scene. Their presence in the Quarto 'History' version may focus the humanist response by introducing voices of pity within the action, yet, although in the Folio 'Tragedy' the tone is different, there is no reason why the reader/audience does not feel directly the same pity and outrage, perhaps even more keenly because the stage spectators are ignoring callously some obvious moral assumptions. The Folio is, then, simply carrying a stage further the Quarto's insistence that Natural Law is a 'need' from within which can be obscured by the existence of question-able positive laws enacted by worldly tyrants, but which can be retrieved by the exercise of human reason and conscience. While the Folio may give us the same number of violations of Natural Law as the Quarto, and fewer affirmations of it, this does not mean that Natural Law is excluded from its orbit. At the same time, Nahum Tate's *Lear* is different from Shakespeare's two versions. Tate eliminated all the doubts, uncertainties, ambivalences, and, in the currently voguish word, 'anxieties' of Shakespeare.

The little group of characters left huddling, exhausted, at the end of both versions of *King Lear* are like the audience in the position of Adam and Eve at the end of Milton's epic. They have witnessed something akin to the tragedy of the Fall of mankind in the evil perpetrated, and they have no refuge in the kind of platitudes and superstition which, for example, Gloucester had fallen back on. 'Speak what we feel, not what we ought to say', whoever says it (Albany in the Quarto, Edgar in the Folio), is a reproof to any glib or easy answer to the violations of Natural Law which we have witnessed: Lear's initial rejection of his loving daughter, Gloucester's failure to trust his son, the blinding of Gloucester, the hanging of Cordelia, and so on. Evil may be dead, but so is good. At the same time, like Adam and Eve, they know these sobered witnesses have the equipment for enlightened moral judgment, and realise also that they will be individually tested in their lonely attempts to follow virtue and shun vice. If they forget the lessons of Natural Law demonstrated by the actions they have witnessed and participated in, they may inadvertently fall themselves, or watch others fall into the blind and tyrannical ways of authority. They have reached a real but fragile point of moral awareness.

Readers and audiences occupy the same position, as, even more pertinently, do critics claiming any 'authority' over such a play. The logic of *King Lear*, with its decisive celebration of virtue over vice and its equally decisive extinction of virtue, folds back to catch in its snare those who would impose any kind of positive law, literary or legal, over Natural Law. As in *Utopia*, no matter how splendid is the prospect of a world based on reason and conscience, that world may not be achievable, because human greed and power-seeking are too deeply entrenched in the existing structures of authority and power: but the effort of trying should still go on. In answer to those who debate whether *King Lear* is an optimistic or a pessimistic play, we might conclude that it is optimistic in so far as Shakespeare believes in the existence, innate in the hearts of human beings, and the supreme importance of, Natural Law; pessimistic in so far as he does not give indications that we may foresee its imminent implementation in the political and legal processes of human society, because those who have power to change the political world for the better, are the 'hard-hearts' sealed against the promptings of Natural Law. If Shakespeare indeed has the transportability between cultures and times that have invited the term 'universality', the source lies not in his presentation of presumed verities, but his unsettling ambivalence about the possibility of ever arriving at such verities. His unerring focus on the central human activities of doing justice and injustice, and the problems each raises, is the central dynamic of all his plays and the reason they are applicable in some way to such diverse cultures. In this focus, the dialectic between Natural Law and positive law is fundamental, and *King Lear* is its powerful exposition.

# 9    Milton and Natural Law

[S]eeing that persuasion certainly is a more winning and more manlike way to keep men in obedience than fear, that to such laws as were of principal moment, there should be used as an induction some well-tempered discourse, shewing how good, how gainful, how happy it must needs be to live according to honesty and justice; which being uttered with those native colours and graces of speech, as true eloquence, the daughter of virtue, can best bestow upon her mother's praises, would so incite, and in a manner charm, the multitude into the love of that which is really good, as to embrace it ever after, not of custom and awe, which most men do, but out of choice and purpose, with true and constant delight. (*The Reason of Church Government*, ii, 439)[1]

A modest but important work by John Milton is known as *On Education*. It was written in 1644 and addressed to Master Samuel Hartlib. Milton's programme for educating the young begins with language, regarded as 'but the instrument conveying to us things useful to be known' (iii, 464). The 'instrument' is like Sidney's version of poetic artifice, a delightful induction in the tradition of Sidney's theory of poetry, as invoked in the headpiece to this chapter:

I shall detain you now no longer in the demonstration of what we should not do, but straight conduct you to a hillside, where I will point you out the right path of a virtuous and noble education; laborious indeed at the first ascent, but else so smooth, so green, so full of goodly prospect, and melodious sounds on every side, that the harp of Orpheus was no more charming. (iii, 467)

Here, again in the Sidney mould, is language as imagery of the natural world, which Milton says is the proper end of knowledge, and he advocates the study of agriculture, astronomy, geography, fortification, architecture, navigation, meteors, minerals, plants, living creatures, and in short all branches of 'natural philosophy'. In offering 'a real tincture of natural knowledge' (iii, 471) the teacher, again like Sidney's poet, has his eye on a training in the contemplation of 'moral good and evil' (iii, 472). A 'sound indoctrinating' (not, for Milton, the pejorative word it has become for us, but rather used in its literal sense of in-teaching) in 'the knowledge of virtue and the hatred of vice' is the direction of the educational programme, and after grasping the capacity for such distinctions the pupil then goes on to law and legal justice. A study of the 'peculiar gifts of nature' leads inexorably towards a capacity for moral reasoning and, by implication, comprehension of Natural Law. Taken as a whole, Milton's account presents the physical laws of nature and Natural Law as linked and self-consistent, and both exist as evidence of God's pre-eminent reason which he has implanted in humanity. His consistency on the issue of Natural Law, which I hope is confirmed by the many quotations I bring to bear, may surprise those who are accustomed to read Milton as a thoroughgoing Calvinist. Even in the later poetry like *Paradise Lost* where we expect and find an increasing pessimism about mankind's moral capacities, there is still a place for Natural Law, a little dimmed perhaps but defiantly and definitely central. Despite his famous phrase about Spenser being a better teacher than Scotus or Aquinas, Milton seems to agree with Aquinas on the central points of Natural Law. He is one writer who consistently links the words reason and conscience as inevitable companions and virtually synonyms. At the very least, as one who trusted his election, he was willing to have faith in his own God-given, innate reason, and conscience as routes to truth.[2]

I should add that Milton was not alone in his age or amongst his political allies in his reliance on Natural Law thinking. In a book which is perhaps already too long, I cannot demonstrate the fact, but the Civil War and Commonwealth periods witnessed a triumphant reassertion of Natural Law, used, rather ironically, by libertarian thinkers such as Lilburne, Walwyn, and Winstanley, instead of by conservatives as is often the case in the sixteenth century and certainly Hooker. The transportation of English radical thought to America in the seventeenth century was to ensure its further survival as Fundamental Law. It is a story that I hope will be told, by another if not myself, that Milton in this respect was broadly 'of his age'.[3]

*On Education* is a benign and reflective work. At another extreme is the impassioned *The Second Defence of the People of England*. Stung by an anonymous attacker's reference to his blindness, Milton retorts with wounded indignation:

if the choice were necessary, I would, sir, prefer my blindness to yours; yours is a cloud spread over the mind, which darkens both the light of reason and of conscience; mine keeps from my view only the coloured surfaces of things, while it leaves me at liberty to contemplate the beauty and stability of virtue and of truth. (i, 239)

His inward eye was always set on absolute justice, and his heart was set on its mode of implementation, Natural Law.

For many radical Protestants living in the sixteenth and seventeenth centuries, life would have been intolerable without a belief in some version of Natural Law. It was necessary for those, like Milton, who opposed existing forms of authority to appeal beyond the legal framework consisting of positive laws made under a monarchical system, to an overarching moral system which conveniently existed in the form of Natural Law. In his belief in such a system, John Milton was a typical example. Living first under a monarchy, which on principle he disapproved of and detested as tending towards tyranny, then under a commonwealth which steadily grew away from his own conception of a democratic republic, and finally under a restored monarchy which made him personally a scapegoat for the failed revolution, Milton was clearly an embattled figure who was, with only relatively brief respites, opposed to worldly and ecclesiastical authority in position during his lifetime. Unlike, for example, Marvell, Milton was always prepared publicly to defend his views on the most controversial subjects such as regicide (Milton would probably prefer the term tyrannicide, but so sweeping was his condemnation of royalty to become, that the wider word is justified), reform of ecclesiastical government, and reform of the divorce laws. Driven by a passionate belief in the rightness of his conscience, and in the sanctity of human reason, it is not surprising that he makes constant reference to Natural Law in justification of liberty.

### Politics

*The Tenure of Kings and Magistrates* (1648–9) remains Milton's most controversial statement. Written as a justification of the execution of Charles I, made against not only royalists but also some republicans such as the Presbyterians, the work in unequivocal fashion endorses political assassination under certain circumstances. The subtitle is a characteristically forthright and explicit statement of belief, asserting that the work proves 'That it is lawful, and hath been held so through all ages, for any, who have the power, to call to account a tyrant, or wicked king, and after due conviction, to depose, and put him to death, if the ordinary magistrate have neglected, or denied to do it. And that they who of late so much blame deposing, are the men that did it themselves.' The first sentence declares Milton's reliance on reason against the authority of 'custom', the distractions of sentimentality and even common law which would have condemned as treason and murder the killing of any British king:

If men within themselves would be governed by reason, and not generally give up their understanding to a double tyranny of custom from without, and blind affections within, they would discern better what it is to favour and uphold the tyrant of a nation. (ii, 3)

He then asserts that reason can be either undermined by an 'inward vicious rule' of a tendency to choose evil, or alternatively supported by a tendency towards 'virtue and true worth'. Those practising virtue are the friends of freedom who oppose tyranny in all its forms, while those practising evil are accustomed to love only license under the name of freedom. In his division of people into the elect and non-elect, those who innately know and follow Natural Law and those whose instincts for justice have been permanently clouded by the Fall, Milton is simply following Luther and Calvin, as we would expect of a radical Protestant. On the question of judging who is a tyrant, Milton chooses to leave the matter to magistrates ('at least to the uprighter sort of them') and the people, or at least those of the people 'in whom faction least hath prevailed above the law of nature and right reason' (ii, 7). Milton consistently resolved a perennial problem facing all radical political theorists in Britain by maintaining that the common good of the people was not necessarily the same as the will of the majority, since many are kept ignorant of the truth, or else live in a state which would now be called false consciousness of their own real interests: hence his insistence on governance by a wise élite representing the true interests of the people, rather than democracy, rule by the majority. Any faith in majority rule which he may have harboured would have finally been shattered on the Restoration. At the heart of his political argument is the conviction that kings and indeed all rulers are 'by the bond of nature and of covenant' (ii, 10) entrusted with power only within the terms based on the allegiance of the people and on their willingness to execute those laws to which the people assent. Milton is firm in his opinion on the point concerning human authority which had divided Natural Law theorists: rulers are under the Law of Nature and accountable to the people governed:

It being thus manifest, that the power of kings and magistrates is nothing else but what is only derivative, transferred, and committed to them in trust from the people to the common good of them all, in whom the power yet remains fundamentally, and cannot be taken from them, without a violation of their natural birthright. (ii, 11)

'A prince is bound to the laws' he says, and 'on the authority of law the authority of a prince depends, and to the laws ought to submit' (ii, 14). He could not condone Cornwall's version of personal rule by positive law in *King Lear*. In general terms, then, a tyrant is one who does not respect either the law (which, we remember, is held always to be consistent with Natural Law unless it is against reason and conscience, in which case it is no law) or the 'common good' which is a central yardstick of Natural Law. Even tyrants themselves 'by a kind of natural instinct' (ii, 21) hate and fear 'the true church and Saints of God' who uphold truth and virtue. On the matter of the basis of the covenant between ruler and people, Milton again invokes the more general state of nature:

No understanding man can be ignorant, that covenants are ever made according to the present state of persons and of things; and have ever the more general laws of nature and of reason included in them, though not expressed. (ii, 30)

The inference that the guidance offered by Natural Law will differ according to circumstances ('according to the present state of persons and of things') is an orthodoxy that Saint Thomas Aquinas, whom Milton sometimes quotes, would approve. Finally in this pamphlet, Milton turns against his opponents what they claim as the natural right of individual self-defence, by transferring it to a collective level:

They [Milton's opponents] tell us, that the law of nature justifies any man to defend himself, even against the king in person: let them shew us then, why the same law may not justify much more a state or whole people, to do justice upon him, against whom each private man may lawfully defend himself; seeing all kind of justice done is a defence to good men, as well as a punishment to bad; and justice done upon a tyrant is no more but the necessary self-defence of a whole commonwealth. (ii, 44)

After many centuries of uninterrupted monarchical rule, the events leading to the deposition and execution of Charles I and the abolition of the monarchy were, at least until the Restoration, the most traumatic in British history, and Milton does not hedge or prevaricate. He justifies the events by overt appeal to the Law of Nature.

In 1651 Milton returned to the fray on the question of the execution of Charles I, when he wrote *A Defence of the English People*, published in Latin purposefully since part of its intended effect was to arouse to revolution other European countries labouring under monarchies. While other prose works by Milton were written under his own initiative, this, as he readily and even proudly admits, was commissioned by the commonwealth as an official statement made against Charles II's hireling advocate, the Frenchman Claudius Salmasius who was respected as one of the most learned classical scholars in Europe. Milton's response is perhaps the most powerful piece of political oratory recorded in English history, since he annihilates the logic, argument, scholarship, and even presumed honesty of Salmasius in sustained invective which turns against that scholar hundreds of internal inconsistencies, contradictions, and instances of simple bad learning in his work. Salmasius died three years later, apparently a broken man. Milton answers every point, substantial and trivial, made by the defender of monarchy, his tone switching constantly from crashing sobriety to corrosive sarcasm and wit. He left so little leeway for counter-blasts that it must be considered an act of folly when Charles hired two other writers who published anonymously against Milton and provoked his even more merciless onslaught in *The Second Defence of the People of England* (1654). The sheer power of the first *Defence* made it top of the list of proscribed books under Restoration decree.

Milton begins his argument with a reiteration of the reasons 'by what law, by what right and justice' the judges condemned Charles I to death, 'viz. that whatever things are for the universal good of the whole state, are for that reason lawful and just' (i, 15). Charles proved himself a tyrant by his actions, Milton argues, and the duly constituted law-making authority brought judgment against him. What Milton regards as the compellingly rational argument adopted by the judges is authority in itself: 'No law that is grounded upon a reason expressly set down in the law itself obligeth further than the reason of it extends' (i, 68). Reason itself provides the most convincing authority for any law, irrespective of written laws, regal authority, or custom, 'For the law, says Cicero in his Philippics, is no other than a rule of well-grounded reason, derived from God himself, enjoining whatever is just and right, and forbidding the contrary' (i, 71). This is an assertion of full-blooded Natural Law with a vengeance. Since its expression is so central a tenet of Natural Law thinking, Milton regards as a literally heaven-sent opportunity the fact that Salmasius had the temerity to try to defend monarchy itself as 'natural' under Natural Law. Chapter V of Milton's work slays this view by piling up example on example of legitimate, non-monarchical systems of ruling, and of examples where monarchs have been overthrown or assassinated because of their demonstrated tyranny against their own people. Milton accepts Salmasius' assumption about Natural Law that it 'respected the universal good of all mankind' (i, 110), and proceeds to argue that a nation has as a natural right of self-defence, 'that right which nature has given the people for their own preservation' (i, 116), a legitimate sanction against a tyrant. He challenges Salmasius:

Produce any rule of nature, or natural justice, by which inferior criminals ought to be punished, but kings and princes to go unpunished; and not only so, but though guilty of the greatest crimes imaginable, be had in reverence and almost adored. (i, 112)

A provocative statement in the seventeenth century, with factions attempting to install an orthodoxy of divine right of kings, this statement in itself reflects our modern law, not for the last time showing that Milton's faith in eventual vindication was well founded. If a person in authority instructs others to commit a crime, or in some way colludes with this crime, then that authority, even if he be a supreme ruler, must be tried at law and punished in an appropriate way. Milton's central point from Natural Law has entered the current of twentieth-century law. Milton shows awareness of the teaching of Aquinas when he concedes that 'Nature teaches us of two evils to choose the least: and to bear with oppression, as long as there is a necessity of so doing' (*ibid.*), but he asks rhetorically why this should mean 'that tyrants have some right by the law of nature to oppress their subjects, and go unpunished, because, as circumstances may fall out, it may sometimes be a less mischief to bear with them than to remove them?' (i, 116). In modern political terms, in a democracy the people may not directly prosecute their rulers for their moral shortcomings, but they can await an election and vote them out of office. There are many arguments advanced by Milton for his cause in *A Defence of The People of England*, but the central one is encapsulated in his phrase 'what nature and right reason dictates': 'viz. that it is very agreeable to the law of nature, that tyrants should be punished; and that all nations, by the instinct of nature, have punished them' (i, 119).

In his other defences of liberty, Milton uses the rhetoric of Natural Law as a basic foundation for his argument. In *Areopagitica* (1644), the inspirational tract in defence of freedom of publishing, he comes close to asserting the principle of allegory underpinning Spenser's *The Faerie Queene* and of 'true fictions'. Writing itself, if it is based on truth, can be the worldly encoding of the persuasive, reasoning faculty which is at the heart of Natural Law, and will compel consent from any reasonable reader.

as good almost kill a man as kill a good book: who kills a man kills a reasonable creature, God's image; but he who destroys a good book, kills reason itself, kills the image of God, as it were, in the eye. Many a man lives a burden to the earth; but a good book is the precious life-blood of a master-spirit, embalmed and treasured up on purpose to a life beyond life. It is true, no age can restore a life, whereof, perhaps, there is no great loss; and revolutions of ages do not oft recover the loss of a rejected truth, for the want of which whole nations fare the worse ... whereof the execution ends not in the slaying of an elemental life, but strikes at the ethereal and fifth essence, the breath of reason itself; slays an immortality rather than a life. (ii, 55)

The drawback of unrestricted publishing is that many evil and misleading books can be published, but consistent with his views on liberty, Milton relies on man's 'gift of reason to be his own chooser', and to recognise an evil book from a virtuous one. 'When God gave [Adam] reason, he gave him freedom to choose, for reason is but choosing' (ii, 74).

To unsympathetic readers of Milton, 'reason' may seem a talismanic, catchall word used by him as a substitute for what he personally considers to be right. However, the word, probably Milton's most important one, needs to be considered in the context of his total *œuvre* and the galaxy of meanings supplied by contemporaries. For example, Arthur E. Barker quotes the amplified definition given by William Chillingworth who exhorted Protestants to follow 'right reason, grounded on divine revelation and common notions written by God in the hearts of all men, and deducing according to the never-failing rules of logic, consequent deductions from them.'[4] Milton does not stress 'divine revelation' so much as reading of scripture, but he would endorse Chillingworth's general emphasis upon a mode of thinking which excludes appeals to custom, prejudice, external authority (other than the Bible), mystique, ceremony, uncritical 'faith', and leaps of imagination, and which includes straightforward logic and common sense that inevitably compel the agreement of all thinking people. Robert Hoopes' book, *Right Reason in the English Renaissance*, which culminates in Milton, calls it 'the practical art of righteous living':[5]

if there is one aspect which in [Milton's] work receives more concentrated attention and articulation than in the work of his predecessors (save Spenser), it is right reason regarded as the principle and means of moral control in the daily life of man. (*Right Reason*, p. 190)

In these terms, derived from the abstract definition of Natural Law and expressed virtually as a truism, it is hard to see anybody disagreeing. That Milton believed so firmly in his own powers of reason does not mean he claimed his ideas to be immune from the kind of critical scrutiny which he advocates of anybody else's, and it simply returns us to a fact which has constantly been stressed in this book: the ground-rules of Natural Law are almost irrefutably straightforward to the point of circularity, but their application to contemporary events and problems is endlessly problematical.

As elsewhere, Milton asserts that the knowledge of good is interwoven with the knowledge of evil and that 'a fugitive and cloistered virtue unexercised and unbreathed' (ii, 68) cannot be as healthy as one that is exposed to all shades of opinion and left free to choose. His concept of the Fall is that it gives us at least experience of evil which must inform all our moral considerations. Milton, of course, is shrewdly aware that his own writings, and *Areopagitica* in particular, can be unpopular even to a regime he generally supports, and licensing of publications would be a hindrance to his own statements. His 'reading' of Spenser's figure of the untongued poet would assert, not that the poet had told an untruth, but that he may have told a truth which the ruling monarch or government did not like to hear.

That the magnificent statement on liberty of publication quoted above is grounded in Natural Law is self-evident, for Milton is equating 'good' books with reason itself, and furthermore an immortal kind of truth taught only by conscience, that outlasts temporal authorities and may be neglected or opposed in its own time. His 'fifth essence' is closely allied to Aquinas' statement of Natural Law as the human participation in the eternal life of morality. Later in the work he mentions his meeting with Galileo, the almost symbolic figure of one who (increasingly shakily, admittedly) maintained against authority the most 'natural' truth of all, the daily circulation of the earth around the sun, and he invokes also the works of his friend in parliament, the jurist Selden, who wrote a long tract on Natural Law:[6]

[his] volume of natural and national laws proves, not only by great authorities brought together, but by exquisite reasons and theorems almost mathematically demonstrative, that all opinions, yea, errors, known, read and collated, are of main service and assistance toward the speedy attainment of what is truest. (ii, 66)

Even the detection of errors and mistakes can be a step on the path to truth, a premise which Francis Bacon, no friend to Protestants of Milton's colour (although sometimes quoted approvingly by Milton), had already endorsed.

It must have taken courage to write *The Tenure of Kings and Magistrates, A Defence of the People of England* and *Areopagitica*, for the execution of Charles was by no means universally popular, and the Commonwealth, at its most radical, saw restriction on publication as a survival tactic. A more narrowly 'career politician' of the time would regard supplying outright support for deposing a king, let alone assassinating him, as giving a hostage to fortune, should the regime change again. Also, he would see licensing of publications and censorship as a necessity for the survival of the new state by which he was employed. Milton's affirmative and lofty tone indicates that he believed so strongly in the rightness of his arguments and in the perpetuity of the Commonwealth's cause, that he could afford to make straightforward statements based on 'reason', secure in the knowledge that he would be vindicated by posterity. He was, in fact, to suffer for his principled stands, for in 1660 he was pursued, put in fear of assassination, and eventually imprisoned for his 'treasonous' statements. His books were publicly burned, the most material kind of censorship that one could imagine, and no doubt the bitterest blow to one who had supported freedom of publication so staunchly.

It is interesting, and somewhat tragic, to contrast the message and tone of these earlier works with his output in 1659, the year in which partisans of the Stuarts clawed back popular support and a restoration of the exiled monarchy rose over Milton's horizon like a black storm-cloud. *The Ready and Easy Way to Establish A Free Commonwealth, and the excellence thereof, compared with the inconveniences and dangers of read-mitting kingship in this nation*, if anything, exhibits even greater courage and conviction than the *Tenure*, since once again he was in a minority and this time ominously on what increasingly looked certain to be the 'losing' side. The pamphlet is fuelled not by the earlier, self-assured and lofty confidence, but by controlled anger and passion against those who were reneging on 'the solemn engagement, wherein we all forswore kingship' (ii, 110). These turncoats, argues Milton, are willing to tie themselves to 'statutes which for the most part are mere positive laws, neither natural nor moral' which can 'by any parliament, for just and serious considerations, without scruple ... be at any time repealed' (ii, 111). Milton once again pins his colours to the flag of Natural Law as the only legitimate authority for a free country, although in this case it can be argued he was compelled to do so because common law could not be used. Those in parliament, he says, are

not bound by any statute of preceding parliaments, but by the law of nature only, which is the only law of laws truly and properly to all mankind fundamental; the beginning and the end of all government; to which no parliament or people that will thoroughly reform, but may and must have recourse ... (*ibid.*)

'A free commonwealth' rests on the liberty and 'civil rights and advancements of every person according to his merit' (ii, 135), that is, the unrestricted development of each individual according to his or her nature as established by Natural Law. By definition these conditions, Milton argues, cannot be fulfilled under a monarchy, since 'kingship, though looking big, yet indeed most pusillanimous, full of fears, full of jealousies, startled at every umbrage' is too mistrustful to allow such freedom to flourish. Even the revered Queen Elizabeth, 'though herself accounted so good a protestant, so moderate, so confident of her subjects' love' (ii, 134) held back the cause of Protestant reform by imprisoning and persecuting its proposers. It is this kind of personal attack on a virtual English Protestant icon, absent from *The Tenure*, and yet marking *The Ready and Easy Way*, which Milton justifies again by reference to Camden. His most intense anger is reserved for those 'backsliders' who 'are so affected as to prostitute religion and liberty to the vain and groundless apprehension, that nothing but kingship can restore trade' (ii, 137), stating that, on the contrary, restoration of monarchy will bring England back into 'foreign and domestic slavery', a reference to Charles II's exile in France and Scotland, and the inevitable isolation from Protestant countries which Restoration would bring. At the end of the pamphlet Milton adopts the stance of the Mosaic prophet:

> Thus much I should perhaps have said, though I was sure I should have spoken only to trees and stones; and had none to cry to, but with the prophet, 'Oh earth, earth, earth!' to tell the very soil itself, what her perverse inhabitants are deaf to. (ii, 138)

Even the imagery of earth, 'grounding' the argument in nature, is consistent with the fundamental stand taken by Milton on Natural Law, and he despairingly foresees a kind of historical inevitability overtaking events, akin to a natural force like the biblical flood. He fears 'to what a precipice of destruction the deluge of this epidemic madness would hurry us, through the general defection of a misguided and abused multitude', who are 'choosing them a captain back for Egypt'. He lived to see the fulfilment of this gloomy prophecy but not his more optimistic anticipation of the British people coming to their senses in a partial return to 'The Good old Cause' (ii, 138). This was to occur in 1688 with the second eviction of the Stuarts and the assertion of parliament's law-making supremacy in the Grand Proclamation, events which became known, misleadingly, as The Glorious Revolution.

### Religion

It could be said that all Milton's writings are, to some extent, political, in that they use rhetoric to persuade the reader to accept a Protestant, republican ideology. He would have argued, however, that the ideology was driven ultimately by religious convictions which could, with the exercise of reason, be applied and lived out in the context of secular society and political institutions. For him the commandment 'all the law is fulfilled in one word, even in this, Thou shalt love thy neighbour as thyself' (Galatians v. 14), or 'he that loveth another hath fulfilled the law; love is the fulfilling of the law' (Romans, xiii. 8, 10) was not an abstract, theological point but a *credo* for living, under whose terms he believed society should be organised. At the same time, some works are less immediately political, in that their occasion was not some momentous event in political life, but rather the fruit of reflection, the exercise of reason on basic religious concerns. Such is the treatise *On the Christian Doctrine, compiled from the Scriptures alone, (Doctrina Christiana)* published posthumously.[7] Although its existence was known long before, the Latin text was discovered as late as 1823. It is quite likely that it was written between 1655 and 1658 when, due to his blindness, Milton was superannuated and not employed in public business. This is the period in which he is believed to have begun *Paradise Lost*, and indeed *The Christian Doctrine* provides keys for understanding the epic, for his preoccupations with original sin and free will are fully expounded. The evident optimism and reflectiveness of the work would suggest that Milton wrote it before 1659, when a new sense of alarm and increasing bitterness began to enter all his works.

At the centre of *The Christian Doctrine* lies an unswerving commitment to a Miltonic version of Natural Law:

Seeing, however, that man was made in the image of God, and had the whole law of nature so implanted and innate in him, that he needed no precept to enforce its observance, it follows, that if he received any additional commands, whether respecting the tree of knowledge, or the institution of marriage, these commands formed no part of the law of nature, which is sufficient of itself to teach whatever is agreeable to right reason, that is to say, whatever is intrinsically good. (iv, 222)

The claim to derive everything in the book 'from the Scriptures alone' which Milton regards as an encodement of pre-existing Natural Law, leads him duly to quote, and requote at least four more times, Jeremiah xxxi. 33, 34: 'I will put my law in their inward parts, and write it in their hearts; and will be their God, and they shall be my people' (iv, 343, 378 and *passim*).[8] The quotation undoubtedly gives scriptural authority, but its content throws the actual process of decision-making on the consciences of the 'people'. The sentiment is repeated in one of Milton's favourite quotations, 'the work of the Law, written in their hearts, their conscience also bearing witness' (Romans, 2.15): and in Isaiah lix. 21, Joel ii. 28, Hebrews viii. 10, each of which Milton also invokes (iv, 384). For the seventeenth-century Puritan, these older, Mosaic texts had primal authority. Sometimes Milton uses the word conscience to express the same idea of an 'inward' law: 'By the law is here meant, in the first place, that rule of conscience which is innate, and engraven upon the mind of man' (iv, 253), but so often does he use also the phrase the Law of Nature with the same force that they seem interchangeable terms, and he makes it clear that such Law was available even before Christianity, let alone the Bible.

The problem for Milton, as for others who ponder the problem, is how, if humanity is innately endowed with knowledge of 'whatever is intrinsically good', we manage to stray into evil. The answer for him, of course, as for Calvin in even more decisive terms, lay in the momentous event of the Fall, the act of original sin. After this, the 'innate' knowledge still latently exists, but in all but the 'regenerate' it is somehow impaired or dimmed:

The unwritten law is no other than that law of nature given originally to Adam, and of which a certain remnant, or imperfect illumination, still dwells in the hearts of all mankind; which, in the regenerate, under the influence of the Holy Spirit, is daily tending towards a renewal of its primitive brightness. (iv, 378)

It is the expression of optimism in the phrase 'its primitive brightness' which Milton was to find ever harder to muster after the events that led to the Restoration in 1660. In the same passage, he accepts, like Hooker before him, that the law of nature is in *all* humanity, pagans, prechristians and Christians alike. He quotes Romans ii. 14, 15:

the Gentiles, which have not the law, do by nature the things contained in the law, these having not the law, are a law unto themselves; which show the work of the law written in their hearts. (*ibid.*)

Milton's assertion that some can innately obey the law while others cannot, shows the influence of Luther and Calvin, but the idea of those who possess Natural Law being 'a law unto themselves' is consistent with the Natural Law origins in Aristotle and Cicero, of which Milton was certainly aware, and it is not inconsistent with the teaching of Aquinas. Generally speaking, Milton shows more consistent faith in the workings of inner Natural Law than either Calvin or Spenser.

In Milton's art and ideology as in his theology, the 'impairment' caused by the fall of Adam and Eve is of crucial importance. It is what explains not only the existence of sin in the world, but also of free will, and for this reason alone there is a 'fortunate' aspect to what otherwise seems a human disaster. For Milton as for Spenser, before the Fall 'it was the disposition of man to do what was right, as a being naturally good and holy', 'led by a natural impulse, independently of the divine command' (iv, 221), but since the Fall it is hard work to recover the clear light of conscience and its law. It is work for the faculty of reason rather than of faith, so in this we are on our own, without God's direct guidance. Artegall is not simply a knight in shining armour, but also everyman, needing to struggle in his mission to bring justice to the fallen world. Spenser emphasises divine grace, and Milton gives it a role to play, but Milton still believes in human reason as the route to truth. In *Comus* this doctrine is at its most explicit, since the Lady and her brothers use reason to refute libertinism, and the only area in which the Lady requires divine grace is not in revelation of truth, but in simply freeing her from her state of *physical* paralysis: her will remains undefiled. Milton's real emphasis is on the necessity for free will in choosing virtue or vice, since God, having given us reason, knowledge and conscience, trusts us to use them, rather than coercing us willy-nilly into a virtuous course of action. He 'decreed nothing absolutely, which he left in the power of free agents' (i. 31), and vice exists more as a test of one's grasp of Natural Law than as an innate quality. Reason works by contrast and by full knowledge:

It was called the tree of knowledge of good and evil from the event; for since Adam tasted it, we not only know evil, but we know good only by means of evil. For it is by evil that virtue is chiefly exercised, and shines with greater brightness. (iv, 222)

Death itself which was introduced by the Fall, 'consists, first, in the loss, or at least in the obscuration to a great extent of that right reason which enabled man to discern the chief good, and in which consisted as it were the life of the understanding' (iv, 265).

Milton himself anticipated the army of literary critics who have asserted that this makes his God into a cruel and hypocritical figure, and pre-empted them by asserting,

On the contrary, it would be much more unworthy of God, that man should nominally enjoy a liberty of which he was virtually deprived, which would be the case were that liberty to be oppressed or even obscured under the pretext of some sophistical necessity of immutability or infallibility, though not of compulsion. (iv, 36)

True liberty must include the possibility of choosing evil, as *Areopagitica* had explicitly asserted. In this reasoning, the ever-present safety net is Natural Law. Man has been given the innate ability to solve moral problems virtuously, and he is allowed full liberty either to use this ability or to neglect it. If there were not Natural Law we would be marooned without a rudder, but if there were no free will to choose, then we would be less than creatures at liberty. At times Milton does go as far as to say that to do evil is as 'natural' as to do good, since it is equally a choice available to humanity because of our human, natural, and fallen condition. In following this line, Milton is drawing on the distinction made by Sidney that, for example, sexual desire is 'natural' and instinctive, but it may not always be in accordance with Natural Law. It is indeed the 'sin' 'which is common to all' because the original parents were first guilty of 'evil concupiscence' and by their transgression transmitted it 'in the shape of an innate propensity to sin' (iv, 259), and it is the classic case where reason may be overthrown by passion, and innate Natural Law clouded over. However, there is a strong tendency to say that, even if Natural Law and vice may both have their roots in human nature itself, yet by definition, since man has free choice, knowledge of Natural Law is a prior or sovereign quality. This would explain why in *Paradise Lost* Adam and Eve feel guilt so quickly after their torrid postlapsarian lovemaking, as the higher law asserts itself immediately. As in Sidney's case in *Arcadia*, there is a tendency in Milton to have it both ways on the issue of sexuality: it is 'natural', but whether Natural or not, depends on circumstances. But both Sidney and Milton would assert in justification that nature can be either unbridled and purely physical in its carnality (since sexual desire is experienced as an instinct operating in animals as in people), unreason epitomised, or it can be in accord with 'right reason' and conscience, in which case it is consistent with Natural Law and the capacity for rational choices which distinguishes people from animals. He is, of course, no 1960s' sexual liberationist or even a seventeenth-century Ranter, and would confine the lawful operation of sex to consecrated marriage. He is certainly not the first or the last to be somewhat ambivalent about the ways in which morality operates within the field of sexuality. He tends to have it both ways again by making marriage, in the words of James Turner, 'paradoxically more ascetic and more erotic'.[9] Milton also wavers over the more general question of whether man innately inclines towards good or evil. Unlike Aquinas, and in agreement with many of his contemporary Puritans, he generally tends to think the worse, and to regard virtue as something that must be struggled for rather than found easily. After reading Selden he seems to have accepted that man's fallen imperfections are part of his nature, and that amongst our innate qualities is potential for good and evil equally. This may represent a weakening of Aquinas' trust in innate good, compelled by Milton's assertion of choice, but it does not deny the fundamental theory of Natural Law.

*The Christian Doctrine*, the work Milton described as 'my best and richest possession'[10] is a great treasure-trove of ideas for those who seek to understand Milton's works, all of which can be seen to anticipate or swim in the wake of its reasoning. It is the abstract definition of problems which are dynamically presented elsewhere in his prose and poetry, and it acts as a guide towards understanding what he means by all-important terms such as free will and the Fall. At its firmest level of foundation, lies the notion of Natural Law. In this, as Joan S. Bennett argues, Milton and other radical writers of the time were the true, orthodox heirs to Hooker's theology of 'right reason', operating in a new context, no matter how Hooker himself would have detested the radicals' political ideologies:

In order to survive, the powerful root of the Christian humanist tradition in England had to undergo a radicalization of its external form. Originally aristocratic, by the mid-seventeenth century it had become Puritan.[11]

Hooker would certainly, if he had had the chance, have wished to disown such heirs as the Puritan radicals, but Milton's tribe ensured the survival of Natural Law thinking at least until 1660.

### Divorce

Another of the unpopular stands Milton took was against the divorce laws which allowed only adultery as the main cause for divorce.[12] Milton advocated divorce by mutual consent in his address to parliament later published as *The Doctrine and Discipline of Divorce* and augmented in other publications. Some have suspected that, like Henry VIII, Milton was simply pursuing his own personal self-interest in his desire to be divorced without the sordid involvement of adultery, but none the less the address is pitched at the level of disinterested reasoning for the most part devoid of personal motivation, and it is perfectly consistent with all the beliefs he held dearest. It must also be acknowledged that, although it has taken more than three centuries, Milton's logic has now at last been enshrined in legislation outside Catholic countries just as firmly as his belief that rulers are accountable to their people and should be punished for criminal offences. It seems that Milton's brand of reason and conscience must have some efficacy over a long enough run, almost three centuries in these cases. Once again Milton's primary appeal is to Natural Law as a higher order of unity:

For Milton's conception of matrimony as a harmony of souls and wills is a direct result of his conviction of universal order ... True marriage in Milton is an emblem of natural order, just as, to the divines, it was an emblem of the authority of Christ over the church. And although the human institution of marriage violated the order of nature, the possibility of its amendment gave man the opportunity to create a reflection of that order, to follow in his laws as closely as possible the internal disposition of things.[13]

Milton begins by suggesting the untrustworthiness of uncritical 'custom' as a basis for law, and he urges radical rethinking of laws along the lines of reason and conscience as routes towards virtue. He argues that human law should as little 'bind that which God hath loosened, as to loosen that which he hath bound' (iii, 175), reasserting the God-given gifts of 'reason, charity, nature' and the requirement that law should allow the self-development of the individual, with divine insight and benignity measured out to the proportion of each mind and spirit, each temper and disposition created so different each from other, and yet by the skill of wise conducting, all to become uniform in virtue. (iii, 177)

It is not necessary to summarise all the reasons advanced by Milton for divorce by mutual consent in his long and detailed argument, except to draw out the basis in Natural Law upon which he works. Chapter X is written to prove 'that to prohibit Divorce sought for natural Causes, is against Nature' (iii, 206) and argues that the existing law (allowing divorce only on grounds of adultery) is 'as respectless of human nature as it is of religion'. Milton consistently argues that the first (but not the only) rationale for marriage is lifelong companionship sustained by mutual affection, 'the helps and comforts of domestic life', and that the begetting and rearing of children was secondary, an emphasis which John Halkett has persuasively argued was virtually unique for his time.[14] Milton says it is an 'incongruity, a greater violence to the reverend secret of love' to 'force a mixture of minds that cannot unite'. Emotional compatibilities, the 'hidden efficacy of love and hatred' are 'not moral but natural' (iii, 207) and therefore should be guided not by restrictive, positive law, but with an eye to particular circumstances as Natural Law advocates. Observance of 'the law of nature and equity imprinted in us' (iii, 227) should be the main grounds on which divorce is judged, and Milton goes to massive lengths to show there is nothing in the scriptures that suggests God has legislated on this area where 'natural' and therefore rational, conscientious and individual rather than general, religious criteria should apply. 'And what is against nature is against law, if soundest philosophy abuse us not' (iii, 236). He makes the clever point that, if adultery is proscribed as a religious sin (and by the law in 1650, as we have seen), then it should be punished, rather than be rewarded as the sole cause of what most would regard as liberation from a loveless marriage. Furthermore, he argues from the fact that many continue in an adulterous marriage, as evidence that such exercise of freedom of choice is considered proper 'as being of unquestionable right and reason in the law of nature' (iii, 239). The law, he argues, is radically confused. The overriding considerations for the institution which 'is most ancient and merely natural' (iii, 265) should be freedom of choice, conscience, which is not criminally enforceable (iii, 258 and 263), equity not rigour (*ibid.*) and charity which is 'not a matter of law' (iii, 264). Once again Milton refers approvingly to *Of the Law of Nature and of Nations* written by Selden, 'a great man in wisdom, equity, and justice' to give authority to the guiding 'clear light of nature in us'. There is even an odd forecast of Freudian psychiatry in Milton's suggestion that to hinder or repress 'those deep and serious regresses of nature in a reasonable soul' (iii, 265) will force nature into perverse directions. He could be describing the inner state of Shakespeare's Angelo, strict man of the law who legislates on human sexuality while lusting after Isabella:

Let us not be thus overcurious to strain at atoms, and yet to stop every vent and cranny of permissive liberty, lest nature, wanting those needful pores and breathing-places, which God hath not debarred our weakness, either suddenly break out into some wide rupture of open vice and frantic heresy, or else inwardly fester with repining and blasphemous thoughts, under an unreasonable and fruitless rigour of unwarranted law. (iii, 272)

As in the case of Spenser, we must be aware of a mote in Milton's eye, and once again it stems from a blinkered, masculinist perspective which is strong enough even to override his assertion of equality and individual liberty. For this we may blame the overwhelming burden of patriarchal tradition rather than Milton himself. At first Milton seems liberal in saying that for divorce to be granted 'not for men, but to release afflicted wives' is 'not only a dispensation, but a merciful law' (iii, 247), which would avoid 'senseless cruelty'. But, to modern eyes, he backslides when he takes his argument a further stage. After reasonably pointing out that divorce should not be exclusively granted 'for relief of wives rather than of husbands' he makes a statement about the supremacy of men which is unpleasant but all too typical of his times:

who can be ignorant, that woman was created for man, and not man for woman, and that a husband may be injured as insufferably in marriage as a wife? What an injury is it after wedlock not to be beloved! what to be slighted! what to be contended with in point of house-rule who shall be the head; not for any parity of wisdom, for that were something reasonable, but out of a female pride! 'I suffer not,' saith St. Paul, 'the woman to usurp authority over the man.' If the apostle could not suffer it, into what mould is he mortified that can? (iii, 247)

The sentiments are particularly cruel since divorced women had far more to lose economically than men. He is also locked into a discriminatory reading of original sin which, as we see in *Paradise Lost*, not only places prime blame on Eve, but also, following Luther and Calvin, places the harshest interpretation upon the consequences of the Fall for women. The attitude is summed up by a chapter heading in Fortescue's rather obsessively misogynist *On the Law of Nature*, 'Woman is subject to the Man, provided she obey him in respect of any kind of Dominion.'[15] It is ironic that if Milton in this case had not been seduced by the 'custom' enshrined in authority such as St Paul's and the hardline Reformation writers', and instead carried through his otherwise relentlessly consistent assertion of human equality based on Natural Law, he would have been a friend to modern feminism rather than counted amongst its foes.[16] None the less, Milton does assert a countervailing emphasis on companionship in marriage, and therefore places himself on the road to equality, and above all he argues that 'wedded love' in the prelapsarian world, recoverable after the Fall, is 'Founded in Reason, Loyal, Just and Pure, Relations dear' (*Paradise Lost*, iv, 750–7). Both Adam and Eve equally must exercise individual free will in choosing between good and evil, and this exercise of reason and conscience is not an exclusively male domain.

### 'Paradise Lost'

It may require justification apparently to relegate the works of poetry which have remained Milton's claim to fame as an appendage to his prose. However, judging from the sheer amount of scholarship, labour, and rhetorical craftsmanship in Milton's prose, it would seem on the face of it that he did not regard prose as a dishonourable or necessarily inferior medium. Equally, the fact that he espoused causes that were often against his own government, or downright unpopular, indicates that he was no time-serving politician doing a job of parliamentary propaganda, while awaiting the opportunity to return to his poetic calling. Milton expressed pride in what he calls 'the zeal which I shewed, and the dangers which I run for the liberty which I love' (i, 240), and it is at least arguable that his famous reference in *Smectymnuus* to his efforts in prose as being from his left hand was not only an early statement before the political race became arduous, but also the kind of decorous undervaluing of public service which was expected and customary at the time, followed, for example, by Cromwell himself, if we may believe Marvell's poems. Alternatively, it could be argued that because he was so hard-pressed to produce polemics, the creative energy which would have fuelled poetry went instead into prose, creating a kind of prose poetry, most evident in *Areopagitica*. It seems clear that in his prose Milton is setting down clearly and soberly his own beliefs and attitudes, and if this is the case the ideas expressed must be of supreme importance as a context for understanding his works in the more allusive, fictional, and indirect mode of poetry.

For much the same reasons – the disastrous train of events which shattered Milton's political dream for England and endangered his own safety – Milton also subtly diluted his belief in the whole theory of Natural Law. Where he had previously been confident of its availability in the human mind, in his poetry he moves gradually towards the Calvinist view that it is benighted and obscured. His view, however, was maintained resolutely that Natural Law existed, that it was imprinted on the human heart, and that it could, with effort, be retrieved by individuals. All the evidence suggests that *Paradise Lost*, written to 'justify the ways of God to man', was intended as a beleaguered but powerful attempt to restore such sight and insight to humanity. This impulse, as we shall see, underpins the overall tone of muted but insistent confidence against powerful odds.

For all Protestants the main aim was to tell unadorned truth. In such an enterprise, prose could be seen (at least in the innocence of a world before postmodernism, when belief in universals and in language as a stable signifier could more or less be assumed) as a medium that can work through sober statement, while poetry is by definition an act of fiction and its imagery one of adornment. Or at least, to put it another way, lies and illusions are more nakedly exposed in prose than in the form which, as Plato had reminded them all, was based on figurative representation and therefore on a lie. Protestant writers such as Sidney, Spenser, Herbert, Milton, Marvell, and Bunyan worried about the unavoidably fictive basis for poetry, and felt compelled to accept the distinction between true and false poetry, like true and false dreams, to justify rationally their choice of poetry and metaphor as a medium for 'truthful' writing, in the way that Sidney, among others, theorised. The most important point, perhaps, is that it would appear from the chronology of his works that Milton abandoned prose and resorted to poetry only when he realised, with good reason, that the particular ruling body was inimical to straightforward expression in prose of his version of truth. It is significant that he wrote exclusively in what he regarded as the literally truth-telling medium of prose during the 1640s and 50s when he felt relatively safe within a system which at least espoused liberty for radical Protestants and one which, through his official involvement in it, he hoped to influence towards ever more libertarian policies. However, he expressed himself in poetry, the figuratively truth-telling 'as-if' medium of fiction, before and after the commonwealth period, when conditions of royalist hostility to his beliefs prevailed. If unadorned truths in prose were to be proscribed and burned, it was a natural move to adopt an allegorical or fictive mode, simply in order to be read. The pattern of Milton's output demonstrates once again the particular Renaissance understandings of fiction and rhetoric that run through this book. He uses poetic fiction in the way that lawyers used legal fictions: to solve with a degree of covertness problems that could not be solved openly within an existing framework, in this case political. If authority would not accept certain conclusions, no matter how cogently presented in prose, then the writers had to resort to other means of expression, and convince readers at the more emotional level of exemplification of a moral system in a fictional narrative. By choosing, at least after the Restoration, to dramatise and fictionalise events from the Bible, Milton further safeguarded himself because it was the one book universally regarded as 'true'. The other point to be made is the obvious one that poetry, being a more directly imaginative medium, allows some things to be said which could not be expressed in discursive, literal prose: what life was like before the Fall, for example.

Obviously, as I implied in an aside above, recent theory would quite properly confirm that it is not only poetry that speaks in codes and uses fictions, for prose is equally a construction of rhetoric, where pathos, the emotional sympathy of the reader, is the goal. If the question were put to him as one about the power of rhetoric in the service of rational persuasion, Milton might agree, and like Sidney he could rest, not on a distinction between prose and poetry, but between statement and narrative. Even in the apparently factual work *The History of Britain*, begun shortly before the Restoration but finished afterwards, Milton manages to heroicise a figure like Canute, who learned from the natural force of the sea 'the weak and frivolous power of a king' (v, 367) before the 'eternal laws', and who abjured court-flatterers and the crown, thus turning the whole narrative of events into a grim allegory of England's impending second fall, as well as an echo of *King Lear*. The final pages of this work are a bitter and moving denunciation of the Anglo-Saxons who ignored Edward's warnings and chose to 'take the yoke of an outlandish conqueror' (v, 392), the Norman William, just as Milton could see in his own day 'the revolution of like calamities' taking place.

If Milton's concept of fictions resembles Sidney's, at least in some ways, so the strategy of his poetic rhetoric is like Spenser's, drawing the reader into participating with inner moral laws by having to make choices and judgments which are not necessarily presented coercively or spelled out openly. The 'false dissembler' Satan is 'unperceived' by most who hear his plausible speeches, 'For neither man nor angel can discern Hypocrisy, the only evil that walks Invisible, except to God alone' (*Paradise Lost*, iii, 680–2). Many are taken in by Satan's apparent use of reason, most importantly Eve, and Milton leaves a lot of work for the reader to do in order to see through his winning but false logic, just as Shakespeare requires audiences to see with some difficulty that the logic of the great persuader, Iago, is flawed by its basis in surmise rather than observation. Even a multitude of later readers, including the Romantic poets Shelley and Blake in their famous assertion that Milton was of the devil's party without knowing it, were exercising the free choice so vaunted by Milton, to judge exactly contrary to Milton's intentions.

Milton, of course, gives many signposts to his true message: he celebrates reason and puts it into the mouth of God, Michael and Raphael, expecting that we will inspect and find lacking the glozing, deceitful use of rhetoric, logical *lacunae*, and false turnings in Satan's statements, all the 'calumnious art Of counterfeited truth' (v, 770–1). Unpleasant imagery attached to Satan gives the game away too, as does the constant harping on his assumption of 'regal' power with 'monarchal pride' which, to anybody knowing Milton's politics, would betray immediately the fact that Satan is no true, righteous rebel, but rather a would-be tyrant. Like his own God, Milton can say that at least virtuous readers possess through the inward imprint of Natural Law the equipment to judge aright. Those whose reason has been clouded by the very Fall that Milton is narrating, may follow Satan's path, but if they do so they have chosen their destiny with free choice. Like his use of poetic fiction as a vehicle, this deployment of rhetoric may be a safety device to disarm those who would accuse him of treasonous statements, and it is also consistent, not only with Spenser's use of poetic allegory as an educative experience for the reader, but also with Milton's own overall, moral view of the liberty of human choice after the Fall. After disobeying the one positive law given by God (do not eat the apple from the tree of knowledge), Adam and Eve and all succeeding human beings must undertake the much harder task of searching within themselves to find what is right and wrong according to Natural Law.

The approach adopted here, then, is to regard Milton's poetry not so much as an appendage to the prose but as a more guarded, 'coded' and fictional expression of the same ideas that we find in the pamphlets and addresses, transposed into poetry, either because it was dangerous to speak openly, or more simply because any more candid expression would not be published and thus not be read.[17] If there is any validity to the popular view that the poetry is more 'valuable' than the prose, it rests on the premise that the transposition into verse requires a rhetorical intensification and conscious universalisation into mythic vehicles, of matter which otherwise could be dismissed as 'opinion' and propaganda. It allows also imaginative speculation about the past and the future, unfettered by what Sidney called the 'bare was' of history and the unknowability of the future. Milton himself, in praising poetry for being 'simple, sensuous and passionate' may be saying it is a higher form than prose, certainly one more immediately acting on the emotions, but he is not saying that prose is not important in being the appropriate vehicle for some kinds of messages. There is a strength gained. Natural Law, for example, becomes not just an abstract idea used as a court of appeal, but rather an enactment or demonstration of moral principles generated from interaction between people in dynamic relationships through a narrative, and involving the reader's capacities to exercise reason and conscience in making judgments.

These themes are present in *Paradise Lost* in a manner consistent with his prose although advanced with less optimism. Similar interpretations could be made of *Paradise Regained*, *Samson Agonistes*, and even the earlier *Comus* and *Lycidas*, but *Paradise Lost* encompasses discussion of Natural Law in a more comprehensive fashion than the others.[18] Throughout *Paradise Lost* we find Milton's customary messages clearly if pithily presented. In the stately opening where Milton proposes in his 'advent'rous song' to pursue 'Things unattempted yet in prose or rhyme' (i, 13–16) he is wearing the mantle of one who is able to speak directly from a knowledge of Natural Law, law given to man as a mediating channel for eternal law, and he claims even higher authority if he can trust in inspiration from God:

> what in me is dark
> Illumine, what is low raise and support;
> That to the highth of this great argument
> I may assert Eternal Providence,
> And justify the ways of God to men.                    (i, 22–6)

Unlike the stern figure emerging from Milton's prose, the God of *Paradise Lost* is like a god of equity, one who excels 'In mercy and justice both', 'But mercy first and last shall brightest shine' (iii, 132–3). This makes his jurisdiction akin to Aquinas' concept of Natural Law, and to English equity, although Milton would not accept the background of royal prerogative behind the Court of Chancery, and was, besides, no great public supporter of Aquinas as an authority. Adam correctly reasons that God must be merciful, since it would be unjust if he were to be infinitely vindictive against a creature which, at the very least, is part of his own created, material world: 'that were to extend His sentence beyond dust and Nature's law' (x, 804–5). Raphael has the superior knowledge able to hint at the idea of Natural Law as a medium through which mankind can participate in the eternal:

> what surmounts the reach
> Of human sense, I shall delineate so,
> By likening spiritual to corporal forms,
> As may express them best; though what if Earth
> Be but the shadow of Heaven, and things therein
> Each to other like, more than on earth is thought?      (v, 571–6)

Excluding nobody from his mercy, God foresees the Fall of mankind and proposes to give people not only reason and free choice but 'peace Of conscience, which the law by ceremonies Cannot appease' (xii, 296–8):

> And I will place within them as a guide
> My umpire Conscience, whom if they will hear,
> Light after light well used they shall attain,
> And to the end persisting, safe arrive.                      (iii, 194–7)

This draws upon one of Milton's favoured quotations from Jeremiah, 'I will put my law in their inward parts, and write it in their hearts', as does the later phrase concerning faith, anticipating the coming of Christ:

> but from heav'n
> He to his own a Comforter will send,
> The promise of the Father, who shall dwell,
> His Spirit, within them, and the law of faith
> Working through love, upon their hearts shall write,
> To guide them in all truth, and also arm
> With spiritual armour . . .                                    (xii, 485–91)

The qualification should immediately be added, as throughout this chapter, that, while Milton says that *all* people are given these inward gifts, only some are able to draw upon them in a relatively direct way. For the rest of us, as Calvin and Luther maintained, there must be struggle and uncertainty in rediscovering the clouded capacities. But the explicitness and clarity of Milton's words should force us to rethink any assumption that he is an orthodox Calvinist in believing in the unregenerate nature of fallen man. The archangel Michael speaks of 'high justice' according to 'the law of God' in terms reminiscent again of Luther and Calvin who maintained charity or love as the centre of justice:

> The law of God exact he shall fulfill
> Both by obedience and by love, though love
> Alone fulfill the law.                                        (xii, 402–4)
> . . . add love,
> By name to come called charity, the soul
> Of all the rest . . .                                          (xii, 583)

After the Fall God explains to Christ that he can no longer allow men and women to live in paradise for 'The law I gave to Nature him forbids' (xi, 49). Mankind's sin cannot be allowed to corrupt the very essence of nature, although, as I have stressed throughout, Milton does consistently show a belief in the innate ability of man to choose according to Natural Law. Where Milton differs from Calvinists in degree on this point, is his belief in the possibility of redemption, the regaining of paradise through the rediscovery of Natural Law. The gate is not permanently shut.

So far, these quotations are in line with Milton's prose assertions.

Where the poetry goes further, however, perhaps as an indulgence encouraged and sanctioned by the form, is in representing nature itself, the world of 'natural philosophy', collaborating and enshrining the moral laws at work in paradise and in the world after the Fall, as if 'true' poetry is able itself to collaborate with or enact Natural Law, in the sense suggested by Aquinas. In a moving and beautiful passage Milton invokes 'the book of knowledge fair' inscribed in nature which to him in his blindness (and probably imprisonment) is cut off from his physical senses:

> Thus feed on thoughts that voluntary move
> Harmonious numbers, as the wakeful bird
> Sings darkling, and in shadiest covert hid
> Tunes her nocturnal note. Thus with the year
> Seasons return; but not to me returns
> Day, or the sweet approach of ev'n or morn,
> Or sight of vernal bloom, or summer's rose,
> Or flocks, or herds, or human face divine;
> But cloud instead, and ever-during dark
> Surrounds me, from the cheerful ways of men
> Cut off, and for the book of knowledge fair
> Presented with a universal blank
> Of Nature's works to me expunged and razed,
> And wisdom at one entrance quite shut out.
> So much the rather thou, celestial Light,
> Shine inward, and the mind through all her powers
> Irradiate, there plant eyes, all mist from thence
> Purge and disperse, that I may see and tell
> Of things invisible to mortal sight.                     (iii, 37–55)

Nature's book of knowledge is presented as a model of diurnal rhythms and harmonies, having an equivalent within the human heart which can retrieve from its own resources an inward light. Throughout *Paradise Lost* nature is a part of the moral order. The idyllic scene of prelapsarian innocence is marked by Adam's and Eve's unforced respect for and participation in the principles of growth in burgeoning nature (iv, 205–535) which mirrors their own mutual aid. 'Nature's whole wealth' (iv, 207) surrounds Adam and Eve, who are themselves 'natural' in their unselfconscious nakedness, Eve's hair imaged as 'hyacinthine locks', the golden locks in ringlets that wave 'as the vine curls her tendrils' (iv, 305–7). They spend the day working in perfect concord with nature and with each other, and they sleep when darkness comes, like the growth around them. The 'innocent' love-making scene, a Miltonic depiction of companionship within marriage rather than lust or the conscious desire to propagate, is enwombed by supportive and protective plants and flowers (iv, 688–775), rather like a Samuel Palmer painting. The moment of the Fall itself is seen not only as the betrayal of reason, collaborativeness and innocent freedom, but of nature itself:

> So saying, her rash hand in evil hour
> Forth reaching to the fruit, she plucked, she eat.
> Earth felt the wound, and Nature from her seat
> Sighing through all her works gave signs of woe,
> That all was lost.                                                    (ix, 780–4)
> Earth trembled from her entrails, as again
> In pangs, and Nature gave a second groan;
> Sky loured and, muttering thunder, some sad drops
> Wept at completing of the mortal sin
> Original; . . .                                                        (ix, 1000–4)

Nature's innocence survives the Fall in a way that can shame men:

> If chance the radiant sun with farewell sweet
> Extend his ev'ning beam, the fields revive,
> The birds their notes renew, and bleating herds
> Attest their joy, that hill and valley rings.
> O shame to men! Devil with devil damned
> Firm concord holds, men only disagree
> Of creatures rational, though under hope
> Of heavenly grace; and God proclaiming peace,
> Yet live in hatred, enmity, and strife
> Among themselves, and levy cruel wars,
> Wasting the earth, each other to destroy.                             (ii, 492–502)

Michael, in showing to Adam the future of the world, forecasts first a guarded revival of a state of innocence or at least days spent 'in joy unblamed' and peace; until a second Satan, Nimrod, shall arise and significantly practise the kingly 'sport' of hunting, of preying off nature:

> till one shall rise
> Of proud ambitious heart, who not content
> Will arrogate dominion undeserved
> Over his brethren, and quite dispossess
> Concord and law of Nature from the earth;
> Hunting (and men, not beasts shall be his game)
> With war and hostile snare such as refuse
> Subjection to his empire tyrannous
> A mighty hunter thence he shall be styled.                            (xii, 25–33)

It is no coincidence that the Stuarts had always been renowned for hunting, an activity traditionally despised by humanists such as More and Milton, and in this passage we can glimpse Milton's bitterness at the second political fall that had occurred to Britain at the Restoration.

Admittedly, in *Paradise Lost* we do not find the assertive confidence in Natural Law and the optimism that was evident in Milton's earlier prose works and in *Comus*. His own experiences cannot fail to have made him more cautious, and perhaps more pessimistic. To this extent, by the time of the later poetry, he is more Calvinist in his attitude to the problems involved in believing Natural Law to be innate and recoverable. But recoverable it still is, no matter how hard is the effort. The conclusion of *Paradise Lost* is marked not so much by the tone of 'cold pessimism' detected by Bennett in Milton's later works, but by a hard-won and highly qualified hope out of general sadness. This note is struck in the uneasy serenity of evening mist rising from a river as the labourer, once more brought into some relationship with nature's rhythms, returns home. It is struck in the 'natural tears' shed by Adam and Eve, and in the final image of the human beings now alone and fearful, but at least returning to an ethic of mutual aid and with the capacity to choose their destinies with reference to the Law of Nature, imprinted on their hearts, sadly dimmed to their spiritual insight, but undoubtedly still there:

> The world was all before them, where to choose
> Their place of rest, and Providence their guide:
> They hand in hand, with wand'ring steps and slow,
> Through Eden took their solitary way.                    (xii, 646-9)

# Epilogue: Hobbes and the demise of classical Natural Law

One small event in 1651 probably did more in the long run to eclipse Milton's reputation and the traditional notion of Natural Law upon which he relied than did any institution such as kingship. This was the publication of Thomas Hobbes' *Leviathan*,[1] a book which came to cast an enormous ideological shadow over post-Restoration thought right up to the present day. Indeed, Hobbes has been seen, rightly or wrongly, as the grandfather of the politics of political materialism and pragmatism, the economy of market forces,[2] of possessive individualism, all of which dominated Britain and the USA in the 1980s, as well as of the totalitarianism of 1930s' Germany, Italy, and Japan. Hobbes missed no opportunity to castigate those collectively instrumental in his own time in pursuing civil war, 'thinking it a work of merit to kill, or depose, or to rebel against, the Sovereign Power', but more than this it is his complete redefinition of Natural Law that served gradually to counter the ideas we have been examining. His influence was strengthened later by Bentham, whose corrosive attitude to legal fictions we have observed, and who dismissed Blackstone's version of Natural Law as a 'formidable non-entity' and its reasoning as a 'labyrinth of confusion'.[3]

It is tempting to say sweepingly, as many do, that Hobbes, with Bentham's collaboration, killed Natural Law, and there is some truth in saying he killed at least what it had been up to 1650.

In the hands of Hobbes, therefore, the natural law became, paradoxically enough, a useless law, compressed into the single legal form of the social and governmental contract of subjection ... the extreme consequence of the proposition that law is will.[4]

However, he too argues from a belief in Natural Law, and it must be admitted that his definitions and descriptions are far more detailed than any proposed before him. In reading *Leviathan* we come into contact with a profoundly sceptical mind which is determined to exclude from political science any concept which is less than precise and certain. It may be more cogent to argue, as does Norberto Bobbio, that far from destroying Natural Law, Hobbes pioneered modern Natural Law theory, which has agreed with its medieval counterpart that the right to life is inalienable, but has developed this maxim by assuming not that human beings are sociable by nature, but that they are selfish, isolated individuals,[5] and need protection from each other. This has led to the rather bizarre result of such phenomena as the carrying of guns being justified as 'freedom of the individual', and racial vilification being condoned as 'individual freedom of speech'.

In Hobbes' thought, the first casualty of classical Natural Law theory is conscience: 'Hobbes does not believe in freedom of conscience'.[6] He does not deny the concept of a 'consciousness' which all men hold in common and he says that 'it was and ever will be reputed a very Evil act, for any man to speak against his *Conscience*; or to corrupt or force another so to do' (p. 132), but he deplores the practice which has developed of using 'the same word metaphorically, for the knowledge of their own secret facts, and secret thoughts' in justification of individual opinions:

And last of all, men vehemently in love with their own opinions, (though never so absurd,) and obstinately bent to maintain them, gave those their opinions also that reverenced name of Conscience, as if they would have it seem unlawful, to change or speak against them; and so pretend to know they are true, when they know at most, but that they think so. (*Ibid.*)

This is a sideswipe at Puritans such as Milton who set such stock on individual conscience against external authority, even while, ironically, the words echo both Calvin and Luther who were quoted in earlier chapters saying very similar things about the variability and untrustworthiness of individual consciences. Indeed, one of the things which this book has shown by continual qualification of its central thesis, is that since the Reformation there had been a tradition alive and available which was sceptical of Natural Law in Aquinas' optimistic formulations. Hobbes magisterially restated the contrary argument in its entirety, so powerfully that few chose afterwards to return to Aquinas with any confidence.

After conscience, the second casualty in Hobbes' onslaught, is reason, again as understood by earlier Natural Law theorists. In place of their understanding based on reason as leading us to essential truth, what is reasonable given the primal law of doing unto others only what one would have done unto us, Hobbes substituted a more restrictive sense of reason as calculation, the exercise of deductive logic, based on his beloved geometry and arithmetic. If an argument does not begin from generally agreed naming of things and proceed along the lines of

'*Reckoning* (that is, Adding and Subtracting)' towards 'certainty' which will be unanimously approved, then it cannot be called rational. If Hobbes is to apply these senses of reason and conscience to the substance of Natural Law, it is bound to become very different from Aquinas' and Milton's concept, and in effect, disturbingly close to its opposite.

Hobbes begins from a vision of the individual in society which, it is no exaggeration to say, is diametrically opposed to that held by classical Natural Law theorists. Whereas they stressed a *desire* to contribute to the public good as the major plank of Natural Law, Hobbes presupposes that although 'peace' is paramount, such a *desire* cannot be presupposed. Rather, he argues that men will not be good to one another unless either it is in their own self-interests or they are compelled by a sovereign body to be so. A central passage in *Leviathan* asserts that the desire for peace can be defined only in terms of individual fears and hopes which are largely negative and without idealism:

The Passions that incline men to Peace, are Fear of Death; Desire of such things as are necessary to commodious living; and a Hope by their Industry to obtain them. And Reason suggesteth convenient Articles of Peace, upon which men may be drawn to agreement. These Articles, are they, which otherwise are called the Laws of Nature. (p. 188)

In his discussion, Hobbes sharply reproves those (such as Selden) who in his view confuse Natural Rights (*Jus Naturale*) and Natural Law (*Lex Naturalis*). The former he squarely defines in individualistic terms as 'the Liberty each man hath, to use his own power, as he will himself, for the preservation of his own Nature' (p. 189). Natural Law on the other hand, is a limitation on liberty, because it determines what cannot be done ('shun evil') and binds men to its terms as to an obligation. Hovering behind these definitions is Hobbes' bleak, ruthlessly individualistic vision of the 'state of nature': 'the condition of Man ... is a condition of War of every one against every one' and as long as this is so then nobody can live in security without guaranteed constraints from something outside themselves. Freedom of the individual becomes a far more effective route to the survival of humanity than reliance on fellow-feeling or altruism. His version of Law of Nature, then, is an absolute code which ensures that the preservation of one person's life is not at the expense of another's. People must be *forced* to survive mutually, since they would not do so under their own volition. It is akin to the terms of a truce or ceasefire in war. The two fundamental Laws of Nature are '*to seek Peace, and follow it*' and '*By all means we can, to defend our selves*' – again, the order-based, conservative, and individualistic attitude of those who today argue that citizens should have the right to carry guns. For Hobbes there is no potential conflict between these two, given his overall metaphor of life as a state of war and of men engaged in constant competition. Rather, the one is a check on the other and vice versa. These precepts enable Hobbes to redefine the traditional golden rule as 'That a man be willing ... to be contented with so much liberty against other men, as he would allow other men against himself' (p. 190). He then goes on to tabulate, with far more precision than anybody before, the other Laws of Nature: Justice '(*That men perform their Covenants made*); Gratitude (*That a man which receiveth Benefit from another of mere Grace, Endeavour that he which giveth it, have no reasonable cause to repent him of his good will*)'; 'Compleasance', '(*that every man strive to accommodate himself to the rest*)', and so on, to the requirements of equality and equity. There is even grudging provision for some kind of communalism, for the twelfth Law is '*that such things as cannot be divided, be enjoyed in Common, if it can be*'. Hobbes then reasserts the traditional claim of Natural Law to be eternal, but without the assumption that it resides in the human heart:

The Laws of Nature are Immutable and Eternal; For Injustice, Ingratitude, Arrogance, Pride, Iniquity, Acception of persons, and the rest, can never be made lawful. (p. 215)

All the time, Hobbes' basic aim is to justify absolute monarchy, in the terms set by Cornwall, Gonoril, and Regan: the monarch's will is law, and there is no appeal beyond this.

If a Raphael Hythlodaeus or Aquinas, for example, were to read the sections in *Leviathan* dealing with Natural Law, they would find the experience very baffling. Virtually every conclusion arrived at by Hobbes is exemplary and could compel only assent from all writers from Aquinas to Milton on grounds of strict logic. However, they are derived from an axiom which would be implacably rejected by many earlier thinkers, and they lead to a position justifying absolute power by a sovereign or sovereign body which effectively has as much power as the Christian God who is supposed to have handed down Natural Law. While earlier thinkers hypothesised that people living in a 'natural state' would draw consistently on *inner*, God-given resources of reason and conscience to perform altruistically for the community's good, the Hobbesian state of nature is one of vicious individualism and cut-throat competition, where Natural Law needs to be imposed from outside through positive law in order to compel peace:

For the Laws of Nature (as *Justice, Equity, Modesty, Mercy*, and (in sum) *doing to others, as we would be done to*), of themselves, without the terror of some Power, to cause them to be observed, are contrary to our natural Passions, that carry us to Partiality, Pride, Revenge, and the like. And Covenants, without The Sword, are but Words, and of no strength to secure a man at all. (p. 220)

He paints a nightmarish picture of man in a state of nature as a cynical community without an absolute power, riven with insecurity, theft, growing inequality, cruelty, murder and invasion. No wonder 'the life of man' in a state of nature is described by Hobbes in his memorable phrase as 'solitary, poor, nasty, brutish, and short' (p. 186). The harsh and stern judgments on man's innate fallibility by Calvin are brought to the surface, as is Luther's nominalism, contrary to classical Natural Law's belief that its impulse lies within the human heart and mind. And unlike Luther and Calvin, Hobbes does not except even a body of elect.

We are back almost full circle to the discussion broached in More's *Utopia* about the radical differences created by ideological disagreement, but here the debate is taken about as far as it can go. The nature of underlying assumptions about the world governs subsequent chains of reasoning, and in this case it seems little short of an almost impossible coincidence that final agreement can be reached by the communitarians and the libertarians on the content of Natural Law, since they disagree so radically on whether virtue is compelled from within or without, whether survival of the community or the individual is paramount. Ironically, it was the communitarians (at least as defined in this book) who inadvertently allowed Hobbes' assumptions to dominate cultural discourse. Sidney and Shakespeare, by depicting love as a compulsive feeling that overrides public morality and restrictiveness, show the potential for self-seeking and indvidualistic motives to creep in and take advantage of the vulnerability of communitarian idealism. *King Lear*, while demonstrating so vibrantly virtues of compassion and social altruism, also disconcertingly provides characters who adopt the Hobbesian position that the human world is not *naturally* like this, and that in reality humanity must perforce prey on itself, like creatures of the deep, unless restrained by strong execution of positive law. Indeed, the most telling symptom of the post-Restoration understanding of *King Lear* lies in the fact that Nahum Tate, when he rewrote the play in 1681, opened with Edmund's soliloquy, 'Thou, nature, art my goddess', thus reorientating the play in the wake of Hobbes. Thomas More, if his intention really was to show the supreme merits of living in a state of utopian communism, gives enough evidence of a 'real world' of Machiavellian statecraft to leave Utopia literally nowhere, as an unrealisable fantasy. Even Milton, by his hesitancies over the exact nature of original sin, gives Hobbes ammunition for arguing that Puritan conscience is no more than a rationalised opinion. This leaves Spenser, whose authoritarian, positive law-based analysis seemed so out of step with that of his contemporaries, holding a position which derived from Calvin and culminated in Hobbes.

Hobbes caused a profound revolution (or reaction) in western thinking whose implications reverberate down to the present day. He so successfully and radically confused the traditional understanding of Natural Law that it could never recover, but was destined to exist at best in uncertainty and at worst in dark limbo, unspoken by anybody of note until the late twentieth century. In literary theory after 1660, one consequence was that poetic justice, understood as something instinctive and shared by readers, became disengaged from Natural Law, and instead became akin to Hobbes' supreme sovereign, forcibly coercing recalcitrant 'human nature' away from its incorrigible ways into a sanitised and over-easy moral *schema* of punishment for the guilty, reward for the innocent. Accordingly, all of Shakespeare's plays except *Othello* and *1 Henry IV* were literally rewritten to conform to the expectations of a prescriptive moral code, and ironically to turn him, as Michael Dobson demonstrates, into 'an Enlightenment Cultural hero'.[7] All the moral complexities and ethical participation of an audience making judgments in *Love's Labour's Lost*, *Measure for Measure* and *King Lear*, or the notion of a reader making conscientious judgments as advised in Milton's *Areopagitica*, were swept away in favour of a formal law imposed by the writer (or rather his policeman, the critic) in a newly self-styled 'age of Reason'. 'Nature' itself has a different meaning in literature in a post-Hobbesian age, as is illustrated by a male character in Dryden's *The Enchanted Island* who asserts that for men 'the state of nature' is one of 'war of all against all'.[8] Superficially there is no change in the *terms* of literary theory, since it draws on Aristotelian terminology, and it is even called neo-classicism as if it were a straight revival:

And besides the *purging* of the *passions*, something must stick by observing that constant order, that harmony and beauty of Providence, that necessary relation and chain, whereby the causes and the effects, the virtues and rewards, the vices and their punishments are proportion'd and link'd together, how deep and dark soever are laid the springs and however intricate and involv'd are their operations.[9]

Despite the lip-service to the deep and dark springs of moral evaluation, their intricate and involved operation, there is a disjunction between theory and practice when Rymer, notoriously, came to explain *Othello* by harping on the disobedience of Desdemona: 'the silly woman' (p. 233), her carelessness with linen, and her purported speech modes: 'No woman bred out of a pig-sty could talk so meanly' (p. 248). Rymer condemns the moral patterning of Shakespeare: 'If this be our end, what boots it to be virtuous?' (p. 252), and 'our Poet, against all Justice and Reason, against all Law, Humanity, and Nature, in a barbarous, arbitrary way, executes and makes havock of his subjects' (p. 253). What is evident is not so much crassness, as new and different implied content to words like justice, reason, humanity, and nature, the nomenclature of Natural Law without its substance. Justice has become a simplistic apportioning of rewards and punishments according to prescriptive and dogmatic rules, issued by a sovereign body. Reason has become equated with cause-and-effect rather than practical moral analysis. Humanity and nature are lumped together as talismans of moral *exempla*. No concepts of equity as reasonableness (let alone charity, mercy or even common sense), or conscience, seem available. Not so significant is the Renaissance context of the rhetoric of affective pathos, which awakens the audience's moral outrage, not against the playwright (Rymer's target), but at the shocking injustices against an innocent woman perpetrated by Iago and by his tragically impressionable and vulnerable agent and gull, Othello. Rymer is working from logic and moral certitudes, rather than applying humane reasoning and conscience to the turbulent, fluctuating pattern of Shakespeare's play, and he is also, incidentally, drawing a very sharp distinction between the literary artefact where such rules apply, and 'life', where they do not.

Similarly, Collier uses the rhetoric of Natural Law without its Renaissance conceptual subtlety. Certainly he says that conscience should 'go true' in literature, but he comments on how 'dangerous' it is 'when Vice is varnish'd over with Pleasure, and comes in the Shape of Convenience' for then 'Reason [is] suborn'd against it self'.[10] Admittedly he is speaking not of Shakespeare but of Dryden, but he gives no hint of accepting the earlier theory that audiences and readers are capable and strongly invited to make moral judgments themselves, by way of exercising their innate understanding of the Aquinian version of Natural Law. He may insist that 'Instruction is the principal Design of both [tragedy and comedy]', but his version of instruction is one that leaves no room for a dynamic relationship between audience/reader and the literary action, but asserts from above a set of rules. Under this scheme, Milton would be dismissed for having made Satan too attractive, opening the way for Blake and Shelley to mount their argument. Like Rymer, Collier is writing from a set of Hobbesian assumptions, that people are ignorant, morally corrupt, and need coercive authority to make them distinguish right from wrong: the dramatist for him is as the monarch for Hobbes, a necessary and coercive, authoritarian moralist. The crucial place of Hobbes in a history of the writing and interpretation of English drama and literature has yet to be written.

We live in a post-Hobbesian state, and modern criticism has generally read Renaissance texts from his point of view, assuming that people are 'naturally' wicked, that villains are by definition more attractive than the virtuous because they often get the most colourful poetry, and that the only way some kind of virtue can be introduced into the world is by coercion. Milton would have been horrified to hear the Romantics proclaiming the moral authority of Satan in *Paradise Lost* or modern critics praising the rhetoric of Comus' flawed logic over the Lady's rationality, as I believe More would have at least been bemused to hear generations of teachers, students and even critics proclaim knowingly that Hythlodaeus is advocating practices that deny 'human nature', such as not adorning oneself with rich clothing and maximising social equality by eliminating competition and its root cause, private property.

A Rubicon was crossed with the reception of Hobbes into western thinking. In Thomas Kuhn's term, a paradigm shift was effected, which changed the world as we see and interpret it. This is why a book such as the present one might seem obstinately perverse in trying to recuperate a pre-modern concept of Natural Law, since upon the texts I have examined, so many layers of Hobbesian interpretations have been placed like smothering blankets. Once again, I must emphasise I am not suggesting that Hobbes initiated scepticism, or that before him Natural Law was agreeably monolithic and undisputed, but that, from our vantage-point, 'reading backwards', his presence causes severe difficulties in comprehending earlier attitudes.

In the field of law itself, the Anglo-American world lives, whether we like it or not, in the wake of Victorian Britain, when, as Weber argues, law became an instrumentality of the state, designed to reconcile conflicting interests, shorn of metaphysical, transcendent, or moral reference except in so far as political bodies may choose to address such dimensions. To return to our starting-point, Natural Law can be derided and ignored by common law and legislatures. The only area in which Natural Law arguments sometimes receive notice is when the legitimacy of a government and the authority of its lawmaking powers under unique circumstances are questioned, as happened, for example, tragically after the event, when Nazi law was retrospectively annulled. All this in itself does not prove Natural Law does not exist,[11] or that it is not a cultural inheritance, or that it is irrevocably lost as a mode of thinking. Indeed, in some fields there are signs of change in the 1990s, and the inveterately optimistic may feel that the wheel of paradigm is shifting slowly but surely once again. In jurisprudential quarters, Natural Law is once again a respectable and increasingly mainstream topic for discussion as a bastion against the whimsicalities and changes of political fashions. Proposals for Bills of Rights and Citizens' Charters are seen as potential vote-winners in elections in western countries, and although they are couched in individualistic terms there is at least evidence that fundamental questions are being re-addressed. Sharp practices of 'big business' which used to be condoned as 'natural', competitive behaviour, are being flushed out and condemned, turning the tide against the habit of hero-worshipping millionaires as exemplary individualists. Even at governmental levels, a new urgency and seriousness has entered the debate about preserving the environment for future custody, rather than exploiting it for short-term, individual profit, or using the logic of various 'freedoms' to exploit private property as justification. Even the specific language of Aquinas is being used by people who have almost certainly never read him, that we hold property only in stewardship, and must do no more than 'use' it accordingly, with some view to the 'needs' of future generations. Technological advances are increasingly suspected rather than hailed, as news of the dangers of radioactive waste and accidents 'leaks' out, and as the irrationality of reliance upon genocidal nuclear weapons for 'defensive' purposes is increasingly recognised. All these perceptions stem from the reactivation of human faculties which the Renaissance Natural Law theorists held supreme: reason, conscience, equity; placing community 'needs' above the individual's liberties, co-operation and mutual survival above competition and self-destruction, people above institutions. Above all, as the stakes of human survival, which was at the heart of Natural Law, come to be perceived as so high, the term crucial to Natural Law, 'necessity', is returning to moral and political debate. If such a paradigm shift is occurring, and if this book has moved one stone as the boulders begin to roll, then it will have confirmed that we can still learn from history, historical jurisprudence, and imaginative literature of the Renaissance and its cultural sources, if we are willing to listen and to read with our minds open to earlier understandings.

# Appendix: Aquinas on the right to own private property[*]

Aquinas' deliberations on the right to own private property provide a good example of his dialectical reasoning which is the same in every section of the *Summa Theologica*. First he always presents the argument against, usually in three statements:

It would seem that private property is not lawful. For whatever is contrary to the natural law is unlawful. Now according to the natural law all things are held in common, and the possession of property is contrary to this community of goods. Therefore it is unlawful for any man to appropriate any external thing to himself. Secondly, the words of the rich man already quoted are expounded by Basil (Homily on Luke xii, 18) as follows: the rich who reckon that the common goods they have seized are their own properties are like those who go in advance to the theatre excluding others and appropriating to themselves what is intended for common use. Now it would be unlawful to obstruct others from laying their hands on common goods. Therefore it is unlawful to appropriate to oneself what belongs to the community.

Thirdly, Ambrose says, (*Sermo lxix, de tempore*) and he is quoted in the Decretals: (Dist. xivii) let no man call his own that which is common. That he is speaking of external things appears from the context. Therefore it seems unlawful for a man to appropriate an external thing to himself.

Next he presents the orthodox argument for private property, and it must be said that, in contrast to the firm and lucid arguments against, the one given for seems limp and glib, the kind of arid use of logical cleverness which has given Aquinas' followers, the 'schoolmen' a bad name. But Aquinas himself expresses neither approval nor disapproval:

But on the contrary Augustine writes of the Apostolics, or those who gave themselves that name with extreme arrogance, who did not admit into communion persons who use marriage or possess property of their own, people such as monks and many clerics in the Catholic Church. The reason why these Apostolics were heretics was that they separated themselves from the Church by allowing no hope of salvation to those who enjoyed the use of these things which they themselves went without. Therefore it is erroneous to maintain that it is unlawful for a man to possess property.

[*] All quotations are from *Summa*, 29–29e.

252

Aquinas next states his own position, and it repays patient analysis:

In explanation let me declare that two elements enter into human competence in appropriating external things, the administration and the enjoyment. The first is the power to take care of them and manage them, and here it is lawful for one man to possess property: indeed it is necessary for human living and on three grounds. First, because each man is more careful in looking after what is in his own charge than what is common to many or to all; in the latter case each would shirk the work and leave to another that which concerns the community, as we see when there is a great number of servants. Secondly, because human affairs are conducted in a more orderly fashion when each man is charged with taking care of some particular thing himself, whereas there would be confusion if anyone took charge of anything indeterminately. Thirdly, because a more peaceful state is preserved when each man is contented with what is his own. Hence we observe that quarrels arise more frequently among people who share in common and without division of goods.

The second element in human competence concerns the enjoyment of material things. Here man ought to possess them, not as his own, but as common, to the extent of being ready to communicate them to others in their need. Hence St Paul says: *Charge the rich of this world to give easily, to communicate to others, &c.* (1 Tim. vi. 17–18).

Despite its apparent – if hedging – approval of private property, Aquinas could be cited by Raphael as supporting utopian 'communism'. Boiled down to an essence, Aquinas is saying that a man may own an object so long as he is properly using it as a good steward for God. When he is not using it (or presumably is misusing it for purposes unrelated to 'human benefit') then he ought to give it to others who 'need' it. Raphael's whole argument insists that need and use are the primary, not secondary considerations. Those who need and can use things should have possession of them, and 'The Utopians think it is hardly right to take what they don't need away from people who do need it' (p. 61). The question of ownership need not then be addressed, since it is at best provisional and temporary, indistinguishable from possession. Property is held in common by mankind as a corporate stewardship, and may be distributed into private hands according to Aquinas' own priorities of proper, rational utilisation of the object, and of personal need. Within this general framework Raphael shoots a hole in Aquinas' apparently persuasive example that 'each man is more careful in looking after what is in his own charge than what is common to all' by saying that this is a loose or confused use of the phrase 'common to all'. The whole utopian scheme is founded on the twin premises that, if property is regarded as common to all, then only those who need or can best use objects will be entitled to them or actually want them, and that by eliminating the concept of ownership we automatically and self-evidently eliminate the sins of greed and laziness referred to by Aquinas. Raphael himself points out, in what appears to be a direct refutation of one of Aquinas' points, that it is not common ownership which leads to squabbles, but private property which creates contested titles, 'innumerable and interminable lawsuits, fresh ones every day'. Although the utopian system would put lawyers out of work, More himself, when he became chancellor, inherited an enormous backlog of cases in all the legal courts which, he might have wryly noticed, would be alleviated by a dose of utopianism.

A utopian reading of Aquinas, then, would say that his overall answer to his question is exactly the utopian's answer, and that he has been sidetracked by anecdotal example into not strictly following the force of his own logic to its root. Aquinas finally offers replies to each of the first three objections, but again utopians could use his words. He states that,

Community of goods is attributed to the natural law, not in the sense that natural law dictates that all possessions should be common and that nothing should be possessed as one's own, but in the sense that the division of possessions is not made by natural law but by human agreement, which belongs to positive law.

# Notes

PREFACE

1 Richard Hooker, *Ecclesiastical Polity*, I. viii. 9.
2 Norberto Bobbio, *Thomas Hobbes and the Natural Law Tradition*, trans. Daniela Gobetti (Chicago and London, 1993, first pub. in Italian, 1989), p. 2.
3 Jeffrey Stout, 'Truth, Natural Law, and Ethical Theory', in *Natural Law Theory: Contemporary Essays*, ed. Robert P. George (Oxford, 1992), pp. 71–104, p. 72.
4 *The Idea of Conscience in Renaissance Tragedy* (London and New York, 1990).
5 *The High Design: English Renaissance Tragedy and the Natural Law* (Lexington, Kentucky, 1970).
6 Robert Hoopes, *Right Reason in the English Renaissance* (Cambridge, Massachusetts, 1962).
7 Constance Jordan, *Renaissance Feminism: Literary Texts and Political Models* (Ithaca and London, 1990), p. 66.


1 NATURAL LAW IN HISTORY AND RENAISSANCE LITERATURE

1 *The Dictionary of English Law*, ed. Earl Jowitt and Clifford Walsh (London, 1959).
2 *Summa*, 1a 2ae, 95, 2. All quotations from Aquinas, unless otherwise signalled, come from St Thomas Aquinas, *Summa Theologiae* (London and New York in 61 vols., 1963–81), especially vol. 28.
3 A. P. d'Entrèves, *Natural Law: An Historical Survey* (London, 1951) p. 7. In many ways I acknowledge this work as the one that made me think of writing this book.
4 Hugo Grotius, *De Jure Belli ac Pacis Libri Tres* (1625) I. I. xii. I, trans. F. W. Kelsey (New York, 1964): see Stephen Buckle, *Natural Law and the Theory of Property: Grotius to Hume* (Oxford, 1991), p. 5.
5 Francis Bacon, *Of the Coulers of Good and Evill. A Fragment (1597)*, in *The Works of Francis Bacon*, ed. James Spedding *et al.* (London, 1859), vol. 7.
6 George C. Herndl, *The High Design: English Renaissance Tragedy and the Natural Law* (Lexington, 1970), p. 86.
7 Robert Hoopes, *Right Reason in the English Renaissance* (Cambridge, Massachusetts, 1962), p. 5.

8    'Just as even God cannot cause that two times two should not make four, so He cannot cause that that which is intrinsicially evil be not evil.' *De Jure Belli ac Pacis*, I. i. x. quoted d'Entrèves, *Natural Law*, p. 53.

9    *Natural Law and Natural Rights* (Oxford, 1980), p. 351. I attendeded Finnis' lectures on jurisprudence at Adelaide University in 1971, which were an early version of his book, and they made me aware of Natural Law for the first time.

10   *Treatise of Human Nature,* III. ii, 'Of Justice and Injustice', quoted in Hart *Concept of Law*, p. 187.

11   *Biathanatos*, vol. 1. p. 36.

12   McCabe, *Incest, Drama and Nature's Law 1550–1700* (Cambridge, 1993).

13   *Ibid.,* p. 60.

14   'Upon Appleton House', stanza 73.

15   F. C. Copleston, *Aquinas* (Harmondsworth, 1955), p. 214.

16   Heinrich A. Rommen, *The Natural Law: A Study in Legal and Social History and Philosophy* , trans. Thomas R. Hanley (London, 1947), p. 82.

17   'Letter from Birmingham City Jail', in *A Testament of Hope: The Essential Writings of Martin Luther King Jr.*, ed. James Melvin Washington (San Francisco, 1986), p. 293.

18   A. P. d'Entrèves, *Natural Law*, pp. 84–7.

19   See Introduction by M. A. Screech to his edition of *The Essays of Michel de Montaigne* (London, 1987).

20   Montaigne, *Essays*, p. 201.

21   Herndl, *The High Design*, p. 287, quoting from 'Apology for Raymond de Sebonde'.

22   'On the affection of fathers for their children'.

23   Hoopes, *Right Reason*, pp. 163–4. But see the outstanding and virtually definitive book by Stephen Gaukroger, *Descartes: An Intellectual Biography* (Oxford, 1995), who finds no concern whatsoever with scepticism in Descartes' writing before 1630, no evidence of a sceptical crisis of any kind. 'His interest in scepticism was relatively late, and took shape in the context of providing a metaphysical legitimation of his natural philosophy'; and even then scepticism was not used to assert the separation of the material and metaphysical, but to establish the natural as metaphysical (pp. 11–12).

24   H. L. A. Hart, *The Concept of Law* (Oxford, 1961), pp. 181–95.

25   *Appeal cases* [1915] 120–51, Local Government Board v. Arlidge, Lord Shaw, p.138.

26   *Ridge v. Baldwin* [1963] 2 All ER 66 at 71.

27   See Geoffrey A. Flick, *Natural Justice: Principles and Practical Applications* (second edition, Sydney, 1984).

28   See, for example, Robert Nozick, *Anarchy, State, and Utopia* (Oxford, 1974).

29   See the debates in John Rawls, *A Theory of Justice* (Oxford, 1971) and Stephen Mulhall and Adam Swift, *Liberals and Communitarians* (Oxford, 1992).

30   I am referring to the curious phenomenon of the Natural Law Party which has stood candidates in elections at least in Britain and Australia and probably elsewhere in the 1990s. It is, I should add, very different from the version of Natural Law dealt with in this book.

31 Although Fuller believes agreement could be reached on a kind of 'meta-law', laws about how to make laws. See Lon L. Fuller, *The Morality of Law* (New Haven and London, 1964).

32 Aquinas, *Summa*, vol. 28, p. 165.

33 George W. Keeton, *Shakespeare's Legal and Political Background* (London, 1967), p. 67.

## 2 THE HERITAGE OF CLASSICAL LAW

1 Quotations are from *Early Greek Philosophy*, translated and edited by Jonathan Barnes (Harmondsworth, 1987), p. 115.

2 Published in German in 1936, translated by Thomas R. Hanley (London, 1947).

3 Rommen, *Natural Law*, pp. 7 and 8.

4 See Rosalie Colie, *Paradoxica Epidemica: The Renaissance Tradition of Paradox* (Princeton, New Jersey, 1966).

5 *The Works of Aristotle,* ed. W. D. Ross (Oxford, 1915), vol. 9.

6 Eden, Kathy, *Poetic and Legal Fiction in the Aristotelian Tradition* (Princeton, New Jersey, 1986).

7 *De Legibus*, trans. C. W. Keyes (Loeb Classical Library), *Cicero*, vol. 28, (Cambridge Massachusetts and London, 1977), pp. 318–19.

8 *De Re Publica*, XXII, p. 211.

9 See John F. Danby, *Shakespeare's Doctrine of Nature. A Study of 'King Lear'* (London, 1949).

10 See *The Elements of Roman Law with a translation of Institutes of Justinian*, by R. W. Lee (fourth edition, London, 1956), pp. 25–7.

11 Barry Nicholas, *An Introduction to Roman Law* (Oxford, 1962), p. 35.

12 *Ibid.*, p. 54.

13 Lee, *Elements*, p. 43.

14 *Ibid.*, p. 44.

15 J. Walter Jones, *Historical Introduction to the Theory of Law* (Oxford, 1940), p. 103.

16 Nicholas, *Introduction*, pp. 54–9.

17 Finnis, *Natural Law and Natural Rights* (above) deals thoroughly with this issue.

18 Quoted Rommen, *Natural Law*, pp. 12–13, from George Young's translation.

19 Harold J. Berman, *Law and Revolution: The Formation of the Western Legal Tradition* (Cambridge, Massachusetts, 1983), p. 143.

20 *Ibid.*, p. 145.

21 *Ibid.*, p. 146.

22 Finnis, *Natural Law and Natural Rights*, pp. 401–2.

23 On this concept, see Robert A. Greene, 'Synderesis, the Spark of Conscience, in the English Renaissance', *Journal of the History of Ideas*, 52 (1991), 195–219, and John S. Wilks, *The Idea of Conscience in Renaissance Tragedy* (London and New York, 1990).

24 Rawls' 'goodness as rationality', p. 423; Finnis' 'practical reasonableness'. See also Hoopes, *Right Reason (passim)*.

25 The phrase is Finnis', *Natural Law and Natural Rights*, p. 94.

26  Rommen, *Natural Law*, p. 51.

27  Appendix to *Summa*, p. 171.

28  *Ibid*, p. 168, referring to *Summa* 1a 2ae, 85, 1 and 2.

29  1–11, 1. 95, a. 2c; trans. Finnis, *Natural Law and Natural Rights*, p. 284.

30  Herndl discusses Platonism and the Renaissance in its relation to Natural Law, at various points in his book, *The High Design: English Renaissance Tragedy and the Natural Law* (Lexington, 1970).

31  Gilby, Commentary in Aquinas edition, p. 167.

32  Francis Oakley, 'Medieval Theories of Natural Law: William of Ockham and the Significance of the Voluntarist Tradition', *Natural Law Forum*, 6 (1961), 65–83. I am cheered by Alister E. McGrath in *Reformation Thought: An Introduction* (second edition, Oxford and Cambridge, USA, 1993) who acknowledges the 'utter tedium' and irreducible complexity of distinctions between different types of Scholasticism (p. 71).

33  McCabe, *Incest, Drama and Nature's Law*, pp. 59–60; given that McCabe is examining not the theory itself but one very volatile application of it in incest, his conclusions are understandable.

34  Appendix to Aquinas edition, p. 169.

35  J. Walter Jones, *Historical Introduction to the Theory of Law* (Oxford, 1940), p. 105.

36  Finnis, *Natural Law and Natural Rights*, pp. 43–4.

37  Luther, *The Works of Martin Luther* (Philadelphia, 1930), pp. 16, 22.

38  Quoted from *Martin Luther*, ed. John Dillenberger (New York, 1961), p. 401.

39  *Works,* 13, pp. 160–1.

40  'Secular Authority: To What Extent it Should be Obeyed', *Works,* 3, 231–71.

41  C. A. Patrides, *Milton and the Christian Tradition* (Oxford, 1966), p. 101.

42  The edition used here is *Calvin: Institutes of the Christian Religion*, ed. John T. McNeill (in 2 vols., Philadelphia, 1967).

43  *Institutes*, 2. 8. 1.

44  *Institutes*, 2. 2. 18.

45  Commentary on Genesis, 26:10; William J. Bouwsma, *John Calvin: A Sixteenth Century Portrait* (New York and Oxford, 1988), p. 75.

46  *Institutes*, 4. 10. 3.

47  *Ibid.*, 4. 10. 5

48  McCabe, *Incest, Drama and Nature's Law*, p. 62.

49  Commentary on Leviticus, 18:6.

50  Bouwsma, *John Calvin*, p. 75. See also John T. McNeill, 'Natural Law in the Teaching of the Reformers', *Journal of Religion,* 26 (1946), 168–82.

51  Greene, 'Synderesis', p. 203.

52  *Institutes*, quoted in Greene 'Synderesis', p. 205.

53  *Institutes*, 4. 10. 5.

54  Wilks, *The Idea of Conscience*, p. 26.

55  Herndl, *The High Design*, p. 159 and *passim*.

3  THE RECEPTION OF NATURAL LAW IN RENAISSANCE ENGLAND

1  *Bracton on the Laws and Customs of England*, ed. George E. Woodbine, trans. Samuel E. Thorne (Cambridge, Massachusetts, 1968).

2  Rot. Parl. v. 6226.
3  Sir John Fortescue, *De Natura Legis Naturae*, reprinted in 1869 by Thomas (Fortescue) Lord Clermont, ed. David S. Berkowitz and Samuel E. Thorne (New York and London, 1980), p. 193.
4  Richard O'Sullivan, 'The Natural Law and Common Law', *University of Notre Dame Natural Law Proceedings*, 3 (1950), pp. 9–44.
5  R. C. van Caenegem, *The Birth of the English Common Law* (second edition, Cambridge, 1973, 1988).
6  Sir Charles Ogilvie, *The King's Government and the Common Law 1471–1641* (Oxford, 1958), p. 40.
7  S. F. C. Milsom, *Historical Foundations of the Common Law* (London, 1969), p. 83.
8  Maria L. Cioni, *Women and Law in Elizabethan England. With Particular Reference to the Court of Chancery*, PhD (1974) for Cambridge University, (reprinted New York and London, 1985).
9  *Sir Edward Coke and the Grievances of the Commonwealth* (Manchester, 1979).
10 See Louis A. Knafla, *Law and Politics in Jacobean England: The Tracts of Lord Chancelllor Ellesmere* (Cambridge, 1977), pp. 160–1.
11 Ogilvie, *The King's Government and the Common Law*, p. 90.
12 Milsom, *Historical Foundations*, p. 84
13 Louis A. Knafla, *Law and Politics in Jacobean England* (Cambridge, 1977), p. 216.
14 Coke upon Littleton 976, Michael Lobbon, *The Common Law and English Jurisprudence 1760–1850* (Oxford, 1991), p. 4.
15 Gough, *Fundamental Law in English Constitutional History* (Oxford, 1955, 1961), chapter 3 on Coke and Natural Law.
16 1530, quoted in Ogilvie, *The King's Government and the Common Law*, p. 30.
17 S. E. Thorne, *Essays in English Legal History* (London and Ronceverte, 1985), p. 209 no reference given.
18 Francis Bacon, *The Elements of the Common Laws of England* (London, 1630), B2v.
19 Cioni, *Women and Law in Elizabethan England*, p. 6.
20 'Twelve Silly Men? The Trial at Assizes, 1560–1670', in Green, *Twelve Good Men and True. The Criminal Trial Jury in England, 1200–1800*, ed. J. S. Cockburn and Thomas A. Green (Princeton, New Jersey, 1988), pp. 158–81.
21 *Ibid.*, p. 376 and *passim*. For further analysis see Thomas Andrew Green, *Verdict According to Conscience: Perspectives on the English Criminal Trial Jury, 1200–1800* (Chicago and London, 1985).
22 Green, *Twelve Good Men and True*, chapter 5, especially pp. 166–7.
23 Saint German, *Doctor and Student*, ed. T. F. T. Plucknett and J. L. Barton (Selden Society, London, 1974).
24 See Martin Wiggins, *Journeymen in Murder: The Assassin in English Renaissance Drama* (Oxford, 1991).
25 Paul Vinogradoff, 'Reason and Conscience in Sixteenth–Century Jurisprudence', *Law Quarterly Review*, 24 (1908), pp. 373–84, p. 377.
26 Milsom, *Historical Foundations of the Common Law*, p. 80.
27 *2 State Trials*, 663–4.

28  See Richard J. Terrill, 'William Lambarde: Elizabethan Humanist and Legal Historian', *Journal of Legal History*, 6 (1985), 157–78.

29  W. Nicholas Knight, 'Equity, *The Merchant of Venice* and William Lambarde', *Shakespeare Survey*, 27 (1974), 93–104.

30  Preface and first four books published in 1593, the rest posthumously in 1648 and 1661–2.

31  Edition used is Richard Hooker, *Of the Laws of Ecclesiastical Polity: An Abridged Edition*, ed. A. S. McGrade and Brian Vickers (London, 1975).

32  See the excellent account given by W. D. J. Cargill Thompson, 'The Philosopher of the "Politic Society": Richard Hooker as a Political Thinker', in *Studies in Richard Hooker: Essays Preliminary to an Edition of his Works*, ed. W. Speed Hill (Cleveland and London, 1972), pp. 3–76.

33  John S. Marshall, *Hooker and the Anglican Tradition: An Historical and Theological Study of Hooker's Ecclesiastical Polity* (London, 1963), p. 12.

34  See H. C. Porter, 'Hooker, The Tudor Constitution, and the *Via Media*', in W. Speed Hill (ed.), *Studies in Richard Hooker* (above), pp. 77–116.

35  'Throughout the *Laws*, Hooker borrowed freely from a wide range of writers, and his debt to Aquinas was certainly no greater than his debt to Aristotle or Whitgift', writes W. D. J. Cargill Thompson in 'The Philosopher of the "Politic Society" ' (above), p. 22.

36  *A Learned Sermon of the Nature of Pride*, Oxford, 1612, p. 5; quoted Patrides, *Milton and the Christian Tradition* (Oxford, 1966), p. 83.

37  Francis Bacon, *The Advancement of Learning* and *New Atlantis*, ed. Arthur Johnston (Oxford, 1974), pp. 200–1.

38  Try as I might, I could not shape my analysis of Spenser's *The Faerie Queene*, Book 5 into a chapter on its own. This surprised me, because it is a complete work dealing with the material of this book, but still it defied overall structuring in the terms I am adopting. After the twentieth draft I exploded the chapter and sent shards and splinters flying into other sections of the book and beyond.

39  Michael O'Connell in A. C. Hamilton, *The Spenser Encyclopedia* (Toronto and London, 1990), p. 281.

40  For an analysis that focuses on Artegall's human weaknesses, see T. K. Dunseath, *Spenser's Allegory of Justice in Book Five of 'The Faerie Queene'* (Princeton, New Jersey, 1976).

41  Jane Aptekar in *Icons of Justice: Iconography and Thematic Imagery in Book V of 'The Faerie Queene'* (New York, 1969) argues for the centrality of the Hercules allusion.

42  See Donald Cheney, *Spenser's Image of Nature: Wild Man and Shepherd in 'The Faerie Queene'* (New Haven and London, 1966), for fuller analysis of this *topos*, although he does not analyse Natural Law in any detail.

43  In A. C. Hamilton *The Spenser Encyclopedia* (Toronto and London, 1990), p. 281.

44  See Cioni, *Women and Law in Elizabethan England* (above).

45  'The Narrative Unity of Book V of *The Faerie Queene*: "That part of Justice which is Equity" ', *Review of English Studies*, n.s., 21 (1970), 267–94, p. 292.

46  See Cioni, *Women and Law in Elizabethan England* (above).

47 Donald Cheney, *Spenser's Image of Nature: Wild Man and Shepherd in 'The Faerie Queene'* (New Haven and London, 1966), p. 160.

48 Perhaps I am too harsh on Spenser's attitude to women. For a counter-statement, see Pamela Joseph Benson, *The Invention of the Renaissance Woman: The Challenge of Female Independence in the Literature and Thought of Italy and England* (Pennsylvania, 1992), chapter 11. Benson reads Book V as primarily allegorising the superiority of feminine rule over masculine, but she seems to me to gloss over some of the problems raised in the text.

49 This makes Pamela Joseph Benson's judgment questionable, though it has a superficial appeal: 'Mercilla, the ideal representative of the alternate feminine order in power, simultaneously enforces justice and feels "the wretched plight" of her whom she must judge, unlike Artegall, who is consumed by his "zeale of Iustice"' (V. ix. 49). Benson, *the Invention of the Renaissance Woman*, p. 304. The problem is that Mercilla does not really 'enforce justice'.

50 Cheney, *Spenser's Image of Nature*, p. 167.

51 *Ibid.*, p. 160.

4  LAW AND LITERATURE IN SIXTEENTH-CENTURY ENGLAND

1 Puttenham: *The Arte of English Poesie*, 1589, quoted G. Gregory Smith, *Elizabethan Critical Essays*, (2 vols. 1904), vol. 2, pp. 7–8; modernised spelling adopted here as elsewhere.

2 George Puttenham, *The Arte of English Poesie*, ed. Gladys Doidge Willcox and Alice Walker (Cambridge, 1936) p. xxii.

3 Wilfrid R. Prest, *The Inns of Court under Elizabeth I and the Early Stuarts 1590–1640* (London, 1972).

4 S. F. Johnson, *Early Elizabethan Tragedies of the Inns of Court* (Harvard Dissertations in American and English Literature, ed. Stephen Orgel: New York and London, 1987).

5 Philip J. Finkelpearl, *John Marston of the Middle Temple. An Elizabethan Dramatist in his Social Setting* (Cambridge, Massachusetts, 1969).

6 Johnson, *Early Elizabethan Tragedy*, p. 6.

7 'Gascoigne's Woodmanship', *The Posies*, ed. John W Cunliffe (Cambridge, 1907), p. 348.

8 Finkelpearl, *John Marston*, p. 24 .

9 Francis Lenton, *Characterismi* (1631) sig. F4, quoted in Prest, *Inns of Court*, pp. 137–8.

10 Sir Richard Baker, *A Chronicle of the Kings of England* (London, 1696), p. 450 quoted Finkelpearl, *John Marston*, p. 29.

11 Robert Potter, 'Divine and Human Justice', in *Aspects of Early English Drama*, ed. Paula Neuss (Cambridge, 1983), pp. 129–141, p. 133.

12 J. H. Baker, *An Introduction to English Legal History* (London, 1971), pp. 88–90.

13 *The Mirror for Magistrates*, ed. Lily B. Campbell (Cambridge, 1938). Page references are to this edition.

14 (Princeton, New Jersey, 1988).

15 See the voluminous books by James J. Murphy, cited in the Bibliography.

16 Brian Vickers, '"The Power of Persuasion": Images of the Orator, Elyot to

Shakespeare', in *Renaissance Eloquence*, ed. James J. Murphy, pp. 411–35, pp. 876ff.

17  Kathy Eden, *Poetic and Legal Fiction in the Aristotelian Tradition* (Princeton, New Jersey, 1986).

18  Potter, 'Divine and Human Justice', p. 134.

19  For a slight difference of opinion on this matter, compare Eden's account with that of Martin Wiggins, *Journeymen in Murder: The Assassin in English Renaissance Drama* (Oxford, 1991).

20  *De Ratione Dicendi*, Loeb edition, ed. Harry Caplan (London and Cambridge, Massachusetts, 1954), p. 5.

21  *Institutio Oratoria*, Loeb edition, ed. H. E. Butler (London and Cambridge Massachusetts, in 4 vols., 1920), vol. 1, p. 339.

22  See Vickers, 'The Power of Persuasion'.

23  Murphy, *Renaissance Rhetoric*, p. 90.

24  *Ibid.*, p. 58.

25  Facsimile, (Amsterdam, 1977).

26  Ed. R. H. Bowers, (Gainesville, 1962).

27  Johnson, *Early Elizabethan Tragedies*, pp. 518ff.

28  See R. S. White, *Innocent Victims: Poetic Injustice in Shakespearean Tragedy* (second edition, London, 1986).

29  R. J. Schoeck, 'Rhetoric and Law in Sixteenth-Century England', *Studies in Philology*, 50 (1953),110–27, p. 119.

30  Jeremy Bentham, *The Theory of Fictions*, ed. C. K. Ogden (London, 1932), Appendix A, p. 141.

31  Coke used this phrase – *fictio cessat ubi cessat aequitas … in omni fictione inest aequitas naturalis*, but he was preceded by Bartolus, the report of *Liford's Case*, and Blackstone: see Jones, *Historical Introduction to the Theory of Law*, p. 164, fn.

32  Peter Birks, 'Fictions Ancient and Modern', *The Legal Mind. Essays of Tony Honoré*, ed. Neil MacCormick and Peter Birks (Oxford, 1986), pp. 83–101.

33  Jones, *Historical Introduction to the Theory of Law*, p. 173.

34  Lon L. Fuller, *Legal Fictions* (Stanford, California, 1967), p. 9.

35  Earl Jowitt and Clifford Walsh, *The Dictionary of English Law* (London, 1959).

36  P. G. Osborn, *A Concise Law Dictionary* (London, 1964).

37  Lee, *Roman Law* (see chapter 2, n. 10, above) p. 9.

38  Gaius 3. 194: (my italics), quoted Birks, 'Fictions Ancient and Modern', p. 86.

39  On the general topic of legal and poetic fictions, see Owen Barfield, 'Poetic Diction and Legal Fiction' in *Essays Presented to Charles Williams*, ed. C. S. Lewis (Oxford, 1947).

40  The classic statement on this subject is F. W. Maitland's *The Forms of Action at Common Law* (Cambridge, 1954).

41  Milson, *Historical Foundations of the Common Law*, pp. 56–7, p. 137 and *passim*.

42  Bentham, *Theory of Fictions*, p. 147, fn.

43  Hans Vaihinger, *Philosophie des Als Ob*, trans. C. K. Ogden, *The Philosophy of 'As If'* (London, 1924).

44  Birks 'Fictions Ancient and Modern', p. 84.

45 See again Barfield, 'Poetic Diction and Legal Fiction'.

46 Gregory Smith, *Elizabethan Critical Essays*, vol. 1, p. 45.

47 John Rainolds, *Oratio in Laudem Artis Poeticae,* English trans. Walter Allen Jr., Introduction and commentary William Ringler (Princeton, 1940), p. 43.

48 Sir Philip Sidney, *A Defence of Poetry* in *Miscellaneous Prose of Sir Philip Sidney* ed. Katherine Duncan-Jones and Jan van Dorsten (Oxford, 1973). All page references in this section are to this edition.

49 *The Registry of Admissions to Gray's Inn, 1521–1889,* by Joseph Foster (Hansard, London, 1859), p. 37.

50 *Dictionary of National Biography*, vol. 18, p. 220.

51 Katherine Duncan-Jones, *Sir Philip Sidney. Courtier Poet* ( London, 1991), p. 39.

52 S. Parnell Kerr, 'Philip Sidney: Graian', *Graya,* 41 (1955), 48–52.

53 See A. P. d'Entrèves, *Natural Law: An Historical Survey*, p. 86.

54 For a thorough examination of the idea of poet as maker, see S. K. Heninger Jr., *Sidney and Spenser: The Poet as Maker* (Pennsylvania and London, 1989).

55 For more on this subject, see Eden, *Poetic and Legal Fiction* throughout.

56 Aquinas, *Summa*, Art. 1, Qu. 93, d'Entrèves' selection.

57 S. K. Heninger, *Sidney and Spenser: The Poet as Maker* (Pennsylvania and London, 1989), p. 290.

58 The case of the unfortunate John Stubbs who suffered this fate is most recently summarised in Leonard Tennenhouse's *Power on Display: The Politics of Shakespeare's Genres* (Methuen, New York and London, 1986).

59 See the chapter on Spenser in David Norbrook, *Poetry and Politics in the English Renaissance* (Routledge, London, 1984).

60 See John N. King, *Spenser's Poetry and the Reformation Tradition* (Princeton, New Jersey, 1990).

61 Eden, *Poetic and Legal Fiction*, pp. 47–8.

5 MORE'S *UTOPIA*

1 The text quoted is Thomas More, *Utopia*, ed. George M. Logan and Robert M. Adams (Cambridge, 1989).

2 See the excellent introduction by J. H. Hexter to St Thomas More, *Utopia, The Complete Works of St Thomas More*, ed. Edward Surtz S.J., and J. H. Hexter (New Haven and London, 1965), vol. 4. Alistair Fox in *Utopia: an Elusive Vision* (New York, 1993), surveys the range of approaches, as (more selctively) does George M. Logan in 'Interpreting *Utopia*: Ten Recent Studies and The Modern Critical Traditions', *Moreana*, 31 (1994), pp. 204–58.

3 Stephen Greenblatt, *Renaissance Self-Fashioning from More to Shakespeare* (Chicago, 1980).

4 Quentin Skinner, *Foundations of Modern Political Thought* (in 2 vols., Cambridge, 1978), vol. 1, p. 216.

5 Alistair Fox, *'Utopia': An Elusive Vision* (New York, 1993).

6 *The German Ideology,* ed. and trans. S. Ryazanskaya, London, 1965, p.50: quoted by Dominic Baker-Smith, *More's 'Utopia'* (London, 1991).

7 George Woodcock, *Anarchism* (Harmondsworth, 1963), *passim*.

8  *Lyfe of St Thomas More* (reprinted Oxford, 1935), p. 22.
9  R. J. Schoeck, 'Common Law and Canon Law' in *St Thomas More: Action and Contemplation*, ed. Richard S. Sylvester (New Haven and London, 1972), pp. 17–55.
10 Hexter, *Utopia*, p. xv.
11 Baker-Smith, *More's 'Utopia'*, chapter 6.
12 Edmund Spenser, *A View of the Present State of Ireland*, ed. W. L. Renwick (Clarendon Press, Oxford, 1970), pp. 82–3.
13 *Republic*, Loeb edition, 311.
14 Loeb edition 739 B–D.
15 *Pol.* II, 2:1263a26, 38–9: quoted Finnis, *Natural Law and Natural Rights*, p. 171.
16 *Octavia*, u. 402: see Buckle, *Natural Law and the Theory of Property* (Oxford, 1991), p. 12.
17 I found this snippet of information in the unusual context of the *Guardian*, 27 July 92, in the 'Notes and Queries' column.
18 Hexter, *Utopia*, p. cx.
19 *Erasmi Opera Omnia*, vol. 2, cols. 13–17; quoted in Martin Fleisher, *Radical Reform and Political Persuasion in the Life and Writings of Thomas More* (Geneva, 1973), p. 42. Fleisher's book has been very helpful in writing this section.
20 Fleisher, *Political Persuasion*, p. 42, quoting Lupton, *Colet,* p. 134.
21 *Ibid.* p. 44.
22 Skinner, *Foundations of Modern Political Thought*, vol. 1, p. 153.
23 *Winstanley. The Law of Freedom and Other Writings*, ed. Christopher Hill (Cambridge, 1973, 1983), p. 36.
24 Buckle in *Natural Law and the Theory of Property* barely mentions Aquinas; his concentration, however, is on Grotius and his successors.
25 For more detail about Aquinas' rather ambiguous chain of reasoning on this issue, see Appendix.
26 Roger Deakins, 'The Tudor Prose Dialogue: Genre and Anti-Genre', *Studes in English Literature*, 20 (1980), 5–23.

6 'LOVE IS THE FULFILLING OF THE LAW': *ARCADIA*, AND *LOVE'S LABOUR'S LOST*

1  *The Fire of Love and the Mending of Life*, chapter 29. I am grateful to Joanna Thompson for supplying this quotation.
2  See Richard A. McCabe, *Incest, Drama and Nature's Law 1550–1700*.
3  References in the text are to Sir Philip Sidney, *The Old Arcadia*, ed. Katherine Duncan-Jones (Oxford, 1985): this text was established by Jean Robertson, *The Countess of Pembroke's Arcadia (The Old Arcadia)* (Oxford, 1973).
4  The differences between the 'Old' and 'New' versions are irrelevant to this book.
5  See Walter R. Davis, *A Map of Arcadia: Sidney's Romance in Its Tradition* (New Haven and London, 1965).
6  See Richard Lanham, *The Old Arcadia* (New Haven and London, 1965).
7  This partly refutes the very Calvinist reading by Elizabeth Dipple, ' "Unjust Justice" in the *Old Arcadia*', *Studies in English Literature* 10 (1970), 83–101.

8  Jordan, *Renaissance Feminism*, pp. 237, 234.
9  Nancy Lindheim in *The Structures of Sidney's 'Arcadia'* (Toronto, 1982), pp. 160ff., makes a distinction between circumstances meriting equity as a genuinely 'ethical justice', and mercy, which she sees more or less as a verdict of guilty, set aside on grounds of extra-legal intervention.
10  S. K. Heninger, *Sidney and Spenser: The Poet as Maker* (Pennsylvania and London, 1989), p. 460.
11  References in the text are to William Shakespeare, *Love's Labour's Lost*, ed. G. R. Hibbard, The Oxford Shakespeare (Oxford and New York, 1990).
12  Northrop Frye, *A Natural Perspective. The Development of Shakespearean Comedy and Romance* (New York, 1965), pp. 73–4.
13  'Shakespearean Comedy and Northrop Frye', *Essays in Criticism*, 22 (1972), 33–40.
14  William Shakespeare, *Love's Labour's Lost*, ed. Richard David, The Arden Shakespeare (London, fifth edition, 1956), p. xxvii.
15  *Gesta Grayorum*, ed. Desmond Bland, p. 88.
16  *Ibid.*, pp. xx–xxii.
17  Johnson, *Early Elizabethan Tragedies of the Inns of Court*, p. 26.
18  *Ibid.*, p. 28.
19  A. Wigfall Green, *The Inns of Court and Early English Drama* (Yale University Press, New Haven, London, Oxford, 1931), p. 32.
20  See R. S. White, 'Oaths and the Anticomic Spirit in *Love's Labour's Lost*', in *Shakespeare and some Others*, ed. Alan Brissenden (Adelaide, 1976), pp. 11–29, some of which is used here.
21  John Selden, *Table Talk* (London, 1689), pp. 86–7.

7  'HOT TEMPER LEAPS O'ER A COLD DECREE': *THE MERCHANT OF VENICE* AND *MEASURE FOR MEASURE*

1  References in the text are to William Shakespeare, *The Complete Works*, ed. Stanley Wells and Gary Taylor (Oxford, 1986).
2  O. Hood Philips, 'The Law Relating to Shakespeare 1564–1964', *Law Quarterly Review*, 80 (1964), 172–202 and 399–430.
3  Keeton, *Shakespeare's Legal and Political Background*, pp. 144.
4  Maxine MacKay, '*The Merchant of Venice*: A Reflection of the Early Conflict Between Courts of Law and Courts of Equity', *Shakespeare Quarterly*, 15 (1964), 371–5.
5  W. Nicholas Knight, 'Equity, *The Merchant of Venice* and William Lambarde', *Shakespeare Survey*, 27 (1974), 93–104.
6  Mark Edwin Andrews, *Law versus Equity in The Merchant of Venice. A Legalization of Act IV, Scene 1* (Boulder, Colorado, 1965).
7  B. J. Sokol, '*The Merchant of Venice* and the Law Merchant', *Renaissance Studies*, 6 (1992), 60–7, p. 66.
8  Cheney, *Spenser's Image of Nature* (New Haven, Connecticut, 1966), p. 158.
9  John D. Euce, 'Shakespeare and the Legal Process: four Essays', *Virginia Law Review*, 61 (1975), 390–433.
10  Andrews, *Law versus Equity*, p. 43.

11  See E. W. Ives, 'The Law and the the Lawyers', *Shakespeare Survey*, 17 (1964), pp. 72–86.

12  References in the text are to *Measure for Measure*, ed. Brian Gibbons (Cambridge, 1991).

13  Keith Thomas, 'The Puritans and Adultery. The Act of 1650 Reconsidered', *Puritans and Revolutionaries. Essays in Seventeenth Century History Presented to Christopher Hill*, ed. Donald Pennington and Keith Thomas (Oxford, 1978), pp. 257–82.

14  *A Perambulation of Kent* (1596), quoted Thomas, *Puritans and Adultery*, p. 265.

15  Quoted from an unsympathetic Thomas Edwards in A. L. Morton, *The Ranters: Religious Radicalism in the English Revolution* (London), p. 23; spelling modernised here.

16  Quoted Andrews, *Law versus Equity*, p. 33.

17  For a thorough examination of the ins and outs of *sponsalia de praesenti* and *de futuro*, see Margaret Loftus Ranald, who sweeps up all earlier discussions, but oddly enough does not look at *Measure for Measure*, in *Shakespeare and His Social Context* (New York, 1987), and the more incisive discussion by Anne Barton in ' "Wrying but a little": marriage, law and sexuality in the plays of Shakespeare', in *Essays, Mainly Shakespearean* (Cambridge, 1994), pp. 3–30.

18  See Leah Marcus, *Puzzling Shakespeare: Local Reading and Its Discontents* (Berkeley, Los Angeles, London, 1988) for topicality of the play.

19  Horst Ruthrof, *Pandora and Occam: On the Limits of Language and Literature* (Bloomington and Indianapolis, 1992), p. 146.

20  *Ibid.*, p. 147.

21  As does, for example, G. Wilson Knight in '*Measure for Measure* and the Gospels', *The Wheel of Fire* (London, 1949), pp. 73–96.

22  See Richard Wilson, 'The Quality of Mercy: Discipline and Punishment in Shakespearian Comedy', *The Seventeenth Century*, 5 (1990), 1–42.

23  Donna B. Hamilton uses the text of William Perkins' *A Case of Conscience* (1592) to reinforce this point, in *Shakespeare and the Politics of Protestant England* (Hemel Hempstead, 1992), p. 186.

24  Again, Donna B. Hamilton is one critic who agrees that a central point of *Measure for Measure* is that it 'condemns laws which oppress subjects, and celebrates by contrast actions by rulers that "use the law to protect life and liberty" and so, by implication, to maintain the liberties of the subject which had been guaranteed, the common lawyers had argued, by Magna Carta'; *Shakespeare and the Politics of Protestant England*, pp. 114–15.

8  SHAKESPEARE'S *THE HISTORY OF KING LEAR*

1  This chapter draws freely from my previous publications, *Innocent Victims: Poetic Injustice in Shakespearean Tragedy* (second edition, Athlone Press, London, 1985), chapter 8, and '*King Lear* and Philosophical Anarchism', *English*, 37 (1988), 181–200. I am not sure whether it is encouraging or dismaying that we go on discovering much later what we were trying to say on earlier occasions. In this case, research into Natural Law has clarified and

simplified my thoughts on the play, and in no way reverses them. I also owe debts to John Danby, William Hazlitt, A. C. Bradley, G. Wilson Knight, and William Elton.

2  William Shakespeare, *The Complete Works* (Oxford, 1986) p. 1025. Quotations taken from this edition.

3  Edited by Gary Taylor and Michael Warren, Oxford Shakespeare Studies (Oxford, 1983).

4  Christopher Wortham, 'Ghostly Presences: Dr Faustus meets King Lear', *Meridian*, 14 (1995), 65–74.

5  *A Concise Law Dictionary*, ed. P. G. Osborn (London, 1964).

6  John Donne's imagery is full of 'anatomy', and it was, after all, the age of William Harvey's discovery of the circulation of blood. See Devon L. Hodges' fascinating little book, *Renaissance Fictions of Anatomy* (Amherst, 1985).

7  John D. Euce, 'Shakespeare and the Legal Process: four Essays', *Virginia Law Review*, 61 (1975), 390–433.

8  John Rawls, *A Theory of Justice* (Oxford, 1971). Rawls' book, while not dealing directly with Natural Law, has been a continuing influence behind this book.

9  Cotterell, *The Politics of Jurisprudence*, p. 143. I should point out, in defence of quoting at third hand, that Cotterell's book is an excellent 'Critical Introduction' which works largely through quotations, many of which are useful here.

10  Cotterell, *The Politics of Jurisprudence*, p. 131, quoting Fuller.

11  My analysis differs markedly from John Danby's in *Shakespeare's Doctrine of Nature. A Study of 'King Lear'* (London, 1949), although I readily admit my general indebtedness to this book. Although he does not ignore Natural Law, his main analysis deals with what I have called 'natural philosophy'.

12  Among the many accounts of this contentious issue, see J. C. Maxwell, 'The Technique of Invocation in *King Lear*', *Modern Language Review*, 45 (1950), 142–7; Barbara Everett, 'The New King Lear' in *Critical Quarterly*, 2 (1960), 325–9; and compare William Elton, *King Lear and the Gods* (San Marino, California, 1966).

13  It has sometimes been argued that one actor doubled for Cordelia and the Fool. I find it very implausible that these two characters were played by the same actor, since both roles are identified with specialist actors, a professional comedian and a boy actor respectively.

14  For the topicality of this issue in James I's reign, see Leah Marcus, *Puzzling Shakespeare* (above, chapter 7, note 18).

15  See Michael Goldman, *Shakespeare and the Energies of Drama* (Princeton, New Jersey, 1972), pp. 94ff., for a graphic description of the kind of beggar's persona Edgar asumes.

16  Edmond N. Cahn, *The Sense of Injustice: An Anthropocentric View of Law* (New York and London, 1949).

9  MILTON AND NATURAL LAW

1  The edition quoted throughout is John Milton, *The Prose Works* in 5 vols., ed. various hands (London, 1870–3). This is hardly a 'state of art' modern

edition, but has sentimental value to me and was edited with passion and precision. I have also learned much from the commentaries in the magisterial Yale edition, *The Complete Prose Works of John Milton*, ed. Don M. Wolfe (New Haven, 1953–83). I realise how foolhardy it is to stray into the minefield of Miltonic theology, where almost all points, major and minor, are hotly contested between a range of Protestant and Catholic positions, and also Jewish: see Jason P. Rosenblatt, *Torah and Law in 'Paradise Lost'* (Princeton, New Jersey, 1994). My argument necessarily diminishes the Calvinist influence on Natural Law, which many others have seen as central, with the consequence that *Paradise Lost* is seen not as an example of Calvin's notion of the reprobate nature of man after the Fall, but as 'the supreme comedy of Christian liberty' (Rosenblatt, *Torah and Law*, p. 234), which is closer to my position than to a Calvinist reading. At the risk of alienating all shades of opinion, I base my argument simply on 'the words on the page', the actual evidence of Milton's statements, hoping enough is quoted to make a convincing case that mine is at least one of many possible.

2  Joan S. Bennett makes a similar point by analysing the influence of Hooker on Milton on the subject of 'right reason': *Reviving Liberty: Radical Christian Humanism in Milton's Great Poems* (Cambridge, Massachusetts, and London, 1989). See also Hoopes, *Right Reason*, chapter 10.

3  See, for example, Pauline Gregg, *Free-Born John: A Biography of John Lilburne* (London, 1961) and Nigel Smith, *Perfection Proclaimed: Language and Literature in English Radical Religion 1640–1660* (Oxford, 1989) *passim*; and see throughout the anthology David Wootton, (ed.), *Divine Right and Democracy: An Anthology of Writing in Stuart England* (Harmondsworth, 1986).

4  Arthur E. Barker, *Milton and the Puritan Dilemma 1641–1660* (Toronto and London, 1942), p. 82; Chillingworth, *The Religion of Protestants a Safe Way to Salvation* (1638).

5  Hoopes, *Right Reason*, p. 193 and throughout.

6  John Selden, *De Iure Naturali et Gentium* (London, 1639/1640), available in the Bodleian Library but not translated from Latin. So far as I can see, the only person who has fought his way through the 'tortuous' Latin is Jason P. Rosenblatt, *Torah and Law*, who describes Selden as 'Milton's Chief Rabbi', and Selden's books certainly are immensely learned in Rabbinical law. The connection between Jewish law and Puritan beliefs is very plausible, given the Puritans' repeated emphasis on going back to Mosaic law.

7  See William B. Hunter's 'The Provenance of the *Christian Doctrine*: Addenda from the Bishop of Salisbury', *Studies in English Literature* 33 (1993), 191–207 and Gordon Campbell's 'The Authorship of *De Doctrina Christiana*', *Milton Quarterly*, 26 (1992), 129–30, on the argument that Milton did not write *The Christian Doctrine*.

8  See Michael Bauman, *A Scripture Index to John Milton's Christian Doctrine* (Binghampton, New York, 1989).

9  See James Turner, *One Flesh: Paradisal Marriage and Sexual Relations in the Age of Milton* (Oxford, 1987), p. 208.

10  See Barker, pp. 217 and 384–5 fn2.

11  Bennett, *Reviving Liberty*, p. 13.

12 On this area see the authoritative book by John Halkett, *Milton and the Idea of Matrimony: A Study of the Divorce Tracts and 'Paradise Lost'* (New Haven and London, 1970).

13 *Ibid.*, p. 57.

14 Halkett argues against William and Malleville Haller, 'The Puritan Art of Loving', *Huntington Library Quarterly*, 5 (1942), 235–72, who argue that Puritans in general shared this belief.

15 Fortescue, *On the Law of Nature*, chapter 46.

16 This does not address the cogent argument sometimes put, that Eve was the first 'feminist' in disobeying patriarchal commands and questioning its structures: Lucy Newlyn, *Paradise Lost and the Romantic Reader* (Oxford, 1993), chapter 5, sets out some of the arguments. The case has often been put that Milton is not rigidly patriarchal in his treatment of Eve, and that he imbues her with individual rationality: for just one example, see Kay Gilliland Stevenson's 'Eve's Place in *Paradise Lost*', *Milton Quarterly*, 20 (1988), 126–7.

17 See Christopher Hill, to which my approach is indebted, *Milton and the English Revolution* (Harmondsworth, 1978).

18 I do not advance any ambitious, overall reading of Milton's poetry as allegories of his times, although such readings can, and have, been made.

EPILOGUE: HOBBES AND THE DEMISE OF CLASSICAL NATURAL LAW

1 Quotations in the text are to Thomas Hobbes, *Leviathan*, ed. C. B. Macpherson (Harmondsworth, 1968).

2 C. B. Macpherson, *The Political Theory of Possessive Individualism* (Oxford 1962).

3 Cotterrell, *The Politics of Jurisprudence*, p. 122.

4 Rommen, *The Natural Law*, p. 85.

5 Norberto Bobbio, *Thomas Hobbes and the Natural Law Tradition*, chapter 5, especially pp. 151–2.

6 *Ibid.*, p. 70.

7 Michael Dobson, *The Making of the National Poet: Shakespeare, Adaptation and Authorship, 1660–1769* (Oxford, 1992).

8 Quoted by Dobson, *ibid.*, p. 50, who also finds this attitude 'Hobbesian'.

9 Thomas Rymer, *The Tragedies of the Last Age Consider'd and Examin'd by the Practice of the Auncients and by the Common Sense of All Ages* (1678), Spingarn, ii, p. 207: Rymer's italics.

10 *A Short View of the Immorality and Profaneness of the English Stage* (1698).

11 Finnis, *Natural Law and Natural Rights*, p. 24.

# Select bibliography

Andrews, Mark Edwin. *Law versus Equity in The Merchant of Venice. A Legalization of Act IV, Scene 1* (Boulder, Colorado, 1965).

Anon. *The Life and Death of Jack Straw*, ed. Kenneth Muir and F. P. Wilson, Malone Society Reprints (Oxford, 1957).

Aptekar, Jane. *Icons of Justice: Iconography and Thematic Imagery in Book V of 'The Faerie Queene'* (New York, 1969).

Aquinas, St Thomas. *Summa Theologiae* (London and New York, in 61 vols., 1963–81), especially vol. 28.

*Aquinas: Selected Political Writings*, ed. A. P. d'Entrèves, trans. J. G. Dawson (Oxford, 1970).

Aristotle. *Ethica Nicomachea, The Works of Aristotle*, trans. and ed. W. D. Ross (Oxford, 1915).

Babington, Anthony. *The Rule of Law in Britain from the Roman Occupation to the Present Day. The Only Liberty* (Chichester and London, 1978).

Bacon, Francis. *The Advancement of Learning* and *New Atlantis*, ed. Arthur Johnston (Oxford, 1974), pp. 200–1.

    *Of the Coulers of Good and Evill. A Fragment (1597)*, in *The Works of Francis Bacon*, ed. James Spedding *et al.* (London, 1859), vol. 7.

    *The Elements of the Common Laws of England* (1630) (facsimile, Amsterdam and New York, 1969).

Baker, J. H. *An Introduction to English Legal History* (London, 1971).

Baker-Smith, Dominic. *More's 'Utopia'* (London, 1991).

    *Thomas More and Plato's Voyage* (Cardiff, 1978).

Barfield, Owen. 'Poetic Diction and Legal Fiction', in *Essays Presented to Charles Williams*, ed. C. S. Lewis (Oxford, 1947).

Barker, Arthur E. *Milton and the Puritan Dilemma 1641–1660* (Toronto and London, 1942).

Barton, D. Plunket, Benham, Charles, and Watt, Francis. *The Story of Our Inns of Court* (London, n.d.)

Bauman, Michael. *A Scripture Index to John Milton's Christian Doctrine* (Binghampton, New York, 1989).

Baylor, Michael G. (ed. and trans.). *The Radical Reformation* (Cambridge, 1991).

Bennett, Joan S. *Reviving Liberty: Radical Christian Humanism in Milton's Great Poems* (Cambridge, Massachusetts and London, 1989).

Benson, Pamela Joseph. *The Invention of the Renaissance Woman: The Challenge of Female Independence in the Literature and Thought of Italy and England* (Pennsylvania, 1992).

Bentham, Jeremy. *The Theory of Fictions*, ed. C. K. Ogden (London, 1932).

Berman, Harold J. *Law and Revolution: The Formation of the Western Legal Tradition* (Cambridge, Massachusetts and London, 1983).

Birks, Peter. 'Fictions Ancient and Modern', in *The Legal Mind. Essays of Tony Honore*, ed. Neil MacCormick and Peter Birks (Oxford, 1986), pp. 83–101.

Bland, D. S. 'Rhetoric and the Law Student in Sixteenth-Century England', *Studies in Philology*, 54 (1957), 498–508.

Bland, Desmond (ed.). *Gesta Grayorum*, English Reprints Series (Liverpool, 1968).

Bobbio, Norberto. *Thomas Hobbes and the Natural Law Tradition*, trans. Daniela Gobetti (Chicago and London, 1993; first pub. in Italian, 1989).

Bourke, Vernon J. 'Two Approaches of Natural Law', *Natural Law Forum*, 1 (1956), 92–6.

Bouwsma, William J. *John Calvin: A Sixteenth Century Portrait* (New York and Oxford, 1988).

*Bracton on the Laws and Customs of England*, vol. 2, ed. George E. Woodbine, trans. Samuel E. Thorne (Cambridge, Massuchesetts, 1968).

Bradshaw, Brendan. 'Edmund Spenser on Justice and Mercy', in *The Writer as Witness: Literature as Historical Evidence*, ed. Tom Dunne, Historical Studies XVI (Cork, 1987), pp. 76–89.

Buckle, Stephen. *Natural Law and the Theory of Property: Grotius to Hume* (Oxford, 1991).

Cahn, Edmond N. *The Sense of Injustice: An Anthropocentric View of Law* (New York and London, 1949).

Calvin, John. *Institutes of the Christian Religion*, ed. John T. McNeill (in 2 vols., Philadelphia, 1967).

Charlesworth, Hilary. 'The New Jurisprudences', in *Beyond the Disciplines: The New Humanities*, ed. K. K. Ruthven, Occasional Paper No. 13 from the Australian Academy of the Humanities Symposium 1991 (Canberra, 1992).

Cheney, Donald. *Spenser's Image of Nature: Wild Man and Shepherd in 'The Faerie Queene'* (New Haven and London, 1966).

Cioni, Maria L. *Women and Law in Elizabethan England. With Particular Reference to the Court of Chancery*, PhD (1974) for Cambridge University (New York and London, 1985).

Cockburn, J. S., and Green, Thomas A. *Twelve Good Men and True: The Criminal Trial Jury in England, 1200–1800* (Princeton, New Jersey, 1988).

Cohen, Ronald L. *Justice. Views from the Social Sciences* (New York and London, 1986).

Copleston, F. C. *Aquinas* (Harmondsworth, 1955).

Cotterell, Roger. *The Politics of Jurisprudence: A Critical Introduction to Legal Philosophy* (London and Edinburgh, 1989).

Coughlan, Patricia. *Spenser and Ireland: An Interdisciplinary Perspective* (Cork, 1989).

Cox, Leonard. *The Arte or Crafte of Rhetoryke* (London, 1524?), facsimile (Theatrum Orbis Terrarum, Amsterdam, New Jersey, 1977).

Daley, A. Stuart. 'Shakespeare's Corin, Almsgiver and Faithful Feeder', *English Language Notes*, 27 (1990), 4–21.

Danby, John F. *Shakespeare's Doctrine of Nature. A Study of 'King Lear'* (London, 1949).

David, Rene, and Brierley, John C. *Major Legal Systems in the World Today* (London, 1985, third edition; first edition in French, 1964, first English edition, 1966).

Davies, Brian. *The Thought of Thomas Aquinas* (Oxford, 1992).

Davies, J. C. *Utopia and the Ideal Society* (Cambridge, 1981).

Davis, Walter R. *A Map of Arcadia: Sidney's Romance in Its Tradition* (New Haven and London, 1965).

Davitt, Thomas E. 'St Thomas Aquinas and the Natural Law', in Arthur L. Harding, *Origins of the Natural Law Tradition*.

Deakins, Roger. 'The Tudor Prose Dialogue: Genre and Anti-Genre', *Studies in English Literature*, 20 (1980), 5–23.

Dipple, Elizabeth. ' "Unjust Justice" in the *Old Arcadia*', *Studies in English Literature*, 10 (1970), 83–101.

Dobson, Michael. *The Making of the National Poet: Shakespeare, Adaptation and Authorship, 1660–1769* (Oxford, 1992).

Doddridge, John. *The Lawyers Light* (London, 1629).

Duncan-Jones, Katherine. *Sir Philip Sidney. Courtier Poet* (London, 1991).

Dunseath, T. K. *Spenser's Allegory of Justice in Book Five of 'The Faerie Queene'* (Princeton, New Jersey, 1976).

Eco, Umberto. 'In Praise of St Thomas', in *Travels in Hyperreality*, trans. William Weaver (San Diego, New York, London, 1986).

Eden, Kathy. *Poetic and Legal Fiction in the Aristotelian Tradition* (Princeton, New Jersey, 1986).

El-Gabalawy, Saad. 'Christian Communism in *Utopia, King Lear*, and *Comus*', *University of Toronto Quarterly*, 47 (1978), 228–238.

Elyot, Sir Thomas. *The Boke Named The Gouernour*, in 2 vols., ed. H. H. S. Croft (London, 1883).

d'Entrèves, A. P. *Natural Law: An Historical Survey* (London, 1951).

'The Case for Natural Law Re-examined', *Natural Law Forum*, 1 (1956), 5–52.

Euce, John D. 'Shakespeare and the Legal Process: Four Essays', *Virginia Law Review*, 61 (1975), 390–433.

Faulkner, Robert K. *Richard Hooker and the Politics of a Christian England* (Berkeley, Los Angeles, London, 1981).

Fifoot, C. H. S. *History and Sources of the Common Law: Tort and Contract* (London, 1949).

Finkelpearl, Philip J. *John Marston of the Middle Temple. An Elizabethan Dramatist in his Social Setting* (Cambridge, Massachusetts, 1969).

Finnis, John. *Natural Law and Natural Rights* (Oxford, 1980).

Fleisher, Martin. *Radical Reform and Political Persuasion in the Life and Writings of Thomas More* (Geneva, 1973).

Fletcher, Angus. *The Prophetic Moment: An Essay on Spenser* (Chicago and London, 1971).

Flick, Geoffrey A. *Natural Justice: Principles and Practical Application* (Sydney, second edition, 1984).

Fortescue, Sir John. *De Natura Legis Naturae*, reprinted in 1869 by Thomas

(Fortescue) Lord Clermont, ed. David S. Berkowitz and Samuel E. Thorne (New York and London, 1980).

Fox, Alistair. *Utopia. An Elusive Vision* (New York, 1993).

Frye, Northrop. *A Natural Perspective. The Development of Shakespearean Comedy and Romance* (New York, 1965).

Fuller, Lon L. *The Morality of Law* (New Haven and London, 1964). *Legal Fictions* (Stanford, California, 1967).

Gaukroger, Stephen. *Descartes: An Intellectual Biography* (Oxford, 1995).

George, Robert P. *Natural Law Theory: Contemporary Essays* (Oxford, 1992).

German, Saint Christopher. *Doctor and Student*, ed. T. F. T. Plucknett and J. L. Barton (Selden Society, London, 1974).

*Gesta Grayorum*, ed. W. W. Greg. Malone Society Reprints (Oxford, 1914).

Godwin, George. *The Middle Temple: The Society and Fellowship* (London, 1954).

Goodrich, Peter. *Languages of Law. From Logics of Memory to Nomadic Masks* (London, 1987).

Gough, J. W. *Fundamental Law in English Constitutional History* (Oxford, 1955, 1961).

Graziani, René. 'Elizabeth at Isis Church', *Publications of the Modern Language Association*, 79 (1964), 376–89.

Green, A. Wigfall. *The Inns of Court and Early English Drama* (New Haven, London, Oxford, 1931).

Green, Thomas Andrew. *Verdict According to Conscience: Perspectives on the English Criminal Trial Jury, 1200–1800* (Chicago and London, 1985).

Greenblatt, Stephen. *Renaissance Self-Fashioning from More to Shakespeare* (Chicago, 1980).

Greene, Robert A. 'Synderesis, the Spark of Conscience, in the English Renaissance', *Journal of the History of Ideas*, 52 (1991), 195–219.

Halkett, John. *Milton and the Idea of Matrimony: A Study of the Divorce Tracts and 'Paradise Lost'* (New Haven and London, 1970).

Halliwell, Stephen. *Aristotle's Poetics: A Study of Philosophical Criticism* (London, 1986).

Hamilton, A. C. *The Spenser Encyclopedia* (Toronto and London, 1990).

Hamilton, Donna B. *Shakespeare and the Politics of Protestant England* (Hemel Hempstead, 1992).

Harding, Alan. *A Social History of English Law* (Gloucester, Massachusetts, 1973).

Harding, Arthur L. *Origins of the Natural Law Tradition* (Dallas, 1954).

Harris, J. W. *Legal Philosophies* (London, 1980).

Hart, H. L. A. *The Concept of Law* (Oxford, 1961).

Hayes, T. Wilson. *Winstanley the Digger: A Literary Analysis of Radical Ideas in the English Revolution* (Cambridge, Massachusetts, 1979).

Heninger, S. K. Jr. *Sidney and Spenser: The Poet as Maker* (Pennsylvania and London, 1989).

Herndl, George C. *The High Design: English Renaissance Tragedy and the Natural Law* (Lexington, Kentucky, 1970).

Hexter, J. H. *More's Utopia: The Biography of an Idea* (Princeton, New Jersey, 1952).

Hill, Christopher. *Puritanism and Revolution* (London, 1958).
  *Milton and the English Revolution* (Harmondsworth, 1978).
Hill, W. Speed (ed.). *Studies in Richard Hooker: Essays Preliminary to an Edition of his Works* (Cleveland and London, 1972).
Hobbes, Thomas. *Leviathan*, ed. C. B. Macpherson (Harmondsworth, 1968).
Hodges, Devon L. *Renaissance Fictions of Anatomy* (Amherst, 1985).
Holdsworth, W. S. *History of English Law* (in 16 vols., London, 1903–64).
Hooker, Richard. *Of the Laws of Ecclesiastical Polity: An Abridged Edition*, ed. A. S. McGrade and Brian Vickers (London, 1975).
Hoopes, Robert. *Right Reason in the English Renaissance* (Cambridge, Massachusetts, 1962).
Howell, Wilbur Samuel. *Logic and Rhetoric in England, 1500–1700* (Princeton, New Jersey, 1956).
Hunter, William B. (ed.). *A Milton Encyclopedia* (Lewisburg, 1978), vol. 4.
Hutcheson, Hon. Joseph C. Jr. 'The Natural Law and the Right to Property', *University of Notre Dame Natural Law Institute Proceedings*, iv (1951), pp. 43–73.
Ives, E. W. 'The Law and the the Lawyers', *Shakespeare Survey*, 17 (1964), 72–86.
James, John S. *Stroud's Judicial Dictionary of Words and Phrases* (fourth edition, London, 1973), vol. 3.
Johnson, S. F. *Early Elizabethan Tragedies of the Inns of Court* (Harvard Dissertations in American and English Literature, ed. Stephen Orgel: New York and London, 1987).
Jones, J. Walter. *Historical Introduction to the Theory of Law* (Oxford, 1940).
Jones, W. J. *The Elizabethan Court of Chancery* (Oxford, 1967).
Jordan, Constance. *Renaissance Feminism: Literary Texts and Political Models* (Ithaca and London, 1990).
Jowitt, Earl, and Walsh, Clifford. *The Dictionary of English Law* (London, 1959).
Keeton, George W. *Shakespeare's Legal and Political Background* (London, 1967).
Kerr, S. Parnell. 'Philip Sidney: Graian', *Graya*, 41 (1955), 48–52.
Knafla, Louis A. *Law and Politics in Jacobean England: The Tracts of Lord Chancellor Ellesmere* (Cambridge, 1977).
Knight, W. Nicholas. 'Equity, *The Merchant of Venice* and William Lambarde', *Shakespeare Survey*, 27 (1974), 93–104.
  'The Narrative Unity of Book V of *The Faerie Queene*: "That Part of Justice which is Equity" ', *Review of English Studies*, n.s. 21 (1970), 267–94.
Kropokin, Prince Peter. *Mutual Aid* (Harmondsworth, 1939).
Lambarde, William. *Archeion or, A Discourse upon the High Courts of Justice in England* (1635; MS 1591), ed. C. H. McIlwain and Paul L. Ward (Cambridge, Massachusetts, 1957).
Leyden, von W. *Aristotle on Equality and Justice: His Political Argument* (London, 1985).
Lindheim, Nancy. *The Structures of Sidney's 'Arcadia'* (Toronto, 1982).
Lobban, Michael. *The Common Law and English Jurisprudence 1760–1850* (Oxford, 1991).
Lodge, Thomas. *Defence of Poetry* (1579), in *Elizabethan Critical Essays*, ed. G. Gregory Smith, vol. 1, pp. 61–86.

Logan, George M. 'Interpreting *Utopia*: Ten Recent Studies and the Modern Critical Traditions', *Moreana*, 31 (1994), 203–58.

Lord Lloyd of Hampstead, and Freeman, M. D. A. *Lloyd's Introduction to Jurisprudence* (London, fifth edition, 1985).

Lucas, J. R. *On Justice* (Oxford, 1980).

Lumb, R. D. 'Natural Law and Positive Law: The doctrines of Aquinas and Suarez Compared with Later Theories' (D.Phil, Oxford, unpublished, 1958).

Luther, Martin. *The Works of Martin Luther: 'The Philadelphia Edition'* (Philadelphia, 1930), especially vol. 3.

*Luther's Works*, ed. Jaroslav Pelikan (in 56 vols., Saint Louis, 1958–86), especially vols. 13 and 16.

McCabe, Bernard. 'Francis Bacon and the Natural Law Tradition', *Natural Law Forum*, 9 (1964), 111–21.

McCabe, Richard A. *Incest, Drama and Nature's Law 1550–1700* (Cambridge, 1993).

McGinn, Donald J. 'The Precise Angelo', in *Joseph Quincy Adams Memorial Studies*, ed. James G. McManaway, Giles E. Dawson, and Edwin E. Willoughby (Washington, 1948) pp. 129–39.

McIlwain, Charles Howard. *The High Court of Parliament and its Supremacy: An Historical Essay on the Boundaries between Legislation and Adjudication in England* (New Haven, 1910).

MacKay, Maxine. '*The Merchant of Venice*: A Reflection of the Early Conflict Between Courts of Law and Courts of Equity', *Shakespeare Quarterly*, 15 (1964), 371–5.

Macpherson, C. B. *The Political Theory of Possessive Individualism* (Oxford 1962).

Maine, Sir Henry. *Ancient Law: Its Connection with the Early History of Society and its Relation to Modern Ideas*, Notes by Sir Frederick Pollock (London, 1906; first pub. 1861).

Marc'Hadour, Germain. 'Thomas More's Spirituality', *St Thomas More: Action and Contemplation*, ed. Richard S. Sylvester (New Haven and London, 1972), pp. 125–59.

Marius, Richard. *Thomas More: A Biography* (London and Melbourne, 1984).

Marrian, F. J. M. *Shakespeare at Grays Inn – a tentative theory* (self-printed, 1967).

Marshall, John S. *Hooker and the Anglican Tradition: An Historical and Theological Study of Hooker's Ecclesiastical Polity* (London, 1963).

'Richard Hooker and the Origins of American Constitutionalism', *Origins of the Natural Law Tradition* (Dallas, 1954), pp. 46–68.

Meyer, Hans. *The Philosophy of St Thomas Aquinas*, trans. Rev. Frederic Eckhoff, (London, 1944).

Miller, David. *Social Justice* (Oxford, 1976).

Milsom, S. F. C. *Historical Foundations of the Common Law* (London, 1969).

Milton, John. *The Prose Works* in 5 vols., ed. various hands (London, 1870–3).

*The Complete Prose Works of John Milton*, ed. Don M. Wolfe (New Haven, 1953–1983).

*Milton, Poetical Works*, ed. Douglas Bush (Oxford, 1966).

*The Mirror for Magistrates*, ed. Lily B. Campbell (Cambridge, 1938).

Montaigne, Michel de. *The Complete Essays*, ed. M. A. Screech (London, 1987).

Morawetz, Thomas, (ed.). *Justice*, The International Library of Essays in Law and Legal Theory (Aldershot, 1991).

More, St Thomas. *Utopia, The Complete Works of St Thomas More*, ed. Edward Surtz S.J., and J. H. Hexter (New Haven and London, 1965), vol. 4.

　*Utopia*, ed. George M. Logan and Robert M. Adams (Cambridge, 1989).

Mulhall, Stephen, and Swift, Adam. *Liberals and Communitarians* (Oxford, 1992).

Murphy, James J. *Rhetoric in the Middle Ages. A History of Rhetorical Theory from Saint Augustine to the Renaissance* (Berkeley, Los Angeles, London, 1974).

　*Renaissance Rhetoric. A Short-Title Catalogue of Works on Rhetorical Theory from the Beginning of Printing to A.D. 1700* (New York and London, 1981).

Murphy, James J. (ed.). *Renaissance Eloquence: Studies in the Theory and Practice of Renaissance Rhetoric* (Los Angeles and London, 1983).

Norbrook, David. *Poetry and Politics in the English Renaissance* (London, 1984).

Noyes, C. Reinold. *The Institution of Property. A Study of the Development, Substance and Arrangement of the System of Property in Modern Anglo-American Law* (New York, Toronto, London, 1936).

Nozick, Robert, *Anarchy, State, and Utopia* (Oxford, 1974).

Oakley, Francis. 'Medieval Theories of Natural Law: William of Ockham and the Significance of the Voluntarist Tradition', *Natural Law Forum*, 6 (1961), 65–83.

Ogilvie, Sir Charles. *The King's Government and the Common Law 1471–1641* (Oxford, 1958).

O'Sullivan, Richard. 'The Natural Law and Common Law', *University of Notre Dame Natural Law Proceedings*, 3 (1950), 9–44.

Patrides, C. A. *Milton and the Christian Tradition* (Oxford, 1966).

Peacham, Henry. *The Garden of Eloquence* (1577), facsimile of 1593 edition, introduced by William G. Crane (Gainsville, Florida, 1954).

Phillips, James E. 'Renaissance Concepts of Justice and the Structure of *The Faerie Queen*, Book V', *Huntingdon Library Quarterly*, 33 (1970), 103–120.

Philips, O. Hood. 'The Law Relating to Shakespeare 1564–1964', *Law Quarterly Review*, 80 (1964), 172–202 and 399–430.

Plato. *The Republic*, Loeb edition, trans. Paul Shorey (London and Cambridge, Massachusetts, 1953).

Plucknett, T. F. T. *A Concise History of the Common Law* (London,1956).

Pollock, Sir Frederick, and Maitland, F. W. *The History of English Law before Edward I* (second edition, Cambridge, 1923).

Posner, Richard A. *Law and Literature: A Misunderstood Relation* (Cambridge, Massachusetts, London, 1988).

Postema, Gerald J. *Bentham and the Common Law Tradition* (Oxford, 1986).

Potter, Robert, 'Divine and Human Justice'. *Aspects of Early English Drama*, ed. Paula Neuss (Cambridge, 1983), pp. 129–141.

Poynet, John. *A Short Treatise of politike power and of the true Obedience which subiectes owe to kynges and other ciuile Gouernours, with an Exhortation to al true naturall Englishe men* (London, 1556).

Prest, Wilfrid R. *The Inns of Court under Elizabeth 1 and the Early Stuarts 1590–1640* (London, 1972).

  *The Rise of the Barristers. A Social History of the English Bar 1590–1640* (Oxford, 1986).

Puttenham, George. *The Arte of English Poesie*, ed. Gladys Doidge Willcox and Alice Walker (Cambridge, 1936).

Rainolds, John. *Oratio in Laudem Artis Poeticae,* English trans. Walter Allen Jr., Introduction and commentary William Ringler (Princeton, 1940).

Raitiere, Martin N. 'More's *Utopia* and *The City of God*', *Studies in the Renaissance*, 20 (1973), 144–68.

Rawls, John. *A Theory of Justice* (Oxford, 1971).

Rommen, Heinrich A. *The Natural Law: A Study in Legal and Social History and Philosophy*, trans. Thomas R. Hanley (London, 1947).

Rosenblatt, Jason P. *Torah and Law in 'Paradise Lost'* (Princeton, New Jersey, 1994).

Ruthrof, Horst. *Pandora and Occam: On the Limits of Language and Literature* (Bloomington and Indianapolis, 1992).

Schoeck, Richard J. 'Lawyers and Rhetoric in Sixteenth–Century England', in *Renaissance Rhetoric*, ed. James J. Murphy, pp. 274–91.

  'Thomas More and Lincoln's Inn Revels', *Philological Quarterly*, 29 (1950), 426–30.

  'Rhetoric and Law in Sixteenth-Century England', *Studies in Philology*, 50 (1953), 110–27.

  'Canon Law in England on the Eve of the Reformation', *Mediaeval Studies*, 25 (1963), 125–47.

  'Common Law and Canon Law', in *St Thomas More: Action and Contemplation*, ed. Richard S. Sylvester (New Haven and London, 1972), pp. 17–55.

Selden, John. *De Iure Naturali et Gentium* (London, 1639/1640), Bodleian Library.

Shakespeare, William. *The Complete Works*, ed. Stanley Wells and Gary Taylor (Oxford, 1986).

  *Measure for Measure*, ed. Brian Gibbons (Cambridge, 1991).

  *Love's Labour's Lost*, ed. Richard David, The Arden Shakespeare (fifth edition, London, 1956).

  *Love's Labour's Lost*, ed. G. R. Hibbard, The Oxford Shakespeare (Oxford and New York, 1990).

Shklar, Judith N. *The Faces of Injustice* (New Haven and London, 1990).

Shuger, Debora K. *Sacred Rhetoric: The Christian Grand Style in the English Renaissance* (Princeton, New Jersey, 1988).

Sidney, Sir Philip. *The Old Arcadia*, ed. Katherine Duncan-Jones and Jean Robertson (Oxford and New York, 1985).

  *A Defence of Poetry*, in *Miscellaneous Prose of Sir Philip Sidney*, ed. Katherine Duncan-Jones and Jan van Dorsten (Oxford, 1973).

Sisson, C. J. *Shakespeare's Tragic Justice* (London, 1963).

Skinner, Quentin. 'More's *Utopia*', *Past and Present*, 38 (1967), 153–68.

  *Foundations of Modern Political Thought* (in 2 vols., Cambridge, 1978).

  'Sir Thomas More's *Utopia* and the Language of Renaissance Humanism', ed. Anthony Pagden, *The Languages of Political Theory in Early-Modern Europe* (Cambridge, 1987), pp. 123–57.

Smith, G. Gregory (ed). *Elizabethan Critical Essays* (2 vols. London, 1904).

Smith, Nigel. *Perfection Proclaimed: Language and Literature in English Radical Religion 1640–1660* (Oxford, 1989).

'Forms of Kingship in *King Lear*', in *Critical Essays on 'King Lear'*, ed. Linda Cookson and Bryan Loughrey (Harlow, n.d.).

'The Charge of Atheism and the Language of Radical Speculation, 1640–1660', in *Atheism from the Reformation to the Enlightenment*, ed. Michael Hunter and David Wooton (Oxford, 1992), 131–158.

Smith, Sir Thomas, (attrib.). *A Discourse of the Commonwealth of this Realm of England*, ed. Mary Dewar (Folger Documents of Tudor and Stuart Civilization, Charlottesville, 1969).

Sokol, B. J. '*The Merchant of Venice* and the Law Merchant', *Renaissance Studies*, 6 (1992), 60–7.

Spenser, Edmund. *The Faerie Queene*, ed. Thomas P. Roche Jr. and C. Patrick O'Donnell Jr. (Harmondsworth, 1978).

*A View of the Present State of Ireland*, ed. W. L. Renwick (Oxford, 1970).

Stillman, Robert E. 'Justice and the "Good Word", in Sidney's *The Lady of May'*, *Studies in English Literature*, 24 (1984), pp. 23–38.

Sturm, Douglas. 'Natural Law' entry in *The Encyclopedia of Religion*, ed. Mircea Eliade (New York and London, 1987), vol. 10, pp. 318–24.

Terrill, Richard J. 'William Lambarde: Elizabethan Humanist and Legal Historian', *Journal of Legal History*, 6 (1985), 157–78.

'Humanism and Rhetoric in Legal Education: The Contribution of Sir John Dodderidge (1555–1628)', *Journal of Legal History*, 2 (1981), 30–44.

Thomas, Keith. 'The Puritans and Adultery. The Act of 1650 Reconsidered', *Puritans and Revoutionaries. Essays in Seventeenth Century History Presented to Christopher Hill*, ed. Donald Pennington and Keith Thomas (Oxford, 1978), pp. 257–82.

Thorne, S. E. *Essays in English Legal History* (London and Ronceverte, 1985).

Tonkin, Humphrey. *The Faerie Queene* (London, 1989).

Trigg, Roger. *Ideas of Human Nature: An Historical Introduction* (Oxford, 1988).

Tuck, Richard. *Natural Rights Theories* (Cambridge, 1979).

Turner, James Grantham. *One Flesh: Paradisal Marriage and Sexual Relations in the Age of Milton* (Oxford, 1987).

Vaihinger, Hans. *Philosophie des Als Ob*, trans. C. K. Ogden, *The Philosophy of 'As If'* (London, 1924).

van Caenegem, R. C. *The Birth of the English Common Law* (second edition, Cambridge, 1973, 1988).

Veall, Donald. *The Popular Movement for Law Reform 1640–1660* (Oxford, 1970).

Vickers, Brian. ' "The Power of Persuasion": Images of the Orator, Elyot to Shakespeare', in *Renaissance Eloquence*, ed. James J, Murphy, pp. 411–35.

Vinogradoff, Paul. 'Reason and conscience in Sixteenth-Century Jurisprudence', *Law Quarterly Review*, 24 (1908), 373–84.

Wallace, Malcolm William. *The Life of Sir Philip Sidney* (Cambridge, 1915).

Weinred, Lloyd L. *Natural Law and Justice* (Cambridge, Massachusetts, 1987).

Weston, Corinne Comstock, and Greenberg, Janelle Renfrow. *Subjects and*

*Sovereigns: The Grand Controversy over Legal Sovereignty in Stuart England* (Cambridge, 1981).

White, Frederic [*sic*] R. *Famous Utopias of the Renaissance* (New York, 1966).

White, R. S. 'Oaths and the Anticomic Spirit in *Love's Labour's Lost*', in *Shakespeare and Some Others*, ed. Alan Brissenden (Adelaide, 1976), pp. 11–29.

*Innocent Victims: Poetic Injustice in Shakespearean Tragedy* (second edition, London, 1986).

White, Stephen D. *Sir Edward Coke and the Grievances of the Commonwealth* (Manchester, 1979).

Wiggins, Martin. *Journeymen in Murder: The Assassin in English Renaissance Drama* (Oxford, 1991).

Wilks, John S. *The Idea of Conscience in Renaissance Tragedy* (New York, 1990).

Wilson, Richard. 'The Quality of Mercy: Discipline and Punishment in Shakespearian Comedy', *The Seventeenth Century*, 5 (1990), 1–42.

Wilson, Thomas. *The Arte of Rhetorique* (1553), facsimile introduced by Robert Hood Bowers (Gainesville, Florida, 1962).

*Winstanley. The Law of Freedom and Other Writings*, ed. Christopher Hill (Cambridge, 1973, 1983).

Wootton, David, (ed.). *Divine Right and Democracy: An Anthology of Writing in Stuart England* (Harmondsworth, 1986).

Young, G. M. 'Shakespeare and the Termers', Annual Shakespeare Lecture for the British Academy, *Proceedings of the British Academy*, 33 (1947).

# Index